THE
Mail-Order
BRIDES
COLLECTION

9 Historical Stories of Marriage that Precedes Love

THE
Mail-Order
BRIDES
COLLECTION

Kathleen Y'Barbo,
Megan Besing, Noelle Marchand, Donna Schlachter,
Sherri Shackelford, Michelle Shocklee,
Ann Shorey, Liz Tolsma, Jennifer Uhlarik

BARBOUR BOOKS
An Imprint of Barbour Publishing, Inc.

Perfect for the Preacher ©2018 by Megan Besing
The Outlaw's Inconvenient Bride ©2018 by Noelle Marchand
Train Ride to Heartbreak ©2018 by Donna Schlachter
Mail-Order Proxy ©2018 by Sherri Shackelford
To Heal Thy Heart ©2018 by Michelle Shocklee
Miss-Delivered Mail ©2018 by Ann Shorey
A Fairy-Tale Bride ©2018 by Liz Tolsma
The Brigand and the Bride ©2018 by Jennifer Uhlarik
The Mail-Order Mistake ©2018 by Kathleen Y'Barbo

Print ISBN 978-1-68322-444-0

eBook Editions:
Adobe Digital Edition (.epub) 978-1-68322-446-4
Kindle and MobiPocket Edition (.prc) 978-1-68322-445-7

All scripture quotations are taken from the King James Version of the Bible.

This book is a work of fiction. Names, characters, places, and incidents are either products of the author's imagination or used fictitiously. Any similarity to actual people, organizations, and/or events is purely coincidental.

Published by Barbour Books, an imprint of Barbour Publishing, Inc., 1810 Barbour Drive, Uhrichsville, OH 44683, www.barbourbooks.com

Our mission is to inspire the world with the life-changing message of the Bible.

 Member of the
Evangelical Christian
Publishers Association

Printed in Canada.

Contents

Perfect for the Preacher

by Megan Besing

Dedication

To my husband: my love, my best friend, my happily-ever-after.

Acknowledgments

Abigail Wilson, God knew I needed you as my critique partner and friend. #Iheartyou. Wouldn't want to do this without you. Thanks for who you are and all you do. Peggy Trotter, so many hats you wear, including author, but I treasure you most as my mom. Thanks to you and Dad for your Christ-like examples. Kerry Johnson, you are lovely indeed. Thanks for stretching me to write better. Karen Collier, Amanda Stevens, and Serena Chase you've all had a major impact on my writing journey. Jessica Kirkland, thanks for being my agent and believing in me, especially when I don't. To my husband, thanks for dragging me to all those bookstores. You were right, reading is fabulous. My kiddos who love me just for being their mom. Barbour Publishing, you make dreams come true. To my Savior, THANK YOU. May my words, stories, life bring you honor, glory, and praise.

Chapter 1

Sophie Ross worried the edges of the secondhand Bible on her lap. If only she'd been the one to have worn out its leather binding, she might not have the baggage that she did—literally—the carpetbag tucked beneath the pew served as a reminder of how important today was.

It shamed her to admit she wasn't hearing much of the sermon. Her focus remained on the preacher himself. His description was exactly as he'd written.

Brown hair on the verge of blond. Medium build, a bump on the bridge of my nose from when my brother swung a stick that bruised my face for weeks.

Not that the bump appeared visible from her seat in the back. She peered over an array of bonnets and hats with flowers and feathers and, quite possibly, one topped by a bird's nest with speckled eggs. Sophie smoothed her faded calico dress. Her shined boots didn't compare to the silk dresses and lace gloves across the aisle.

After the closing song, those in attendance flocked to the exit with more gusto than was sung during any of the hymns. No one noticed her in the corner. Neither had anyone greeted her upon arrival. Of course she'd snuck in as services began. Nerves had twisted her stomach early in the morning, even though she knew God had this whole situation under control. He'd lined everything up when she needed it most. But who wouldn't be a little anxious about meeting the man she was about to spend the rest of her life with?

Sunshine flooded in the opened doors, swirling around the vaulted ceiling and highlighting the ornate stained-glass windows, much fancier than Pastor T's sanctuary. She shook her head. A sanctuary—a church—didn't belong to one preacher or another. They were all God's. Only God's.

At last Sophie's fiancé stood before her. This was it. The start of a new forever. He extended his hand in greeting. "Glad to have you join us for service today. I'm Pastor Amos Lowry." His grip was strong and sure, and to her surprise, she didn't hesitate or even flinch. God was indeed answering her prayers. Every last one.

He released her hand and cleared his throat. "Are you in town visiting family?"

Right. She hadn't sent a photograph of herself. He couldn't recognize someone he'd never seen before. "I'm Miss Ross."

No recognition registered on his face. She leaned against the pew back in front of her. They'd only exchanged five letters after she'd answered his ad. It was fine that he didn't recognize her name, even when she couldn't imagine forgetting his. Those two words had been floating around her mind for weeks.

Sophie tucked a wayward curl behind her ear. "I'm. . ." She licked her lips. Why was this so difficult to say? "I'm Sophie Ross, your mail-order bride."

"My mail-order bride? You're. . ." He squinted as if trying to make her into someone else. Was her description inaccurate? She'd written exactly what Mrs. T suggested, even though Sophie never would have called her eyes—lovely, of all things. They were too large. Too dark brown to be considered pleasant. But Mrs. T had insisted.

Doubt, or something close to worry, flashed in his eyes that held a thin green ring around their acorn center. His eyes, on the other hand, were quite lovely indeed. He glanced toward the front of the sanctuary where people mingled and the pianist organized her music.

"I'm sorry." She dipped her chin. "I thought you were agreeable to. . .us." The last part barely audible with her lips trembling. She resisted the urge to tug his latest letter out and show him the words she'd memorized. What had given her hope for a normal future.

As long as you know what will be expected of a preacher's wife, and you're still willing, I'd very much appreciate you arriving once you've had time to put your affairs in order.

Hours were spent probing Mrs. T on all things preacher-wife-like, and after much prayer, Sophie decided she could, with the Lord's help, become such a spouse. One who prayed and cooked for those in need. Be considerate of the extra time the church would take from her and her husband's moments together. She understood that money probably would remain tight for their family. Marrying a preacher may not be agreeable to every woman, but for Sophie, it was the safest route.

But no proof of his promise on paper matched the message expressed on his face. In person, willingness or not, she wasn't what he hoped for. How could she have thought she, of all people, would make a suitable preacher's wife?

"I'll go." She reached for her carpetbag, the one she should have kept at the boardinghouse. When she'd arrived yesterday, Amos was away visiting a family. She'd had enough for room and board for two nights. However, Momma had trained her to never allow her valuables out of sight. Considering this was all she had left, Sophie couldn't afford to go against her upbringing at least on this one particular matter.

The handle slipped from her grip and fell with a thump. Where would she go? Anywhere but near that obscene building she was raised in, and she couldn't go back and stay with Pastor T and his wife. Not with the sudden death of their son-in-law, and their daughter and grandchildren returning to live with them.

"No. No." He grabbed her carpetbag off the polished wooden floor and placed it on the pew separating them. His hands found hers, surrounding them in warmth. "Please stay. I held every intention of making a grander impression on you. . .m–my bride." He pressed his lips together as if the words tasted funny.

"I'm the one who must apologize. I was only caught off guard. I believed you'd write again to tell me of your date of arrival. I had planned on sending funds for your travels . . . ." His fingers shifted, almost linking in between a few of hers. His touch didn't bring fear, but rather a gentle promise of safety. A hope of a true home waiting where she could put everything behind her. "But I'm glad you're here now."

"Then. . .we're still to wed?"

"Indeed. If you'll have me?"

"Pastor Amos?" A tiny speck of a woman stood at the end of the pew. The feather on the side of her hat very well may have been taller than the woman herself. White gloves concealed everything up to her wrists. A patchwork of wrinkles outlined her eyes, the only clue hinting at an older age.

Amos released Sophie and backpedaled as far as the pew behind him would allow.

"Will you still be joining us for the midday meal?"

If Sophie had known Amos any better, or at all, she'd believe she'd caught him grimacing. But with the feather woman's wide grin, apparently, she hadn't noticed the way he'd crinkled his nose.

"Ah, yes. Your generous invitation. Would it be possible. . ." Amos rubbed the bump on his nose. "What I mean to say—"

"I think he's worried about your cooking, Margaret." A bearded man stepped beside the feather lady, patting his thick stomach. "You've nothing to worry about, Pastor Amos. My wife can't mess up beef stew and cornbread. Her persimmon pudding on the other hand. . ." He let out a low whistle.

"William, please. That was one time. Surely, I've made up for that awful moment. Even your mother forgave me for serving such a burnt dish."

William chuckled, his stomach jiggling, proving he was doing more than fine on his wife's cooking. "Tell that to Dusty. That dog still cowers when we bring a bucket of persimmons into the house."

"I'm sure you're a fine cook, Mrs. Olmstead. However, something's come up. Arrived, really." Amos stole a peek at Sophie, his face unreadable, but at least there was no scowl. "A personal—"

Margaret's eyes grew large, her gaze darting back and forth between Sophie and Amos. She thumped her knuckles against William's chest. "Is this who I think it is?"

William's beard pulled upward as he chewed in his bottom lip. He stilled Margaret's knocking fingers. "I don't know why you're asking me?"

She rose on tiptoes and tugged on William's ear. "When will you learn to use these? The good Lord knows He's gone near blessed ya with an acre of them. You were at the pastor interviews. Hmm? This must be her. The pastor's future wife."

"Depends on the vote." A gruff male voice carried across the sanctuary. From the corner, a man marched toward their group, the spurs on his boots echoing with each rattled step. Graying whiskers covered his chin and a mole rode on top of his left eyebrow. He took in all of Sophie the way men had assessed Momma in her work attire.

Sophie shivered and crossed her arms over her chest.

William grunted. "Majority will rule, Hanson. You've already swayed the preacher into ordering a wife. So you see, even you can't say he's not the perfect man for the job."

A vote? Wasn't Amos already their pastor? The church wasn't going to vote on their upcoming marriage, were they? Mrs. T never discussed anything on that church matter. Amos' first letter explained why he desired to obtain a wife quickly, but he failed to mention she'd have to be approved of—by more than just him.

Margaret clapped, the feather on her hat wavering like a pendulum on a grandfather clock. "That's it." She pointed at Amos, as if Hanson hadn't added a layer of tension. "That's why you were trying to get out of your invitation to lunch. Not because of my cooking, William. You thought you'd be rude asking to bring your intended along with you." She clucked her tongue. "Have no fear. Ha! See what I did there? Your sermon being on the fear of the Lord. Which was intriguing and profound. Anyhow, I've got plenty of stew."

She clapped her hands twice more as if she might break into a jig. Did church people do that sort of thing? Sophie wasn't certain of all the rules yet. Pastor T had assured her she knew all the important ones. She hoped so.

"I'm the luckiest lady in the church." Margaret continued on, without kicking up her heels. "What an opportunity to be the first to get to know our soon-to-be pastor's wife. What a fit the quilting circle will make when they discover I got to feed you first."

"Humph," Hanson grumbled.

William arched his shoulders. "Would you like to join us for some stew, Hanson? Oliver and Ruby, too. As my wife said, we've got plenty." The few other families circulating the sanctuary stopped their conversations. The whole room seemed to be leaning in, waiting for Hanson's answer.

"Hardly." He gave Sophie one more glance-over before stomping away and slamming the church doors behind him.

William shifted closer to Amos. "Don't worry about Hanson. And I believe if you give everyone a quick introduction, the crowd will get what they stayed for, and we can be on our way to eat that stew."

Amos smiled, but his jaw was clenched. "Welcome to Hilltop Chapel, Sophie. These are the elders and their families. Well, most of them." He introduced them, their names bouncing around Sophie's mind. She'd met so many new people, learned so many things since Pastor T found her kneeling near Momma's grave and offered her a life outside the saloon. How would she ever remember it all? "And this is Sophie Ross, my fiancée."

Margaret sighed. "Ahh, I remember the good ol' days of courting. Pastor Amos, don't forget women like flowers and gifts and walks and compliments." She shot William a heated look before beaming at Sophie. "But you won't have any trouble coming up with compliments like William. Sophie here's a beauty. Truly." The other wives nodded, murmuring their agreement. After a moment, Margaret's brows narrowed, and she put her fists on her hips. "Pastor Amos, isn't she a beauty?"

Amos blinked twice before loosening his tie. "Yes. Of course. Sophie, you look. . ." The tiniest bead of sweat etched on his brow as his lips worked silently.

Sympathy clutched at her uneasy middle. The poor man. Nothing like putting him on the spot. She shook her head. He didn't have to give her a compliment. Didn't have to do any of those things Margaret listed off. He'd pledged to marry her. Nothing else was required, especially in front of all these strangers.

"You're more than I dared to pray for," he whispered.

How wrong she'd been. She did need to hear those words. His approval settled in her heart, much richer praise than hearing anything concerning her appearance, because she'd seen firsthand how quickly outward beauty faded.

"All right." William rubbed his palms together. "Dinnertime."

The knot that had awoken Sophie this morning tightened at the thought of food. *Lord, please let these nerves go away soon.*

Amos gave her a crooked grin as if he, too, had been praying the same thing. Maybe it wasn't doubt she'd seen earlier in his eyes, but a mirror of her own nerves. What a gift God had given her, a man who could overlook her upbringing. Now, if only the congregation would agree.

Chapter 2

Amos craned his neck, feeling much like a schoolboy. If only his mail-order bride had been seated across from him instead of beside. Sophie Ross—his Sophie—was beautiful. Her description in her letters hadn't done her justice.

I'm of average height. Slender. Honey hair and have a dusting of freckles that frame my lovely brown eyes.

Why would she ever have needed to answer a mail-order ad? God had blessed him. There was no simple way around it.

In the Olmstead's kitchen, they huddled near the center of the long table. A white oblong doily separated William and Margaret from him and Sophie like a path through the Red Sea. Four other chairs sat against the wall as if being punished. A Bible, proudly displayed, rested on a shelf. Was that a glare from the sunlight, or was there dust on the cover? Perhaps their daily reading Bible was in a handier location.

Amos managed a spoonful of food. On any other day, the meal would have been a welcomed treat. Mrs. Olmstead knew how to liven up beef stew. However, how was he supposed to get to know his future wife when the dinner table topics centered around a dog's intestinal issues, and why Margaret chose not to include carrots in today's menu?

Speaking of the Olmstead's dog, he nudged his wet nose against Amos' elbow. With his grayish-brown coloring, there was no guessing why he'd been named Dusty. The dog wagged his tail and whined, his pleading eyes set on Amos' next bite.

"Dusty. Corner. Get on over." William pointed to a faded patchwork quilt, child-sized, that lay over a flattened pillow.

The dog might as well have Amos' share with the way nerves were attacking his body, preventing him from enjoying the food. He should have asked to reschedule their invitation, but he couldn't afford to be rude. Olmstead had been his biggest supporter during his interviews. Amos resisted the urge to yank off his tie. At least the meal provided ample time to consider how to make a better start with Sophie.

He ground his teeth against another tasty lump of stew. He should have been there to pick her up from the stagecoach. Or had she arrived on the train? Or both? Where was she staying, and most importantly, how does one go about wooing their intended? Amos took a drink and accidently moved his leg too far to the left, brushing against Sophie's dress.

She sucked in a breath.

"Excuse me." Had the thought of him near sent her in a panic? With all her beauty, maybe he hadn't measured up to her expectations?

Her cheeks turned pink. No, perhaps nerves, like him? He prayed that's all it was.

Margaret crumbled a piece of cornbread into her stew. "Have I managed to mess up the meal? Everyone's hardly eating."

William tilted his bowl and downed the rest of its contents. A belch loud enough to rival the church bells announced his satisfaction. "It's more than fine."

Amos waited for a reaction from Sophie, but she didn't seem fazed by William's lack of table manners. Pauline's quick tongue would have lashed William before he'd had a chance to close his mouth. Perhaps God had done him right by allowing his childhood friend to reject his offer of marriage. Of course God knew better. At the time he'd disagreed, but now. . .

"So when's the wedding? I assume it will be after service. That way all the families won't have to make more than one trip into town for the week."

"Marg, easy. These two might want to get to know each other first."

"Get to know each other?" She batted at his words. "They'll have the rest of their lives for that. What this town needs is a wedding. It's been much too dull around here." Margaret leaned forward, her focus on Amos. "Will it be this Sunday or the next?"

Amos automatically looked to Sophie. That was a good sign, right? He was already receptive toward his future helpmate. This fiancé-husband stuff wouldn't be too difficult. Would it?

Sophie's long lashes fluttered. She really had the perfect amount of freckles.

William cleared his throat, a smirk on his face.

Right. There had been a question. "Well, I . . ."

"I imagine they'll have to wait until Pastor Gable can return a trip here, dear. It's not like Amos can go and perform his own wedding. He'd planned on returning for a visit next month."

"Well. That may work. It would give the quilting circle a chance to finish our project. Oh, I think you two are going to love it. We may have just enough time to finish for the wedding night."

The air in the room grew so thick Amos drew his napkin to his face.

Margaret's brows pinched. "Are you all right?"

Amos wiped his forehead. As long as there was no more talk of the wedding night. Amos loosened his tie. He hadn't even thought to discuss that in his letters. Would theirs be a marriage in name only? He hoped not.

"Sophie?" Margaret asked, not looking at him.

Sophie's coloring had vanished. Her fingers clinched the collar of her dress. What a horrible fiancé he was turning out to be. He should be more focused on Sophie, not himself.

Amos took her free hand and rubbed his thumb along her smooth skin.

Sophie stared at their joined hands. "Shall I return closer to the wedding then?" Her voice fell into a whisper.

Return? But she'd only just gotten here. What if she left and changed her mind? Then where would that leave him? If Hanson had his way, Amos would never become their permanent pastor. Great. Now he was only thinking of his bride as a means to an end. But wasn't she? That's why he'd placed the ad for a wife in the first place, to prove to the board he held a maturity level beyond his boyish appearance and age.

"No, I never want you to leave." She was more than the way to achieve the church he'd wanted since his youth. Out of all the women who could have answered him, she was the one God had picked. His desire to know her better was further proof, and he couldn't do that if she left.

Her lips pulled up on one side. Amos wished she'd meet his gaze again.

"Ahhh. Now that is romantic. William, you should be writing this down. We may be old, but I'd still appreciate words such as those."

"You know I love you."

"A little reminding never hurt anyone. Surely, Pastor Gable could sneak away from the orphanage sooner, couldn't he? You can't let Sophie spend weeks at the boarding-house. Why, that Eleanor can make divine cookies, sure, but those biscuits of hers are as solid as rocks. I don't know how her guests manage to survive breakfast." She tapped on the table with her knuckles and grinned. "I have the grandest of ideas. Sophie can stay with us. William, my biscuits are some of the fluffiest, aren't they?"

"They are, but—"

"The quilting circle's gonna be downright envious. With me feeding you first, and now you staying here, this is too exciting. Do you need to fetch your other bags, or is it just the one until your trunk arrives? Do you want your biscuits with honey or butter or—or I don't have to make biscuits at all. I could bake bread or rolls or—"

"Marg, air." William took an exaggerated breath, his beard wiggling as he exhaled. "The room's full of it, sugar. Now's the time to take your share before you run clean out."

Margaret's narrow shoulders bounced up and down, too quick to have taken much of a breather.

"Good." He turned to Sophie. "You're welcome to stay with us. It will be our pleasure." He nodded at Amos. "In fact it would do our. . .the spare room good to have life in it again. It's yours as long as need be."

Amos crossed his arms. "Thank you, but—"

"Yes."

Amos frowned at Sophie's answer.

She nibbled her lip.

William rose and took hold of Margaret's elbow, lifting her from her seat. "We're going to go feed the table scraps to the hogs. We'll be back in a few moments." He ushered her outside, and the door slapped shut behind them.

Dusty sat up from his spot in the corner. His ears perked as if expecting to witness something exciting. Sophie fiddled with the carpetbag she'd insisted on putting under her chair.

Amos ran a hand through his hair. Would this become their first disagreement? Was it bad if they argued before they wed? On the very day they met. "Sophie—I don't think it best to take advantage of a member's kindness. Not sure how that would appear to the board before the vote."

She glanced at her hands. The floor. The doily. What was she thinking behind those big, dark eyes? "I—" Were those tears she blinked away? "I don't have money to pay for tomorrow night's room and board. Or beyond. I didn't. . . I mean. . . I don't have enough. I'm sorry. You're right, of course, about the vote. I should have waited to come. I–I'll think of something else."

She thought she'd have to pay for her nights at the inn? He scooted sideways in his chair until his knees touched hers. This time neither of them jerked away. "I know I haven't done a fair job of showing you yet, but I promise to take care of all your needs, Sophie. That's my job as your. . .as your husband. I'll pay your room and board until Pastor Gable arrives."

"Now Margaret. . ." William's voice was cut off by the opening of the door.

Once inside, Margaret pushed her shoulders back, making her appear almost tall with them seated. "I know it's none of my business, but—"

"You're right on that account." William said, slinking in behind her. He scooped more stew into his bowl.

Margaret clasped her fingers together. "Hilltop Chapel is a church that strives to help those in need. The Lord has blessed us, so we're required to bless others. Please let Sophie stay here. The elders will not frown upon you taking us up on our offer. If anything, they'll wonder why you didn't, and may think pride might be involved in your hindrance to accept. And trust me, it's best to keep Hanson far away from anything resembling a reason to send you on your way."

William wiped at his mustache. "What she says is true."

Amos sighed.

Margaret raised her hands toward the ceiling. "I'm taking that as a yes, Pastor Amos."

Dusty, not wanting to miss the celebrating, let out a bark that rattled the dishes.

"Let's see," Margaret drummed her fingers on her chin, "should I bake. . ."

Her voice faded as Amos watched Sophie's once quivering lips raise in a smile. He took her hand and pressed his lips to her skin. So this was what God intended within a marriage. The joy in making another happy.

She went rigid from his touch, and he dropped her hand. Perhaps he knew far too little about wooing Sophie after all.

Chapter 3

Sophie pushed the last of her pins into her tucked braid. The oval mirror revealed a woman ready for the day. She prayed she was.

The morning streamed inside the borrowed bedroom, providing more light than the small lamp on the bedside table. She still wasn't used to having a room with a window or one that had a ceiling tall enough to walk under without having to hunch over. Her so-called room growing up had been nothing more than storage in the attic of the saloon. Too cold in the winter and hot in the summer, but Momma had been wise to put her far from all the happenings of the night.

At Pastor and Mrs. T's house, the sunrise had been hindered by their bedframe. It had felt odd sleeping on a pallet in their bedroom, but during the weeks she'd been there, where space lacked, the faith and hope shared, well. . .it saved her life. Without them she never would have known the freeing power of Jesus. Which was why Sophie had to repay them by leaving. She didn't know how their daughter and her two little ones were going to fit inside that two-room house, but unlike Sophie, they didn't have any other options.

After reading her Bible, Sophie unfolded the second letter Amos had sent. The creased pages complained about being straightened, but she needed to study. To remember all the things he wrote, things he enjoyed, disliked. It was more than that though. She loved the snippets of his past. A far cry from her own, him having a father, a brother, a mother, one who'd been a respectable member of society.

Scanning Amos' words until she got to the middle paragraph, she read, hearing his voice in her head.

Upon my decision to attend seminary, I asked Pauline, my childhood sweetheart-of-sorts, to wait for me. Upon completion of my studies, we'd be wed. Or so I offered as much. She, however, for reasons beyond my understanding, sneered at the idea of becoming a minister's wife. Sadly, I do believe she thought it beneath her.

Noise outside paused her reading. Margaret and William had been in the kitchen earlier, but she hadn't wanted to interrupt their alone time. The new noise sounded like wheels and shuffling of horse hooves. She peaked from behind the curtain. A wagon sat in front of the Olmstead's home with Amos holding the reins.

Margaret beat her to the front door. "Good morning, Pastor Amos." Without her Sunday hat with that feather, Sophie easily saw over her head. "What're you doing on the milk run?" Margaret put her hands on her hips. "Eugene's not with ya?"

"He asked me to do his deliveries this morning." Amos ambled up the path to the front porch. All dressed like he had yesterday, as if he were about to stand in front of the pulpit, ready to give another sermon. Perhaps today she would be a better listener.

"Hope Eugene's not sick." William's voice boomed from the side yard. His heavy footsteps creaked over the porch boards until his profile was in view through the window. He must have already been at the barn with the pigs.

"No doubt that fox is more than fine. Probably roping in someone else to do his work. Forgot to warn you about him. Well, no need to stop here and waste more of your morning. We get milk from our own Tessa."

"Don't imagine that's why he's here, Marg." William's stomach jiggled with his throaty chuckle. "Couldn't stay away from his Sophie."

"I don't blame him. She is a keeper, that one."

Amos' face turned red, but his eyes smiled when he noticed her standing in the entryway behind Margaret.

Margaret followed his line of sight, and faced Sophie. "Well, good morning to you, too." The older woman studied her clothing with her eyebrows drawn together.

Sophie hoped her hair was behaving. She really could have used another pin or two to keep her braid more secure.

"I hadn't heard you wake. Quiet as a mouse you are."

William hooked his arms around Margaret's shoulders, blocking Sophie's view of Amos. "Marg, why don't you join me for a cup of coffee?"

"But we already. . .ah." She winked at Sophie as they made their way toward the kitchen. "What a splendid idea."

Amos adjusted his tie. "Mornin'."

Sophie touched the back of her hair. Her braids remained obedient. "Morning."

Dusty brushed against her skirt and then sat in between them like a guard dog. Except his tail swooshed, and he panted happily. He'd have to work on his threatening demeanor.

"I was wondering. . .since. . .I mean. . ." Amos bent over and scratched Dusty behind his ears. "You look nice today."

Was he talking to the dog or her?

"Not that you didn't look nice yesterday. Because you did. Look nice that is. Both yesterday. And today." He rocked on the balls of his feet and stole a glance at her.

Was it good that her fiancé was nervous around her? She pressed a hand to a flutter in her stomach. Apparently, the feelings were mutual.

On the road, the horse snorted, and the loaded wagon jilted forward a bit. Glass jars clanked together. Amos looked ready to run and grab hold of the reins, whether from the movement of the horse or from talking with her, she wasn't sure.

"Would you like to join me on the milk deliveries?" Amos still eyed the wagon, as if asking it the question. It would be nice if he'd peek at her again. Eyes often told the truth of the heart before a person was brave enough to speak it. Did he truly wish for her to go, or was he merely being considerate?

"Of course she would." Margaret burst through the doorway and thrust a covered basket into Sophie's side. "I packed you both a snack." She pulled Sophie along with her and threw the blanket draped across her shoulder into the back of the wagon beside one of the milk crates. "You can stop after you deliver at the Flemings'. Eugene gave you instructions about them, didn't he? I'm sure he did."

She nearly had to jump to give the horse a love-pat. "There's a field near there with a lovely shade tree. I've always wished William would take a notion to see it as the perfect picnic spot. What a sight the sun would be streaming through those dangly branches. Alas, I'll have to live my romantic notations through the both of you."

"May I help you up, Sophie?"

Sophie wanted nothing more than to spend the day with Amos, to prove that she could be the spouse he desired. Or rather, required. "I don't need a picnic," she whispered, taking his offered hand. "You probably have other pressing needs of the church to attend to today."

"The most pressing need of Hilltop this morning appears to be helping one of the elders deliver the milk." Amos covered a yawn. "And I would love some company."

"Isn't that sweet. You two have fun now. And Amos, you come on back over for supper. I'm making chuck wagon. If that don't tickle your fancy none, then I'll fry up some apricot fritters." Margaret waved until William stomped over and tugged her inside.

"He's on the board. . .this Eugene you're helping? For the vote?" The vote for her to be able to be Amos' bride.

Amos nodded, waiting until she was settled, and then strode to his side of the wagon. "This will be a good way for the congregation to see us serving the community and church members."

Sophie steadied herself on the seat, more so from the reminder of Amos' words than from the jarring start of the horse and wagon. Last night when he'd kissed her—well, her hand—she'd been surprised. Surprised that his touch hadn't stirred any awful memories. Then again, no man had ever kissed her before, not even on that horrid night. But it did make her wonder what he'd expect of her on their wedding night.

Amos loosened his grip as the wagon clattered down the road and turned slightly toward her, almost as if he felt her pain and was about to reach out and take her hand in his again. Last night while trying to sleep, she contemplated Amos' actions during supper, and she'd settled on him only holding and kissing her hand because Margaret and William were watching, encouraging their courtship. After all, William was on the board, too. The amount of people to impress seemed a heavier burden today, especially when she'd arrived thinking Amos was the only one needed to approve of her.

She laced her fingers, resting them on her lap, and blocked out thoughts of the past. God had wiped all that clean, and had given her a safe future with Amos. Hadn't He?

Words from Amos' first letter floated in her mind.

I need a God-fearing bride as soon as possible. Marriage will affirm my level of commitment to the church and will show that my maturity is beyond that of my youthful appearance.

Amos undoubtedly had received dozens of responses to his ad, but he'd written back to her. Pastor T had said God would always provide for her, and He had. Sophie couldn't lose this chance at a better future with an amiable, Christian man. God would help her through everything that would be required of her as a wife.

Lord, make me into a good pastor's wife. Give me wisdom.

But she must focus her sight on the first hurdle: keeping those at Hilltop Chapel happy, especially before the vote.

Amos finished his share of the lemonade Margaret had packed. Their morning milk delivery had been productive in two ways: the deliveries were complete, and Sophie had shown desirable qualities for a preacher's wife. She'd hopped off the wagon at each and every house without complaint. Her smile never drooped, and everyone seemed receptive of her. He wished Eugene delivered to more of the elders' houses. If only they could see their future pastor's wife in action. God had indeed chosen the perfect bride and helpmate for him.

Yes, everything had gone smoothly, except the one thing he'd hoped to accomplish hadn't happened—alone time with Sophie. Someone was always catching a ride on their wagon during their route, stealing the conversation. He should be grateful for the warm welcome Sophie was receiving. However, why did she feel the need to invite the Fleming children to their picnic? Was she not wanting to get to know him as much as he wanted to get to know her? Would they ever be alone enough to talk through what kind of marriage they each wanted?

The willow tree's branches danced around them. The smallest Fleming boy snuggled on Sophie's lap. His two older sisters, who had all followed them for their picnic stop, were squished up beside Sophie. The older boy sat right in front with his legs stretched, leaning in for Sophie's Bible story.

The blanket Margaret sent would have been the right size for the two of them; however, with it being shared by five, it left Amos resting against the tree trunk. Despite the scratchy bark digging into his back, it was the perfect spot to watch Sophie's eyes light up, shining like fresh coffee. Her dainty fingers swirled through the air as she relayed the story of Jonah and the whale.

She explained it to the children in a way that he wouldn't—couldn't— have. After spending two weeks studying the short book at seminary, he wasn't sure he would have left out all the fine details, details that would have passed over the children's heads, especially since the Fleming family hadn't attended a single service the past year. Or so Eugene had said after he'd pounded on the parsonage's door, waking Amos at four this morning. He claimed that going on the milk delivery would provide Amos a chance to grow his flock.

Amos scratched the stubble on his chin. Eugene had been right. It had been a good opportunity to show kindness, but he hoped he wouldn't have to do it every morning— the getting up at four part anyway.

The older Fleming boy scoffed. "That won't ever happen to me." He rubbed his palm against his ear. A bug crawled toward his thin legs, and he flicked it away. "There's no fish big enough around here to swallow me."

The youngest boy shook his head. His featherlight hair stood tall with the breeze. "Yeah–huh. Samuel said his brother caught one this big down on the river." He held his arms wide, looking from one end of his finger tips to the other.

"He also said you's was a baby when we's went frogging last night, and you's stayed home."

The youngest boy crossed his arms. His lip pushed out. "I wasn't no baby. Momma said I wasn't to go."

" 'Cause you scared of the dark."

"No, huh. Am not."

"Baa–bee. Tommy's a baby." He covered his eyes then shoved his hands wide. "Boo!"

The youngest shuddered in Sophie's arms.

Sophie clicked her tongue. "George, whether there is a fish large enough to swallow you or not isn't the point of the story."

Amos pushed off the ground and stood. He should have paid more attention to the children. He hadn't caught any of their names, but Sophie had. God knew he needed help with names. Hopefully Sophie was good at remembering faces, too.

"I know." The girl with the braids raised her hand, stretching taller. "It's that we're supposed to listen and obey. Like how you're supposed to listen to Momma when she tells you to stop picking on Tommy."

The other girl stuck out her tongue. "Yeah, George."

"I wasn't picking on him. I was telling the truth."

"God wants us to listen even when it's hard and even when we don't want to." Sophie patted George's knee. A wisp of dust from his dirty pants floated into the air.

George sprang up. "Time to go. Like her said." He tipped his chin at Sophie. "We gots to obey, and Pa said we gots chores."

Before running off, the three older children grabbed the food Sophie held out, pieces of bread, an apple, and something else wrapped inside a piece of cloth. Unlike his siblings, Tommy rested his head on Sophie's shoulder, not appearing to be going anywhere anytime soon.

"I wanna 'nother stor–wey."

Sophie gave the boy a squeeze. "I would be glad to tell you another. Maybe one about a lion?"

The boy nodded and swatted at his cotton hair, sending it away from his bright blue eyes.

"But, like Jonah should have done the first time, you need to obey, too. We'll do the lion story soon." She tapped the end of his rounded nose.

"You's promise?"

"I do. But you know even if I forget my promise—"

"I won't let you's forget."

Sophie hadn't laughed much, but Amos needed to make sure she did it more because it looked good on her. As did her holding a child. She'd want children, right? He wanted to be a father. . .eventually.

"Even if I do break my promise, there's someone who never breaks a promise. Someone we can always trust."

"The one from the whale stor—wey?"

"Yes, God. And He loves us very much."

Tommy's eyebrows pulled together. "He's real?"

"So very real." She placed her hand over her heart. "He—"

"Tom—mey!" One of the girls called. "Pa says you gots to do the fishing for supper."

Tommy snatched the apple left lying on the blanket. "Sees you soon, Mrs. Sophie." He took a bite from the apple, talking around his chewing. "I gots to obey. Don't want the real God to swallow me at the creek."

When he'd dashed away, Sophie's shoulders hunched. "That wasn't actually what I was getting at."

Amos parted some branches like curtains, finally getting his chance to be near. "You planted a seed. God's the one who grows and waters." He made sure to avoid the muddy footprints left on the blanket.

"You were great with them." Here might be the best opportunity to discuss future children of their own. He hoped his words wouldn't offend, but if Pauline's dismissal had taught him anything, it was never to assume, no matter how things appeared on the surface.

He ran his knuckles across his cheek. His face plumb itched. It'd been years since he hadn't shaved first thing in the morning. "Do you. . ." He tucked his long legs underneath him. "Since. . ." Why was his throat dry? He drank half the container of lemonade. Must be that stupid tie. He yanked at the tight knot, but it didn't budge.

"May I?" Her fingers touched his, and he stilled. "Why do you wear this all the time if you don't like it? It's plain to see that your tie and you aren't the best of friends."

He rolled the silken material into a circle. He didn't hate it exactly. Ma had made it for him when he first announced he wanted to become a preacher. Pa had thumped him on the back and said how proud he was.

"We had to wear them at seminary. Thought it would help show the Hilltop members. . ." He shrugged. "To look the part." To make the best impression. Ever since they'd funded his hometown church's rebuilding after a fire, he was determined to show his gratitude and become their pastor one day. And that day was now.

"Like how you needed a wife. To act the part of a good pastor?"

Not *good*, per say, for scripture says that no one was good, but capable, yes. He wanted to appear to be a capable preacher, because he was.

He should go ahead and ask if she wanted children. Even preachers wanted. . .well, husband rights and all that. They needed to discuss those topics before they wed, but above all, he desired to remove that look of disappointment. Like the idea of marrying her was as uncomfortable as wearing his constricting tie. It wasn't in the least.

Hanson had stated Amos didn't even look old enough to get married. To prove he was ready for such a responsibility as shepherding a large congregation and to keep Hanson happy, Amos placed the mail-order bride ad like many of the elders had suggested. Yet Amos was also getting married because he wanted to.

He may appear younger than his twenty-two years, but with his training and love for Christ, he was ready for Hilltop. Plus, watching his folks had embedded the longing for a loving, built-in friendship. They made marriage look easy.

She lifted the edge of his tie only inches from where his fingers had once rested. "Pastor T didn't wear one every day. When we met, he was covered in dirt from head to toe. His appearance didn't hinder God from using him. It probably helped."

She was right, of course. What he wore shouldn't matter, but his mind was already off in another direction. She had mentioned so little about herself, he was eager for more. The letter she'd sent after her first reply had been but half a page and had only really answered the questions he had for her in his previous letter. "Pastor T? You were quite close to him?" Was this preacher a younger man? Had she had feelings for him at one point?

A wrinkle appeared on her forehead and something like hurt flashed in her eyes. She nodded and picked at a string on the blanket. "He saved my life."

Chapter 4

Sophie held her yellow dress up to her neck. A loose thread on its hem danced along the floor. She shook her head. Her flowered calico would have to do. One couldn't wear anything in need of actual stitching to meet those in the quilting circle.

A knock sounded, but as always, Margaret didn't wait for Sophie's response. The door swung open, thumping against the dresser. A different hat, with a feather twice the size of the one from Sunday, completed Margaret's navy skirt and buttoned blouse. "You look darling. Everything's all packed for the day, only waiting on you." She wrinkled her nose. Never a good sign.

"Should I wear something else?" Not that she had many other options. Would Amos be embarrassed if she wore the same dress twice in a row to see the ladies of the church? She bit the edge of her thumbnail and glanced at her carpetbag. No help would be found hiding in there. If only she'd gotten to bring Momma's trunk. There would have been a few salvageable pieces. An apron at least. Perhaps she'd been too hasty about burning her favorite skirt the week before. That stain would have washed. The rip mendable. . .

Heat flushed her body and the room tilted to the side. Sophie leaned into the dresser for balance. Her vision darkened even though her eyes were open.

A cool glass was pushed into her hand. Sophie blinked away the stars. She focused on the water trembling inside the cup.

"Child, you're shaking." Margaret helped bring the glass to her lips. "That's a girl. Drink. Go on."

The water seeped down her throat, extinguishing the dryness, but not the flamed memory. She thought God had healed her completely. Especially after she'd felt so comfortable in Amos' presence, and her dreams had been pleasant since she'd arrived.

Moisture on the outside of the glass pooled together. Much like how she needed to compose herself. No more thoughts about Momma's things or her old clothing. What was done was done. There could be no more remembering that night and what it had cost.

"Maybe you need to stay home?" Margaret felt Sophie's forehead then held both cheeks in her palms.

Sophie forced a smile and ended her silent plea with God for His continual assistance. She had to meet the church ladies. She had to earn their votes, or rather their husband's votes. Becoming a preacher's wife had to work. She couldn't go back and stay with Pastor and Mrs. T now that their daughter and grandchildren were coming back home. And the saloon wasn't an option. What if Junior decided she hadn't paid enough and came looking for her a second time. . . .

The room tilted again.

She unlocked her knees. "I—I'm fine. Promise." Or she would be with God's help. And Amos'. She was a new woman. Pastor T had assured her, and she knew it to be true. All because of the cost paid on the cross.

Sophie swallowed another sip of water and set down the glass. "Is this dress all right? I wasn't sure what to wear."

"Didn't you hear me earlier? You look darling. But with your figure you could wear a flour sack, and it'd still manage to bring out those beautiful brown eyes." Margaret covered her mouth. "Goodness. That didn't sound proper. There's nothing wrong with wearing clothes made from flour sacks. Not at all. We even make them for the orphans." She shook her head, the giant feather bouncing along for the ride. "Margaret Luella Olmstead." She grunted at the ceiling. "Forgive me, Lord."

Margaret's cold hand wrapped around Sophie's wrist. "We shouldn't keep the circle waiting. They're already fit to be tied because I've fed and housed you, and all some of them got was a quick introduction after service." She stopped. The feather on her hat drifted back, tickling Sophie's nose. "Unless you are truly unwell?"

Sophie waited for the urge to sneeze to pass. "I'm sure it's only nerves."

"There's nothing to be nervous about. These are some of the finest ladies around. And Mrs. Grouse is sure to bring her apple dumplings. They plum melt in your mouth, and that ain't no lie."

With the sewing kit and the leftover apricot fritters from last night in hand, the walk to the boardinghouse was shorter than Sophie remembered. Two quilt frames were set up on the large porch. A pair of oaks shaded a semicircle of mismatched chairs that faced the steps. Only two seats were available, and they weren't side by side.

Margaret hooked her arm around Sophie's. It seemed half the church was here, and all the ladies watched her and Margaret arrive. "Good morning. As most of you know, this here is our Sophie."

The ladies near threw down their needles and rushed over. Sophie hadn't been involved in such a commotion since she'd snuck down the stairs two years ago and witnessed the saloon owner, Clyde, kick out the spirited King brothers for sabotaging a round of Faro.

As Sophie was ushered into a chair, the tray of fritters disappeared from her grip, and instead a plate of cookies appeared on her lap.

"—and that's how I became famous for my. . ."

"You can't be famous for something as simple as cookies." Another voice near shouted.

Sophie hugged her fingers around the beautiful porcelain plate, afraid the quilting circle would crush them both.

"And why not? Go on, dearie." A button-nose lady stuck her face in front of Sophie's. Her breath smelled like lemons. "Give them a taste. That will prove to Eleanor my cookies are the softest this side of the Ohio River."

Eleanor? The one with the hard-as-rock biscuits? When Sophie had stayed at the boardinghouse she'd skipped the breakfast to make it to church on time, and it had been an elderly man who had shown her to a room. Was Eleanor the one in the green or flower-patterned dress?

"Ladies. We're here to quilt." Sophie heard Margaret, but her short stature left her lost in the swarm.

"Quite right, and to get to know our new pastor's wife, who you've been hogging."

Seated on the ground under the nearest tree, a redheaded girl, not much younger than Sophie, crossed her arms. A smug look on her face. "Do you play the piano?"

"Oh." Sophie covered her mouth as a crumb of cookie landed on the ground. The bite may have been soft, but it didn't seem to want to go down. Everyone stopped their elbowing and turned their eyes on her. Even the heated breeze quieted for Sophie's response.

The correct answer was written all over the ladies' faces, and Sophie wanted desperately to speak a lie. Why hadn't Sophie thought about how Mrs. T played at service every week? Why did she think she could become a preacher's wife? "I don't. I'm terribly sorry." How long would it take her to learn?

A tall woman clumped down the steps with a pitcher of lemonade in her hands. "Wait. What did I miss?" The crowd parted and meandered back to their original chairs. But not a soul looked prepared to return to their stitching anytime soon. The younger girl stormed toward the boardinghouse. She sent one more glare over her shoulder before disappearing inside.

The button-nosed lady seated across the circle patted her chest and scowled at Sophie. "She doesn't play the piano."

The lemonade woman's eyes widened. "No." How she made such a small word draw out into three syllables, Sophie hadn't the slightest. And apparently, the woman lost the ability to shut her mouth. "Surely, as a preacher's wife, you can indeed play the piano?"

"Ladies." Margaret arrived behind her, placing her hands on the back of Sophie's chair as if to offer support. Good thing, because she needed it. Oh, how Sophie wished the chair beside her was open so Margaret could weather this storm near her. "We have at least four pianists in our congregation, not counting the learning children. And I don't think you are eager to find a replacement for your bench on Sunday morning quite yet? Am I right, Judith?"

"Well, no, but I. . ." Judith bustled, the lemonade sloshing inside the crystal pitcher. Her nose rose so high it seemed she was trying to guess what someone planned to cook for supper. "Through the years, *all* of Hillside's preacher wives have. . ."

Sophie's cheeks heated. She eyed the lemonade pitcher. Perhaps she could take it and press it to her face? This would have been an excellent moment to have had one of Momma's fans. How was she going to convince these women she had to be voted in as their pastor's wife? She had to marry Amos. Her future depended on it.

An elderly woman hobbled over. Her weathered skin was spotted and wrinkled, but her eyes sparked with life. She tapped her cane on the grass. "You cats are scaring this poor girl to death. Honey." She tilted Sophie's chin upward. "My name's Beulah." Her smile was missing two top teeth, but it wasn't lacking warmth. "Do you know how to stitch? Before you answer that, Hilltop Chapel may be known for its quilts, but there's no shame in not knowing how to sew. We've been blessed to have plenty who can teach. Isn't that right, Linda?"

The button-nose lady sat up straighter. "Yes, ma'am. Mrs. Grouse taught me how to improve my blind stitch. We're a church who gives their knowledge, their time, and their quilts, of course." She smiled proudly, but then her face paled, and she blinked at Sophie. "I'm sorry about before." She whispered. "Margaret and Mrs. Grouse are right. We don't need another pianist."

Sophie set her plate under her chair and grabbed a needle from an opened kit. There was no need for an apology. Heaven knows worse things had been said about her than not being able to play an instrument. "Will you show me where I'll be most needed?"

Linda's smile returned. "It would be an honor."

"There. That sounds like a hearty Hilltop welcome. Now, hop to it. We've got children who need blankets. If we finish four by sunset, I'll make everyone some of my apple dumplings."

And just like that, Beulah had the women silenced and their needles darting. The old woman gave Sophie a slight case of homesickness. Not for her old attic room or even for Momma, but for Mrs. T and her daily encouragement. "Us newcomers have to stick together."

Sophie couldn't help the confusion she felt line her face.

"It seems like yesterday I was like you. Trying to find my chair in this hen circle. I, too, was a mail-order bride." She patted Sophie's shoulder. A slight aged tremble made her nod appear more like a swinging motion. "There's your chair, and trust me, once you're in, you're in."

Margaret raised her needle in the air as if to toast in agreement with Beulah. As long as she had Beulah and Margaret on her side, things would go smoothly. After all, the Lord knew they had to.

If only He'd remove the nervous flutter threatening her stomach. Shouldn't it be growing weaker instead of gaining strength?

On their evening walk, Sophie rolled her tight shoulders. She and Amos approached the Olmstead's house, their alone time disappearing like their conversation had. Amos hadn't once asked any more about her past or Pastor T. How could he not have understood who Pastor T was from her letters? Had he not cherished her words as she had his?

Sophie bit her lip and braved asking Amos about her ruining Hillside's tradition. "Do you think the board is upset about my lack of piano skills?"

He chuckled until he read her expression. "Nothing was said in seminary about the need for me to marry a pianist. A God-fearing woman, yes, but your lack of piano skills wouldn't be a good enough reason to break my promise to wed you, even to Hillside. Unless. . ." His arm tensed under her fingers. "Are *you* wanting released from our pledge? From the engagement?"

Sophie pressed her free hand to her chest. It didn't quite erase the sharp pain of panic. He wasn't serious, was he? How could anyone not want Amos to marry them? His childhood sweetheart had been a fool to reject him. He was honest, and dependable, and loved the Lord. And. . .she felt her cheeks blush as she took in his handsome profile.

She forced her voice steady. "I'm looking forward to being your wife." Even if that meant taking piano lessons or learning to juggle fire.

Once they ascended the porch steps, Amos set his hazel eyes on hers with an intensity that stole her breath. She prayed he liked the idea of marrying her because of who she was, and not only to please a congregation that wanted him to be married—to anyone.

He cleared his throat. "May I. . .since we. . . Could I kiss you good night, Sophie?"

Her gaze dropped to Amos' mouth then back to his eyes. He wanted to kiss her? Her heart thumped in time with the fluttering in her stomach. The very thing that hadn't stopped since he'd asked if she wanted to take a stroll after supper.

She squeezed her fingers around a handful of the fabric on her dress. "Mmm–hmm."

A bug buzzed near her ear, and the steady clipping of Dusty's claws on the porch set her nerves ablaze. Should she say something else? All she managed to do was swallow.

Amos clasped her hand and brought it to his lips. He brushed them against her skin, just as he'd done the first day she'd arrived.

It was lovely. And perfect. And disappointing.

The front door flew open. Margaret held up a wooden spoon. "Perfect timing." She waved the spoon toward the kitchen. "Doughnuts are done, and William's already had half the batch. If the two of you don't hurry, there won't be any left."

"Actually, Margaret," Amos said, "I think I need to head back to the parsonage. I have some things to attend to."

"Oh." Margaret said with a huff, her smile slipping away.

William filled the doorway, wiping a crumb from his beard. "More for me then. We should have visitors stay with us more often. You've not cooked me doughnuts in forever." William steered Margaret back toward the kitchen. "We'll leave you two to your good night."

Amos traced his thumb in a circle on her hand, a gesture she could get used to. Was that her who sighed?

"Thank you for walking with me." His voice low, his thumb still tracing.

"Mmm–hmm." Really? That's all she could say?

Amos released her and shoved his hands into his pockets. "Well. Until tomorrow." He did sigh. "Actually, I have a pretty full schedule. I'm sorry, but—"

"You don't have to apologize." Disappointment almost made her dizzy, but she tightened her features to keep it from showing. She needed to remember the church came first.

His eyes seemed darker, deeper tonight under the dimming sun. He nodded. "It's a good night then, and I'll see you soon."

"Good night, Amos."

"Night, Sophie." He rocked forward once, twice, and then retreated down the steps.

Dusty whined and followed at his heels. The smell of Margaret's dessert danced in the air. Amos paused before he reached the end of the grass. He wiped his palm down his face and then marched back.

Sophie curled her toes in her boots. Had he changed his mind about the piano thing? She couldn't read his reaction when he avoided her eyes.

Stopping inches away, he ran his knuckles along her cheek. His gentle, inviting touch was so different from her memories that she didn't flinch when he erased the space between them. He lowered his lips to hers. There was no past, only the present. Right now, in the safe arms of Amos—her future.

Her first kiss.

And it was perfect.

"Good night, my Sophie." His voice was barely louder than her drumming heartbeat. She never wanted to miss him saying her name like that again. *My Sophie.* "I'll miss seeing you in the morning."

"Mmm–hmm." Was he holding her up? He had to be. Her legs were numb. Did all kisses do that?

He kissed her on the forehead then took two steps away. "It's getting late."

Sophie gained control of her legs and turned the door handle. "I'll. . ." Her lips tingled. "See you soon."

His crooked grin made her stomach do another round of flutters. "Mmm–hmm." His voice rumbled in his chest.

Sophie tucked a piece of hair behind her ear and crossed the threshold. She closed the door, pressing her back against it. Her fingertips rested on her grin, feeling its foreign shape on her face. Becoming a mail-order bride was by far the best thing that ever happened to her. Well, almost. But not much could beat giving away her first kiss to her soon-to-be husband.

If only that wasn't one of the last "firsts" she had to offer him.

Chapter 5

Amos finally figured out how to be a good fiancé. He'd just skip it.

"I think we're going to move up the wedding." His folks would be disappointed to miss their eldest son's wedding, but the way Sophie leaned into him during their parting last evening, he was confident she wouldn't oppose the idea.

William stopped the bucket in his hands before a drop splashed into the trough. The momma hog snorted in disapproval, hopefully from the lack of water. "Hadn't heard Pastor Gable was coming in earlier."

The wind shifted, and Amos wrinkled his nose. One didn't have to see the hogs to know they were near. After setting the scrap bucket near the gate, Amos covered a yawn. It wasn't the anticipation of another milk run that had kept him up. But the lack of sleep was worth it because it earned him a plan. "Thought Sophie and I could travel his way. Save him a trip, or we could head to the nearest town and—"

William raised his brows and emptied the bucket of water. "Now you know plain well Margaret has her heart set on Hilltop celebrating your wedding."

Momma hog dipped her snout into the water, and air bubbles filled the trough. She lifted her head with a more encouraging expression than William's. If only Margaret would let Amos and Sophie get a word in to each other during dinner. Discussing flowers and lace and cakes wasn't particularly helpful in establishing a relationship.

"It's not exactly her wedding."

William stepped into the pen and the piglets raced toward him. His boots sank into the muck, right where Amos should be for saying such a rude comment.

Two slurping steps later, William surprised him with a smirk. "Right you are, boy."

Amos ground his jaw. *Boy?* He looked young, however, that didn't mean the Lord hadn't given him wisdom and the ability to make his own decisions. Good decisions. Like having Sophie as his wife come this time next week, or better yet—tomorrow.

"You're anxious, and the two of you seem well suited. But you can wait a couple more weeks, can't you? It would look better to the whole congregation if you did. The elders may be doing the actual casting of ballots, but. . ."

William plucked the littlest piglet, flipping him over, and held him like an infant. "A little marriage advice." He rubbed the piglet's ears as if it were Dusty. "A husband always takes his wife's nag—" He glanced at the back porch. "Her helpful and constant suggestions. But anyone worth his salt will consider his wife's opinions. The quilting circle doesn't have you and Sophie's bridal quilt complete. And you know what that means."

Amos kicked at an escaped mud clump on his side of the fence. It's not like he and Sophie couldn't use the quilt on another night. Or several other nights. Unfortunately,

William was right. Amos needed every vote. His longing to lead Hilltop's congregation was worth the long weeks, even if he could hardly wait to make Sophie his.

Hilltop was any preacher's ideal church. What kind of people volunteered to help those they've never met, miles away? None of the area churches had offered aid to his burnt hometown church, but Hilltop had sent enough funds to completely rebuild.

It wasn't fate that on the very week Amos finished his seminary studies, Hilltop's pastor moved to Kentucky to further help the orphanage their church assisted. It was God providing opportunity. Now if only Amos could get more of them to bring their Bibles to service. But maybe they'd given those away, too? He'd settle on them agreeing to a midweek service along with Sundays.

"William." Eugene's voice interrupted the noise of the hogs as they rolled and scampered about. The wiry, gray-haired milkman bent over near the lean-to shielding the fattened hogs. After he stopped gulping air as if it were molasses, he spared a glance Amos' way. "Hanson's holding an elders' meeting."

A growl rumbled in William's chest. The piglet in his arms squirmed and the others fled from around his ankles. "Lord, help me. That man. . .he ain't what he used to be." William set the piglet near its momma, before slamming the gate shut. "Let's get to it. Can't wait to see what he's come up with this time."

Amos pumped his arms to keep up. At their pace, it was as if they were heading for battle. Maybe that's why Eugene was sweating? The white church did look a bit like a surrender flag high on the hill. William kept grumbling, and Amos did what he could—prayed. If only he knew exactly what he was praying for.

Come to find out, it was convenient the elders were meeting. They may have to vote on replacing the front doors the way William barreled through them.

"What's this all about, Hanson? This isn't protocol." Mud splattered off William's boots, raining down on the floor. Poor Beulah. How did that woman in her age manage to shine those boards on her hands and knees? The second time this week he'd caught her hard at work, even though the wood was already as clean as Margaret's serving platter.

Hanson stood behind the pulpit. He murmured something that sounded like, "Be happy you're here at all." He pointed to Amos. "Lowry, stay outside."

William blocked Amos' chest with his arm, as if they were seated on a buckboard and William was protecting a child during a sudden stop. "If this is an elders' meeting, Pastor Amos should be included. This will soon be his church."

Hanson narrowed his eyes. "Have it your way, William. But your way is about to end."

Amos followed William to the third row. Where did Hanson's anger stem from? Amos had jumped through all the hoops Hanson had set up. Agreed to the trial months as temporary pastor. Had referral letters from other preachers sent—all required five of them. Endured three grueling interrogations that these men called interviews. Had even secured a mail-order bride just to prove his ability to become their full-time preacher.

Hanson propped both elbows on the podium. "Remember how I wanted a deeper background check on Lowry but not a one of you listened?"

William stood. "This is how we're starting the meeting?"

"We don't need all your legal mumbo jumbo. Everyone can tell we're all accounted for." Hanson shot a glare at Amos. "Even have an extra."

"Perhaps I'll start with prayer?" No one protested, unless Hanson's crossing of arms counted, but before Amos could bow his head, Hanson stepped in front of the podium and started.

"Sent my boy to check on Lowry's hometown and to that seminary he claimed he went to." Hanson ran his tongue over his teeth. "Lowry told the truth."

Who would have guessed the word *truth* could sound as if someone had died of dysentery?

A man in the front row rose. He was some relation to the family who ran the barber shop, a cousin, or maybe a son-in-law? "I left Nancy's side for that?" He slapped a cap onto his balding head. "If I miss her giving birth for a meeting we didn't need, she'll have both our hides."

If Sophie were here, she'd have remembered the man's name. Didn't it start with a *V*? Victor or Vernon, maybe?

"Sit down, Willes."

Willes? Yes, it was Vernon. Nancy and Vernon Willes, because *Willes* in Amos' memory meant Nancy "*wills*" have another baby soon. They always sat on the second to last row on the left. Amos could tell exactly where each of the men in the room sat during service, but for the life of him couldn't name half of them. Quite a thorn in his side for a preacher to have such a problem.

Amos sent up another prayer thanking God for Sophie and her knack for faces and names. Yesterday on their way to visit with the Fleming children, she'd patiently explained how to tell between the girls: Beth and Bertha. Amos would have never thought to inspect their earlobes.

"I wouldn't think to bring you here for nothing. I told you all. Lowry's the wrong preacher for Hilltop from the start. Now you'll see I'm correct. If a man can't even get his bride right, how can anyone trust him with the matters of this church?"

Amos' gut clenched. How dare he bring Sophie into this?

William cleared his throat. "Hanson. You best watch yourself. Miss Ross is—"

"A sin-infested saloon girl." Hanson nodded at the collective gasp from the four packed rows. "That's right, men. And I will not allow my church to be drug through the mud because this—this naive, blinded-by-pretty-looks preacher. . . For the hundredth time, he's too young. Too inexperienced. A pastor's wife should be one of upstanding, moral conduct. All of which a saloon girl is not. I re-propose we offer the pastorship to Emerson Pokis. He's twenty years Lowry's senior. And his wife plays the piano."

Amos pressed his back against the pew and glared at the piano. He pried his grip from the board beneath him. Never would he have guessed a member of Hilltop would stoop to lying to get their way.

"Why do we need another piano player? We already got Judith and Miss Hays, and I think even Mrs. . . . ." The middle-aged man whose seat during service was next to the middle window flinched when Hanson slapped his palm on the podium.

Hanson's nostrils flared, and the mole above his eyebrow seemed to grow. "A. Saloon. Girl. Is there corn in your ears? You want to go to a church where your wives and daughters are being mentored by a dance-hall girl?"

William leaned over. "You know anything about this?"

Amos closed his mouth and shook his head. His Sophie. . .a. . .he reached for his tie, but it wasn't there. He hadn't worn one since Sophie told him her pastor T hadn't. Something must be hindering his ability to breathe. He loosened his collar.

It didn't help.

"If what Hanson says is true, then Pastor Amos can order himself a new bride from the other applicants he received. It's not his fault this woman was a—a. . .well, you know." The pianist's husband squared his shoulders. "Pastor Amos shouldn't be tarnished because of that woman. I still vote to keep him on as a candidate."

"Agreed. His sermons are quicker than Pastor Gable's ever were." Someone said from the fourth row. "I've not fallen asleep once during Pastor Amos'."

The shortest man in Hilltop's congregation raised his hand. It almost cleared the top of William's head. "I have a cousin twice removed on the other side of the river. She's a good church girl. She's not too old for Pastor Amos." His voice deep and low, a contradiction to his short statue. "Not if he hurries."

Amos slid his knuckles down his thighs. Pauline had been a good churchgoing girl, too, and look where that led him. Not that it mattered. He was not going to choose a new bride. He wanted Sophie. God had sent her to him.

Before he could stand, a hand squeezed his shoulder, holding him in his pew. "Wait a minute there, son. Let these menfolk handle this."

Son? Menfolk? Would the congregation view him differently after the vote, and not as someone they had to watch over? William hadn't even let him defend himself.

William placed his finger and thumb in his mouth and produced an ear-piercing whistle. Then again, the man did handle Hanson better than most. But wasn't Amos there to shepherd them? Not the other way around. "Hanson, do you have proof of your accusation?"

That's how William wanted to handle things? By further pursuing the lie Hanson created?

"I had my boy stop by the place where Miss Ross hailed from."

How'd he know Sophie's information? Grasping for straws anyway possible, that's all this was. Amos shook his head.

The postmaster sent a nervous squint over his shoulder. So much for confidentiality concerning him and Sophie's letters.

"So, it's Oliver's word against the. . ." Vernon blinked and removed his cap again. "Miss Ross'?"

Hanson huffed. His whiskered cheeks grew as round as a gathering squirrel's. "And half her town. Won't be hard to receive an official statement from their sheriff. I'm sure of it. I'll even pay for the wire myself."

Amos rubbed his numbing palms together. What if Sophie had been a lady of the night? Maybe she didn't have the best past for a preacher's wife, but that's what it was—past. God had the power to wash clean all her sin, just as He did all the men in here. And then there was always Hosea and Gomer's story in the Bible to consider.

Plus, Amos would never find a flawless candidate to become a preacher's wife like they wanted. One didn't exist.

He used the back of the pew in front of him to help him stand. "I'm not giving up on Sophie."

William patted his back so heartily Amos pitched forward. "I think what Pastor Amos is trying to say is even if Miss Sophie's past wasn't what we anticipated, she isn't on that path anymore."

Amos held in his own growl and slumped back down. Why did William always jump in and save him? The congregation would never seek him for spiritual council if he couldn't show himself capable.

"She could be waiting until after the wedding to return to her heathen ways. Then our reputation would be ruined. We can't trust her."

All the voices piled together. "Then we'd hire ourselves a new pastor. No harm done."

Everyone's except Hanson's. His held the most venom. "Or we hire someone else now." The words echoed across the vaulted ceiling. "Save the church a stained reputation. Imagine her influence on our womenfolk."

Amos massaged his temples. Indeed, he had marched his way into a battle. With all this talk of the women in the congregation, what about Hanson's? His redheaded daughter, Ruby, had all but snubbed him when Amos first introduced himself weeks ago. He'd not met Hanson's wife yet. Had she passed? It would explain a few things. He should discuss it with William, but all Amos wanted to do was hightail it to Sophie. Not because he had to know all about her past sins. But it had been a whole day since he'd seen her. When he'd finally finished preparing Sunday's sermon notes, she and Margaret hadn't returned from delivering a batch of cookies to the girl who'd broken her arm.

The thought of kissing Sophie again hadn't been far from his mind. Which meant he couldn't—wouldn't—order himself another bride. Sophie had already become a part of him. That's why when she arrived and first introduced herself without her Christian name, he hadn't recognized it. After receiving her first letter she had simply become—his Sophie.

"Everyone in favor of keeping Pastor Lowry as potential candidate for our pulpit, say, 'Aye.'" A handful of those responded. "Those opposed?" A few nays sounded.

"Willes?" Hanson sputtered. "Really?"

"The aye's have it by three. Two refused to vote. And I counted Hanson in already as a no. Thought that was a given."

"Thanks, Charles. All right. Pastor Amos' official vote for pastorship remains on schedule for the first of the month when Pastor Gable arrives."

Well, one good thing came from this meeting. The pianist husband's name was Charles.

"Whoa." Hanson gripped his belt. The butt of a pistol sparkled in the dimming light. "You all know what you voted for? To keep a wretch as a potential preacher's wife."

That was more than enough. "She's not a wretch. She's my intended. And a child of—"

"You're wrong, Lowry. Trust me, you better not hitch yourself to such a woman. You'll regret it."

"Enough, Hanson. You had your say. Meeting's adjourned." William's bushy beard covered much of his clenched jawline, but his tone wasn't missed.

While the elders may still have Amos set to become their preacher, the snarl Hanson produced dropped the victory to its deathbed. Amos shut his eyes. Becoming a pastor to a church who won't heed to his council. . . Was that what he'd always dreamed of?

Chapter 6

Amos extended his elbow past the entryway. "You ready?" He looked at Sophie like she was an answered prayer, but they both knew she wasn't. Not anymore. Her fingernails dug into her palms. "Are you sure?"

Dusty's tail swayed, brushing up against Amos' pant leg and the house. Amos' lips tugged a bit to the side. "Yes. I'm ready." His full smile had gone missing since the elders' meeting. "Question was, are you?" He peered around her. "Do we need to help Margaret carry any last items to church?"

Sophie steadied herself against the doorframe. She shouldn't have skipped breakfast. Dusty agreed, because he inched closer and gave a low-pitched whine. "No. Margaret and William took everything earlier. I mean. Are you sure. . ." She stared at his shoes. Dusty put his nose on her arm. "I won't blame you. . .you know, since Hanson. . ."

Amos lifted her hand and traced his thumb along her skin. Tingles danced up her arm before settling in her stomach. Would she ever find another man like Amos? Who was she kidding? A preacher was the only type of man who would have accepted her upbringing.

"Sophie." Even the way he spoke her name made the flutters ignite again. "I pledged to marry you. God never breaks His promises, and I strive to be more like Him each day."

"But—"

"We've already talked this through. Do you still hold to your admission that you wrote to me explaining your background?"

Sophie nodded. Mrs. T had been with her when she'd sent the letters off. So how did only her first response and last letter arrive?

"Sophie Anne Ross." Amos dropped onto his knee. "I prayed for a bride, and I was sent you. Many days and nights were spent praying for you. For us. And even after Hanson tried. . ." He exhaled. "God's still in control here. You are the one He has for me." He placed his other hand over his heart. "Your upbringing wasn't something you chose. You aren't accountable for your mother's actions. Only your own. The Bible is clear on that."

"Then we are still to wed?"

Standing, he opened her palm and placed a kiss inside. "If you'll still have me." He fisted her fingers, as if wrapping the kiss inside like a gift—one of a decent future.

Even if she had any other options, she wouldn't want them. He was her calm after the storm of life she'd lived. "Always," she whispered.

"Excellent." He really was handsome, more so when he smiled.

Walking along Main Street, Shipley's General Store had its closed sign flipped in the window. The whole town had packed up and gone to today's church social. If only they'd all come back for Sunday's sermon. Laughter and the aroma of fish reached her nose before Hilltop came into view. Sophie's stomach grumbled but not of hunger. Strange.

The lawn surrounding the hill had its grass covered by an arrangement of blankets and a few makeshift tables. The fire with the kettles of lard were located near the largest shaded area. Margaret had explained that Hilltop Chapel's fish fry was more than a social gathering. Even though some of the town's folk were in need, they didn't want to be exposed as not having enough. Those who wanted extra funds could bring in their catch and get paid, and if they stayed and helped to clean and filet the fish, then an extra nickel was earned. The members of Hilltop had the calendar full of such events. Maybe that's why they vetoed Amos' suggestion of adding a Bible service to the middle of the week.

Margaret met them as they neared. "Here." She handed Sophie a glass of tea. "You look parched. Would you like to go with me to visit the ladies?" She tilted her chin to where most of the quilting circle had gathered on blankets on the flattest part of the church lawn. All their eyes were locked onto Sophie.

News about her upbringing no doubt surprised them, but like Amos had mentioned more than once, she wasn't responsible for her momma's actions. If only they'd agree. Beulah had said she'd already earned her chair. . . . Sophie wiped her forehead. Hopefully, there'd be time to win them over. How much longer until Pastor Gable arrived, anyway?

Amos' nose crinkled. "Would the ladies mind if I keep her with me for a bit longer? Especially since I'll be busy most of the day tomorrow reviewing the sermon. I've found that I can't get too much of her company."

Margaret fanned her face. "How precious. But Sophie, you'd be the only lady over by the kettles. It's the men's duty today; however, maybe. . ." She grimaced at the ladies. "They may need some more time to adjust to Sophie's. . . Well, how about I come rescue you from the men in a bit? We still need to line up the desserts for the auction. Oh, and don't forget, I made an additional carrot cake to keep at home for us to have tonight after the social."

Amos pushed his sleeves up to his elbows and then flipped his tie over his shoulders. He'd gone back to wearing one after the elders' meeting. Did those men realize what control they held? "Let's go try our hands at some frying."

The heat of the day would have been warm enough, but adding the fire and bubbling lard, Amos couldn't keep his sleeves rolled up high enough. Vernon draped his arm around Amos' shoulder, the temperatures apparently not affecting him. "Don't you worry about Hanson." And then there was the smolder from all the gossip. "He can't sway us. In fact, if you want to choose *not* to get married, I can discuss it with the rest of the board. They might be in favor of keeping you even if you're unmarried."

Amos reached for Sophie's hand. Did he not see her standing right next to him? How his statement might make her feel? "We're getting wed when Pastor Gable arrives."

William dropped the rest of the fish into the angry grease. He placed the empty bowl under Vernon's nose. "Mind getting me another load?"

Before Vernon answered, Sophie grabbed the bowl. "It'd be my pleasure, William."

Amos stepped with her, but she shook her head, leaning near his ear. All at once he no longer cared if it was 200 degrees, he wanted her beside him forever. "You stay. Visit. I just need. . ." The rest of her words were said with her eyes.

He placed what he hoped was a comforting hand on the small of her back before she headed down the hill for the cleaning station.

Thankfully the men's conversation turned to more pleasing topics—how to properly filet fish and which methods worked best for a breached calf. They chuckled after one of Eugene's stories, and Amos felt a tug on the back of his shirt. He turned to find Tommy Fleming.

The boy's eyes were filled with worry. Maybe he hadn't turned in his catch of the day yet. That didn't matter. Amos would buy the fish himself if needed.

"Preacher man. Your missus needs ya real bad."

Amos' legs buckled. His Sophie? He sprinted ahead of Tommy and found Sophie on her knees, halfway up the hill. The requested cleaned fish spilt all over the ground with Beth Fleming squatted, caressing Sophie's back.

He dropped to his knees. "What's wrong? Did you fall? Sophie, are you hurt?" Her breathing was labored, and she was pale, way too pale.

"Pastor Amos, might I be of service?" The town's doctor stood before him, blocking out the sun's bright light. "My office is across the way."

Thanks, God. For always sending what is needed.

"I'm fine." Sophie licked her lips. "I need to get the fish back to William. George said he hadn't had any yet." When she motioned at the bowl, she gagged. Her hand trembled as she covered her mouth.

"You think you can help me carry your fiancée?" The doc's white eyebrows lowered. "From the symptoms I'm witnessing, she needs to be removed from the sun as soon as possible."

Any other moment, he'd enjoy scooping Sophie up and drawing her near, but instead Amos prayed his shaking legs would carry them both.

Inside the office, the doc opened a bag on the counter. "Fetch me a wet cloth for her head and a glass of water. Rags are by the sink in the kitchen." By the time he arrived back beside Sophie, the doc took the items and asked him to wait in the front room.

"I'll stay with her." He grasped her limp hand inside of his.

The doc didn't meet his eyes. "I, ahhh. . .upon asking some further questions. What I mean to say is. . .there needs to be a more thorough examination completed."

Amos crossed his arms and widened his stance.

"One an unmarried man. . .shouldn't witness. Please. Have a seat. I'm sure it's nothing. Your. . ." Something on the far wall gained his attention. "*She* probably only requires some rest in the cooler air."

If that was the truth, then why was he doing a more detailed examination? And what type of examination was it exactly? And what was so interesting on that cream-colored wall?

The room spun, but Sophie couldn't stop shaking her head. Doc McCormick had to be wrong.

Her—with child?

Closing her eyes, her mind slipped to the evil of a night she'd tried to erase. The darkened saloon staircase, being shoved toward the brothel rooms. . . If only Clyde had heard her screams over his spirited patrons.

Sophie laid her hand over her nose and mouth as if she could still smell the alcohol on Junior's breath. His spit-filled slurs louder in her memory than ever before. The sound of her skirt ripping.

She sucked in a breath.

Lord, how could You have allowed me to bear a constant reminder of that awful night?

Junior had said she owed his father, Clyde, for allowing her and Momma to live there despite the fact that Momma had been too sick to perform. But Clyde, the saloon owner, had been the closest thing to a father figure until Pastor T. He had never asked questions when Momma lied year after year on Sophie's birthday. She'd wink and say Sophie was below eighteen and too young to work the house. Clyde would never have required her to pay in the way Junior had enforced.

Hot tears dropped onto her hand. Her face wet. But that town would forever see her as Junior had. How Hanson did. As nothing more than a saloon girl whether she ever worked as one or not. What would become of her? Amos deserved to marry an unstained woman.

A handkerchief fell onto her lap, and she heard Doc McCormick slip from the room. What did he think of her? Nothing good. She rubbed a hand over her flat stomach. How much longer until the world could tell? If the church members reacted to the news of her upbringing as they had, would they now shun her completely?

She'd need to get another fresh start, a place where no one knew her. Would God be upset if she lied and said that she was widowed? Then her baby wouldn't grow up as she had, plagued by her mother's past doings. Except unlike Momma, it wasn't Sophie's fault she'd become pregnant. However, people would not care about that small detail. They'd make their own assumptions and figure her to be a liar. But how was she going to leave without any money?

The floor boards groaned in the hall. Amos paused in the doorway with Doc McCormick behind him. Even through her blurred vision, his emotions were clear. His expression filled with shock and disgust and disappointment. All things she deserved.

She bit her lip and hugged her arms to her chest.

Lord, You are the creator of all things. Why did You open my womb after Junior destroyed me? Why bring me here at all?

An unsteady whimper slipped out, and she rested her head in her palms to muffle her disgrace.

Arms circled around her, and she shuddered, but Amos didn't release her or stop his whispering prayers. She allowed herself to be guided by his support and joined in praying. Not with any words. The tears heating her cheeks and the pounding of her heartbeat in her ears were all she could offer.

But it was enough.

She may no longer be marrying Amos, but he'd help her like Pastor T had. That's what preachers did. God, being ever gracious, would provide her with a future. Just not the one she'd prayed for.

Amos' shirt hung wet against him from Sophie's tears. Tears that meant she was undeniably pregnant. His Sophie was with child—another man's child.

He summited the last burst of jealousy before finally whispering an amen. Sophie raised her head off his chest. Her beautiful brown eyes wouldn't meet his.

His back cracked as he arched his shoulders. It shouldn't take disaster to bring him to his knees. Sure, he'd prayed for his future bride, but nothing like this.

The doc cleared his throat. "Can I offer anyone a glass of water?"

Sophie's focus remained on the floor. If only the help she needed could be found in the bottom of a glass, but life wasn't that easy or simple. If it were, his fiancée would not have been raised in a saloon, Amos swallowed around the lump in his throat, or arrived pregnant. "No, thank you. Do you mind if we have a private word?"

He slid his hands in his pockets, jiggling a few coins. "I don't have any pressing patients. The miss can rest. Here, if you prefer. It would be best. . .in her condition to do so." Now there were two people avoiding his gaze.

After the door clicked shut, Amos pulled a chair from the corner and placed it in front of her. He sat, tapping his thumb and finger against his thigh. "In the letter that never arrived, had you spoken of. . ." He gestured toward her stomach.

She shook her head.

Amos crossed and uncrossed his ankles. She'd lied to him, or at least omitted the truth. Amos put his elbows on his knees. "And you've never been married?"

She shut her eyes, another round of tears running down her face.

He stood, sending the chair scooting into the wall. He'd been so sure God had sent him Sophie to be his bride. Hers was the first letter to respond to his ad. Had God changed His mind? Or was He using Amos like He had the prophet Hosea, with his marriage to Gomer? Was his and Sophie's marriage to be some kind of example, too? Did God still work in that kind of way?

A commotion came from the front entry. The room's door opened, knocking into a washbasin, which wobbled and crashed onto the floor.

"You trying to ruin our church, boy?" Hanson's boots clinked with determination, William and another elder not far behind.

Amos left the broken pitcher pieces and stepped in front of Sophie.

Hanson poked his finger against Amos' chest. "I said you were too young. But no one listened to me. Now look what happened. You couldn't even wait to have her legal before God."

Wait. He thought. . . Amos' neck burned, whether from embarrassment or anger or both. How could Hanson think he and Sophie had. . .? She hadn't even been here long enough to. . .

"Wait a minute, Hanson."

Hanson narrowed his eyes at William. "I've been right so far concerning Miss Ross"—spit flew from his mouth as he hissed her last name. "Fine." All his hatred returned to Amos. "Is your intended with child?" He wiped his mouth. "There's no need to add lying to your sins. Fleming's boy heard McCormick tell you she was."

"Gentlemen." Doc edged forward, sweeping the broken pieces toward the wall. "Is this really the way we speak on such private matters?" Why couldn't this rational man be on the church board?

"When it comes to hiring a sinful preacher, there are no private matters. Pack your bags, Lowry. There won't even be a need to vote. You won't be our preacher. Not at Hilltop Chapel. I can promise you that."

Chapter 7

Sophie pretended to be asleep when Margaret tiptoed in and laid a tray on the bed. After Amos practically hauled her back to the Olmsted's house, Sophie tried to obey Doc McCormick's advice to rest, but her mind would have none of it.

She pushed aside the slice of carrot cake and picked up her Bible. Amos had taken all the heat for her. How could Hanson assume it was his? She would never have knowingly put Amos in such an awful predicament. Still, what would become of her now? If Pastor and Mrs. T didn't have room for her along with their daughter and kids in their house, how would they have room for an additional child? Her child.

She pressed a hand to her stomach.

"No, no." Margaret's voice drifted through the other side of her door. And then another lady's reply. Someone Sophie couldn't quite decipher.

"Because she's resting. That's why." Sophie pictured Margaret with her fists placed on her hip, making her tiny frame appear larger than she was. The perfect person to have on her side. Other than Amos. Sophie blinked away tears. Amos had fled as soon as her feet hit the porch.

Sophie inched to the door.

"Of course it's not Pastor Amos' child. Goodness ladies, it's as if you know nothing about the matter of birth, and each of you've had your fair share. She's only been here—"

"Good. Then he may have a chance at staying." That sounded like Judith? "But he cannot marry her." Her words pierced Sophie, jabbing her heart. Oh, how the truth hurt.

"And how can you let her remain under your roof? She'll bring sin into this house."

"You're willing to help the poor in our town, and the orphans in Kentucky, but when one of our own is in need, you turn your head?"

"She is not one of our own. She is an immoral woman. How dare she bring our church's name down with her? And Pastor Amos with her, too."

Was Judith right? Would she shame the Olmsteads if she stayed? Was that why Pastor and Mrs. T's son-in-law was killed in a wagon accident? Because she'd brought sin into their family's lives?

She grabbed her carpetbag, shoving her Bible inside. She couldn't let that happen to the Olmsteads, or worse, to the man she'd grown to love.

After hearing the news of Sophie's pregnancy, Amos had been certain nothing else would shock him. However, watching Sophie dangle her second leg out of the Olmstead's opened window proved him wrong. He blinked at the sight before him. "What are you doing?" Had he been dropped into a dime novel? Maybe then the events of the day would make more sense.

Sophie muffled her yelp of surprise with her hand, but when she did, her grip on the windowsill loosened, and she fell to the ground.

Amos rushed across the yard and picked her up. "Are you all right?" He helped her stand, inspecting her limbs, face, her stomach where her unborn child grew. Then glanced at Olmstead's window she'd just fallen from.

Dusty trotted around the corner of the house, ears on alert. His tail wound back and forth when he noticed Amos.

Sophie bent and clutched her carpetbag. "There's no way the congregation will ever vote for me to marry you, and I don't want to bring sin upon the Olmsteads and—"

He held up his hand, his tongue too slow to address all her statements—her wrong statements. "The church wasn't going to vote on you."

"But the vote—"

"Was for me to become their pastor. It wasn't official yet. These past months have been a trial run." He pried the bag from her fingers. "No one but God will tell me who I can or can't marry."

"You and I both know it can't be me. I'm unworthy to be a preacher's wife."

"Are you. . ." Amos cleared his throat. "Are you going back to the. . ." He stole another glance at her stomach. "To the father?"

She bumped into the house. Her chest heaved with a ragged breath.

"It wasn't like that—"

"Are you willing to flee from your old self? Confess your sins?"

"Well, yes, but—"

"Then I'm going to marry you, Sophie. God sent me you." He had been a coward to have dropped her off at the Olmstead's earlier. But after all the elders and their wives showed up at the clinic, Sophie had turned as white as that broken washbasin, and he couldn't think straight with all the yelling. There was a right way to deal with problems and sin in church, and they weren't going about it the correct way. Plus, he needed time alone with God, and knew that Margaret would help protect his Sophie.

"Hilltop will still have you. Just not me. I couldn't have been the only option you had from your mail-order ad. You can marry someone else."

True, she wasn't, but like Abraham's servant sent to find a bride for Isaac had prayed and received a sign, so had Amos. "I don't want anyone else. I prayed that the bride God had for me would write to me first. My bride is you. You answered first."

Her eyes dimmed. "What if God said no to giving you your sign? Maybe He didn't like your request. Or maybe He did provide you a sign, but what if the postmaster accidently held the correct bride's letter a day before handing it over? What if—"

"Your response was the only one I received in the first two weeks."

"You can't marry me. You're a preacher. I was raised in a saloon. By a dance-hall girl. And I'm. . .expecting," she struggled to say through her tears. "Hilltop won't let you. I'll just bring sin into their church."

And there was the other thing he needed to address. He dropped her bag and laced his fingers through hers. "Honey, sin's already in their church. Sin's everywhere in the world, because we live here. We don't become perfect even after God rescues us. Sophie, I made a promise to marry you."

"And I'm releasing you of your promise." She stepped away as Dusty shuffled under her feet. "You can't have Hilltop and me, and I know which one you need to choose."

So did he.

He left her standing there and knocked hard on the Olmstead's front door. His knuckles throbbed. A second later the door opened, and Margaret and William stood with guilty looks. Had they heard everything? The fluttering curtains in the open window provided the answer.

"William, I need. . .I need. . ." He needed air. Ripping off his tie, he enjoyed a deep breath.

Sophie hugged her arms to her chest. She looked so fragile. Afraid. How long until she started to show? It wouldn't matter. The peace he'd received after spending the afternoon on his knees filled him again.

He turned back to the unnaturally silent Olmsteads. "Can I borrow your wagon? And try not to allow Hanson to boot me out just yet. There's something we need to do first."

On the buckboard, Sophie clung to the only thing that made any sense—her carpetbag. "I don't understand."

William's horse was a head shorter than Eugene's, but it didn't hinder their speed. Two startled bunnies hopped off the path, their white tails disappearing into the brush.

Amos squinted at the trail ahead. "What's not to understand? You're my mail-order bride, and we're getting married. No more waiting on Pastor Gable. We'll head to your Pastor T. Suppose we could search for a closer circuit preacher, but thought you'd enjoy seeing home again."

Home? Neither the saloon nor Pastor T's house were home anymore. She gripped the handles tighter until her fingernails dug into her skin. What if she saw Junior again?

"Sophie, honey, what's wrong?"

"I can't."

He lowered his eyebrows, his jaw clenched. "Can't what? Can't marry me?"

That's what she should admit for his sake, then Hillside would hire him, but her lips remained shut.

With a steady tug, Amos slowed the wagon. Dust floated overhead as he set the brake. The horse chomped at her bit and stomped her foot. Even the horse knew not to be thrilled with Sophie.

Amos rested the reins on his thighs. "Now's the time to get out of this. . .if that's what you want?" He swept his thumb along her skin as he always did. Tingles whisked to her heart. He was wrong. There was no reason to return anywhere. Home was no longer a place, it was him.

"But it's not what I want." He inhaled deeply. "Once we say I do, there's no getting away from me, and we'll need to be able to trust and talk to each other."

Her knees knocked together. "I can't go back there. If I see Junior again—" She'd what? God proved faithful. He'd get her through that, too, and she did miss Pastor and Mrs. T. Amos would be along. She trusted him to help protect her.

"Is Junior the. . .father?" He swallowed. "How long had you two stopped. . .sparking before you answered my ad?"

"Sp–spark. . .?" Where was the air her lungs needed?

"Help me understand."

"That man." Tears stung her eyes. "Was never. . ." She bent forward, one hand on her stomach, the other holding her upright on the seat. The carpetbag fell beside her feet on the buckboard. "Would never be the. . ." He didn't deserve to be connected to the word *father*. "He attacked me. Said I owed him." Even though the sun shined, her vision blurred to night.

Amos' arm circled her waist, strong and steady. Holding her up. "Honey, I think you need to start at the beginning."

Chapter 8

Hilltop's back stoop framed a swaying cornfield. Amos' leg brushed Sophie's. Maybe they could skip what lay ahead and just enjoy God's creation as their worship service. She squeezed his hand, as her lips moved silently in prayer.

After all she'd been through, her heart remained tender to God. He truly was a miracle worker. If only she'd have confided in him sooner. As to why Amos hadn't thought to head back to seminary to find another preacher before yesterday, he hadn't a clue. But God's timing was always perfect.

The back door opened and William's beard was the first thing in sight, followed by his stomach. "It's time."

Amos froze in the door frame, shielding Sophie. She didn't need to suffer any more of their scorn. He had to give this sermon—his last here, but he didn't have to bring Sophie to watch.

She ducked under his arm and the entire congregation gasped. Never had Amos felt unwelcomed inside a sanctuary, until now. They'd known he was returning, but apparently William led them to believe he had taken Sophie away, never to return. Or had they only wrongly assumed—again.

On the first pew on the right-hand side, Sophie sat, straightened her new skirt he'd bought her, and then gave him an encouraging smile. When he didn't move, she bowed her head.

"What's the meaning of this?" Hanson stood and crossed his arms. His snarling comment pierced the silence.

In the fourth row, Linda nudged her husband. Her finger pointed at Sophie. Whispers spread like a single spark engulfing dry grass. Traditionally, a few hymns and a prayer or two came before the sermon. Amos glanced at the wide-eyed pianist, Judith. Now that he wasn't staying, he'd finally figured out most everyone's names. God's humor. Another unsolvable mystery.

Amos wiped his palms and opened his Bible to Revelation, chapter two. "The church in Ephesus was praised for their diligence in service. Hilltop shares in that honor with your care for the orphans and the poor. Like them, you've been wise in your quest for prohibiting false prophets, making sure I, your potential pastor, was doctrinally sound. But..." He read aloud a few more verses of scripture. "Do you also share what the church in Ephesus had forgotten? What started their journey of faith? Forgiveness. Love. An increasing relationship with Christ?"

"I'm afraid you've been too quick to assume." He paused, nodding to the front row. "And too slow about listening to the one God was possibly assigning over you." He pointed to himself. He also shared their guilt. He'd failed in shepherding them well because he'd been too concerned about how he looked on the outside. Wanting their votes more than spiritual growth.

"I don't understand?" Vernon called. "Why's she back?"

Eugene shook his finger. "If you want a chance at pastoring our church, you will end this engagement."

Amos sighed, taking in the sanctuary he'd once coveted to have as his own. He'd been sure Hilltop *needed* him to be their pastor as much as he wanted to be. But they only needed God.

Scripture mentions pride comes before the fall. Good thing God specialized in restoration. "Our engagement ended when I married Sophie yesterday. And I withdraw my candidacy to become Hilltop's preacher. We'll be moved out of the parsonage by morning."

A teary-eyed Margaret dropped off a basket of cinnamon biscuits to the parsonage. After hugs, thank-yous, and a promise to drop by tomorrow before they left, Amos ate just enough to keep his stomach from complaining. Sophie sat at the table picking at her food while he did another sweep through the house. Not much left to pack besides a few daily items.

He gathered his Bible and tie, the silk material reminding him of home. There was a little good news in all this. His folks would now get to meet Sophie sooner. A noise sounding like gunshots made Amos dump everything into his trunk. A few whooping hollers followed, and if Amos wasn't mistaken, half the town may have just galloped away on horseback.

"What was that?" Sophie spoke his thoughts aloud.

Amos peered out the parsonage's front window. Vernon sprinted his way through the dust with his hand covering his cap. When Amos cracked open the front door, Vernon slid to a stop, waving for him to follow. "Bandits ransacked Shipley's General Store! They picked up two ladies and sped away."

Sophie gasped, pressing a hand to her chest, and rested against his filled black trunk.

The church bells announced the urgent call for help. Amos opened the door wider. "You got another horse?"

Vernon nodded. "Eugene's saddling up all he's got. Come on."

"Sophie—"

She ran into his arms and kissed him hard on the mouth. Twice. "Be careful. I'll be praying. You better come back to me. You hear?"

He took in her beauty, both inside and out. How could anyone have ever thought his wife wasn't the right bride for him? "I love you," he whispered against her neck.

She pulled back, her brown eyes wide. Her lips parted, ready for her next words. She'd repeated *love* in her vows, but his heart was eager to hear it for real.

William burst into the kitchen. The back door slammed into the wall. A broom fell to the floor, booming almost as loud as the gunshots. "Eleanor and her daughter are both safe. Disheveled, but safe. Apparently, Eleanor throws a mean elbow to the nose."

Vernon swiped off his cap. "Good. Then those vermin can have whatever they stole.

No point in riding against their guns. I say, let the Lord provide justice."

William wiped his mouth with the back of his hand. "Hanson's daughter's still missing."

Through the stained-glass windows, blue and purple rays shone upon the altar. Sophie's prayers ran dry hours ago, but the sunset remained diligent. The church door opened and banged shut. Sophie rose from her kneeling position. A redheaded girl had her back against the door.

Thank You, Lord.

Hanson's daughter, Ruby, was safe.

Ruby erupted into tears and slid to the floor.

Or maybe not?

With shaky hands, Ruby tugged at something on her skirt. No, something was missing from her skirt. A tear had been sliced down the middle exposing Ruby's knees. Wisps of hair stuck to her wet cheeks. The girl's braids looked as if she'd wallowed in the straw, and her nostrils flared like a frightened stallion.

"Are you hurt?" Sophie pushed through a wave of dizziness and moved her numb legs forward. Wrong question. There were more than physical scars that wounded a person. Like Sophie's own memories. "We've been praying for you. Your father—"

Ruby pulled in her knees and wrapped her skirt around them, covering her exposed skin. "I won't be his treasure anymore."

"Whose treasure?" Sophie knelt, leaving space between them. "Ruby. Your father's going to be thrilled you're safe. He organized the search party to find you."

Tears pooled along her lashes, and she thumped her head back against the door. "He used to call me his little Ruby, his favorite treasure. Now I can't be anyone's treasure. Ever." A sob coursed through her like a hiccup. "Papa told me to stay away from him, but I. . . He said he wanted to go on a walk."

"Him who?"

She lowered her chin onto her knees. "He started winking at me when he came into town the past few weeks. Said he was figuring on buying property here. Papa caught him once and told me to stay away. But I—I. . ." she covered her lips. "He kissed my hand. . . and. . .those riders thundered in with their guns in the air, and he. . ." A whimper escaped. "I thought he was trying to save me." She gulped in air as if it were a cup of water, and coughs interrupted her tears. "He shoved me behind the blacksmith's fence yard." Her eyes stared beyond Sophie with a glazed quality. "He drew a knife. It wasn't to protect me."

Sophie reached to comfort but stopped, remembering a touch of any kind may harm more than help.

Lord, guide me. How do I help Ruby without getting sucked back into those evil memories?

Ruby's lips quivered. "Papa found me after the church bell sounded the second time." She rocked side to side. "Said no daughter of his would be a loose woman. He said I had always been too much like Ma."

Like her mother?

"W–what am I supposed to do now?"

"God always provides hope." Everything inside Sophie warned her to remain quiet, but Amos had been right. She needed to share the burdens trapped inside her. They didn't define her. "You've heard the rumors about me, but it's not all truth. A man attacked me, too. But God. . .washes everything away. You'll be clean. Everyone has a fresh start in Him."

"You." Her eyes narrowed like on the day she'd asked if Sophie could play the piano. "Your baby isn't. . ." She licked her lips. Her voice softened. "Thought you were a saloon girl? Papa said you were a. . .a. . .sort of like my mother. Except she never dressed in red; she just ran away with Papa's youngest cousin." She wiped her cheek with her palm. "That's why he hated Pastor Amos so much. He reminded him of Leon, 'cause he's so young. Papa's still so angry at what Ma did to him. To us. Even after all these years."

Now wasn't the time to sift through Hanson's resentment toward her and Amos, but things were starting to become clearer. "God loves us despite our past. Despite how people perceive us. He loved me when I thought I was unlovable. And He loves you, too." Sophie ran her fingers along her stomach. Her baby was a gift no matter how he or she came to be. "Amos and I are leaving in the morning. You can come with us. Amos will explain what God's love is all about."

"No." Amos' voice shot to her. When had he snuck in through the back? She smiled. Didn't matter. He was safe.

Thank You, Lord.

"Sophie's done a far better job of living out the scriptures as of late than I have. She'll do a fine job explaining it all to you, Ruby."

Amos bent and kissed Sophie's forehead. Never would she tire of his gentle, reassuring touch. Without saying the words, she knew what that slow blink and side smile meant. Who would have ever thought a girl raised in a saloon would one day have the chance to love a preacher? Only a big God—One who redeemed and forgave—could take her earlier life and turn it into something beautiful.

A knock rattled the front door. Vernon poked his head inside. "Nobody is going anywhere. If you can forgive us, we want you to stay Pastor Amos. Please."

"Sophie, too!" Another higher voice called.

Ruby scooted over as a handful of church members shouldered inside.

"You were right." Vernon tucked his chin. "We've been fixated on the wrong things. Yes, we need to help the needy and the orphaned, but we have forgotten our first love—the Lord. Please say you'll stay?"

Amos searched Sophie's eyes as his hand found hers. "We'll pray about it."

"What about Ruby? Hanson has—"

"She'll stay with us." Margaret took off her apron and draped it over Ruby. With Ruby in her curled position, there was no way to tell her dress had been sliced. How much had everyone heard? "It makes perfect sense. We miss having younger ones in the house. Of course, we'll keep praying Hanson comes around, but like Sophie said, God sees your heart, dear girl."

"And you. . ." Margaret wrapped Sophie into a hug. "Why didn't you tell us what happened? Oh, my dear, dear, sweet child, I'm so sorry. Please say you'll forgive us for our judgmental ways."

Chapter 9

The new faces inside Hilltop's sanctuary had grown in number over the past few months. Almost making up for the empty seat on the fifth row, left-hand side. Almost.

During the closing hymn, two women slipped in. The thinner woman, wearing a frayed dress, turned to leave, but the tall one in silk, took her by the arm and plopped them into the last pew.

Amos didn't have to beckon Sophie, she was already nearing his side. He extended his hand, welcoming the women. "Mornin'. I'm Pastor Amos. Good of you to join us."

The one in silk placed her hand over her chest, failing to mask the amount of exposed skin. A bruise covered the cheek of the one in the frayed dress. No smile. She stared at Amos' hand. "Is this Hilltop Chapel?"

"Sophie's Hilltop?" The one in silk bit the edge of her painted lips. Her gaze darted around before landing on Sophie's swollen stomach. Her fingers twisted around the tip of a curl hanging around her shoulders.

"This church is the Lord's. But yes, I am Sophie. Can my husband and I help you in any way?"

"Irene?" a woman asked behind them.

The woman in silk stilled her fingers. She peered around Sophie. "Emeline?"

Emeline had showed up a few weeks ago, following the rumors of a church who'd helped girls like her. She flung her arms around Irene. "I'm so glad you're here. You said you'd never come."

"In your letter, you said. . .you felt clean. I want that. . . . If I can?"

Emeline sniffled and looked to Sophie. "Can she stay?"

Irene reached for the woman beside her. "Cora, too. I found her at the last train station. Both her cheeks were black and blue."

"How about we talk things out over some food?" Sophie rested her hand under her stomach, supporting her soon-to-be child—their child. How Amos hoped he or she had Sophie's big brown eyes.

"I heard the word *food*." Margaret and her bouncing hat feather squeezed into the pew right next to Emeline. "It's my turn to provide meals this week."

"I've got the Bible devotions." Linda waved a hanky from the front of the sanctuary.

Beulah hobbled over. "And it's my week to house these fine ladies. Welcome. Welcome."

Amos left the women to argue over the details of their newest ministry. No woman was unworthy of what they'd all been given—a chance at a relationship with Christ.

Word about Sophie and what she'd endured hadn't taken long to spread. Women with an array of backgrounds had been arriving ever since, hungry for God's grace. Love. His forgiveness.

Speaking of forgiveness...

A familiar jangle of spurs quieted those around him. Even Judith stopped her playing of "Safe in the Arms of Jesus." Hanson's silhouette blocked some of the morning's light. Was the entire room holding their breath, or only him? Amos really wanted Judith to keep playing. The hymn's lyrics running through his mind would be helpful right about now.

Hanson shifted his weight, glancing between Amos, Sophie, and other points around the sanctuary, probably searching for Ruby. But he wouldn't find her here. Unfortunately, running from problems seemed to be one of their inherited family traits.

Hanson lowered his gaze. "I'm sorry."

William clapped once before rubbing his palms together. "All right, everyone. Let's help get Miss Irene and Miss Cora settled." He gestured at the back door, and everyone except Amos and Sophie obeyed. Slowly. But obeyed, nonetheless.

Hanson removed his Stetson. He ran his fingertips along its brim. "I don't know how, but somehow I landed up north." He cleared his throat. "A wise preacher by the name of Theodore Tettleton helped me let go of the bitterness that was buried." Hanson tapped his chest. "I've said and done some mighty awful things. I'm sorry. If you could..." He wiped at his nose. "Your Pastor T is a real fine man of God, Sophie. He seemed to believe that you could...maybe.... What I mean to ask is..."

Sophie marched, or rather waddled, forward and extended her hand. "Good day, sir. My name's Sophie Lowry. It's a pleasure to meet you, Mr....?"

Amos drew alongside, placing his hand on her lower back. Hanson's gaze met his. A wobbly smile lifted his lips, and he took Sophie's offering. "Name's Hanson." He combed back his hair that looked a mite grayer than when he'd left. "She's gonna make you a fine preacher's wife."

Amos wrapped his arm around Sophie's waist, and she snuggled into his side. "She already has." Hanson may have prodded Amos into ordering himself a mail-order bride, but it was God who chose him the perfect one.

Megan Besing adores reading, writing, and reviewing stories with happily-ever-afters. Her own writing has received many awards, including being a multi-category finalist in ACFW's *Genesis* and a winner of MCRW's *Melody of Love* contest. She lives in Indiana with her husband and their children where she dreams of the beach and drinks way too many vanilla Cokes. Connect with Megan at www.meganbesing.com.

The Outlaw's Inconvenient Bride

by Noelle Marchand

Chapter 1

Wyatt Coulter had done some things he wasn't proud of to fit in with the Hidden Springs gang, but tricking an unsuspecting woman into captivity and ruination was where he drew the line. The last thing he wanted was to let an innocent bystander get caught in the crossfire, and there would be plenty of it if the gang ever found out his true identity. Luke Bellamy—undercover detective.

His task for the last year had been to provide reconnaissance on the Renegade Gang and their many associates to Pinkerton's National Detective Agency. Once Pinkerton was satisfied with the information Luke collected, they'd move to the final stage of their plan in which every member of the gang would be captured and pay for their various crimes. Until then, Luke lived and breathed only as Wyatt Coulter—an outlaw rumored to have murdered a man back in Texas before fleeing to Wyoming, where he'd racked up an impressive record of petty crimes and gained skill as a cattle rustler. Wyatt Coulter grinned and lifted a shot glass in the air. "To the groom!"

The whole saloon echoed, "To the groom!"

Wyatt's slender, auburn-haired fellow gang member, Wild Dog Jack, slid from the bar stool and slumped into a bow. He straightened with a snap that sent him careening sideways into a saloon girl. Millie dodged out of the way to let him fall flat on his back then glared down at the fresh-faced outlaw with a look of pure fury. Laughing, Jack grabbed her by the arm and pulled her down beside him for a kiss.

Petey Stanwyck weaved through the tables with a whiskey glass lifted. "To the minister!"

"To the minister!" Wyatt echoed along with everyone else.

Petey winked and turned his white collar around so it mimicked a clergyman's. With his dark suit, slicked back hair, and sainted expression, Petey would have looked every bit the minister if he hadn't stopped in his tracks to guzzle a beer. Jack finally let Millie loose and yelled, "I need a drink!"

Wyatt handed Jack the untouched shot glass he was holding then helped Millie stand. Noticing the tears in the girl's kohl-lined eyes, he ushered her to the bar and mumbled under the loud toasting, "You all right, Millie?"

"I'm fine." The young blond blinked a few times until her blue eyes cleared.

Wyatt shook his head. "Why didn't you take Jack up on his offer to live in the valley with us?"

Her chin lifted haughtily. "And be snowed into that canyon from November to March with no one for company other than a bunch of ne'er-do-wells? I don't think so. There's a reason the only person who would agree to that is some fool-headed mail-order bride who doesn't know any better. I just can't figure out why Jack has to be the one who marries her. He's the youngest of the lot. Shouldn't he be able to live free a while longer?"

Jack sidled up beside her, clinging to her waist like it was the only thing keeping him standing. It probably was. "I get the bride because it was my bright idea to begin with. Ain't that right, Wyatt?"

Millie snarled. "Oh, I'm sure it was, you lily-livered polecat."

The train whistle blew announcing the bride's arrival, but the hollow sound barely pierced through tinny piano and riotous laughter filling the saloon. Jack was too busy trying to sweet-talk Millie to notice. Waiting until Jack was distracted by another drink, Wyatt leaned closer to Millie. "The train is here. Why don't you take Jack upstairs and sober him up a little while I take care of the bride?"

She stilled, searched his gaze with something akin to hope. A smile touched her red-painted lips. She winked. "Don't you worry, Wyatt Coulter. I'll sober him up plenty."

A quick nod from him sealed their alliance. It didn't take much convincing for Millie to get Jack up the stairs with a bottle of whiskey in hand. Wyatt waited until the door closed behind them before slipping out of the Silver Spurs Saloon to the main street of Hidden Springs. Only then did he let even a hint of relief flow through him. Everything had gone according to plan. Now, all he had to do was send the bride-to-be on her way and get back to his assignment with no distractions, complications, or innocent women to worry about. How hard could that be?

Mariah Snow had promised her dying mother that she would marry a good man. Three years had passed before she had found a way to escape the life she'd been living and keep that promise, but today it was finally going to happen. Jackson Wilde was a respectable foreman on a ranch in Wyoming with a letter of introduction and recommendation from the local minister, Peter Stanwyck.

Jackson had even sent her a tintype of him dressed in his Sunday best. He was a dashing young man with classic, boyish features who'd dared to smile despite the photographer's insistence that he at least pretend to be serious. His letters had been witty, sweet, and heartrending as he'd told her how his father had died when he was only a young boy, leaving him to fend for himself in the harsh world. Only a year younger than her at nineteen, he'd climbed to the revered position of ranch foreman through skill and determination.

She couldn't say she'd fallen in love with her husband-to-be quite yet, but she was well on her way. That was far more than she'd hoped for when she'd first desperately combed through the classifieds of every newspaper she could get her hands on in search of some way of escape. Thankfully, her stepbrothers' interest in Wyoming cattle prices had paid off for her. They'd never expect her to run so far away from home.

Nor were they likely to try to venture this far outside their realm of influence. She was safe. She was ready to start over. And, as much as she loved her stepbrothers, she'd be more than happy to never see their faces again if it meant she was finally free of their ever-watchful, overprotective eyes.

Catching sight of her reflection in the train's window, she smoothed down her hair and repositioned her jaunty hat as the train pulled into the station. Traveling light was imperative for a quick getaway so one satchel held all the possessions she had left in the world. She clutched it tightly as she stepped from the train onto the station's platform as one of only three passengers to disembark.

A gaily painted sign took up most of the train station's wall proclaiming, WELCOME TO HIDDEN SPRINGS!

Well, at least it tried to. Some audacious prankster had blocked out most of the letters in the word "Springs" so the sign actually read, "Welcome to Hidden Sins!"

Hardly appropriate for a town boasting not one, but three churches. She frowned. *Someone really ought to fix that.*

"Beggin' your pardon, miss." The distinguished-looking conductor tipped his hat to her with concern in his brown eyes. "Will someone be coming here to meet you?"

"Yes, my intended should be here any moment." She scanned the faces of the few men milling about, but none of them matched the tintype she carried.

"Very good, miss." He nodded then walked over to speak to the engineer before returning. "We'll wait a few minutes to make sure you meet your intended."

"Oh, that's very kind of y'all, but there's no need."

He shook his head. "I reckon there is plenty of need in a town like this."

"What do you mean 'a town like this'?"

"Why, Hidden Springs. . . Well. . . It's *Hidden Springs*, miss. Such a lady as yourself shouldn't walk around unaccompanied. Don't fret, though. The train was a few minutes early. I'm sure your gentleman is on the way." He excused himself to speak with a passenger who'd called for him on the train.

Mariah gave her head a little shake. How very odd that the conductor would have such a negative view of a town Jackson had described so glowingly. The poor conductor must be dreadfully mistaken. Surely, he must be.

The sound of a throat clearing spun her around toward the horrid sign again. She took a quick step back at the imposing gentleman standing before her. Actually, "dusty cowpoke" might be a more accurate description.

Everything about him seemed chiseled from steel and granite, from his silver eyes and strong, angular jaw to the wide breadth of his shoulders and imposing height. The thick waves of his rich brown hair stirred in the breeze, providing the only measure of softness to his determined visage. There was nothing disrespectful in his gaze, despite the way it traveled over her like he was committing every bit of her to memory. "Miss Mariah Snow?"

Drawing her shoulders back, she lifted her chin along with an eyebrow. "And you are?"

"Wyatt Coulter, at your service. I'm here on behalf of your intended. Jack won't be coming. In fact, it's best you forget the whole scheme." He opened his hand to flash a few silver dollars, which he unceremoniously pressed into her palm. "This is for your trouble and to get you back home. Thank you for coming. Have a good day."

Her mouth fell open. She reached out to snag the sleeve of his coat before he could finish turning on his heel. "Just a moment."

He paused, glancing down at her hand. "You have questions?"

An incredulous laugh slipped from her throat. "I certainly do. Where is Jackson Wilde?"

"He's unavailable, I'm afraid."

"Unavailable?" She searched his face but couldn't read him. "What does that mean? Is he dead?"

"No."

"Paralyzed?"

"No, ma'am."

"Then what possible excuse—"

"He's drunk."

Her eyebrows lifted. She released his coat. "Drunk?"

"Yes, a state that afflicts him anytime he's in town." He took a small step closer to her. Lowering his voice, his tone softened. "Please listen to me, Miss Snow. Know that I speak to you as one of Jack's closest friends. As such, I can honestly say you deserve better—much better. Whatever he may have told you, in fact, *everything* he has told you about himself is a lie. The best thing you could possibly do is get on the train and go right back to where you came from."

How much bleaker a scene could a man paint? Surely Miss Snow would see reason, take the money, and go back home. Instead, she stood with tawny eyes so piercing and perceptive they seemed to see into his very soul as they searched for the truth. This once and only this once, he let it shine through. Willing her to know he was more than Wyatt Coulter. He was a good man—or at least tried to be. The son of a preacher, he'd been raised to treat women with honor and respect. She could trust him, trust his word.

Her dark brown lashes fluttered closed then pressed against her cheeks. Any other woman might have swooned, argued, or cried at having her hopes dashed and plans so thoroughly ruined. Instead, Mariah Snow gave the tiniest little head shake that sent the wavy tendrils beside her ears trembling. She opened her eyes to reveal an odd mixture of determination and helplessness. "I can't. There's no home to go back to."

"Then take the money. Start over somewhere else."

"How? Start over at what? You can't send me away. I have nowhere else to go. No money of my own." She glanced down at the coins he'd given her. "This will run out soon. Then what will I do? How will I live?"

He reached into his pocket to see if there was anything more he could give her. There was nothing left other than what he'd been given to buy supplies for the gang. "I have nothing more to give you."

"I don't want anything from you." She gave him back the coins and lifted her chin. "I demand to see my groom."

"You *demand*?" He glanced at the conductor waiting a respectful distance away. "But the train—"

The conductor glanced at his pocket watch. "Four minutes, sir, then we've got to pull out."

"Hurry." Impatience fueling his movements, Wyatt took Miss Snow's suitcase then caught her arm to rush down the sidewalk toward the saloon. "That's the only train coming through today and you've got to be on it when it leaves."

She lifted her skirt away from the mud caking the streets as she trotted beside him. Hopefully, Millie had the situation in hand, but even if Jack was on the loose, he'd been in no shape for a ceremony. One quick look would prove that to Miss Snow. She'd be begging him to take her back to the train. He slowed down a bit as they passed a house of ill-repute, wanting the lady to get an honest view of the kind of town she'd stumbled into.

Rounding the corner, he nearly bumped into Rosie, the Silver Spur's proprietress. "Sorry, Rosie."

"That's all right. I wouldn't go in there, sugar. Not unless you want a black eye. Petey started another brawl." Rosie smiled wryly then took in a long drag of a cigar as she eyed Miss Snow. "Is this the blushing bride?"

Not if he could help it. He peered over the swinging door at the melee happening inside. "Yes, ma'am. She needs to see Jack. I guess we'll go around the back."

"Wouldn't do that either. Millie's tending to him upstairs. He always did have a soft spot for her."

He glanced toward Miss Snow to find her noticeably paler than when he'd last bothered to look at her. Pink flushed her cheeks. She looked ready to be sick. Good. He took her arm again. "Let's get you back on the train."

Finally, her eyes began to water. "I can't go back. I won't."

Rosie straightened with new interest. "You looking for a job, little missy? Pretty face and figure like yours would be welcome at my place. I'd start you out downstairs serving drinks, then—"

Two men tumbled through the window next to Miss Snow. Instinctively, Wyatt pulled her into his arms, turning to block her from the flying glass as he sheltered her between his body and the wooden wall of the saloon. Rosie let out a scream of outrage. "You idiots! How many times have I told you not to throw people through my window, Petey Stanwyck?"

Wyatt instinctively covered Miss Snow's ears as Rosie let out a tirade of curses so foul it would've made a sailor blush. Miss Snow's fingers clutched his jacket with trembling fingers. This close, he could see Rosie was right. Miss Snow was pretty—awfully pretty. She was also younger and far more vulnerable than her courage and determination had led him to believe.

Her innocent brown eyes stared back at him. They filled with tears that escaped to tangle in her lashes like tiny, pure diamonds. Something in him shifted then clicked into place.

Her whisper seemed to echo over every other sound. "Oh, what am I going to do?"

The answer rose up in him so right and true and unmistakable the fact that it was also crazy and foolhardy seemed unimportant. There was only one way to keep this woman safe, to right the wrong done to her by the gang, and, hopefully, one day give her the better life she so obviously longed for. Uncovering her ears, he braced his hands on the wall behind her and spoke the only words that would do any of that. "Marry me."

Chapter 2

She'd married a stranger.

Of course, she hadn't had much of a choice, and it wasn't like that hadn't been the plan to begin with, so what did it matter who specifically the stranger was? It mattered that it wasn't Jackson Wilde. Or should she call him Wild Dog Jack, the name everyone else in Hidden Springs seemed to know him by? She'd never laid eyes on the man. She hadn't wanted or needed to by the time Rosie had laid out how fortunate Mariah was to be marrying Wyatt Coulter instead of Wild Dog.

Apparently, if gossip was to be believed, Wyatt never condescended to visit anyone upstairs at the Silver Spurs Saloon or any of the three other brothels in town. That made him a gem of a man—comparatively speaking. Although, as far as character references went, a madam wasn't exactly the most sterling of endorsements.

Yet, here she was. Mariah *Coulter*. Sharing a saddle with her husband while a mule packed with supplies plodded behind them.

Wyatt had promised to protect her, treat her with caring and respect. All of that before they'd said their vows in front of a justice of the peace who'd assured them repeatedly that he didn't want any trouble. No wonder the town was. . . Well, *Hidden Springs*. It couldn't even be Hidden Sins, because no one was hiding anything. Except for Wild Dog, of course, but even his treachery had come to light.

"Better hold on tight, Miss—uh, Mariah." Removing her hand from where it clutched his brown coat, Wyatt moved it to his waist. "The trail is going to get rough."

A grimace pulled at her lips. Husband or not, she'd been raised to keep her distance from men, to refuse them even a chance to mistake any of her actions as encouraging their affections. It felt purely odd to wrap her arms around this man's waist. It was also entirely necessary, for as soon as she did, Wyatt guided the horse down a steep, treeless hillside to wade through the shallow depths of a lazy flowing brook.

She'd seen her share of beautiful scenery while growing up in Texas, but nothing like the gray mountains that loomed ever closer. The landscape was so pure, untouched, and peaceful. So different from the town they'd left behind. This seemed like the perfect opportunity to get to know her husband better, but he'd hardly spoken a word since they'd left Hidden Springs behind.

Then again, she certainly didn't want to delve into her own past. He'd already told her he was taking her to the ranch where he worked as a hand. What else was there to say?

The clomping of hooves on the flat, rock-hewn banks of the creek echoed around them to fill the silence as they entered the canyon. They rode through a maze of twisting, turning corridors that would have made even the most skilled tracker hopelessly lost—not that there would be any signs to follow with the ground as hard as it was.

The corridor tightened to a narrow pass and forced them back into the brook. A man could disappear in a place like this and never be heard from again. Every muscle in her body tensed. Was that the point? Did Wyatt want them to disappear?

The path seemed to come to a dead end boasting of nothing but a few large trees. The horse picked its way over the roots then made a sharp right turn through a slot smaller than a wagon into a corridor that widened out again. What kind of ranch would—

A face appeared over the edge of the canyon wall then disappeared. Her fingers dug into Wyatt's waist. Her voice came out in a hoarse whisper. "Indian."

"What?"

"There's an Indian on the top of the ridge. I saw him."

Wyatt nodded, the essence of calm. "Where about?"

"Left side. Twenty yards ahead of us."

His right hand hovered near the gun at his hip. "Stay behind me."

As if she had anywhere else to go. She might be a sitting duck, but she didn't have to be a lame duck. "Give me a gun."

"No."

There was no time to argue. The Indian emerged on the rim of the canyon with his bow drawn and aimed directly at them. She reached for the gun on Wyatt's left hip. Rather than drawing his weapon, Wyatt wrestled the gun from her hand. A single word of warning rang from his lips. "Woman!"

"Wyatt! Shoot, you fool!" She sent a panicked glance upward, but the Indian hadn't moved an inch. She reached for Wyatt's other gun. "He's going to kill us!"

Laughter washed down over them, filling the canyon as the Indian lowered his weapon to brace his hands on his knees. Wyatt knocked her hand away from his gun then swung down from his mount. He reached up to pull her down beside him. His gray eyes were as hard and flinty as granite. "Never touch my gun. Do you understand me?"

"Yes," she said distractedly as she watched the Indian climb down the side of the canyon with his bow on his shoulder. "I'm guessing that must be a friend of yours."

"Well, we aren't dead, are we?"

"No thanks to you and your slow reflexes."

His eyes narrowed, but he turned to the buckskin-clad man approaching them with a harshly spoken, "Hawk."

Laughing dark eyes surveyed Mariah. "You stole Wild Dog's bride and his bride nearly stole your guns. Seems about right, my friend."

"I wouldn't call it stealing, exactly. The lady made her choice." Wyatt turned to her with something she'd almost call humor in his gaze. Maybe even a little bit of warmth. "Didn't you, Mariah?"

Biting back a reply, she simply offered a smile. She wanted to tell him not to feel too honored. After all, she hadn't had much of a choice. However, she'd pushed him far enough over the last few minutes, especially since she knew very little about his temperament. She nodded to Wyatt's compadre. "Mr. Hawk."

"It's just Hawk, little lady." The amusement tilting his lips turned a bit wry. "Wild Dog isn't happy. He's about two hours behind you and riding like the devil. Better take this matter to the General before he catches up."

"You work on the same ranch as Wild—as Jackson?"

Hawk's eyebrows lifted. "Seems there's a lot you haven't told your bride, Wyatt. She is your bride, isn't she?"

"She's mine all right and don't you forget it. C'mon, Mariah. We've got to get going." He mounted the roan then reached down and pulled her up behind him.

"I'm not the one you should be worried about," Hawk called. His laughter chased them down the hillside now interspersed with rocks, grass, and trees. Still, her husband didn't bother to speak to her.

She had no problem squeezing his waist now. Maybe it would loosen his tongue. "What did Hawk mean? What else haven't you told me, Wyatt Coulter?"

"Well, to start with, Jack and I work on the same outfit."

"How. . .awkward. I'm guessing he's the one you're supposed to be worrying about?"

Wyatt shrugged. "He's likely to be angry that you married me even though it was his own fault for getting drunk and going off with Millie. Course, I might have encouraged him some."

"You encouraged him? Why?"

"I already told you. Friend or not, he wasn't good enough for you. None of that has changed."

She shook her head. "So you just up and married me?"

"No. I tried to send you home. You wouldn't go."

She pulled in a deep breath. "That's just perfect."

He threw a challenging look over his shoulder. "It was either that or let you work for Rosie and her ilk, so you're welcome."

Well, he wasn't wrong. She was grateful to him—as much as she hated to admit it. "Who's the general Hawk mentioned?"

"Our boss. He wanted one of his hands to get married so he could have a housekeeper."

"So I'll still have the same job on this place? Cooking and cleaning and the like?"

"Yes, you'll simply be married to a different man. A better man. The best one here."

She let out a short laugh. "And humble too."

"You have no idea what. . ." He shook his head. "You'll see that I'm right."

The trees cleared, revealing a green, verdant valley. It encircled a milky blue lake that abutted a mountain range of craggy peaks both beautiful and forbidding. Feeling as though she'd forgotten how to breathe, she pulled in a gasp. "Oh, my."

A hint of a smile filled Wyatt's voice. "Sometimes I forget how beautiful this place is."

"How long have you lived here?"

"About a year."

"And before that?"

"All over. I traveled a lot."

She caught sight of several log cabin homes and a small barn interspersed among the trees peppering the valley. "Which cabin is ours?"

"I've been living in the bunkhouse so we'll have to see what the General says."

"Is he really a general?"

"We call him that out of respect since he fought in the war. Don't ask him a lot of questions, all right? He's not much of a talker. Best let me explain everything. I'm not sure how he'll react to the changes I made in his plans."

She lifted her shoulder in a shrug. "As long as he gets a housekeeper, what does it matter?"

"I'm hoping it won't."

He raised a hand to wave at the lanky blond cowboy who sat whittling on a porch step. The man tipped his head back to stare at them for a moment. Brushing the wood shavings off his clothes, he went into the two-story cabin then returned a moment later to lean against the porch railing. A Negro cowboy emerged next and paused near the top of the porch step. He crossed his arms and watched them with a bemused smile on his face.

An older man strode past him to stand on the grass with his hands on his hips. Gray hair whitening at the temples, his commanding air left little doubt which of the men claimed the moniker of General. He frowned as they dismounted. "Where is Jack?"

"About two hours behind me." Wyatt took Mariah's hand and met her gaze with a faint smile before turning back to the men. "I'd like all of you to meet Mariah. . . Coulter."

Shocked silence filled the air. The blond man recovered first. "What?"

The General's eyes narrowed. "*You* married her?"

"Why?" the third man asked.

The question seemed to stump Wyatt, who momentarily floundered. Mariah lifted her chin. "Jackson was too drunk to meet me at the train station. Wyatt tried to convince me—"

Wyatt's grip on her hand tightened almost painfully. "I'll tell it, honey. I tried to convince her to stay and give Jack a chance, but he'd gone upstairs with Millie. Mariah decided she wouldn't have him. The only way to keep her here was to marry her myself, so that's what I did. I've got the papers to prove it."

He released her hand only long enough to pull their marriage license from his saddlebag and give it to the General. The man looked it over, lifting his eyebrows. "It certainly looks official."

"It is, sir."

The General handed the paper to the Negro, who read it before handing it off to the blond man. Wyatt tucked the marriage license back in his saddlebag then everyone seemed to hold their breath waiting for their leader to decide what was to be done about the change in plans. Finally, the General gave an approving nod. "We don't call you 'The Fixer' for nothing, Wyatt. I appreciate you stepping in and getting the job done. I'll need to have a talk with Jack once he gets here. Meanwhile, you and your lady can have the cabin I'd promised him."

Wyatt nodded then caught the horse's reins again. "Come on, Mariah. Let's get you settled in."

"Wait," she whispered. "You didn't finish the introduction. I don't know any of their names."

Wariness flashed over Wyatt's features, but the Negro man stepped forward with a charming smile and dancing brown eyes. "How rude of you, Wyatt. I'm Jasper Douglas. You can call me Jasper or Dodger."

"Dodger?"

"It's an old nickname of mine."

She nodded dumbly. Dodger Douglas? *The* Dodger Douglas? Renowned horse thief, cattle rustler, counterfeiter, and train robber? Surely not. The name... The man... It had to be a coincidence.

The blond man straightened and lifted his chin to stare down the sharp angles of his nose at her. His pale blue eyes seemed to threaten and smolder. "Blade. Blade Turner."

She swallowed hard then glanced down to the sheathed knives encircling his waist. There were so many of them that his guns seemed like an afterthought. Every one of them shouted he was *that* Blade Turner. The one who'd helped Dodger Douglas pull off the Laramie Bank Robbery with the rest of the Renegades. Which would make the older man General—

"Galen Lorde at your service, ma'am."

"Mister—" She forced a smile to her lips and corrected herself. "General, thank you for your hospitality."

He lifted a silver eyebrow. "Well, now, I wouldn't call it hospitality, exactly. More like an opportunity. Do your job. Do it well. We won't have a problem. You can start by cooking dinner tonight."

"Yes, sir." She couldn't look at her lying scoundrel of a husband. "Wyatt, I'd like to see the cabin now if that's all right."

"I'll show you the way."

Everything had changed when Wyatt had said those vows to Mariah. He simply hadn't realized it until this moment. There would be no more late nights in the bunkhouse swapping stories with the other outlaws, which would make it much harder to collect confessions. He'd be the odd one out. The only one with a woman—one he'd didn't intend to share.

It could easily become a dangerous dynamic. Yet, he'd chosen his path. There would be no turning back. Somehow he'd find a way to get Blade to admit he'd murdered a saloon girl in Abilene and learn where the gang had hidden the money from the Laramie bank robbery—if there was any left of it. He'd already gotten confessions from Galen Lorde, Jack, and Dodger concerning their most serious crimes.

Of course, he'd been a witness to the gang's cattle rustling since he'd signed on with the crew. He'd kept careful records of the transactions in the form of a log book for Lorde. The General appreciated knowing how many cattle he'd stolen from whom and where he'd sold the animals. So would Pinkerton and the state of Wyoming.

Wyatt couldn't afford to lose the valuable inroads he'd made with the gang. Nor could he allow them any hint he wasn't exactly who he'd said he was. That meant the one glimpse he'd given Mariah of Luke Bellamy in Hidden Springs would have to be the last. Somehow he had to make her believe he was just as much a desperado as everyone else on the crew while also showing her that she was safe with him and could trust him completely. She'd likely have to do that very thing to get out of this gang with her life and her honor intact. In fact, life with the gang would be so much easier and safer for both of them if she learned to follow any order he gave to the letter.

There was only one way to make a strong-willed woman like Mariah come to heel. He had to make her fall in love with him. The kind of love that made a woman devoted, loyal, and true. The kind that made her so foggy-headed she'd think the man she loved could do no wrong and if he did it was justifiable. Something to make her pliable.

That way, she'd be peaceable, unobtrusive, and, hopefully, nearly forgotten by the rest of the gang, allowing Wyatt to finish his assignment without incident. Yet, eager to follow him out of this forsaken valley at a moment's notice. It could work. It had to.

Mariah slammed the door behind them, dropped her traveling bag on the table, then planted her hands on her hips. "*Renegades!* The whole lot of you are good-for-nothing Renegades!"

Then again, this particular part of the mission might be easier said than done. Nevertheless, Wyatt held back a smile. Affecting a cocky tone, he raised a brow. "So you've heard of us. I'm flattered."

"Well, I've never heard of *you*, so don't be." She lifted her chin, brown eyes flashing. "What is your name again?"

"Wyatt Coulter, ma'am," he said with an unerring politeness that he hoped from the bottom of his heart was as irritating as he meant it to be. "You'd best get used to it, since you share it."

"Ha!" She pulled a chair from the table and sank into it while staring him down. "Is that even your real name?"

He shrugged. "Only one I'll own."

"And the one on the marriage certificate." A hint of triumph mixed with wariness in her voice. "You do realize that means we aren't truly married, don't you?"

He sat on the bed. "We're as married as you're going to get. Well. . .almost."

Her hand slid toward the satchel, which likely meant she had a peashooter tucked inside, especially considering the way she'd wrestled for his gun. "If you think for one moment that I'm sharing a bed with you, you are out of your ever-loving mind."

That was a good thing, seeing as she was right. They were definitely not married. He had no intention of acting like they were. At least, not beyond what was necessary to keep up appearances with the rest of the gang. "Far be it from me to force a lady to do anything she doesn't want to, but it's in your best interest to keep our sleeping arrangements between the two of us."

There was no fear in her voice. Simply bafflement. "You. . . You'll really leave me alone?"

"Contrary to what you might think, I am a gentleman. I'll sleep on a mat near the door." He chanced crossing the expanse between them to go on one knee. Ignoring her suspicious, closed-off expression, he covered the hand near the satchel. "Let's get one thing straight. I am the only thing standing between you and every other man in the gang who wouldn't hesitate to misuse you. You're under my protection. Our 'marriage' is sanctioned by the General, which is likely the only reason besides my reputation with a gun that the men might stay away from you."

"*Might?*"

"Stick close to me."

"Because you'll protect me?"

He held her gaze and gave a firm nod. "With my life."

She didn't back down or look away. "And who'll protect me from you?"

"I'm no threat to you. Even if I were, I have a feeling you could handle yourself. It's probably a good thing for me that you won't have to." He tilted his head toward the bag. "What do you shoot?"

She hesitated, likely weighing the value of revealing her hand. "Colt .45, of course."

He smiled approvingly. "Good. That'll do some damage. Keep it on you even while you cook and clean. All right?"

She gave a nod. "Why do they call you 'The Fixer'?"

He corralled a nearby chair and pulled it close enough that their knees nearly touched. Did she realize he was still holding her hand? He was tempted to brush his thumb across the back of it but didn't want to push his luck yet. There would be plenty of time to build a connection with her. Rushing it would help no one. "I've a talent for keeping folks out of trouble and solving problems. I clean up messes, whether that involves situations or evidence or—"

"People?" Challenge rang in her voice.

It was always best to tell the truth as much as possible since it made the lies he'd likely be forced to tell more believable. "Only when necessary."

A bitter little laugh escaped her throat. Shaking her head, she looked away. "Of course."

Wyatt tilted his head to survey her. She was an odd little thing, wasn't she? As innocent as she had seemed at first, there was a hardness to her he hadn't expected. Maybe even a worldliness. Beneath that, was a tired resolution, as if she'd heard this all before, not once but a thousand times. What was her story? "Where are you from?"

A cautious look filled her tawny eyes. "Didn't Jackson tell you?"

Maybe, but Wyatt had been so caught up in trying to prevent the marriage that he hadn't let the information imprint on his mind like it should have. Some detective he was. "Jack might have mentioned it, but seeing as I wasn't planning to marry you myself, I guess I didn't pay as much attention as I should have."

"I'm from Texas."

He waited for her to continue. When she didn't, he prodded, "Where about?"

"El Paso. What about you?"

"A boring little town in the Hill Country." He'd get into the rest of his cover story with her later. "Any family?"

"No." She bit her lip then modified, "Not anymore."

Did that mean they were all dead, or that she had disassociated herself from them? He'd come back to that later. "How did you live before this?"

"On a ranch as a cook and housekeeper. I wasn't a saloon girl. Nor did I work in a brothel, if that's what you're thinking."

"Never even crossed my mind. Just trying to get to know you."

She tossed him a suspicious look again then took in the rest of the cabin. The Fulton gang had stayed here a few months ago on their way to Utah. He'd sent word and the authorities had caught the gang when they'd left Utah for California. Despite the gang's reputation for being rowdy and violent, they'd left the cabin relatively clean. Still, there wasn't much else to recommend the place besides four solid walls with a window facing north and another facing south.

Both windows were trimmed with curtains so old and dusty they'd probably been hung by the frontier family that had settled here then abandoned the valley after a rockslide had made the main pass through the canyon impenetrable. A table and chairs, stove, dresser, and trunk were the only pieces of furniture in the one-room cabin besides the large bed. It was covered in a quilt and blanket that hadn't seen a good washing in a long time and sorely needed one.

Outlaws couldn't afford to be choosy when it came to good hideouts. Wyatt's "bride," however, deserved better. Apparently, Mariah agreed. She rolled up her sleeves, pulled an apron from her suitcase, and went to work cleaning the cabin. He didn't lift a finger to help. Instead, he grabbed a deck of cards from his saddlebag to play a game of solitaire. The longer he kept her in this cabin with him, the more legitimate their marriage would appear and the safer they both would be.

Chapter 3

Why?

She'd prayed. She'd hoped. She'd waited and believed her life was finally going to change for the better. Instead, she was in almost exactly the same situation she'd been trying to leave behind. Only now it was worse. To this gang of outlaws, she wasn't the pure, untouchable "Snow Wescott," whose stepbrothers would shoot any man who dared look at her. She was Mrs. Wyatt "The Fixer" Coulter, which meant the outlaws had no qualms about watching her like she was the last piece of pie in a two-hundred-mile radius.

Ignoring them, she set a pot of coffee on the stove in the ranch house. The woodbox was empty, as usual. It was Jack's responsibility to keep it full, but he never seemed to get around to it. Or maybe he was simply trying to keep his distance after the shaming he'd received from the rest of the gang for nearly messing up their plot—and it had been a plot, to be sure.

Jack's utter disbelief that Wyatt had officially married her instead of simply fooling her into a life of sin spoke volumes about the true intentions behind his proposal. And he hadn't been the only one with nefarious intentions. Blade was especially angry at Jack. Apparently, he'd been hoping for a chance at wooing her when Jack tired of her. It was enough to make a woman sick to her stomach. Beyond that, she was madder than she'd ever been in her life at the Renegades, her no-good stepbrothers for putting her in a situation where she had to leave home, her dearly departed mother for marrying Henry Wescott and maybe even. . . Maybe even God.

She'd been loyal to Him through thick and thin. In return, He'd led her here. Or had she led herself? Had she been so desperate for a way out that she'd taken the first opportunity that made sense whether He liked it or not? She held back a groan. She didn't know anymore. It was all so confusing. So hopeless.

With the coffeepot on the stove's warmer, she stepped outside and grabbed the ax, then paused to stare at the mountains looming on the other side of the lake. There had to be a way through them. In time, she might be able to gather enough supplies to hike over them. How long would it take? Days? Weeks? It was already September. She had a feeling winter would set in soon. Hardly the best time to climb a mountain. A better plan might be to try to escape through the canyon, even if it meant getting lost in its maze.

A horse neighed in the corral like a message from God Almighty. Of course! The horses knew the way out. Perhaps she could trust one of them to take her safely through the canyon and back to town. From there she'd go to. . . Well. . . Right now, she wasn't sure where she'd go, but she'd find a place.

Setting a log on the block, she began chopping into it as the kitchen door opened. It would be Wyatt, of course. He hardly ever let her out of his sight. Even when he was working on the books and pouring over maps with Galen Lorde, he kept the door to the ranch office open so he could see her moving about the house. To be honest, she'd come to count on it.

Setting the ax aside, she glanced over to meet his gaze. Only it wasn't him. In fact, it was someone she'd never seen before. The grandfatherly-looking fellow with white bushy hair smiled at her as he passed by with a book tucked under one arm and a cinnamon roll in each hand. "Good food. Thank you, Mariah."

"You're welcome." Wide-eyed, she watched him amble away.

Another voice sounded from the doorway. "That's Doc Tillman."

She spun to face Jack. "Who?"

"A war friend of the General's. He was a field doctor. Sawed off one too many limbs and lost his mind. He likes to amble about. Comes and goes as he pleases between here and Hawk's nest."

"Hawk's nest?"

"Hawk has a tepee out there somewhere in the wilderness. He prefers to live the old Shoshone way rather than bunk with the rest of us. Can't say I blame him, but it must get awfully lonely out there." Jack pulled in a deep breath. "Speaking of lonely, I'm sorry I didn't come for you when your train arrived."

"I'm glad you didn't."

He gave a soft laugh. "Taken a liking to Wyatt, have you?"

She shrugged. "Well enough."

"You're not in love with him."

"Nor was I in love with you." She turned away from him and placed a new log on the block.

Jack's hand covered hers on the ax handle. "I'll do it. It's my job anyway."

She tried to release it into his grasp, but he didn't let go of her. Instead, he took a step closer. "I made a mistake, Mariah. Do you forgive me?"

Eyes narrowing, she glanced down at his hand. "Let go of me."

He released her. "Do you?"

"What could it possibly matter to you?"

"You matter to me. I meant what I said in those letters. Everything we shared was real. If you'd rather be with me, all you have to do is say so."

He couldn't be serious. Yet, the sincerity on his face said otherwise. Barely holding back a laugh at the ridiculousness of the situation, she shook her head then met his gaze. "That is never going to happen."

His lips flattened into a line. Content to leave it at that, she tried to step past him, but he caught her arm and jerked her to his chest, angling for a kiss. Her knee lifted. An ominous click sounded behind them, making them both freeze. Steel laced Wyatt's voice. "You heard the lady. Her answer is no. Unhand her."

Jack pushed her away from him. She only stumbled a step before Wyatt steadied her. He slid past her until he and Jack were toe to toe. "Touch my wife again and I *will* pull this trigger. Do you understand me?"

Jack's jaw flexed. He stared right back at Wyatt then threw down the ax and walked toward the barn. She watched him go and blew out a frustrated breath. "He still didn't chop any blasted firewood."

Wyatt sent her an amused look before tucking his gun back in its holster and taking the ax in hand. "Are you all right?"

"Fine. I appreciate the assistance, but I could have handled him."

"I don't doubt it." A half smile touched his lips.

Crossing her arms, she watched as he split the wood in a single strike. She wasn't entirely sure what to make of Wyatt. He'd slept in a bedroll on the floor without any complaints or innuendos for the past three nights. As much as she hated to admit it, he was starting to grow on her a little. That was probably because he'd been telling her the truth when they'd ridden into the valley. He certainly seemed to be the best man here. Unfortunately, that wasn't saying much.

She wanted to ask him what he was on the run for, because surely he must be wanted somewhere to hole up in a place like this. Yet she wasn't sure she wanted to know. It would be so much nicer to think of him as the somewhat kindly outlaw who'd kept the wolves at bay before she escaped this awful place. And she would escape. It would only take a few more days—three at the most—to lull him into a false sense of security. Then she'd put her plan into motion and find her way out of here.

Wyatt had expected Mariah to try to escape at some point. In fact, he would have been disappointed if she hadn't. But, *this*? This was just stupid.

He maintained a sleep-laden rhythm to his breathing and watched beneath his lashes while she shimmied out the cabin window into the night. He held his breath as soon as she dropped out of sight, then listened to her quiet footfalls circle the cabin and head south. Shaking his head, he eased out of the cabin and tracked her to the barn where she bribed a sure-footed roan into cooperating with a few sugar cubes and some sweet-talking.

Wyatt gave her a couple minutes head start then hopped onto a palomino that could lap the roan when it came to speed. Mariah led her horse right up to the canyon's opening. Her horse balked a little, and Wyatt couldn't blame it. The canyon was a frightening place at night and more than one mountain lion had been known to stalk its walls.

A wild neigh was all the warning he received before the roan shot past him back into the valley with Mariah clinging to the saddle like a burr on a blanket. Racing after her, Wyatt plucked the woman from her horse and sat her in front of him on the saddle. He didn't say a word as he herded the spooked horse away from the cabins so it wouldn't disturb the other men. The roan calmed quickly once they reached the lakeshore. The same could not be said for the woman.

Mariah's hands clenched the saddle horn, but the rest of her body trembled like a leaf in the wind. He dismounted then lifted her down as well. She immediately pulled away.

Stalking downhill, she stopped at the edge of the lake and slid her hands into the pockets of— Were those his denim pants? She'd rolled up the legs and hitched up the britches with a bit of rope, but they were definitely his pants. They looked absolutely ridiculous on her as did the oversized plaid shirt she wore. Had she been trying to disguise herself as a drifter?

Holding back a chuckle, he watched her sit down on the grass near the edge of the lake. She brought her legs to her chest, wrapped her arms around them, and rested her forehead on her knees as though she wanted to curl inside herself and disappear. The anger she'd been carrying like a shield for the last few days seemed to have burned out, leaving only defeat.

Perhaps she'd finally be open to connecting with him. He claimed the spot beside her but waited for her to speak first. Her voice was steady and resigned. "There's no way out of here, is there?"

"I can think of at least two off the top of my head. Neither of them involves you getting yourself killed in the middle of the night."

Eyes wide, she turned to search his face in the moonlight. "There are two other ways out of here? I don't suppose you'd tell me what they are?"

He braced his palms behind him on the grass. "You could have told me there was something you desperately needed from town. A feminine something or other only you could pick out yourself. I would have eventually taken you there to get the item. You could have escaped, taken a train to. . . Where were you headed with the money you took from my secret stash before climbing out the window?"

"I wasn't sure yet." She sighed. "What's the other way out?"

"You could have asked me to take you away from here."

She gave a soft, skeptical laugh. "Would you have done it?"

He tucked his hands behind his head and lay back on the grass to consider the question. Would he have found a way to sneak her out of here? He couldn't. Not without causing the gang to doubt his loyalty. Already, Jack had stopped talking to him unless absolutely necessary and Blade seemed to seethe with a quiet jealousy that made Wyatt wary. He shook his head. "Right now, it isn't possible."

Lying down on her side, she rested her head in her hand as she stared at him. "But someday?"

He had to give her something—some bit of hope to get her through this. "Gangs don't stay together forever, Mariah."

"I know."

His brow furrowed. "You do?"

"Well, I've. . . I've read about outlaws in the papers same as everyone."

No doubt she never thought she'd be living among one. Taking her hand in his, he rested it on his chest. "I know this might seem like a bleak situation to you, but it won't last forever. You don't belong to the Renegades. You belong with me. You go where I go."

"I go where you go," she repeated softly as she stared down at where her hand rested in his grasp. Her tumultuous gaze met his. "Then can't we go somewhere else? Somewhere no one knows you. We could start over together."

He barely held back a smile at her enthusiasm. "Why? So you could take my advice and run away from me as soon as we get to civilization? Isn't that exactly what you would do?"

She let out a frustrated sigh. "How did you become an outlaw anyway? Can't you just do a little time in prison and start over as a new man?"

"Just do a little time in prison?" This time he didn't bother to hold in his chuckle. "You make it sound so harmless."

She sat up and crossed her arms. "Well, maybe what you did wasn't so harmless and you deserve it. What *did* you do, Wyatt? You know I could ask any of the other outlaws. They'd tell me with no hesitation. I'd rather hear it from you."

It was a fair point. If she asked anyone else, they'd tell her the cover story he'd established. The one where a simple, relatively harmless robbery had accidentally ended in murder and sent him on the run. It wasn't true. Not one bit of it. Yet, he'd never had a problem bandying it around. . .until now.

Telling her would serve no real purpose. It would only cause more distance to grow between them. That was the last thing he wanted at this point. For her safety and his, she needed to be loyal to him. He needed to make a move now. He sat up to cup that stubborn chin of hers. "Don't ask them. Don't ask me. If you want me to start over, then let it begin here and now."

"You would do that?" she asked with a mix of skepticism and disbelief. "You would really change for me?"

He nodded. "Who do you want me to be, Mariah?"

"Honestly?" She glanced toward the lake for a long moment then turned back to him with her guard finally lowered. "I want you to be someone who loves God, someone who loves me more than you love danger or violence or the next job. Is that possible for you, Wyatt? If not, you have no right to keep me here. Especially if Wyatt Coulter isn't your true name and our marriage isn't legal."

"I know God. I've strayed, but I do know Him. Or, I did. Once." It was true enough. It was hard to maintain faith when he lived among those consumed by greed, violence, and death. Harder still, when simply owning a Bible could blow a carefully constructed cover. He'd told himself long ago he was doing all of this to serve God, to see justice done. Yet how could that be true when the work he was doing for God only seemed to take him further and further from God?

She caught his wrist. "Then get to know Him again. Love Him. Love me. Put my interests first. That's what the Bible says a husband should do for his wife—sacrifice himself, give himself up for her as Christ did the Church."

He barely managed to hide a frown. Loving her was out of the question, but maybe she was right about everything else. Maybe this was the right moment to start over. He'd write to his contact and ask to be pulled off this investigation then take Mariah with him when he left. He could help her start a new life somewhere unencumbered by her fake marriage to him. It's what she deserved. More than that, it was the right thing to do.

He took Mariah's hand in his and gave it a gentle squeeze. "I'll try, Mariah. I promise you, I'll try."

She seemed to be weighing him, weighing his words. "I believe you."

For a man who made his living through deceit, whether it was for a good cause or not, those three small words seemed too good to be true. Yet she really meant them. They burrowed down deep inside of him, past every disguise, right to the heart of him. They made him want to be a better man, one worthy of the belief she had placed in him and the trust he was determined to earn.

Amid all the deceit and the veneer that had made up his world for so long, she seemed like the only real thing here. Her and the God he'd drifted so far from. He might not be able to reach out and touch God, but he could touch Mariah. So he did. Staring into her eyes, he traced a shaft of moonlight across her cheek. She stilled but didn't move away.

He needed to make a moment here, find a way to forge their bond deeper, inspire affection. His lifted his head toward hers, but she pulled away, going so far as to stand and wrap her arms around herself. "This is a kind of prison for me. You know that, don't you?"

"It doesn't have to be." He stood up beside her. "It could be a refuge."

She sent him a disbelieving look. "Not with the Renegades for company."

"I promised to protect you from them, and I will. Maybe this isn't the life you were hoping for, but surely it has its moments. Look around. Without thinking of this place as a prison, just look." He waited as she took in the bright moon hovering in the sky among a million stars, mountains blanketed by the deep blue of night, and the vast lake where still, dark waters shimmered with starlight.

Something within her seemed to relax enough to let a soft smile shine through. "It's pretty. I'll admit to that much."

He could say the same of her and more, but she didn't seem like the kind of woman to respond to flattery. Forthrightness would likely serve him better. "Mariah, I'd like to kiss you."

She stilled. The soft sound of the wind whispering across the lake filled the silence as she considered his request. Finally, she turned to look at him. "Why?"

That was Mariah, all right. No feigned bashfulness. Not a hint of alarm. Just pure curiosity and confrontation. He searched himself for the answer she demanded. Why did he want to kiss her? Because it was a part of his job. A means to an end. Was that really all there was to it?

Maybe. Maybe not. He shrugged. "You've got moonlight in your hair."

Her eyebrows lifted as a hint of amusement set her voice lilting. "I've got moonlight in my hair?"

He nodded, touching the loose waves that reflected the light. "Besides, you're still here—not lying dead in the canyon somewhere."

Her eyes narrowed. He smiled for the first time in what felt like ages. Her long lashes blinked in surprise as her gaze drifted to his mouth and lingered there. "So what?"

He pressed his advantage, taking a step closer. "It seems like the right thing to do right about now, wouldn't you say?"

"I suppose one kiss might be acceptable in a setting like this." Warning filled her voice. "*One* kiss. That's all."

He placed his hands on the curve of her waist. "Yes, ma'am."

Chapter 4

Mariah stood at the kitchen sink a week later running a soapy cloth over the last dirty plate. The midday sun poured through the windows of the General's house, but her mind was filled with moonlight, stars reflecting off a still lake and a soft breeze whispering through the trees. Wyatt's fingers sliding into her hair as he deepened the kiss, lingering until they were both breathless. Yet he'd kept his word by respecting her request. One kiss.

That was all that had transpired. Nothing more. Nothing less.

A few days later, General Lorde had sent him out to do... Well, she wasn't sure what Wyatt was doing out there in the world beyond this valley. Likely stealing or robbing. Maybe even killing. Or being killed. Blade and Jack had gone with him. Their absence was a relief. There was no mistaking that. It was nice to be able to walk around without Blade's cold eyes following her every move or fearing Jack might waylay her for another attempt at sweet-talking her into trading her husband for him.

Still, she couldn't help wondering if Wyatt was safe in their company. Would they betray him simply to get him out of the way? What would happen to her if they did? If Wyatt didn't come back...

She closed her eyes against the thought, not even wanting to consider what might happen. Shaking her head, she rinsed off a tin plate and set it on the drying rack. The sound of shuffling cards paused for a moment then started again. "Mariah, come play a hand with us."

She turned to lean back against the sink and met Dodger's friendly smile with a doubtful one of her own. Galen Lorde didn't echo the invitation, but he didn't protest it either. Instead, he lit his pipe then looked at her with a hint of challenge in his gaze. He wanted her to bond with the men, did he? She knew the tactic well enough. Make a newcomer earn his or her place in the gang. Let them form some affection or at least a sense of belonging to the other members. Thereby making that person far less likely to turn state's witness if given the chance.

Tilting her head, she eyed Dodger's fancy shuffling. "What game are y'all playing?"

"We call it matchstick poker. It's like regular poker except we play for matchsticks instead of money." He began dealing the cards for the three of them. "Come on. I'll teach you how."

She'd been playing poker since the summer she'd turned twelve and moved in with her stepfamily. Nonetheless, she let Dodger have the pleasure of teaching her all over again since he seemed so eager to help. She lost the first hand on purpose then set about trouncing them both with a doddering innocence that kept them from guessing she'd ever played the game before. Four hands in, Doc Tillman opened the front door and peeped in to announce, "The boys are riding in."

Everything within her stilled. Wyatt was back? The General let out a grunt. "Right on time. Mariah. It's your turn."

She forced her distracted gaze back to her cards as Doc disappeared outside, closing the door behind him. "Two cards, please."

Dodger dealt her two more. It seemed an eternity before the front door opened again. She deflated at the sight of Blade and retrained her eyes on her cards. General Lorde cleared his throat. "Blade, come and take Mariah's place before she bursts."

She met the General's kind blue eyes with a thankful smile then set her cards face-down on the table before hurrying out to join Doc Tillman on the porch. The white-haired fellow stood at the railing with his black doctor's bag at the ready. Concern filled her. "Is someone hurt?"

"Don't know yet." He opened his bag and pulled out a handkerchief, studiously unfolding it to reveal three of the sugar cookies she'd baked two days ago. He took a large bite of one. "Blade said he didn't need my help, but you never know. The others might."

She eyed his doctor's bag. "Do you have any. . .um. . .medical instruments in your bag, Doc Tillman?"

"Pshaw, missy." He sent her a disdainful look. "What do you take me for?"

"Is that—does that mean yes? You do have medical equipment?"

He leaned his hip into the porch railing and stared her down with flinty blue eyes. "Now, listen here. I ain't half as crazy as those young pups make me out to be. Course, I've got medical equipment in this bag, and I know how to use it. Ask any one of the gangs who come through here all battered up and bloody. They'll tell you who set them to rights. It was Doc Tillman. That's who."

"My apologies. I shouldn't have doubted you."

He gave a firm nod then narrowed his eyes at Jack, who exited the barn and walked toward them favoring his left arm. "What happened to you?"

Jack grinned at them both. "Coyotes."

"Two-legged or four?"

"Both." Jack gave her a once-over as he climbed the porch steps. "Hello, Miss Mariah. You're a sight for sore eyes."

"Hello, Jack." Nervousness filled her stomach. "Did Wyatt ride in with y'all?"

"Sure did. He's in the barn, but I'm sure he'll be right happy to see you. I know I am."

She ignored his flirtation, knowing he was mostly doing it to needle Wyatt even if her husband wasn't there to witness it. With all the other men accounted for except Hawk, who hardly showed his face anyway, Mariah deemed it safe enough to walk over to the barn and greet her husband—*fake* husband. Though why she felt inspired to do so was a mystery to her.

Relief filled her at the sight of him standing in the sunlight with one shoulder leaning against the open doors of the corral. Glancing down at the letter in his hands, he gave a frustrated shake of his head then stared out at the mountains. Mariah pulled in a steeling breath. "Bad news?"

He spun to face her. His gray eyes lit up and a smile curved his mouth. Folding the letter into his pocket, he reached out his hand then met her halfway to claim hers. That oddly perceptive gaze of his seemed to scour and catalog every inch of her as he spoke in low tones. "My sister says it's best for me to stay put for now."

Her heart leaped in her chest. "You were thinking of going somewhere?"

"Thought you might could use a trip."

Her free hand squeezed his arm. "Oh, Wyatt, truly?"

He nodded. "But we can't go. Not yet. No one can know we're even thinking of it, understand?"

"I understand."

He cupped her cheek and let his thumb trace her smile. "How'd you manage without me?"

Releasing his arm, she took a step back, though she couldn't go far with her hand still tucked in his. "I managed fine."

"The men didn't give you any trouble?"

"No trouble at all."

"Good. I brought you something. Come and see." He led her over to where his saddlebag rested on the gate of a nearby stall. He pulled a brown paper package from the bag and handed it to her. "Go on. Open it."

She gave him a curious smile as she untied the string. Peeling back the folded paper revealed a length of lace. He shrugged. "I know it's impractical out here, but every bride should have a bit of white lace. There's more."

There was definitely more. Something hard and square rested beneath the lace. It turned out to be two small books. "Oh, Wyatt, a book of Psalms and a New Testament. I love them! Thank you."

"I hope you don't mind if I read them now and then too."

"Mind? Of course, I won't mind. We'll share them." She hugged them to her chest. "This means so much to me, Wyatt."

"I'm glad you like them. Best keep this between us, though. We don't want the other men to think I'm going soft." Taking the books from her, he slid them back into the saddlebag then took her arms and boldly draped them around his neck. He caught her waist between his hands and leveled his silver eyes at her. Sincerity filled his low voice. "I missed you."

Her rebellious heart fluttered, but she knew better than to let herself be charmed. As much as she wanted to be able to trust him, he was an outlaw. She had no idea what he'd been doing. Nor whom he'd been with. Perhaps he'd found affection elsewhere. The thought left her cold, but she'd be foolish not to at least consider it.

Just because that madam in town didn't know about him having a woman didn't necessarily mean there wasn't one. She knew how outlaws could be after they'd successfully finished a job—far too ready to celebrate with any woman who was willing.

She couldn't help but give him a doubtful look. "Are you sure you weren't too busy with someone else?"

"With someone—" Storm clouds filled his eyes. "I would never be unfaithful to you, Mariah. How could I, when I can't stop thinking about you or our kiss? All the while I was gone, I was wishing I was with you, waiting until I could see you again, wanting to hold you, and. . ." A hint of frustration flashed across his face, followed by desperation. "Honey, didn't you think about me at all while I was gone?"

"Maybe a little," she admitted in a reluctant whisper.

The firm line of his mouth hitched upward at the corner. "And you missed me?"

It was more of a demand than a question so she treated it as such. Arching her eyebrows in surprise, she batted her lashes innocently. "Did I? Hmm. Oh, I don't know, Wyatt. What was there to miss?"

He tugged her into a kiss without so much as a by-your-leave. He was here. He was safe. He was hers—sort of. So she may have kissed him back a little. All right, more than a little. She didn't exactly limit him to one kiss either. Not that he asked about a limit before kissing her again. She let him kiss her once more before sliding her hands down to his chest and pushing him away. "You shouldn't—"

"*I* shouldn't?" He grinned at her.

"*We* shouldn't kiss like that. We aren't married. Not if your name isn't legally Wyatt Coulter."

He was quiet for a moment. Catching her hands, he tugged her into an embrace. "Suppose I took you into town right now, had the justice of the peace draw up the papers with my legal name. Would you marry me again?"

Would she? Her heart whispered a silent yes, even as reason screamed no. She should run from him, from all of this, the second she had the chance. She wanted to lie and say yes, make him bring her into town, take out on the next train, but she couldn't mislead him in this. No matter how much she should. "Wyatt. . ."

"I thought not." He kissed her temple. "Maybe one day. . . One day your answer might be different."

She searched his gaze. "So you'll keep me here against my will until it changes?"

"Where is it you want to go?"

"Away from here."

He shook his head. "Be specific, Mariah. If you left here without me, where would you go?"

"Without you?" Why did her foolish heart lurch at the mere thought of it? She sighed. "Wyatt, you know I have nowhere to go."

"I know." His lips formed a straight line again. Concern furrowed his brow. Finally, he framed her face with his hands and looked deep into her eyes. "Sweetheart, when are you going to realize the safest place for you to be is right here?" He pulled her into a hug. "I promise you on my life. It's *right here*."

She hesitated for a moment, then her rigid body relaxed into his and she held on tight. She believed him. Truly. Deep down. He would protect her. He would help her. One day, God willing, they'd leave this life behind for something new.

He really shouldn't kiss Mariah so often. It was unprofessional. She trusted him now, so it was also unnecessary. Not to mention unwise. Her kisses had a way of making him lose focus, turning his mind and his priorities topsy-turvy. Right now he should be thinking about a way to finally capture the entire Renegade gang. Instead, he was thinking about Mariah. That scrappy, no holding back, tell it like it is, mischievous, innocent yet jaded woman was turning his brain to mush. It had to stop, and it had to stop now.

He ignored the glass of whiskey the Silver Slipper's burly bartender slid to him. Surveying his surroundings, his jaw tightened as he realized that for once nearly the whole Renegade gang was right here, ripe for arresting—if he wasn't so outnumbered. Rarely did the General ever let the whole gang leave the valley at once. If Wyatt had known this would happen, he would have called for reinforcements, but the General never let his right hand know what the left hand was doing.

After two weeks at home with Mariah, Wyatt had been sent to mop up behind Blade, Dodger, and Jack, who'd rustled nearly two hundred head of cattle. Hiding trails, mending cut fences, and the like until the only trace of the gang was the ink on Wyatt's ledger. Meanwhile, the General had done something to come into money on his own and left his lair to do it. Wyatt needed to ferret out what the General's crime was, but the General and Rosie were deep in conversation.

Try as he might, Wyatt couldn't hear them over the tinny piano. There would likely be an opportunity to talk to the General at some point this evening. However, the longer Wyatt waited, the less likely he was to make it to the valley before nightfall. Mariah would be waiting and worrying. Wyatt would be worrying too, because even though Doc Tillman seemed to harbor some grandfatherly affection for Mariah, the man wasn't altogether sane.

The only other person left at the valley was Hawk. The gatekeeper to the hideout didn't pay much attention to what went on inside the safety of the valley. If there was trouble, he'd notice, but how soon?

A man slid onto the stool on Wyatt's right. Another claimed the stool on his left. Wyatt caught a glimpse of their faces in the mirror behind the bar. Familiar. Both of them. Too familiar.

The man on his right met his gaze. Blue eyes. Ruddy brown hair. A full beard that didn't quite cover the faint, jagged scar trailing down his cheek. Wyatt had studied the man's wanted poster enough to know exactly who he was. Colin "The Killer" Wescott—murderer of six men and one woman, bank robber, train robber, horse thief, and older brother of the man seated on Wyatt's left. A quick glance at that man confirmed he was indeed Dave Wescott. Dave didn't quite have his brother's penchant for killing, but he'd joined in with the bank robbing, train robbing, and horse thieving eagerly enough.

The Renegades had a reputation. There was no mistaking that, but recently they'd stuck to cattle rustling. In Wyoming rustlers came a dime a dozen. The gang's true value lay in their connections to the other gangs who passed through their hideout. On the other hand, the Wescott brothers—they were legends. All they had to do was show up and folks would hand over fistfuls of cash to see them gone. The bounties on their heads had sent plenty of bounty hunters after them. Four of them had gotten close enough to die for their efforts.

The brothers and their gang were Texas's problem. What on earth were they doing in Wyoming? Seeking new territory? Apparently they had business with him. Otherwise, they wouldn't have surrounded him or keep staring at him. The best way to get out of this alive was to make friends with them. He motioned the bartender over. "First one is in on me."

The men gave their orders to the bartender then Dave grinned. "Right kindly of you."

"Don't mention it." He threw back his whiskey because it would look strange if he didn't.

Colin did the same with his then leaned an elbow on the bar. "Is your name Wyatt Coulter?"

"Who wants to know?"

"I'm Colin. This here is Dave. Rosie pointed you out. She says you might know something about our missing sister."

Snow Wescott—assumed to be an aider and abettor to the Wescott gang. Although rarely seen in public, she was reported to be a beauty. The newspaper painted her as everything from an angel to a hellion. Wyatt shook his head. "I don't know anything about anyone's sister. You might want to talk to my friend Jack. He's the resident lady-killer."

"No." Colin's eyes seemed to pierce through to his very soul. "I don't want to talk to a lady-killer. I want to talk to the kind of man who's looking to marry a woman."

Wyatt frowned. "You do know you aren't making a lick of sense, don't you, Colin?"

Dave chuckled. "He's got you there, Colin. What my brother is trying to say is we think you might have married our sister."

"What?"

"Show him the picture, Col."

Colin placed a tintype on the bar. Wyatt snatched it up. Unsmiling and solemn, his wife stared back at him in black and white. Mariah Snow. Snow Wescott.

Colin growled, "You recognize her."

He'd been too stunned to hide his reaction. He could lie, say that he'd seen her in passing, but Rosie had already confirmed he'd married this woman. No wonder Mariah—Snow—hadn't wanted to go home. Her home was the Wescott gang hideout. So much about her suddenly made sense. Even so, he shook his head in disbelief. "This can't be my wife."

Dave grinned. "Fooled you, did she? What did she say her name was?"

"Mariah Snow."

"Well, she didn't lie," Dave said as he motioned for a refill. "That's her real name, all right. She's our stepsister. Her ma married into our family when Mariah was twelve. We called her Snow as a pet name. The papers just assumed she was a Wescott."

Wyatt glanced back and forth between the brothers. "Wescott?"

Either Colin didn't buy into the surprise in Wyatt's voice or he didn't care. "Where is she?"

"She's safe."

Colin tipped his head in the direction of the canyon. "Tucked inside the Renegades' hidey-hole? Take us to her."

As Mariah's almost-husband and friend, he didn't want to let either of them near her. After all, she'd run from them for a reason. Yet, as a man sworn to uphold the law, he couldn't let the Wescott brothers go without trying to capture them or trying to discover information that would lead to their capture. In fact, if he could wire his superiors and let them know the brothers were in the area. . . "I'll try, but it isn't completely up to me. Stay here."

Wyatt caught the General's attention and they met near the back of the saloon. He explained the situation while the General eyed the two men in question. "You're sure they're really her brothers?"

"They have her picture. I can't imagine why else they would come all this way."

"Well, it can't be simply to talk to her. You must know they're here to take her away from you, from all of us. The question is, how many of us would they be willing to kill to do it?"

"Do you think they'd check their weapons with Hawk?"

"It's the only way I'd let them into our camp." Lorde scanned the room. "They could be detectives, you know, pretending to be the Wescott brothers to worm their way into our hideout."

Wyatt shook his head. "I've seen their pictures in the paper and read descriptions of both of them. They're the Wescotts, all right."

"To be safe, we'll have Mariah identify them after they check their weapons with Hawk. I'll round up the boys for the ride back to the valley. We want the Wescotts outnumbered. You let them know our terms. If Mariah doesn't want to see them, they're out. I'm not keen on losing my cook, so I hope you're ready to fight for her."

He nodded. "I'm ready."

"Well, then. Let's give you your chance."

Chapter 5

She'd thought one week without Wyatt was bad. Two weeks was torture. She'd spent most of her time doing chores, playing solitaire, reading books from Doc Tillman's expansive library, and listening to the old fellow's war stories. If she heard one more tale ending with someone losing a limb, she might lose her mind.

She jumped as the front door banged open and Jack stepped inside. Joy and relief filled her. The men must be back. She dropped her knife into the large bowl of potatoes she was slicing then rinsed her hands in the sink. No need to smell like raw potatoes when greeting her husband—almost-husband. "Supper won't be ready for another hour or so, I'm afraid."

Jack sank onto a kitchen chair and frowned. "No rush. It's just me for now. Millie and I had a fight so I came back early. The rest of the men had business in town."

"Oh."

"Well, you needn't sound so disappointed." He took one of the dry potatoes out of the bushel and rubbed the dirt from the skin. "Your guard dog will be here soon enough."

She let the comment pass, knowing he was likely still sore about whatever happened between him and Millie. Grabbing the knife from the bowl, she settled back in the chair catty-corner from him and went back to slicing potatoes. He drummed his fingers on the table impatiently. "Where's Doc?"

"On a ramble, I guess."

He nodded then stared off toward the fireplace and grimaced. "Why are women so blamed unreasonable?"

"What happened with Millie, Jack?"

"She wants to marry me."

Hiding a smile at his horrified tone, she carried the bowl to the sink. "Well, why don't you? You obviously care about her."

"I don't give a fig about Millie." He was quiet for a moment, then she felt his chest brush against her back as his hand trailed up her arm. "You have to believe me."

"What are you doing?" Spinning to face him, she tried to sidestep away from him, but he braced his hands on either side of the counter behind her.

"It's you I want." The smell of liquor filled what little air remained between them. His green eyes traced her features desperately. "Can't you see that?"

A cold feeling washed over her, filling her voice with a warning. "Jack."

"Give us a chance." He pressed against her, pinning her to the counter, then caught her jaw in an unyielding grip and kissed her.

She squirmed and pushed away from his chest until she was free of his demanding lips. "Let go of me!"

He let go only long enough to grab her waist and sit her on the counter. Sending her a sultry look, he smiled. "You'll like this. I promise."

She slapped at his face, kicked his chest, and screamed, "I said stop!"

He ducked away from her firestorm. Sliding off the counter, she raced out the front door. Jack and his laughter chased after her. If she could lock herself in her cabin until Wyatt arrived—Jack tackled her legs. Her palms met the hard-packed ground. Twisting to face him, she screamed and tried to kick her legs free, but he straddled her. He covered her mouth with one hand then blocked a blow to his face with the other. "Stop fighting me, you wildcat!"

She bit his hand. Hard. He jerked it away with a laugh. "Fine. Scream all you want. There's no one around to hear you."

He dodged her bared nails then caught her hands and pinned them over her head. A gunshot rang out. Jack froze. A look of bewilderment replaced his smile. He released her hands to touch the hole that had appeared in his shirt on his right shoulder. His fingers came away with blood. "I've been shot."

Taking advantage of his distraction, she struck his nose with the heel of her hand as hard as she could. He cried out and toppled off her. She scrambled away from him as horses thundered into the yard and encircled them.

"What do you think you're doing?" General Lorde yelled as he dropped from his horse and started pummeling Jack with his fists. "What were my orders concerning Mariah?"

Jack held up his hands but otherwise didn't try to defend himself. "Stop! Please."

General Lorde ignored him. "*What were my orders?*"

"To leave her alone." Jack curled into a ball.

General Lorde kicked him one last time. "My apologies, Mariah. I'll make sure he's packed up and gone within the hour."

Mariah flinched as a gentle hand touched her shoulder. Glancing up, she met her husband's fierce, concerned gaze. Her eyes filled with tears of relief. "Wyatt."

Wyatt scooped Mariah into his arms. Her arms went around his neck and she buried her face in his shoulder. That was enough to give her enraged brothers pause as they moved toward her. Wyatt held her closer. Dave gave him a shallow nod then murmured something to Colin. Wyatt didn't wait a second longer to stride into the cabin he shared with Mariah. He leaned back on the door to shut it behind them.

Mariah tensed. "Wait. Put me down."

He immediately released her. She hurried over to the door and slid the bar into place, locking them in. No, locking everyone else out. That became obvious as she stood frozen in place, her breath heaving in her chest—no doubt going over a thousand scenarios of what might have happened if the rest of the gang hadn't ridden in when they did. "Mariah."

She slowly turned and lifted her gaze to meet his. In two steps, she was in his arms again, trembling and clinging to him with all her might. His heart felt near to bursting, but it shouldn't. None of this was supposed to be real. She wasn't truly his wife. She was just a girl he was supposed to protect. Someone with deep connections to two notorious criminals.

He needed to refocus on his assignment, take her statement, add whatever she said to Jack's list of crimes, and. . .

Swallowing hard, he shook his head and, just for now, blocked out everything but the fact that Mariah was in his arms. She was safe. On some level, she cared for him. He could hold on to that, even if it was all he ever truly had of her. Eventually, she stopped shaking. He swept her into his arms again. Sitting on the edge of the bed, he set her on his knee then captured her gaze. "Will you tell me what happened?"

It would have been tempting for her to gloss over any uncomfortable and personal aspects of the attack. Yet Wyatt believed her account to be complete, which meant the attack hadn't progressed as far as he'd first feared. That was a relief. After she finished, her hand traced the planes of his shoulder then rested at his nape. "Say something."

"I'm sorry."

Her brow furrowed in confusion. "*You're* sorry?"

He lowered his gaze to the plank floor. "I promised to protect you. I should have been here."

"Stop blaming yourself. I could just as easily say I shouldn't have been so friendly with him. It's only—well, somehow, I got complacent. I should have known better than to trust an outlaw." That familiar, jaded expression crossed her face, then her eyes widened and she winced. "I didn't mean. . ."

He smiled. "You didn't offend me. You're right. No one in the gang is trustworthy."

"Except you."

"Except me," he echoed softly. If only that was true. He shook his head. "You are definitely wrong about one thing, though."

"What's that?"

"In no way, shape, or form is what happened your fault. Once you realized what he was after, you told him to stop. He didn't. That's on him. I'm betting he's regretting it about now. If not, I'll—"

"Wyatt." Mariah's hand covered the fist he hadn't even realized he'd made. "Leave it to General Lorde. He seemed to have it in hand."

Not to mention her brothers. He pulled in a deep breath. "Mariah, there's something we need to discuss."

Wariness filled her eyes. "Is something wrong?"

A fist pounded on their front door, making her jump. Her eyes widened as Colin's voice called through the wood. "Coulter, we're done waiting! We demand to see our sister!"

Mariah's mouth dropped open. Standing, she stared at the front door then turned to face Wyatt as betrayal swept through her. Her voice came out in a rushed whisper.

"You brought my brothers here? Are you out of your mind? Do you have any idea who they are?"

A hint of amusement glinted in his eyes. "Oh, they introduced themselves."

"Of course they did," she said with a frustrated sigh.

"Mariah?" Dave called. "Are you coming out here or are we coming in there?"

"I'll come out. Give me a few minutes, though. I'll meet you at General Lorde's house."

Colin sounded decidedly cross. "Fine, but hurry up."

Wyatt lifted a brow as their footsteps faded away, then reached out a hand to her. "So you're a member of the Wescott gang."

"I wouldn't say that." She took his hand and he tugged her onto his knee again. "Leastwise, not by choice. My mother married their father when I was twelve. She didn't know he was an outlaw until after they said 'I do.'"

He smiled. "That sounds familiar."

"Colin was fourteen. Dave was twelve. They desperately wanted a ma, since theirs had been dead for ten years. The Wescott men treated us like we were queens, angels, and saints all wrapped up into one. Everything was wonderful except for the fact that the Wescotts were wild, violent, and greedy with everyone else and we were hardly ever allowed to leave the ranch. Ma got sick and died three years ago. Their pa soon followed. That's when the boys took over the gang."

"And you?" He released her hand and let his slide along her arm comfortingly, distractingly. He still hadn't kissed her hello. They'd had more urgent things to deal with. That didn't stop her gaze from straying to his lips as he asked, "What did you do for the gang?"

She sighed. "I didn't do anything *for* the gang. I kept house same as I do here until I was able to get away."

He frowned then lifted her hand to kiss her palm. "Why couldn't you leave freely?"

"They wouldn't let me. They said it wasn't safe. According to them, there are too many outlaws and lawmen waiting to take advantage of me or settle the score. Besides, I had to wait until the timing was right, until I had someplace to go. Some way to start over without anyone knowing about my past or my brothers."

He tilted his head. "So you were protecting them?"

"No," she said firmly, in case he had any illusions as to where she stood when it came to the law. Sadly, that wasn't on the same side as him. Heaviness settled over her heart and blurred her eyes with tears. "They've done awful things—especially Colin. I know one day they'll have to pay for all of it. Maybe even with their lives. I can't protect them from that."

He rubbed a circle on her back. "Why didn't you tell me?"

"They're hardly the type of in-laws a prospective husband hopes for. Besides, I wanted to leave all that behind. You can understand that, can't you?"

"I understand." He was quiet for a moment, no doubt sorting through all these new revelations. "What about you and your brothers? Did they continue to treat you well after your parents died? Are y'all close?"

"They treated me as they always did. We get along well, but I'm not sure I'd say we're close. They have a lot of secrets—most of which I'd rather not know."

He nodded. "Anything else I should be aware of before we face them?"

"Two things. First, you'd better let me handle them. Second. . ." She pressed a kiss as soft and fleeting as a butterfly upon his lips. "I missed you horribly, almost-husband."

A softness she'd never seen before entered his eyes. "I missed you too."

His lingering kiss proved it before he stood and set her on her feet. "I memorized a few psalms while I was gone."

Memorizing scripture while rustling cattle? That had to be a first. She reached for her gun—not that she intended to use it, but she'd rather have it on her than off especially after what had happened with Jack. "That's wonderful. Which one is your favorite?"

" 'Whither shall I go from thy spirit? Or whither shall I flee from thy presence? If I ascend up into heaven, thou art there: if I make my bed in hell, behold, thou art there.' " His serious gaze met hers. "I've been making my bed in hell for a long time, Mariah. The fact that I'm still alive on this dangerous path I've taken makes me think God's been protecting me all this time, even though I've strayed from Him, even though I didn't always believe it or see it. He was my—what does Isaiah say? My 'rear guard.' "

"I'm glad, Wyatt. I'd. . . I'd like to believe that's true for me too."

Concern filled his gaze. "You don't?"

She shrugged. "So much of my life was chosen for me. Then when I did have a choice, I ended up in almost exactly the same place—only worse in some ways. At least no one in the Wescott gang ever tried to attack me. I can't help but think maybe God wasn't with me when I made that choice."

"He was."

She gave a watery little laugh. "How do you know that?"

"Because he led you to me." Her heart melted as he took her arms and gently pulled her closer. "Sweetheart, I won't let you go back to that life. I'm going to get us both out of here. Trust me. Trust that the God you've been leading me back to has a plan to rescue you even if you can't see it and are afraid to believe it. He does. I promise you He does."

His words filled her heart with a hope she hadn't felt since she'd arrived in Hidden Springs. The faith he exuded wrapped her in warmth and made her want to soak in it like a flower would the sun. Something true and genuine shone in his eyes, making her search them deeper. Her words came out in a breathless whisper. "Who are you?"

Just like that, Wyatt's eyes shuttered then closed. He pulled in a deep breath and met her gaze, guarded once again. "Someone who wants a new start."

There was more to it than that. She could feel it in her bones. Sliding her arms around his waist, she hugged him tight then tilted her head back to meet his gaze as more questions formed on her lips. He claimed her mouth with a possessive kiss that took her breath away. Distracting her. Always distracting her. Why was that?

He deepened the kiss and, as usual, she let her questions fade away. . . . At least, for now.

Chapter 6

He was slipping.

Never before had Wyatt had such a hard time staying in character. Then again, he wasn't altogether sure where the characters stopped and Luke Bellamy began. He always maintained his true personality. It was his history and his name that changed from time to time. And, his values.

What if lack of skill wasn't the reason Mariah was starting to see through the veneer of Wyatt Coulter? What if, in truth, he wanted her to know—to care about Luke Bellamy?

He hoped not, because that would be the easiest way to get himself killed. And where would that leave Mariah? Trapped in the life she so badly wanted to be free from. He needed everyone to believe he was exactly who he said he was—especially now that her brothers were here.

Apparently, they hadn't been appraised of Mariah's plan to take point on this discussion. Other than the initial "What were you thinking?" and "How could you leave us?" questions, they'd aimed their ire at him. He couldn't blame them. He felt sick to his stomach now that the shock of Jack's attack on Mariah had waned and they were all faced with the reality of what could have happened.

Perhaps they were right. Perhaps Wyatt ought to be shot for failing to protect Mariah. Colin lifted a gun that seemingly materialized out of nowhere. Mariah jumped in front of Wyatt yelling, "No!"

"Mariah!" Wyatt grabbed her by the waist and spun around to shield her.

"I love him!"

So intent was he in bracing for the bullets that it took a moment for her words to register. When they did, he froze. Their eyes met. Hers widened as though just realizing what she'd revealed. He pulled her into the General's study and closed the door on the fracas in the living room, letting the rest of the gang sort out exactly how Colin had smuggled in a gun, how to restrain him, and what was to be done about the infraction.

Winded for reasons he couldn't define, Wyatt stared down at her in bewilderment. "You love me? Or did you only say that to stop your brothers from killing me?"

He'd given her an out. They both knew it. Part of him hoped she'd take it. This would all be so much simpler if she did. Instead, her voice turned soft and vulnerable. "I. . .I love you."

He didn't believe it. He couldn't. How could she love him? She didn't even know his— Her hand settled on his arms, stilling his racing thoughts. A sad little smile touched her lips as she shifted closer. Her whispered words answered his thoughts all too perfectly. "No matter what your name is."

"Luke," he said quietly. "My name is Luke."

He might as well have said, "I love you too." That's what it meant, didn't it? Trusting her that much. Being willing to lay down his life for her, not because she was a potential witness or an informant under his protection, but because she was Mariah. The woman he loved. The one he wanted with him when the rest of the world faded away. She seemed to understand, for her eyes lit from within and her smile spread into something new and glorious.

He thought for sure she'd say his name then, but she didn't. Instead, her lips pressed together and she gave him a single nod. All but saying, "Whatever your secret is, I'll keep it."

But she couldn't understand what that meant. Not really. Otherwise, she'd know that one day soon, he'd be responsible for the incarceration of everyone in the next room and, most likely, the hanging of at least one of the men she called brother. Could she love him even then? Trust him after that day?

A knock sounded on the door and Dodger's voice filtered through the wood. "Come on out. We've got him tied up."

Wyatt exited first, to find Colin already working to untie himself from his chair. Dave leaned against a nearby wall shaking his head at his older brother. Colin sent Dave an irritated look. "Aren't you going to help me?"

Dave rolled his eyes. "And get tied up myself? No, thank you. Mariah, why'd you have to go and fall for an outlaw after all we've done to keep them at bay? What would your mama say?"

"My mama would hardly be one to talk. Bless her outlaw-loving soul. Besides, I tried not to marry an outlaw and this is where I ended up. Maybe it's fate."

"I don't care who you married," Colin growled. "I care that you're not going back with us. Who's going to look after us while you're living out here?"

Dave shrugged. "I guess we could always order our own brides."

Mariah's eyes widened in horror. "Dave Wescott, don't you dare."

Colin got one hand free then started on the other. "Wyatt, you could go back to Texas with us. Join the Wescott gang. After all, you're practically family now."

Pinkerton would love that. Unfortunately for Wyatt's boss, Mariah was having none of it. Her hands went to her hips. "Wyatt Coulter, if you join the Wescott gang, it will be without me."

Wyatt shrugged, not letting one bit of his relief show. "Well now, that wouldn't do at all, Mariah."

"I thought not," she said with an adorable little smirk.

Dave sighed. "This has been a fine waste of time."

"It doesn't have to be." Colin freed himself from the restraints completely. "While we were in Laramie, I did a little digging. There's a payroll due there in five days. It'll be guarded, so it's too big a job for me and Dave to handle alone. But if we team up with you guys. . . Well, let's just say it'll be worth it for all of us. What do you say, Renegades? Who's up for a little fun?"

General Lorde glanced at his men to gauge their interest. Dodger nodded. Blade shook his head no. It was majority rule, so everyone looked to Wyatt, including Mariah. This could be the chance he had been looking for to get all of the Renegades out of the valley and capture the Wescott brothers to boot. He had no hesitations whatsoever in nodding his agreement. "I'm in."

General Lorde confirmed, "We're all in."

He's in? He's *in*? After everything Wyatt had told her, he was going to ride out there with her brothers and get himself killed? For what? More money? The thrill of danger? Had anything she'd said to him made any difference at all? Or had he simply told her what she wanted to hear to keep her from leaving with her brothers? As if she'd ever do that.

With a frustrated sigh and tears smarting her eyes, she hopped onto the last boulder large enough to sit on. Dave, who'd been left behind to guard her while Wyatt, Colin, and General Lorde scouted out the job, was right on her heels. He settled next to her on the smooth boulder and they let their feet dangle in the cool water below. "Do you really love Wyatt, Mariah?"

"Yes." Although, not for the first time, she was starting to wish she didn't.

He shook his head in disbelief and seemed to remark more to himself than to her, "No hesitation, even knowing he's a killer."

A chill washed over her, stealing her breath. Wyatt's warning not to ask about his past drifted through her mind, but she couldn't deny the dread that made her eyes search Dave's. Her voice came out softly, haltingly. "A killer? What do you mean, Dave? What has he done?"

"He killed a man during a train robbery back in Texas. That's why he's on the run." He frowned. "Didn't you know that?"

"I. . .didn't know the details."

"Well, he did. I remembered it as soon as I heard his name. It was in the newspapers at the time. Mariah, you know as well as I do it doesn't matter if a man kills one person or seven. After the first one, it's all over. You're marked for the hangman's noose. The rest of your life will be spent in hidey-holes or on the run. I thought you wanted more for yourself. Isn't that why you left us?"

"It's exactly why."

"Well, you won't get it with Wyatt Coulter." His gaze snagged on something behind her and muttered, "Speak of the devil."

She turned to see Wyatt walking along the bank of the creek toward them. Dave waved then backtracked over the boulders to meet with him. The two spoke for a few seconds before Dave left her with Wyatt. She stood and wrapped her arms around her waist but kept her back toward him as her ears tracked his every step toward her. She stiffened when his hands settled on her arms from behind. His sigh tickled her ear. "You're still angry with me for agreeing to this job?"

"Yes."

"Don't be." He kissed the nape of her neck, which only made her angrier.

She spun to face him and lost her balance. Tumbling backward, she grabbed his shirt to steady herself but only succeeded in pulling him into the cold lake with her. She freed herself from their tangled limbs and shot to the surface, gasping in a breath of air. He popped up beside her with a drowned chuckle. "That wasn't nice, Mariah."

"You can't kiss me and expect all of our problems to go away."

He stilled for a moment then began treading water again. "We have problems?"

"Is it true?" she asked through chattering teeth. "Did you kill a man down in Texas? Is that why you're on the run?"

Wyatt's gaze turned stormy. "I thought you weren't going to ask about my past."

"I didn't have to ask. Someone told me. And that isn't the denial I was hoping for."

"No, I suppose it wasn't." He heaved himself onto the boulder and reached down to pull her up beside him before meeting her gaze again. "I can't deny I've killed before. I'm not proud of it, but it had to be done. God has forgiven me."

She wrapped her arms around her shivering body, determined not to move from this spot until they'd had it out. "But the law won't."

"I am—" He pressed his lips together then shook his head. "It doesn't change anything. I'm still going to get us both out of this gang. I've already told General Lorde this is my last time riding with the Renegades. He wasn't too keen on that or the idea of you leaving, but he feels like he owes you something after what happened with Jack, so he'll let us go once the job is done."

Relief mixed with frustration. "Well, I'm glad for that, but why can't we go now? You don't need to help them rob the train."

"Yes, I do. That's the cost of your freedom. I have to help them with the last job. After that, I promise I'll be done with all of this forever."

"But you've already committed so many crimes. If you get caught—"

"Mariah." He waited until her panicked gaze met his calm one. "Trust me."

Trust him? How could she when he was asking her to live the rest of her life with him on the run? As unsure as she'd been about God's plan for her life, she knew that couldn't be it. Ultimately, her trust shouldn't be in Wyatt, anyway. It was supposed to be in God. He was the only one who could truly rescue her from all of this.

Mariah pulled in a deep breath then said the only thing that would satisfy everyone. "I trust You."

Ear pressed to the cold, steel rail, Wyatt listened as a low hum filled his ear. "Train's coming."

General Lorde tossed his cigar aside and ground it with his boot. "Light it up."

Wyatt smashed his lantern into the logs, saplings, rocks, and boulders the gang had piled onto the tracks. The fishy smell of whale oil filled the murky purple air of twilight as orange flames sizzled and spread. Tossing the lantern onto the pile, Wyatt backed away from the tracks, pulling a kerchief over the bottom half of his face and melting into the woods where the rest of the gang lay in wait.

The ground rumbled as a train thundered around a curve in the track. Sparks flew as its brakes screeched, and steam hissed before it finally came to a stop. The gang sprang from the woods. Wyatt, tasked with subduing the rear brakeman, dashed toward the caboose. He immediately recognized the brakeman as an old Pinkerton friend of his. Wyatt held up his hands in surrender. "James."

James pulled down Wyatt's kerchief to confirm his identity then practically threw him into the dimly lit caboose. Wyatt's immediate supervisor managed to catch him. The short, stocky man grasped Wyatt's lapels. "We've got the rest of the gang taken care of. There's no way they're getting away, but you need to escape. Go back to the valley. Clear it out and shut it down. Bring in all of the aiders, abettors, and harborers."

That wasn't what they'd agreed to in Wyatt's last letter to his "sister," but there wasn't time to argue, which was probably exactly why Stevens was relaying the orders now. "You want Doc Tillman and Hawk?"

"And Snow Wescott."

"Snow? Why? Is there a warrant out for her that I was unaware of?"

"We don't need a warrant. We have probable cause. Bring her in."

Bring her in.

This was not what Wyatt had planned. Nor was it what he'd promised Mariah. It certainly wasn't what he'd hoped for. . .and he *had* hoped. As much as he'd tried not to acknowledge it, he'd hoped he and Mariah would have a future beyond this job. Now she'd likely never want to see him again. Why would she? Not only would he be the man who'd put one brother in prison and sent the other to the hangman's noose, but he'd also be the man who'd arrested her and possibly sent her to jail as well.

"Luke, did you hear me?"

That's right. He wasn't Wyatt Coulter anymore. He was Detective Luke Bellamy. A man who had prayed and believed that God would work all of this out for good. A man who had made a promise to the woman he loved. A man who kept his word. He couldn't give up now. Not when he was so close to receiving everything he'd prayed for—not only for himself but for Mariah.

Courage filled him as his gaze connected with Stevens's. "I heard you, sir, but those charges won't hold up before a judge. My testimony and that of her brothers will make that clear. Mariah Snow is a victim of circumstances, nothing more. Dragging her into the courts will cause undue harm to her and irreparable damage to her reputation once it's revealed she has been living as the unlawful wife of a Pinkerton agent for the past several weeks."

Stevens's face clouded, but Luke continued on. "Although nothing untoward happened between the two of us during the investigation, it wouldn't reflect well on the agency. After the debacle with the James' gang, I'm sure the last thing Pinkerton wants right now is more bad press."

"That's true," Stevens admitted.

"Miss Snow is of far more value to us as an informant and state's witness."

"You think she would cooperate with us?"

"I'm certain of it."

Luke sent up a silent prayer during Stevens's quiet moment of deliberation. Finally, the man nodded. "Fine, but I still need you to bring her in for questioning and arrest the other two. Someone will contact you on the way back to the valley with more details. You have your orders. Now, go!"

"Yes, sir." Luke scanned the suspiciously quiet track then slipped back into the woods. Taking all the horses with him in case one of the outlaws did manage to escape, he waited until he was several miles away before letting out a celebratory whoop. "Thank You, Lord!"

Now he just had to break the news to Mariah about her brothers and the rest of the gang, secure her cooperation, and somehow convince her they still had a future together. Those were daunting tasks, to be sure. However, after what he'd overcome with his supervisor, it didn't seem quite as impossible as he'd once thought.

Two other Pinkertons met him on the trail. They took him to an old abandoned log cabin where they spent a few hours planning their next operation. At dawn, they rode to Hidden Springs, where a wire confirmed the Wescott brothers and the Renegade gang had all been successfully captured at the attempted train robbery. Thankfully, that meant Luke wouldn't be riding into a trap. With wounds painted on his right leg and left arm, he rode through the twisting, turning canyon, toward the valley.

Hawk descended down the cliff face looking sick at the sight before him. "What happened?"

Luke swallowed hard then spoke as though every breath was a labor. "The train was full of soldiers headed for Fort Laramie. It was madness. They captured everyone but me, Dave, and the General. We made a run for it. Got shot up pretty bad. Dave didn't last long. General Lorde was breathing until dawn."

Hawk let out a curse then glanced at the limp bodies that were covered in blankets and draped over horses. "Did you get any money out of it at least?"

"Couldn't get near the safe." Luke pressed a hand to his side, allowing the "blood" there to begin seeping through his clothes. "Where's Doc?"

"On a ramble, as usual. I'll get him for you. Meet you at the house."

"Wait." Luke pulled in a shaky breath. "Help me store these bodies out of sight. I don't want Mariah to see them until I have a chance to break the news about her brothers."

"All right, let's get them into the valley first." After Hawk quizzed him about the robbery and the possibility of a posse headed their way, they finally made it into the valley. Luke dismounted to help Hawk cut the bodies down from their saddles then returned to his horse. Hawk froze. "Did you hear that?"

"What?"

"One of them groaned."

"That's impossible. They're both dead."

"I'm telling you, Wyatt. One of them groaned. We've got to unroll them and check." Hawk knelt beside the nearest body, cut the ropes binding the blanket, then tossed his knife aside to unroll them. Luke stepped up behind Hawk and covered the man's nose and mouth with a cloth dipped in chloroform. Hawk struggled for a moment or two, but Luke held fast. Finally, Hawk went limp. Luke cuffed him then quickly unrolled the "bodies." Gray-haired Pinkerton Detective Henry Henderson pulled in a deep breath. "Took you long enough. I was surely about to expire."

"Couldn't have gone any faster without tipping him off."

They unrolled Jacob Miller, whose pale, freckled face had turned red. The man grimaced. "Man, it was getting warm in there. Henry, are you still up to going after Doc, or would you prefer I do it?"

"I'm fine. You guard Hawk. Stick to the plan. Right, Luke?"

"Right. I'll be back with the girl in a few minutes. If you aren't back by then, Henry, I'll come looking." With a confirming nod, they parted ways. Luke took the time to change clothes, not wanting to alarm Mariah into acting out of the norm. He found her behind their cabin, taking laundry down from the line. He pulled in a steeling breath then couldn't help but smile. "Mariah."

Heart lurching in her chest, Mariah fortified herself against her husband's voice, his presence, his charm, his kisses. None of that was going to work on her today. He'd promised he'd take her away from this place, and she was holding him to it. Once she was free, she'd find work as a maid or a shopkeeper or a cook—it didn't matter how hard or lowly as long as it was honest and respectable. As for Wyatt. . .

Well, she'd likely never see him again. She'd miss him terribly, but there was nothing else she could do. Even so, she was determined to make their last moments together sweet. She spun to face him with a smile. "Wyatt."

The vulnerability in his eyes gave her pause then made her step into his arms and whisper, "Luke."

He held her closer and kissed her cheek. "How are you?"

"Fine." She pulled away enough to survey him. "Are you hurt?"

"No."

"My brothers?"

A shadow passed through his gray eyes. "Captured."

Her breath stilled in her chest. "Captured?"

"Along with the rest of the Renegades. It was a trap."

"A trap? But. . . How did you escape?"

"It wasn't hard." His jaw tightened a little as though he was bracing for something. "You see, Mariah, I'm the one who set the trap."

She took a step back. "*You* did?"

He unbuttoned his shirt pocket, pulled out a badge, and gave it to her. "I'm a detective—a Pinkerton to be exact. I've been working undercover on a reconnaissance mission to infiltrate the Renegades' hideouts, gather confessions of their crimes, take note of the comings and goings of visiting gangs, and determine the best possible way to capture them."

"You're a. . ." *Detective?* Wyatt—No, *Luke* was a detective. Eyes widening, she thrust the badge back into his hands. "You need to go. Now. Doc is on a ramble, but if he comes back and finds out—"

He shook his head as he tucked the badge back in his pocket. "Doc is being arrested as we speak. Hawk has already been captured. They'll both be transported to the nearest jail."

She stilled. "And me? What do you intend to do with me? Will I be arrested and put in jail?"

"I'd like to bring you in for questioning. I believe you can provide information of interest concerning the Renegade gang and perhaps even shed some light on where we might find the rest of the Wescott gang. Would you be willing to do that?"

"Yes." She bit her lip. "I'm afraid I may not know very much. My brothers kept most of their business to themselves and you probably have far better information concerning what the Renegades have been doing."

Gentleness filled his eyes. "You may know more than you think. Even things that seem small or insignificant could prove helpful."

She nodded then hesitantly asked, "So I'm not going to be arrested or put in jail?"

"I'm not arresting you. And, unless there is something you haven't told me about your depth of involvement with the Wescott gang. . ." He waited until she shook her head before continuing. "There should be no reason for you to be charged with a crime. Besides, you're much more valuable to us as a witness."

"I see." Mind reeling, she tried to make sense of everything that had happened, cast it in its true light. "So our marriage. . . What happened between us. . . None of it was real?"

His eyes spoke of something warm, pure, and sweet. "It was real."

"How could it be?" She lifted her chin. "You deceived me."

"I had no choice. To do anything less would have put both our lives in more danger. You had to believe I was exactly who and what I said I was. If not, the men would have sensed something was off. As it was, I did the best I could by you. I tried to keep you safe. I know you have every right to be angry with me for not telling you the truth about who I am, but I've never lied to you about my feelings. I love you, Mariah."

Her breath caught in her throat at the words he'd never officially said to her before. "You love me?"

"Yes. Those feelings are real. *Everything* we shared is real." He seemed nervous for the first time since she'd met him. "I promised to take you out of this valley and help you find a new life. I plan on keeping that promise no matter what, but I want you to know I'm turning in my badge. I'm ready to settle down. Make a home somewhere. Live an honest life with the woman I love. With you. If you'll have me. What do you say, Mariah? Will you marry me again? For real this time."

She searched his face for the man with whom she'd shared kisses, a cabin, and her heart. He stared right back at her. Still strong. Still steady. Yet somehow more open and vulnerable than ever before. No longer Wyatt. Only Luke.

In his eyes, she saw everything she'd wanted, everything she'd hoped to find when she'd started out on her journey to become a mail-order bride. Love. Safety. Hope. A future—and a good one. One they could make their own. One better than should be possible for her.

God had come through. He'd made the crooked places straight, worked things out, rescued her just as He'd promised. Just as Luke had assured her He would. Now that the time had come, was she ready to live in His promise?

Smiling, she nodded, unable to wait another instant. "I say yes, Luke Bellamy. With all my heart, yes!"

Noelle Marchand is an award-winning author who graduated summa cum laude from Houston Baptist University with a BA in Mass Communication and Speech Communication. Her love of literature began as a child when she would spend hours reading under the covers long after she was supposed to be asleep. At fifteen, she completed her first novel. Since then, she has continued to pursue her writing dreams. In her free time, she enjoys spending time with family, learning about history, and watching classic cinema.

Train Ride to Heartbreak

by Donna Schlachter

Dedication

Dedicated first and foremost to God—without Him,
no story is worth telling.
To Patrick, who is the evidence of God's love for me.
To my agent, Terrie Wolf, who believes in me always.
And to Word Crafters Critique Group—you know who you are!

Thou hast turned for me my mourning into dancing:
thou hast put off my sackcloth, and girded me with gladness.
Psalm 30:11

Chapter 1

Mary Johannson plunged reddened hands into the dishwater and scrubbed at a crusty spot on the chipped china plate.

In the yard, the vicar, shoulders slumped from the cares of his congregation, held a small child in his arms while two toddlers clutched his pant leg. And Matron Dominus, the imposing head of the Meadowvale Orphan's Home, towered over the small group huddled before her.

Mary checked the plate. Satisfied it would pass muster, she dipped it into the rinse bucket and set the piece into the dish rack to air-dry. Next she set a burnt oatmeal pot into the water to soak while she dried her hands on her apron and surveyed the scene outside.

The vicar nodded and turned to walk the gravel path he'd traversed just minutes before, the wee ones in tow as he hoisted the child to his other hip for the mile-long trip back. No doubt he was waiting for space to open in the orphanage.

Her space.

Mary would turn eighteen in two months. And despite her desire to escape the confines of the orphanage, she wasn't excited about making her own way in the world. The last girl who aged out—as the other orphans called the act of turning eighteen—now worked at the saloon.

And everybody knew what kind of girls worked there.

Mary swiped at the scarred worktable set in the middle of the kitchen floor, her washrag sweeping crumbs into her hand. She still needed to finish the dishes and report to Matron Dominus for her next order for the day.

By the time she returned to the sink, the vicar and his charges were out of sight.

But Matron Dominus stood outside the tiny window staring in at her.

Checking up on her, no doubt. Making certain she wasn't lollygagging. An activity all the residents indulged in. According to Matron.

Mary hurried through the rest of the washing up. She swept the floor, put a pot of beans on to soak for supper, and shooed the cat out from under the stove. After checking the dampers to make certain the range wouldn't needlessly heat the kitchen—another of Matron's accusations—she hung her apron on a nail beside the back door.

Stepping out into the fresh air, Mary drew a deep breath and leaned against the clapboard siding. Perhaps she could work at the seamstress shop. She was a fair hand with a needle and thread. Or maybe the general store.

"Mary Johannson."

The screech like a rooster with its tail caught in a gate startled her, and she straightened. But in her haste, she overbalanced and stepped forward to catch herself, hooking her toe in the hem of her dress, which she'd let down just last week to a more respectable length.

The sound of rending cloth filled her ears as the ground slammed toward her. She got her hands out in front of her just in time to prevent mashing her nose into the soil. The toes of Matron Dominus's boots filled her vision.

Mary pushed herself to her feet, wincing at an ache in her lower back not there a moment before. Tears blurred her vision when she checked her dress—she had a three-inch rip just above the hem.

"Are you lollygagging about? Sunbathing? Do you think you're on the Riviera?"

Despite her imposing height and girth, the matron's voice—particularly when she was upset—resembled the irksome peacock Mary had once seen in the zoo in Philadelphia. Why God would create such a beautiful bird with such a nasty voice was beyond her.

But if what Matron said was true, He'd created Mary, too, only to have her burned by the flames that killed the rest of her family. Angry red scars ran from her forearms to halfway up her neck, and a collar of white tissue, the result of an inept doctor sewing her back together again, ringed her neck and inched toward her ears.

No, if God really loved her, He wouldn't have allowed that to happen.

She raised her eyes to meet the matron's. "Were you looking for me?"

"I was looking for the responsible child I thought you were." The matron planted her fists into doughy hips. "Perhaps I was mistaken."

"I've finished in the kitchen and was coming to find you. You said you needed me to go into town for supplies."

"Perhaps I should send Tom."

A smile tickled Mary's lips. "If you send Tom, he shall spill your sugar, drop your eggs, and the butter will be melted before he gets back."

The matron peered at her. "Get your shawl and meet me in the office. I have a list."

Minutes later, Mary set off for town, Matron's list and coins in her reticule and the warning to be back in time to prepare lunch for serving at noon ringing in her ears. She shrugged the kinks out of her neck. The sun told her it was already ten. A mile's walk to and from town would take more than half an hour. Three stops on the list would take at least another half hour.

That should leave her enough time to stop at the library and check out a book or two. And maybe she could ask about possibilities for work at some of the shops. Two months wasn't a long time.

She would plan. She would prepare.

She would not end up at the saloon.

Heartbreak, California

John Stewart stretched an arm across the pillow, reaching for Sophia.

But the bed was cold. Empty.

His wife was gone.

Every morning for the past three months, he'd done the same thing, only to awaken to the heartrending realization anew that this was his life now.

In the room next door, one of his two young daughters stirred. With only a year separating them, he still couldn't tell their cries apart. At six and eighteen months, they needed their mother.

The woman who dreamed of them long before they were born. Who prayed for them while she carried them inside her. Who rejoiced over them when they arrived.

And who begged God to spare her so she could see her girls grown to the point where they wouldn't need her so much.

So why didn't God listen? Why didn't He understand that when John prayed, he wasn't asking for himself?

John sat up and grabbed his faded dungarees from where he'd tossed them the previous evening. Or early this morning. Since Sophia's passing, he'd learned an important lesson—the fewer hours he spent in bed, the fewer hours to toss and turn, angry at God, asking questions that wouldn't be answered.

So he took to going to bed later and rising earlier. The girls demanded so much time and energy that those additional hours were critical.

John slipped on his boots, mud and manure caked around the heel. He sighed again. Sophia wouldn't have let him past the back door with boots like that.

She'd have house slippers ready. She'd have a meal on the table, the girls in clean clothes, coffee boiling on the stove, line-fresh sheets on their bed.

She made their house a home.

She made their home a sanctuary.

But no more.

He shrugged into his shirt, splashed water on his face from the bowl on the dresser, and glanced at his reflection in the mirror. Stubble dotted his chin and cheeks, but shaving could wait another day. The girls wouldn't notice, and he was fairly certain neither his horse nor his foreman would complain.

He pasted on a smile and exited the sleeping room, heading for the girls.

Another day to get through.

Somehow.

Mary clutched her market basket closer. She lingered inside the store, admiring the bolts of material, fingering the lace and ribbons. What beautiful gowns she could stitch from such quality fabrics. When she got her first pay packet, she'd buy a length of material and make herself a new dress. Nothing fancy. But no more hand-me-downs. Perhaps she'd splurge on pearl buttons instead of plain ones. She checked the price and sighed.

Probably not. Pearl cost three cents more.

The Winchester clock in the shop gonged the half hour, and Mary tugged her hat down in preparation for exiting the store. Already eleven. She would barely get back in time at this rate.

She switched her basket to the other arm and stepped into the sunshine, pausing to allow her eyes time to adjust. An elderly man sat on a bench outside the store, reading a newspaper.

A large block advertisement headed NOTICE caught her attention, and she permitted herself one more minute. She could walk faster and make up the time easily.

Wanted: young women for marriage. All expenses paid. Come to California for love and adventure. Reply below.

She stepped back. What a silly notion. Imagine traveling to California to marry a man she'd never met. Why, that was crazy. It was foolhardy. It was—

The answer to her dilemma.

She could at least inquire as to who these men were. Given her current situation—a scarred orphan with no prospects—she couldn't be too choosy. And if she was lucky, perhaps love would come later.

At this point, she didn't care. She memorized the address then headed back to the orphanage.

She would not end up in the saloon.

An hour later, John's older daughter, Maggie, slurped milk from a tin cup, a dribble of white running down the side of her mouth. He added laundry to his mental to-do list. Sadie plunged her hands into her porridge then smeared it across her face, giggling. Maggie made faces at her sister, who burbled in delight.

"Maggie, eat your porridge."

"Don't like."

"It's good for you." He swiped a hand through his hair, which needed cutting. Another thing for his list. "Eat."

"Want Mommy."

If asking for their mother would bring her back, he would join in his daughter's lament and call Sophia back from wherever she was. Heaven, Sophia—and the pastor and most of the town—would say.

But John wasn't so sure. Living here on earth with him and their daughters should have been heaven enough for her.

What more did she want?

And what did her leaving say about him? Their marriage? Their children?

Not enough. That's what.

The sound of a wagon in the dusty yard drew his attention. Who would visit at this hour unless it was bad news?

He glanced at Maggie. "Watch your sister for a minute."

Maggie's face lit up. "I be Mommy."

He left the kitchen and headed for the front door, a mighty slab of oak shipped from Missouri to keep his family safe.

But the door hadn't done its job.

He stepped onto the front porch.

The pastor pulled his team to a halt, engaged the brake, and jumped down. "Good morning, John. Fine day the Lord has made."

"Morning, Pastor. What brings you out here?"

Tim Jenkins, a few years older than John's twenty-seven, helped his wife down before walking to the rear of the wagon and letting down the tailgate. "Got some fresh vegetables and fruit here. Well, not so fresh, perhaps. But Marcus at the general store had more than he could sell, so he gave it to me."

John stood his ground at the top step. "Don't need charity."

"Not charity." The pastor tipped a bushel basket of apples, onions, carrots, and cabbage forward to show him. "Hoping I could trade for some eggs?"

Sophia's hens were the best layers in the county, maybe in the state. She swore it was because she sang to them every day. John wasn't sure about that, particularly since he didn't serenade the stupid creatures and yet they maintained their overproduction even now. "I think we could manage that." He stepped back. "Forgive my rudeness, Mrs. Jenkins." He tipped his head to the pastor's wife. "Come in. We're just finishing breakfast."

The pastor's wife scurried up the steps. "Don't want to interrupt, but I've been longing to see your girls." She pulled a candy stick from her purse. "Got a little something for them here, too. If you don't mind?"

"And John, perhaps we could have a little chat out here while the wife sees to the girls?"

John sighed. He knew this wasn't as simple as a food exchange. "Sure. Go on in, ma'am. They're in the kitchen."

He waited until the door closed then indicated the chairs set on the porch. Chairs he'd made for Sophia. He sat in her red chair, unwilling to allow anybody—even the pastor, who was a great friend to them during her sickness—to take her place.

The pastor set his basket near the door then sank into John's blue chair. He pulled a sheet of paper from inside his jacket. "We've missed you in church."

"Been busy."

The pastor nodded. " 'Spect so."

"Probably won't be back anytime soon."

The pastor scooted his chair around to face him. "Sophia was a great believer in God and His redeeming love for us."

"I ain't Sophia." As soon as the words left his mouth, John wished he could swallow them back. Saying it aloud made the truth too real. He dropped his gaze. "Sorry, Pastor."

"I understand. You're still hurting."

John met the man's eyes. "What do you understand? Your wife isn't dead. You aren't left alone to raise two young'uns. You don't sleep in a cold, empty bed every night and wake up every morning living all over again the fact that she's gone."

The pastor leaned forward, elbows on his knees. "My first wife died three months after we married. We didn't have children, but I do know about loss."

John sat back, stunned at the man's words. "Did you know God then?"

"Thought I did."

"Thought you did? What kind of an answer is that?"

The pastor straightened. "I knew about Him. But I didn't truly get to know Him until I went through that time."

A wry chuckle escaped John's lips. "So now you're going to tell me I need to go through this pain so I can get closer to God?" He stood and paced the porch. "If that's what God needs to make me love Him, I don't want any part of Him."

"That's not how God works." The pastor gestured to the empty chair. "Sit. There's something I want to talk to you about."

John complied, his arms folded across his chest. "Don't want to hear anything about my churchgoing. Or lack of."

"Not why I'm here." The pastor unfolded the sheet of paper. "I helped some men in town put an advertisement in an eastern newspaper."

"For what?"

"For wives. And we had a good response. After the men made their choices, another letter came in. Sounds like you two would be a perfect match."

John snorted. What kind of a woman answered a newspaper notice? "Why? Did she lose her husband? She have small children?"

"No. She lost her entire family."

Chapter 2

Mary's hands shook as she accepted the letter from the postmistress. Less than a month since she responded to the notice in the newspaper. She still owed Matron the penny for the postage, and the woman reminded her almost every day of her debt.

Along with mention of the "three wee ones" still waiting for a place. Her beady eyes bored into Mary's soul as she spoke the words.

Well, with any luck, Mary would leave in another month. If this letter was what she hoped—when had she begun hoping again?—she could tell Matron today.

She settled onto the bench outside the post office and laid her market basket to one side. She checked the return address. Heartbreak, California.

What tragedy gave the town such a name? A failed mine, perhaps? Indian raid? She shivered. She'd heard about the dangers of the Wild West, read about it in novels from the town's tiny library. Landslides. Snowstorms. Floods.

She slid a finger beneath the flap and opened the envelope. Perhaps the man she'd written to—the pastor—would say they didn't need her. Didn't want her. Already had all the women they needed.

She swallowed hard. Being rejected from afar, sight unseen, should be easier.

But it wasn't.

She glanced up and down the street. While waiting for a reply from California, she'd checked the reputable businesses in town. None were hiring right now. Or rather, they weren't hiring her. She either didn't have enough experience—the mercantile—or they didn't like the looks of her—the seamstress, who at least had the good grace to blush and apologize that her clientele were genteel women who might be offended by Mary's scars.

She unfolded the single sheet of paper and checked the signature at the end of the brief note.

John Stewart.

Not the pastor, then.

Her heart pounded in her ears like a drum in the Fourth of July parade. Nothing fancy. Just the facts. A widower with two small children. Looking for a woman to raise his children until the oldest could run the home. Twelve years. Nothing more.

Nothing more.

Underlined three times.

And in case she didn't understand, he went on to say theirs would be a contract

105

marriage. Separate sleeping quarters. He would make no further demands on her.

No further demands?

Heat rushed up her neck and cheeks as understanding dawned on her.

Well, wasn't this what she wanted? A way out of her current situation. No illusions about love. And in twelve years, she could walk away, free as a bird.

If that's what he wanted, then that would suit her fine.

He concluded by saying he would wire her the train ticket to use at her leisure. Detailed instructions on finding Heartbreak. Send a telegram when she was on her way. Plan to marry the same day since they couldn't stay in his home together unwed.

She folded the paper and tucked it into its envelope. Well, that was that.

She would reply today, telling him she accepted his proposal and would leave for California in a month's time. That should please Matron.

Thirty days. The number of days before she started what now felt like a twelve-year sentence rather than a release date.

John dismounted at the train depot and untied his carpetbag from behind the saddle then handed the reins over to his foreman. "Thanks for riding in with me to take the horse back."

Martin tipped his head. "No problem, Boss. Glad to help."

"And don't forget, the pastor's wife will come by around ten to pick up the girls. Make sure Maggie takes her dolly, and Sadie likes that blue blanket."

Martin patted his shirt pocket. "Got all the details here, Boss."

John nodded. "Just talking to delay getting on the train."

"Well, it won't wait forever for you. Enjoy your visit with Sophia's folks."

John hefted his bag to his other hand and tossed his foreman a smile he didn't feel. "And don't forget—"

The train whistle drowned out the rest of his words. Just as well. Not like he hadn't told the man everything at least a dozen times in the past two weeks.

What was he thinking? Traveling to see Sophia's parents seemed so important when he'd penned the letter to Miss Johannson. Now, he doubted his motives.

Was he trying to convince them? Or himself?

Mary stomped her foot, unable to stand Matron's deep, heaving sighs one more minute. "Fine. I'll leave tomorrow. You can tell the vicar the children may come here first thing."

"But what of your arrangement, dear? Can you arrive in California so early?"

"Mr. Stewart said to come as soon as I could. His children need a mother. I will send a telegram from town tomorrow so he knows I am coming. The train ride will take three or four days at least."

The children were sad Mary was leaving, but Tom was the most grieved. "Oh, Mary, what will happen to us? I can't cook or clean. I'm no good in the house, and Matron will expect me to be you. Can't you wait until I'm older?"

His pleading eyes almost changed her mind, but she stood firm. Even if she wanted to change her plans, she couldn't.

Mr. John Stewart needed a mother for his children.

And Matron wanted her room.

"I'm sorry, Tom, but I must go. I must leave in two weeks, anyway. So it's not much difference."

The boy laid a hand on her arm. "I shall miss you."

"And I you."

"Will you write to me?"

"I shall be very busy. But I will try."

Her halfhearted promise seemed to satisfy the boy, but Mary knew the truth of it. None of the boys and girls who left were ever heard from again. Once they stepped outside the gate, they seemed to simply fall off the face of the earth.

Would it be the same for her? Despite what she'd learned in school about the earth being round, maybe the scholars were wrong and Columbus was correct. Perhaps the world was flat, and if she traveled too far from Groverton, she'd step off the edge and disappear forever.

At this point, she didn't care.

She would leave.

Tomorrow.

John stared out the window of the passenger car heading west, wishing for the hundredth time he hadn't listened to the pastor. Exhausted from his responsibilities with the girls and the ranch, he'd agreed to take the slower train from Sophia's parents' to allow him time to refresh and renew for his new life ahead.

Seemed he was using a lot of energy getting accustomed to a new life every time he turned around. First the new life with his second daughter. The new way of life when Sophia fell ill. Then this brand-new, unfamiliar life when she died so suddenly.

And now? Preparing to be a bridegroom for the second time.

Except this time, to a woman he didn't know. Didn't love. Couldn't truly envision spending the rest of his life with.

Well, he didn't need to spend the rest of his life with her.

He simply needed to get through the next twelve years. Then she could leave, and he could finish raising his daughters.

The train rounded a bend and jolted him back to the present.

Outside, oak and cottonwood trees had adopted their autumn colors. Reds, oranges, and yellows brightened an otherwise browning landscape. Cattle, their black hides contrasting with the brown, mirrored his thoughts.

Black and dark. Like his mood.

He should have taken the direct train. He would be home now, running his ranch, preparing for this woman from Pennsylvania.

Not that he had anything to prepare. Martin agreed to set up her sleeping quarters in the girls' room. Although, his foreman had raised his eyebrows in question of that particular instruction.

John smiled at the memory of his response. "I want her to get to know the girls quickly so we can settle in right away."

His foreman was not fooled.

And no matter how many times John told himself he was doing this for his daughters, he wondered about his motives. What if this woman was as beautiful as Sophia? He shook his head. No. He would not fall in love with another woman. No matter what, Sophia was his one and only. To love another would be to dishonor her life. And her death.

And he couldn't imagine partaking of the physical side of a marriage relationship with a woman he didn't—couldn't—love simply because she was beautiful.

He settled into his seat, crossed his arms over his chest, and tipped his hat down. But his mind wouldn't quiet as he recalled his visit with Sophia's parents. Although still saddened by their daughter's death, they understood his need for a mother for the girls. They insisted he wasn't dishonoring their daughter's memory. They looked forward to welcoming this woman into their granddaughters' lives.

But still there was a slight hesitancy in their attitude. And then he realized why.

They were afraid of losing this final connection with their daughter.

He hastened to assure them they were welcome to visit anytime. This woman was an orphan, so his daughters still needed them as grandparents. They were family.

Unlike Miss Johannson, who never would be.

He shifted in his seat as the train whistle blew, alerting him to yet another stop along the way. The next big city was Chicago, then St. Louis, Denver, Albuquerque, and in three days' time, Bakersfield. Martin would be there with a wagon, and he'd travel the few miles home to Heartbreak.

How ironic he lived in a town with a name that so perfectly reflected the state of his life.

Chapter 3

Mary sighed. Would nothing go right today? Her stomach rumbled. She'd not eaten since midday yesterday. And she was exhausted.

Matron's gift, amounting to seventy-four cents, was not enough to buy meals every day. Despite the rocking motion of the train, she hadn't closed her eyes for more than a few minutes over the past two days. A succession of travelers came and went through the passenger car, some she might like to know better. Some she was glad kept to themselves.

The conductor made his way down the aisle. The grizzled dark-skinned man named Thomas nodded. "Good morning, Miss. Next stop is Clarkesville. Small town, but it has a diner at the train depot. We'll be there for about thirty minutes. Should be enough time to get something to eat. Cheap and good. Tell them Thomas sent you. They'll throw in a piece of pie for free."

She smiled. "Thank you, Thomas."

He handed her a magazine. "Found this on a seat back yonder. Thought you might like something to read to pass the time."

She accepted his offering. "I would. Thank you for thinking of me."

"Not often I see such a brave woman as you heading west to make a new life. Not many would do what you're doin'. No, siree. That's a fact."

He passed down the aisle, checking tickets and answering questions from the dozen or so passengers. If not for Thomas, she didn't know what she'd have done. She missed her original train in Chicago and didn't know what to do or where to go.

And then along came Thomas, pushing a cartload of luggage, mopping his brow despite the cooler temperatures. He stopped and listened to her tale of slow trains and cattle crossing the tracks and waiting for a passenger at the previous station.

He nodded then directed her to another platform. "You go on over there, miss. That there is my train. I'll be with you in a few minutes. We can't get you to Heartbreak on that train, but we can get you to Bakersfield, and Heartbreak is only a few miles down the road."

At his words, her heart sank to the tips of her dusty boots. Already feeling she was on precarious footing with Mr. Stewart, she had no desire to put him out. "Are you certain there is nothing else I can do?"

He shook his head. "Sorry, miss, but that fast train only goes once a week. I guess if'n you want to stay here in Chicagoland for a week that would be fine. But you'll get where you're going faster if'n you take my suggestion."

And so here she was, on Thomas's train, as he called it, headed west.

She glanced at the magazine. Romance stories. Her breath quickened. Such an exotic find. She studied Thomas's back as he disappeared through the door and into the next car. He was a good man. She hoped Mr. Stewart was half as good as the old conductor.

Mary opened the magazine to the first page. She'd had little time to herself in the orphanage, squirreling away a nub of a candle so she could read in her room late at night. She'd read every book in the town's tiny library at least twice, including the encyclopedia.

But a real, honest-to-goodness magazine she didn't have to share with anybody else? That was a treasure beyond comparison. And she would enjoy every single word.

This was probably the only romance she would ever know.

John gritted his teeth. The pastor was wrong. There was nothing relaxing about this train ride. Besides the fact they stopped at every backwater town and cattle crossing, he had to change trains yet again.

He picked up his carpetbag, exited the train, crossed the platform, and followed the sign for Bakersfield.

That was the other thing he hadn't realized when he booked this trip: he could go east out of Heartbreak, but apparently the train didn't make the return trip. Not without a weeklong layover in Chicago.

John handed his bag to the porter, an older, stooped Negro, who nodded and smiled, thanking him for riding with him. John held back the sharp retort itching on the end of his tongue for release. It wasn't the old man's fault he had to change trains.

He climbed the three steps and hesitated. Left or right? With no assigned seating, the only question was which car would be quieter. He'd had his fill of crying kids and snoring men.

He glanced through the door of the car on his left. A woman reading a magazine, and two men playing cards. On the right, a woman with three children who ran up and down the aisle.

Left it was.

Inside this car, he sat in the second row. The woman was to his right, and the card players were behind him. He propped his feet on the seat facing him, crossed his legs at the ankles, tipped his hat over his face, and closed his eyes. With any luck, he'd have a good long rest before the conductor woke him for dinner.

But while his body screamed for sleep, his mind wouldn't settle. He worried about his daughters. He fretted over how Martin was handling things on the ranch. Sure, he was experienced. Sure, he'd managed things before when John was preoccupied with Sophia's illness.

But he'd always been there in case Martin had a question. Now he was hundreds if not thousands of miles away. What if a cow went into a breech labor? What if a steer broke through the fence again and ended up in the mire? What if—

He snapped his head up. He could "what if" himself to death. John drew a deep breath and settled his chin on his chest. No matter how bad things got in Heartbreak, there wasn't one thing he could do about it. He might as well relax.

Pages rustled beside him, and he glanced at the woman reading the magazine. Pink tinged her cheeks, and her mouth formed a tiny "o" as though she was reading something pleasing. He couldn't make out the cover of the magazine from this angle, but he doubted it was a Sears catalog. She was much too engrossed in it.

The irony of the situation didn't escape him. Here he was, caught up in worrying about what was happening in the real world—his real world—beyond the confines of this train, and there was this young woman purposely losing herself in the make-believe world of her reading material.

He envied her.

At the touch on her shoulder, Mary looked up into the wizened face of Thomas. "Yes?"

"Excuse me, miss. But I came to tell you we won't be stopping any more this evening. We's a little behind schedule, and the engineer says we got to make up some time."

"Thank you, Thomas. I appreciate you letting me know."

"Because we won't be a-stopping, the engineer opened up the dining car to all the passengers for free. So if'n you want to head that way, I'll give you a head start."

She patted his hand. "You are most kind."

"Thank you, miss."

Mary tucked her magazine into her purse and headed toward the dining car. Without the money to buy a meal aboard the train, she'd only smelled the food and heard the stories of the wonderful offerings from other passengers. The opportunity to eat at no charge was too good to miss.

Along the way, she noted the other passengers, wondering if any would make good traveling companions. There were several families with children, a couple who gazed into each other's eyes so intently they must be on their honeymoon, and several dandies, complete with cravats and monocles. Probably traveling gamblers. Two older couples dozed in their seats, and several younger men, working class judging by their calloused hands and rough clothing, occupied the other cars she passed through.

She selected a table for two in the farthest corner of the dining car and slid across the leather seat so she faced the rest of the tables. Perhaps she could pass the time—and the miles—by watching her fellow passengers.

A waiter took her food order then set a steaming cup of coffee before her with a large jug of cream and a bowl of sugar cubes. She applied both generously to her beverage—she couldn't recall the last time she enjoyed sugar at the orphanage—and sipped. Delicious.

The door behind her opened, and about twenty people hurried in. One man by himself glanced at the empty seat across from her and then at her. She offered a timid smile, not wanting to encourage him, but at least wanting to acknowledge him.

His eyes traveled up, ending at her neck. His cheeks flushed, and he turned away.

She tugged at the collar of her dress. Perhaps she should skip her meal and return to the safety of her car. If she kept her nose buried in her magazine, nobody would bother her.

The door at the far end of the car opened, and she glanced up. Three men from her car—two traveling together and a lone passenger—strolled in. The pair chose a table near the middle of the dining room, where they sat and chatted amiably.

Now every seat was filled.

Except the one across from her.

Mary shrank into her seat and pulled her magazine from her purse. If she was engrossed in her magazine, the final passenger might decide to let her sit by herself. At the very least, he wouldn't try to strike up a conversation with her.

A shadow fell across the table. She looked up.

A cowboy, his face tanned by the sun and wind, hands calloused by hard work, wrinkles where there should have been laugh lines, stood before her.

Just like the sad soul in the magazine, he now occupied flesh and bone.

In the story, that cowboy had lost hope, and the heroine—a woman of virtue and gentleness—loved this cowboy right out of his misery.

And out of the story had stepped this man. Not handsome by most standards, there was a longing and an intensity about him that called to her.

This man had deep wounds, invisible to everybody but her.

John waited a couple of extra heartbeats for the young woman to acknowledge him as he stood beside her table. There were no empty seats, and he hoped he wasn't breaking some secret rule about asking a single diner to share their table.

The waiter appeared beside him at that moment and set a plate of lamb chops with parsley potatoes and baby carrots before the woman, who nodded her thanks. The waiter then turned to him. "Take a seat here, sir. It's the only empty seat."

Heat rushed up John's cheeks as the woman studied him through slitted eyes, her mouth twitching. He waited an extra minute, hoping she would invite him to join her, but she busied herself with her meal.

He sat, feeling like ten kinds of a fool. She didn't want him there.

The waiter stood beside him again, notepad in hand. "The special is the lamb chops. Or you can have steak and kidney pie."

"Don't like kidney. I'll have the lamb."

"Very good choice, sir. And coffee?"

"Yes. Thank you."

He studied her as she ate. While not as beautiful as Sophia, there was a deep sadness, perhaps related to the scars on her neck, that called to him. Her chin was more pointed than Sophia's, her hair less golden and more brown, her eyes closer together yet large and clear.

Finally, he could keep silent no longer. "You were reading."

"You were sleeping."

This was an unexpected response. In his limited experience, most women were glad to keep a conversation going for ten minutes or more, jumping from topic to topic.

Either this woman had the social graces of a weathervane, or she was sparring with him, as it were.

He tried again while she sipped her coffee. "Are you heading toward or away from something?"

A moment of panic crossed her face as she glanced from side to side and her mouth pursed into that attractive little "o" again before she answered. "Both."

Well, two could play that game. "Me, too."

She tipped her head in question. "Both?"

"Yes."

The waiter set his dinner and coffee before him, and John forked a potato into his mouth like he hadn't eaten in a week. Within two minutes, his plate was empty. He glanced up.

She studied him. Her food, growing cold on her plate, no longer interested her as much as he did.

Well, two could play that game, too.

He dumped four sugar cubes into his coffee, stirred the liquid, and drank, making great slurping noises before setting the empty cup in its saucer while he stared at her over the rim.

A smile tickled at the corners of her mouth.

He set his cup down and allowed a smile to mirror hers.

She covered her mouth with her napkin and chuckled into the white folds. After a minute or so, she wiped her eyes. "Sorry. That was very impolite of me. But you should have seen the look on the waiter's face. I thought he was going to have an apoplectic fit."

"Probably confirmed everything he knows about cowboys. We're not suitable company for respectable folk." He tipped his head. "I'm John, by the way."

There. That same moment of—of panic? Fear? Surprise?—passed over her face, but she recovered quickly and returned the nod. "Mary."

Mary. The same name as the woman he would wed in less than two weeks. He shrugged off the similarity. Mary was a common name. A poll of the passengers on the train would likely reveal most had a Mary in their family. And he'd probably find two or three women with the same name.

Still, he sobered as he reminded himself he was on this train, heading home, to ready his household and his heart to wed.

If she was half the woman this Mary was, he'd have little to complain about.

Chapter 4

Pushed and jostled by the large number of passengers around her, Mary boarded the train again in Denver, eager to be on her way. As she made her way to her seat—the one she called hers—the woman with her three small children clambered up the steps ahead of her.

She felt like she'd spent a lifetime on this rattling box of glass, wood, and metal that hissed at her now like an angry serpent, and they'd been aboard the train even longer.

The woman's shoulders slumped, and dark circles under her eyes bespoke sleepless nights of watching over her children. Their faces were marred with the jam bun they'd just consumed like hungry ravens in the depot diner, and their clothing was wrinkled and dirty.

The youngest, a little girl with a head full of curly, blond hair, whimpered something to her mother, who sighed and picked her up.

Mary studied the woman's actions, searing them into her mind. Soon she would be a mother, and although she'd spent much of her life at an orphanage full of young ones, she'd not been their sole support and care.

Most of the other passengers were already seated, and she worried she might have to share with another, but no, she was in luck. Her seat was still empty. The woman and children continued down the passageway toward the rear of the car. She slid onto the wooden bench and clutched her purse to her bosom as she considered her situation.

What had she been thinking? That she could insert herself into Mr. Stewart's life and instantly become mother to his children? She knew some about caring for children, but judging by the actions of this woman before her, she knew nothing about mothering.

Her magazine pressed into her ribs, and she pulled it out of her reticule. How foolish she'd been to imagine such would—or could—be hers. More likely she was bound for a life of drudgery and hard work. A life of runny noses and dirty clothes. A life devoid of love.

Heels on the wooden planking of the car roused her. John, her fellow diner from dinner the previous day, the man who occupied more of her thoughts lately than was proper, strode toward her, and for a moment, their eyes met. Her heart leaped, pounding against her rib cage like a lioness struggling to escape its cage.

He sat behind her, bringing with him a whiff of fresh air and the lingering scent of bacon and eggs. Her mouth watered at the memory of him seated at the counter in the diner, sipping coffee and digging into his breakfast. Her day-old bun, purchased from the bakery next door, churned along with her watered-down tea.

From behind, the children chattered and bickered in a friendly tone, nothing mean about them. And then their steps neared. Mary turned in her seat as the train lurched forward. The middle child fell and bumped his head.

The older brother picked him up and brushed him off. "Don't be such a crybaby. We can sit on the floor if we have to."

But his words didn't comfort the boy, who tipped his head back and wailed all the more. His mother, standing in the aisle behind him, gathered him into her arms, but the child wouldn't be consoled. "Don't wanna sit on floor. Wanna sit in chair."

Mary glanced around. Every seat was occupied. Perhaps she could share?

But before she could respond, movement behind her caught her attention, and John stood. "Please, ma'am, take my seat."

"Oh, I couldn't."

"There are no full seats available."

The woman's cheeks flushed. "Thank you, sir."

He stepped aside and the children piled in, then their mother perched on the end of the bench. They finally settled and the boy stopped crying when allowed to sit nearest the window.

The man stood at Mary's elbow. "Ma'am."

She lowered her gaze. "Sir."

When he sat, their elbows touched, and she shrank against the outside wall. But not before a tingling sensation traveled all the way from her fingertips to her shoulder.

While the sensation was unknown to her, it wasn't unwelcome.

John shifted, crossing his legs at the ankles. These seats were too narrow to share, even with a woman as tiny as the one who sat stiffly beside him. She hadn't relaxed for one minute in the past three hours but sat with her right shoulder pressed against the window like she wished she could escape.

Thomas waddled down the passageway, checking tickets and chatting with the passengers. The farther west they traveled, the more labored the elderly man's breathing became.

When he drew near, John nodded his greetings. "G'mornin', Thomas. How are you doing today?"

A sheen of perspiration covered the conductor's face. "Fair to middlin', Mr. John."

John quirked his chin toward the door of the car. "Can I walk with you a bit? Need to stretch my legs."

A grin split Thomas's dark face. "Sure would like that, Mr. John."

John stood then turned to Miss Mary. "Save my seat, would you?"

She nodded but still didn't look at him.

He followed Thomas toward the rear of the train then stood with him on a platform. The scenery sped past, not much more than a blur enveloped in smoke from the engine. Thomas gripped the railing and leaned over, coughing.

John placed a hand on the man's shoulder. "You're having trouble breathing."

The older man straightened and nodded. "The higher I go, the less air there is."

"You need to rest."

"Can't. The boss man is lookin' for a reason to retire me. Got to keep working."

"How can I help?"

Thomas smiled at him. "No need for that. And if the boss man ever caught me—"

"Then we'll have to be smarter than the boss man." He clapped Thomas on the back. "Please, you'll be doing me a favor. I've been cooped up in this bean can for days. I'm going to get fat and lazy if I don't do something."

Thomas stared at him a long time, and for a moment, John was certain he would turn down his offer. Then he nodded slowly. "Fine. I gots to move some things in the baggage car for the passengers getting off at Albuquerque."

For the next two hours, John shifted what seemed like a ton of suitcases, crates, boxes, and carpetbags. Sweat poured down his back and face despite the chill air of the mountain passes the train labored through. But it felt good.

Job done, he straightened and breathed deep of the fresh mountain air.

Thomas sat on a crate, hands on his knees, and swiped at his forehead with a handkerchief. "Thanks so much for your help, Mr. John."

"No, thank you for letting me work off some of my frustration and worry."

"That's fine, then. We both accomplished somethin'. I thank the good Lord for sendin' you to me."

"I don't think God was involved."

Thomas shook his head. "No, sir. God has His holy fingers in everything we do."

"He's not interested in me."

"God is protectin' you all the time. You just don't see it."

John gritted his teeth to keep from screaming. "He didn't do anything but sit back and watch my wife die. He didn't care about our two young children."

Thomas stared at him for several heartbeats. "You got a heap of hurtin' inside you, Mr. John. If'n you don't let God take care of it, it'll eat you up."

John snorted. "Well, He ignored her prayers. A lot of other people were praying, too, including the pastor. What kind of a God doesn't listen to the prayers of a pastor?"

The conductor shook his head. "Just 'cuz He don't answer the way we want don't mean He's not a-listenin'. That's two different things, Mr. John."

"Why wouldn't He do something for my daughters?"

"I don't know all the answers, Mr. John. But I know the One who does."

John stood. "If God listens to you, maybe you could ask Him to watch over my children."

"I'd be right proud to do that on your behalf. For now."

"For now?"

"Sure. It's kind of like when you're a young'un. Your pa teaches you how to saddle your horse. Then he helps you. Then he expects you to do it on your own. That's what prayer is like. At some point, you gots to take responsibility for your own prayers."

John headed back to his seat as thoughts of Thomas's God whirled through his head. How could a person believe in a God who didn't answer prayer? Didn't intercede

when He could? No. He didn't need God.

He needed a mother for his children. And he'd taken care of that, all on his own.

Although John was easy on the eyes and smelled good, Mary pushed away the thoughts of him that intruded on her daydreams. He'd been gone for a while, most likely as an excuse not to sit next to her. He was as stiff as winter-dried dungarees fresh off the line, and the cat must have bitten off his tongue.

Not that she knew what she'd say if he did speak. Maybe the next time they sat together, she'd ask about his family. Where he was from. Where he was headed.

She shook her head. She'd do no such thing. She'd do what she always did around men. Sit silently and let him do all the talking. Voices caught her attention. She peeked over her shoulder.

He was coming her way. Torn between her heart's desire to know him better and her head telling her she was engaged to another, she waited.

And listened.

"Thanks for your help, Mr. John."

"Enjoyed our time together."

"Will you think on what we talked about?"

"I will, Thomas."

"And I'll be praying for your little ones."

Her heart caught in her throat.

Little ones.

He was married.

Time to forget her foolish daydreams and put some distance between her and this man.

Which would prove difficult since they were stuck on this train.

In the same seat.

John slid onto the bench. Miss Mary pressed against the window again. He shook his head. What was it with women that made them such a mystery?

Not that it mattered. Once he arrived in Bakersfield, they'd go their separate ways, and he'd never see her again.

He stared out the window to his left, past the two men playing cards on the small table between them. The scenery outside flashed past. The train took a southern turn after leaving Denver toward Albuquerque then Flagstaff. With any luck, later tonight they'd head west and be in Bakersfield the day after tomorrow.

They left the valley and began a tortuous climb up the mountainside. Their travel slowed, and plumes of black smoke from the engines obscured his vision. He looked to his right, past the profile of the young woman sitting still as a statue beside him. Nothing but air on the other side.

As he listened, the rumble of the wheels echoed against the rock, reverberating through the boards beneath his feet. Finally, the train crested the apex and descended into the next valley.

His eyes drooped and his chin dropped to his chest, only to be startled awake when Thomas hurried through the door into the car.

"Brace yourselves, folks!" Using the backs of the seats for support, the conductor traveled the length of the car with amazing speed. "Gonna come to a stop real quick here. Brace yourselves."

John raised a hand to stop the man, but Thomas shrugged off the touch. "Got to keep movin'. Got to tell the other passengers."

Miss Mary gathered her purse into her arms, her magazine tucked under an arm. She grasped the seat in front of her and turned to him, the color draining from her cheeks. "Goodness. What's going on?"

John shook his head. "Don't know."

He planted his feet solidly on the floor, knees braced against the next seat. The train whistle blew, four long blasts, as the train slowed. He glanced out the window again. Sparks flew from the friction of the wheels on the rails. The engineer engaged the brakes full on.

The force of the train stopping pulled at him, and he eyed Miss Mary. Her arms strained beneath the thin fabric of her dress, and her clenched jaw muscles communicated her effort to remain upright. He hadn't noticed her strength—he'd thought her frail, petite.

His Sophia was strong, too, but womanly in all the right places. Able to take care of herself, yet welcoming of a helping hand. Capable when it came to tending the house and the children, she always managed to make him feel he was more than man enough for her.

He swallowed back the lump in his throat as tears burned his eyes.

He had no misconceptions. Sophia was gone, and to expect any woman to replace her was both foolish and fruitless.

The sun dropped below the horizon like a stone in a pond. Within minutes, twilight settled on the stalled train like a wet blanket.

Mary peered through the gloom and around the bend in the track ahead. Five men stripped to their waists labored to move the rock and rubble blocking their progress. Mr. John had been out there for the past several hours, chipping away. When they started, it looked like a house camped across the rails. Now they'd whittled down the remaining section to perhaps a few hundred pounds.

The conductor perched on the seat across from her, the one vacated by the two card-playing companions who toiled alongside Mr. John, the fireman, and another able-bodied man from the car up ahead. Several others took turns but soon returned, winded from both the effort and the elevation. Thomas tossed a few shovels full of rubble but quickly tired. Mr. John sent him back. Judging by the sweat running down the man's face, she was glad for it. His breathing, deep and chesty, hadn't returned to normal even these hours later.

Using the trunk of a tree as a lever, the last large boulder rolled off the track and onto the gravel bank. The men straightened from their work, clapped each other on the back, and headed for the train. Within minutes, they were on their way again, the engine straining to pull the cars up and over yet another pass.

Mary settled back in her seat. Mr. John would return, and he would be exhausted and famished. She dug into her purse. Perhaps she could find enough coins to purchase his dinner as thanks for his work. Apart from the fireman, who was getting paid for the work, Mr. John was the only man who'd stayed out there the entire time.

She counted the few bits of change. She had enough for his dinner—the most expensive meal of the day—with none left over to eat for the remainder of the journey.

Two full days without food. She sighed. She could do it.

She owed him that much.

Chapter 5

John woke the next day stiff and sore. Funny how a few days of no work made a man soft and lazy. One of the three children sitting several rows behind coughed, and he opened his eyes.

That didn't sound good.

He recalled when Maggie had a bad cold, and this one sounded worse than hers.

In fact, this one reminded him of—

Mary nudged him in the ribs with her elbow. "Excuse me. I need to get out, please."

He sighed and stood, every joint and muscle protesting. He glanced out the window as she pressed past him, her shoulder brushing against his chest. White covered the ground as far as the eye could see.

But her touch was enough to make him feel as though he were ablaze.

He shook his head at his foolishness and turned as she made her way down the aisle, swaying with the movement of the train.

If she were sashaying on a dance floor, she couldn't look any prettier.

No matter that her dress was limp and wrinkled, and tendrils of hair escaped the knots and twists designed to contain those waves. So unlike Sophia's hair, yet he'd shoved his hands into his pockets to keep from reaching over and touching them to see if they were as soft as they looked.

Mary paused at the place where the woman and her children sat and placed her hand against one child's forehead. Concern drew her brow down, and she tested the other two siblings, one of whom coughed. She spoke to the mother, who shook her head, but Mary persisted, and finally the woman nodded. Mary gathered the middle child in her arms and headed toward him.

She paused and set the child in her seat. "The other children aren't feeling well. It's probably too late, but since this one doesn't have a fever, I felt it best to separate them. No point in spreading it around if it's contagious."

He squinted at her. "If?"

"Can you keep an eye on Trevor while I help with the others?"

"I don't know anything about taking care of sick children."

She planted her hands on her hips, reminding him for all the world of Sophia before she started to speak her mind about something. "Thomas said you have children."

"I do, but—"

"Then you know enough." She pointed to the seat. "Sit."

The boy beside him knelt on the seat and swayed from side to side in time with the train's movement. Occasionally he bumped John's arm. John reached over to steady the child, who took that as an invitation to sit on his lap. Within minutes, his head slumped onto John's chest, and his steady, rhythmic breathing indicated he'd fallen asleep.

Looking down at the pale skin, the blue veins against the white eyelids, John marveled at this tiny creature who trusted him enough to collapse into his embrace.

Is that what Thomas meant when he said God protected His children? John longed to hand over his problems to somebody—or Someone—more capable than himself.

But for now, this boy depended on him.

Mary rocked the little girl in her arms, the child's body hot as an ember. Sweat glistened on the girl's forehead and upper lip, but her hands and feet were cold to the touch.

Mary glanced over at the mother, who held the oldest child. His eyes, dark-circled and sunken, stared back at her. He breathed heavily through dry, cracked lips, erupting into a long, hollow cough like a sick coonhound every few minutes. His mother stroked his hair and whispered in his ear, but if he heard or understood, he made no indication.

They needed to get to Flagstaff—and a doctor—as soon as possible.

Instead, they were slowing once again. Surely not another landslide. They'd been out of the mountains for several hours. Outside, snowflakes danced against the windows. Frost patterns from the extreme difference in temperatures marred her view. Thomas had been through the car several times ensuring passengers had a blanket for their feet or a hot beverage for their insides.

And here he came again, bearing a tray of steaming bowls. He paused at the seats ahead of her, offering his wares. Her mouth watered at the scent of chicken soup. She'd not eaten much, preferring to leave the larger portion for the men who'd worked all day. Given the lateness of the train, the engineer opened the dining car again, but their supply of food wasn't unlimited.

Passengers accepted a bowl, a spoon, and a napkin, but again no money traded hands.

Was it possible the food was still without cost?

When Thomas reached her, he nodded at the little one in her arms. "How she doin'?"

Mary stared at the child. "Not good. Her cough has eased a little, but I'm very worried about her breathing. How long before Flagstaff?"

Thomas shook his head. "According to the schedule, we was due there three hours ago. We're still six hours out in miles. And the snow is gettin' worse."

"Is that why we're slowing?"

He nodded. "We might not be able to keep goin'." The train lurched, and he clutched at his tray. "Another drift across the tracks, mayhaps." One side of his mouth turned up in a wry smile. "Can I leave you a bowl? Compliments of the company."

She scooted over on the seat. "That sounds good. Maybe I can get Cassie to eat."

"Don't share a spoon. You don't want what she's got."

Now it was Mary's turn to smile. "A little late for that. She's been coughing all over me for hours." She cuddled the child closer. "But I should be okay. I had whooping cough when I was younger."

"If that's what it is, you got no guarantee. One of my young'uns had it three times, Miss Mary. Only God can keep you safe this time around."

"Well, He's not likely worried about me. I'd much rather He focus His attention on these children."

Thomas patted her shoulder, his large, meaty hand transmitting his care and concern like a warm hug. "He can look after you and these young'uns alike, Miss Mary. No job too big for Him."

Mary nodded and looked out the window again. Nothing but white.

If God was looking for something to do, He might think about getting them to Flagstaff.

John set Trevor on the seat and covered him with a blanket then dozed off for a few minutes, awaking to find the train wasn't moving. A quick check out the window—after he scraped the frost off with a fingernail—confirmed what he already knew.

They weren't going anywhere.

He strode through the three cars ahead then stepped through the door to the outdoors. A bitter wind whipped around the train, blowing up small snow-tornadoes that pelted him with shards of ice, stinging his face and neck. Holding a ladder, he peered around the train.

Up ahead, in front of the engine, stood a knot of men, including Thomas, huddled against the cold, snow collecting on their shoulders. He hopped down and made his way through thigh-deep drifts.

The engineer shook his head, his brim cap with the telltale stripes slicing through the frigid air. "I'm telling you, we aren't going anywhere. This train is up to its axles in snow and ice."

The fireman, his face black from coal, leaned on his shovel. "So what are we going to do? Wait for spring? We can't sit here."

The engineer shrugged. "We'll have to send someone back the track. Holbrook is closer than Flagstaff, and the storm is bound to be worse up ahead. It's moving west."

John stepped forward. "I'll go."

Another man who'd been helpful in moving the rockslide joined him. "You can't go alone. I'll go, too."

The fireman nodded. "Makes sense. I'll stay here and keep the firebox going. We can move passengers forward to stay warm."

The engineer turned to Thomas. "How long can we hold out?"

Thomas pulled a notebook from his pocket and peered at the figures. "Dinin' car says they have enough food for almost two days if we cut rations. We can melt snow in the engine for water. We'll need to dig a facilities pit. But what are we goin' to do with the ones who are sick?"

The engineer peered at Thomas. "Sick? With what?"

"Whoopin' cough, we think. Two young'uns in the fourth car."

The engineer and fireman argued between themselves. After listening for several minutes, John raised a hand, and the men fell silent. "Fit us out with warm clothes, food, and a gun. We'll head for Holbrook. We should be able to cover twenty-five miles in six hours."

"Think again." The engineer pointed to the track behind them. "You might be able to make it that quick in the summer. But there's almost a foot of snow on the track. And if you go off-track to cut miles, you'll be breaking new trail. Could take you twelve hours or more."

Twelve hours. In unfamiliar country. And if they got lost, or injured—but somebody had to go. He looked to his fellow volunteer. "Still willing to go?"

"If you are."

John nodded. "Good enough for me. Get our supplies. Quick. I want to get on the way within twenty minutes."

No point standing around burning daylight.

The two men tromped away from the train on hastily constructed snowshoes while the able-bodied passengers crowded the windows on that side of the train.

Mary couldn't bear to watch. When she learned of Mr. John's plans to traverse the rough countryside between them and Holbrook, it took every ounce of strength not to scream out.

Now that he was gone, her chest ached as though the air had been sucked out of her life. But she had no time to fret, no energy for worry. She had patients to care for.

Eli and Cassie had taken a turn for the worse, and their mother, worn out from caring for them, distraught over the recent death of her husband, and mightily afraid of what the future held for her and her family, appeared lethargic and disinterested today, leaving Mary to their full care.

With Mr. John gone, Trevor needed someone to watch him. The other passengers, concerned he may be contagious, refused to take the little tyke under their wing, so he played on the floor at her feet.

Thomas waddled down the aisle, a tray in his hands. "Soup for the young'uns."

Mary swabbed a damp cloth over Eli's forehead. "I can't get them to eat. Sorry you went to the trouble."

He set the food on the seat across from her. "Maybe Trevor is hungry."

Trevor climbed up in her lap. She held the bowl, and he finished every drop. Then he laid his head on her chest and within minutes was asleep.

Mary set him carefully on the seat opposite, glad for a respite from his constant activity and questions. Traveling by train was hard on the children. Nowhere to play, no place to run and work off their energy. Surrounded by adults, reading the same books over and over, playing the same quiet games.

Thomas returned from the car behind, his brow pulled down. He settled onto the seat in front of her and sighed. "I just don't know what's wrong with folks."

"What's the problem?"

He quirked his head toward the rear of the train. "Some of them folks back there got a notion that these here young'uns is dangerous to the rest of us because they're ailin'. I told them it's nothin' to worry about, but someone started a rumor about yellow fever."

"That's not what they have."

He held up a hand in surrender. "They won't listen. They want to put the children and their mother—and you—off'n the train."

"But it's too cold out there."

"They say you can build a fire and a shelter. 'Keep them warm and fed out there, before the rest of us catch it.' That's what they're sayin'."

"Can you gather the passengers in the forward car?"

He brightened. "That's a good idea. The engineer said they'd be warmer up there anyways. If'n I say they gots to move, we can keep them away from the young'uns."

She smiled and patted his hand. "Thank you. I'll come and talk to them."

"Give me a few minutes. I'll let you know when I'm ready."

For the next twenty minutes or so, Mary tended to her charges. Eli and Cassie seemed to be holding their own, but their mother wasn't. Her breathing worsened, and she coughed more frequently, long, drawn-out coughs that left her breathless. Her temperature soared, and she went from violent cold chills to severe sweats and back within minutes.

Finally, Thomas came to the front of the car and beckoned to her. "Ever'body is gathered in the front two cars. I'll open the doors so you can talk to them all at the same time. They's a portico to protect you from the weather."

She nodded. "Trevor, come with me."

He grasped her hand and toddled along behind her. When she entered the second car, all conversation fell silent. And when Thomas opened the doors between the cars, the passengers forward turned around and stared.

She cleared her throat softly. "Ladies and gentlemen, I want to settle your concerns. The children have whooping cough, not yellow fever."

A woman from the first car spoke up. "Are you a doctor?"

"No, but I know the difference."

A man sitting near her stood. "But whooping cough can kill ya, can't it?"

"It can, but that usually only happens to the very old and the very young who don't get good care."

Another woman: "What kind of care can you give?"

A young man with a large Adam's apple called out: "You got any drugs to help them?"

"No, I don't. But—"

With that, everybody started talking at once. Mary sank onto the nearest seat, her head pounding. She rubbed her eyes.

At a shout from nearby, the crowd quieted. "If'n you don't have anythin' good to say, keep still."

She looked up. Old Thomas stood on the seat opposite her, his cap with the gold braid held high over his head like a signal lamp. Trevor climbed into her lap and nestled against her.

Thomas continued. "This here is what we's gonna do. We's gonna move them that ain't sick to these two cars. Them what's sick will be in the third car. Miss Mary has generously offered to watch over the sick until the men get back with a doctor and supplies." He stared at each passenger in turn. "Anybody got anythin' else to say?"

Despite some grumbling and whispering, his solution solved the two problems Mary was most familiar with: not me, and not here. She sighed. So long as not too many passengers sickened, she should be able to handle the work.

She stood. "Thank you for your help. If you could spare extra blankets, pillows, clothing, tea, and soup, the children and their mother will appreciate it."

More grumbling followed her suggestion.

As she made her way back to the third car, Trevor in tow, she glanced through a frosted window. John and the other man, Peter, had been gone for several hours. How far had they gotten? The wind blew a snow devil across the landscape, and she shivered.

She paused and closed her eyes. *Lord, please protect Mr. John and bring him back safe. He has a wife and children who need him. God, forgive me for not letting You into my life. If You need to take somebody, take me. Nobody will miss me.*

Chapter 6

John slogged through the thigh-deep snow, with Peter close behind. Both pairs of makeshift snowshoes had broken more than an hour before, so they followed a riverbed running approximately parallel to the tracks. Ice made the going treacherous, and several times they slipped on rocks beneath the snow.

Peter's breathing labored, coming in wheezy gasps. John slowed his pace to accommodate his companion's. After a few hundred yards, Peter caught his breath again, and they moved on at a more brisk pace.

After several hours, John checked the position of the sun—around two in the afternoon. They still had more than half the distance to go. They needed to keep moving. But he had no more strength, and his breathing rasped over near-frozen lips. He bent over, hands on his knees.

Peter came up from behind. "Let me go first for a while. Break trail for you for a change."

John nodded, too weary to object.

Peter dug into his pack and handed him a wrapped package. "Eat a sandwich."

"Not hungry."

"You need your strength."

His friend spoke well, and John unwrapped the food with numb fingers, broke off a corner, and put it into his mouth. The flavors of salty ham and hearty bread exploded in his mouth. Surely a king couldn't have eaten better. He soon finished the rest and tucked the wrapper in his pocket.

Another half a mile and they crossed the small river, the crust of ice bending and creaking beneath their weight.

Safe on the other side, John surveyed the terrain. "Should we look for the tracks again?"

Peter shrugged. "Surely the river will eventually go through or near a town."

John nodded. "Sounds good."

He tucked down into his jacket, shrugged his pack into a more comfortable position, and trudged on through the snow, keeping the water to their left. Ice formed around his nose and lips, making breathing difficult. He cupped chilled hands around his mouth, trying to thaw out his fingers and melt the ice from his face.

As they slipped and slid along the treacherous terrain, he thought about things meant to warm him from the inside. Sophia. His daughters.

Miss Mary.

His travel today was much like his journey over the past three months. Being a widower wasn't something he'd prepared for. He was in unfamiliar territory here and in his life in Heartbreak. Sophia said anything was bearable if God was there. He didn't know about that, but she'd been very much at peace in her last days, knowing the end was near.

But would God welcome him back after the way he'd treated Him when Sophia fell ill? Deciding he had nothing to lose, he held his arms out wide in surrender. *God, if You can hear me, we need help. Miss Mary needs Your help. And the kids on the train, too.*

His prayer, exhaled in a vapor of breath, was carried off by a strong breeze. Straight to the ears of God, he hoped.

Miss Mary's face flashed across his mind, propelling him forward. How strange to meet a woman with the same name as his fiancée. Why had they never exchanged surnames? Maybe he didn't want to know her better. She might tell him he was making a mistake. And he didn't want to fall in love with a woman he could never have.

While his logical mind struggled to explain away his feelings for this woman, his heart ached with the knowledge that in a few days they would part ways in Bakersfield, and he would never see her again.

Mary's eyes felt like they were glued shut, and she struggled to open them. A shaft of sunlight seeped through a small circle in the frost-covered window, splaying across her lap, warming her legs. She patted her hair back into some semblance of order and pressed her hands down the length of her skirt, trying to iron out the wrinkles while she worked out her sleepy state.

The third car, which she initially occupied with the children and their mother, was now filled to overflowing with the sick. In fact, so many passengers were ill that they put those with the worst symptoms into the fourth car, while those recovering were with her.

The rest of the passengers huddled in the front two cars, most not even checking on their own sick family and friends. With less than a couple hours of sleep in the last two days, and more than twenty people under her care, Mary wasn't certain she could continue. Thomas was the only person who offered his help, but he'd fallen ill during the night, too.

One of the passengers set trays of tea and soup on the landing between the cars. She fetched the food and distributed it to those able to eat, forcing warm liquid through parched lips. Once some of the healthy patients became ill, their attitudes changed, and she'd heard no more murmuring about throwing her and the sick from the train.

As she made her rounds among the patients, she wondered how Mr. John fared. Funny how he shared his name with the man she would soon marry. A man she'd barely thought of since meeting Her John.

Her breath caught in her throat. *Her John.* She'd taken to thinking of him in those terms since he left to get help. What did that say about her? That she was unworthy of the undoubtedly fine man in Heartbreak, California, who awaited her.

She ran a practiced hand across Eli's forehead. Cool to the touch. His fever broke last night. One less patient to worry about.

Cassie, curled up on the seat next to her older brother, sat up and swiped her hair from her face. "Hungry." She looked around. "Where Momma?"

"I'm going to check on her now." She stroked the girl's cheek. "Feeling better? You must be, if you're hungry."

"Hmm-mmm."

She turned to Trevor, perched on the seat across the aisle. "Can you get the tray from outside the door?" Mary pointed. "Give a little tea and soup to those who are awake, then share the rest with your sister."

Mary headed toward the car where the most ill were housed. But first, she paused on the landing between the cars and drew in several deep breaths. Yesterday, an older woman had died.

There could be more this morning.

She stepped inside and checked her patients. Several seemed less hot this morning, which was a good sign. One seemed a little worse, but the rest held their own. Mrs. McGee, the children's mother and first patient to be moved into this car, was in the last seat. Mary stepped around arms and legs splayed in the aisle and pasted on a smile.

No point in letting her see worry—no!

The woman lay on her back, eyes open. Around her mouth, blue-tinged skin. A mottled hand hung uncovered over the edge of the seat.

Mary sank to the edge of the seat, the grip on her emotions slipping away like sand through her fingers. A lump formed in her throat, threatening to cut off her breathing. How could she tell the children?

If only she were in a position to take them herself. Could she even hope Mr. Stewart might be compassionate enough to adopt them? Unlikely. He had two daughters. He didn't need more children. He expected nothing of her other than to raise his children.

Mary covered Mrs. McGee's face with a blanket. Her John would be back soon, and he would help move the body.

Her John was good and kind.

Completely unlike Mr. Stewart.

Mary returned to the third car, berating herself for her ill will toward a man she'd never met. She didn't know Mr. Stewart any more than she knew Her John. Sure, he was polite, helpful, strong, willing to help. But what was he like in his everyday life?

She returned to the third car and paused. What were the children doing? Their heads were bowed, their little hands folded in prayer.

Eli led them. "God, thank You for this food. Thank You for keeping Trevor safe while we were sick, and thank You for making us well. God, we love You, and we know You'll make Momma not be sick. And thanks for Miss Mary. She must be one of those angels Momma tells us about. Amen."

Mary's vision clouded as they dug into their thin soup and lukewarm tea. These children had nothing, yet they had everything—one another and a childlike faith. They talked to God like He was sitting there beside them.

She wanted that.

She sat in the seat in front of the three and turned to face them. "How are you doing?"

Trevor shoved a small square of bread into his mouth, his cheeks puffed like a chipmunk's. "Good."

Eli smiled at his brother. "They found some bread. And sugar for the tea."

"Good."

Trevor studied her a long minute. "How's Momma?"

Mary drew a calming breath. "Not so well. Where are you traveling?"

Eli set his spoon down. "Momma's brother is the foreman on a large ranch near Bakersfield. We're going to live with him until Momma gets back on her feet. Then we'll live in town, and Momma said we can go to school and play with other kids."

"That's nice. What's your uncle's name?"

"Uncle Marty." He turned to look back at the other car. "Where's Momma?"

"Well, it's like this—"

Trevor's face paled. "Did Momma die?"

Mary dropped her gaze. "Yes, she did."

Cassie swallowed her bread. "Momma dead?"

Eli patted his sister's hand. "She's in heaven now, with Poppa. But we're going to be all right. We'll live with Uncle Marty. And when I get all grown up, I'll get me a job in town. And a house with a bedroom for each of us."

A smile lit Trevor's face. "No more sharing?"

"No more sharing."

The three huddled together, inventing and reinventing their future, while Mary checked her other patients.

The children would be fine. They'd live in Bakersfield, and she'd live in Heartbreak. She'd probably never see them again, but they would be well loved and well taken care of.

They'd have more than she ever had.

In fact, with their faith in God, they already did.

Chapter 7

The sun had been down for hours, and John, blindly following Peter, looked up, squinting through eyes almost frozen shut.

Was that light on the horizon?

No, the moon was playing tricks on him.

He checked the night sky.

Except there was no moon tonight. Or if there was, it didn't penetrate the clouds.

He paused and held his breath a moment. Tinny music drifted on the night air toward him. "Peter, the town!"

Gathering his final reserves of strength, he broke into a trot, Peter close behind. The music came from a saloon, and he staggered up the three steps from street level, across the wooden boardwalk, and pushed in through the swinging doors. Pausing to allow his eyes to adjust to the bright lighting, he surveyed the room.

Drowsy drunks leaned on the bar, soiled doves wove among the tables or sat on the laps of the male patrons, and in the far corner, a piano player belted out the latest tunes. Behind the bar, a couple of black-vested men filled glasses and collected payment.

John stepped up to the bar and signaled to get someone's attention.

A barkeep nodded in his direction. "What can I get you, stranger?"

He licked frozen lips that didn't want to form words. "Help."

The man surveyed him. "Looks like you've come a long ways."

Peter burst through the door, crossed the room, and pounded on the bar. "We need help."

The man stopped his bustling at Peter's shout. "What's that?"

John tried again. "The train is stuck on the tracks. Folks are sick. Where's the doc?"

Within minutes, several groups of townspeople prepared sleighs and filled them with medical supplies under the direction of the town doctor. A couple of women organized a clothing drive, and the owner of the mercantile opened to provide food, blankets, and clothing. As people bustled back and forth, John leaned against the railing of the saloon and, as seemed to happen more and more in recent days, his thoughts went to Miss Mary.

Not the woman he would marry in less than a month.

He'd thought little of Miss Johannson over the past few days, other than to rue the day he agreed to wed her. Not wholeheartedly, of course. Hoping to dissuade her with his covenant marriage requirements. He wanted a mother for his daughters. He wanted company around the ranch, someone to talk to on long winter evenings.

That could be Miss Johannson.

But he also wanted someone to fill his soul, make him laugh, make him look forward to coming home at the end of a long day, someone to wake up next to each morning. Someone he could love passionately.

That was Miss Mary.

If only he'd met her before responding to this other woman.

The doors opened and the elderly doctor stood in the opening. "Mr. Stewart?"

"That's me."

"We're ready to leave."

"Me, too."

"Wanted to be certain to take the right medicine. Somebody said whooping cough?"

"Right. Fever, sweats, chills, sleeping all the time, long whoopy cough like a hound dog with its tail caught in a door."

The medical man smiled. "Sounds like whooping cough. I'll bring syrup of garlic."

In less than an hour, with sleighs loaded, they headed toward the train. Horses snorted and blew out great clouds of vapor, and the men chatted congenially as they covered the snowy ground. Wagons creaked and shuddered over the frozen ground while John marveled at the good natures of these strangers.

The sun was fully over the horizon by the time they reached their destination. John urged his mount into a lope. The beast responded despite its weariness, and within a couple of minutes, John reined the creature in just behind the fire car.

He jumped off and handed the reins to the fireman who stood there, leaning on his shovel. The man nodded at him, his eyes fixed on the men and sleighs following close behind. "Wasn't sure you'd make it."

"Me neither." John jerked a thumb over his shoulder. "We've got enough food and supplies for a small army. The good people of Holbrook came through."

The man leaned his shovel against the side of the train. "I'll see if they need help."

John scanned the windows, hoping to see her leaning out, calling his name. When he saw no movement, he chided himself for his foolish thoughts. She was likely sleeping. Or tending patients. Or—

He turned to the fireman. "How have things been?"

The man hung his head and nudged at a clump of snow. "Fair to middlin'. We lost a few."

John boarded the train and pushed through the door of the first car. "Miss Mary? Where is Miss Mary?"

Passengers looked up, their faces lighting with recognition. Several stood in the aisle to ask questions, but he didn't have time for their queries.

There was only one person he wanted to see.

And she wasn't in this car.

He pressed on toward the next car.

She had to be there.

But she wasn't.

His heart raced like a runaway steer, thrumming and pounding so he couldn't hear himself think. In the third car, the three children sat side by side in one seat, the oldest boy reading a story.

A younger woman leaned against the glass, her husband's head in her lap, as she hummed softly. A couple of older men wrapped in blankets at a table played cards, almost as they'd been when he left.

"Where is Mary?"

One of the pair raised a hand in greeting. "Good to see you back safe and sound, John."

"Thanks." He scanned the few passengers in this third car. "Where is she?"

The other fellow shrugged. "Haven't seen her this morning. But she wasn't looking none too good yesterday."

No.

John's heart screamed even as his mouth refused to work. He scanned every seat then looked to the final car. "What's back there?"

The woman followed his gaze. "The ones what ain't going to make it."

He continued on, needing to know but not wanting to see what his heart feared would be his next new reality. Having had a glimpse at second love, would he leave this train alone?

He steeled his resolve. What a cruel trick this supposedly loving God had played on him. To show him that another love was possible, only to snatch her from him.

But he wouldn't stop until he found her. "Mary, where are you?"

He checked every seat, scanned every face.

And on the last seat, he saw her. There was no mistaking the untidy bun of hair that always seemed askew, or the faded traveling dress even more rumpled and dusty than he'd thought possible.

She lay facedown across another woman whose eyes were open and fixed.

"No!"

He dropped to his knees beside Mary and gathered her into his arms. Her cheeks were pale and a bead of sweat decorated her brow. Had he waited too long to tell her of his love? No, as long as he had breath in him, he would tell her.

He pressed his lips to her ear and inhaled the scent of her hair, her skin. "Mary, I love you. Do you hear me? I loved you since I first saw you reading that silly romance magazine. I loved you when you took the children under your care. I loved you when you ate dinner with me. And if you'll give me another chance, I'll love you with every fiber of my being for as long as I live."

He touched his lips to her cheek, heat rising in his face at the brazenness of his actions. Imagine, John Stewart holding a woman in public, whispering sweet endearments into her ear, kissing her.

And if possible, he'd kiss her back to life. He drew her close and tucked her head beneath his chin. "God, if you'll give me another chance, I won't let her slip away. I promise."

Pressure built in his chest, pushing between them. Startled, he opened his eyes.

To see her staring back at him. "You're smothering me."

"Mary!"

She smiled, weakly to be sure, but the corners of her mouth turned up. "I was dreaming God brought you back to me."

He cuddled her—more gently this time. "And He did. He certainly did."

Answered prayer was one thing, but a direction for her future was sorely lacking.

Mary sighed. The children would live with their uncle. John would return to his wife and children.

Everybody on this train had a plan.

Except her.

High winds came through overnight, blowing the tracks clear, and already the sun melted what little remained. The dead were loaded into the baggage car, to be offloaded at Flagstaff and returned to their families or buried locally. The rescue party headed back to Holbrook amid the shouts and cheers of the passengers.

And John sat across from her as though nothing had changed.

In fact, if she didn't know better, her recovery had confounded his plans. Once he was certain she was all right, he'd not said one word to her.

What of the words of love he'd whispered in her ear? Or had she dreamed that? She glanced at him from the corner of her eye. He appeared to be asleep. Well, he had every right to rest. He'd been awake almost as long as she had, in much harsher circumstances. Except his refusal to talk to her in the few minutes after he helped her to her feet was frustrating. His words still warmed her heart—and her cheeks—and she was certain she'd blushed.

And so she should. She was practically a married woman. Engaged, to be sure. To a man she didn't love.

She loved Her John.

What to do? She could send a telegram to Mr. Stewart. Tell him she wasn't coming. Could she nullify an engagement in that manner, or could the insufferable man hold her to their contract?

In the meantime, she had a couple of patients recovering in the third car, along with the children to care for. The ill fared well under the doctor's care. She was glad he was here, relieving her of some of her duties, and giving her more time—and energy—to think.

Not that she really needed the time. She'd already decided. She would send a telegram breaking her engagement and asking Mr. Stewart to send his reply to Barstow. That should give him enough time to answer.

If he chose not to release her, that would be her answer. And she would continue her train ride to Heartbreak.

Because marrying Mr. Stewart would certainly break her heart.

Chapter 8

Feeling as though he were roping an oversized calf to the ground with his bare hands, John grappled with his dilemma most of that day. Surely he was making the right decision to ignore Miss Mary. After all, he was the same as married to another. And calling off his engagement to Miss Johannson would be awkward and embarrassing. Everybody in town knew he was planning to wed the woman from out east, and to turn up in Heartbreak with a different woman on his arm would look—and feel—dishonest.

How would he feel if he received a telegram from Miss Johannson telling him she'd fallen in love with another man?

To be honest, happy.

He sighed. Truth was, he wasn't certain how Miss Mary felt about him. Once he realized what he'd done—and said—he kept his distance. In fact, rather than face her across a table in the dining car, he spent the last hours digesting his sandwich.

John looked up as Thomas entered the car bearing a tray of cups and a coffeepot. The old man made a good recovery under the doctor's care. Even his breathing seemed better now.

Thomas paused beside him. "Morning, Mr. John. Coffee?"

"Thank you, Thomas. Feeling better?"

The old man smiled, his teeth a white slash against his dark skin. "Oh yes, Mr. John. Sure do. Thank you for askin'." He glanced two seats back and across the way to where Miss Mary sat with the three children. "If'n you don't mind me askin', did you and Miss Mary have a fallin' out?"

John struggled to keep his voice and his expression neutral. "Nothing like that. She just needs to focus on the children."

"Uh-huh." The conductor's tone told John he didn't believe him. "And what about you?"

"Me?"

"Don't turn those gray eyes on me, all innocent lookin' like that. You know what I mean."

John sipped his coffee, glancing over his cup at the subject of their conversation. The old man was too astute by half.

Thomas grunted something under his breath and moved down the aisle, pausing at each passenger in turn, until he reached Miss Mary. He spoke, and she looked over toward John, then back at Thomas.

The old man better not be matchmaking.

Miss Mary accepted a coffee, and Thomas continued through the car. When he reached the end, he entered the final car where the doctor and the recovering patients resided. After a few minutes, he returned to gather up empty cups.

Thomas slowed but continued on when John wouldn't meet his gaze. John suspected the older man would take every opportunity to poke and prod, ask questions, and grunt under his breath.

He was correct in his reluctance to call off his engagement.

So why didn't he feel better about his choice?

Mary set aside the romance magazine. She was no longer naive enough to think true love was anything like these stories.

Eli, tired of reading the same book to his siblings, napped, his head lolling against her arm. Trevor and Cassie played cat's cradle with a length of yarn.

Thomas strolled the aisle, calling out the next station. "Flagstaff up next. Flagstaff, Arizona Territory, coming up. Twenty minutes. Flagstaff."

His singsong refrain churned the butterflies in her stomach. Maybe she should reconsider. She could marry Mr. Stewart and live unhappily ever after. Well, perhaps she was putting too grim a face on it. She was certain she would grow to love his children.

Or she could break off her engagement, hope Her John felt the same way about her, and—she gasped. What had she been thinking? It didn't matter what he felt. He had a wife and children. He wasn't going to ride off into the sunset with her. No matter how many cheesy romance magazines she read, her story wouldn't have a happy ending.

Where once she was content to marry without love, now that she'd tasted the emotion, she couldn't settle for anything less.

She knew what she had to do.

She would send the telegram.

She closed her eyes to ask for help to compose the words that were certain to hurt Mr. Stewart in the short run but surely would set him free to find true love.

She prayed silently, pouring out her heart.

God, if You're there, please help me. I've made a promise that I must now break. Not only because I've experienced what I thought would never be mine, but because I realize I'm not being fair to Mr. Stewart. Please help me write words that release both of us from our arrangement. She paused, the lump in her throat threatening to choke her. She swallowed hard. *God, I've tried to run my life. And I've made a mess of it. Please, God, take control, and let me just rest in You. Amen.*

She opened her eyes and a tear slid down her cheek.

Two difficult decisions made.

John stepped out of the Flagstaff depot, shielding his eyes against the midday sun. Farther down the platform, Miss Mary and the children strolled, hand in hand. The little girl broke away, toddled over to a clump of pansies in a pot, and reached in to pluck one.

Her older brother hurried over and snatched her hand away. "No, Cassie. If you pick it, it will die."

His words echoed John's feelings.

Which should have assuaged his conscience over what he'd just done.

Even now, his telegram was click-clacking its way across wires and through telegraph key machines to a small town in Pennsylvania, telling a certain Miss Mary Johannson not to make the trip to California.

PLANS HAVE CHANGED. *Stop.* DO NOT COME. *Stop.* APOLOGIES. *Stop.* CONFIRM RECEIPT TO BARSTOW. *Stop.* JOHN STEWART.

Plans have changed, indeed. Miss Johannson's plans hadn't.

His decision had to do with his impossible comparison of every woman to Sophia. And none had passed muster—except one.

But Miss Mary hadn't spoken to him in days. Most likely, the embarrassing episode of kissing and sweet endearments had chilled any feelings she might have held for him. What had gotten into him?

He followed her with his eyes, begging her wordlessly to speak to him. To notice him. To ask him what he'd meant by the words spoken in her ear during her semiconscious state.

She turned and stared at him.

Had she read his mind?

After several long moments, she gathered the children and headed in his direction. If he wanted to speak with her, now was the time.

He tipped his hat in greeting. "Hello."

She smiled at him. "Children, say hello to Mr. John. He saved the train."

Heat crept up his neck at her words. "It wasn't me. Took a whole town." Time to change the subject. "Saw you go into the telegraph office earlier. Not bad news, I hope?"

She glanced at the young ones. "Eli, take your brother and sister to the train. Thomas will help you board." She watched while the three complied. "I made a difficult decision today."

Having made his own hard choice, he commiserated with her. "That can be quite draining."

"I was traveling to California to—to meet someone. I sent a telegram saying my plans had changed."

His heart leaped in his chest. Now was his chance to tell her. But he couldn't. Until he received a response, he was still engaged. "I see why you are distressed."

"Did you send a telegram to your wife?"

"She's dead."

Her hand flew to her throat. "I'm so sorry. Thomas said he was praying for your children."

"I'm engaged to be married. Which is as binding as a marriage."

A tiny flicker of some expression—hope? Delight?—vanished at his words.

The whistle blew, piercing his thoughts, and he nodded toward the train. "Your carriage awaits you, Miss Mary."

His fingers itched to offer his hand, but he held back. Touching her now might convince his heart to pursue their relationship before he was truly free.

As for him, he would tuck his heart into his pocket, even as he prayed she could see inside him and feel the same for him as he felt for her.

Mary trailed the children into the dining car, searching for a table for four. Or at least for three. Cassie and Trevor could share the space of an adult, but Eli insisted on his own chair. Because of the delays in travel due to the weather, the snow, and the passengers' illness, the engineer had approved the opening of the dining car for every meal at no charge.

Which was one thing she didn't have to worry about. Feeding three growing children was hard enough when food was plenty and a kitchen was available. Keeping them filled on stale biscuits and day-old sandwiches would have been next to impossible.

Cassie spotted Mr. John and toddled toward him, holding out her hands to be picked up and cuddled. Mary smiled at the picture. He clearly enjoyed being around small children, and Cassie wasn't shy with anybody. He scooped the child onto his lap and bounced her several times, laughing at the child's cooing.

Then he looked up and saw her. He froze as he stared at her. His jaw clenched and unclenched, then he set Cassie down.

Cassie, oblivious to what just happened, returned. Mary scooped her up and hugged her close, studying John over the top of the child's head. He glanced at her then returned to his breakfast and his dining companions.

What was wrong with the man?

His news about his engagement dashed any hopes about a future with him. What did he think of her, breaking her own engagement?

And why did he speak words of love into her ear? Probably the stress of the situation. After all, why would he have any feelings for her? They barely knew each other.

She pointed to a table in the corner. "Over there, children."

They clambered into a U-shaped booth, and she perched on a chair on the outside, feeling like a warden keeping the prisoners contained.

The waiter set their soup before them, and Mary pushed the bowl toward Trevor. "You eat first. Make sure it's not too hot."

The boy dug in, slurping up spoonfuls, dribbling some down the front of his shirt, much the worse for wear given the five days on the train. Mary sighed. She had no facilities to wash and dry clothes and had given up trying to keep the children's clothes clean. She swiped their hands and faces several times a day with a damp handkerchief, planning to discard the dingy gray linen once she handed them over to their uncle.

Once again, the thought of leaving them created a hole in her heart. What would she do now that she didn't have to go to Heartbreak? Stay in Bakersfield? Work until she earned enough to continue to the ocean? It would be nice to see the

Pacific. Dip her toes into the water.

Trevor pushed the empty bowl away. He swiped his hand across his mouth. "Sorry, Miss Mary. I was so hungry I ate it all."

Mary smiled. "That's okay. I wasn't really hungry."

The truth was, her stomach grumbled constantly from lack of food, and her dress hung loose in areas it hadn't when she boarded the train.

When the waiter brought the sandwiches, however, she took her half and passed the plate to Trevor. "Chicken salad. My favorite."

Eli looked up from his own half sandwich. "You said yesterday that egg salad was your favorite."

Trevor giggled. "And the day before, roast beef was the best of all."

Mary smiled at them in turn then took a bite, savoring the creamy filling. It had been a long time since her sparse breakfast of tea and toast. "They're all my favorite."

A shadow fell across the table, and she looked up. A man in a dark suit, somewhat wrinkled and dusty, stood beside her.

She set her sandwich down. "Can I help you?"

"A few of us are finding the miles tedious, and we were talking about setting up a Bible study of sorts. Nothing fancy. Just a group of us asking questions, breaking up the time a little. John suggested perhaps you'd like to join us?"

Mary twisted in her seat and looked toward Mr. John. Although indirect, it was the first interaction they'd had in two days. "I'd like that. I'll have more questions than answers, I'm afraid."

The man smiled. "That's fine. I'm a preacher heading for Sacramento. You can keep me in practice for my new flock. Shall we say in an hour?"

"Fine."

She went back to finishing her sandwich, but her mind was miles ahead. She would be in the same car, sitting in a small group, sharing the Bible. She hadn't opened the book since her Sunday school days and wasn't certain she remembered much of what she'd learned then.

But Mr. John would be there.

Indeed, he'd suggested she be there.

She hesitated. Did he want her company?

Or did he simply assume she needed schooling in the Bible?

While he waited for the other passengers to join him in the dining car for the Bible study, John stared at the door, willing Miss Mary to walk through. To smile at him. To—to what?

What had he been thinking to suggest the preacher ask Miss Mary to join them? Would she misconstrue his intentions?

Speaking of which, what were his intentions?

Footsteps approached, and he held his breath.

When the door opened to reveal the preacher, he exhaled.

Maybe she wouldn't come.

Maybe she'd changed her mind.

After all, she'd changed her mind about meeting someone in California. Surely a decision not to attend a Bible study wasn't nearly so great.

The preacher sat across from him. "Good to see you showed up. Particularly since it was your idea."

John had no response for the man.

The lump in his throat wouldn't let him answer.

For the doors had opened again.

And the woman of his thoughts walked through.

She sat beside the preacher. "So sorry I'm late."

The older man patted her arm. "I just got here myself."

John swiped damp palms on his thighs. "And I've only been here a minute or so."

Which wasn't entirely true.

He'd sat, waiting for *her*, about forty minutes. Hoping against hope she might appear early. Perhaps they'd have a little time together. Alone.

He chided himself for thinking of being alone with her. Those were not gentlemanly thoughts toward a woman he wasn't married to.

"The children were a little more unruly than usual. They didn't like me leaving them. Reminded them of their mother's illness and passing, I suppose."

The preacher opened his Bible. "I can see where that might be the case."

She smiled at John. "But when I told them I was going to learn about God, they settled down on the promise I would share with them on my return."

The preacher nodded. "Then we should start."

For the next hour, John struggled to keep his mind on the story of how Nicodemus came to Jesus at night and asked about being born again. But hearing the preacher explain the passage now, John realized he needed this born-again experience to complete his relationship with Christ.

The preacher closed his Bible. "Any other questions?"

John nodded. "How do I get what Nicodemus wanted?"

Miss Mary giggled. "I was going to ask the same thing."

The preacher grinned. "Well, that was quick."

John shook his head. "God has been working on me this entire train ride."

Miss Mary wrung her hands together. "Me also."

"Then let's join hands and pray." The preacher set his Bible down and bowed his head. "Dear Lord, thank You for these young people who are listening to Your voice. Hear them now, Lord, as they silently confess their sin to You and express their need for Your saving grace."

The preacher continued, but John heard nothing except the crashing thunder of his heart as he held Miss Mary's hand.

He wasn't sure he could explain it, but something had changed in their relationship.

And regardless of whether she was the woman for him, one thing was certain: they were now brother and sister in the Lord.

Chapter 9

Mary peered through the window as the train rounded another bend on its way toward Bakersfield. Another couple of hours and she would be at her final destination.

No. Her next destination.

She'd not stay here long. As soon as she had enough money to buy a ticket, she'd leave.

When the train stopped for lunch at Barstow, her first order of business—after getting the children something to eat—was to check at the telegraph office. There was no response from Mr. Stewart.

She checked on the children in the seat next to hers, but they dozed, their tummies full and their minds exhausted with the monotony of the train. Mary glanced up when the door at the end of the car opened and Thomas stepped through.

He tossed her one of his signature smiles. "Good morning, miss. Gettin' nearer by the mile." He quirked his chin toward her charges. " 'Spect you'll be missin' these little ones."

Her eyes misted, and a lump grew in her throat. "I will."

Thomas studied her a long moment. "Yes, miss, I 'spect it's occupied your thoughts a great deal." He patted her shoulder. "Came to tell you the preacher is having one more Bible study in the dining car before we reach Bakersfield in about two hours. Thought you might like to join them."

Her first inclination was to demur and stay away from the man who occupied her thoughts, but her hunger for the Word of God overrode her hurting heart. If the preacher was correct, only God could ease her heartache and fill her with all she needed. Thinking Mr. John—or any other man, for that matter—could be everything she needed was unfair and unrighteous.

She pressed the wrinkles from her skirt and checked her reflection in the window. "Am I presentable?"

The conductor grinned. "Yes'm, you is always presentable."

He offered her a hand, which she accepted, and she stood. "Thank you, Thomas. I shall miss you."

"Aw, Miss Mary, you can come visit me anytime. You know where to find me."

She shuddered. "After this adventure, I may find another way to travel. Perhaps someday we will be able to fly like the birds."

He chuckled. "Not until we get our angel wings, Miss Mary."

She made her way to the dining car and joined the preacher, Mr. John, and another woman and two men gathered around a table. Despite the upheaval in her life and the turmoil in her heart, an unexplainable peace settled on her instantly, and she bowed her head to join the others in prayer.

The preacher was right. Where two or more gathered, God was in their midst.

And she needed Him more than ever if she was going to follow through on her plan to leave the only man she'd ever loved.

Despite his closed eyes and intent focus on the preacher's words, John sensed the instant Miss Mary entered the car. He couldn't see her, and she didn't sit next to him, but he knew she was there.

He was attuned to her as though they'd been married for years.

Just as he'd been with Sophia. Knowing her thoughts before she spoke. Able to finish her sentences, and she, his.

The preacher said the "amen," then John raised his head and opened his eyes.

And caught her staring at him.

His heart leaped, but when she looked away, his happiness escaped like a leaky balloon.

The preacher cleared his throat. "Today we're going to talk about joy. Joy is not dependent on our circumstances, whereas happiness is. To be happy, a complicated set of parameters has to be in place. What makes me happy may not make you happy. Happiness is a lot like your sense of humor. You might think a situation is funny but somebody else doesn't. Does that make sense?"

One of the men nodded. "Sure. It's like me and my wife. She laughs at the silliest things, like one of the kids brings a few weeds into the house, but I think the kid should be doing his chores and not wasting time."

The preacher nodded. "Exactly. But I bet you get a kick out of seeing a new calf born, while your wife doesn't."

"Sure. She knows we need the calves, but it doesn't make her happy."

John leaned forward. "So explain how happiness and joy are different, Preacher."

The older man tapped his own chest. "Joy comes from within, while happiness comes from outside. Joy comes from knowing God is in control no matter what. You can have joy in the midst of a huge problem, like a mudslide, or a tornado, or a sickness."

John sat back and thought about that. He'd surely lacked joy when Sophia got sick. All he could think about was her leaving him and their daughters, going somewhere better, and him left behind to hurt, to grieve, to wake up in a cold bed.

He shook his head. "I don't see how knowing God is in control could give a body joy in bad times."

The preacher studied him a long moment. "You lost your wife, didn't you?"

John nodded. "Right. There was no joy in that."

"But perhaps if you'd known God then like you know Him now, you could see how He was working in the midst of that struggle to bring about something good. Can you think of just one good thing that came out of that?"

Words to deny the preacher's teaching flew to his tongue, but then he met Miss Mary's eyes. Yes, something good had come from Sophia's passing. He'd never have met Miss Mary otherwise. Never known he could love again. Never known he could look forward to a future with any kind of—of joy. "Yes."

The preacher nodded. He glanced at each person around the table in turn. "No doubt you all can come up with the same answer."

Each one nodded and agreed their outlook had changed in recent days.

Even Miss Mary.

But what had changed for her?

Did that smile on her lips have anything to do with him?

The train whistle blew, and Mary gathered her reticule and carpetbag. She turned to Eli, who urged the children down the aisle. "Sit down, Eli, until the train stops."

"Miss Mary, getting these two anywhere is like herding cats." He swatted Trevor's backside. "Have you got your satchel? I told you to look after your own stuff."

Trevor stopped and turned around, his bottom lip jutting out. "Don't smack me, Eli. That hurts my feelings." He rubbed at the back of his britches. "And my butt."

Mary laughed. "No slapping. No hard words. Let's sit until the train stops. We don't want to fall and skin our knees."

The three perched on one seat and waited, albeit not patiently. Elbows in ribs and whispered threats mingled with complaints proved what she'd known all along—as much as she loved them and thought them extra special, they were simply three ordinary children tired of this adventure and ready to move on to the next.

Much like herself. She was more than ready to be off this train. She'd find cheap housing for a few weeks and a job to pay enough for her to move on. Shouldn't be difficult. She had many skills that should be in demand in the rugged West.

The train slowed and houses came into view on both sides of the track. The children pressed against the glass, now arguing over who should sit next to the window, over who saw what, and over which house was their uncle's.

Mary smiled. What she wouldn't give to have her future all planned out as they did. Or as Mr. John did. But she'd not heard him utter one word about love or special feelings for this woman. Perhaps love wasn't so important for men. Maybe they could be satisfied so long as someone cooked and cleaned and raised the children for them.

After all, wasn't that Mr. Stewart's offer?

The train stopped amid the squealing of brakes and iron wheels on the rails. A great cloud of steam enveloped the train and the station but was soon carried off on the breeze. The children pushed past the other passengers, and Mary hurried to keep up with them.

Outside, Mr. John stood on the platform. He lowered each child to the wooden surface and then offered a hand to assist her. She hesitated, unsure whether she could risk her heart to one more assault, but his smile communicated simple help and nothing more.

She slipped her fingers into his and stepped down.

A young woman stepped out of the shadowy interior of the depot station, a toddler by one hand, a baby in her arms. Mr. John hurried to them, swung the toddler in the air then kissed the wee one. His fiancée was beautiful.

A pang of loneliness and longing filled Mary's chest, pushing out any happiness she felt at finally being off the train.

Mr. John returned to their little group and introduced the children—and then her—to his daughters. Maggie was a delight, obviously thrilled at her father's return. Little Sadie simply stared into his face and touched his cheek then his nose.

The young woman sidled over to join them, and Mr. John turned to her. "This is Mrs. Jenkins, the pastor's wife. They've been taking care of the girls."

Not his fiancée.

Another man stood nearby, scanning the dismounting passengers but dismissing them quickly. He hurried over to Mr. John, and the two men had a quick interchange.

The man, obviously a cowboy, tipped his hat to Mrs. Jenkins and then to Mary. "The conductor says you know about my sister, Mrs. McGee?"

She swallowed. "I'm sorry. Mrs. McGee became ill on the train and passed away. We buried her in Flagstaff, Arizona Territory. The townspeople took up a collection and put a marker on her grave." She wrapped an arm around the shoulders of her three charges. "These are her children."

His smile fell away. "I'm sure sorry to hear that. I was hopin' her life here would be happy. She's had a hard time since her husband passed." He cleared his throat and drew a deep breath then crouched down until he was at eye level with the children. "Let me see. You're the tallest, so you're Eli, right?"

The boy nodded, his eyes wide.

"I'm your uncle Marty." He turned to the other two. "You must be Cassie and Trevor."

Cassie rushed into his arms while Trevor held back and gripped Mary's skirts. Mary pried his fingers free and inched him toward his uncle. "Say hello."

The man held out a hand which the boy accepted. "Your momma says you're all real smart." He gathered the three close. "I'm sure goin' to need your help." Their uncle stood and faced Mr. John. "Looks like I'll have my hands full."

Mr. John clapped the man on the back. "We'll do fine. Sorry about your sister but glad the children got here safe and sound, thanks to Miss Mary."

Mary was confused. "You know each other?"

Mr. John nodded. "Sure. Martin is my foreman."

Mary breathed a sigh of relief. God surely was in control. Knowing these children were going with their uncle, a man who obviously loved them, and with a man of such character as Mr. John, was more than she could have imagined possible.

She gathered her carpetbag into both hands. "I'll leave you to getting home."

Martin pulled a paper from his shirt pocket. "Before I forget, this came while you were gone."

John took the sheet and read it then stood still as a statue. He turned to her, his face aglow as he held the paper toward her. "This changes everything."

She took the telegram, afraid to read it.

Afraid not to.

It was her telegram, sent to Mr. John Stewart. Canceling their engagement.

Not only did Her John and Mr. Stewart share the same name, they were the same man.

And although it looked like she was taking a train ride to heartbreak, God had other plans.

A trickle of sweat dribbled down John's back. The weight of the world had lifted from his shoulders. Now there was no reason he couldn't tell Miss Mary exactly how he felt about her.

But how to speak his heart before she disappeared from his life forever?

Perhaps his actions could speak loud enough for her to hear.

He drew a deep breath and dropped to one knee in front of half the town. "Miss Mary, please say you'll marry me."

"On one condition."

He looked up. He would fly to the moon and back if she asked. "Say the word."

"You must promise me more than twelve years. When I marry, it will be for love and forever."

Twelve years? What in tarnation was the woman talking about? Of course he meant for them to—

Mary. *His* Mary.

Feeling like ten kinds of a fool, he stood. "Do you mean—"

She nodded, a grin belying the unshed tears filling her eyes.

"How long have you known?"

"Since I saw my telegram."

He grabbed her around the waist and whirled her in circles, much to the consternation of those passing by. Mary squealed and held her hat with one hand while the other gripped his neck.

When he was done, he set her down delicately. Had he overdone it? Perhaps she was so embarrassed she'd never say yes.

"I'm sorry, Mary. I didn't mean to—"

"Yes, yes, a thousand times, yes."

Pastor Jenkins slipped in between them and cleared his throat softly. "I think we'd best get to planning a wedding for tomorrow."

Mrs. Jenkins stepped forward and took Mary by the hand. "You'll stay with us tonight, of course. I can lend you my wedding dress, if that will suit you."

Mary nodded. "I'd like that."

John's heart raced with anticipation as his friends led her away. He would see her again tomorrow. And the next day. And every day after that. While they might live the rest of their lives in Heartbreak, and go through some bad times together—he wasn't foolish enough to think they would be immune to the ebb and flow of life—one thing was certain: with their hearts united in God, and their lives united through marriage, there was much joy ahead for them.

Donna Schlachter lives in Colorado, where the Wild West still lives. She travels extensively for research, choosing her locations based on local stories told by local people. She is a member of American Christian Fiction Writers and Sisters in Crime, and facilitates a local critique group. One of her favorite activities is planning her next road trip with hubby, Patrick, along as chauffeur and photographer. Donna has published twelve books under her own name and that of her alter ego, Leeann Betts, and she has ghostwritten five books. You can follow her at www.HiStoryThruTheAges.wordpress.com and on Facebook at www.fb.me/DonnaSchlachterAuthor or Twitter at www.Twitter.com /DonnaSchlachter.

Mail-Order Proxy

by Sherri Shackelford

Chapter 1

The groom was missing.

Delia Lawrence peered at the watch pinned to her bodice, noting that time had neither quickened nor slowed since she'd last checked. "I cannot think of anything worse than spending the rest of one's life in such an isolated settlement," she mused to the man sitting beside her. "I'd go mad living and dying in obscurity."

Nearly the entire town of Tobacco Bend had converged in the makeshift courtroom. The saloon was narrow and long with a raised platform at the far end. The stage was framed by tattered red velvet curtains trimmed in ragged gold tassels. Keeping watch for the groom, she'd assumed her vigil on a bench set against the back wall.

The air was perfumed with hops, unwashed bodies, and stale cigar smoke. A lone cockroach scuttled along the baseboard.

Delia clutched her velvet reticule in her gloved hands and tucked her boots together. On the raised stage, the haggard justice of the peace sat behind a desk scattered with papers, a half-empty whiskey bottle at his elbow. A line of people seeking mediation for their legal disputes waited on the stairs and snaked a path through tables crowded with curious spectators.

"I loathe disorganization and ineptitude," the soldier muttered tersely. "This whole event would be exceedingly more efficient if the justice of the peace was sober."

"Indubitably," Delia replied.

The man turned his gaze on her. Though sitting, he was clearly much taller. Her head barely reached his shoulder. He wore a smart military uniform in a crisp shade of blue, with shiny brass buttons and gold braiding. His gun belt was strapped securely around his lean waist. The red stripe on his trousers disappeared into glossy, black knee boots below his muscular thighs.

Delia caught herself doing something she rarely did. She stared at the man.

His features were harsh but not unpleasing. He had thick, dark eyebrows over chicory brown eyes and a square jaw softened by the barest hint of a dimple. His hawkish nose had healed crookedly from a past break, and she sensed his neatly trimmed mustache was an affectation to age his youthful visage.

His brow furrowed. "You don't belong here, lady."

"Neither do you."

"Touché, miss."

"I wasn't attempting to spar with you, sir. Merely stating the obvious." She pressed her starched handkerchief against her nose, inhaling the comforting scent of a lavender sachet. "You're the only gentleman here who smells as though he's bathed in the past month, and you aren't scowling as though you'd relish a brawl."

The man's cheeks puffed with air then relaxed. "Not the most suitable topic of conversation among strangers, if you don't mind my saying."

"No. I don't mind you saying."

She'd never mastered the art of casual banter. Though her two younger sisters had no trouble understanding the subtle undertones of human conversation, Delia had always struggled. She took people at their word, and expected them to do the same.

The man held out his hand. "Colonel Sean Morgan. At your service, madam."

She clasped his fingers. "Adelia Lawrence. Everyone calls me Delia."

"Wait—"

"Are you—"

The two of them spoke in unison.

The colonel reached into his breast pocket and retrieved a slender photograph with rough edges. "This was the only photograph my brother had of his fiancée. Do you recognize this woman?"

Delia studied the familiar face.

All three sisters had originally posed, though Becky had clumsily torn herself from the group. Photographs were expensive, and Becky didn't have the money for a solitary portrait. "She's my sister, Becky."

"That answers my first question." The colonel scrubbed a hand down his face. "Where is she?"

Delia narrowed her gaze. "Then you're related to my sister's fiancé?"

"I'm Paul's brother."

Delia swiveled in her seat and her booted feet stuttered over the sticky, beer-soaked floor. "My sister sprained her ankle at the last train stop. She sent me ahead to serve as proxy, since the justice of the peace isn't known for his reliability."

She and the soldier flicked a glance in the general direction of the drunken man on the platform. According to Becky, her fiancé, Paul, couldn't leave the ranch for long periods of time during calving season. The engaged couple was at the mercy of the inebriated justice of the peace. A man who kept a spotty schedule and only appeared in town once every three or four months, with little or no notice.

The colonel's expression shifted. "When I didn't see anyone who matched the photograph, I assumed your sister had changed her mind about the marriage."

"You assumed wrong. Becky is quite determined." Delia searched the noisy saloon once more. "Where is your brother? I presume the men of your family honor their word."

Waiting on Becky had already pushed Delia behind schedule. A missing groom put a serious damper on her plans. Whatever happened, those two had to marry for the next step in her strategy to succeed.

"You needn't doubt my brother's word." The colonel squared his shoulders. "Paul contracted the chicken pox and he's still in quarantine. Since I had the illness as a child, I escaped the outbreak. He sent me ahead to marry his fiancée by proxy and escort her back to his ranch."

Delia huffed. Events never seemed to progress in a straight line with Becky. "Well this is a conundrum."

She pressed her lips together. Leave it to Becky to engage herself to a man who hadn't developed immunity to the illness as a child.

Their father had only agreed to let her accompany Becky as far as Tobacco Bend. He had no clue as to the rest of her plans, and she was keeping it that way. An absent groom was an unnecessary complication.

"Now what?" The colonel lifted his hands heavenward. "I doubt the justice of the peace will perform a double proxy wedding."

Delia mentally scrolled through the numerous possibilities, discarding several ideas as unfeasible or unnecessarily complicated, before settling on a solution. "Since both Paul and Becky are indisposed, it's up to us to facilitate the marriage."

"I don't see how. All of this is highly irregular. I prefer we stick to the plan."

"Then it's time we make a new plan."

Because Delia wasn't adept at reading emotions on people's faces, she'd become skilled at reading less tangible signs. When her mother was angry with her father, she inevitably served boiled red cabbage—a meal her father loathed. Her sister, Violet, took twice as long arranging her hair on the mornings when the groceries were delivered, and always managed to be decoratively ensconced in the kitchen when the handsome delivery boy knocked on the rear door.

"I preferred the old plan," the colonel grumbled.

"My father gave me very strict instructions. He said to ensure that Becky was married quickly because God gave folks ten fingers in order to count to nine months."

"They barely knew each other a week!" A flush spread up the colonel's neck. "Is your sister expecting a child?

"Not yet. Apparently, Becky's correspondence with your brother was rather descriptive."

"I can venture a guess."

"If you're only guessing, I'd rather you didn't articulate. I prefer to deal in facts."

"Thank the stars for small favors," he said.

"Personally, I don't understand why anyone would travel all this way to marry a man they've only known briefly during a holiday, but then I've never understood all the fuss my sisters make about falling in love. Violet, my youngest sister, falls in love at least once a month. She's currently infatuated with the grocer's son."

While watching her sisters tumble in and out of love, Delia had studied the benefits thoroughly, and women were far better off staying single. Once a woman married, her rights transferred to her husband. She'd yet to find a situation where the woman benefited in liberties and privileges in wedlock. Her own mother had given up a successful career as a nurse upon marrying her father. The idea of surrendering the chance to save lives in exchange for washing and pressing a man's suits for the rest of one's life was baffling.

Marriage, for a man, meant little difference in circumstances. Marriage, for women, meant dying in obscurity with nothing but a stack of neatly ironed trousers to show for one's troubles. Delia shuddered. She craved something infinitely more substantial for her legacy.

The colonel absently rubbed the scar on the side of his nose. "Their marriage must be postponed. I'm due back to my unit immediately. I can't sit around and wait for your sister to arrive."

"You can't blame Becky entirely. Don't forget the quarantine."

"Serves him right." The colonel snorted. "Paul has always been far too impulsive. Your sister is fortunate the circumstances are unfeasible. Did he mention in his letters that he's barely making a living on that failing cattle ranch?"

"Becky was extremely heartened when he purchased land."

"He paid too much for a worthless bit of scrub. No one sells a thriving business. But would he listen? No. Then to send for a woman he'd met once. Ridiculous." The colonel gazed at her, and his lip curled ever so slightly. "Is your sister anything like you?"

"Yes. Well, um, I suppose. We were all raised together."

"Then she wouldn't last the winter in Montana. Paul has his hands full already. Adding a woman to the mix is imprudent and foolish."

A knot of anger formed in Delia's stomach. "Are you saying women are foolish?"

"No. I'm saying men are foolish for letting themselves be distracted from their goals by a pretty face."

"Then women are merely a distraction?"

"Only if they're allowed to be."

"And you'd never let yourself be distracted by a woman, I presume?"

"You're awfully eager to see your sister wed." The colonel rested his elbow on his bent knee. "Aren't you the least bit concerned that your sister is attaching herself to a man she's only met once? Briefly? By proxy? I'm a stranger to both of you."

"Whether or not I care doesn't matter." Delia ignored the reoccurring twinge of guilt that had been plaguing her for the length of the journey. "Becky is quite head-strong. Father only agreed to the marriage because he finally decided that Becky might as well be her husband's problem rather than his own. We wouldn't be sitting in this filthy saloon if Becky was the sort of person who made sensible decisions." And if the two brothers were anything alike, Becky was in for a rude awakening. "I hope your brother wasn't expecting a biddable wife."

"My brother deserves whatever he gets." The colonel scoffed. "Much like your sister, he has an alarming tendency to leap before he looks."

Delia had been accused of stubborn pride on more than one occasion. She preferred to think herself as determined. The colonel's callous dismal of her sister firmed her resolve. Women were assets, not distractions.

"I keep my word." Delia sat up straighter. "I promised my sister I'd see her married, and that's what I intend to do. What about you, Colonel Morgan? You made a promise to your brother. Are you a man of your word?"

The saloon door banged open, and a robust woman appeared. She sported a rat's nest of gray hair piled atop her head and a stained apron wrapped around her ample waist. She held a pot in one hand, and a wooden spoon in the other. "Ifin' y'all want lunch, you'd best come now. I'm only serving until one o'clock."

The elderly woman capped her declaration with a vigorous pounding on the back of the pot. Delia winced and rubbed her ear. Heads swiveled and there was an almost audible grinding of mental gears as the men pondered losing their place in line over missing out on lunch. Considering the size of the town, there weren't many alternate choices for a hot meal. After a long pause, a stampede of boots filed out the door. The saloon soon emptied, leaving only a smattering of litigants behind.

The justice of the peace remained, a lonely figure on the now-empty stage.

"Here's our chance!" Delia leaped to her feet and snatched the colonel's hand. "We'll tell him the truth, and take our chances."

The colonel remained as immovable as a bronze statue of a war hero. "No."

Delia set her jaw. She'd been taking orders from her father for the past twenty-one years. For the first time in her life, she was free, and she wasn't letting this stubborn man drag her back into submission. "We'll just see about that."

Sean grasped his hat and dusted the brim. His brother had embroiled him in one of his crazy schemes for the last time. He'd only agreed to come this far because he hadn't expected Becky to arrive for the wedding. What woman in her right mind agreed to marry a man she'd met only once? He slanted a glance at Miss Lawrence. Eccentricity must run in the family.

The aggravating woman was completely out of place in the grimy saloon. She wore an expensive satin dress in burnt umber over a matching checked underskirt. Her feathered hat was worthless against the sun, and the thin fabric of her matching gloves was suitable only for decoration. She stood out like a gold piece in a bag full of plug nickels. She needed a bodyguard, not a proxy, but protecting greenhorns was a distraction he avoided whenever possible.

Sean replaced his hat. "There isn't going to be a marriage today. Neither the bride nor the groom is available. I suggest you return to your sister. If she still feels the same way next fall, perhaps you can try again."

"Then you're going back on your word?" Miss Lawrence challenged. "I expected better of a soldier."

A flush of heat swept through his body. No one questioned his integrity. No one. He wasn't the youngest man since the War Between the States to be promoted to colonel because he lacked veracity. No one challenged his honor. Least of all this slip of woman who had no business traipsing through the wilderness dressed as though she were the guest of honor at a tea party.

A blistering set down balanced on the tip of his tongue, and Sean took a deep, fortifying breath. He'd never lost his head in battle, and he wasn't letting his legendary control slide because of Miss Lawrence. Besides, her determination to see her sister wed didn't quite ring true.

He sensed she was hiding something, and her perfidy was her weakness. "If you think you can convince the justice of the peace to agree to a double proxy wedding, then be my guest. Tell him our story."

There was no merit in such a crazy scheme. Surely even the drunken justice of the peace had commonsense reasoning skills.

Miss Lawrence's hazel eyes glinted. "I'm certain once I explain the circumstances, the justice of the peace will agree."

"The truth, however," Sean amended. "No altering the facts. No lies."

Rules, much like the chain of command, were set in place for a reason.

The glint in her striking eyes was challenging. "Deal."

As the petite brunette charged ahead, a twinge of unease scuttled over him. Constructing the telegraph lines across the territory of Montana had tested his endurance to the breaking point. He was exhausted but near enough to his goal to ignore his discomfort. Thus far, his weary unit had battled the weather, Indians, raging rivers, and wild animals. Not to mention territorial settlers who didn't appreciate a bevy of men and equipment plodding over their land to reach the easement the army had negotiated alongside the railroad tracks.

Their worst skirmish had been with an outlaw named Littlebury Helm, the current leader of the Innocents Gang. The outlaws had earned the nickname because their code phrase had once been, ironically, "I am innocent." They'd stolen horses and gear and killed two of his men during a botched raid on their unit's supplies. Sean had promised to complete the line by the end of the month, despite the outlaws, and he'd never gone back on a promise. Once he finished, he was going after Littlebury Helm. That promise was personal.

He must have hesitated, because Miss Lawrence tugged on his hand. "You can't change your mind."

"I hadn't planned on it."

As they made their way toward the raised platform, two men jumped in line ahead of them. One of the men had an untrimmed mustache reaching clear to his jaw, and the other wore a fancy bowler hat he'd probably stolen off an unsuspecting prospector from back East.

Sean took advantage of the delay and set the ground rules. "The minute the justice denies our request, I'm leaving for my unit. You understand that, I presume? I'll even give you the fare back to Denver. You and your sister can't stay in Montana alone. It's too dangerous."

While Paul had his heart set on the marriage, he'd have to wait. His brother should be accustomed to disappointment by now. There was no way this lovely distraction could survive more than a few days in Montana, which meant her sister was better off back home in Denver—safe in the bosom of her family.

As the pair of line jumpers argued their case to the justice of the peace, their voices rose and the men gestured frantically. Lest the situation escalate, Sean casually stepped between Miss Lawrence and the feuding litigants. The justice banged his gavel and declared the mustachioed man the winner of the case. The fellow in the incongruent bowler hat scowled and stomped toward an exit door at the rear of the stage.

Without letting the drunken justice of the peace pause for breath, Miss Lawrence rushed forward. "I'm Adelia Lawrence and this is Colonel Sean Morgan. We're here to marry in proxy for our siblings."

The bleary-eyed man thumbed through a stack of papers. "Fill out this form in quadruple. One for each of you. One for each of your siblings."

"Just like that?" Sean elbowed nearer. "You can't be serious!"

Chapter 2

"Call me Elroy." The justice of the peace burped noisily.

"Isn't this highly irregular, *Elroy*?" Sean enunciated the last word through clenched teeth.

"Don't make me no never mind," the justice replied, tugging at a loose thread attached to his fraying shoulder seam. "Long as the paperwork is filed with the county, I don't care who says the words. By the by, the cost for a double proxy marriage is double."

Sean pressed his thumb and forefinger against his eyes until he saw stars. He hadn't considered the fee. The justice was paid by the case. No wonder he was so accommodating.

Sean glared at the man. "You're doubling the fee?"

He'd been neatly hoisted by his own petard. Paying more for the privilege seemed unnecessarily cruel.

Miss Lawrence shot him a triumphant grin. "Price wasn't part of the ground rules."

Sean dutifully counted out the bills and Miss Lawrence followed suit.

"Double the fee for both of ya'," Elroy amended. "You, too, miss."

With only a slight pursing of her full, pink lips, Miss Lawrence retrieved the balance from her flimsy velvet bag. Grumbling, Sean filled out his brother's name and reached for the second document where he dutifully scribed his name in proxy. Beside him, Miss Lawrence did the same. Much to his surprise, her handwriting was crisp and neat with no unnecessary flourishes. Given her looks, he'd anticipated a flowery script with loops and whirls.

Elroy scanned their answers, placed their paperwork haphazardly on the pile at his elbow, and nudged a Bible toward the edge of the table. "Right hand on the cover, left hand in the air."

Miss Lawrence tugged off her glove and touched the Bible first. Sean's hand dwarfed hers, and her fingers trembled. A jolt of pure, masculine pride vibrated through him. Despite her self-certainty, she wasn't completely indifferent to him. If they were marrying for real, he'd slip his hand around her waist and draw her nearer.

Great Scott! Sean snapped to attention. Where had that thought originated?

He recited complicated battle plans of legendary military campaigns in his head. Despite his attempt at distraction, he noted that her fingers were tapered and elegant with a smudge of ink marring her middle knuckle.

Elroy crookedly adjusted his tattered neck cloth. "Do you promise that the answers you have provided here are the truth, the whole truth, and nothing but the truth, so help you God?"

"I do," they both replied in unison.

"Do you. . . Hold on here." Elroy shuffled through the papers once more, his head bent. "Do you, Colonel Sean Lawrence, take Miss Adelia Morgan in proxy matrimony for Mr. Paul Morgan and Miss Rebecca Lawrence?"

Sean ground his back teeth together. "I, Sean Morgan, take Miss Adelia Lawrence, in holy proxy matrimony for Mr. Paul Morgan and Miss Rebecca Lawrence."

"Right, righty then," the justice mumbled. "Do you, Miss, ah, never mind." He tossed the papers back on the pile. "Just repeat what he said. I can't keep the names straight."

Miss Lawrence repeated the words, her voice hushed. Their gazes caught and held. Sean's mouth went dry and heat curled in his stomach. He shook off the odd sensation. They were only saying the words; the marriage had no personal meaning to either of them. They were simply proxies for the true bride and groom. Whatever sense of gravity he felt was simply the result of too little sleep and too many difficulties.

Elroy took a sip from his glass. "Do you both swear to love, honor, and obey each other in sickness and in health, for richer or for poorer, until death do you part?"

"I do," they replied.

"Did you hear that?" Miss Lawrence whispered victoriously near his ear. "The groom has to obey, as well."

"Paul," Sean rectified, grateful the earlier heated awareness had dissipated somewhat. "Paul has to obey. I've got nothing to do with this."

"Let's not get distracted." Elroy hiccupped. "By the powers invested in me by the Territory of Montana, I now pronounce you husband and wife."

"Vested," Sean corrected.

"They ain't invested in you, they're invested in me."

Sean rolled his eyes.

The mustachioed man from the previous case had taken a seat at the bar. He lifted his mug and offered a weak cheer. "Here, here!"

Elroy replaced the Bible in the center of the table and offered a gap-toothed grin. "Would you like to kiss the bride?"

"No!" Miss Lawrence cried, snatching back her hand.

"Proxy marriage," Sean corrected. "Proxy husband and wife."

Much to his surprise, he discovered he wasn't entirely averse to kissing Miss Lawrence. Her lips drew his attention, and his heart thudded in his chest. Sean gave a sharp tug on the hem of his jacket. This physical reaction was both unwanted and unwelcome. Women were of little use to a military man. His own father had given up a thriving career in the army to marry a woman half his age. The pair had subsequently settled in San Francisco, where his father currently repaired clocks for a living. Clocks. How a man could pivot from the battlefield to mind-numbing gears was unfathomable.

"Is that all?" Miss Lawrence asked, her voice clipped. "Are we finished here?"

"That's all." The justice poured a generous two fingers of whiskey into his glass. "Looks like I have time for tipple. Remind me to thank Maud for clearing out the place for lunch."

An uneasy sensation snaked down Sean's spine. He immediately surveyed his surroundings for any signs of a threat. The saloon was nearly empty save for a few blurry-eyed patrons and the mustachioed man at the bar. As Sean's gaze swept over the remaining customers, one of the card player's eyes widened at something on the stage. The hairs on the back of Sean's neck stirred, and he pivoted on his heel.

The man in the fancy bowler hat had returned, and he looked fit to be tied. He snatched Miss Lawrence around the neck and pressed the barrel of his pistol against her temple.

For a split second, Sean's reaction time slowed. Shaking himself free of the unexpected torpor, he rapidly searched for the nearest exits and gauged his best course of action.

Bowler Hat gave Miss Lawrence a shake, fluttering the reddish-brown feather on her hat. "Nobody move."

Spurred from his initial shock, Sean's focus grew icy.

Elroy sprang to his feet, his whiskey bottle clutched against his chest. "Sure thing, mister. Whatever you say. I don't want no trouble."

"I said, nobody move!" Bowler Hat repeated, his harried attention directed at the justice of the peace. "Especially you."

Sean splayed his arms in a placating gesture and stepped toward the man. "Let the woman go. You don't need a hostage."

"Stay out of this, soldier boy." The man tightened his grip and backed up, tugging a stumbling Miss Lawrence before him. "Don't come any closer or I'll shoot her."

"I believe you," Sean soothed. "We're going to help you, aren't we, Elroy?"

The justice nodded eagerly. "Whatever you need, mister."

Bowler Hat gestured with his chin. "That feller over there with the mustache owes me fifty dollars. I don't care what that drunken judge says. I want my fifty dollars."

As though the glass might somehow protect him from a bullet, Mustache Man held his beer stein like a shield before his face.

"Give him the money," Sean directed quietly, a knot of anxiety twisting in his gut.

Mustache Man reluctantly set down the mug. "I won fair and square."

"You ain't holding the gun!" Bowler Hat waved the pistol in the man's general direction. "I make the rules now."

The shouted declaration jolted Mustache Man into action. He frantically dug in his pockets, spilling coins and bills on the floor before clumsily retrieving them. He fumbled to gather the money in his cupped hands and jerked upright.

"Here it is." Mustache Man extended his arms. "Fifty dollars."

"Bring it this way." Bowler Hat gestured with his gun. "Hurry."

Sean flinched. The outlaw was treating the gun far too carelessly considering the proximity of his hostage.

"This is as fast as I can go with my bum knee," Mustache Man grumbled.

The closest door was behind them. If the outlaw exited from the rear of the stage once more, he gained the advantage.

"The stairs," Sean called, pulling Bowler Hat's attention toward him once more. "You're better off leaving through the saloon. You've got a clean exit to the livery if you leave out the front door. If anyone stops you, you've got the woman as insurance."

"I beg your pardon." Miss Lawrence gasped.

"Shut up," Bowler Hat shouted. "Nobody move or the woman gets a bullet. Stay put, all of you. Especially you, soldier boy."

Keeping Miss Lawrence in position as his shield, the outlaw's attention swiveled, searching for any impediment to his escape.

"You don't need me," Miss Lawrence called, her heels scuffing along the floor. "Take your money and leave."

Nausea roiled in Sean's stomach, and he steeled himself against her distress. This was the only way. He kept his gaze fixed on the abductor, his glacial focus never wavering. The moment Bowler Hat ducked his head to traverse the stairs, Sean jerked his gun from his holster.

Miss Lawrence purposefully collapsed, abruptly bringing down her captor. Sean's bullet narrowly missed its mark, splintering the wood behind where the man's torso had been only a moment before.

Elroy's whiskey bottle crashed to the floor. The justice tossed the table onto its side and scurried behind the barricade.

Bowler Hat shrieked and flailed. He and Miss Lawrence tumbled out of view in a flurry of arms and legs and amber skirts. A gun discharged, and the report echoed through the cavernous space.

The acrid scent of gunpowder assaulted Sean's nostrils and his knees went weak.

An ominous silence descended over the saloon.

The air whooshed from Delia's lungs. She frantically struggled beneath the dead weight of the man crushing her. The next instant she was freed, gasping for air, only to be crushed once again. Barely able to open her eyes, she recognized the dark blue suit of the colonel's uniform.

"Were you trying to get yourself killed?" Colonel Morgan demanded, his voice hoarse.

"I saved us." She pushed off from his chest. "Why were you shooting? You might have hit me!"

He didn't loosen his protective hold, and her heart hammered in her chest. Surely this odd, breathless reaction was from her recent brush with death. She certainly wasn't responding to the elusive scent of sandalwood clinging to his wool uniform jacket.

As she clasped his upper arms, the colonel's strong muscles rippled beneath her fingers. Having been raised exclusively with sisters, she hadn't expected a man's arms to be quite this firm. She glanced at the flabby man writhing on the floor. Then again, perhaps the colonel was special.

"I wasn't aiming for you," he said. "I had a plan."

Gracious, the man was nothing but muscle and sinew. Her heart fluttered and her pulse quickened.

She clutched his arms tighter. "How was I supposed to know that?"

The door to the saloon burst open and a whip-thin, dark-haired man with a tin star pinned to his checked shirt appeared. "Did I hear gunfire?"

"Brilliant deduction." Colonel Morgan released her and stood then clasped her hand. "What took you so long?"

"I was eating." The sheriff flicked at a sticky blob on his shirtsleeve. "Until my meal was rudely interrupted, that is."

"What about me?" The prone man groaned, his expensive bowler hat crushed beneath his hip. "I'm dying! I'm bleeding to death here."

Delia struggled upright, but her legs trembled, and her limbs were oddly weak. The colonel hooked his hands beneath her arms and effortlessly hoisted her to her feet. He kept his hold until she was steady, then stepped back. His brisk, impersonal manner infused her with a sense of independence, and she brushed at her skirts with quaking hands. If he had coddled her or attempted to appease her in any way, she feared she might have burst into hysterical tears from the shock of it all. Which simply wouldn't do.

Her abductor groaned. "I can feel the life draining from me. There's a tunnel ahead!"

The sheriff scratched his temple. "What's happened to him?"

"What do you think happened?" The colonel inspected the man's bleeding arm. "I shot him."

Delia pressed her handkerchief over her lips and swayed. She'd never had much of a stomach for gore.

"He's killed me," the man groaned. "I'm going home to meet my maker."

"Only if your maker is the prison warden." The colonel grunted. "I barely winged you. It's not even bleeding anymore."

The sheriff's scratching grew more vigorous. "Why did you shoot him?"

"Because he was attempting to steal fifty dollars from this man." Colonel Morgan indicated the gentleman with the exaggerated mustache cowering near the bar. "While attempting to abduct this woman."

"Is that true, miss?"

"Yes." Delia lifted her chin. "It's true. Ask the justice of the peace if you don't believe us."

With his papers strewn across the raised stage, Elroy cowered behind the table. He peered around his makeshift bunker. "Is everything clear?"

"It's all clear," Delia assured the frightened man.

With a mournful grimace, Elroy shook one of his papers. Ink-tinged whiskey dripped into an oily puddle. "Now that's a real shame. That was a single malt." He glared at the wounded man. "I'm charging you extra for the spilt whiskey."

"You'll never see a dime from Old Pete." The injured man appeared rather robust all of a sudden given his earlier ominous predictions. "That feller still has my fifty dollars."

Delia's tumble down the stairs had left her aching and bruised, and her hat drooped sadly over her face. She adjusted the feathered brim, wincing as she lifted her arm. After securing her hatpin, she sorted through the various discomforts in turn. Though her head throbbed, nothing appeared broken.

The mustachioed man drained his mug of beer in one swallow and gestured with the empty glass. "That military fellow saved the little lady's life."

"Him?" she snapped. "I'm the one who tripped the outlaw down the stairs."

"Near killed me," Old Pete added. "I might have broken my neck."

"Probably you ought to have thought that through, miss." The mustachioed swiped at his mouth with the back of his hand. "Old Pete was still holding the gun. He might have killed someone when you threw him off balance." The man's brow furrowed. "Say, your eye don't look so good."

While the sheriff hovered uncertainly, Colonel Morgan, who had already divested Old Pete of his gun, discovered a knife in the man's boot. With the subsequent loss of each weapon, Old Pete thrashed and griped. The colonel ignored the outlaw's complaints and tied a length of cloth securely around his wounded upper arm.

All of Delia's bumps and bruises screamed for her attention, and she tentatively touched the edge of her eye, feeling a raised lump.

The colonel turned toward her. His face paled and he cupped the side of her cheek, moving her head gently toward the light. "You're developing quite a shiner."

"Old Pete jabbed me with his elbow during the fall," she replied weakly.

The colonel's eyes weren't as dark as she'd thought at first. There were flecks of gold near the pupils, softening the hue. He retrieved a starched handkerchief from his breast pocket and dabbed at the bruised spot. Breathless once more, Delia remained still during his ministrations.

"I should have known you had a plan," she said by way of apology. "As a military man, it's logical you'd react with precision given the situation."

The colonel tilted his head. "You're a very unusual woman, Miss Lawrence."

"You don't have to be unkind."

"Why do you think I'm being unkind?"

"Because people tell me that I'm unusual all the time, but they don't mean it as a compliment."

"I do."

Those two, simple words echoed the proxy vows they'd taken moments before, and her stomach did an odd little flip.

The colonel's expression hardened. "Is there a doctor in this forsaken town?"

"Yes. Fetch the doctor." Releasing his wound, Old Pete pushed upright, his legs stretched out before him. "Call the priest. I need Last Rights."

"You ain't even Catholic." The man with the mustache guffawed. "And there ain't no priest in Tobacco Bend."

"I'm feeling weak. I'm slipping away."

"The doctor isn't for you." The colonel emptied the bullets from the man's gun in a clatter on the bar. "The doctor is for Miss Lawrence."

"I'm not hurt," she insisted. The excitement was wearing off, and her hands trembled uncontrollably. She clenched her fingers into tight fists. She wasn't some namby-pamby woman who fell apart at the first sign of danger. "I'm only bruised. I don't need a doctor. I'd prefer returning to the hotel."

The pungent aroma of gunpowder curdled her stomach. She needed a little time to collect herself. Certainly she'd known of the dangers involved in traveling through the untamed territory; she'd simply underestimated the risk. No matter. With a few adjustments, she'd be on her way once more. She'd set her plan in motion, and there was no going back now. Perhaps she'd even purchase a gun.

She gave the colonel a sidelong glance. She knew nothing about firearms, but she was a quick learner. He might be persuaded to teach her, especially considering they were now related through marriage.

The justice scooted from his hiding place and dusted his knees. "I'll bring paperwork for the marriage by the hotel in the morning."

Since there was only one hotel in Tobacco Bend, there was little use in providing more information.

Despite her protests, the colonel insisted on accompanying her back to her lodging. Once in the hotel, they took a seat among the gathering of chairs and tables that served as the hotel's restaurant, bar, and lobby. For a small fee, the clerk managed to rustle up some ice. Sean wrapped a generous block in his handkerchief and pressed the soothing cold against her rapidly swelling eye.

Oddly exhausted by the unexpected turn of events, she stifled a yawn. "Do you realize that you're my brother-in-law now?"

"Hmm. I don't suppose we'll be seeing much of each other after today." His warm breath puffed against her cheek, raising gooseflesh along her neck. "Your family lives in Denver and I'm stationed all over the country."

"I don't suppose we will."

The idea left her inexplicably melancholy.

He lifted the ice from her temple and leaned back. "What are you hiding, Miss Lawrence? Why are you really here?"

Her heart stalled in her chest before she realized this man had no hold on her. He had no say in her plans.

She tilted her head and gave him a sidelong glance through her good eye. "Why do you ask?"

"Because you obviously didn't come all this way for your sister." He held up his hand to stay her protest. "I don't doubt your loyalty to Becky. But as a man who thrives on completing a task, I can tell when someone is focused on a mission."

"I'm here to interview Littlebury Helm for *The Rocky Mountain News*," she declared, her chin set at a defiant angle.

"Littlebury Helm?" A fury of color suffused the colonel's face. "The murderous outlaw?"

"That's the one."

"Over my dead body."

Chapter 3

"A re you out of your mind?" For the second time in a day, Sean struggled to regain legendary control. "The man is a killer!"

"I've been corresponding with him for months," Miss Lawrence replied matter-of-factly. As though she hadn't just brightly admitted the receiver of that correspondence was a murderous outlaw. "He's finally agreed to an interview in person."

"You've been writing letters to that cold-blooded killer, Miss Lawrence?"

"You might as well call me Delia. We're in-laws, after all," she said. "Littlebury is extremely articulate. But I won't be able to truly understand him unless I can speak with him in person."

She was meeting with an outlaw. In person. Alone.

He felt as though the blood had drained from his body. "What does his ability to articulate a thought have to do with anything?"

"It's part of his story, part of who he is as a person. I'm doing a personal interest exposé for the newspaper. An in-depth story into the life of an outlaw." She splayed her hands as though she were unfurling a banner. "From rancher to outlaw."

"A murderer is not a personal interest story. A personal interest story should evoke sympathy in the reader. Something with orphans or widows or baby animals. Why would anyone want to read drivel about an outlaw?"

"Because people are fascinated with criminals."

A waiter appeared at their table, a piece of paper in one hand and pencil gripped in the other. "What'll you have?"

The man was squat and grizzled with a grease-stained apron, crescents of black beneath his fingernails, and a smile that probably frightened small children.

"What are you serving?" Sean glanced around for a chalked menu.

"Dinner," the waiter said. "Maud serves lunch, and we serve dinner."

"Dinner sounds lovely," Delia said.

Her angelic smile sent a blush over the waiter's cheeks.

Sean rolled his eyes. "Then we'll both take the dinner."

With painstaking precision, the waiter carefully wrote the words *two dinners*.

Sean pressed the ball of his hand against his throbbing temple. "There are only two of us in the restaurant, and there's only one choice for a meal. Perhaps you could simply memorize the order."

The waiter twisted his lips into something that might have been meant to resemble a grin, and Sean recoiled. Definitely a smile only a mother could love.

"I don't tell you how to do your soldiering." The waiter capped his words with a flourish. "Save your advice for your troops."

Delia dropped the hand holding the wrapped piece of ice, revealing her bruised eye. The lid was nearly swollen shut, and Sean winced.

The waiter scowled at Sean. "Takes a real coward to wallop a lady."

"He didn't hit me!" Delia gasped in protest. "This was an accident."

"Sure, lady. Whatever you say." The waiter scowled. "Two dinners."

After he disappeared into the kitchen, Delia leaned closer. "I don't think he believed me. If you're not terribly hungry, I'd forgo dinner. Just in case."

Sean crossed his arms over his chest. He'd given his life to protect those who couldn't defend themselves. Having folks believe he'd abused Delia smarted. He stuck his index finger in his collar and tugged. Let them believe whatever they wanted to believe. He knew the truth. He certainly didn't need the approval of a waiter who had to write down two dinners for the only patrons in the hotel ordering the only meal provided.

His expression softened. "I'd best take another look at your eye."

"Why?"

"Facial bones around the socket are delicate. They might have been injured."

He gently probed the area, but there was no sign of more extensive damage. She didn't complain, though the injury must hurt something fierce.

"Thank you," she said, her voice sounding slightly breathless.

"How do you plan on conducting your interview with Littlebury?" he asked.

"I can't tell you."

"Why not?"

"Because you're a man with an exaggerated attachment to law and order. You'd be compelled to tell the authorities if you knew his whereabouts."

Sean flushed. Her ability to read his thoughts was unnerving. "Why do you think that?" he prevaricated.

"You're a soldier. You like having a plan. You're certainly not going to miss the opportunity to capture an outlaw."

"Perhaps you should reconsider," he said. "The interview is pointless."

"Nonsense. Littlebury is a person, just the same as anyone else. He has a story to tell. Aren't you the least bit curious about his motivation?"

"I'll tell you his motivation," Sean snorted. "Greed. Pure and simple. Greed combined with a lack of morality. Why not tell the story of one of the men he killed? Surely they have a story to tell, as well."

Her expression shifted—a slight wavering that gave him hope.

"I understand your concerns," she said. "And your comments are appreciated, but I'm going to interview Mr. Helm no matter what you say."

The stubborn little minx. Sean admired her dedication, even though she was a fool to risk her life on such a worthless venture. "If you can't tell me where you're meeting, perhaps you can tell me *when* you're meeting this outlaw?"

"Why?"

"So I can make arrangements for your funeral."

"I don't know when exactly." She ignored his provoking comment. "There are difficulties, you understand."

"I imagine law and order is quite tedious in your line of work, Miss Lawrence."

"He's going to send me a telegram stating the parameters for the interview."

"I can't believe you've managed to keep up this correspondence without either of you getting caught." Perhaps admiration wasn't the right word for Delia. Stubborn was the better word. "Let me guess. He's sending the telegram to Tobacco Bend?"

"I didn't say that." Delia's gaze flitted away. "I won't let you trick me into revealing more. We have an elaborate systems of codes to protect us both."

"And you used your sister as cover to make the trip?"

"Becky was determined to marry your brother. I simply exploited the travel to my favor. My father didn't trust Becky traveling alone."

"He should have sent a third person to look after *you*," Sean mumbled. "Preferably a large, dangerous, armed person."

And ugly. Perhaps with a hunchback and a receding hairline. The idea of a handsome, swashbuckling hero as her bodyguard landed like a rock in his stomach. The image changed and he pictured himself galloping to the rescue, her grateful smile beaming over him like heavenly rays. Blinking rapidly, he willed the fantasy away. He mustn't be distracted from ferreting out her plans.

Telegraph operators gossiped worse than widows at a church picnic. He was owed a few favors, and the time had come to collect. As the man who'd brought the telegraph lines safely across the length of the state, he had plenty of contacts. With a few words dropped in the right ears, he'd trap Littlebury Helm and his gang of Innocents. Sean rested his hand over his holster.

Even the ironic name of the gang annoyed him. "Let me capture Littlebury and his men. You can interview them at your leisure while they're safely behind bars."

"They're hardly going to speak with me if they think I've betrayed them." She tsked. "Do you have some sort of personal vendetta against Littlebury?"

"No." Her ability to effortlessly predict the direction of his thoughts was growing increasingly annoying. "I don't believe in vendettas. I do, however, keep my promises."

And he'd promised his two dead soldiers justice.

Delia blinked at him with her good eye, and his blood simmered. He'd been standing ten feet away from her, and he hadn't prevented her injury.

He'd ensure Old Pete was prosecuted to the full extent of the law for that little stunt in the saloon. "And Becky's marriage provided the subterfuge for this plan?"

Since she wasn't giving him the full story, he might as well nip around the edges.

"Merely convenient. With Becky safely married," Delia said, "my father will let me stay in Montana for a few more weeks. Just to help her settle in."

"That's a terrible wedding gift. If your mere presence doesn't put a damper on the honeymoon, your murder is going to end the festivities all together."

She glanced down before lifting her hands. "Oh gracious. I'm only wearing one glove. In all the excitement, I left the other in the saloon. I'd best fetch it."

She half stood and Sean placed a restraining hand on her arm.

"Later," he spoke, his voice more clipped than he'd intended. He wasn't letting her traipse through the saloon alone. By now, the rest of the men had returned from the break with their various grievances simmering just below the surface. There'd be another brawl before day's end. "You're an independent-minded woman. Why beg for your father's permission at all?"

"According to the State of Colorado, he can send the law after me if I leave home without his permission. He's even threatened as much. You don't understand, because you're a man. A woman doesn't have any rights. The only way of escaping my father's authority is by getting married myself."

The mere idea of her marrying another left him inexplicably furious, but he kept his emotions carefully concealed. "Then why not simply find a husband?"

"Ugh." Her nose wrinkled. "You're jesting, I presume."

He wasn't curious for his own purposes. Merely pecking around the edges of her plans while deciding how to quell her motivation.

Motivation.

That was the key to dissuading Delia. She wanted to feel important. She didn't want to die in obscurity. Did she truly want to prove herself to the whole world? Or merely the one person she saw as suppressing her liberties? Her intentions were all too familiar, and he tugged on his collar again.

He'd entered the army at sixteen with a note he'd forged. He'd spent the past dozen years proving he was a better soldier than his father. A better man. What had he gained in all that time? Promotions and medals. He'd also drifted away from his family. He hadn't seen his father in years. He only spoke with Paul when his brother contacted him, and their interactions invariably ended in an argument.

Sean rested his hands on the table. "You don't sound enthused about marriage. Don't let the ceremony this afternoon dissuade you. Usually the firearm is aimed at the groom."

Delia narrowed her gaze. "Gaining a husband is simply trading one authority for another."

"You never know. Maybe you haven't found the right man."

"Widows have much more freedom," she mused. "But I've never been able to figure how to become a widow without being a wife first."

"That is a pickle."

"I know. That's why I'm determined to make a name for myself in the newspaper business."

"You don't have a very high opinion of men, do you, Miss Lawrence?"

"Fine talk from a man who called women foolish distractions."

He winced. Her barb had struck home. "That comment was directed toward my brother. I apologize for disparaging your sister in the process."

"Apology accepted," she said. Tugging off the single glove, she glanced at him from beneath her eyelashes. "You're probably right, though. I don't think Becky has any idea of what it's like living and working on a ranch. Our father is a lawyer and we live quite comfortably. Becky is the middle child, and she's always had sisters to help with the chores. She's never had to manage a household alone. We've always looked out for her. I think we may have smothered her a bit."

Like Sean and Paul, the sisters had been raised beneath the same roof but with shockingly different results.

Sean tented his hands and drummed his fingers together. "You and your sister are both seeking an escape. Which begs the question. Fame and fortune are merely a means to an end for you. Are you running toward something, Miss Lawrence? Or merely running away from yourself?"

Chapter 4

The question caught Delia by surprise.

She curled inside herself, away from the truth. Finding the hidden motivations in others was exhilarating. Looking inside herself was less appealing. She feared the parts of herself she'd hidden from the world. Her mother had been talented. What if Delia never achieved even a modicum of her mother's success? What if she simply wasn't capable?

She took a deep, fortifying breath. "My mother was a nurse. If she'd been born a man, I imagine she'd have been a decorated surgeon."

"I didn't realize they decorated surgeons."

"You may joke all you want because you have choices." Her eyes flashed. "I'm disappointed in you."

"I apologize, Miss Lawrence," the colonel spoke quietly. "I expect I'm going to be doing a lot of apologizing in the next few days."

She feared that given the same opportunities, she'd take the easy path. She feared she wasn't brave at all. She feared she was only good enough to serve as fashion editor on the women's pages. This trip was her test.

"I wouldn't worry too much; you won't be seeing me after today." She infused her voice with a cheery lilt she didn't quite feel. "You're expected back to your unit, aren't you?"

"They're capable men."

The tightening of his lips defied his casual words. Below the table, his heel tapped against the floor. He was jittery and impatient, barely able to contain his tightly leashed energy. Given the choice, he'd choose his army unit over her. He'd make the choice she feared she couldn't.

Her chest tightened. She was growing more like her mother with each passing day. She had one chance at something more. One chance at a life beyond a stack of ironed trousers as her legacy. Her hands trembled and she tightened them. Colonel Sean Morgan was the greatest temptation of all. She'd never had to control her emotions because she'd never been tempted. He lured her away from her goals. He was giving her a glimpse into why her mother had chosen a different future.

The waiter appeared with two plates, saving her from examining her heart further. One of the plates was piled high with sliced beef, mashed potatoes, and a generous river of gravy. The other held the grizzled end of a roast, a tiny mound of potatoes, and barely a trickle of brown sauce.

The waiter gently set the heaping plate before Delia and dropped the second plate out of Sean's reach with a clatter, then politely inquired if Delia needed anything further.

"No, thank you," she replied. "This all looks delicious."

Following his exit, Delia pitched her voice low. "I definitely wouldn't eat that. A few years ago, I interviewed the kitchen staff at the Palace Hotel for my school newspaper. I won't ruin your appetite with the tales of what happens when the staff takes a disliking to one of the patrons. Suffice to say, it's rather unappealing."

Pushing away his plate, Sean offered a tight smile. "You are not meeting with an outlaw."

"There's nothing you can do to stop me." She gestured with her fork. "There's plenty of food on my plate if you'd like some. I can't eat all this."

"I'm your nearest male relative," Sean said. "I forbid you from meeting with an outlaw."

Delia snorted. "According to the laws of Montana, you have absolutely no say in my affairs. Only a husband or a father can prevent me from meeting Mr. Helm."

"How old are you anyway?" he asked.

"Planning my tombstone, as well as my funeral?"

"Perhaps."

"I'm twenty-one."

"I thought you were younger. Although I shouldn't have asked. It's not very gentlemanly."

"It's a number, Colonel Morgan. Nothing more, and nothing less. Withholding or prevaricating isn't going to change the passage of time."

"For the sake of argument, let's assume that you interview Littlebury. What then?"

Her stomach dipped. She'd have to find another, more important, more dramatic story. Becky's marriage and her correspondence with Littlebury Helm had come together in a most fortuitous manner. She'd leaped on the opportunity with no thought as to what lay ahead or behind her.

"Have you ever heard of Nellie Bly?" she asked.

"Can't say that I have."

"Nellie Bly is a female reporter with the *Pittsburgh Dispatch*," Delia said. "She wrote several intriguing articles about the plight of working women. She even took a job in a box factory alongside the other female workers. She immerses herself in her reporting completely. She meets her subjects in person and writes alongside them."

"I've never heard of this paragon."

"That's because she's a woman and women don't get accolades. We're relegated to the women's page and forced to write silly stories about fashion, society, and garden blights. Nellie didn't let them silence her, though. She's made of sterner stuff. She's currently doing a series of articles about the customs of the Mexican people." Delia slapped the table, rattling the flatware. "She's in Mexico. Alone. And she's my age. What have I done? Nothing."

"Mexico is one thing. Risking your life to interview a murderer is quite another," Sean added helpfully. "You can't sell any newspaper if you don't live to tell the tale."

Each day she lived at home she felt as though the rooms were growing smaller and smaller, trapping her.

Delia's head snapped up. "For a woman to escape the fashion pages, she's got to find a story with broad appeal. Something exciting."

"I understand your motives. But if you're abducted and killed or, or, or other things I'm not willing to discuss over supper, then someone else gets your column space. Dead reporters can't write stories."

Delia made a sound of frustration. "You sound like my father."

"Your father sounds like a sensible man. What's wrong with prudent advice?"

"That's just the sort of talk that keeps women trapped into writing about the latest spring fashions. If I have to transcribe another paragraph about Mrs. So-and-so having a party, or whether bustles are getting bigger or smaller, or what vegetables are good for sandy soil, I'll go mad. I want more."

"There's nothing wrong with reporting about gardening. Think of the excitement. The danger. You could be stung by a swarm of wasps or attacked by a rabid gopher."

She planted her elbow on the table and cupped her chin in her hand. "Name one reporter from the fashion pages."

"I don't read the fashion pages."

"Precisely. I'm not going to live and die in obscurity. I'm going to leave my mark on the world."

"Why is that important?"

Sudden emotion burned behind her eyes. She'd always been different from her sisters. She'd always been odd. Her father had doted on the other two. His most common refrain rang in her ears. *"Why can't you be more like your sisters?"* She'd prove that being different wasn't necessarily a bad thing.

Instead of answering, she said, "Why are you in the army?"

"Because, well, because. . ." His face flushed and he tugged on his beard. "We're not talking about me."

"I'm going to be famous."

She hadn't realized she'd said the words aloud until he threw up his hands.

"By winding up in a shallow, unmarked grave? You won't be famous. You'll be forgotten. People only remember the murderers, not their victims."

"I believe we've exhausted the subject." She plucked at her napkin, her head bent. "I was wondering if you'd teach me how to fire a gun."

She held her breath for his answer. Her father had nearly exploded when she'd posed the innocent question.

"Yes. If you insist on pursuing this matter, I will teach you how to fire a weapon."

Her jaw dropped, and she quickly regained her composure. She'd been anticipating more of an argument. Suspicious now, she cast him a sidelong glance. She'd noticed that people often mumbled their agreement merely to end an argument, even if they had no intention of following through.

He was a man of his word, and she'd use that knowledge to her advantage. "Do you promise?"

"I promise."

"Excellent. I'll purchase the firearm immediately. There were more guns for sale at the general store than canned goods."

"A fact that should give you pause. This is dangerous country."

"Don't worry. I'm a quick study. I'm certain I'll be proficient in no time. I'm sure you're anxious to return to your unit. I'll wait in Tobacco Bend until Becky arrives." She smoothed her napkin over her lap. "The doctor said she should be able to travel in a day or so."

"You're waiting alone?" he asked.

Delia frowned. "I forgot to stow a proper companion in my trunk."

"You're young. You have your whole life ahead of you. People love you. Can you imagine how your father will feel if something happens to you?"

"This is growing tiresome."

"I didn't want to do this, but you deserve the untarnished truth." Sean pressed his palms against the table, appearing to collect himself. "Littlebury Helm killed two of my men."

Delia gasped. "I'm sorry. I didn't know."

"Malone died quickly, but Reeves lingered. He was gut shot and there was nothing we could do but wait. They were two good men. Two men who might have done great things. But we'll never know, will we? We'll never know because Littlebury and his gang of Innocents murdered them."

Delia glimpsed the colonel's red-rimmed eyes before he turned away.

She blinked rapidly. "This is important to me."

"I hope you know what you're doing," he said. "I'll cease trying to convince you otherwise."

"I do know what I'm doing. You'll see. Everyone will see."

She didn't know anything of the sort, because the more the colonel spoke, the more she feared she was making a terrible mistake. But if she turned back now, she'd spend the rest of her life bent over an ironing board.

Sean studied a display at the mercantile. Delia had been right about one thing. The General Store had more guns than canned goods. The setting sun streamed through the windows, glinting off her rich, brown hair, and Sean's posture softened. There were pistols and rifles and enough ammunition to start a war with a small country.

Despite the events of the day, she'd attacked her meal with the zeal of a ranch hand after a long shift, then charged ahead to the next task. She was far tougher than he'd assumed earlier. She'd been shaken by events, but she'd recovered quickly. He didn't imagine many women could suffer through a near kidnapping and shootout and still charge ahead with more errands.

She was also determined to put herself in harm's way. Nausea roiled in his stomach. He'd known her less than a day, and already he couldn't imagine his life without her. The world tipped and he steadied himself with a hand on a nearby display. He'd never believed in love at first sight, but he was starting to question a lot of assumptions he'd held previously.

Keeping one eye screwed shut, she peered down the barrel of a Colt .44. "This one looks nice."

Sean tipped the barrel toward the floor. "You are going to drive me into an early grave."

After setting the gun on the counter, Delia signaled for the store clerk. "I'll take this Colt and four boxes of ammunition."

The clerk was one of those nondescript men that lacked any defining features. He had nondescript blond hair, nondescript features, and a nondescript mode of dress. He could have been plucked from this store and dropped into another anywhere in the country without anyone noticing the difference.

"Four boxes of ammunition?" Sean raised two fingers, and the clerk nodded. "Are you planning on interviewing someone or arming a militia?"

"Just a precaution." She added a bag of licorice to her order. Licorice and ammunition. There couldn't be a more fitting commentary on the current situation. "What are you going to do after you finish the telegraph line?"

For starters, he was going to bring the gang of Innocents to justice. "I don't know. We haven't received an assignment yet."

The future stretched before him. There were no challenges left in his career, no mountains left to climb. He'd done all he'd set out to do in the army. He'd made the rank of colonel younger than his father, and he'd soon complete the telegraph line. A task his commanding officer had deemed impossible.

There was always the rank of general. Except another promotion held no appeal. Near as he could tell, outside of a war, generals spent most of their time overseeing the troops. Becoming a general also meant navigating political minefields. He'd never been much for politics.

Delia crouched before the glass counter. "I'll take half a dozen pewter mugs, as well."

"Are you writing a story or setting up house?" he scoffed. "I obviously don't appreciate journalism."

"The mugs are for Paul and Becky." She tossed him a withering glance. "I didn't want to drag a gift halfway across the country."

"Oh. Of course." He leaned over her shoulder. "Add a half dozen of the pewter plates."

Delia graced him with a smile that sent his heart thudding in his chest.

He swallowed around the lump in his throat and turned toward the clerk. "Is there a good place for target practice?"

"Out back. Take the trail to the creek." The nondescript clerk glared, his voice dripping with anger. "You'll see the spot."

Sean glanced over his shoulder, searching for the source of the man's irritation, but the store was empty.

"Is there a problem?" he asked.

"I don't appreciate when a feller hits a woman."

"This was an accident," Delia interrupted, touching her swollen eye. "I brought it on myself."

The clerk scowled. "That's what he'd have you think."

"Let's go." Sean gently urged her away from the counter. At this rate, they'd have him run out of town on a rail. "You're not helping, Miss Lawrence. While I appreciate the protective zeal in this town, we'd best be about our business."

The clerk added several empty bottles in a metal carrier to their order for target practice. Delia counted out her money and placed the empty handgun in her reticule. The barrel stuck out the top and she tightened the tassels.

Sean raised his eyes heavenward and prayed for forbearance. "Let's practice. We only have another hour before dark."

"You're being rather accommodating, all of a sudden." She eyed him, her brows furrowed. "Why?"

"Because learning to fire a gun is the first sensible idea you've had all day."

"Not the first, surely. I recommended that you not eat anything the waiter served."

He wasn't unsympathetic to her plight, merely cautious. Hadn't he set out to prove himself all those years ago? No one had stopped him. Least of all a father distracted by his new wife. Sean had ridden into danger, time and time again, and had risen through the ranks. How would he have reacted if someone had tried to stop him?

He'd have ignored their advice.

Sean took Delia's elbow and guided her down the narrow path. Cicadas called and the wind ruffled through the leaves. The sun was shining and the temperature was ideal. Neither too hot, nor too cold, as though Mother Nature was smiling on them.

Delia blended well with her surroundings. She smelled of spring and her eyes sparkled like a clear, summer's day. His heart swelled and a buoyant joy unlike anything he'd ever known flowed through him.

He doffed his coat and spread the material on a large, flat rock at the edge of the stream then motioned for Delia to sit.

She thanked him and moved her skirts aside before perching on the edge. For the next fifteen minutes, he demonstrated loading and unloading the gun, along with gun safety. Smart and capable, she quickly mastered the task. Satisfied with her progress, he stood and crossed the narrow plank bridge traversing the creek. A raised table had been positioned on the far side, and he set several bottles on the bullet-riddled surface.

He jogged back to where Delia waited. "Now we shoot."

Minding his instructions, she carefully lifted the barrel and aimed. "I'm ready."

"Squeeze slowly. This isn't a showdown. There's going to be a kick."

The gun discharged, and the report echoed around them. Delia staggered back a step and he placed a steadying hand on her shoulder.

"Oh my," she said. "That's powerful."

"You want to try again?"

"Absolutely!"

They ran through nearly an entire carton of bullets, but Delia eventually managed to hit all six bottles. As the sun disappeared over the horizon in a fiery ball, he walked her back to the hotel.

"When are you leaving?" she asked.

"Tomorrow afternoon. You?"

"I'd best visit Becky." Her gaze skittered away. "She's probably desperate for company."

Sean grimaced. "What a sensible plan."

She was intelligent. She was witty. She was beautiful. And she was also lying through her teeth.

Delia packed her satchel and tiptoed down the corridor. The colonel had been far too committed to ending her fledgling career in reporting. While she appreciated his fears for her safety, she wouldn't be dissuaded.

Violet fingers of dawn crept over the horizon, and a cottony morning mist drifted from the mountains and hovered above the tall grasses. A velvety spring breeze gently stirred the leaves. Birds called and the stream gurgled in the distance. Tobacco Bend's one saving grace was the stagecoach depot on the far end of town. Delia checked the watch pinned to her bodice and stifled a yawn. The stagecoach left at a shockingly early hour.

Located outside the livery, the depot was little more than a raised platform featuring a single bench heaped with luggage set before the clapboard building. As she approached, something on the bench moved.

Delia shrieked. The shapeless mound was a man.

The colonel swung his legs around. "Going someplace?"

Chapter 5

"You frightened the wits out of me." Delia dropped her bag and planted her hands on her hips. "I was catching the stagecoach. As is my right."

"Without saying good-bye?" Sean rested one hand against his chest. "I'm hurt."

They'd had such a lovely afternoon, and she hated to spar with him. She'd wanted to leave on a good note. "You can't stop me."

"Oh. But I can."

Something in his expression gave her pause.

She crossed her arms and tapped her foot. "What have you done?"

"I'm afraid all the tickets have been sold. There's no room for you on the stagecoach."

She'd been assured the tickets never sold out. "How can that be?"

"Someone bought them all." He retrieved a sheaf of papers from his pocket. "Me."

"Of all the low-down, no good, dirty, double-dealing, rotten things to do!"

"I'm sensing you're angry."

Delia kicked her bag. Venting her frustration felt good, and she kicked it again. Glass shattered. "Now I've broken my looking glass!"

"You can't blame me for that."

Why hadn't she thought to buy the ticket earlier? She clenched her fists and made a sound of frustration. Staying angry with the man would be far simpler if he didn't look quite so handsome this morning. In lieu of his uniform, he'd donned a charcoal gray suit with a gold watch chain stretched across the matching vest. His cutaway coat highlighted his powerful frame, and the dark color suited his rugged complexion.

"Why aren't you wearing your uniform today?" Delia asked, not quite ready to forgive him.

"Because I'm not here in an official capacity. I'm a civilian."

"What about yesterday?"

An emotion she couldn't quite read flitted across his face. "For the same reason you wore your best dress. For the wedding."

Warmth spread through her chest. Sean might have taken the opportunity to publicly declare his disapproval of the marriage by appearing in his civilian clothing. Yet he'd made the effort to respect his brother's bride over his personal feelings. A rare concession in her experience.

"There's no use standing here," Sean said. "You had to know that I couldn't let you interview an outlaw on your own. We're family now."

She'd been outwitting her father for too long, and she'd grown soft. Sean was a worthier adversary. Not that they were adversaries, exactly. Merely at cross purposes.

"I wasn't going to interview the outlaw." She retrieved her bag and gripped the handle with both hands. "I was traveling to Virginia City in order to check on my sister."

"You weren't hiding from me?" He quirked an eyebrow. "Fleeing with the dawn's early light in the hopes that I'd forget about your dangerous plans? Or perhaps you thought I'd forget all about you. Out of sight is out of mind, and all that."

She ducked her head. "Actually, yes. That's exactly what I planned on doing."

Sean barked out a laugh. "You're the most beautifully unique person I've ever met."

Delia tilted her head.

"That was a compliment," he added quickly.

"I believe you."

"Good. I was planning on sending a note to my brother." He tugged the bag from her fingers. "We'll send a telegram to your sister. She'll want an update on the proceedings."

Probably Delia should insist on carrying her luggage herself, but the handle was digging into her palm. She flexed her fingers, urging blood through the sore appendage.

Sean placed his hand on the small of her back and guided her across the dirt street. "Once I heard you stirring in the room above me, I knew I couldn't leave without saying good-bye. It's the gentlemanly thing to do."

His touch was gentle but firm, and heat burned through the cotton of her beige calico dress.

"You needn't guard me." She climbed the two stairs leading to the boardwalk. "I can take care of myself."

"I know."

She turned and found herself face-to-face with the colonel. The extra height from the boardwalk had her staring directly into his eyes, and his mouth was only a whisper away from hers. She dropped her gaze.

A shocking desire to press her lips against his took hold. She'd never been tempted to kiss a man before, and a giddy sense of excitement infused her with courage. What was the harm in a little experimentation? She grasped his shoulders and settled her lips over his. Liquid heat coursed through her veins.

He remained stock-still, shocked, no doubt, at her forward behavior. From what seemed like a great distance away, she heard a soft thump as her carpetbag hit the ground. His hands slid around her waist and he angled his head, bringing them even closer. All rational thought fled, leaving her confused and disorientated and hungry for something she didn't quite understand.

The touch of his lips was soft and gentle and unlike anything she'd ever imagined. Pressing closer, she reveled in the myriad of sensations heightened by his touch. She gripped his shoulders, her seeking fingers already familiar with the play of muscles. He splayed his hands across her back and caressed her with rough tenderness. Trembling from head to foot, she murmured something incoherent.

The stagecoach rumbled by, kicking up dirt clods. The horses whinnied and the crack of a whip shattered the still air. Sean jerked back and she caught a glimpse of the justice of the peace, staring at them in mute shock through the open window of the stagecoach. The next instant the conveyance passed, and they were alone again.

Numb with shock, and something else she couldn't quite define, Delia tentatively caressed the line of his jaw.

Sean's eyes blazed and he set her away from him. "Please accept my humblest apologies. A gentleman does not kiss a woman on the streets."

Dazed, she retracted her hand. "Actually, I kissed you."

"Inside." He glanced up and down the street. "You and I have some things we need to discuss."

He marched them down the boardwalk.

"Are you angry with me?" she asked, tugging him to a halt. He was breathing as though he'd run a great distance, when they'd only just crossed the street. "I've never kissed a man before and I was curious. I understand why father was worried about Becky now."

He kicked back his hat and raked his fingers through his hair. "You mustn't go around kissing men every time you're curious."

"I don't want to kiss other men. I only want to kiss you."

"I adore your honesty, Delia, but now is not the time."

"Why not?"

He took her elbow and steered her toward the hotel's double doors. "I don't know whether to shake you or hug you sometimes." He glanced over his shoulder "I don't think too many people saw us."

She tugged her lower lip between her teeth. Only the driver, two outriders, the justice of the peace, and whoever else might have been in the stagecoach that morning.

They crossed the lobby and the bleary-eyed clerk glanced up from his newspaper. "The justice of the peace left something for the two of you."

The clerk flopped a large envelope onto the counter and returned his attention to the newspaper.

Delia reached for the packet, and Sean intercepted her grasp. "This must be the marriage certificate."

He tore open the flap and pulled the document from the sleeve. The stench of whiskey wrinkled her nose.

Delia grimaced. "How are we going to explain that smell to Becky and Paul?"

"A casualty of the scuffle yesterday. Elroy must have written on the document before the paper dried completely."

His face paled.

"What is it?" Delia demanded. She peered around his shoulder for a better look. "Did Elroy misspell the names?"

"No." The paper shook violently in Sean's hand. "Elroy spelled the names correctly." His voice was hoarse and he'd gone shockingly peaked.

"What could be that bad?" she demanded. "Let me see."

She snatched the paper and rapidly scanned the words. Her stomach dropped and her knees went weak. "Surely there's been some mistake." She flipped over the document and checked the back then shook the envelope and retrieved a second piece of paper. "What has he done?"

"Apparently, the justice of the peace made a mistake."

"But we were very clear about who was marrying whom."

Sean sniffed the second piece of paper and grimaced. "This is the document you and I filled out. The ink was smudged when the whiskey spilled. He must have mixed up the names when he was transcribing the information."

"This is all a simple mistake. Easily sorted." She pressed two fingers against her temple. There was no need for panic. Mistakes happened all the time. "We'll simply tear up the paperwork. Problem solved."

"I don't think we'll manage that easily."

She reached behind her, searching for a chair or a bench or someplace to sit. Her legs weren't quite functioning. "What do we do?"

"We'd best fetch Elroy and straighten out this mess."

The memory of Elroy's face in the window sent her stomach churning. She pressed her hand over her face then peered through her fingers. In large block letters, the justice of the peace had neatly filled in their names and occupations under the headings of bride and groom.

She stared unseeing into the distance. "Can't we simply tear up the certificate?"

"We'd be tearing up a copy. The justice of the peace has the original. As of now we're married," Sean said grimly. "Legally and bound by law."

"What do you mean you don't know where he's gone?" Sean roared. "Surely you keep some sort of track of the man?"

"He's gone." The sheriff's mouth screwed up, and he lifted one palm. "Just like I said. The stagecoach left not fifteen minutes ago. You must have seen it."

"Yes," Sean mumbled. "I'm aware the stagecoach has left."

As a soldier, he adhered to a strict code of conduct. A gentleman did not disrespect a lady with public displays of affection. Yet that's exactly what he'd done. The instant she'd touched his lips with hers, he'd lost all sense of time and place. Any hint of rational thought had fled, leaving his senses filled with nothing but the ripple of her cotton dress beneath his fingertips and the elusive scent of lavender drifting from her hair.

He tugged on the lapels of his coat. He'd scoffed at his brother for his hasty marriage. He'd harbored a lingering sense of resentment toward his father—only to find himself rendered senseless by a woman. He'd underestimated the distracting power of feminine allures.

For her part, Delia appeared singularly unaffected by the earth-shattering event. She'd pivoted her attention to the problem at hand with brisk, impersonal efficiency. Her lack of concern sparked his annoyance. Wasn't she the least bit moved by their encounter?

She kept her attention focused on a map of the territory pinned to the wall. "Surely Elroy follows a certain routine? People are primarily creatures of habit. There must be some pattern to the man's travels?"

"He comes and goes," the sheriff said.

"We don't have time to chase him across the country," Sean interjected. "We'll wait for him at the courthouse."

He wasn't thinking straight. He needed to breathe. He needed to treat this like a military campaign. He had an objective. Find Elroy and correct the paperwork. If that tact was unsuccessful, they'd do the next best thing.

He snapped his fingers. "If we can't stop the paperwork, we'll get an annulment."

"You gotta live in the territory for at least a year before you can get an annulment," the sheriff said, propping his boots on his desk.

"Well that's an idiotic rule."

"Gets worse." The sheriff crossed his ankles. "You can't get a marriage annulled if you've been married for over a year."

Sean staggered a few feet and dropped onto a chair.

The sheriff flicked his chin with the backs of his fingertips. "The county seat is in Butte. The stagecoach takes the road, but if you're on horseback, you can take a shortcut. There's a railroad bridge over the creek, but the track was never finished. The locals made the bridge fit for horseback. It's a hard day's ride, but you'll beat him there."

"Then that's what I'll do." Sean considered the supplies he'd brought and calculated what else he needed. "No time to waste."

Which left him with the problem of Delia. He didn't trust her out of his sight. Especially after the debacle this morning. When she wasn't chasing after outlaws, she was giving in to her curiosity about kissing. That wasn't the sort of curiosity he was willing to leave unchecked.

"We should go, Delia," he said.

"Not yet." She turned toward the sheriff. "Why is there a child in the jail cell?"

"That's no child." The sheriff chortled. "That there is a runaway."

In his panic over the mistaken marriage, Sean had completely overlooked the waif perched defiantly on a cot in the locked jail cell. The boy was painfully thin with hollow eyes. He wore ill-fitting, tattered trousers that barely reached below his knee. His shirt was an indistinguishable color, the fabric nearly transparent from numerous washings. The boy's mop of unkempt hair was a sandy shade of blond, and his enormous blue eyes dominated his mud-streaked face.

"He's a child." Delia approached the cell. "He shouldn't be locked up like a criminal."

"Well if he didn't want to be in jail, he ought not to have run away," the sheriff said. "Keeping him locked up is the only way to ensure he doesn't run away again before Mr. Pratt comes to fetch him."

"Please focus, Miss Lawrence," Sean directed. "We have our own problems."

Even as he said the words his attention was drawn to the boy. There was no tolerance in his heart for cruelty against children and animals. The boy was undernourished and obviously neglected.

"You might as well call me Delia," she said. "We're married, after all." She turned her back on him and grasped the bars. "What's your name, child?"

"Robert. But I ain't no runaway, ma'am," the boy said. "Mr. Pratt ain't my pa. He just took me from the orphan train because he's lazy and he wants me to do all the work."

"That's awful." She turned toward the sheriff. "Can't you do something?"

"Yeah. I can send him back to Mr. Pratt. You oughta be careful, son. There's worse folks out there. Take that Littlebury Helm. I heard he and his gang were spotted up near the great falls of the Missouri River."

The boy crossed his arms over his chest and scooted back on the cot. "I ain't going back to Mr. Pratt."

Sean digested the new information. With Littlebury north of Tobacco Bend, travel was relatively safe. There were no Indians in the area, and the only outlaws in the vicinity were in the opposite direction.

"Can't we do something?" Delia implored. "He's only a child."

Sean rubbed the back of his neck. The boy deserved better treatment. "I'll contact the commanding officer of the local fort. They take on apprentices." A discouraging thought took hold. "Do you ride?" he asked Delia.

"Tolerably."

Relief flooded through him. "Then you're going with me."

There was only one way to ensure her safety: *never let her out of his sight.*

"I'll only slow you down," she said. "It's better if I stay."

"I have the utmost confidence in your abilities. I couldn't leave you here all by yourself. Think how lonesome you'll be."

"I'm quite independent."

"You'd abandon me on our honeymoon? I'm starting to think you're having second thoughts about this marriage."

Delia released a long-suffering sigh.

The boy remained silent beneath their volley of words, though his eyes were wide and a smile tugged at the edges of his mouth.

The sheriff jangled the enormous ring of keys attached to his belt. "You two seem nice enough. Why don't you just stay married? It's a lot less paperwork."

"No!" Delia paled. "That's out of the question."

"You needn't act as though it's the end of the world. There are worse things that could happen," Sean grumbled. "You could be attacked by fire ants or chased by a hungry bear."

"Those are my alternatives?"

"Merely making a point."

"I'll remember how lucky I am the next time I'm chased by a bear."

"Or attacked by fire ants," Robert chimed in.

"If that's settled," Sean said, "I'll prepare the horses and we can leave immediately. We'll have this straightened out by evening."

"I'll fetch my bags from the hotel," Delia offered far too easily. "And then I'll join you."

Sean glanced askance at her. She was awfully accommodating, given how the morning had started. He considered her escape routes. The stagecoach was gone, and the only other transportation was at the livery. Since he'd be at the livery, as well, that escape was blocked. She was far too smart to leave on foot. Obviously she'd seen the wisdom of his plan and had accepted the inevitable.

He tugged on his jacket lapels. "Thank you for your assistance, Sheriff."

Once outside, Sean blinked as his eyes adjusted to the sun then made his way to the livery. Feeling unaccountably cheerful, he whistled a tune. At least he had a task. A measurable goal. The early summer weather was perfect for travel. Only a few wispy clouds dusted the skies. He was familiar with the trail the sheriff had recommended. Though the trip had challenges, he was confident in Delia's fortitude and his own abilities if anything went wrong.

He wasn't underestimating her again. He'd unfairly chastised her choice of clothing the previous day. He hadn't considered that, much like himself, she'd dressed for the occasion. Today she'd sensibly dressed for travel. She was tough and determined, and he was certain they'd arrive in Butte before nightfall.

After haggling over the cost, he saddled his horse and secured another for Delia.

The livery owner licked his thumb and counted out the bills. "Mind the bridge when you cross the creek. Sometimes the planks over the tracks come loose."

A rare bout of indecision gnawed at him. "Thanks for the tip."

Sean paused with his hands braced against the pommel of his saddle. The comforting scents of leather and animal soothed his conscience. This was the best choice. If he took the long way, he risked missing the justice of the peace. If he took the shortcut, he risked Delia's safety. If he left her behind, she was liable to get herself killed.

The livery door opened and a triangle of light illuminated the hay-strewn floor.

"We'll need another horse," Delia announced.

"I'm not taking a pack animal," Sean volleyed back without turning around. "Take what you can pack in one bag. No more."

Perhaps he'd been precipitous in assuming she was prepared.

"The extra horse isn't for my luggage."

He pivoted on his heel and caught sight of the urchin from the jail cell. "What's he doing here?"

"Howdy, Colonel!" the child offered cheerfully. "Miss Delia says we're trail partners."

Chapter 6

Delia wasn't leaving the child behind. Not when the town of Tobacco Bend was putting neglected children behind bars. The idea was ludicrous.

"He's ours," she stated crisply. "You'd best get used to the idea."

"I don't understand." Sean clutched his head. "What do mean, he's *ours*?"

"Just that. We're his new guardians."

"Says who?"

"Says the sheriff."

She fiddled with a bit of lace on her sleeve. Convincing the sheriff had been a rigorous negotiation. She'd reminded him of the colonel's contacts with important, high-ranking, Montana Territory officials. She might have exaggerated Sean's influence. Then again—she might not have. For all she knew, Sean was quite well connected.

"I have sympathy for his situation." Sean paced before her, his hands threaded behind his back. "I will help as soon as we clear up this misunderstanding with the justice of the peace. I promise."

"I already signed the necessary paperwork."

"You can't do that." He paused. "Can you?"

"I'm fairly certain I can. Because I just did." She patted the boy's shoulder. "Run along, Robert, and pick out a horse."

The colonel resumed his pacing. "This is unacceptable. We're departing on a potentially dangerous journey. I can't risk taking a child."

"He's quite resourceful."

"I'm sure that he is."

"What was I supposed to do?" she pleaded. "Leave him there? Alone?"

"What are you going to do with him once we've caught up with the justice of the peace?"

She avoided his gaze. That part of the plan was still in progress. "I'll think of something."

"I understand that you feel sorry for the boy, but we're not in a position to help him right now. I promise you, I won't forget about his situation."

"I won't risk any further abuse," she said quietly.

Sean's expression sobered. She'd seen the bruises on Robert's back through a tear in his shirt. The evidence of the boy's mistreatment had compelled her to action. The sheriff had treated him as though he was a commodity and not a living soul with thoughts and feelings.

Sean halted and ran the back of his thumbnail along his forehead. "Can he ride?"

"I can ride, mister," Robert declared. "I'm a really good rider."

"Then pick out a horse," Sean said. "There are several in the corral."

Delia rose on her tiptoes and kissed him on the cheek. "I knew you'd understand."

With the resilience of a child, the boy skipped out of the barn.

"How bad is he hurt?" Sean spoke softly, brushing the hair from her forehead. "Can he travel?"

She had a sudden, overwhelming desire to throw herself into the colonel's arms and burrow close, to scuff her cheek against the rough wool of his coat. She wasn't grateful, no, gratitude was far too weak an emotion. She respected him. She admired his willingness to do the right thing, even when he was inconvenienced.

"The abuse isn't recent," Delia said. "He ran away a week ago. The sheriff caught him stealing food from the hotel."

"Poor kid." Sean gently touched the discolored mark on her eye. "We're a battered and bruised bunch."

"It doesn't hurt."

"You're a brave woman, Delia."

"And you're a kind man."

"Then you don't know me very well."

"You'd never abuse a child, I know that much. I'd like to find that Mr. Pratt and give him a piece of my mind." She'd like to give that awful man something more than a piece of her mind, but justice had to wait.

The livery door slid open and she assumed an expression of serenity once more. Robert was remarkably astute at reading emotions. When the sheriff was blustering at her earlier, the boy had sunk back into his cot, as though making himself smaller and less noticeable. The tact had obviously served him well in the past.

Robert led a mule from the corral. The animal appeared past its prime, swaybacked and knobby-kneed, with a stubborn glint in its liquid brown eyes.

"Where'd you find that nag?" Sean led a second horse by the halter. "There's a nice bay gelding in the bunch."

"Nah. I want this one," Robert said. "His name is Fiddler. He ain't pretty, but he's the best animal in the bunch. I figure we don't need speed to go over the pass. We need stamina. He don't need to be pretty to get the job done. Fiddler here will do just fine."

The colonel appeared exasperated but resigned.

He patted the boy on the head. "He'll do fine. That's a good pick."

Delia's heart melted. All her initial assumptions about the colonel had been wrong. Her limited experiences with men had soured her thinking. Those assumptions had woven threads of contempt through her judgement. Bit by bit, step by step, Colonel Morgan was tugging loose the threads, unraveling her expectations. He had her off balance and struggling for purchase.

A half grin on his handsome face, he led a saddled mare to her. "The livery owner promised me that she's docile."

Delia rubbed the animal's soft nose. The horse snuffled and bumped her hand. "We're going to get along just fine, won't we?"

"Stow your gear," Sean said. "The sooner we're on the trail, the better. We'll be in Butte by nightfall."

Delia had pared her belongings down to the bare minimum for the trip. She stuffed her bundle into the saddlebag and stuck her foot in the stirrup.

"Wait," the colonel interrupted. "I'll be right back."

She and Robert exchanged a confused glance.

"I wonder where he's going." Robert stuck his hands in his back pockets. "He was in a hurry before."

The colonel returned twenty minutes later and handed each of them a canteen, a whistle, and a knife.

"Never go anywhere without those three things," he said. "Signal with the whistle if we get separated. Never be without a knife. Water is life around here. There are plenty of streams and rivers in the area, but it's easy to get turned around and lose your direction. We don't have to ride hard, but we have to ride steady."

Delia saluted. "Yes, Colonel Morgan."

With a giggle, Robert followed suit. "Yes, Colonel Morgan."

Sean took their good-natured ribbing in stride. "Mount up, troops."

Delia made a point of mounting by herself. The task accomplished two things. First, by easily mounting the horse, she proved to Sean that she was a competent rider. Second, she didn't have to feel his hands around her waist, which kept her focused. And he was shockingly adept at making her lose focus. His kiss still lingered on her lips, and she absently touched them. The past few days had been illuminating.

Love didn't seem quite as mysterious, and Becky's cross-country trek didn't seem quite as inexplicable after that embrace. Sean had become a bright, shining focus in her thinking. All her thoughts orbited around him. When he was near, she couldn't take her eyes off him. He moved with a clipped, succinct grace, as though there was never a wasted move. She wanted to know more about him. She wanted to know more about his life and his family. When she looked at him, a fierce longing spiraled through her.

She'd barely given Paul a second thought when Becky had declared her undying devotion. Now she viewed Paul as a link to discovering more about Sean.

Her pulse tripped.

That sort of thinking was a sure path to disaster. Sean was distracting her from her goals, and pulling her back into obscurity. She tightened her jaw. She refused to live a life of quiet desperation.

With a surety born of years of experience, the colonel checked the tack on Robert's mule and secured the boy's saddlebag. He patted Robert on the knee and placed the gathered reins in the boy's hands.

"If you get into trouble, let me know. When we ride together, we look out for each other."

Robert squinted one eye. "The lady here says that you ain't the one who hit her."

"Delia," she spoke quickly. "You can call me Delia. The colonel actually saved me from an outlaw. He's quite brave," she added for good measure.

"Don't overvalue me." Sean flashed a wry grin.

"It's good you ain't mean," Robert said. "I don't wanna ride with no feller that would hit a woman."

"All a man has got in this world is the grace of God and his honor. I value both."

Robert sat up straighter in the saddle. "Me, too."

"Then we'll get along just fine."

As Delia watched the exchange, her chest expanded. Robert was a fine boy who deserved a better life. Despite her uncertain future, she'd been compelled to act. If nothing else, she'd send Robert home to her parents in Denver. Her father would initially be livid, but he'd come around to the idea. He was always grousing about the lack of masculinity in the house.

As she considered returning home, a blanket of melancholy descended over her. While there were many similarities between Colorado and the Montana Territory, there were a lot of differences. For the first time in her life she felt free. As though the world was full of possibilities. The mere idea of returning home tightened a band of discomfort around her chest.

Sean mounted his horse with graceful precision. "Let's haul out."

Delia tweaked her skirts over her ankles and adjusted her feet in the stirrups. As a child, she'd been obsessed with horses. She'd spent hours grooming and riding her favorite pony. She'd wept inconsolably two years ago when that pony died, and hadn't ridden since then. Her skills might have rusted, but she'd quickly regain her stamina.

"Don't worry," the colonel said. "We'll be unmarried by sundown."

"Excellent," Delia said, infusing her voice with a cheerful note. "Unmarried by sunset."

She'd never been much for premonitions, but she sensed her life had changed course, for better or for worse, and there was no going back to the person she'd been before.

A wagon plodded past them. The driver had his head bent, blocking the person sitting beside him. He nodded to his passenger in that absent sort of way people nodded when they weren't really listening. The person beside him gestured.

Delia's gaze sharpened. "Becky?"

Sean twisted around. A woman sat in the passenger seat of the wagon passing them. She bore a striking resemblance to Delia, though she looked to be shorter and was slightly plumper.

Delia leaped off her mount and rushed toward the woman. "Becky! How did you get here?"

Yep, definitely a family resemblance. He motioned for Robert. The boy halted beside him.

"I hired this driver," Becky said. "I've been telling him all about Paul."

The driver sighed. "She has."

Becky stared down at her sister. "What are you doing on a horse, Delia? Where are you going? Where's Paul? Who is this man?"

"It's a long story," Delia replied, glancing in his direction.

Sean shrugged. "A small delay won't make much difference at this point."

The sense of urgency he'd felt that morning had faded in the past hour, and a curious lethargy overcame him. The day was sublime. A recent rain had turned the hills green, and the prairie grasses shimmered on the breeze between the buildings. Such beautiful afternoons were rare, why rush the experience?

Since the town consisted of only four establishments, and only one of them was suitable for ladies, Sean directed them all toward the hotel once more. They hitched their horses and went inside. The clerk glanced up from his newspaper and raised an eyebrow.

"Some fellow was looking for you earlier," the clerk declared. "Hank is still serving breakfast ifin' you're hungry."

"Who was looking for me?" Sean asked.

"Some spotted fellow."

He frowned. "A spotted fellow?"

"Yep. He had bits of plaster all over his face."

"Paul? Was the man's name Paul?"

"Mebbe."

Sean muttered an oath. The man had to be Paul. How many other spotted fellows were traveling through the Montana Territory? First Becky, and now Paul. Neither appearance was entirely unexpected. Paul would have left the moment the quarantine was lifted, and Becky sounded equally infatuated. He only hoped his brother had truly waited the correct amount of time and wasn't spreading the plague.

Scrubbing his hands down his face, Sean considered the delay. The shortcut through the valley saved them half a day. They'd probably discover the justice of the peace holding court over a bottle of whiskey in a Butte saloon. What was the hurry?

"We're staying for breakfast," Sean said.

He'd barely finished the sentence when the door slammed open. Paul stood in the entry, his face covered in white plaster dots.

"Becky, you're here!" he declared.

His fiancée's face lit up and she limped toward him, awkwardly maneuvering the crutches. "I'm here, darling."

The two embraced in a passionate clinch. Sean and Delia exchanged a glance.

The clerk lowered his newspaper. "I don't wanna get sick. You'll have to stay outside."

"I'm not contagious anymore." Paul grinned widely. "The doctor gave me a clean bill of health. Is it official? Are we married?"

Delia rang her hands. "Not exactly."

Becky whipped around. "What do you mean?"

They quickly explained the circumstances, and Becky's face crumpled. "We're not married?"

"No," Delia said. "You're not married."

Becky set her jaw. "But *you're* married."

"You needn't say it like an accusation." Delia threw back her shoulders. "I didn't want to be married. This is all a mistake."

Early in his career, Sean had discovered that disaster often led to opportunity. The impassible, swollen river from the spring rain had given his soldiers a much-needed rest while they waited for the water to recede. An avalanche of rocks covering a mountain pass had saved him from certain death when a late spring blizzard had struck. His brother's infatuation with a woman he'd met in Denver had led him to Delia.

Except she didn't appear at all enthusiastic about their nuptials.

"I'm going to put this all to rights." Sean stepped between the two sisters. "Paul can look out for the two of you while I chase down the justice of the peace."

Robert raised his hand. "Can I go with you?"

"No," Sean said. "It's too dangerous."

"Aw, shucks."

The sooner he was on the road, the better. The time had come to leave, yet he hesitated. He didn't know what was holding him back. Except that Delia had not been completely unaffected by their kiss. She'd even instigated the embrace.

He glanced at his reluctant spouse. Events were moving rapidly. Perhaps they all needed to slow down and reflect on the current state of affairs. Delia had chided him about being too attached to a plan once he'd set it in motion, and the criticism was not entirely unfounded.

Perhaps it was time for a new plan.

Robert rubbed his stomach. "I'm kinda hungry."

"Me, too," Delia said.

Paul and Becky had taken a seat on the bench. They held hands, staring into each other's eyes as they laughed and whispered.

The clerk shot them a disgruntled glare and snapped his newspaper back into place.

Becky didn't seem to mind Paul's unsightly appearance, and Sean hadn't seen his brother that happy in a long while. Possibly ever. Montana winters were brutal, and they were also lonely. Becky had gotten herself this far, there was no reason to assume she'd falter beneath the harsh conditions of ranch life. People were often much more resilient than they appeared. He'd had plenty of soldiers in his ranks that didn't look as though they'd last a week, and those men had become fine soldiers.

"We should give them some time alone together," Sean said. "A few extra minutes won't hurt."

A becoming wash of color swept over Delia's face. "Agreed."

They retired to a table as far away from the enamored couple as the space allowed. Hank carefully wrote down their order of three breakfasts, and Sean contained his annoyance lest his meal suffer.

Delia glanced over her shoulder. "I think Becky is going to do just fine on the ranch."

"Agreed," Sean said.

For the first time in a very long time he relished the peace. All his life he'd been driven to prove something. The compulsions of his youth had compelled him, pushing him to the brink of his physical and mental endurance. Without that driving force behind him, he sometimes feared he'd tumble backward into nothing.

Today was different. Today, a sense of peace lifted his spirits. For once in his life he'd enjoy the here and now, and worry about the future later.

"They seem real nice," Robert said. "I wish the two of them had picked me instead of old Mr. Pratt."

Sean blinked rapidly. He'd put himself in competition with his stepmother, and he'd lost the gamble. He'd spent the rest of his life proving he was a better man. With his military service, he'd demonstrated to the world that he was valuable and important. But worthy of what? Of his father's attention? Of his love? He and Paul only had each other, and yet Sean had spent most of his adult life either chastising or ignoring his younger brother. He wasn't any better than his father, and in some ways, he was far worse.

They each wanted to feel as though they mattered. Delia wanted her voice to matter to the world, and Robert wanted his life to matter to someone who loved him. They were three very different people from strikingly different backgrounds, yet their basic desires were the same. Which was more important? The world, or a single human heart?

"You're looking extremely serious." Delia tilted her head. "What are you thinking?"

Her inherit honesty spurred him onward. "Would you rather have your life matter to a thousand people or to one person?"

"That's easy. A thousand people. What about you?"

Robert planted his chin in his hands. "I think it depends on the person. Like if my ma had mattered more to my pa, then maybe he wouldna run off. My uncle took me in for a while, but his wife had a baby and she didn't have no more time for me. Think of how different my life woulda been if I had mattered to her?"

"You matter to me," Delia said quietly. "Very much."

"But you only just met me."

"Then you must be very special."

Robert swiped at his eyes. "That's the nicest thing anyone has ever said to me."

Sean's throat tightened.

Delia patted the boy's leg. She didn't try and comfort him with false platitudes. She listened, and she spoke from the heart.

Sean hung his head. He'd accomplished a great deal in his life. A lot more than most men his age. But had he accomplished what truly mattered? Had he become a better man? The answer remained in the distance, just out of his reach.

Delia flicked a crumb from the table. "What about you, Sean? One person or a thousand?"

A burst of insight shook him to the core. "One person."

One very particular person.

First, though, he had amends to make. Things were going to be different between Sean and his brother. The past twenty-four hours had opened his eyes and his heart. If Paul wanted a bride, if he truly loved Becky, then Sean wasn't giving up until the two of them were wed. He owed his brother that much.

There was a basket of apples sitting on a sideboard, and Robert pointed. "Can I take an apple to Fiddler?"

"Certainly," Delia said. "I'll join you. I need something out of my saddlebag."

Hand in hand, the two of them left. Sean drummed his fingers on the table. He had a mind to try his hand at ranching. Paul needed the help, and there was plenty of land for both of them.

Delia wanted to remain in Montana, near her sister, which meant he'd be seeing her often. Yet she'd made her opinions about marriage quite clear. If he was going to convince her, he'd have to encourage her journalistic work. Even the legendary Nellie Bly hadn't begun her career with outlaws. The reporter had started with a box factory. What was the equivalent of a box factory in Montana?

Sean glanced at Robert's empty chair. Who would harm such an innocent child? He sat up straighter. No one had less of a voice than children. Delia was compassionate and caring. What better voice for the unheard? Even as he formulated the thought in his head, his heart sank.

How did he persuade Delia that learning to love him did not mean living and dying in obscurity?

A shot rang out, and glass shattered.

Chapter 7

Delia shoved Robert. "Get inside!"

The boy hesitated and she gave him another hard push. He dashed into the hotel, and the outlaw caught her around the upper arm.

He pressed the barrel of his gun against her temple. "Don't shoot. I got a hostage."

As he dragged her into the middle of the street, she clawed at the hand clamped around her waist.

This couldn't be happening. Not again. How did one person have this much misfortune?

"Unhand me!" she demanded.

"Let her go, Littlebury," a voice called. "We've got you surrounded."

Delia stilled. This was Littlebury Helm? The scourge of the territory? She craned her neck for a better look at her captor. He was of average height and build, and his stringy blond hair was receding at the temples. His clothing was tattered, and he smelled atrocious. She'd built him into a larger-than-life figure in her head, but he was just a man. A scrawny, smelly man with a gun at her temple.

Sean appeared in the doorway of the saloon and she willed him to stay back. He glanced down the street, and she followed his gaze. A half-dozen soldiers on horseback blocked one end of the street. She whipped around and discovered another half-dozen men on the opposite side.

Sean cupped his hand to the side of his mouth. "Lieutenant Brackett, what are you doing here?"

One of the army riders urged his horse forward a few paces. "We intercepted a rumor that Littlebury Helm had been sending telegrams to Tobacco Bend. The commander authorized us to investigate."

"Shut up!" Littlebury Helm shouted. "Quit your yapping and get me a horse."

"We chased him here," the lieutenant continued. "Nearly had him. I'm sorry, ma'am."

Sean held up his hands. "Let the girl go, and we'll let you leave."

"You're lying!" the outlaw hollered. "You'll never let me leave. I'm taking her with me."

Delia stared at Sean. She'd only just met him, but she was well on her way to falling madly in love with the brave, stubborn man. He'd asked her once if she was running from herself, and she'd avoided providing him with the revealing answer. She'd always been different. She'd never had the easy way of flirting her sister had mastered.

Becky had Paul. Violet had the grocery delivery boy. Delia had always been alone. She'd sought attention and adoration from strangers with her writing. Except the love of a faceless public could never replace the affection of one person. She'd wanted to be important to thousands of people because she didn't think she'd ever earn the love of one person. But love wasn't about earning someone's approval. Love was about opening her heart and letting someone else get to know her, even the flawed bits.

Sean took another step closer. "Darling, if we're going to have a future together, I insist you stop getting yourself in these hostage situations."

Delia's heart leaped. He'd called her darling. "Do we have a future together?"

His dark eyes softened. "Only if you want."

"Then I'll try very hard never to be taken hostage again."

Littlebury made a sound of frustration. "This ain't about the both of you. This is about me. I demand a fresh horse and enough supplies for three days."

"Done," the lieutenant agreed.

Sean gestured. "My horse is right here. I was preparing for a trip. There's enough food and water for at least three days."

"Then get everyone outta here," the outlaw ordered. "Clear the street."

His tight grip made it difficult to breathe, and stars appeared at the edges of Delia's vision. Her heart beat a rapid tattoo in her chest. The men from the army wheeled their horses around. Curtains flicked in the hotel window and she caught the glint of metal from one of the roofs.

His gun outstretched before him, the outlaw dragged her toward the horse. "You're coming with me."

"No!" she protested. "I'm a terrible traveling companion."

She no longer wanted to interview outlaws and put herself in danger. She wanted to live. She wanted to love. She wanted to tell Sean all the things she kept locked in her heart.

"I ain't getting out of this town alive if I leave alone. As soon as I let go of you, they'll shoot me dead."

Sean unraveled the reins of his horse from the hitching post. Delia's gaze flicked between the two men. Sean was out of uniform, and Littlebury didn't appear to see him as a threat.

"The other one, too!" Littlebury shouted.

Keeping his gun trained on her, Littlebury mounted then ordered Delia to do the same.

"Wait," Sean said. "There's something I have to do first."

He caught her around the waist and spun her around. His lips moved hungrily over hers, kissing her with the same pent-up desire she'd felt since the first moment they'd met. It was a kiss of possession, and she reveled in the feel of his touch. There was no hesitancy, no pleading, no entreaty, he was a man making a claim, and she was more than willing to surrender.

He pitched his voice low. "When I give you the signal, duck."

"What's the signal?"

"You'll know."

"Ah, quit it you two," Littlebury groaned. "I'm not playing around. I'll shoot you both to get outta this one-horse town."

Sean easily lifted her into the saddle. "Don't worry."

"I'm not."

The outlaw struggled to control both horses while keeping his gun trained on her. "Don't try anything, or I'll shoot you."

She kept a tight grip on the reins. "I thought you'd be taller."

Littlebury gaped. "What did you just say?"

"I'm Miss Adelia Lawrence."

"The reporter?"

"Yes. And I thought you'd be taller." She smirked. "And smarter."

"Have you taken leave of your senses?"

"No," she declared. "I've changed my mind. I don't want to do a story about you."

"Well, I've changed my mind, too. I don't want to be interviewed."

"Good."

Apparently, no one had noticed that she still clutched her reticule.

A sharp whistle pierced the air. Assuming that was the signal, she ducked. Gunfire sounded and her horse sidestepped and bucked. Thrown off balance, she lost her grip and tumbled to the ground. Littlebury landed beside her.

A growing red stain bloomed across his shoulder. She met his gaze and her pulse kicked. He was alive. The outlaw staggered upright. Disoriented and stumbling in pain, he fired wildly. A bullet hit the ground and dirt pellets exploded into the air.

The horses danced nervously between them. She reached for her reticule, and a hoof grazed her arm.

Littlebury was staggering toward the hotel. Toward Sean.

She closed her hands around the barrel of her gun. Setting her jaw, she took aim. She'd finally found true love, and she wasn't letting some foul-smelling outlaw ruin her future happiness.

The outlaw leveled his gun at Sean's chest.

Hoping the bullet might graze him, he tossed his body to one side. Time slowed and Sean pictured Delia's face. Sorrow tore through him. He should have let her speak before. He should have told her that he loved her. He'd wanted everything to be perfect, and now it was too late. A gunshot sounded and Sean braced for the bullet ripping through his flesh.

Littlebury staggered forward and collapsed on his knees then fell on his face in the dirt.

Delia stood behind him, a smoking gun in her hand.

Sean gaped. The gun drooped from her limp fingers, and he crossed the distance in three strides, catching her in his arms. Behind her, the rest of his unit appeared and mustered around the prone man.

Sean's heartbeat stuttered.

She was safe.

In the short time he'd known her, she'd changed him. He was normally a man who made logical decisions and rarely acted on impulse. When Delia was near, all rational thought fled. A fierce sense of protectiveness gripped him. He'd die for her.

She pressed her forehead against his shoulder. "Did I kill him?"

Sean glanced at the prone man. "Let's just say that I don't think you're going to get that interview."

"I should have listened to you." She sobbed. "He was evil."

Sean took the gun from her limp fingers, and led her toward the hotel. "Are you all right? You fell. Are you hurt?"

"I'm not hurt."

He dusted her sleeves and searched for any sign of injury. She appeared shaken but unharmed, and remarkably robust considering the turmoil of the past forty-eight hours. He led her into the hotel.

"You're bleeding!" She stared at his left shoulder. "Littlebury shot you."

"It's nothing. A scratch."

Becky rushed toward them, but Paul held her back. "Let's give them some time alone together."

Sean flashed his brother a grateful smile and urged Delia to sit. "I have a new idea for a story."

"What's that?"

He knelt before her and took her chilled hands. "An investigation into the phenomenon of love at first sight."

"Are you a believer?" she asked, her voice watery with emotion.

"I am now."

"I think I'm falling in love with you, Sean."

"That's a coincidence. I believe I'm falling in love with you, as well."

All his doubts and fears dissolved. He sought her lips with an ardent passion, as though he'd been waiting his whole life for this single moment.

She pulled away and touched his cheek. "But we've only just met. What if this is simply a passing infatuation brought on by heightened emotion from a dangerous situation?"

"Why don't we stay married long enough to find out?"

"Are you certain?"

"On two conditions."

Her brow furrowed. "What are they?"

"Robert lives with us."

"Agreed."

"And I can't live in a town without a newspaper," he said. "Do you know any good reporters?"

"I might have some connections."

"Then, yes, we can stay married."

Their lips met and their breath mingled. Sean savored the pleasure of the moment and considered their future together with heady anticipation. He wasn't the man he wanted to be, not yet, but he was well on his way. He had a family. He had love. He had Delia.

This wonderful, caring, intelligent, beautiful, and utterly infuriating woman wanted him. Just him. And he wanted nothing more than to be the man she deserved.

Three weeks later, Delia, Sean, Paul, Becky, Violet, and the grocery delivery man stood before the newly ordained reverend of the newly renamed town, Whynot Bend.

Delia's father dabbed at his brow, and her mother reached over Robert, who sat between them, and patted her husband's knee. "Relax, dear; think how much money we're saving getting them married all at once."

"Small consolation," her father mumbled. "Becky is on crutches, Paul is covered in spots, Sean's still bandaged from a bullet wound, and Delia's eye has barely healed. They look like escapees from a hospital ward, not a wedding party."

"Think how easy their marriages will be after having survived their courtships."

"Nothing is ever easy." Delia's father tucked his handkerchief into his suit pocket. "It's a good thing we didn't have any more children, my poor heart can't take it."

Robert looked between the two. "Are you really moving to Montana?"

"I guess I have to," her father grumbled. "There's no one left in Denver, and now the grocer won't even deliver since Violet has married his best delivery boy."

"Then can I call you grandpa?" Robert asked with innocent sincerity.

Her father hastily reached for his handkerchief once more. "You surely can," he said. "You surely can."

Delia glanced over her shoulder at the crowd of people. The entire town of Whynot had turned out for the wedding.

She squeezed Sean's hand. "Are you certain you don't miss the army?"

"How can I miss the army when my wife is better armed than most outlaws? Not to mention, between the chores and the kissing, I don't have time for much else."

Delia giggled.

The reverend cleared his throat with a harried grimace. "I now pronounce you husbands and wives."

Tears of joy filled her eyes. During that awful moment when she thought she might lose him, she'd gotten a glimpse at how bleak and miserable life would be without him by her side. In that instant she'd understood that being loved by the right person was better than being adored by a bevy of strangers.

She still wanted to write stories, and she'd begun a series of articles about the plight of orphan children in the West. She'd even talked her mother into serving as the town midwife, now that all of her daughters were married. Her mother hadn't abandoned her career for her family; she'd simply taken a leave of absence.

Things hadn't turned out the way Delia had planned. They'd turned out infinitely better.

Sean cupped her cheeks. "Do you still think you love me?"

"No." She paused. "I know so."

"What am I going to do with you, Mrs. Morgan?"

"Love me," she said. "Just love me."

Since her debut in 2011, **Sherri Shackelford** has become a highly acclaimed author of nine novels published with Love Inspired Historical. Her debut novel was a finalist in the ACFW Genesis Awards. Her books have earned a Readers' Choice nomination from *Romantic Times* magazine, as well as placing in the National Readers' Choice Awards. She's a member of Romance Writers of America and the Faith, Hope and Love Chapter. A wife and mother of three, Sherri's hobbies include collecting mismatched socks, discovering new ways to avoid cleaning, and standing in the middle of the room while thinking, *Why did I just come in here?* A reformed pessimist and recent hopeful romantic, Sherri has a passion for writing. Her books are fun and fast-paced with plenty of heart and soul.

To Heal Thy Heart

by Michelle Shocklee

Dedication

For my mother-in-law Shirley Shocklee,
a woman of beauty and grace

Chapter 1

Carson Springs, New Mexico Territory
May 1866

A 30-year-old doctor of medicine seeks woman of similar age and aptitude willing to share life and adventure in the rugged landscape of the New Mexico Territory. Sympathetic toward natives and free Negroes. Confederate widows need not apply.

Phoebe Wagner refolded the square of newspaper, its corners worn from her anxious attention throughout the long journey from Kansas City to the northern New Mexico Territory. Had her nerves not been as taut as a grandpa's fiddle strings, she might have enjoyed the breathtaking view from the stage depot platform, where majestic, snowcapped mountains surrounded the tiny village of Carson Springs, set in a pretty valley alive with pine and aspen trees. But as it was, her stomach churned with nervousness—and her deceit—making her ill.

"You sure your intended is coming to meet you, miss? I don't like leaving you here alone."

The stage driver, Mr. Howard, eyed her suspiciously. He'd picked her up in Santa Fe, none too happy to transport a woman traveling alone into what he described as a wilderness only fit for Indians and men like Kit Carson, the famed Union general and frontiersman whose colorful life was depicted in sensational dime novels.

"I'm sure Dr. Preston will arrive posthaste, sir. You needn't concern yourself, although I appreciate it. I'll be fine."

Phoebe hoped the confident smile she forced to her lips convinced the aging man all was well. She needed him to leave before she changed her mind and climbed back into the coach. Mounting doubts that she'd done the right thing by coming piled up like a logjam in the Cimarron River, yet she'd had no other choice.

Mr. Howard checked his watch again. With one last look around the deserted depot, he huffed in resignation. "Well, good luck to you, miss. 'Tis a lucky man you're marrying."

The kind words stabbed Phoebe with shame as she watched him climb onto the stage. Would he declare Dr. Luke Preston lucky if he knew she hadn't been completely honest in her correspondence with the man?

Once settled on the high seat, the driver tipped his hat, slapped the team of horses with the reins, and set off in a cloud of dust. A mixture of regret and relief swept through her, watching the back end of the coach disappear into the thick forest from whence they'd come. Any thoughts of returning to Kansas City vanished with the conveyance, forcing her to continue with the plan she'd set into motion two months earlier when she responded to Dr. Preston's ad. In a matter of hours, she would marry a man she'd never met.

Tears stung her eyes, and she touched the cameo brooch at her collar, her throat thick with remembrance. Danny had looked so handsome in his gray uniform the day he left for war. He'd surprised her with the brooch at the train station, promising to pin it on her dress himself on their wedding day as soon as he returned. How could she have known she'd never see Danny again?

Sniffling, she tucked the bittersweet memories away. To dwell on all she'd lost served no purpose.

"Miss Wagner?"

She looked up to find an older gentleman approach, his white beard reminding her of a drawing she'd seen of Saint Nicholas years ago. Surely this was not Dr. Preston.

"Yes?"

A warm smile crinkled his blue eyes. "My, aren't you a pretty little thing." He nodded with approval. "I'm Reverend Whitaker. Dr. Luke asked me to come in his stead and offer his sincere apology for not meeting you himself. There was a mining accident in the hills earlier with several men injured. He's gone to attend them."

"Oh dear, I do hope the injuries aren't serious."

"I'm afraid it comes with the territory, so to speak. But"—he waved his hand as though to wipe away any unpleasant thoughts—"I'm certain you're quite weary from your travels. Let's get you settled. Eula, my dear wife, left a pot of venison stew simmering in the doctor's cabin as a sort of wedding supper."

The reverend glanced at the two faded carpetbags sitting on the platform next to her. His gaze searched the area. "Is this all your baggage?"

"It is." She was unable to keep embarrassment from staining her cheeks. She needn't tell the kind man how she'd been forced to sell nearly all her possessions after Papa died and the war raged on. The gowns, the silver and china. . .everything. It was all gone.

Reverend Whitaker seemed to sense her discomfort. "I believe that might be the best way to begin a new life. Unencumbered with the past."

She offered a weak smile. The past most definitely encumbered her, but she kept that to herself.

With her bags in hand, Reverend Whitaker led the way to an open carriage harnessed to a mule. "Dr. Luke's cabin isn't far from my own. Eula and I came to the area before the war, hoping to deliver the Gospel message to the natives." He stored her bags behind the seat and helped her up. "Now, with so many former soldiers coming to the mountains to try their hand at mining, we find our mission has changed. Ministering to the hurting hearts of men from both sides seems to be what God has called us to."

A yearning for some of that ministering set an ache in her own heart. While she'd never claim to possess the same soul wounds as a soldier who'd seen and done despicable things, the war and its repercussions had inflicted injury on her, too.

They traveled north through the tiny village with Phoebe giving little notice to the few shops and log buildings lining the rain-rutted street. The nervous flutter in her stomach demanded all her attention. With each beat of her heart and turn of the carriage wheels, her trepidation mounted. Was she truly going through with this? Even now, she was headed to the cabin she would share with a man she'd never before laid eyes on.

Oh, what have I done?

She didn't dare ask for divine help, being that she'd already committed a sin against the man who'd soon become her husband. Not until their vows were spoken would she consider confession. Even then it was doubtful she'd reveal the truth.

As the town gave way to thick forest, the words from Dr. Preston's ad flitted across her mind's eye. She could see them clearly, as though written in big, bold lettering.

Confederate widows need not apply.

I'm not a widow, she reminded herself sternly. But even as the admonition echoed in her conscience, she wished it wasn't true. She longed to be a widow. Danny's widow. If God had given the slightest hint that Danny wouldn't come home, Phoebe wouldn't have let him leave for war without taking his name and knowing him as her husband.

Moisture sprang to her eyes, and she turned so the reverend wouldn't see. With a hand on her empty womb and a deep longing for Danny's child, whom she would never have, she steeled herself against the guilt a few lines in a letter might initiate. She wasn't a widow, therefore she hadn't lied when she stated her marital status. The deception came, however, when Dr. Preston wrote back with an offer for marriage. His words burned into her memory.

I served with the Union Army as a surgeon, seeing firsthand the carnage wrought by the savage Rebels. As I am certain you can understand, the woman I marry must share my opinion on the war and its outcome.

Phoebe worried her bottom lip, recalling how torn she'd been reading that last line. Could she marry a man whose heart was so hardened toward Southerners? Though she'd replied to every ad for marriage in the *Kansas City Gazette*, Dr. Preston was the only one who'd made an offer. With no money and no prospects, she couldn't impose on her father's sister any longer. Aunt Augusta was herself in dire straits, with Confederate currency worthless, her husband long dead, and northern partisans with revenge in their hearts in power. Marriage, Augusta regretfully declared, was the only solution available to Phoebe, and Dr. Preston the only willing groom. With a heaviness that continued to weigh on her, she'd written to accept his proposal, allowing him to assume her sympathies were indeed aligned with his own.

"There's Dr. Luke's cabin."

The reverend's voice returned her to the present. Phoebe took in the log structure with one quick sweep of her eye. To say it was small would be generous. The churning in her stomach intensified, knowing she would share the cramped space with a stranger.

If Reverend Whitaker expected her to comment on her new home, he didn't dwell on her silence. He helped her down then proceeded to carry her bags inside. The delicious aroma of venison stew welcomed them, but under the present circumstances Phoebe wasn't able to appreciate Mrs. Whitaker's labor.

"I'll stir the fire to life." The parson went directly to the rock fireplace and picked up a poker. "Though it's pleasant outside now, once the sun sets, the temperature drops quickly here in the mountains. It's best to get one's chores done early in order to enjoy a quiet evening around a toasty fire."

Phoebe watched all this from her place inside the open door. While the reverend poked around the banked embers, her eyes scanned the tidy but small room. A large bed with a colorful quilt took up considerable space in the far corner. Warmth spread up her neck seeing it there, and she quickly moved her attention elsewhere. In front of the stone hearth sat a bulky overstuffed chair, its arms worn from use. A smaller one, appearing to be brand new, sat beside it. Noting the floral pattern on the fabric, it occurred to her Dr. Preston had probably purchased it for her.

"Dr. Luke said he'd come by my cabin on his way down the mountain," the reverend said, straightening. "Eula and I will be pleased to come over for the ceremony."

Phoebe felt the blood drain from her face. The mere mention of a marriage ceremony was more than her unsettled stomach could take. She whirled out the door and lunged for the clump of foliage beyond the cabin as her stomach emptied itself of the meager meal she'd eaten at the last stage stop.

When her heaves ceased, mortification set in. What must the reverend think? She turned, a ready apology on her lips. But instead of finding disapproval on his weathered face as he stood in the doorway, sympathy shone in his eyes. She accepted the damp cloth he handed her.

"I don't pretend to know your situation, Miss Wagner," he said, kindness in his voice, "but I know the One who does. You and Dr. Luke will be in my prayers as you forge ahead in this new life you've chosen."

Phoebe pressed the cloth to her hot cheek, fighting tears. "Thank you," she whispered.

She watched the reverend drive away, a wave of loneliness engulfing her. He reminded her of Papa. Though nearly two years had passed since her father was killed by Union militants, his voice and words of wisdom often repeated in her mind. What advice would he give her now as she stood in an unfamiliar place, waiting to wed an unknown man? She closed her eyes, straining to listen.

Only the trill of a bird from atop a tall pine filled the silence.

She sighed. Papa could've never imagined her acting in such desperation. But then he couldn't have imagined many of the things that happened during and after the war.

Glancing about the small cabin, she wondered if she should sit and wait for Dr. Preston to arrive. The chair near the fire looked comfortable, but—she cast a longing look to the big bed in the corner—the promise of a soft mattress and pillow seemed far more inviting.

Giving in to her exhaustion, Phoebe closed the door, removed her boots, and crawled onto the quilt. It felt scandalous lying on a bed belonging to a strange man, his masculine scent lingering on the pillow. But as her eyes drifted closed, she reminded herself that man would soon be her husband.

Chapter 2

Luke patted the coarse coat of his mule's thick neck, the sinking sun sending shadows into the small, hay-strewn lean-to behind the cabin. Even with the promise of summer in the lengthening days, a chill had settled over the valley as he rode down the mountain from the mining camp. A warm fire and a belly full of Eula's venison stew sounded good.

"You did well today, ol' boy."

Ulysses munched from the pail of oats Luke held. They'd had a long afternoon, climbing up and down steep mountain trails to get to the injured miners. After a shaft caved in, the four men were fortunate to only have a few broken bones.

Luke watched the animal eat. Despite his longing to settle in for the night, one inescapable obstacle kept him practically hiding out in the musty stall: a strange woman now occupied his home.

He blew out a breath. "What am I supposed to do with a wife I know nothing about?" The mule looked at him. Was that sympathy reflected in its big eyes? "How did I let Reverend Whit talk me into this crazy scheme?"

He shook his head, thinking back to the day he received a letter from Miss Phoebe Wagner in answer to the ad Reverend Whit convinced him to place in the Kansas City newspaper. Hers was the only response that came, and Luke surmised that was due to his stipulation that no Confederate widows need apply. He'd nearly changed his mind about the whole thing, but Reverend Whit reminded him of the benefits of marriage, the least of which were regular meals and warm companionship.

But with Miss Wagner ensconced in his cabin at this very moment, the doubts that had plagued him the past few weeks crept in and made themselves at home in his mind. He didn't possess what it took to be a good husband. Not anymore. Perhaps before the war he might've found happiness in sharing his life with a woman he loved. But the carnage he witnessed on the battlefields and in the surgical tents destroyed any aspirations for peace and contentment in his future for years to come. The nightmares and flashbacks he experienced saw to that. What would Miss Wagner think when he woke her in the middle of the night with his screams?

Ulysses finished the oats. Luke set the empty pail on a shelf, wishing for some other chore that required his attention, but he couldn't delay going inside much longer. Reverend Whit and Eula would arrive within the hour for the ceremony. It seemed best that Luke at least meet his bride before they exchanged vows.

He gave Ulysses one last pat, picked up his medical bag, and exited the lean-to. A basin of cold water and a sliver of lye soap sat on a stand outside the cabin door. Luke put them to use washing his hands and face, noting that no lantern light shone from the small window despite the waning day. He wondered why Miss Wagner sat alone in the darkening room.

Drying his hands on a towel, he glanced about the yard. Had she left the cabin after Reverend Whit dropped her off? The woods weren't a safe place for a woman unfamiliar with the area, especially with evening coming on. Curious, he eased the door open. The delicious aroma of venison stew and an ebbing fire greeted him, but otherwise the cabin appeared deserted. Two carpetbags sat near the door, however, advising him his missing bride hadn't vanished.

He closed the door and moved to light a kerosene lantern. What should he do now? He had no idea where to look for Miss Wagner. He didn't even know what she looked like. Should he check the outhouse? The road to town?

A soft sound came from the bed. Luke whirled around and swallowed hard. There on top of the covers, curled into a ball, slept his bride-to-be. Yellow lantern light touched the smooth planes of her face, highlighting a rosebud mouth and thick lashes lying against pale cheeks.

Luke's gaze traveled unchecked from the top of her golden-haired head, over gentle curves that dipped and rose, down to her stocking-clad feet. His heart thundered in his chest when his gaze arrived at her face again. When he'd stopped at the Whitakers, Reverend Whit assured him Miss Wagner was quite comely. Luke thought the older man was simply being kind, but staring at the woman asleep on his bed, he was certain he'd never seen a lovelier lady in all his born days.

The object of his gawking stirred.

Panicking, Luke looked around the cramped space for. . .for what? A place to hide? Certainly not. This was his home. His cabin. He leaped into his armchair as her eyes opened. From his vantage point by the fire, he watched her frown, her confused expression revealing her disorientation. After a moment, her body sagged back into the mattress, and she squeezed her eyes shut, clutching a brooch at her throat.

Luke decided to make his presence known before she did something that might embarrass them both. He cleared his throat and waited. Miss Wagner's eyes sprang open, and she bounded from the bed, her wide gaze landing on him.

"Oh!" Her fright reminded him of a rabbit caught in a snare.

"Miss Wagner." He stood and nodded politely.

"Dr. Preston," she squeaked. She reached up to investigate her hair with her fingers. Dismay flashed across her face at what she found. Next, her hands moved to smooth the wrinkles her nap had creased in her skirt. When she looked at him again, moisture glistened in eyes the same shade of summer grass. "I must apologize." A catch in her voice ended her speech.

"No need to apologize," Luke said, hoping to ease her distress. "I'm sure you must be tired after such a long journey. I'm the one who should apologize for not being available to meet you in town and making you wait here in the cabin alone."

Her tense shoulders relaxed some. "I do hope the miners' injuries weren't serious."

Her compassion in spite of the awkward situation pleased him. "It'll take some weeks of bed rest, but they'll mend."

She nodded but remained mute with her hands clutched together in an uneasy knot.

Luke glanced at the pot of stew warming over the low embers of the fire. He needed a distraction, anything, to fill the uncomfortable silence. "Are you hungry? Eula Whitaker is an excellent cook." He offered a small smile, finding himself ridiculously nervous in Miss Wagner's presence.

"I don't believe I could eat a thing just now, but thank you."

He nodded. His own stomach had turned rebellious despite his hunger only minutes before. The clock on the mantel told him the Whitakers would arrive soon, so it was best to get on with their introduction.

"Miss Wagner," he said, indicating the small floral armchair he'd purchased last week. "Won't you have a seat? I feel we should get acquainted before the Whitakers arrive."

She moistened her lips and blinked several times before nodding. Luke allowed her to settle in the chair then took a seat in his own. Had he been inclined, he could reach out and take her delicate hand in his. He didn't, of course, but maybe someday he would.

Now, with her green eyes wide and staring at him, Luke's mind went blank. What does one say to a woman he's just met but plans to marry in less than an hour?

"I trust your journey was uneventful?" That seemed safe. Cowardly, but safe.

She nodded again. "Thank you for the fare."

He had so many questions. Why was a woman as attractive as Miss Wagner seeking marriage to a total stranger? She'd surely had suitors lined up at her door. Suspicions swirled through his mind. Without an obvious physical flaw, Luke wondered if it were perhaps a flaw of character that prevented her from finding a suitable husband in Kansas.

"You should know, Miss Wagner, that honesty and trustworthiness are the two most important traits I require in a mate. It doesn't matter to me if you're not a good cook, although I'm looking forward to meals that aren't scorched or cold."

His attempt at humor did little to change the serious expression on her face.

"I believe a married couple should have no secrets between them," he continued, feeling more confident as he lay the foundation for their life together. Perhaps this mail-order marriage wasn't such a wild idea after all. Having a comely wife, with trust as the underpinning of their relationship, might bring the peace and happiness he'd been missing the past five years.

"It will take time for us to come to know each other," he said, offering a gentle smile he hoped conveyed his patience as a husband, "but it seems to me the best marriages often begin with friendship. And the best friends I've ever had were those individuals I knew I could trust beyond a shadow of a doubt."

Luke waited for an amenable response. It didn't come. Instead she stared at him with those luminous eyes, her face pale in the firelight. He reminded himself she was tired and in a strange place. Perhaps she simply needed time to adjust to it all.

The jingle of a wagon sounded from outside, announcing the Whitakers' arrival. "That must be the reverend." He stood to greet their guests.

Phoebe shot a panicked glance to the door, her eyes growing wider, if that were possible. "Dr. Preston, I must tell you—"

"Please, Phoebe, call me Luke. We are, after all, about to become man and wife."

She clutched the cameo pin at her throat, her chest heaving as she stared at him.

Luke waited. "Was there something you wanted to tell me?"

A knock sounded at the door.

Phoebe squeezed her eyes closed for a long moment. When she met his gaze again, she shook her head. "No. It's nothing."

Luke wished they had more time to finish their discussion. Moving to open the door for the Whitakers, he made a mental note to revisit the conversation with her in the coming days. Perhaps by then she'd feel more comfortable talking with him.

But for now, it was time for his mail-order bride to become his wife.

Chapter 3

Mrs. Dr. Luke Preston.

That was the title Reverend Whitaker had addressed Phoebe with as he and Eula took their leave after the brief wedding ceremony. The older couple declined Luke's invitation to stay for the meal, and now the newlyweds sat alone in the deep shadows of the cabin, staring as flames licked the log he'd added to the fire.

Earlier she'd insisted on cleaning the supper dishes while he put the leftover stew in a cold pit outside. She'd hoped he might stay away from the cabin, giving her a few minutes to herself, but he'd returned all too soon. They'd moved to the comfortable armchairs at his suggestion, but after a few stilted attempts at conversation, even he fell silent.

Exhaustion drooped her heavy eyelids, and it took sheer force to keep them from closing. She longed to call an end to this day, yet the mere thought of sharing a marriage bed with her new husband sent a wave of terror rushing through her. Mama went home to heaven long before Phoebe needed to know womanly things, and Aunt Augusta's blunt description of marital unions left her confused and more than a little apprehensive. Would Luke expect a wife knowledgeable in such things?

"It's been a long day."

His deep voice made her jump. Phoebe looked up to find him studying her, firelight dancing in his brown eyes. When she'd awoken from her nap and seen Luke for the first time, his dark coloring and handsome features took her by surprise. Danny's hair and eyes had been light, like her own.

He stood and extended his hand to her. Phoebe's eyes widened as she stared up at him. She couldn't refuse. He was her husband, after all. But surely—

"I imagine you're exhausted. A good night's sleep is what the doctor recommends." The corners of his mouth lifted.

Phoebe stilled. Did he mean they wouldn't. . .?

His warm fingers closed over her icy hand when she shyly placed it in his. As he drew her up, she met his gaze, the question surely shining in her eyes.

"We are married until death do us part," he said softly, his gaze caressing her face in such a way that Phoebe's stomach fluttered unexpectedly. "I'm willing to wait until you're ready."

His meaning was perfectly clear. And much appreciated. "Thank you," she whispered. Their eyes held for a long moment before Luke bent and placed a light kiss on her forehead.

When he released her hand, he moved toward the door. "I'll check on Ulysses and make sure he's settled for the night. You don't need to wait up for me." He turned before going out into the darkness, a relaxed smile on his lips. "Good night, Phoebe."

A mixture of relief, gratitude, and something akin to admiration raced through her after the door closed behind him. Her new husband was not only a doctor, but he was also a gentleman.

After a quick trip to the outhouse, she hurried to undress then tugged on her nightgown. Crawling under the covers on the far edge of the bed, she pulled the quilt up to her chin. The glint from the new gold band on her left hand caught her eye. Tears welled as she stared at the simple piece of jewelry, turning the golden circle blurry.

She rolled onto her side, presenting her back to the door. Unable to keep her eyes open, she gave into her exhaustion, her last thoughts on Danny.

Oh, how she wished it were his ring on her finger.

Sunlight shone through the window above Phoebe's head when she awoke the next morning. The aroma of coffee and bacon filled the cabin, a reminder that she hadn't eaten much for supper last night.

Sitting up, she found herself alone in the small room. Luke's pillow held the indention of his head, so she knew he must have come to bed at some point. She'd never been aware of his presence next to her, though.

Heat filled her cheeks. Her first night as a married woman had come and gone. Things were bound to change between them soon enough, but for now she appreciated the time he gave her to adjust.

Up and dressed, with the quilt spread neatly, she was surprised to find a plate of bacon and eggs warming on the hearth next to a pot of coffee. That Luke had made his own breakfast, as well as hers, while she slept filled her with shame. He no doubt expected his wife to prepare the meals.

She'd just finished the repast when the door opened, letting in a chilly breeze along with her husband.

"Good morning." His easy smile held no condemnation, much to her relief.

"Good morning." She indicated her empty plate. "Thank you for breakfast. I'm sorry I overslept. It won't happen again."

Luke took off his hat and coat and hung them on a peg near the door. He turned to pour himself a cup of coffee. Phoebe could kick herself for not offering to get it for him.

"You needed the rest," he said after taking a sip of the hot liquid.

"I appreciate that, but it's my duty as your wife to tend to the house and the cooking." She didn't mention her other wifely duty.

After a moment, he settled in his chair. "I need to go to the mining camp and check on my patients." He took another sip from the mug, his eyes meeting hers over the rim.

Phoebe perked up, relishing the prospect of having him away from the cabin for the day. She could unpack, do some washing, and become familiar with her tiny new home. She also needed to pen a note to Aunt Augusta to let the older woman know she'd arrived in the New Mexico Territory in one piece.

"I thought you might like to accompany me."

Her plotting came to a crashing halt with his suggestion. "Accompany you?"

"Your letter mentioned your father was a doctor. Did you not ever assist him with his patients?"

Thoughts of Papa spilled into her heart. "I did. I don't know that I was much help, being that I was a young girl, but I enjoyed going with him. After my mother died, it was just the two of us."

"How old were you when she passed?" Compassion shone in his dark eyes.

"Ten. She took to her bed with pneumonia. Papa never got over the fact that he couldn't save her."

Luke nodded. "It's difficult as a doctor to lose a patient. I can only imagine how helpless your father must've felt."

"I hope you haven't lost too many patients," she said, wanting to turn the conversation away from the painful memories of Mama. The look that crossed Luke's face, however, told her the shift didn't please him.

"I was a doctor in the Union Army." His voice took on a hard edge. "I saw thousands of men die, thanks to the brutality of those cowardly Rebels."

Phoebe bit her lip. How foolish could she be to remind him of the war. That was a topic she most definitely didn't wish to discuss.

"I suppose I could come with you," she hurried to say. "To the mining camp, I mean."

The resentment in his eyes brought on by talk of the war vanished. A smile slowly inched its way up his face in its stead. "I would like that."

While Luke gathered the necessary medical supplies from the storage cabinet in the corner, Phoebe packed a simple lunch consisting of more fried bacon and flapjacks.

"We'll go to town later," he said, loading rolls of bandages and small glass bottles of liquids into his black medical bag. "You can purchase the supplies you think we need to cook some decent meals." A lopsided grin tipped his mouth, and Phoebe was struck anew by his handsomeness. "Let's just say my cooking leaves much to be desired."

She smiled halfheartedly at his joke. Her admiration for her attractive husband caused her to feel disloyal to Danny. As irrational as it seemed, considering the circumstances, she didn't want to put Danny's memory aside, no matter that she was now another man's wife. Danny was with her always, in her heart and her mind, and she couldn't let that go. She reached up to grasp the cameo at her throat and closed her eyes, trying to picture his wavy blond hair and dimpled cheeks.

"Is something wrong?"

Her eyes flew open to find Luke very near.

"No, no. I—I'll try to think of some meals to prepare. You'll have to tell me your favorites."

His warm smile left her feeling guilty. She'd need to keep her thoughts of Danny tucked away and only bring them out when she was alone.

They finished their preparations and left the cabin. Tied to the hitching post outside stood an enormous mule.

"This is Ulysses." Luke's affection showed as he rubbed the big animal's neck. "I named him after General Grant. I'm not sure the general would see it as a compliment, but it's meant to honor a great man."

Phoebe nodded when he looked her way but refrained from commenting. After his reaction earlier when speaking of the war, she felt it best they avoid that subject altogether lest she reveal things better left unsaid.

She looked for a wagon or buggy but found the yard empty. "How will we get to the mining camp?"

"Ulysses."

She turned to see if he was genuine. It was then she noticed Ulysses's broad back boasted a saddle. Her eyes widened. "Dr. Preston, surely you don't mean for me to ride that thing, do you?"

His laughter filled the cool morning air. "I do, Mrs. Preston." Bright sunshine sparkled in his brown eyes as his gaze briefly traveled over her attire. She only owned three serviceable dresses, none of which were adequate for riding. "While we're in town, you can order one of those split skirts I've seen women wear when they ride. And whatever underthings you might need, too."

Her face flamed. She'd never discussed unmentionables with a man. Not even Papa.

"But for now"—he went on as though talking about women's fashions was an everyday event—"I figure you can sit in my lap."

Phoebe gulped. "Your lap?"

"Ulysses can easily carry the both of us, but we'll need to get another mule soon. We wouldn't want to wear him out."

Her concern wasn't whether the mule could tolerate their weight. The very thought of being in such proximity to Luke set her heart racing with nerves. "Perhaps I shouldn't go. I wouldn't want to be any trouble."

Disappointment flashed across his face. "I'd very much like you to come." His shoulders slumped a bit. "But I understand if you'd rather stay home."

Home.

His use of that simple word reminded her of the promises she'd made to this man yesterday. They'd stood before God and witnesses and pledged themselves to each other. He was her husband and she, his wife. His helpmeet, as Reverend Whitaker quoted from the book of Genesis during the brief wedding ceremony. A helpmeet should certainly go with her spouse to the mining camp, no matter the crowded form of transportation.

"I'd like to come and help you with your patients."

His countenance brightened, as though a cloud had moved away from the sun, warming her with his obvious pleasure. He easily swung her up into the saddle, leaving both her legs dangling against Ulysses's left side. Before she could make herself comfortable, Luke stepped into the stirrup and squeezed in behind her.

"I'm going to raise you up a bit," he said, his hands circling her waist again. Without so much as a grunt of exertion, he lifted her as though she were light as a child and plunked her backside onto his lap. "There. That's better."

Satisfaction sounded in his voice. She, however, found no such comfort in her awkward position, wedged between the pommel and Luke. His hard chest was pressed against her arm, yet there was no way to avoid it. The muscles in his thighs moved beneath her as he settled into his seat, and her face heated with the intimate arrangement.

"Ready?" he asked, his arms circling her to take hold of the reins. It seemed she was surrounded by Luke.

She refused to let him see her embarrassment and faced forward, her back ramrod straight. "Yes."

With a click of Luke's tongue and a slight nudge from his heels, Ulysses started a slow prod north. Phoebe attempted to keep her body from jostling too much, trying in vain to prevent herself from bumping into Luke. After a few minutes, however, her tense muscles began to cramp, and she knew she couldn't keep this up for very long.

"How far is it to the mining camp?" she asked, hoping they didn't have too many miles to cover.

"It will take us a good hour or more," he said, dashing her hopes. As though sensing her discomfort—and possibly the reasoning behind it—he added with a chuckle, "You'd best settle in and relax."

Recognizing there was no way to avoid touching him, Phoebe let her stiff posture slowly ease. He, in turn, seemed to tighten his arms around her, acting as a brace. Although Ulysses's gait remained plodding, it was good to know Luke wouldn't let her slip off.

Following little more than an animal path tucked in a thick forest of towering pine trees, they gradually began their ascent into the mountains. Snow still capped the uppermost peaks, and Phoebe was thankful she'd worn her coat. The temperature had already begun to drop despite the sun shining on their backs.

"This is some of the prettiest country in the territory." Reverence softened his voice.

She studied her surroundings, finding she agreed. "Living in Kansas, I could have never imagined the grandeur of the Rocky Mountains. They're breathtaking."

"Nor could I, growing up in Indiana."

She turned her head to look at him, surprised by this tidbit of personal information. "My mother's family came from Indiana."

He smiled. "It seems we have quite a few things in common."

Curiosity regarding her new husband sprang up like weeds in a garden. "Do you still have family there?"

"I do. My parents and two sisters, both married with a passel of children that keep my mother occupied."

She smiled at his obvious affection for his family. "What made you come to the New Mexico Territory? It's so far away from Indiana."

A shadow came over his face, and his smile faded. "The war. When it finally ended, I wanted nothing more than to get on my horse and ride as far away from the battlefields as I could."

Phoebe stifled a groan. She'd once again inadvertently brought the subject of war to the surface. She searched her mind for a safer topic. "Papa dreamed of moving to the frontier when he was a young man, but Mama wouldn't leave Kansas. After she died, he lost his desire for adventure."

"How long has it been since you lost your father?"

She looked up toward the mountain peaks, barely visible now through the vast forest of trees. As painful as the war was for Luke to remember, so too was her father's death. The wounds in her heart still felt raw.

"He was murdered in October of 1864."

Her quiet answer put an end to their conversation.

Chapter 4

The mining camp came into view a short time later, appearing as dismal as it had the previous day. Luke felt the first twinge of unease about bringing Phoebe with him clench his gut. He'd been so intent on getting to know his new wife that he'd failed to think ahead to what he was exposing her to. Now with it too late, he saw the camp as she most assuredly would.

With a chill in the air and patches of icy snow clinging to shady areas, the primitive conditions the miners lived in seemed woefully inadequate. Clusters of canvas tents dotted the hillside with not one decent structure among them. Although the men set up camp a mere month ago, having been forced to wait until the majority of winter snow melted, it looked well lived in. Empty bean and meat cans lay where they'd been tossed. Dirty dishes and dirty laundry were strewn about, and mounds of muddy tracks spoke of a recent rain.

Luke brought Ulysses to a halt on the edge of the camp and dismounted. When he looked up to Phoebe, he saw the camp's deplorable conditions reflected in her wide eyes. "I'm sorry. I shouldn't have brought you up here. I guess I wasn't thinking clearly. You stay here while I check on the men. I shouldn't be long."

She glanced at the tents, at the mine openings on the hillside above, then back to Luke. After a moment, determination squared her shoulders.

"I came to help you with your patients, and that's what I intend to do." She held out her hands, waiting for him to help her down.

"Are you sure?" He looked from the mud to her shiny black boots peeking out from beneath the hem of her dress.

"I'm a doctor's wife now. A little dirt won't hurt me."

Pride in her swelled his chest. "All right then." He reached to lift her from the saddle, setting her on the driest patch of ground he could find. After tying Ulysses's reins to a tree branch, he took his medical bag in one hand and offered his other arm to his wife. "Shall we?"

A man approached as they carefully picked their way into camp. Luke recognized him from the previous day. "Doc," the man said, but his attention remained on Phoebe.

"Hello, Mr. Richards. This is Mrs. Preston, my wife. She'll be assisting me today."

Richards' brow arched. "Wife, you say? Didn't know you was married, Doc."

Luke wasn't about to admit he and Phoebe had been married less than twenty-four hours. It wasn't anyone's business, least of all a bunch of rough miners. "How are my patients today?" he asked instead. He took Phoebe by the elbow and moved toward the tent where the injured men were housed.

"Moanin' and complainin'," Richards said, stepping out of their way. "I sure hope you've got some medicine in that bag of yours that will quiet them down."

Luke and Phoebe arrived at the tent, its flap closed, concealing what was inside. "Let me make sure all is well before you come in," he said under his breath. Phoebe nodded and waited outside.

Thankfully the men were fully dressed, most likely for warmth rather than for decency's sake. Luke ushered Phoebe in, and with more efficiency than he could've hoped for, she assisted him in changing bandages, administering pain medicine, and generally lifting the injured men's spirits with her smile and warm words. When Luke finished with the last patient, the men respectfully asked that he bring Phoebe back on his next visit.

With her once again tucked safely onto his lap, he headed Ulysses down the mountain.

"You were wonderful in there," he said, still amazed at how comfortable she seemed in her role as nurse. "If I didn't know better, I would've assumed you were trained in the medical field."

"Thank you."

He couldn't see her face, but he heard pleasure in her voice. Questions regarding her father's medical practice and how she helped were on the tip of his tongue, but their earlier conversation and her revelation about her father's untimely death kept him silent. Perhaps someday she'd feel comfortable speaking of it, but for now he'd respect her privacy.

"There's a small lake not far from here," he said. "I thought we could take our lunch there and enjoy a picnic."

She turned to face him, green eyes shining. "That sounds lovely."

He grinned, steering Ulysses toward the east. Maybe courting one's wife wasn't as complicated as he imagined.

The mountain lake was everything a mountain lake should be. Water clear as glass reflected the azure sky dotted with a few puffy white clouds. Tall pines surrounded the small body of water, with mountain peaks in the background.

Luke dismounted then helped Phoebe. He kept a blanket and canteen of water with him when he traveled into the mountains, never knowing what conditions might come up. He spread the blanket on the grass near the water's edge and set out their simple meal while Phoebe gazed at the splendor around them.

"I don't believe I've ever seen anything so beautiful." Her voice echoed her sense of awe.

Luke nodded, pleased. "I felt the same way when I first saw it. The Pueblo Indians have a lake not far from here called Blue Lake. It's larger than this but just as beautiful."

Phoebe came to sit on the blanket, her attention fastened on him.

"It's a sacred place to them. They believe it's their place of origin, where their ancestors rose up from the earth."

"That's fascinating," Phoebe said, looking out to the crystal water. "Of course we know God created Adam and Eve as the first people, but I can see why the Indians might believe they came from someplace as lovely as this."

They ate their meager lunch, easily conversing about the mining camp, the men, and simply enjoying the glorious day. When it was time to return home, Phoebe took hold of an end of the blanket and they folded it together.

"I'm glad I came today," she said, offering a shy smile when he lifted her into the saddle.

With his hands circling her waist, Luke gazed into eyes he knew he could get lost in. "I'm glad you came, too."

As they rode home, with his wife nestled against his chest, a sense of peace the likes Luke hadn't experienced in five years settled over him. The sun shone brighter. Birdsong sounded sweeter. Even the air tasted fresher.

He grinned at his crazy thoughts. While the sun and birds may not have changed, one thing was certain. He'd slept all night without ever waking to a nightmare, and he couldn't remember the last time that had happened.

Perhaps married life agreed with him after all.

Phoebe found herself humming while she kneaded a mound of dough on the floured table. She hadn't enjoyed fresh-baked bread since leaving Aunt Augusta's, and the promise of it had her mouth watering. She and Luke had gone to town the previous day and stocked their tiny kitchen with all manner of supplies, giving her the confidence she needed to prepare meals her husband would enjoy.

The ease with which she referred to Luke as her husband surprised her. After their trip to the mines, followed by their lakeside picnic two days ago, a warm companionship had formed between them. Her heart still belonged to Danny, but she was finding that Luke had a good heart of his own. His kindness and caring attention to her created an atmosphere in their snug home that vanquished any reservations she had regarding whether she'd done the right thing by coming to New Mexico.

Her thoughts revisited last evening. After a supper of smoked trout and potatoes, which Luke declared tastier than any he'd eaten at the fanciest restaurants in Denver, they'd settled in for a pleasant night around the fire. Luke had several books on a shelf, and Phoebe volunteered to read poetry aloud while he restocked his medical bag. Long after he put the leather case away, they stayed up taking turns reading from the book and discussing the meaning behind the poets' words. It was one of the most pleasurable evenings she could remember.

The sound of mule hooves outside told her Luke had returned. He'd gone to see about purchasing another animal so they wouldn't be required to ride double on Ulysses. She had to admit she'd miss being tucked safely within Luke's strong arms as they traveled through the mountains. She had little experience riding alone, but Luke promised to find the most docile animal in the territory.

Wiping her flour-covered hands on a towel, she moved to the door as Luke entered.

"Oh!" She hurried to avoid getting hit as the portal swung open, but her skirt tangled around her legs, causing her to topple over backward.

In a swift move, Luke caught her before she hit the plank floor. He pulled her up, with the momentum landing her hard against him. "Well now, that's some kind of greeting." Laughter sounded in his voice.

"I suppose I'm head-over-heels happy that you're home," she said, her droll words muffled by the front of his coat. She was rewarded with a deep chuckle rumbling in his chest.

When she moved her head enough to look up at him, she found his brown eyes shining. "I can get used to this kind of welcome every day, Mrs. Preston."

Warmth spread up her neck and spilled onto her cheeks. His hands remained around her waist with their lower bodies flush against each other. Suddenly timid, she looked away. He released her, but it occurred to her it wasn't such a bad thing to find oneself in the arms of a strong, handsome man.

"Were you able to locate another mule?" She kept her back to him until she was certain her face had returned to its natural color.

"I did. Would you like to meet her?"

Phoebe turned. "Her? I assumed you would get another male."

"Mr. Collins, the livery owner, says Dolly is real gentle."

"Dolly." She smiled. "I like that name."

They went outside, where two mules waited. While Ulysses was taller and broader through the shoulders, Dolly was no small animal. The thought of being up so high sent a tremor of apprehension racing through Phoebe. She'd been a child the last time she sat on a horse alone, and even then it hadn't appealed to her.

"I thought we could go for a ride and let you ladies get used to each other." Luke offered an encouraging smile.

Phoebe eyed the dark brown mule. Dolly stood peacefully alongside Ulysses, who kept sniffing his new companion. Doubts wormed their way into Phoebe's stomach. Could she ride such a large animal alone?

"I'm not sure about riding my own mule," she finally said, regret tugging her brow into a frown. He'd gone to a lot of trouble and expense to find Dolly. "Maybe it's not such a good idea for me to go along with you when you see patients." Even she heard the tremor in her voice.

Luke stepped closer, forcing her to look up into his face. He reached to take her hand in his and gave her fingers a slight squeeze. "I'll be right next to you. It won't be that different from riding with me on Ulysses. Besides," he said, grinning, "the men at the mine are expecting you to come back. You wouldn't want to disappoint them, would you?"

She shook her head and glanced at Dolly. "I suppose I can try."

"That's my girl."

Surprised by the affectionate phrase, she looked up to find Luke smiling at her. Was that admiration in his eyes? Butterfly wings fluttered in her stomach under his warm gaze.

"Let me set the dough to rise," she said, breaking eye contact and hurrying toward the cabin entrance. Luke's nearness and her strange reaction to him had her confused.

"Wear your new split skirt," he called after her, bringing a flush to her cheeks again. She nodded and hastily closed the door behind her.

She set the bread dough to rise, draping it with a thin dish towel, then hastened to change into the new riding skirt Luke had insisted she purchase at the mercantile. Mrs. Frank, the mercantile owner's wife, had ordered it last fall for a young miner who planned to bring his bride west. The bride, however, refused to move to such a remote area, forcing the miner to return home before the skirt arrived.

Donning the strange garment, Phoebe felt scandalous preparing to go out in public without her petticoats, even though her chemise and drawers were in place beneath the sturdy wool material. Sewn up the middle to create two separate legs, the split skirt was as close to wearing men's trousers as she'd ever come. She couldn't help but giggle thinking what prim and proper Aunt Augusta would say could she see her niece in such a getup.

When she exited the cabin, more than a little self-conscious, Luke's wide grin spoke his pleasure. "Perfect."

"Thank you," she said, hoping her cheeks didn't give away her embarrassment.

They walked to where Dolly waited. Luke bent and cupped his hands. "I'll hoist you up, since the stirrups might be a bit higher than you can manage."

Phoebe placed a steadying hand on his shoulder, feeling the muscles beneath her fingers ripple as he readied to take on her weight. When her booted foot settled in his hands, he easily lifted her so she could swing her right leg over the saddle. Dolly never flinched.

"Let me adjust the stirrups," he said, doing just that. "We'll ride down to the river."

"I don't remember how to steer," she said, taking up the reins. Dolly bobbed her big head in response.

"Just give a gentle tug, either left or right, or back toward you if you want her to stop." Luke patted Dolly's neck. "She'll follow Ulysses, so you won't have to worry much about directing her where to go." He swung into his saddle. "Ready?"

She gave a halfhearted nod, glancing down to the ground and praying she didn't land in the dust on her backside. "Be a good girl, Dolly," she whispered as Luke and Ulysses started off. True to Luke's prediction, Dolly turned to follow the boys without much coaxing.

Riding side by side with Luke offering encouragement and helpful instructions every so often, they made their way slowly down the path toward the river a mile away. After the first few terrifying minutes, Phoebe began to relax and enjoy the freedom she felt sitting atop her own mule.

"You did well," Luke said when they reached the riverbank.

"I admit it isn't as difficult as I imagined." She leaned to pat Dolly's neck. "We're going to be friends, aren't we, girl?"

"I'll need to add a second stall onto the lean-to now that Ulysses has a friend." His dark eyes danced as he bent near the mule's tall ear and whispered loudly, "I guess our bachelor days are over, old fella." He winked at Phoebe before turning the mule back toward home.

Luke couldn't know how the teasing gesture reminded her of Danny. He'd often winked at her, usually at the most inappropriate times, forcing her to hide her smile behind her hand. The first time she saw him at a dance, he'd winked at her from across the room. She thought him brash and rude, but when he came forward and asked her to dance, she couldn't resist his sparkling blue eyes and dimples.

Oh Danny, how I miss you.

She let Dolly plod along behind Ulysses, the joy of the adventure suddenly gone.

Chapter 5

"Hello in the cabin!"

The call came after breakfast the next morning. Luke glanced up to find Phoebe's eyes wide with alarm where she stood at the washtub, scrubbing their breakfast dishes. He rose from his chair and set aside the medical instruments he'd been examining, trying to determine which should be replaced and what to include in the order he planned to put in with Mr. Frank at the mercantile later that day.

"It's a common practice in these parts," he said, walking to the door. "Folks call out rather than knock to announce themselves."

Relief swept her face. "I see."

Luke opened the door, surprised to find a tall Negro man standing in the yard, holding the reins of an ancient horse. Although free Negroes were slowly drifting into the territory now that the war was over, giving them their long-awaited freedom, seeing one outside his door was unexpected.

"Hello. What can I do for you?"

"You the doc?"

Luke nodded. "I am."

The man's expression went from wary to worried. "It be my wife, Doc. She been trying to birth our young'un for two days now, but it ain't comin'."

Dread washed over Luke. He'd participated in a number of births, so he knew the information this father and husband relayed wasn't good. "Where is your home? I'll get my things and come right away."

The man's broad shoulders sagged with relief. "We be camped down near the river, 'bout a half-mile north of the road." He hesitated. "I ain't got no money to pay you, though."

Luke assured the man he'd be there posthaste despite the lack of funds and returned to the cabin to find Phoebe readying his medical bag.

"I heard." She glanced around the cabin. "I wasn't certain what else you might need for a difficult birth."

"I'd like you to join me," he said, pleased with her efficiency. "I'm sure having another woman near would help ease the mother's discomfort."

Phoebe agreed and hurried to ready herself while Luke saddled the mules. He feared the pace he set might be too fast for her, but she proved determined to stay seated and kept up admirably.

Arriving at the camp, they found the Negro man standing next to a rickety wagon draped with a canvas covering. Luke dismounted then helped Phoebe down.

"This is my wife," he said to the man, realizing how proud he was to introduce Phoebe in such a manner.

"Ma'am," the man said, tipping his hat. "My name's Calvin Mathews. My wife is Julia. We's from Texas. Thought to come try our hand at gold minin'." A soft moan came from the wagon, and he frowned. "Didn't count on the little one, but Julia. . .she be happy 'bout him."

"Let me take a look at your wife." Luke moved to the opening in the canvas at the back of the wagon. Inside the dim interior, he set about examining Calvin's exhausted and barely conscious wife. After a few minutes, he poked his head out the opening.

"The good news is I don't believe anything is obstructing the birth canal." Calvin's brow lifted. "But," Luke continued, not wanting to give false hope to the father, "if my guess is correct, the baby is very large. It's going to take a lot of work to bring him into the world. I'll need some hot water and towels." While Calvin set off to see to the supplies, Luke turned to Phoebe. "The mother is all but unconscious. It'll take both of us to help her deliver the child."

Phoebe's eyes widened, but she nodded. Luke assisted her into the wagon despite the crowded conditions. She took her place at the front toward the driver's seat, with Julia's head resting near her knees.

"Her contractions are weak. When I tell you, lift Julia's shoulders while I push the baby downward."

Phoebe nodded again. He put his hand on Julia's protruding belly, waiting for the next contraction. It came within moments.

"Now," Luke said. He used firm strokes to encourage the baby downward. Phoebe lifted the limp woman's shoulders and settled in behind her, offering words of encouragement while the mother moaned.

They repeated this scenario over and over. Calvin remained outside, peering in occasionally, wringing his hands. Finally, after more than two hours, the baby's head crowned. Julia roused enough to give a great push, clinging to Phoebe's hands as she brought forth her son.

Immediately, Luke began to work on the baby, whose round face appeared blue in the dim light of the wagon. He rubbed the infant with a towel and used his finger to clear the airway. When that didn't work, he turned the baby upside down and smacked his tiny rump.

A beautiful, angry wail was his reward.

Calvin's worried face appeared in the opening. "He be all right?"

"You have a healthy boy, Calvin. My wife is going to clean him up a bit."

Phoebe crawled along the wagon bed to where Luke held the squalling baby. Their gazes locked, and he saw tears glistening in her eyes.

"You saved him," she whispered.

He so desired to kiss her right then, but it was not the time. "I couldn't have done it without you."

After Luke cut the cord, Phoebe wrapped the baby in a blanket and climbed from the wagon with Calvin's assistance. Luke heard their voices outside while he helped Julia complete the birthing process. Once he was satisfied the new mother was out of danger, he climbed down stiffly from the wagon.

"Doc, I can't thank you enough for what you done." Calvin approached, his son cradled in his arms. The baby took in his surroundings with bright, albeit, puffy eyes.

"You have a fine boy there. I'm sure his mama would like to see him now."

Calvin disappeared into the back of the covered wagon. Luke closed his eyes, relieved the potentially life-ending crisis had reached such a joyful resolution.

"You were wonderful in there." Phoebe's soft voice brought his eyes open. She stood next to him, looking as though he'd hung the moon in the sky.

"We make a good team." His gaze caressed her face.

She offered a hesitant smile.

He watched her tidy the camp, admiring the curve of her hips and the way her honey-gold hair fell down her back, tied with a simple ribbon at the base of her neck. He didn't want to rush her, knowing they had the rest of their days to live as man and wife. Although their circumstances required a different kind of courting—couples didn't typically share a bed in courtship—he'd do his best to woo his wife and bide his time.

Because one thing became perfectly clear in Luke's mind.

He was falling in love with Phoebe.

A cool afternoon breeze swept through the open cabin door, bringing with it the sweet scent of pine and sunshine. Phoebe smiled from her place in the comfy chair Luke had purchased before she arrived. Although Kansas held a beauty of its own with its rolling plains and farmland, in the brief time since her arrival in Carson Springs, she found herself captivated by the Rocky Mountains.

Mug in hand, she took a sip of coffee, enjoying the quiet solitude of the cabin. Luke had gone into town to place his order at the mercantile for several medical instruments as well as other supplies he was running low on. He'd invited her along, but Phoebe had declined. The laundry needed washing, and she still hadn't written to Aunt Augusta. Luke nodded in understanding, but she couldn't mistake the disappointment in his eyes.

She sighed and gazed on the beauty beyond the door. It pleased her to know her husband enjoyed her company. When she accepted his proposal for marriage, all manner of terrible scenarios had played across her mind as she traveled west. That Dr. Luke Preston had turned out to be a kind, handsome man was more than she'd hoped for. Their future looked far brighter than she'd dared imagine two months ago.

But marriage to Luke hadn't diminished the one obstacle that kept her from giving herself freely to her new husband. Her heart belonged to Danny. To make the situation more complicated, there was her deceit regarding her Confederate sympathies during the war. Thus far, she'd avoided any talk of which side she'd stood in allegiance with, but she knew that couldn't last throughout the long years of their marriage. And from the few comments he'd made regarding his loathing of all things Confederate, she wasn't certain how Luke would react when he learned his wife's father and fiancé had both supported the South.

Phoebe glanced at the Bible in her lap. It had belonged to Papa, and she could still hear his voice as he read passages each morning before they started their day. Papa hadn't approved of slavery, but his family came from Tennessee, and he felt very strongly that states should govern themselves, even when it came to the issue of slavery. He'd admired President Lincoln though, and Phoebe wondered if perhaps Papa might have been persuaded to change his views had he lived long enough.

Memories of the dark day her father was murdered surfaced in her mind. She closed her eyes against them, but nothing could ever remove the horror she'd felt when she saw his broken body lying in the street when she'd gone in search of him. The war had arrived at their back door, with a battle being raged over the Missouri border. Casualties ran in the thousands, and Papa went to help, tending men from both sides. A witness told her Unionists found him giving aid to a wounded Confederate soldier. They beat him senseless, dragged him through the streets, and left him to die.

A shudder raced through her. Phoebe opened her eyes and wiped at the trail of tears that wet her cheeks. Poor Papa. She counted it a blessing she remained ignorant of the details of how Danny perished. The simple fact that he would never return to her was nearly more than she could bear.

A folded letter peeked out from the pages of the Bible. She took the familiar missive in hand and read the precious words that were practically engraved on her heart:

My darling Phoebe,
I write this from the side of the road as we stop to rest. We are marching north to Pennsylvania, although I can't tell you exactly where. The excitement we feel as we prepare to roust the Federals makes the long march bearable. I consider myself fortunate to be here, when many of our Kansas boys are out West, far from the action. General Lee, it is said, believes this battle could well decide the war, and I wholeheartedly agree.

I think of you often, my darling. Stay busy making preparations for our wedding, for the moment this war is over, I will make you my wife!

Yours forever,
Danny

It was dated June 28, 1863, less than two months after he'd turned eighteen and joined the Confederate States Army. His name had already appeared on the list of soldiers who perished at Gettysburg by the time his letter reached Phoebe.

A noise outside alerted her to Luke's return. She hurried to tuck the folded keepsake back into the book and laid it on the seat of the chair as she stood. One day soon she'd need to make a full confession to her husband, but for now the memories of Danny and her father would remain hers alone.

Luke filled the doorway a few moments later, his arms loaded with brown-paper-wrapped packages.

"I see you're enjoying the glorious day." He smiled as he came inside and deposited his burden on the table.

"I am. I hope you don't mind, but I found a rope in the lean-to and strung it behind the cabin for the laundry." She didn't mention the carrot she snuck to Dolly while searching for something to use as a clothesline.

"I don't mind. When it was just me, I hung my washing from the rafters." At her raised brow, he grinned. "I suppose I'll need to make a permanent place to dry laundry." He glanced at the packages on the table, and his grin widened. "In fact, I'll have to make it extra long to hold all of your clothes."

"Mine?" She frowned. Surely he'd noticed she only owned three dresses.

He picked up the largest of the packages and handed it to her, looking quite pleased with himself.

"What is this?" His behavior puzzled her. She hadn't asked for anything from the store.

"Open it and see."

She carefully removed the paper and gasped. Yards of various colored fabrics spilled onto the table. Blue, yellow, stripped. Some lightweight, some sturdier wool. There was even a length of soft flannel, perfect for a new nightgown.

She stared at the mound of material then looked up at Luke, confused.

He smiled. "I wasn't certain if you sewed for yourself, but Mrs. Frank assures me there is a capable seamstress in town if need be. She put some patterns and sewing items in one of these packages."

Understanding dawned, and Phoebe stilled. "You bought all of this. . .for me?"

"Yes," he said. "Many brides have a trousseau made before their wedding. In our case, yours will come after the ceremony."

She stood openmouthed. His thoughtfulness touched her in the deepest places of her heart. "Thank you."

Their eyes held for a long moment before he leaned toward her. She thought he intended to kiss her, but his lips tenderly brushed her forehead instead, in much the same way he'd done on their wedding night.

"I suppose you'll have to take charge of our reading time in the evenings," she said to cover the rush of emotion his caring gesture and warm kiss wrought. "I'll be happily occupied until winter, I suspect, with all my sewing."

The look of pure satisfaction on Luke's face stayed with her throughout a very enjoyable evening.

Chapter 6

The following morning over a breakfast of warm oatmeal with molasses and butter, Luke said, "I've been thinking about something, and I'd like your opinion."

Phoebe glanced up from her meal, her brow raised with curiosity. "Oh?"

"I'm considering opening an office in town." He paused, gauging her initial reaction. After a look of interest filled her eyes, he continued. "When I first arrived in Carson Springs, I wasn't certain I wanted to put down roots. But now," he said, an involuntary smile forming on his lips as he looked across the table to his wife, "with all that's happened, it feels like the right time to make things permanent."

"I see," she said, her expression thoughtful. "Papa had an office and an examination room on the first floor of our house. Of course we lived in town, making it convenient for patients."

Luke nodded, happy to have a wife who understood the practical side of a doctor's life. "I've thought about simply adding a room to the cabin, but as you say, convenience for the patient is of utmost importance. While I was in town yesterday, I noticed one of the shops is vacant. I'm thinking of renting it."

"Would you keep regular hours?"

"The clinic would be open three or four days a week at first. People could come see me as their needs arise, so there isn't a way to know for certain when someone will require the doctor." He grinned. "You needn't fear about being lonely without me. I'd like you to work alongside me."

After a momentary look of astonishment, the corners of her mouth lifted. "I must admit I've enjoyed accompanying you as you tended your patients. It reminds me of times I spent with Papa." She glanced about the small cabin. "But I wouldn't want to neglect my household responsibilities."

Giving in to his desire, Luke reached across the table and folded her small hand in his. "I promise to help here at home. You might be surprised at how well I can wash dishes or sweep the floor."

His teasing didn't elicit the smile he'd hoped for. Instead, she stared at their hands, blinking several times, almost as though she fought tears. Had he wounded her feelings somehow?

She seemed to gather herself. "I think it sounds like a fine idea." Only the slight tremor in her voice told him something was amiss despite her favorable words. Perhaps later he'd raise the discussion again and watch for any sign as to what might have upset her. It had been long years since he'd dealt with the females in his family on a daily basis.

Thinking back to his youth, he recalled days when his mother ended up in tears, usually due to a misspoken word on his father's part. He'd need to remember women often didn't think like men, which—he grinned—wasn't always a bad thing.

He released her hand and resumed the meal. "I thought to check on the Mathews family this morning. If you'd rather not come, I understand."

She cheered up. "I'd love to see how Julia and the baby are doing."

Pleased, Luke helped clear the table then headed outside to ready the mules, whistling a happy tune. He chuckled when he found the animals cozied up next to each other.

"Looks like the two of you are getting along well," he said. "Maybe you can give me some advice."

Although he jested, as he saddled the animals he wondered if perhaps he did need some advice. Not from a mule, of course, but from someone who knew a thing or two about marriage. Reverend Whit and Eula had celebrated their thirtieth anniversary last fall with a small reception at the church. If anyone could offer sound marital counsel, it would be the man who'd talked him into marriage in the first place. Leading the mules to the front of the cabin, Luke decided he'd go see the Whitakers later that afternoon.

Phoebe joined him in the yard, a bundle in her hands. "I hope you don't mind, but I'd like to give them a bit of the flannel you bought me so Julia can make a few baby things. I also thought she could use some extra nourishment, so I included some bread, bacon, and cheese."

"I don't mind at all," he said. His wife's compassion for others only increased his admiration of her.

The baby's wails came from the wagon and greeted them when they arrived at the sparse camp. "Mornin', Doc. Missus," Calvin said.

"How are the patients today?" Luke asked, dismounting. The crying came to an abrupt halt, telling evidence that it was dinnertime for the little guy. Luke moved to assist Phoebe from the saddle, wishing he could let his hands linger on her narrow waist a bit but knowing she would be embarrassed if he did.

"Julia's still tired, but she be stronger. The little one," Calvin said, grinning, "he gonna wear us both out, he's so feisty."

Luke and Phoebe laughed.

"We brought you a few things," Phoebe said, offering the bundle. "As a gift to celebrate your son's birth."

Calvin hesitated to accept it. "That real nice, Mrs. Doc, but we the ones who owes you fine folks for all you done."

Phoebe smiled easily. "Every baby deserves a few gifts. Why, even the wise men brought gifts to the Baby Jesus."

Dipping his head, Calvin received the package. "Thank you kindly, ma'am."

"Calvin?" Julia called from inside the wagon.

He excused himself and poked his head through the flap. A moment later, he returned holding the baby, who smacked his lips contentedly.

"Oh, he's darling." Phoebe reached to run her finger over the baby's tiny hand. Her reward was having her finger grasped in a firm hold.

Julia peeked out from the back of the wagon then, a shy smile on her face. She looked a sight better than the last time they'd seen her.

After greeting them, Julia's eyes welled with tears. "Like my man said, we can't thank you folks enough for what you done." She looked at Calvin and nodded.

Calvin walked over to Luke and offered the baby. Confused, Luke took the warm bundle in his arms, once again thankful this difficult birth had turned out so well.

"Doc, we ain't got nothin' to give you for helpin' us in our time of need, but we'd be honored to name our boy after you."

Luke stared at the man, shocked by the announcement. "You don't need to do that."

"We want to always remember your kindness toward us. If it weren't for you, I might not have my boy or my wife today." When Luke nodded in acceptance, Calvin grinned. "This here be Preston Mathews."

Luke looked down at the baby, whose eyelids drifted closed. Long lashes rested on plump cheeks. "Preston Mathews." Luke glanced over to Phoebe and found tears glistening in her eyes.

They stayed an hour or so, chatting with the Mathews and enjoying the beautiful riverside setting. When it came time to leave, Phoebe, who cradled Baby Preston in her arms, placed a tender kiss on his cheek before handing him to Julia. Luke watched, mesmerized. A deep longing to see her with a child of their own began to form in his heart. A place he'd thought long dead, destroyed by the things he'd seen and done during the war.

Hope sprang anew, as though little Preston's birth somehow blotted out the ugliness of the past and offered something fresh and unsullied by bloodshed. Hope that the unseen wounds inside him would heal. Hope that his and Phoebe's future held the promise of many children and many years of happiness.

Chapter 7

Sunday morning dawned gray, gloomy, and downright chilly. The sodden sky held the assurance of long hours of rain and made going to town for the service in the chapel problematic, since their only means of transportation were the two mules.

"I may have to look into ordering a buggy," Luke said, standing at the window. Even as he spoke, fat raindrops began to pelt the ground.

The suggestion troubled Phoebe as she spread the quilt neatly over the mattress, fluffing each of their pillows into plump mounds. She would certainly enjoy riding in a buggy instead of jostling along aboard Dolly's back, but the expenses her arrival had cost Luke seemed to mount with each passing day. First her travel fare, then a mule and saddle, then the sewing supplies. While he hadn't uttered one complaint, she worried about their finances, especially after hearing him tell Calvin Mathews payment wasn't necessary. How often did he render medical aid for little to no compensation? Perhaps her concern was due to the dire circumstances Papa's death left her in, but no matter the reason, she was certain their marriage had greatly taxed Luke's funds. The subject wasn't something she felt comfortable broaching with him, however.

But worry nagged her. Were his dwindling funds the reason he felt it necessary to open an office in town? Renting the vacant store would take yet more money.

"I'm sure we can get along without a buggy," she said, hoping her voice didn't betray the concern racing through her.

Luke cast a curious look her way. "Am I to understand you would rather traipse about the countryside on Dolly than in a buggy?" Teasing shone in his dark eyes.

"I simply don't believe you need to go to all that trouble and expense. Dolly and I are getting along quite well."

He moved to stand in front of her. After a moment, he reached for her long braid she'd tossed over her shoulder, rubbing the silky strands between his fingers. A gentle smile stretched his lips as he perused her face. "I am proud of you for adapting so well to riding Dolly, but I don't want my wife soaked to the skin every time it rains."

The possessive way he said *my wife* brought on a wave of nervousness. Would he kiss her? And possibly expect more? He'd said he would wait until she was ready, but she couldn't expect his patience to last forever.

He dropped her braid and moved to his chair near the fireplace. She waited for the relief that should have come, but oddly enough it was disappointment she felt.

"I'll ask Mr. Collins the next time we're in town about a buggy." He spoke as though the matter was settled in his mind.

She went about tidying the small cabin, but the problem at hand was not settled for her. Worry over finances had plagued her every day after Papa died. Living with Aunt Augusta relieved some of the burden, but her aunt's circumstances hadn't been much better. Phoebe tried to find work, but with no skills or experience other than occasionally going with Papa to see patients, coupled with the vast number of women seeking positions due to the war, securing a permanent arrangement had been nearly impossible. If not for the kindness of some of Papa's friends and a few shop owners who'd felt sorry for her, she and Augusta might have starved.

"All right," Luke said, laying aside the newspaper he'd purchased the last time he was in town. "I can see something is troubling you."

Her hands stilled as she reached for the washbasin, planning to empty it and refill the pitcher with fresh water. Turning wary eyes to him, she found him looking directly at her.

"I don't know what you mean," she said.

"You've been wearing a scowl ever since I mentioned purchasing a buggy." He motioned to the chair next to his. "Join me, and let's discuss this."

Feeling like an errant child, Phoebe sat in the floral-print chair.

"Now, why don't you want me to purchase a buggy?" He seemed truly perplexed.

And why shouldn't he be? Wouldn't anyone in their right mind prefer to travel in a buggy than on the back of a mule? It seemed an honest answer was the only solution to the misunderstanding.

"I fear you have spent far too much money on me and my needs as it is," she said quietly, staring at her lap.

A log in the fireplace popped and sizzled in the silence following her declaration.

When he reached for her hand, Phoebe looked up to find a look of pure adoration shining in Luke's eyes. The sight both elated and frightened her.

"Phoebe, you needn't be concerned with our finances," he said, stroking the tender underside of her wrist with his thumb. She didn't miss his use of the word *our*, nor how easily he uttered it. "Every dime I spent getting you here, as well as any expenditures since your arrival, have been more than worth it."

Beguiled by the warm sensations his caresses elicited, she nearly lost track of why she was upset. Shaking her mind clear, she said, "I appreciate everything you've done. I love Dolly, and the material for new dresses is more than I could've hoped for. But. . ." She paused. How could she explain the raw fear that tormented her in the years following Papa's death?

"But what?" His fingers tightened on her hand.

She closed her eyes, praying for the right words. "I can't help but worry you're spending too much," she whispered, opening her eyes, beseeching him to understand she wasn't being nosy but was instead concerned for their future. "I fear we will run out of money, and then what?"

Instead of the annoyance she expected, since wives no doubt were not supposed to question their husband's use of income, compassion filled his face. "My sweet Phoebe." He bent to place a light kiss on her knuckles. "You have nothing to be concerned over.

As a captain in the Union Army, I drew a decent salary and managed to save much of it. And I have my medical practice."

"But the Mathews couldn't pay you for your services, and I suspect they aren't the first. Papa often had poor patients that couldn't pay."

He nodded. "That is true, and like your father, I won't send them away simply because they can't pay."

"I know, and I admire you for it." She bit her lower lip. "It's just that. . ."

"Yes?"

The encouragement she found on his face gave her the confidence to be completely honest. "After Papa was killed, things were very bad. Unbeknownst to me, he'd borrowed money against the house. Far more than I could raise, so the bank called in the note. I had to sell everything. Furniture. Dishes. Even my clothes." A tear slid down her cheek. Luke tenderly wiped it away. "Papa was a good man, but he didn't manage his money well."

Luke stood and drew her up out of the chair. His arms went around her, holding her in a wonderfully protective way she hadn't known since Papa died. With abandon, she clung to him while tears streamed down her face. After long minutes, memories of the awful days she'd endured after Papa's murder faded, replaced by a comfort she hadn't expected to find in this man's arms.

"You never need worry about our financial state," he said into her hair, his breath warm. "I promise I'll be careful with our money, and you can ask to see the ledgers whenever you wish."

With her cheek pressed against his chest and his strong arms wrapped around her, the weight of her worries lifted. For the first time in a long time, Phoebe felt secure.

Luke swung an ax over his shoulder. The log he aimed for split with a resounding *whack*, echoing through the dense woods behind the cabin. Two evenly cut pieces fell on either side of the stump he used as a block, and he bent to pick them up and toss them into a half-full bin attached to the side of the lean-to. Even with spring officially on the calendar, nights in the Rockies were still quite chilly, requiring him to keep their woodbox filled.

Since Phoebe's arrival, they'd used more firewood in one week than he would've used in a month as a single man. But he wasn't complaining. He grinned. The meals she cooked and their cozy evenings in front of the fire were definitely worth the extra effort. Besides, there wasn't anything like splitting logs to give a man some thinking time.

He recalled the sweetness of holding her in his arms earlier. He'd been surprised to hear her confess her worries regarding finances. That her father left her in such dire straits was disappointing. He'd wanted to ask about the murder but thought better of it when he saw her tears. If his suspicions were correct, Dr. Wagner's death had most likely been a result of the war, yet another casualty of the hate-filled Rebels. A fierce protectiveness settled over him, and he silently promised he would never let her down the way her father had.

Leaning the ax against the block, Luke took a handkerchief from his pocket—freshly laundered and neatly folded, he noted—and wiped his brow. Over the past five years, memories of the war had never been far from him, despite his deep desire to forget. The nightmares he'd experienced since riding away from the battlefields had plagued him until he thought he might go mad. If not for Reverend Whitaker and his prayers and sound counsel, Luke wasn't sure what would've become of him.

Glancing toward the cabin, peace the likes of which he hadn't known before washed over him. Never could he have imagined a mail-order bride would bring him the kind of happiness his heart was full of these days. Some months back when Reverend Whit made the suggestion that Luke marry, he'd laughed in the older gent's face. The reverend wasn't offended and simply offered a silly, knowing kind of grin. Weeks later, as Luke grew weary of the nightmares and tormenting memories, Reverend Whit said he believed God wanted to give Luke a wife. Marriage, he declared, was good for a man's soul. Desperate to know that kind of peace, Luke gave in. Who was he to argue with the reverend *and* God?

He thought back to his chat with the good reverend a few days ago. Once again, the man's wisdom and advice had given much encouragement to the newly married husband. Feeling as bashful as a schoolboy, Luke confided about his unconsummated marriage and his promise to Phoebe to wait. Although he hadn't expected Reverend Whit to tease him the way the rough miners might've, he hadn't expected the sheer approval in the reverend's eyes. A woman's heart was a fragile thing, the parson said. Better to capture it completely with tender love than bruise it with lustful passion. The intimacies between a man and his wife needed the foundation of committed love to last through the years ahead. Luke had come away from their meeting more determined than ever to win his wife's heart.

He worked splitting wood for another hour. Just as he reached for the last of the logs, a piercing scream rent the air.

Phoebe!

Luke tossed the ax to the ground and tore around the corner to the front of the cabin.

The sight he beheld sent a chill slicing through him.

Chapter 8

Three native men stood in the yard talking among themselves. A fourth lying on a crudely built stretcher nearby seemed in too much pain to worry about a white woman's fright.

Phoebe hadn't meant to scream. They'd simply taken her by surprise. When the door opened she thought Luke had returned from chopping wood. A difficult stitch in her sewing kept her attention, but when he didn't greet her, she looked up. Instead of her husband, a dark-skinned man dressed in leather stood on the threshold. At her shriek, he'd fled. Now she peeked out the window, realizing she had no idea if Luke owned a gun or what she should do to protect them from these men.

"Hello!"

Luke came into view. He moved slowly toward the men, his hands out as though to show them he wasn't armed. Would they attack him?

The man who'd entered the cabin spoke, his words unintelligible, and motioned toward the man lying on the stretcher. Phoebe kept her attention trained on Luke, noting the calmness in his voice when he told the stranger he would look at his injured friend. Whether they truly understood each other, she couldn't say.

Luke then turned to the cabin. Phoebe cracked the door open with shaky hands. Concern filled his eyes when he saw her. "Are you all right?" he said, his voice low so only she could hear.

She nodded. "They startled me is all."

A slight smile tipped his mouth. "My brave wife. Will you please hand me my medical bag? I don't want to go inside for fear they might think I'm retrieving a gun."

Phoebe hurried to do as he asked. When she handed the black leather satchel to him, she glanced to the waiting men. They seemed genuinely concerned for their friend. Surely they wouldn't harm Luke. The thought of waiting in the cabin alone sent her heart racing, and she made up her mind to assist him, no matter her jumpiness around the native men. Luke had called her brave, hadn't he?

"I'll come with you," she said, the words expressing a bit more courage than she truly felt.

But Luke shook his head. "You stay here." He cast a glance toward the group, who now gathered around the injured man. "They're Apache and mostly at peace with white settlers these days. I don't think they'll cause any trouble. It appears they simply want help for their friend, but I'd feel better knowing you were safe inside the cabin."

She crossed her arms. "And I would feel better standing next to my husband."

Luke's brow rose, then he chuckled. "Is this our first disagreement?"

"No." She tried not to grin. "Because you're going to agree with me."

One dark eyebrow arched. "Remind me never to argue with you." After a moment, he stretched his free hand toward her and she grasped it. "Stay near."

"I intend to," Phoebe said, her stomach knotting as they approached the men. Three pairs of black eyes followed her every move.

Luke knelt beside the injured man, who lay beneath several animal pelts. The leader spoke, motioning toward the patient's legs. Luke pulled back the pelts, and Phoebe gasped at the sight. Sharp white bone protruded from a horrific gash below the knee, and dried blood covered his skin down to his bare foot.

"This is very bad." Luke's hushed voice told her everything she needed to know. "If I'm to set the bone properly and sew the wound closed, I must administer chloroform. The pain would be unbearable without it. The problem is his friends might believe I'm doing him harm if they see him lose consciousness. They can be superstitious about bad medicine."

Phoebe peeked at the three men, all watching intently from a few steps away. She drew closer to Luke and whispered, "I could offer them some refreshment. That would give you time to administer the chloroform without them being aware."

Luke frowned. "I can't ask you to do that."

"You aren't asking. It's the only way to draw them aside so you can get to work."

Their gazes held for a long moment. Phoebe wasn't keen on the idea, but there wasn't another option. Luke had to administer the medication without the men being aware of what he was doing.

"All right," he finally said, looking none too happy about it. "But serve it outside. I don't want them in the cabin."

Phoebe nodded then stood. She hurried to the house under the full attention of the three fierce-looking strangers, wondering what to serve their unexpected guests. She'd baked bread the previous day and had a jar of strawberry preserves Mrs. Frank had encouraged her to purchase. That and some coffee would have to suffice.

A few minutes later, she walked out the door carrying her largest cast-iron skillet with the meager offerings inside. The men immediately became curious. Phoebe sneaked a glance at Luke, who sent her an encouraging wink before she walked in the opposite direction from where the injured man lay. A large boulder near a cluster of aspen trees would make a fine table, and she headed toward it. Setting the pan on the rock, she turned to the men, who continued to watch her rather than Luke.

"For you," she said, forcing a smile to her trembling lips. Using hand motions, she tried to convey her intentions. "For you. To eat."

The leader's brow rose. He said something to his companions and moved toward her. The other men followed. From the corner of her eye—for she didn't dare look directly at Luke—she saw him hastily take a small bottle and cloth from his medical bag. It was up to her to keep the native men's attention away from their injured friend in order to give Luke time to administer the sleeping agent and set the bone.

Swallowing her fear, Phoebe offered what she hoped was a pleasant smile. "I'm sorry I don't have something more filling than bread, jam, and coffee."

The men drew in close. Although she'd seen various Indian tribe members at a distance while she lived in Kansas, she'd never spoken to one. When she motioned they were welcome to the refreshments, the leader slowly reached to take a slice of bread spread with preserves while his friends watched with interest. He took a small bite, chewed, and broke into a grin. He said something to the others, which must have been positive, for they each reached for a slice. Soon the three were seated on the grass, engrossed in eating the simple repast and sipping coffee. They never glanced in Luke's direction.

When Luke finally stood and gave her a nod, she breathed a sigh of relief.

He rinsed his hands in the basin of water he'd set beside him and walked to the group. "I've done all I can."

The men rose and made their way to their injured friend. The chloroform was just beginning to wear off, for the patient seemed groggy. Touching the snowy white bandage, the leader carefully examined Luke's work. Phoebe held her breath, praying he was satisfied enough to take his companions and leave.

Seemingly pleased, he spoke to Luke, motioning toward the west. Then he turned his attention to her. After a long moment under his intense observation, he reached into the front of his shirt, pulled out a braided leather necklace with a large turquoise stone dangling from it, and handed it to her.

She glanced from the necklace to the giver to Luke, uncertain what to do.

"He's returning your generosity," Luke said, putting his arm around her waist. "It would offend him if you refused it."

Surprised by the kind gesture, she accepted the gift. "Thank you."

The man spoke in his own language then said to Luke, "Good woman."

Luke nodded his thanks.

The men each took hold of the stretcher and departed. Luke and Phoebe watched them until they disappeared into the woods.

When they were out of sight, Phoebe glanced down to the necklace. "Will they return?"

"I don't think so," Luke said, his hand still resting on her hip. "From the little I could understand, they live in the mountains west of here." He tightened his hold on her. "I'm very proud of you."

His praise sent a tingling sensation racing through her.

They walked toward the cabin. "How about we check on the Mathews?" he said, opening the door for her. "Then we could take a picnic lunch to the lake. I'd say we've earned it after a morning like this."

Phoebe was only too happy to agree.

"Looks like a storm is coming," Luke said to himself. He studied the sky above the lake. Where white puffs of cotton had floated aimlessly a few hours ago, dark, ominous clouds blotted out the warm sunshine, and a cool breeze held the scent of rain. He glanced at Phoebe curled on the blanket, dozing on their impromptu lazy afternoon. He hated to wake her, since he'd thoroughly enjoyed the uninterrupted opportunity to drink in her lovely features without her being aware.

She gave a sleepy sigh before her eyes slowly opened. "I can't believe I went to sleep." Rising to a sitting position, she offered an embarrassed grin. "You've probably been ready to return home for ages."

"Not at all," Luke said, admiring the rosy blush on her cheeks. "The view held me captive."

They hurried to pack their picnic items as the wind picked up. Ulysses and Dolly tugged at their leads, eager to get to their warm stable. Luke hoisted Phoebe into the saddle, wrapping the blanket around her for protection, then vaulted onto Ulysses. They'd only traveled a short distance when the heavens opened with a torrent of rain. He chided himself for lingering at the lake.

When the cabin came into view, Luke practically flew from the saddle to help Phoebe dismount. She was shivering as he carried her through the door. "I'll get a fire going then tend the animals."

"No," she said, seeming to shrink farther into the wet blanket. "Get them out of the weather. I'll be fine until you get back."

Luke rushed outside and quickly had the mules unsaddled and happily munching on fresh hay. The rain hadn't let up, and he received another drenching as he ran for the cabin. He found Phoebe kneeling before the fireplace, the smell of smoke evidence of her failed attempts to light the kindling.

"Let me do that," he said. In a matter of minutes, he had a good-sized blaze going. He turned to his wife, who continued to tremble with sporadic shivers. "You best get out of those wet things. We wouldn't want you taking sick."

"At least. . .I'm married. . .to a doctor," she said, her teeth chattering as she scooted closer to the fire.

Luke chuckled and rose. "Then you'd best heed the doctor's orders." He retrieved a towel from the washstand and draped it over her hair, patting gently to absorb the excess moisture. Her long braid dripped water, and he carefully squeezed it with the towel.

All the while, he was keenly aware of everything about her. Her creamy skin dotted with raindrops. The rise and fall of her chest as her breath grew more rapid. When she looked up to him with large, luminous eyes, he couldn't stop himself from kissing her upturned mouth.

Warm. Soft. Sweet. Everything he knew she would be. He dropped the towel and let his hands cup her face, drawing her deeper into the kiss. When he felt her respond, he pulled her into an embrace, his desire for his wife filling every inch of him.

All too soon, however, she stiffened and pulled away. He caught a glimpse of her flushed cheeks as she turned her back to him. "I–I'm so cold."

Disappointment washed over him. The warmth of a marital bed seemed the perfect solution to her chill, but he'd promised to give her time. After all, they had their entire lives to live as husband and wife. "I'll check the mules while you change. A cup of hot tea would help you warm up, too."

She sent him a shy look over her shoulder. "Thank you, Luke."

He dashed back into the downpour, a smile firmly in place despite the nasty turn in the weather. His wife's rebuff wouldn't discourage him. He just had to be patient.

It was only a matter of time before Phoebe Wagner Preston would be his true wife.

Chapter 9

Phoebe awoke the next morning to bright sunshine dancing across the colorful quilt, the cabin silent. She vaguely remembered Luke whispering to her while it was still dark, informing her that he was going hunting. Over a pot of vegetable stew the previous night, she'd offhandedly remarked how nice it would be to have some venison. As though her wish were his command, Luke determined he'd do his best to track down a deer today.

Stretching, she rose and completed her morning toilette, her husband occupying her thoughts. Their kiss, especially, had her mind awhirl. The tenderness of his touch. The strength of his arms around her. It felt so wonderful to be in his warm embrace with the foul weather outside and a toasty fire within. She'd almost let herself be carried away by the passion of the moment, until, that is, memories of Danny's kisses stole in, bringing with them a sense of betrayal.

She glanced out the window to the beautiful day and sighed. Last night she'd lain awake long after Luke's even breathing told her he was asleep. Although it was too dark to see him, his nearness filled her with the kind of contentment she hadn't experienced since Danny died. The love she and Danny had shared could never be replaced, but she was Luke's wife now. She couldn't deny her attraction to her husband. Not only was he strong and handsome, but his compassion for others moved her deeply, to the point she knew she could fall in love with him if she allowed herself.

But what of their differences regarding the war? She had yet to tell him about Danny or her father's murder. Could he forgive her for withholding the truth from him, before and after their wedding?

"*Tell him today,*" the Lord seemed to whisper.

The gold band on her finger caught her eye. She knew what she had to do.

Taking her Bible from the shelf, she removed Danny's letter and read the precious words one last time. Bittersweet memories of their days together flooded her mind and heart. She would always love him, but it was time to let him go.

With determination, she walked to the fireplace. Low flames licked the stack of logs Luke left burning so the cabin would be warm and cozy when she awoke. Pressing the letter to her heart, she closed her eyes. "Good-bye, Danny."

As she knelt to toss the missive into the fire, the door opened.

"Good morning," Luke said, smiling when he came in and leaned his rifle against the wall.

Quickly, she tucked the letter back into the Bible and set the book on the table.

Now wasn't the time to explain about Danny. "Good morning. You were up early."

Luke closed the door and removed his coat, hanging it on a peg. "Yes, but unfortunately I didn't see any traces of deer. I'll need to take Ulysses and head east. The terrain isn't so mountainous, which offers better grazing for the herds of mule deer."

"You needn't go to so much trouble," she said. "We have plenty of supplies."

He came to her and lifted her hand to his warm lips. "My bride wants venison, so venison she shall have."

His mouth lingered close to her skin, and his warm breath sent a flutter racing through her. She wondered if he might kiss her again, recognizing the hope that rose in her at the possibility. Her response, she knew, would be so very different than yesterday's.

As though sensing the change in her, Luke closed the gap between them. He moistened his lips, searching her face. "Phoebe?"

She held her breath, her eyes fixed on his. Could she give herself to this man? The way a wife gives herself to her husband?

Her heart throbbed in answer.

He rubbed her cheek with his thumb. "Phoebe, I—"

A noise came from outside, followed by, "Doc! Doc, you home?" Someone pounded on the portal.

Luke closed his eyes, emitting what sounded like a growl. Tickled by his obvious frustration, Phoebe quickly moved away, lest he see her grinning and think she was happy about the interruption. Little did he know her disappointment matched his.

When Luke flung the door open, a ragged-looking young man stood in the yard. "Doc, you gotta come to the mining camp. It's my brother. He's awful sick and burning up with fever."

Phoebe heard the Southern drawl in the man's voice. When she peeked over Luke's shoulder to the visitor, she found him to be not much older than herself with worry in his blue eyes. But it was the dirty, gray jacket he wore that captured her attention. There was no mistaking the Confederate uniform.

Her husband's back stiffened. "I can't help you." His terse reply shocked her. When he moved to close the door, the young man braced it open.

"Please, Doc," he said. "James is the only family I got left. I can pay you. We got lucky and found some gold before he took sick."

"I said I won't help you."

Phoebe stared at Luke, confused by his hard refusal. "Why ever not?"

He turned to look at her, a dark scowl in place of the gentle passion she'd seen only a few moments ago. "Because he's a *Rebel*," he spat. "I won't help the very men responsible for the deaths I witnessed. For the shattered bodies I had to try to put back together. Who knows how many Union lives this man and his brother destroyed." He turned back to the stranger, whose face had gone pale. "You'll find no help here."

Luke slammed the door with so much force the cabin shook. Phoebe gaped at him, stunned. Gone was the compassionate doctor who'd tended an Apache warrior and a free Negro woman. In his place stood an angry, resentful man.

"Luke," she said, searching for the right words, "the war is over. Men on both sides did terrible things. We must put the past behind us and move forward. You're a doctor. Helping that man's brother is the right and honorable thing to do."

"You speak to me of honor? Of forgetting?" His mouth formed an ugly snarl. "You weren't there. You didn't see the carnage left by Rebels like that man and his brother. I did. Those are images I will never forget. Or forgive."

Anger of her own welled up and spilled over. "My father was murdered by Unionists, all because he offered aid to wounded Confederate soldiers when the war arrived in Missouri. They didn't care that he'd tended dozens of Union soldiers, as well. Instead of being grateful for his help, they beat him, tied him up, and dragged him through the streets where they left him to die. So you see, Dr. Preston"—her voice rose as a hot tear fell from her lashes—"you aren't the only one who has suffered."

With angry strides, she moved around him and yanked her coat from the peg by the door. "If you won't help that man's brother, I will."

Phoebe left the cabin, slamming the door with as much force as Luke had moments before. Thankfully the stranger hadn't gone far. The poor fellow stood beside his mule a short distance from the cabin, seemingly not knowing what to do next.

"Sir," she called. "I'll help you. I'm not a doctor, but I've assisted my father and husband with patients."

Relief washed over his face. "Thank you, ma'am."

While Phoebe saddled Dolly, she prayed Luke would relent and come with her. But when she rode out of the yard, the cabin door remained closed. Headed into the mountains, she couldn't shut out the fear that Luke's heart would be closed too, once he learned of her Confederate ties.

Luke stared into the smoldering fire, brooding from where he'd sat since Phoebe stormed from the cabin an hour ago. His anger had ebbed, with frustration and a dozen questions taking its place.

Why couldn't she understand his reasons for not treating the sick Reb?

Why would Unionists kill her father?

He'd been surprised to learn the circumstances of Dr. Wagner's death. Sadly, the man would be alive today had he refused to treat Confederate soldiers.

But even as Luke thought this, a stab of guilt pierced him. When he'd become a doctor, he hadn't done so in order to deny treatment to those needing it. He'd prided himself on offering medical help to Negroes and whites alike before the battles began. But war changed a man. He'd witnessed so much death and destruction, all at the hands of the Rebels, that he simply could not and would not give one of them assistance.

Yet the look of disappointment in Phoebe's eyes when he refused to help the Reb inflicted a pain far greater than any war memory could. What must she think of him? And what kind of husband allowed his wife to ride off with a stranger to a mining camp, of all places? He may resent helping the sick man, but he should've never allowed his wife to go off without him.

An urgency brought him to his feet. Phoebe needed him. Grabbing his medical bag from the table, he accidentally knocked her Bible to the floor. A paper fell out when he bent to retrieve the book. Glancing at it, he saw it was a letter. Not one to read someone else's mail, he was about to return it to the pages of the book when the salutation caught his attention.

My darling Phoebe.

His blood ran cold as his eyes involuntarily scanned the neat script of a love letter, written to his wife from the Confederate soldier she'd planned to marry when the war ended.

Anger at her betrayal washed over him like a raging mountain river.

What a fool! He, a Union doctor, had fallen in love with a Confederate sympathizer. The author of the letter surely must have died in the war, leaving her at the mercy of a lonely, foolish Yankee. No wonder she rebuffed his attempts to woo her.

His breath came in hard gasps. Dark, ominous images crept in, flashing across his mind. Cries of fallen soldiers. Screams from the men under his knife. Blood everywhere.

Luke squeezed his eyes closed. "No! God, no!"

The letter fell to the floor.

Chapter 10

After seeing to Dolly's care, Phoebe approached the cabin with trepidation. Their long trek up and down the mountain to tend the sick miner had worn them both out, but her worry over Luke and what he'd say had her nerves raw.

All morning she'd hoped he would come riding into the mining camp, give her that smile she'd come to adore, and say he was sorry for his poor behavior. But he hadn't come, and she'd had to tend the sick man herself. Thankfully, with cider vinegar bartered from an old miner who wanted her to look at his bad tooth, along with cool compresses and lots of water, the man's fever loosened its grip. Paul, the brother who'd come for help, gave her a good-sized gold nugget for her trouble. She contemplated refusing it, but in the end decided she might be in need of money should Luke toss her out for her blatant defiance.

Breathing a prayer for courage, she reached for the latch. The door swung open, revealing an empty cabin. Luke wasn't there. Belatedly, she realized Ulysses hadn't been in the lean-to. She'd been so focused on the confrontation she anticipated, she hadn't noticed the big animal's absence.

She had no idea where Luke had gone or when he would return. What should she do to keep her mind occupied while she waited? A glance toward her kitchen supplies gave her an idea. Perhaps she could whip up something sweet as a sort of peace offering. Surely they could talk things out over a delicious slice of molasses cake.

With a plan in mind, she started for the shelves but noticed a paper lying on the plank floor. Her heart nearly stopped when she recognized Danny's letter. Picking it up, she glanced to where her Bible rested on the table. Had the missive simply fallen out? More importantly, had Luke seen it?

Knowing now was the time to finish what she'd started that morning, she hurried to the fireplace. A few red embers were all that remained of the fire, but they would suffice. She placed a light kiss on Danny's signature then carefully set the paper on the hot coals. It flamed and was gone in moments.

With the door to the past closed for good, Phoebe determined to do everything she could to salvage her marriage. She wanted a life with Luke and prayed the damage she'd done today would heal.

The cake batter was nearly finished when she heard someone outside. Her stomach fluttered with anticipation, and she moved to greet her husband.

But it wasn't Luke.

"Reverend Whitaker," she said, masking her disappointment at finding the parson in her yard. A glance at the darkening sky told her another storm was approaching.

"You're welcome to come inside, but Luke isn't home. I hope he'll return soon as it looks like we might receive more rain."

Her polite banter was met with a troubled frown.

"Is something wrong, Reverend?"

"I am afraid so, Phoebe."

His somber tone set her heart pounding. "Luke?"

Reverend Whitaker nodded. "He's safe, but he's at the church in a very bad state of mind."

She closed her eyes. "This is my fault. I should've never gone to the mining camp." When she looked at the reverend, she saw understanding in his eyes. "He told you what happened?"

"Yes." He paused a moment before adding, "He also mentioned a letter he found." There was no reproach in his voice.

"He read Danny's letter." Tears choked her throat. "I never meant to hurt him. I planned to burn the letter this morning, before we argued."

The kindly man nodded. "Your husband needs you now."

"I'm sure he hates me, Reverend. I haven't been honest with him."

"He loves you, Phoebe. The question is, do you love him?"

She blinked, the answer suddenly so obvious. "Yes! Yes, I do love him."

"Then tell him."

Declining the reverend's offer to accompany her to the church, Phoebe flew to the lean-to and saddled Dolly.

"Hurry, girl," she shouted, urging the mule into a run.

Thunder in the distance and a chill in the air told of the approaching storm, but she didn't care. Luke needed her.

When the church finally came into view at the edge of town, she tied Dolly next to Ulysses as fat drops began to pelt the ground. She hurried up the whitewashed steps and entered the dim building. A breath of relief escaped when she saw Luke in the front pew, hunched over with his head in his hands.

"You shouldn't have come out in the storm, Reverend Whit," he muttered. "My mood is as black as the sky, and nothing you say will change that."

Phoebe moved up the aisle, her heart heavy knowing she was the cause of his pain. More than anything, she wanted to wrap her arms around him and tell him she was sorry. "It's me, Luke," she said softly when she drew up beside him.

He sprang to his feet, his hair disheveled and a wild look to his eyes. "What are you doing here?"

"Reverend Whitaker came by the cabin and told me where you were. I was worried."

He gave a humorless laugh. "Why would you be worried about me? I've never mattered to you before."

The words cut like a knife. "That isn't true. I care very much."

"As much as you cared for your precious Danny? Yes, I know all about your Reb." He glanced to the brooch at her throat, and she realized she should've stopped wearing it the day she married Luke.

"I'm sorry I didn't tell you about Danny," she whispered. "I wanted to, but—"

"But you knew I wouldn't marry you. Isn't that it?"

Phoebe bit her bottom lip then nodded. "Yes."

"Finally, some honesty."

They stood in silence, with so much to say yet not knowing where to begin.

Tell him, Reverend Whitaker had said.

She reached for his hands, finding them cold to her touch. He frowned when she brought them to her heart.

"Before the war, I gave my heart to Danny," she said, her eyes pleading with him to understand. "He wasn't a Confederate soldier then. He was a boy I loved. When he died, I didn't think I could ever love again, but. . ." Her pulse thrummed. Whether Luke could forgive her or not, she had to risk it all and tell him the truth. "But I love you, Luke. *You* are my husband, and I love you."

The storm raged outside with rain splashing against the windows and thunder shaking the small building. But it was the storm she saw in Luke's eyes that frightened her.

Could he ever forgive her?

Luke stared at Phoebe. Dared he believe her? She'd lied since before she arrived in Carson Springs. Was she now saying what she must to keep him from throwing her out?

He closed his eyes, feeling the beat of her heart beneath his fingers.

The joke was on him, and he knew it.

He couldn't throw her out, even if every word that came from her mouth was a lie. He loved her. God help him, he loved her. When he looked at her again, he saw tears glistening in her eyes.

"Can't we start again, Luke?" she whispered, her grip on his hands tightening. "Right here, in the church, with God as our witness."

"That's mighty bold talk, don't you think? With God as our witness, there can't be any secrets between us. Are you prepared for that?"

She nodded. "I am. I've asked God to forgive me for not being honest with you, and He has. Now I'm asking you to forgive me, too."

A flash of lightning rent the sky, illuminating Phoebe's hopeful face. In that moment, Luke realized the dark thoughts that had tormented him all afternoon had fled the moment she entered the church. In the same way the nightmares he'd lived with had abated on his wedding night. God, he acknowledged, had sent him a beautiful wife in answer to his prayers for healing despite his undeserving. Despite his own sin and failings.

How could he refuse to forgive her when he himself had been forgiven so much?

"Can you forgive me, Phoebe?" he said, dropping to his knees with her hands gripped in his own. "I've been a fool."

She knelt in front of him, the tears on her cheeks shiny in the waning light. "No more than I."

"I love you, Phoebe. More than I could've ever dreamed possible."

She moved forward until there was but a breath between them. "I love you, too. Let's go home, my husband."

The kiss they shared was filled with hope, healing, and the promise of new beginnings.

Michelle Shocklee is the author of *The Planter's Daughter* and *The Widow of Rose Hill*, the first two books in the historical romance series The Women of Rose Hill. She has stories in numerous Chicken Soup for the Soul books and writes an inspirational blog. With both her sons grown, she and her husband of thirty-plus years enjoy poking around historical sites, museums, and antique stores near their home in Tennessee. Connect with her at www.MichelleShocklee.com.

Miss-Delivered Mail

by Ann Shorey

Chapter 1

Waters Grove, Illinois
1884

Waters Grove simmered in an unseasonable May hot spell. Horses' heads drooped as they waited at hitching rails in front of stores. Few ladies were out shopping, but that suited Helena Erickson just fine.

At twenty-five years old and single, with pale blond hair framing what Helena believed to be an unattractive face, she'd grown tired of ignoring the pitying glances of girls she'd known all her life. They pushed baby carriages and led children by the hand as they ventured from millinery to dressmaker to grocer on the wide streets surrounding the town square. Their smug expressions telegraphed the superiority of their status as married women.

Her prospects for marriage in Waters Grove had dwindled to zero, unless she counted old Mr. Holmes, who'd marry anyone who'd have him. Helena jutted her chin in the air. She hoped by her brisk stride she'd give the impression of being too busy for idle conversation.

She turned right at the corner of Central Avenue and Reed Street and hurried down the block toward her family's modest frame dwelling. Once inside, she dropped her parcels on the table, thankful it would be a couple of hours before her father returned from work. She'd have time to tidy the downstairs.

After sweeping the rooms, she turned toward the back door then halted with the dustpan midway toward the waste bin.

A crumpled envelope lay on top of the accumulated trash.

What on earth? It hadn't been there earlier.

She placed the dustpan to one side and plucked the envelope from its resting place. The address read "Miss Felicia Trimble." As far as she knew, no one by that name lived in Waters Grove. Why would such a letter be in the Ericksons' trash? Beyond curious, she opened the envelope. A folded sheet of paper was tucked inside.

When she drew out the paper, several pasteboard rectangles slipped from the fold and fluttered to the floor. She flipped open the page. It wasn't as though she was snooping. She needed to solve the mystery.

Dear Miss Felicia,
Forgive me for addressing you in such a familiar manner, but since we are to be married I trust you will understand.
*   Enclosed are your tickets for the journey from Waters Grove through Chicago to Spalding, my home in Washington Territory. Based on your agreement to my*

proposal of marriage, I shall be awaiting your arrival on May 26 next.

Yours in sincerity,
Daniel McNabb

She bent to retrieve the tickets. Somewhere, a Miss Felicia Trimble was expecting this letter. The best thing to do would be to return the letter to the post office. The postmaster might know if someone with that name. . . She stopped and stared at the address on the envelope. #6 Reed Street. This house. Her house.

Helena frowned. Reed Street meandered all the way out toward farmland. Obviously, Mr. McNabb copied the address incorrectly. There'd still be time before supper to walk to the post office if she left now. As she folded the letter around the tickets, the screen door slammed shut and her younger brother burst into the kitchen.

"You found that letter?" He guffawed. "Funny, eh? I answered his advertisement for a joke. Never thought he'd fall for it." He plucked the envelope from her fingers. " 'Felicia Trimble'—sounds like a dance-hall girl."

Helena snatched the letter back. "Joseph Erickson! This isn't a joke, it's cruel." She leaned against the table in the center of the kitchen. "Mr. McNabb spent good money to buy these tickets. You must send them back to him and apologize."

"No."

"I'll tell Pa."

"Go ahead. I'm sixteen. He can't make me do nothing." His gaze hardened. "Anyways, Pa won't care. He don't care about nothing since Ma died—'cept maybe that job of his." He brushed past her and stomped up the stairs.

Heart pounding, she dropped onto a chair. Joseph was right about Pa. Without their mother's cheerful presence, he'd retreated into silence. He ate the food Helena prepared, read the *Daily News*, then climbed the stairs to bed. At daylight he left for the lumberyard.

The pasteboard rectangles burned in her fingers. Tickets to Washington Territory. A homesteader needing a wife. She crossed the room and called up the stairs. "Joe, did you send a picture?"

"Course not."

"What did you tell him?"

"None of your business." His bedroom door slammed.

Fine, then. He'd probably written about housekeeping skills and a taste for adventure. If Mr. McNabb was desperate enough to advertise for a bride, he likely wouldn't be choosy.

Daniel McNabb stood at the door of his cabin, his face lifted to the spring sunshine. A soft breeze stroked the rolling grassland covering the prairie. God willing, by next year he'd be able to prove up his claim and purchase a land patent.

He and his brother had plowed a ten-acre patch for wheat the first year they'd taken up their claim. Now, after years of hard work, forty acres of sprouted wheat greeted his eyes. He felt sure his new bride would be happy living so far from town, since he'd taken pains to describe his homestead land. Her eager reply had convinced him. Felicia Trimble was the bride for him.

Before going to the springhouse for water, he turned back for another look at the interior of the cabin. A table and two chairs, braided rug, cookstove, and a separate bedroom. Everything a woman could want. He'd even hung muslin curtains over the window next to the door.

A hollow feeling in his chest stole his satisfaction with the cabin. If only his brother—Daniel shook his head. He wouldn't think about Ross now. Why spoil the day?

In two weeks, Felicia would be here and his new life would begin.

After a silent supper, Helena bent over a basin scrubbing flecks of burned potatoes from a cast-iron skillet. She'd spent more time dreaming about leaving Waters Grove than she had paying attention to the stove. Thankfully, Pa hadn't complained. But then, he never did.

She rested the cleaned pan on the drainboard and looked around the room, trying to imagine what conveniences a homesteader's kitchen might hold. A reliable cookstove? An icebox? Then she laughed at herself. Wondering about a kitchen when she hadn't met the man. Hadn't even decided to use the tickets.

"Are you done dawdling? Lamp oil isn't free, you know."

Helena spun around when she heard her father's voice. "Yes, Pa." She reached above the table and turned off the lamp, leaving the room in semidarkness. A faint twilight glow from the window over the sink sketched a path to the foot of the stairs.

"Well, then. Good night." His stockinged feet brushed against the treads as he mounted the steps.

Her fingertips touched the envelope in her apron pocket. The printed tickets indicated a departure date of May twenty-first. Today was the fifteenth. She had one week to decide.

Chapter 2

Helena spent much of the next day gathering courage to speak to her father. Her chores passed in a blur of sweeping, dusting, and scrubbing while her mind traveled to Washington Territory. So far away. So filled with opportunity for a better life. Yet if Pa said no, she wasn't prepared to defy him.

After storing the cleaning supplies, she checked on the beef and vegetable stew simmering at the back of the stove. As soon as Pa and Joseph returned from work, she'd pop biscuits in the oven. The warm cinnamon fragrance of Pa's favorite dessert, blackberry jam cake, swirled through the kitchen.

He said little during the meal. Helena choked down a few bites of food, her throat too tight to swallow. Her thoughts spun. How could she explain where she got the tickets without starting a row with her brother? She sagged with relief when Joseph banged out the back door to spend time with his friends.

She cleared the supper dishes and then placed the cake in the center of the table. A small smile cracked her father's solemn features. "Is that blackberry cake?"

"It is." She slid a generous slice onto a small plate and handed him his dessert. While he ate she pretended to be busy at the sink, but as soon as she heard him lay down his fork, she spun around.

"More cake, Pa?"

"No, I've had plenty."

"Coffee?"

He cocked an eyebrow at her. "What is it? You're acting like your Ma used to. You got something to tell me?"

"Yes." Helena drew a deep breath. "Yesterday, I found a letter in the trash bin." She told him about Joseph's deception, the letter, and the tickets, holding up her hand in a "wait" gesture when his mouth dropped open. "I'm an old maid, Pa. I want to use those tickets, go to Washington Territory, and be Mr. McNabb's bride."

Her father stared at her.

She hurried on, running her words together. "I've thought of nothing else since yesterday. This is my best chance. But I don't want to leave without your blessing. Please, Pa."

Head bent, he put his fist to his lips and closed his eyes. After a long moment, he looked up. She could tell by the set of his jaw he'd made a decision.

"You sure about this?"

"Yes." Heat raced through her body. She held her breath and prayed she wouldn't faint.

He pushed himself up from his chair. "Go, then. You have my permission."

His permission. Not his blessing. She rubbed her chest as though she could erase the pain in her heart.

Helena paced back and forth across the parlor in her father's house. His armchair rested next to a small table containing a lamp and several copies of the *Daily News*. A rose-colored sofa—her mother's choice—sat facing a braided rug in the center of the room. Polished shelves in one corner displayed knickknacks—teacups, a souvenir fan from a trip to Chicago, and a porcelain figurine of a girl with a basket of flowers.

The train would have to leave without her in the morning. She couldn't do this. She'd find a way to repay Mr. McNabb.

No.

She'd be on the train, headed west. Away from a colorless life to one of promise. She stopped pacing next to the corner shelf to trail her fingers over a pink and gold teacup and saucer. Of everything in the collection, Helena loved those the most. Maybe it was the gold handle, or the golden fleur-de-lis painted on the pink china. She lifted the delicate cup. Her mother had brought the set from her family home when she married Pa.

A tear splashed on the gold rim. Helena blinked hard and then picked up the matching saucer. Now it would be her turn.

Helena sent a critical glance at her reflection in the cheval mirror in her bedroom. She wore her best travel costume, one she'd remade from her mother's wardrobe. The pointed bodice dipped over a pleated dark green moiré-patterned skirt. She'd curled her blond hair into a fashionable fringe on her forehead then settled an embroidered bonnet over the chignon at the back of her head.

She lifted her valise containing a shawl, toiletries, and a change of clothes. The balance of her belongings were packed in her trunk, which her father had already placed in the back of their wagon. No trace of her presence remained in the room.

"I don't have all day," Pa hollered. "Boss only gave me a couple hours off."

"Yes, Pa." She hurried out to the waiting wagon, settling beside Joseph. Her father slapped the reins across the horse's back.

Dust swirled behind them as they traveled toward the station. Helena clutched her gloved hands together in her lap, praying they'd see no one she knew when they arrived. She'd not told anyone she was leaving. Bad enough that Joseph treated her as though she'd taken leave of her senses—she didn't relish facing the same reaction from townsfolk.

She uttered a relieved sigh when they arrived. Several families were gathered on the platform, but no familiar faces. A small boy tugged at his mother's hand, apparently eager to run along the tracks. Two men stood engrossed in conversation. At the far end of the building, the stationmaster held out his watch as he stared along the rails.

Her heart hammered when her father touched her elbow and guided her to a position near the station entrance. In a few minutes, she'd be leaving Waters Grove. After an hour's ride on the Short Line railroad, she'd transfer to an overland train in Chicago for the trip to eastern Washington.

"Sure you're not going to change your mind?" Pa's tone sounded more like checking the weather, rather than hoping she'd stay.

"My mind's made up. I'll write to you when I arrive."

He shuffled his feet. "Thing is, we're leaving soon. Me and Joe, that is."

A plume of black smoke arose in the distance. The vibration from the tracks grew louder, matching the roaring in her ears. She tightened her grip on the handle of her valise. "How. . . How can you be leaving? Where will you go?"

"To Chicago. Lots more work there. We'll take a room in a boardinghouse. Couldn't do that if you weren't going west."

Her world shifted. Somewhere in the back of her mind she'd believed she could always come home to Waters Grove. She stared at her father, speechless.

After a moment, her brother spoke. "Don't look so shocked. You're not the only one who wants out of here."

"But. . . How will I know where you are?"

"We'll get word to you once we're settled."

The bell on the locomotive clanged. Steam billowed from beneath the wheels as the train braked to a stop. Once the departing passengers disembarked, it would be Helena's turn to board.

Pa gave her an awkward pat on the shoulder. "Don't worry none. We'll be fine."

But what about me? she wanted to scream. If only he'd put his arms around her this one time. Instead he picked up her valise and handed it to the conductor.

Helena stumbled into a passenger car, chin thrust high. She didn't look back. With no home to return to, she'd make this marriage work, no matter what.

Chapter 3

The bouquet of wildflowers Daniel held drooped in the heat. His companion, Reverend Philip Marley, slipped out of his black frock coat and draped it over his arm. He stepped toward the shaded portion of Spalding's modest railroad depot.

"We don't have to stand here in the sun."

Daniel followed him for a moment then returned to the edge of the platform to peer along the tracks. If Felicia saw him waiting there, she'd know how eager he felt about their marriage. Insects chirped in the bunchgrass surrounding the station, but try as he might, Daniel couldn't hear the rumbling of a locomotive.

"Train's late." He returned to the preacher's side.

"Not by much, is my guess. See there?" He pointed to the south end of the platform, where the stationmaster pushed a baggage cart toward the rails.

A Northern Pacific train rumbled around a low hill then barreled straight into the station. Brakes squealed as the cars came to a sweeping halt.

Daniel studied the three passenger cars, wondering which one carried Felicia. He turned to Reverend Marley. "Appreciate you coming with me. Soon as we get Miss Trimble's bags, we'll go straight to the church so you can marry us." He knew he'd repeated the plan more than once, but he couldn't think of anything else to say. After wiping his sweating palms on his trousers, he removed his hat and ran his fingers through his hair.

"Settle down, son. She'll be here in a moment." The reverend clapped his hand on Daniel's shoulder.

A few passengers disembarked and strode into the depot or out to waiting buggies. No Felicia. After another minute dragged by, a slender blond woman stepped into the sunlight. She dropped a valise at her feet and surveyed the platform with one hand shading her eyes.

"She's beautiful." Daniel spoke in a whisper. "She looks like an angel, standing there in the sunlight."

"You're quite the poet," his companion said. "Is that your bride?"

"No. According to her letters, Miss Trimble has red hair, and she's more full-figured. My intended must still be on the train."

The station agent pushed the loaded baggage cart past them. No one else disembarked. In another few moments the locomotive bell clanged and the Northern Pacific continued its journey west.

Daniel's heart seized. Had Felicia not received the tickets? Did she miss the train?

Worse yet, had she deceived him? He'd spent almost all the profit from last year's wheat harvest to purchase her fare. He cringed to think he'd told everyone who would listen that today he would be bringing home a bride.

His face burned. Daniel McNabb—the biggest fool in eastern Washington.

Helena squinted into the brilliant sun at two men who stood side by side next to the depot. They were of similar height, about six feet. The man on the left had wide shoulders that strained at the cut of his fawn-colored sack coat. He clutched a bouquet of drooping flowers in one broad fist. His hawk-nosed companion appeared to be the older of the two, judging from his gray mustache. She hoped the one holding the flowers was Daniel McNabb, but if so, why wasn't he coming forward to greet her? What if neither of them was Daniel? Then what would she do?

After a moment's pause, she stepped forward. "Excuse me. Is one of you gentlemen Mr. McNabb?" Her heart drummed.

The younger man tipped his wide-brimmed hat, revealing slicked-down red hair. His deep-brown eyes met her gaze. "That would be me, miss. How do you know my name?"

She'd rehearsed how she'd explain she wasn't Felicia Trimble, but now that the moment had arrived she couldn't remember what she'd planned to say. Fingers trembling, she opened her handbag and gave him his letter. "I'm here in answer to this."

"You're not Felicia. She said she has red hair and—" He cleared his throat. "Where did you get this?"

"I can explain if you will listen."

"D'you take me for a fool? Listen to what?"

"Give the lady a chance." The older man removed his hat and bent in a half bow. "I'm Reverend Marley, friend of the family. We expected a Miss Trimble to arrive today. She gave you her tickets?"

Grateful for the preacher's kind tone, Helena dipped her head and mumbled, "Not exactly."

Daniel clenched his hands at his sides. "I thought not." He dropped the wilted bouquet on the platform and kicked it aside.

"I found your letter in the trash." Her voice wavered. "My brother wrote to you for a joke. When you sent the tickets he threw them out."

"Threw them out. Nearly a year's profits. A joke." He took several steps away then wheeled around to face her. "So why are you here? To laugh?"

"No, Mr. McNabb. You advertised for a bride. That's why I'm here."

"I don't even know your name. The letters said she's a schoolteacher. Are you?"

Her shoulders sagged. There had to be some way to rescue this situation, but she couldn't imagine what it might be. No telling what else Joseph had written in his letters. She'd been beyond naive to believe she could take a fictitious person's place. Of course Mr. McNabb wouldn't marry a stranger. She blew out a breath.

"My name is Helena Erickson. I'm not a schoolteacher, but I am a hard worker."

He snorted. "That's not important now. Reverend Marley came here to marry Felicia and me so I could take her to my farm. Now I don't know what to do."

Many of the stops along the trip west had featured overnight hotel accommodations for travelers. A quick glance beyond the depot revealed nothing more than a dusty street dotted with a few shacks. Her plan lay in shreds. She couldn't have made a bigger mistake if she'd tried.

Chapter 4

Daniel turned toward Reverend Marley. "What if the Hallidays don't have room?"

"Only one way to find out. The turnoff to their place isn't too far ahead." He hooked one arm over the back of the seat. "Be glad to get out of this sun for a spell."

The buggy swayed on the rutted track leading east from Spalding to farmland beyond. Miss Erickson shared the narrow rear bench with her trunk and valise. She hadn't said a word once Daniel and the preacher discussed asking his neighbor to take her in.

He felt guilty about foisting her off on the Hallidays, but this late in the day no other solution came to mind. Tomorrow he'd find better lodging for her. His chestnut gelding stepped along with a lively trot, no doubt believing he was headed for the barn.

Daniel pulled up on the reins, guiding the animal onto a narrow lane leading to the Hallidays' cabin. As soon as the buggy halted, the cabin door flew open.

Sarah Halliday stepped onto the covered porch. "Daniel! I want to meet your bride." She bustled toward them, strands of honey-brown hair flying loose from the bun at the back of her head. Before he could respond, she reached the buggy and peeked around the trunk at Miss Erickson.

"I'm your neighbor, dear. Come in and refresh yourself. You must be plumb worn out after all those days on the train."

Miss Erickson leaned forward. "Thank you, ma'am, but—"

"She's not my bride." Daniel hopped down and wrapped the reins around the hitching rail. "There's been a mistake."

Sarah glanced from him to Reverend Marley and then back to Miss Erickson. She quirked an eyebrow. "Come in, anyway. This poor girl looks downright peaked. Must be some story."

"Thank you, Miz Halliday." Reverend Marley offered his hand to help Miss Erickson from the buggy then followed their hostess along a stone pathway.

Daniel trailed behind. Miss Erickson looked done in, for a fact. His anger had subsided enough for feelings of pity to emerge, but he ignored them. She'd brought this on herself. If she was concerned about those tickets, why didn't she simply send them back?

Once inside, Sarah drew a chair away from a rectangular table near the kitchen area in the main room. "Come here and sit, dear. What did you say your name was?"

"I'm Helena Erickson, ma'am." A blush colored her fair skin. "I'm grateful for your kindness."

"Pish. It's nothing." Sarah crossed to a shelf, placed four cups on the table, then filled them with water from a gray crockery pitcher. After seating herself next to Miss Erickson, she fixed her gaze on Daniel and Reverend Marley. "Now, tell me what this is all about."

Daniel stared into his cup. He couldn't find the words to describe his bitter disappointment. First Ross, now this.

After a moment, the reverend stood. "To come straight to the point, Miz Halliday, this young lady is not Daniel's intended. The circumstances are unclear, but we're here to ask if you and Will could put her up overnight. She obviously can't be at Daniel's cabin since they're not married."

Miss Erickson dropped her gaze to her lap.

Sarah placed her hand on the girl's arm. "We'd be happy to. We're so far from family here that it's a treat to have a visitor."

"It's settled then." Daniel sprang to his feet. "Tomorrow I'll find a better situation for her." He strode to the door, thankful to be relieved of Miss Erickson, if only for the night.

She told him she was a hard worker. He'd knock on every door in town. He'd find someone who needed help in return for room and board.

Helena followed Mrs. Halliday behind a partition opposite the kitchen to three sleeping areas divided by further partitions. She carried her bonnet and valise. Mr. McNabb had left her trunk in his buggy, no doubt to signal her stay in Spalding was only temporary. No matter what he planned, she wouldn't—couldn't—go back to Waters Grove. She'd be sure to make that clear when he returned for her tomorrow.

Mrs. Halliday stepped into one of the rooms. The space held a narrow bed topped with a double pink coverlet quilted in a star pattern. A bureau graced the far end of the room, two dresses hung from pegs on the wall, and a round rag rug covered the wooden floor. "This is Beth's room. She's thirteen. Our son, Grant, is sixteen. You'll meet them soon. They're both out helping their father. We'll decide who sleeps where when they come in."

Helena's eyes burned with unshed tears. The girl who slept in this room was blessed to have a mother like Mrs. Halliday.

The older woman settled on the edge of the bed and patted the space beside her. "Come tell me what Daniel avoided saying. You didn't just pop up here like a mushroom."

Tears momentarily at bay, Helena sank onto the soft coverlet. "I found the train tickets in our trash bin." She told Mrs. Halliday about her brother's cruel prank and why she made her subsequent decision. "I didn't know about all the lies he put in his letters. I thought it would work to come here as Mr. McNabb's mail-order bride." Tears slid down her cheeks. "Then as I was leaving, my father told me they were moving to Chicago." She drew a shuddering breath. "Now I don't even know where they are."

Mrs. Halliday slipped her arm around Helena's waist. "Did you pray about this before you left?"

"Not very much. It seemed like a gift from heaven to find the tickets."

"Maybe it was a test, not a gift." Mrs. Halliday spoke in a gentle voice. Her expression held no condemnation.

"A test?" Helena swallowed. "What do you mean?"

"Are you trusting the Lord for your future? Or did you run ahead of Him?" A moment of silence passed, then she rose. "There's water in the pitcher on the bureau. After you've refreshed yourself, I'd welcome your company while I prepare supper."

Mrs. Halliday's questions echoed in Helena's mind while she splashed cold water on her tear-stained cheeks. *Did you pray about this?* In truth, she had not. Praying had died with her mother.

After a restless night, Daniel sat on his doorstep nursing a cup of coffee. Dawn swirled golden light over wisps of cirrus clouds. He'd imagined he'd be eating breakfast with his bride this morning. Instead, he'd be spending time searching for a place for Miss Erickson to live while he saved enough funds to send her back to Illinois.

His rudeness to her stung his conscience. When he closed his eyes, he pictured the flush covering her fair skin when she confessed her deception. True, she used tickets meant for someone else, but she didn't steal them. She didn't claim to be Miss Trimble even for a moment. Now he wondered why someone as pretty as Miss Erickson would be willing to leave the comforts of an established town to marry a struggling homesteader. He wished he'd asked.

He huffed out a breath and stepped inside to place his empty cup in the kitchen washbasin. First he'd tend to his chores then go to Spalding and find lodging for her. Several boardinghouses had sprung up with the influx of settlers seeking land. Should be an easy matter to find a proprietor who'd be glad to rent a room in exchange for help with cleaning. Then he'd have time to transport Miss Erickson and her trunk into town before evening.

Helena carried a bowl of potatoes to the supper table. Mr. Halliday shot her a teasing grin from his seat next to his son, Grant. From his slicked-back dark hair to his tanned skin and muscular forearms, the young man was the image of his father.

"So my Sarah's put you to work already."

Mrs. Halliday matched his wide smile. "I told her she was our guest, but she's as stubborn as you are. Insisted on helping."

"It's the least I could do," Helena said. "You are beyond kind to allow me to stay here. Mr. McNabb promised he'd come for me today, but he didn't."

The Hallidays' daughter, Beth, patted the empty chair next to her. "Please sit by me. I'm happy he hasn't come. It's nice to have a big sister for a change."

Helena bowed her head as Mr. Halliday spoke a blessing on the meal. While he prayed, she clenched her hands in her lap, feeling lost. She hadn't expected to live in a log cabin instead of a real house. Beth told her that Mr. McNabb's cabin was just like theirs except for the sleeping arrangements. With a blush, she whispered that he had just one bed.

The quiet of the prairie also unnerved her. By comparison, Waters Grove hummed with noise—horses and buggies clopping by on the street, locomotives rumbling through twice a day, dogs barking, children playing. Helena hadn't noticed how much sounds were part of her life until she experienced today's silence, broken only by the occasional screech of a hawk or caw of a crow.

With a start, she realized Mrs. Halliday was speaking to her.

"It's not dark yet. Daniel may still arrive." She reached across the table to pat Helena's hand. "But if he doesn't, don't you worry. Beth won't mind giving up her bed for another night, would you, dear?"

"No. I like Helena."

Although her heart warmed at the girl's words, Helena gazed across at Grant. "You are the one who's displaced. I'm so sorry."

He forked fried venison onto his plate then set the platter down with a thump. "Pa can tell you, I'm happy sleeping in the barn loft. I already had a bed fixed up there."

"Trick is keeping him from sleeping there when he's supposed to be tending to chores." Mr. Halliday's eyes crinkled at the corners as he poked his son's shoulder.

The banter between father and son took Helena back to Pa and Joseph. She swallowed a lump in her throat as a stab of loneliness reminded her how far she'd traveled from Illinois. Managing a smile at the two of them, she took a tiny bite of potato.

Where was Mr. McNabb? Yesterday, he couldn't wait to be rid of her. She feared he'd abandoned her to the care of this kind family.

Chapter 5

Daniel trudged to the door of the Hallidays' cabin. On the road from town he tried rehearsing what he might say, but nothing could describe the quandary in which he found himself.

Sarah opened the door at his knock then flung it wide. "Daniel. I knew you'd get here sooner or later. Come in. Helena—Miss Erickson—can be ready quickly."

At the sound of her name Miss Erickson paused at her task, dish towel in hand. His heart twisted when he noticed the glow in her eyes.

She draped the towel over a hook. "It will only take me a minute to pack my things."

"Hold on." He held out his hands, palms up. "I've tried every boardinghouse in Spalding. I can't find a reputable one that will take a single lady."

"But. . .there must be someplace I could stay. I'll find work. I'll save every penny. I'll earn my own train fare out of Spalding." She gripped the back of a chair, a pink flush covering her cheeks. "I know my situation isn't your worry, but the sooner I can get a job, the sooner I can be out of your life."

"Miss Erickson, I'll provide the tickets as soon as harvest is in. Train fare isn't your concern."

"Yes, it is." She lifted her chin. "I've brought trouble on all of you." Her gaze swept past him to rest on Sarah. "I know I can make my plans succeed."

Sarah shook her head. "Spalding isn't like the towns you're used to. With all the miners coming through on their way to Idaho, you'd be exposed to a rough element."

Grief jolted through Daniel at her words.

She must have noticed his expression. "I'm so sorry!" She rested her hand on his arm. "Please forgive me."

"Of course." He berated himself for his weakness. Whenever he thought he'd conquered his memories, they rose up, snakelike, to attack. He took a deep breath and looked down at Sarah's worried face.

"Can I impose on you another night? I don't know what else to do."

Miss Erickson moved around the table and stopped in front of him, hands clasped at her waist. Tendrils of pale blond hair curled loose around her ears. Up close, her eyes were the blue of a sun-warmed lake.

"Mr. McNabb, there's no need to speak as though I'm not in the room. If Mr. and Mrs. Halliday will have me, I'd be pleased to spend another night here. Beyond that, we'll see."

Speechless, he tugged at his collar, aware of the heat that suffused his face. Despite her soft voice, this little lady could probably hold her own with prospectors who swarmed through Spalding.

Sarah clapped her hands. "It's settled, then. Helena stays."

"Thank you." Daniel and Miss Erickson spoke in unison. Her lips curved in a smile when she glanced up at him.

"I do appreciate the effort you've made to help me. I won't forget your courtesy."

"Yes. Well. . ." Feeling dismissed, he nodded at Sarah and then stepped out into the dusk.

Miss Erickson claimed if she found work she'd be out of his life soon. Now he wondered if he wanted her out of his life at all. Perhaps he'd been too hasty.

After breakfast the next morning, Helena returned to Beth's room. The cabin had settled into a lull with Grant and Beth outside helping Mr. Halliday, and Sarah mending a shirt at the kitchen table.

Helena pondered her limited wardrobe. Mr. McNabb still had her trunk, which left her with either her green pleated travel suit or the brown and gray plaid everyday dress she currently wore. She shook her head. To make the best impression, she'd have to wear the travel suit despite the promise of another warm day.

Her black boots tapped the floorboards when she reentered the living area. Sarah glanced up, eyebrows raised.

"What on earth! You're going somewhere?"

"To Spalding to find work. I've made up my mind. Once I save enough, I can leave for Spokane Falls. I saw the city from the train on the way here. It's much bigger than Waters Grove and bound to have opportunities for lodging and jobs."

Sarah stood, dropped the shirt on the tabletop, and gave Helena a one-armed hug. "Please don't feel you're in the way here. We truly enjoy your company." She chuckled. "When I was a girl in Illinois, visitors might stay for weeks at my folks' farm. You're welcome for as long as you wish. Daniel promised he'd buy your ticket home after the wheat harvest."

"I don't want him to do that. I plan to buy my own ticket and be gone before harvesttime." Helena leaned against Sarah's shoulder, relishing her motherly touch. "My coming here has cost him enough already." She took a step toward the door. "Spalding is only two miles east, isn't it?"

"Two miles through dust an inch thick. If you wait until noon, Will can give you a ride in the wagon."

"You're kind to offer, but I don't want to take him from his work. I'm used to walking."

The road to town followed a straight line east, bordered by undulating hills covered with tufts of green grass. Small yellow sunflowers, purple lupine, and a cone-shaped white flower Helena didn't recognize flourished on the prairie. Few trees dotted the horizon.

After the first mile, perspiration trickled down her temples. As far as she could see, there wasn't a spot of shade anywhere on her route. One more thing to get used to out here.

Waters Grove had lived up to its name, with tree-lined streets stretching in every direction. She shook her head at the memory. Waters Grove wasn't home anymore.

Once she neared Spalding, the jingle of harnesses and rattle of wagons smothered the silence of the prairie. She stepped up onto a boardwalk lining a street crowded with false-fronted businesses. Signs outside the buildings advertised a laundry, a lawyer's office, and a market. As she walked farther, she spotted a café.

After stepping into shade offered by an overhanging roof on a mercantile, Helena noticed a sign on a drugstore across the wide street advertising liquors, groceries, and mine supplies. Noise from a saloon blatted through a set of swinging doors nearby.

" 'Scuse me, lady." Two men pushed past her from the open door of the mercantile. They carried wooden boxes to a wagon tied at a hitching rail then turned and reentered the building. Helena wrinkled her nose at the heavy smell of sweat that followed them. She stepped to one side and watched as they finished loading their wagon, unhitched their team, and joined a steady flow moving east on Spalding's main thoroughfare.

After a moment's decision, she backtracked to the café. Time spent cooking for her father and brother ought to qualify her for work in a kitchen. She entered, darting a quick look around the room. Faded blue-checked cloths covered four long tables. Matching fabric covered the single window. A chalkboard on the wall advertised the day's menu—beefsteak, fried potatoes, boiled greens. Coffee included. The only thing missing was customers to eat the food.

Puzzled, she turned toward the rear of the dining area at the same moment the door to the kitchen opened and a skinny man wearing stains on his shirt from the day's menu frowned at her. "Breakfast's six to nine. Dinner's at noon. Come back then." He took a step away then cocked his head at her. "You're dressed mighty fancy to be walking around Spalding this time o' day. You new here?"

Helena squared her shoulders. May as well ask and get it over with. "Yes, sir. I'm looking for a job and wondered if you need a cook."

"No need to call me 'sir.' Name's Oliver Austen, but folks call me Oily, for some reason. And I don't need a cook."

She pasted a small smile on her lips so he wouldn't see her disappointment. Silly of her to walk off the street and think she'd find work immediately. "I'm sorry to bother you. I'll be on my way."

"Wait. Can you serve tables?"

"Yes." Hope tingled up her spine.

"Girl I had quit on me yesterday. Plates and cutlery need to be set out. You want to start now, I'll give you a dollar a day." His gaze traveled from her silk bonnet to the pleated hem of her skirt. "Best wrap a towel around yourself and dress better tomorrow. And take off that hat."

A genuine smile lifted her lips after he returned to the kitchen. At a dollar a day, she'd have enough for a ticket to Spokane Falls long before harvesttime.

"Hey, girlie, come 'ere. We're outta potatoes."

"Over here, beefsteak's gone."

Helena hurried to answer the man who hollered for potatoes. When she reached over to lift the empty bowl, he leaned back in his chair and ran his hand over her hip. "You're a lot better lookin' than the last one Oily had in here."

Ignoring his comment, she jerked away from his reach then turned toward the men who wanted more beefsteak. Try as she might, she couldn't avoid the hands that grabbed at her. Men dressed in dusty denim and stained work shirts filled seats at all four tables.

Nausea rose in her throat as the odor of greasy fried meat combined with sweat circled the room like a thick fog. She returned to the kitchen with dragging steps and plunked the crockery platter and bowl next to the range.

Oily shook his head. "I counted them steaks—one apiece. No more." He shoveled several scoops of browned potatoes onto both the bowl and platter. "This'll fill 'em up. Pour more coffee. Be time to close soon anyways."

The men grumbled when she returned without beefsteak, but apparently they were used to Oily's ways and piled the fried potatoes on their plates. Carrying the oversize coffee boiler in both hands, Helena approached the tables, shuddering when men patted her backside as she leaned over to pour their coffee.

Once Oily locked the door after the last patron left, Helena sank onto a kitchen chair and closed her eyes. She couldn't remember when she'd been so tired. Her slim black boots were fashionable for train travel, but after three hours on her feet her toes throbbed. The thought of the walk back to the Hallidays' cabin loomed ahead like a judgment.

"Soon as you wash them dishes, you can go."

Oily had told her she was to serve tables. He didn't say a word about scullery work. Helena surveyed the lopsided stacks of greasy crockery piled next to a basin. Beneath her makeshift apron, she tightened her hands into fists.

"Yes, sir."

Chapter 6

Helena limped along the road leading to the Hallidays' farm. The route, which appeared so promising that morning, now seemed endless. Dusty flowers, limp grass, no birds.

She knew when she relayed the day's events to Sarah, the first thing the older woman would ask was, "Did you pray about it?"

She kicked at a pebble on the road. Once again, she hadn't prayed. Like the ticket to Spalding, Oily's offer seemed like a gift from heaven. And like the ticket, perhaps the offer was a test. Then she thought of the silver dollar in her handbag and lifted her chin. *What's done is done.*

A cloud of dust arose far down the road. As she squinted into the sun, the shape of a horse-drawn buggy emerged from the glare. She recognized Daniel McNabb's horse—a chestnut with black points.

She picked up her pace and strode purposefully ahead, ignoring the pain in her feet. Mr. McNabb didn't care about her problems. She'd acknowledge him with a wave and keep walking when he passed by.

As the buggy drew abreast of her, he jerked up on the reins. "Whoa, Ranger." She jumped out of the way when his horse sidestepped at the sudden stop.

"Miss Erickson? What are you doing out here?"

"Walking to Hallidays'." She kept her voice matter-of-fact, as though a walk to his neighbors' cabin in the heat of the afternoon was nothing unusual.

He leaned toward her from his perch on the buggy seat. "Get in. I'll take you there." A frown creased brows over deep-set eyes the color of melted chocolate.

Her heart gave an extra thump. If she didn't know better, she'd think he felt concerned for her welfare. "But you're going in the opposite direction."

"That's easily corrected." He patted the leather upholstery. "I'd help you up, but I need to hold the horse steady."

As soon as she seated herself next to him, he guided the animal in a wide half circle and headed west, holding the reins loosely in his broad hands. The rolled-up sleeves on his shirt gave her a glimpse of his strong forearms. She forced herself to look away. Mr. McNabb was simply being kind, nothing else.

He tipped his head in her direction. "It's not my business, but why are you out walking on such a warm day?"

"You're right, it's not your business." As soon as the words left her mouth, she regretted her sharp tone. "Forgive me. I didn't mean to be rude."

A slight smile lifted his lips. "Forgiven. Now will you answer my question?"

"I went to Spalding to find a job, and I succeeded. When you came along, I was on my way back to the Hallidays' cabin."

Silence hung between them for a moment. She hoped he wouldn't ask her where she went to work. Her job in the café was far from what she'd hoped for.

"Where'd you go to work?"

She lowered her head and mumbled, "A café next to the market."

"Oily's place?" He straightened on the seat, staring at her. "You didn't."

"I did. I told you I would earn my own train fare."

"Yes, but Oily's?" His jaw tightened.

The warmth between them cooled to studied politeness. When they arrived at the Hallidays' cabin, he tied his horse to the rail and helped her from the buggy. Her heart jolted when his calloused palm wrapped around her hand. She swallowed hard, summoning all her willpower not to squeeze his hand in return.

She moved toward the cabin then paused, using the hitching rail as a barrier between them. "I notice my trunk is no longer in your wagon. As soon as it's convenient, would you please bring it to me? I have need of my belongings." Her words were an understatement. After a hot day wrapped in her green wool travel suit, she didn't intend to wear the garment again until she boarded a train for Spokane Falls.

Mr. McNabb leaned against a buggy wheel, his face flushed. "I set the thing in the barn yesterday and then clean forgot it." He scrubbed his chin with his fist. "I'm sorry. I'll get your trunk here after supper tonight."

"Thank you." She walked toward the door, her sore toes forgotten for the moment. Tomorrow morning she'd wear one of the cotton dresses she brought from Waters Grove, along with comfortable shoes.

Better yet, she'd see Mr. McNabb one more time today.

Sarah and Helena stood side by side, peeling vegetables for a stew simmering on the range. After splashing her face with cool water and changing into her brown and gray plaid dress, Helena felt somewhat renewed after the hours at Oily's. So far, Sarah hadn't asked about her day, other than to cluck her tongue when Helena limped past her into Beth's room to change her clothes.

She gripped the knife she held, wondering how to broach the subject of lodging. Now that she'd found work, she'd need a permanent place to live until she left for Spokane Falls. Her throat tightened. This cabin and this family already felt like home.

Sarah dropped carrot chunks into the pot then drew two chairs away from the table. "Let's rest for a few minutes. I'm burning with curiosity. You said you found a job. Where is it?"

After experiencing Mr. McNabb's reaction, Helena lifted her chin before replying. "I was hired to serve tables in a café next to the market. Breakfast and—"

"Not Oily's!"

"Well, yes."

Sarah grabbed Helena's hands. "That's no place for a lady. He hires girls who like to . . .let's say 'flirt' with the men. His patrons expect to take liberties."

Her encounters with Oily's customers played across Helena's mind. From the other woman's words, she realized allowing the familiarity the men displayed was the reason Oily paid so well. Her stomach churned.

"I need the money he pays me," she whispered. "I'll only have to put up with the men for a couple of months." As she spoke, she felt her words fall around her like flames, singeing her conscience. Tears trickled over her cheeks. "Oh, Sarah, what am I saying! I left an unhappy life in Waters Grove, and now I've created something far worse here."

She fled to Beth's room and curled up on the bed, burying her face in the pillow to muffle her sobs. Oily expected her at six tomorrow morning. She cringed away from the thought of serving breakfast while allowing herself to be fondled by anyone who wanted to touch her.

The first prayer she'd uttered since her mother died burst from her lips. "Lord, help me!"

Daniel led his horse into its stall and poured a measure of grain into a trough. Without intending to, he glanced toward the empty stalls at the rear of the solid log structure. Although six months had passed, Daniel still expected to look up and see his brother caring for their draft horses. One decision that could never be taken back had changed everything.

He raked his fingers through his hair and strode to where he'd left Miss Erickson's trunk inside the open barn door. The memory of her crimson face when he saw her limping along the road wouldn't leave his mind. It was a wonder she hadn't collapsed from the heat.

One thing he'd say for her, she was determined. The kind of woman needed out here. As quickly as the thought arose, he dismissed the notion. He said he'd pay her fare back to Illinois, and he'd keep his word, no matter how much her ivory skin and cloud-like hair haunted his hours.

If he had enough money, he'd pay her fare right now rather than see her serve tables at Oily's. Everyone in Spalding knew the stories about that place, yet in her innocence she'd walked into Oily's web.

He grabbed her trunk and heaved it into the back of his buggy.

Helena savored bites of her dried-apple pie. After her afternoon at Oily's, the sweet treat helped dim the memory of men and greasy food odors. Mr. Halliday lifted his gaze from his plate to give her an appreciative smile.

"Sarah tells me I have you to thank for this pie."

"I'm happy to help. I feel I've done so little to thank you for allowing me to stay here."

Smile lines creased his weathered cheeks. He lifted his fork in a salute. "Pie like this, you can stay as long as you want."

Sarah shook her head at him. "Will, you make it sound like you never get dessert." Her chuckle took the sting from her comment.

"Guess I better mind my tongue, eh?" He winked at Helena.

Silent mealtimes with her father and brother left her unsure of how to respond. Helena couldn't remember a time when her father had winked at her, or teased her as Mr. Halliday did. She drew a breath. "Well, sir—"

"Sorry to be late." Mr. McNabb stood framed in the open doorway. "Got Miss Erickson's trunk out in the wagon." He tipped his head toward her. "Tell me where you want it and I'll fetch it in."

Her chair screeched on the wooden floor as she jumped to her feet, an embarrassed flush warming her cheeks. She hadn't taken into account the limited space in the small cabin. As far as she could tell, there wasn't room anywhere to put her trunk. Her gaze landed on Mr. Halliday.

"Sir? Should I ask him to take my belongings to the barn?"

"Absolutely not. You're our guest, not one of the horses." He chuckled at his own humor. "Daniel, put the trunk over there inside the door. I'll take care of it later."

Helena stood next to the rocking chair beneath the cabin window, watching while Mr. McNabb came through the door with his burden. She wrapped her arms around her middle as a sensation of loss swept through her.

If only they'd met under different circumstances.

Chapter 7

That evening, Mr. Halliday maneuvered Helena's trunk into a tiny spot next to her bed and bid her good night. She heard his and Sarah's voices murmuring from their room across the cabin.

Unable to sleep, she lit a lamp and opened the domed top of the trunk to expose her belongings. Her heart bumped in her throat at the sight of folded linens she'd packed from her bridal chest. Instead of being a bride, she'd be what? An old maid living in Spokane Falls, far from everyone. She clenched her fists until her nails dug into her palms.

"Take no thought for the morrow." Her grip relaxed. "Yes, Lord," she whispered. On her knees, she searched for her mother's gold-trimmed teacup and saucer, praying they were unharmed. Dropping linens, towels, and dresses beside her on the bed, she continued to burrow through her possessions. When she reached the center of the chest, she felt the outline of a cup. She sucked in a breath. Gently, she peeled back the shawl she'd used as padding and grasped her prize. Lamplight bounced off the gold fleur-de-lis pattern.

Tears clouded her vision. She'd packed the pink china with such high hopes, and ended up serving tables in an unsavory café. Those tickets were definitely a test, not a gift. After placing the teacup and saucer on the bureau, she blew out the lamp.

Helena awakened to the sound of utensils clinking against pottery. Dim light filtered from the kitchen area. Without a window in her room, she couldn't guess the time, but she hoped she hadn't slept through breakfast. She stepped into her gray and brown plaid dress, fastened the buttons, then peered into the tiny mirror above the bureau while she twisted her hair into a bun. After slipping on her shoes, she hurried to the main room.

"Good morning, Helena. You're just in time." Sarah turned from the range, holding a platter of flapjacks. "Eggs will be ready in a moment." Grant and Beth greeted her with mischievous smiles, as though they shared a secret.

Helena glanced from one smiling face to another. "Where's Mr. Halliday? He's usually the first one up, isn't he?"

"He had to take care of early chores. I'll keep his food warm. The rest of you go ahead." Keeping her back turned, Sarah slid a filled plate into the oven.

Helena hesitated. Brilliant sunshine flared through the window, painting the room with shades of gold and orange. "Perhaps I'd better be on my way. I told Mr.

Austen—Oily—that I'd be there at six."

When Beth snickered, Grant elbowed her in the side. "Eat your breakfast and hush." He looked up at Helena. "Mama makes good flapjacks. You'll have plenty of time."

At Beth's laughter, Helena's skin crawled with humiliation. Even a girl as young as Beth knew what she faced at Oily's. She kept her head down so they wouldn't see the tears that stung her eyes. Hand trembling, she forked a single flapjack onto her plate, managing to chew and swallow.

In spite of Grant's assurance about the time, she finished her portion quickly, thanked Sarah for the meal, and hurried out the door. Cool morning air carried the sweet scent of grasses. When she looked back over her shoulder, the rows of young leaves in the Hallidays' wheat fields glowed green in the spreading sunlight.

Sarah had told her that Mr. McNabb also raised wheat. Imagine living in a little cabin and working alongside him to prove up their claim. Helena bit her lip. She wished she'd never come to Spalding. The knowledge of what she'd missed would forever dim the luster of anything her future might hold.

A puff of air pushed her bonnet forward, and when she resettled the wide-brimmed hat over her hair, she noticed a man on horseback galloping toward her. In moments, Mr. Halliday reined the animal to a stop and shot her a broad smile.

"Hoped I'd catch you before you left, but this'll do."

"What's wrong?" She choked out the question over the pounding of her heart.

He slid from the horse to stand facing her. "Not one thing. Contrariwise, I have good news—you don't work at Oily's any longer."

"What?"

His grin grew wider. "I just came from there. Told him you were not coming back, ever. Then I went down the street to Wolford's Mercantile. Horace admitted he could use some help."

Dizziness threatened to topple her. She reached out to place a steadying hand on the horse's neck. "I. . .I don't know what to say. Why would you do this for me?"

"I look at you, I see my Beth in a few years. I pray someone would help her if she found herself in a—" He lifted his hat and raked his fingers through his graying hair. "Let's say, a bad situation."

Helena fought for composure. Through a mist of tears, the morning appeared brighter, the grass greener, and the flowers more colorful. A meadowlark sang as it glided overhead.

"Saying thank you doesn't seem like enough, Mr. Halliday. I'm truly grateful."

"Glad to do it." His face reddened. "I'm not used to being 'mister' all the time. How about you call me Uncle Will?"

"Thank you. I'd be honored." Her voice hitched on a sob.

Leading his horse, he walked beside her as they returned to the cabin.

Later that morning, Uncle Will took Helena's elbow and escorted her through the entrance to Wolford's Mercantile. Mingled aromas of pickles, kerosene, leather, and who knew what else met them inside. Once over the threshold, he whispered next to her ear. "That's Horace up on the ladder back there. He's expecting you."

A pulse fluttered in her throat. She'd do her best to please the storekeeper so Uncle Will would have no cause to regret helping her. While they waited, Mr. Wolford hung the lantern he held from a rafter and clambered down to greet them. With his drooping mustache and tired eyes, he reminded her of a basset hound one of her Illinois neighbors owned. She ducked her head to hide a quick smile.

"This the young lady you mentioned?" Mr. Wolford spoke in a high-pitched voice that carried a tone of skepticism. "Looks too puny to be much help around here."

"She'll soon prove you wrong." Uncle Will gave her elbow a slight squeeze.

Helena lifted her chin. "I'm a hard worker, sir. Sweeping, dusting, keeping your shelves tidy—I can do all that. If you wish, I can tend to your accounts. My father—"

"Don't need no one to trifle with my accounts. If you're ready to work, there's a crate of crockery open in the back. Find a good place and stack the plates on a shelf."

She bowed her head. "Yes, sir."

After thanking Uncle Will for escorting her to town, she walked toward the rear of the building, passing countertops covered with jars of candy, boxes of cigars, and numerous small items. The floor-to-ceiling shelves seemed to be bursting with goods. *Could be that's why Mr. Wolford hasn't unpacked the crockery.* Near the crate she noticed a bare space between rolls of colorful calico and an assortment of patent medicines. She pushed the open container toward the shelf and reached inside for the first plate.

Shoppers came and went, but apparently Mr. Wolford didn't intend to allow her to help him with customers. He kept her busy arranging merchandise in the dim interior. Fine, then. This was better than serving tables at Oily's. She bent to arrange the nail bins beneath the shelves holding tools. If nails were in order according to size, people would have an easier time making a selection.

"Miss Erickson." She spun around at the sound of his voice.

"Yes, sir?"

"Time to lock up." His gaze traveled over the shelves she'd tidied, then moved down to the bins at her feet. One corner of his mustache twitched in a near smile. "Looks like you'll work out. Pay is four dollars a week. Course since this is Thursday, and tomorrow's Decoration Day, I'll give you two dollars on Saturday."

"Thank you. I'll be here."

He grunted acknowledgement, strode to the front door, and held it open for her. She followed, pausing when she noticed copies of *The Spokane Falls Review* stacked on the counter.

"Excuse me, sir, may I purchase a newspaper?"

"That's last week's. Just take one." The smile in his eyes belied his gruff response.

With the paper folded under one arm, she hurried out the door, eager to return to the Hallidays' and begin making plans.

Chapter 8

Daniel passed beneath the flag flying at the entrance to the small Grand Army of the Republic cemetery. Rows of graves marked with either simple wooden crosses or carved headstones created a boundary between the cemetery and the rear of Spalding's only church. Several families had already arrived to tidy and decorate graves of Union soldiers who had ties to the community.

He turned to his left, his goal an upright stone with a cross engraved above the words:

ROSS MCNABB
DIED
DEC. 10 A.D. 1883
AGED 37 Y'S, 6 M'S & 1 DAY

Daniel carried no flowers. Ross would laugh at him for strewing flowers over his grave. When he reached the stone he removed his hat and bowed his head.

"Should've been me, Ross. We were partners, meant to be a team." Fresh grief for his brother choked him. He took a deep breath and continued. "You'd be proud to see this year's wheat. It's coming in good. I'll prove up our claim next year." He stood for another moment, as though expecting a response, then wiped his eyes with the back of his hand.

As he stepped away, he noticed people nearby arranging wildflower bouquets on three side-by-side graves. Taking a second look, he recognized Will's family—and Miss Erickson. She glanced up and saw him at the same moment. Her cheeks pinked.

"Good day, Mr. McNabb."

"Good day to you." Pretty girl like that, shame she'd decided to serve tables at that disreputable café. He wondered why Oily had allowed her time away. Normally he kept his doors open every day but Sunday.

Will raised his hand in greeting. "We brought a picnic. Join us."

"Oh, yes, do." Sarah gave him a bright smile. She placed the bouquet she held beneath a wooden cross next to her feet. "The food's in the wagon. We'll eat in the churchyard." After taking a final glance at her handiwork, she led the way out of the cemetery.

Beth and Miss Erickson followed her, with Will, Grant, and Daniel at the rear of the procession. The ladies spread a quilt over the grass and then waited while he helped carry food hampers from Hallidays' buckboard.

After Sarah unpacked bowls filled with fried chicken, beet salad, and biscuits, she dipped into a smaller basket and drew out a square cake covered with caramel-colored icing. "Helena made this for us. It has blackberry jam inside." She patted a space between her and Miss Erickson. "Come, sit."

He sat cross-legged on the edge of the quilt. Surely Sarah wasn't matchmaking after knowing how Miss Erickson came to be in Spalding in the first place. But, matchmaking or not, he couldn't sit there like a lump. He should make polite conversation.

"That looks tasty. I haven't had a bite of cake in some time."

A pleased expression crossed Miss Erickson's face. "I hope you like it. Blackberry cake is my father's favorite." He had to scoot closer to hear her soft voice.

It occurred to him to ask how her father felt about her traveling so far from home, but he decided the question might be too personal. He rubbed his damp palms on his trouser legs, telling himself the cause wasn't Miss Erickson's nearness. The sun overhead would make anyone sweat.

When Will turned the conversation to comments about the cemetery and the veterans represented there, Daniel relaxed and focused on his plate.

Helena stole a glance at Mr. McNabb as she lifted a buttered biscuit to her mouth. Her hand trembled. Every time she thought she'd managed to put him out of her mind, circumstances brought them together again. If only she'd been the one he'd proposed to.

A silent moment passed while she cast about for something to say. Then, with a nod toward the cemetery entrance, she asked, "Mr. McNabb, did you know one of the veterans buried there?"

He choked on a mouthful of food.

The Hallidays all gaped at her. Sarah reached over and clasped Helena's free hand then turned her full attention to Mr. McNabb.

"I'm sorry, Daniel. We haven't mentioned anything about—"

"Don't apologize, Sarah. It's my story to tell." He set his half-filled plate on the quilt, his gaze landing on Helena. "My brother, Ross, is buried here. He survived the war but passed on last winter. It was. . .a terrible waste."

Her throat tightened at the pain in his eyes. "I'm so sorry. That was a thoughtless question."

"Not at all. It's natural to wonder." He rose, thanked Sarah for the meal, and strode toward his horse.

Moisture stung Helena's eyes as she watched him ride away. "Oh my goodness, the poor man. I had no idea. I just wanted to be friendly."

Sarah slid closer to her and slipped her arm around Helena's waist. "Don't reproach yourself, dear. Daniel won't talk to anybody about his brother's death. I think he'd feel much better if he had someone who would to listen to him. We hoped—" She cupped her free hand over her mouth. "Never mind."

"I know what you're thinking." A tear slid down her cheek. "You hoped he would have a bride by now. Instead, I arrived."

"It's been a blessing to have you with us." Sarah pulled her into a hug. "I'm thankful you're here."

Beth hurried to Helena's side. "We're all thankful. Please don't cry."

Sniffling, Helena leaned against Sarah and brushed the tears away. As kind as the Hallidays were, she looked forward to the day she could leave. She had no place in this community.

Chapter 9

Daniel leaned on a hoe while watching a buckboard rattle down the track toward his cabin. A woman held the reins. In the time it took him to prop the tool against the fence, Sarah Halliday reached the hitching post and clambered from the wagon.

"I brought you some bread, just baked this morning." She held a towel-wrapped bundle toward him.

"Mighty kind of you." He dusted his hands on the sides of his trousers then reached out to take the loaves. He gestured toward his shaded porch. "Come out of the sun for a few minutes. I just fetched water from the spring—it's still cold. Then you can tell me what really brings you here."

Sarah chuckled as she stepped up onto the porch. "Now, why would you say that?"

"Maybe 'cause you haven't brought food by since Ross. . .passed." He carried the bread inside and returned with two water-filled tumblers. After seating himself next to her, he sent her a searching glance. "Does Will need help with something? You know I'm happy to lend a hand."

"I'm here to talk about you, not Will." She took a sip of her water. "We haven't seen you in church for weeks. Fact is, we haven't seen you on the road since Decoration Day. I know you like to keep to yourself, but no church? No trips to town? Did Miss Erickson upset you that much last month?"

He shifted in his chair and stared out at his garden patch. Sometimes Sarah treated him as though he were no older than her son. His stomach muscles tightened. From experience, he knew she'd continue to probe until she felt satisfied with his answers. He huffed out a breath.

"Miss Erickson's question hasn't kept me from town."

"Then what has?"

"I don't like passing by the café, knowing she works for Oily to earn money to leave. It's my fault she's here. I've brought her to ruin. I never—"

Sarah set her glass down with a thump. "She only worked there the one time. Will put a stop to it the next morning."

Relief washed over him, cool as spring water. He strode to the edge of the porch and stood with his back to her. He'd imagined her sullied by Oily's rough clientele, when she was—

A board creaked when he swung around to face Sarah. "Then where is she?"

"Living with us. She's helping Mr. Wolford at the mercantile, and he seems pleased with her work." She sent him a pitying glance. "You can't hide out here forever. As I recall, your birthday is at the end of this week."

"On Saturday, the twenty-eighth. How did you know?"

"Women remember these things. Come for supper. And leave your guilt at home."

"Yes, ma'am." His face burned while he unhitched her horse, helped her into the buckboard, and watched the dust rise as she traveled back to her farm.

Truth be told, his supplies were running low. Time for a trip to the mercantile.

Mr. Wolford paused at the entrance. "You sure you're able to deal with customers while I'm at the bank?"

Helena subdued a tickle of excitement. For weeks, while stocking shelves and sweeping floors, she'd hoped for this opportunity. Now she'd have a chance to show him her capabilities. She smiled and nodded. "Yes, sir. Please don't worry."

After he left, she moved behind the counter to stand between the coffee mill and the scales. The door stood open to catch what little breeze might blow through. Horses and wagons passed by in both directions, but this late in the day shoppers had apparently decided to stay at home. She drummed her fingers on the countertop. *Please, Lord, just one customer.*

Slow minutes ticked by. To occupy her time, she opened the display case beneath the scales and bent down to arrange wind-up toys, harmonicas, and china dolls in some semblance of order. At this season of the year, few children received a new plaything, but by Christmas she knew little hands would be pressed to the front of the case.

She bit her lip. It wouldn't do to become too attached to this tiny community. By Christmas, she'd be in Spokane Falls. Someone else would sell these toys to eager children.

"Is anyone here?" A male voice interrupted her thoughts.

"Yes, one moment." Helena jumped to her feet and froze. Mr. McNabb stood inside the door, a sheet of paper in his hand. Her pulse raced. She'd been sure they'd never meet again after her thoughtless remark at the cemetery.

He touched the brim of his hat, a half smile playing across his lips. "Miss Erickson. I need a few items. Is Mr. Wolford here?"

"He stepped out for a bit. I can help you." She swallowed the squeak in her voice. "May I see your list?"

His fingers brushed hers when he handed her the paper. To hide her heated cheeks, she dipped her head as she read aloud. "Coffee, salt, flour, beans, sugar. Cartridges, powder, birdshot. Goodness, quite a list." She felt herself flush a second time. She shouldn't make personal comments.

"I've been. . .distracted. Let things run out."

"Tell me how much you need of the bulk items and we'll have this together in no time. I'm sure you already know where the ammunition is kept." She did her best to imitate Mr. Wolford's brisk manner.

Mr. McNabb blinked then told her the quantities he needed. As soon as he finished speaking, she bustled toward a row of bins and began filling bags with his supplies. All too soon, she had his purchases totaled and wrapped.

She added the amount of the sale to the day's ledger page. "Thank you." She used her best Mr. Wolford voice as she handed him his change.

He jingled the coins from hand to hand. Cleared his throat. "I don't suppose you'd like me to take you home after closing. I'm going that way."

She hesitated a long moment before lifting her gaze to meet his.

"That would be fine. Thank you."

On Saturday, the savory aroma of stewed chicken greeted Helena when she entered the Hallidays' cabin after work. Sarah stood in the kitchen area cutting strips of dough into short pieces. She glanced up from her task.

"You're just in time. Daniel will be here soon."

Helena tensed. Mr. McNabb never had supper with them. She folded her arms across her waist and stepped next to the aproned woman. "I hope you're not matchmaking." She kept a smile on her lips to take the harshness from her words. "You know I plan to leave in August."

"I do know that." The knife Sarah held made rhythmic bumping sounds as a pile of noodles accumulated on the cutting board. She paused to look at Helena. "Today's his birthday. It didn't seem right to leave the poor man alone in his cabin. He'll be missing his brother. They always celebrated their birthdays together."

"I'm sorry, Sarah. I spoke without thinking."

"Nothing to be sorry for, dear. I have been known to indulge in matchmaking from time to time." She patted Helena's shoulder with a floury hand. "Now you might want to take a moment to tidy your hair and splash on a bit of rosewater."

Helena suppressed a smile as she turned toward her room. Birthday or not, Sarah sounded like a matchmaker.

Within the next half hour, Uncle Will, Beth, and Grant had washed at the basin on the porch and escorted Mr. McNabb to the festive meal. The fragrance of chicken and noodles rose from a tureen at one end of the table. Bowls of nutmeg squash and boiled new potatoes rested between a plate of sliced bread and one of fresh butter.

The tantalizing meal did nothing to settle the butterflies in Helena's stomach. She hadn't expected Sarah to seat her next to Mr. McNabb, but Sarah insisted. While Uncle Will said grace, Helena prayed she could calm down enough to eat.

As food was handed from one to another around the table, she sensed Mr. McNabb's eyes on her. He took up the tureen.

"I'll hold this while you serve yourself. It's heavy."

Helena murmured her thanks and ladled a small portion onto her plate. His kindness left her feeling unsettled, as did his plans to buy her ticket to Illinois. He owed her nothing. As soon as wheat harvest commenced, she'd leave for Spokane Falls. If he believed she returned to Illinois, so much the better.

Family chatter rose and fell during the meal, providing a welcome distraction. She tried not to notice how Mr. McNabb's damp red hair curled at the back of his neck. Or the way his blue chambray shirt stretched over his broad shoulders.

She excused herself to clear the table as soon as everyone finished. While she stacked soiled dishes in the basin, Sarah bustled over to a round tin box near the stove. The cover clattered to one side when she opened the container and lifted out a dessert.

With a flourish, she placed the caramel-frosted cake in front of Daniel. "Happy birthday!" Her blue eyes twinkled at Helena. "Would you mind serving, since it's your recipe?"

"I'd be happy to." She hoped Sarah heard the note of wry amusement in her voice. Not matchmaking, indeed.

After everyone received a slice, Helena tasted the jam-swirled cake, savoring the mixture of caramel icing and tart blackberry preserves. "This is delicious, Sarah."

"Indeed it is." Daniel rested his fork on his plate. "Best I ever ate."

Uncle Will reared back in his chair. "This is just a sample. Helena treats us to her cooking every Sunday." He patted his stomach. "She and Sarah are quite a pair at the stove."

Beth and Grant added their enthusiastic praise as they passed their plates for second servings.

Helena stifled a groan. The Hallidays were dear people, but Mr. McNabb couldn't possibly be interested in her cooking abilities, or anything else about her for that matter.

At bedtime, Beth followed Helena into her room. Helena watched as Beth moved the folded newspaper to one side and laid a gentle finger on the pink and gold cup and saucer atop the bureau.

"These are so pretty."

"They were my mother's. I put them there to remind me of her." She paused. Maybe the girl resented giving up her space in the small cabin. "But this is really your room. Would you like me to put them away?"

"Oh, no. We don't have many pretty things anymore. When we came from Illinois, we only had one wagon to carry all our belongings. Mama cried when she had to leave so much behind."

Helena sat on the edge of the bed and patted the space beside her.

Beth nestled close. "I like having you here. I wish you'd stay." She pointed at the newspaper. "I hope you don't think I was snooping, but when I put my clean clothes away I saw you had circled some advertisements. That's *The Spokane Falls Review*—are you going there?"

Her woebegone expression tore at Helena's heart. She slipped her arm around Beth's waist. "Yes. As soon as I earn enough money. I circled advertisements for rooms to rent so I know how much I'll need."

"Is that why you give Mama a dollar each Saturday? To live here?"

"It's only right, Beth. Groceries cost money."

"If you have to pay anyway, why not stay here?" Beth stood, giving her a knowing smile. "I see how Mr. McNabb watches you. I think he's sorry he didn't take you for his bride."

Helena shook her head. "I doubt that very much. You know he's planning to buy my train ticket as soon as the harvest comes in."

"Maybe he's changed his mind." Beth moved to the doorway. "I think you should pray about it. Good night, Helena."

After she left, Helena stared down at her hands. Life seemed so simple to a thirteen-year-old. Just because Mr. McNabb enjoyed her cake recipe didn't mean he'd changed his mind.

Chapter 10

Helena tucked the newspaper into her satchel when she left for work the following Monday. Two of the advertisements for rooms looked promising. When she had an opportunity, she'd go to the post office and send letters of inquiry.

Mr. Wolford greeted her at the door of the mercantile. A smile lifted his droopy mustache. "You did a fine job when I was gone last week. The ledger balanced and the store is in good order."

"Thank you, sir. I'm glad you were pleased."

"Indeed I am." He stepped away to hold the door for her then followed her inside as she placed her satchel behind a counter. When she looked up, he was studying her with a thoughtful expression. "Would you be able to manage things here for a few weeks? Just for part of each day?" When she hesitated, he hurried on. "I'd add another dollar a week to your salary, of course."

The extra money would assure her of enough funds to make a new start in Spokane Falls. Then her mind flitted over rough miners who came in for supplies, homesteaders who asked for credit until crops came in, and housewives who haggled over every penny. Waiting on customers was one thing, but being responsible for the business was a great deal more.

She sucked in a deep breath. Beth suggested she pray about leaving. Perhaps the opportunity to earn extra money was her answer. "Thank you for your confidence in me. When will I start?"

"This afternoon. Mrs. Wolford is ill, and I need to be at home more to tend to her."

"Gracious. I'll do my best for you, sir."

"I'll be counting on you." He strode to the stairs at the rear of the store and climbed to the loft where he kept extra merchandise. Dust motes sifted down between the planks as he moved about overhead.

Helena lifted her chin. Managing a mercantile hadn't been in her plans when she boarded the train in Illinois. She prayed this wasn't another test.

With Mr. Wolford's permission, Helena used her dinnertime to walk to the post office. "One block east," he'd said. "In a white clapboard house across from the church. Walk on in—there's no sign out front."

While she waited for a break in the flow of horses and wagons before crossing the wide thoroughfare in front of the mercantile, she smiled at the idea of a post office located in someone's house. In Waters Grove, the postal service had a proper building with a sign next to the door. Everything here appeared to have been constructed in haste as settlers flocked in to homestead land. Spalding represented the change she'd hoped for. What she hadn't expected was having to leave.

After hurrying across the road, she circled to the next block. Her heart sank at the sight of three white clapboard houses across the street from the church. Which door to enter?

She squared her shoulders and considered the house directly facing the church. If this were the wrong one, she'd already have narrowed her choices by a third. She marched up the walkway, climbed the porch steps, and opened the door. The hinges emitted a protesting squeak. Instead of entering a parlor or a sitting room, a bulky rolltop desk, occupying most of the opposite wall, met her eyes. The space smelled of paper and dust. A tall counter stood beneath a window on the east side. Two inkwells, pens, and paper rested on top.

She startled when a pocket door next to the desk slid back and a tall blond man stepped through the opening.

"Mail hasn't come through yet this week. Try again Wednesday."

"I was hoping to purchase writing materials from you. I need to send two letters." She pointed to the stacked paper on the table. "This is the post office, isn't it?"

"You must be new here." His hazel eyes shone from his tanned face. "I'm Cliff Kendrick. Welcome to Spalding's post office."

She relaxed at the warmth in his voice. "Thank you. I'm Helena Erickson."

"I hope there's a 'miss' in front of your name."

"Why would you ask such a question?" Her voice cooled several degrees.

"Beg your pardon. Unmarried ladies are rare in these parts."

The room seemed to shrink. This might be a post office, but it was also a private home and she was alone with a man who towered over her. She sidled toward the writing table. "Would you please excuse me while I dash off two brief letters? My employer will come looking for me if I don't return soon."

His face reddened. "Certainly. I'll post them for you as soon as the mail wagon arrives." He retreated to a space next to the desk and stared at his boots.

Her pen scratched over the paper as she composed brief inquiries to rooming houses in Spokane Falls. She addressed the envelopes and handed them to Mr. Kendrick.

After tearing two stamps from a sheet on the desktop, he licked the backs then pasted them on the envelopes. "Four cents for the stamps, and four cents for the writing materials. Please." He spoke in clipped tones.

"Thank you." Helena placed the coins in his open palm. "Do you know how long it takes for mail delivery between here and Spokane Falls?"

"Mail service is tri-weekly." His warm grin returned. "If it doesn't come through one week, they try again the next."

Despite her efforts to remain aloof, a giggle bubbled up. "I'll remember that. Thank you." She turned toward the entrance.

He stepped around her and held the door open. "Pleasure meeting you. Who did you say your employer was?"

"Mr. Wol—" Her hand flew to her mouth. "I didn't say. Good day, Mr. Kendrick."

Daniel hefted split pine rails into the back of his farm wagon. He wiped sweat from his forehead, grateful for the shade of the forested canyon. With this load he'd have enough material to build a long-overdue fence next to his barn. A breeze sighed through the long needles on the ponderosas, trailing a resin scent in its wake.

He flopped down on the soft ground to catch his breath before driving the wagon the eight miles to his homestead. This task had been easier with Ross's help.

Everything had been easier.

Hunger rumbled his stomach. If he had a wife, she would have packed a picnic basket and come with him. Maybe there'd be a blackberry cake in the basket. He closed his eyes, imagining Miss Erickson's moonlight-colored hair falling around her shoulders as she served his food. His eyes flew open. *Stop dreaming, McNabb. She can't wait to get away from you.*

Nevertheless, on the return trip to his cabin his thoughts jumped to winning her heart. Nothing overt. He didn't want to chase her off—again. Her resourceful character and serene beauty had proved over and over that he'd made a fatal mistake by failing to listen to her explanation when she arrived. Now that he wanted her as his bride he had no idea where to start.

He fell into bed that night, exhausted. The rails were stacked, he'd cleared the ground where the fence would be built, but instead of planning tomorrow's workday, he decided to visit the mercantile as soon as it opened in the morning.

At first light, he heated water for a bath. No reason he couldn't bathe on a Tuesday instead of Saturday. Wood chips floated on the water as he scrubbed yesterday's toil from his hair.

He dressed in clean clothes, stepped into polished boots, and strode out to saddle Ranger. His wheat crop glowed green in the clear morning air. He nodded with satisfaction at the maturing plants, already heading and ready for pollination. Another five or six weeks and he could begin the harvest. In the meantime, he'd do all he could to win Helena's heart.

Daniel whistled as he rode to town. Such a fine day for new beginnings. The door to the mercantile stood open when he tied Ranger to the hitching rail. He bounded onto the board sidewalk and strode into the building, stopping short when he saw Miss Erickson in conversation with a tall man who had his back to the entrance. A smile lit her face.

Daniel cleared his throat, but she didn't seem to notice him. Instead, she poured coffee beans into the mill.

"You said a pound?" She lifted her gaze to the man's face.

"Yes, please, Miss Erickson."

Was it his imagination, or did her customer stress the word 'miss'? A high-pitched sound rose from the grinder as she cranked the handle, drowning out further conversation. Daniel stepped to the counter while she scooped fragrant coffee into a paper bag. He narrowed his eyes when he recognized Cliff Kendrick, the postmaster, one of Spalding's many bachelors.

"McNabb, isn't it? No mail for you lately. Hope that saves you a trip."

"Appreciate that." He didn't need Kendrick to tell him he had no mail. The only letters he'd received over the past months were from Felicia Trimble—or rather, Miss Erickson's brother. A fresh wave of discouragement rocked him. If only they'd met some other way, he'd be courting her by now.

After Helena gave the postmaster his purchase, he placed his free hand on the counter. "May I see you home this evening?" He glanced at Mr. McNabb and lowered his voice. "Tell me what time you leave and I'll be here."

Her face warmed. Mr. Kendrick was practically a stranger. One visit to the post office didn't make them friends. Too much could happen on the lonely stretch of road from town to the Hallidays' cabin. "No, thank you."

"Then how about letting me escort you to the Fourth of July celebration this Friday?"

"Thank you, but, no."

"Why not?"

"We don't know each other at all."

"Spending time together is how we'll get acquainted."

Mr. McNabb folded his arms across his broad chest. "She said no. Maybe you'd better head back to the post office." He spoke in a low growl.

"Maybe you'd better tend to your own business."

"Gentlemen, please." She frowned at both of them. "If you're going to argue, do it elsewhere."

The postmaster tipped his hat. "I'll come back when you're not busy." With a glare in Mr. McNabb's direction, he stomped out the door.

As soon as he left, she jammed her hands on her hips. "You didn't need to do that. I'm quite capable of taking care of myself." Inside, she felt a tiny thrill that he cared enough to defend her.

"I'll remember that next time." A muscle twitched in his jaw.

"There won't be a next time."

He held up his hand, palm out. "Let's move on, please. I'm here to purchase a couple pounds of sixteen-penny nails."

"Right back here." She led the way to the nail bins, relieved that the tension between them had eased. To lighten the mood, she paused and turned to him with a smile. "Sixteens are big nails. What are you building?"

"A fence beside my barn. Going to get a cow and have to keep her in."

"A cow." She suppressed a chuckle at the image of his strong hands juggling milk pans and churning butter. "So you'll need milk pails and so forth?" From his stunned expression, she surmised he hadn't thought beyond obtaining the animal.

He rubbed his chin. "Well, not today. Have to get the cow first."

"Absolutely. Nails today, pails another time." A smile lifted her lips. "Nails are right over there."

She turned away when a man entered carrying a wooden crate. "Please excuse me,

Mr. McNabb. Just bring your purchase to the front when you're ready." With quick steps she hurried toward her next customer. From his dusty clothing to his scraggly beard, he looked like one more person hoping to strike gold in Idaho.

He gave her an approving glance as she approached. "You the owner's daughter?"

"No, sir. I'm his employee. Mr. Wolford will return later this afternoon."

"No matter. You look like you'll do fine." He dropped the crate at his feet and handed her a wrinkled page obviously torn from a newspaper. "Here's what I need to set up in Mullan."

She noticed dirt caked beneath his fingernails when she plucked the paper from his hands. The printed sheet contained two columns headed "Prospector's Supply List." After scanning the columns, she looked up at him. "I haven't seen a list like this before. Where did you get it?"

"Baker City paper, down in Oregon. Placer mines there petered out, but Mullan's coming on strong. I aim to get rich."

Helena nodded toward the crate. "You'll need another box to hold all of this."

"Then pick what'll fit. I'll make do."

"Gold pan, gold scales, bacon, flour. . ." Her voice trailed off as she read to the bottom of one column then focused on the next. "Boots, stockings, two blankets—"

"Make that one blanket, and forget the stockings."

"But, sir—"

Mr. McNabb stepped next to her. "Excuse the interruption. You'll need those blankets. Mountain winters are bitter cold." His intense expression set her customer back a pace. "Don't skimp on waterproof boots or heavy underwear, either."

The man snorted. "It must be ninety-five degrees today and you're blathering about heavy underwear?"

"Winter comes quick in the mountains."

"Fill the crate, miss. I can't pay for no more." He shoved his thumbs in the front pockets of his canvas trousers. "And step lively. We're burning daylight."

Mr. McNabb shook his head and strode to the back of the building without further comment.

Drawing a deep breath, Helena carried items from the shelves and packed all she could into the wooden crate, completing the order by tucking a thick woolen blanket over the top. When she told the man his total, he tightened his jaw and counted the exact amount into her palm. Then he slung the filled container onto one shoulder and marched to a horse and wagon tied in front of the boardwalk.

After he left, she walked to the rear of the store. "I pray he finds enough gold to buy more supplies. Thank you for trying to help, Mr. McNabb."

He turned around, face pale. "Wish he'd listened." His color returned as a smile crinkled the corners of his eyes. "At any rate, would you please call me Daniel? We've known each other for several weeks now."

"I feel unworthy, considering how we met."

"Then let's start today. Call me Daniel."

Her heart bloomed at his kindness. "All right. . .Daniel. I'm Helena."

Chapter 11

On Friday, Helena rose early to help prepare food for their Fourth of July picnic. She decided to wear her blue gingham dress, and on impulse tied a red scarf around her waist as a sash. Carrying her apron, she hurried out to the kitchen area, where the fragrance of vanilla and cinnamon rose from a tray of doughnuts cooling beneath the window.

"Don't you look festive!" Sarah gave her a one-armed hug and returned to slicing baked ham into sandwich-sized portions. "Beth and Grant are out finishing their chores. I saved the cucumber salad for you to make. Everything's on the table."

As Helena completed tossing sliced vegetables with vinegar and sugar, Uncle Will strode into the room dressed in his cavalry uniform. The heels of his shiny black boots rapped on the plank floor as he crossed to Sarah's side. "I'll be hitching the wagon now. Daniel should be here soon."

His wife paused in her task to smile up at him. "You'll be the best-looking soldier in the parade. You're still the handsome man I met twenty years ago."

"And you're still the prettiest girl in town." He squeezed her shoulder and strode out the door.

Helena's heart twisted at the obvious love the two of them shared. Would she ever find someone who cared that much for her? She gave the vegetables an extra-vigorous stir, splashing drops of vinegar on her apron.

Her mind skipped back to Uncle Will's first statement. "Sarah, did he say Daniel was coming with us?"

"It's Daniel now, is it?" Sarah smiled then pulled out a chair and sat facing Helena. "He asked if he could join our family today, and of course we said yes. This is a big step for Daniel—last year his brother marched with Will and the other veterans. I pray he's overcoming his grief."

Helena tugged the picnic hamper toward her and placed the salad inside. "I'll watch what I say, so I don't raise any sad memories for him. I'm still embarrassed by his reaction to my question at the cemetery on Decoration Day."

"You couldn't have known." Sarah returned to her work area. After wrapping the platter of sandwiches in a towel, she set them beside the bowl of salad then put the tray of doughnuts on top and covered everything with a red-checked cloth. "As soon as Will comes around with the wagon, we'll be on our way."

A tickle of anticipation bubbled up inside Helena. She loved patriotic displays on the Fourth of July. Even if the one in Spalding would be smaller than celebrations in

282

Waters Grove, the sound of a brass band and marching feet never failed to thrill her. She folded her apron over the back of a chair just as Grant and Beth dashed past on their way to change from work clothes to town clothes.

Harnesses jingled outside. In a couple of minutes Uncle Will appeared in the doorway with Daniel at his heels. Daniel's face brightened when he saw her.

"Miss—" He coughed. "I mean, Helena. Will and Sarah are going to be crowded with the food and all. Would you do me the honor of riding with me in my buggy?"

Sarah gave Helena a little nudge toward Daniel. "See you at the picnic grounds."

He held out his elbow and she stepped forward to rest her hand on his forearm.

A speaker's platform wrapped in red, white, and blue bunting decorated the picnic grounds. The Stars and Stripes sagged on a flagpole next to the platform, waiting for a breeze to show off its bright colors.

Daniel guided his buggy to an open space on a hitching rail, his heart thudding at Helena's nearness. His fingers itched to touch one of the wisps of silvery-blond hair that had escaped from beneath her bonnet. From her rigid posture at the far side of the buggy seat, he knew she wasn't interested in him in any romantic way. He was the Hallidays' neighbor, and that was that.

After tucking two blankets from the rear seat under his arm, he strode toward a shaded arbor. Helena beamed at him. "How thoughtful of you to bring extra blankets. I didn't notice whether Sarah set any out or not."

He flushed at her praise. "Looked like she made plenty of food. Figured the least I could do was provide places to sit." In the silence that followed, he grasped one of the blankets to spread on the ground.

"Let me help." Helena's fingers brushed his when she reached for the second one. The softness of her touch felt like a caress.

Warmth shot through his body. To hide his reaction, he bent over, squared the blankets against each other, then lifted his hat and wiped sweat from his forehead.

She watched him with a puzzled expression on her face. "Did I lay them out wrong?"

"No! No, of course not." How could he explain to her that precision was his refuge when he felt uncomfortable? Even more, how could he confess that her presence was the cause of his discomfort?

Helena turned from Daniel's flushed face to survey the groups of people gathering on the grounds. He'd been uneasy ever since leaving the Hallidays' cabin, no doubt dreading the ordeal of today's parade. She wished she knew what to say to ease his sorrow.

She released a relieved breath at the sight of Sarah and her children coming toward them carrying the picnic food. Beth reached her first and grabbed her hand.

"As soon as we can, let's go find a good place to watch the parade. Papa's already gone to join the other veterans."

The sound of drums and trumpets rolled over the crowd. Before following Beth, Helena reached out and grasped Daniel's arm. If the veterans' march were to disturb him, she wanted to be by his side.

Trumpets flashed in the sun as the perspiring band passed the reviewing stand. Helena's heart thrilled to the drumbeat pounding out "The Battle Hymn of the Republic." Following the band, veterans marched by in military formation.

She felt the muscles in Daniel's arm tense. When he pulled off his hat and held it over his heart, she stepped closer, fighting back a desire to slip her arm around him. Hard as she tried to ignore her feelings, she loved him and wished to be his bride.

When the music faded away, the clang of the bell on the eastbound Northern Pacific train could be heard from the nearby depot. The ground rumbled and cars clashed together as the engine left the station.

Another month and she'd be on that train and out of his life.

Chapter 12

With Mr. Wolford's permission, Helena left the mercantile before closing time to visit the post office. Three weeks had passed since she'd sent her inquiries to Spokane Falls. By now she should have the hoped-for responses.

She unfurled her parasol against the relentless July sun and crossed to the next block. A few wilting flowers sagged in front of homes along the street. For a moment, she imagined the flowers she'd cultivate in front of Daniel's cabin if she were his wife.

Helena shook her head. *You're wasting time with daydreams.* She marched up the steps of the post office, wishing she could stop thinking about him.

Mr. Kendrick rose from a chair in front of the rolltop desk as soon as she entered. "Miss Erickson. You've been on my mind."

"I hope that's because you have some mail for me."

"Part of the reason." He fanned through a tray and handed her two envelopes.

"Thank you." A quick glance revealed Spokane Falls postmarks. Concealing her curiosity, she tucked them in her bag before turning to leave.

"Not so fast." He put his arm against the wall, blocking her path to the door. "Another letter came you should know about."

She lifted her chin. "Then give it to me, please."

"Can't do that. It's not yours."

"Mr. Kendrick, I won't stand here and play guessing games with you. Please let me pass."

He dropped his arm, but didn't step away from the entrance. "I saw you with McNabb at the Fourth of July celebration. Figured I should tell you there's a letter here addressed to Mrs. Daniel McNabb." A crooked grin lifted his mouth. "Did you know he had a wife?"

She put her hand on the writing table to keep from swaying. A pulse pounded in her throat. "That's not possible."

"Apparently it is." He moved closer. "Guess I'm not the only fellow you don't know all that well."

She pushed past him and ran out the door, afraid she would be sick. Shouldn't Daniel have told her he'd been married? What happened to the first Mrs. McNabb?

Helena stalked past homes and businesses, her mind whirling. All this time, she'd borne the guilt of deceiving Daniel, when he'd been the deceiver. Should she confront him?

She paid little attention to horses and wagons raising dust along her route to the Hallidays' cabin. When she stepped off the end of the boardwalk, her boots sank into the fine powdered soil, deep as sand on a lakeshore.

As she trudged through the dust, she felt as wilted as the flowers she'd passed. Once she reached the Hallidays', she'd read the letters from Spokane Falls and choose a rooming house. In two more weeks she'd buy her train ticket. She'd make her plans work—she always had.

At the sound of hoofbeats, she paused to look over her shoulder.

"Helena, did you forget me?" Daniel brought his buggy to a stop next to her. "I told you I'd take you home this evening."

"Something came up. I had some. . .disturbing news." Despite her dislike of confrontation, her simmering anger erupted. She glared at him. "I learned today you have a wife."

His head jerked back. "What? Where did you hear that?"

"From Mr. Kendrick. He has a letter addressed to her."

He smacked his palm on the seat beside him. "Get in. We're going to the post office."

Once he turned the buggy around, he urged Ranger to a trot. Helena wrapped her arms around her middle and stared straight ahead. She couldn't wait to hear how he'd explain himself after Mr. Kendrick gave him the letter.

From her seat in the buggy, Helena heard men's voices escalating through the open door of the post office. Daniel's deep bass tones rolled over Mr. Kendrick's replies. After a minute or two, Daniel stomped out of the building, an envelope clutched in his hand. He vaulted into the buggy and turned east.

Helena gripped the edge of the seat. "Where are we going?"

"Picnic grounds. We can talk there."

He guided the horse off the main street, stopping behind the speaker's platform. His lips were pressed in a thin line.

The envelope he held crinkled when he turned to face her. "Because a letter came for a Mrs. McNabb, Kendrick told you I have a wife and you believed him?"

"Yes." She stammered her reply.

"I'm sorry to ask, but why do you care?"

Her mouth dropped open. Truly, why did she care? Daniel planned to send her back to Illinois. He didn't love her and certainly didn't plan to marry her. She fiddled with a stray thread on her skirt while she pondered a response.

"I guess because. . .because you seem so honest. It stunned me that you would avoid such an important issue."

Smile lines crinkled around his eyes as he handed her the envelope. The words "Mrs. Daniel McNabb" were written in flowing Spencerian script—her brother Joseph's handwriting.

"I believe this is intended for you." A wide grin spread over his face. "Looks like it's from Felicia Trimble."

Helena felt sure he could sense the heat radiating from her face. Bad enough she'd as good as accused him of dishonesty, but worse, she'd allowed her feelings for him to show. "Forgive me, Daniel. I had no way to let Joseph know we didn't marry. He and Pa went to Chicago soon after I left Waters Grove." She straightened her shoulders and pretended her interest lay in opening the envelope. "I never expected to hear from them. Pa's not like that." She drew out a single sheet of paper. "I'm anxious to learn how they are."

"I understand." The tenderness in his voice spread over her like a balm. "I'd give anything to be able to hear from my brother."

"Oh! I didn't think." She jammed her brother's letter into its envelope.

Daniel rested his hand over hers and stared off into the distance for a moment. "Don't apologize. It's time I stopped hiding behind my grief."

She raised a questioning glance to his face. "Hiding?"

His grip tightened. "Ross's death was my fault. We'd planned to build a house on our claim but didn't have the funds. I got the idea to take our team and wagon and deliver freight to miners in Idaho. The road over the mountains is treacherous, especially in the snow, so the pay's good. Ross insisted on going in my place. . . ." His voice trailed off.

Her hand ached beneath his strong fingers, but she didn't try to free herself. He'd chosen her to help him heal.

He shook his head as though awaking from a long sleep. "On his last trip, the wagon slid off the steep road, pulling Ross and the team down the mountainside. Days later, another freighter spotted them, but by then Ross was dead. Frozen to death." He set his jaw in a tight line. "My fault. Should've been me."

"Daniel, no." She fought back tears. "Sarah told me that he was quite a bit older than you. If he insisted, could you have stopped him? Was freighting something he enjoyed?"

"He did like teamster work. After the war he hauled freight until we decided to come here and file on a homestead." His grip relaxed and he leaned back on the seat. "Thank you. You've given me a great deal to think about."

Her heart sang at his words. A small redemption, but a redemption nevertheless. She hoped he'd remember her kindly after she left.

Chapter 13

Uncle Will's wheat crop was ready for harvest by mid-August. He took one of his teams and left for the Palouse country to help other farmers, with the understanding that they'd be back to share the work and equipment on the Hallidays' acreage as well. Daniel's fields were part of the work-sharing agreement.

The time had come.

Golden wheat stalks swayed in a gentle breeze as Helena walked toward Spalding past cultivated land. She told herself that the heaviness in her heart had nothing to do with the prospect of leaving Daniel and the Hallidays in less than a week.

When she reached the main route through town, she turned south to follow railroad tracks toward the depot. Ten weeks of work. Now she'd spend most of her savings on a ticket to Spokane Falls. Thankfully, one of the replies to her query about lodging offered a room at a dollar a week—two, with meals. Helena believed she'd have a job in no time once she arrived. She'd write to Joseph and her father in Chicago as soon as she was settled.

She swallowed tears as she mounted the steps of the wood-frame train station. Benches lined three walls inside the dimly lit room, with the stationmaster's window on the fourth. The clicking of a telegraph key sounded loud in the small space. She peered through the window at a bald man hunched over a desk, his index finger tapping out a message.

"Excuse me, sir."

He glanced over his shoulder. "Be with you in a moment." After several more taps, he walked to the window. "You here to send a message?"

"No, sir. I'd like to purchase a ticket to Spokane Falls on Friday's train."

"One-way or round-trip?"

The finality of her decision brought a lump to her throat. "One-way." Her voice wavered.

His bushy eyebrows shot up. "Ain't you the gal who works at Wolford's? He know you're leaving?"

"Yes, sir. He knows."

The stationmaster selected a pasteboard strip with "Northern Pacific" printed at the top in bold black letters. He dipped a pen in an inkwell and wrote Friday's date below the destination. "That'll be twenty-nine dollars, miss."

Helena counted the fare onto the ledge outside his window, the clink of the coins nailing her decision in place.

She grabbed her ticket and hurried into the sunshine. Four more days.

Daniel waited on his porch as the rattle of harnesses and rumble of machinery moved up the lane toward his wheat crop. Daybreak flared in the eastern sky, lighting the way for a dozen horses and a grain header. Ripened wheat stretched full and heavy toward the rising sun.

He rubbed the back of his neck. Now he could buy Helena the ticket he'd promised. After seeing her eagerness when she received her brother's letter, he knew he had to let her go.

Will met him at the foot of the steps. "Soon as you're ready, we'll begin." He gestured toward the men holding horses in place. "Grant's out there with one of the teams. Sarah and Beth will be over later with the noon meal."

"Appreciate the help." Daniel hesitated. "Don't suppose Helena's coming, is she?"

"It's Thursday. She's at the mercantile." Will chuckled. "Now, if she were your wife, she'd be right here cooking for the threshing crew."

Daniel tugged his hat lower on his forehead. No matter how much he wished, she wasn't his wife. The sooner he bought her ticket, the sooner he'd be spared seeing her and knowing she couldn't be his.

The two men joined the others as they positioned the header toward the first row of grain then lined the horses across the back of the machine. At a command from the drivers, the teams pushed and the cutting reel turned. Moving down the row, the sickle bar chewed its way through the standing wheat. A warm toast fragrance rose from the stalks as they were carried onto a canvas platform beside the machine.

Daniel jumped up behind the cutting reel to guide the harvested wheat into a following wagon. "Let's move faster," he hollered to the drivers. "I want to finish today."

Helena dawdled at her task of arranging canned peaches on a shelf in the food section of the mercantile. She'd finally learned where Mr. Wolford kept everything, and prided herself on being able to lead customers straight to whatever they wanted. She'd miss his gruff manner, which hid a candy-soft heart.

"You about finished there? The missus sent over some of her ginger cookies as a going-away gift. Having you look after the store while she was sick was a blessing from God. Don't know how we would have managed without you."

"I was happy to help, considering you were kind enough to take the risk of hiring me."

Mr. Wolford placed a towel-covered dish on the counter. "It hasn't been easy keeping your departure a secret."

She rested her hand on his forearm for a brief moment. "I'll tell the Hallidays in the morning. It's better for all of us not to suffer drawn-out good-byes."

"If you say so." He cleared his throat. "Sarah's going to be mighty upset to see you go."

"I'll miss the whole family." Helena didn't mention that keeping the news from Daniel was her most important reason. She planned to be on a train headed east before he purchased the promised ticket to Illinois.

She drew a ragged breath and bit into a cookie, enjoying the mingled sweet and spicy flavors. "Tell Mrs. Wolford thank you. These are delicious."

The bell over the door jingled as a man dressed in patched overalls stepped inside. Ignoring Helena, he turned to Mr. Wolford. "Over at the stable, they told me I could get a new ax from you. Someone stole mine off my wagon."

"Miss Erickson can show you where they are."

She subdued a pleased smile. "Right this way, sir. The tools are—"

The door banged open, hitting the wall.

"Helena! Come quick. Mama needs you." Beth ran to her and grabbed her hand. "Daniel's hurt. Papa went for the doctor in Cheney."

Helena's knees buckled. She grabbed the counter for balance as she sought Mr. Wolford's eyes.

"May I?"

"Go. I'll help the customer."

Beth tugged Helena toward the hitching rail, where the family's old mare waited. "We'll have to ride double. Papa's got the buggy and the teams are still at Daniel's." She stuck her foot into a stirrup and sprang into the saddle.

Helena bunched her skirt between her knees, put her foot in the stirrup, and pulled herself up behind Beth. As soon as she wrapped her arms around the girl, Beth turned the horse west and kicked her feet into the animal's side.

"Giddup, Belle."

Belle's giddup was at best a fast walk, but at least they were moving. Helena leaned close to Beth's ear. "Where is he? What happened?"

"He fell off the header. The sickle bar cut him up pretty bad. Blood everywhere. He might've broken a leg, too." Her chest rose and fell as she took a deep breath. "They have him in back of a wagon out of the sun. Mama's doctoring him, but she needs help."

Helena rested her forehead on Beth's shoulder. One more consequence of her headstrong decision. If Daniel weren't so determined to buy her ticket, this wouldn't have happened. *Lord, please let him be all right. Heal his wounds.*

Daniel struggled to open his eyes. Something was wrong with the left one—everything looked black. He lifted his hand to his head, but soft fingers clasped his and held them still.

"Daniel?"

The vision in his right eye cleared to reveal Helena's angelic face smiling down at him. He tried to speak through a weight pressing against his lower lip. " 'Elena. Where am I? Wha' happened?"

She looked over her shoulder. "Sarah. He's awake."

"Praise God!" Sarah appeared next to Helena. "You fell off the header. Doc's been here and stitched you up. Your ankle's hurt bad, but not broken. You're in bed and you need to stay there."

Images of harvesters working in his wheat crop filled his mind. If he fell off the header, that meant they weren't finished. He pushed himself up on one elbow. "Got to get back to work. Wasting daylight." His words emerged garbled.

Helena shook her head. "It's dark outside. Harvest's done."

"Done? How?"

Chair legs rasped across the floor and in a moment Sarah sat next to him. "The men finished a couple hours ago. Your grain's on the way to the thresher. You had a good crop."

She patted his shoulder. "I'm going home now that you're awake. Helena will be with you until Grant comes. He'll stay the night." Her heels tapped as she left the room.

When he turned his head to follow the sound, the familiar sight of his bureau with his comb and brush centered in front of Ross's picture met his eyes. His bedroom window reflected lamp glow over Helena's soft blond hair.

He put his hand to his face. Bandages covered his lower lip, half his face, and wrapped around his forehead. "What's under all this?"

Tears glistened in Helena's eyes. "When you fell, you gashed your cheek, cut your lip, and tore your eyebrow and your ear." She bowed her head. "Daniel, this wouldn't have happened if I hadn't used your tickets to come here. I'm so, so sorry."

He tried to deny her words by shaking his head, but she stopped him, resting a gentle hand on his bandages.

"Please let me speak. When I found those tickets, they seemed to be a gift from heaven. I wanted so much to be your chosen bride. So I used them, hoping you would accept me in spite of my brother's deception." Her voice trembled. "But I didn't stop to consider the possible consequences. You wouldn't have had your fall if you weren't hurrying to raise money to send me back—isn't that true?"

"Maybe. But—"

The cabin door opened. "Helena?" Daniel recognized Grant's voice.

"In here." She bent over the bed and placed a kiss on the top of Daniel's head. "I pray the day comes that you'll think of me with forgiveness in your heart. Good-bye, Daniel." With a whirl of her wide skirts, she hurried away.

He flopped back on the pillow. He wanted to chase after her and tell her he loved her, but he was as good as tied to this bed. The only consolation was she couldn't leave town until he bought her ticket. He knew she couldn't have earned the fare to Illinois in the three short months she'd been in Spalding.

He had time to win her heart.

Chapter 14

Late morning sun glittered over vacant Northern Pacific tracks. Helena's trunk waited on the baggage cart at the edge of the platform.

Beth clung to her, sobbing. "You can't leave. We're sisters."

"It breaks my heart to leave you, but I can't stay." Helena hugged her close. "You need your room back."

"I don't want my room! It's plain without the pretty cup and your dresses."

"Winter's coming. Grant isn't going to want to sleep in the barn forever." She tried to force a smile past her trembling lips.

Sarah moved next to them, her eyes red and puffy. "It's made such a difference to have you here. I wish things—"

"So do I. You have no idea how much." Helena wrapped her arms around Sarah and held her tight. Over Sarah's shoulder she saw Uncle Will twisting his hat brim around between his broad fingers. A pained expression wrote itself over his countenance when black smoke spiraled on the western horizon.

Within minutes, the engine squealed to a stop. Helena felt as though her heart were being torn from her body. The consequences of her deception seemed never-ending. She drew in a deep breath then turned to embrace each of the Hallidays. "I'll write to you. All the time."

As soon as the conductor appeared at the door of one of the passenger cars, she gripped her ticket between her fingers, lifted her valise, and fled up the steps. Moving through the first car, she settled in one of the seats toward the back, her anguish held in check by the slenderest of threads. She needed time alone.

When the train lurched into motion, she wrapped her arms around her body and rocked with the swaying of the car. *Lord, be with me. Lead me, guide me. I'm listening.*

The door between cars opened and closed. Helena straightened and held out her ticket as the conductor's steps thumped behind her.

"Excuse me, ma'am. Is this seat taken?"

Her breath stopped. Next to the opposite bench, a tall man, face swathed in bandages, leaned on crutches.

"Daniel! How did you—"

"Grant helped."

Smile lines fanned out from the deep-brown eye visible above the dressings. "It's time to start over, Helena." Balancing with care in the moving car, he reached for her hands and drew her to her feet. "I love you and can't let you go. Consider this your welcome to Washington Territory as my bride—if you'll have me."

"Oh, Daniel, a thousand times, yes!" She lifted her face toward his, and by careful manipulating, managed to kiss him above the bandages.

He held her close with his free arm. "We'll get off at the next stop and go back. Reverend Marley is waiting."

Helena felt she could soar above the train and fly back to Spalding. She had no doubt this was the answer to her prayer. Marriage to Daniel was the gift from heaven that God had been leading her to all along.

Ann Shorey has been a full-time writer for over twenty years. She made her fiction debut with *The Edge of Light*, Book One in the At Home in Beldon Grove series. Her latest releases include *Love's Sweet Beginning*, the third book in the Sisters at Heart series, and several novellas. Ann and her husband make their home in southwestern Oregon.

A Fairy-Tale Bride

by Liz Tolsma

Chapter 1

Cuento, East Texas
May 1867

Next stop, Cuento. Cuento, next stop." The conductor swayed down the aisle as the train rushed over the Texas prairie toward Nora Green's new life.

Nora turned to Maude Palmer, her traveling companion and stepsister. "This is where we get off and meet our soon-to-be husbands. Are you ready?"

Maude patted her dark, upswept hair and frowned. Actually, the frown was a permanent feature on her face. "I only hope my fiancé is good looking. I couldn't stand to spend the rest of my days with an ugly man. Could you imagine?"

Her new husband's face was the least of Nora's worries. More than the unpleasantness of his countenance, what would life be like if his personality was disagreeable? "Maybe this wasn't a good idea."

"And what would you have had us do? The war robbed us of our husbands and our homes. Neither of us has any family left. Those Yankees took everything we had. New spouses are the only way we're going to survive."

Four years had dimmed the ache in Nora's chest at the mention of Richard. What would their life have been like had he lived? Children? A new, large home? Servants? She shook her head. No use in pondering any of that. Her Virginia existence was over. In a few hours, she would be Mrs. J. M. Griffin and have a fresh start. A home and security. Maybe not the love she thought she had shared with Robert, but perhaps companionship.

"Mrs. Wade Yates. That has a nice ring to it."

"And four stepchildren."

"They'll be busy with school and chores. Wade promised they are well behaved and good mannered. I wouldn't have come west without that assurance."

No, Maude wasn't the maternal type. Desperation over their financial circumstances drove her to answer the advertisement for a mail-order bride. Since Maude was her only family, Nora found herself a match in the same town and followed her stepsister. "You might discover you like the children."

Maude snorted. "Highly unlikely. That was one thing Frank did right. He never gave me babies." She rose and pulled her carpetbag from the rack above their seats.

Nora pressed her nose to the window as the train raced toward their destination. She giggled.

"What's so funny?"

"Nothing." She giggled some more, even though her hands shook as she smoothed down her gray traveling suit. Soon to be her wedding gown. What had she done? Was it too late to turn around and head back East?

The train slowed and pulled along the platform. Would her new husband lie to her like her old one had? Nora covered her mouth, trying to stifle her nerves. She had to contain herself before the man thought her insane. A few people stood scattered outside the station, either greeting arrivals or preparing to begin their journey. Among those waiting must be J. M. Griffin and Wade Yates.

Maude joined her at the window. "Stop that nervous laughing. It drives me crazy. Nothing is funny. Now, which do you suppose are our grooms? Wade must be that tall gentleman with the bowler hat. The one with his back to us. He's broad and well built. The one in the coveralls can't be him."

"Neither of them may be our fiancés." Nora's stomach jumped around her midsection, even as she tittered.

"Will you please stop laughing? You'll scare off your intended, and then what will become of you?"

Nora bit the inside of her cheek. "I can't help it."

"You'd better. I'll not have you ruining my chances for a respectable life."

The brakes squealed as the train halted in front of the small station not much bigger than some outhouses. A lone bench sat in front of the weather-worn structure. Though the area grew cotton like Virginia, the similarities ended there. The wide, flat prairie stretched on forever.

Nora retrieved her reticule from the seat and followed Maude as she sashayed down the aisle. Another giggle bubbled in her throat, but she choked it back. "Wait." She grabbed Maude by the arm. "I'm not sure I can go through with this."

Maude spun around, her dark wide skirt swishing. "If you don't want to, fine. But I'm going to marry Wade. You can go back to Virginia if you want. But you have no home to go to and no money to get there. What will you do to support yourself?"

"I. . .I don't know." Before he walked off to war, Richard told her about a stash of money in a bag under the floorboards for her to use if he never returned. The day she discovered his name on the casualty list, she also discovered his lie. The bag contained nothing but air.

"That's what I thought." With another swing of her dress, Maude trekked the rest of the way down the aisle with Nora in her wake.

A gust of hot, humid air greeted Nora as she stepped through the door. She gulped. Time to meet her new husband.

Across the prairie, the train's whistle sounded, and a shudder raced through Josiah Abbot as he stood on the platform. His soon-to-be bride was on that train. His stump ached, and he shifted his weight from his prosthetic leg. He lifted his bowler hat, slicked back his hair, and replaced the hat. "I don't know about this, Wade. This might not have been our brightest idea ever. Why did I allow you to talk me into placing an advertisement for a mail-order bride?"

"You've always liked my plans. Moving to Texas was a good one. The cotton has done well."

"If we hadn't liked it here, we could have gone elsewhere. If I don't like my bride, I'm stuck with her forever." He wiped his damp hands on his pants.

"You enjoyed her letters well enough."

"That's true, but you can present yourself however you want to in a letter. She sounded sweet and gentle, a fine Christian widow, but how do I know that's true? She might be a spiteful, hateful shrew."

Wade thumped him on the back. "I'm not sure she'd be able to hide a personality like that, even in a well-formulated letter. She'll be fine. I'm not nervous about meeting Maude."

"Because you're desperate for a mother for your little hooligans. I hope she can handle them."

"She told me she loves children and she's good with them."

"Don't believe everything you see in print."

"You mean the way you used your initials and your mother's maiden name instead of your own?"

"I was scared."

"Of what?"

"I don't know. The shield of anonymity gave me the courage to write that first letter."

"You'll have to tell her she's going to be Mrs. Abbot and not Mrs. Griffin."

Among other things.

The engine chugged into the station and belched one last puff of steam as it stopped. Any moment now, she would appear on the step and walk into his life. His stomach clenched. "What am I going to do when she finds out about my leg?"

"You should have told her before this. Besides, what do you have to be worried about? Your wooden leg is as good as any flesh and blood one. You do the farm chores yourself. There's nothing you can't do with it. Up until now, it hasn't kept you from anything."

"But what is she going to think of me when she sees me, you know, without it?" Heat raced up his neck and into his cheeks. Good thing his beard hid the blush.

"She'll think you're a brave man who made a great sacrifice for his country. She's a fellow Virginian, so she'll be proud of you and how you fought."

Blood whooshed in his ears. "What if she—"

"Just stop it. Stand tall and proud. Be kind and loving, and everything will work out."

"Is that your plan?"

"Sure is. No one can resist my charms. Libby couldn't." Wade tugged on his denim overalls.

"Honestly, I never did understand what she saw in you." Josiah managed to crack a smile.

"Wait. Look. There's movement inside. I think they're coming."

A woman appeared on the train steps, her dress and her hair dark, as well as her countenance. She pinched her lips together as she scanned the few people gathered along the tracks. Then she turned. "Hurry up, Nora. Don't be so poky."

So that was Wade's bride.

Josiah might just be sick to his stomach.

A moment later, another woman, presumably Nora, stepped out of the train carriage.

She sucked the breath from his lungs. Hair the color of maple syrup parted in the middle and pulled back. An oval face. Full, pink lips. A soft smile. A simple gray dress that accentuated her tiny waist.

In other words, sheer perfection.

His heart bucked in his chest like an untamed bronco. "I can't do this. She'll never have me. Tell her I couldn't make it. That I'm terribly ill or something. Don't let her know I was here. She's not for me." He strode from the tracks as fast as he could.

He rounded the building and leaned against it for support. She was beautiful. Everything he had ever hoped for in a wife. Maybe more.

Once she found out about his injury, she would want nothing to do with him. He'd seen it before his prosthesis. Stares. Questions. Pity.

Nothing he wanted from his wife.

Chapter 2

Nora swooped down the steps behind Maude and almost ran into her when she screeched to a halt. Maude peered over her shoulder at her. "Wonder which ones are ours?"

Nora shrugged and stifled a nervous giggle. Only one man remained on the platform, the one in the overalls. His companion must have boarded the train.

The lone man approached them. "Are you Mrs. Green and Mrs. Palmer?"

Maude peered down her nose at him. "We are. If you could direct us to the men who were to meet us, we would be most grateful."

He held out his hand to shake Maude's but dropped it to his side when she made no move to reciprocate. "Which one of you is Maude?"

Maude answered with a sniff. "I am."

"I'm Wade Yates, your husband-to-be." His grin stretched from Cuento to Dallas.

Maude sucked in her breath. "You're Wade?"

"Yes, ma'am, I am. Very pleased to make your acquaintance. You must be exhausted from such a long journey. Let me take your bags. The preacher's wife is opening her home to you ladies so you can refresh yourselves before the ceremony."

Nora stepped from behind Maude, a colony of butterflies whizzing about in her stomach and laughter on her lips. "Excuse me, sir. I'm Nora Green, J. M.'s intended."

Wade cracked his knuckles and cleared his throat. "Well, um, you see, Mrs. Green, um, well, it's like this. He isn't coming."

She stumbled backward, her breath catching in her throat. "What do you mean, he isn't coming?"

"See, he's real shy, and after he sent you the train fare, he changed his mind about having a wife. He likes the seclusion of his ranch and decided to keep everything just the way it is. He's awful sorry and sends his apologies."

"He's not going to marry me?" She slumped.

"Afraid not."

Maude's shrill voice pierced Nora's fog. "Where is she going to go, then? What is the gentleman prepared to do for her?"

"I'll speak to him about getting you train fare back to Virginia."

"That won't do me any good. I have no home there anymore. I've lost everything."

"Family?" Wade scratched his eyebrow.

Nora shook her head.

He brightened. "You can stay with Maude and me."

Good heavens, did he know what he was suggesting?

Maude shook her head with such vigor her little hat should have flown off her head. "She will not stay with us. I'm not sure I'm going to marry you."

Nora's fingernails bit into her palms. "You have to wed him. What else will we do? Everything is gone to the debt collectors."

"Hush." Maude spit the words at Nora. "He doesn't need to know our business."

"If you're to be his wife, he does."

"I'm not marrying him."

Nora focused on Wade. "Could you excuse us for a moment, please?"

"Certainly." With one nod, he backed away. "I'll get your trunks loaded into the wagon."

Maude stomped her foot. "You will leave them where they are."

Behind her stepsister's back, Nora pointed to the trunks piled against the station and motioned for him to take them. He slunk away. She grabbed Maude by the upper arms and swung her around. "Be reasonable. Since my groom deserted me, you have to marry Wade." She swallowed around the lump in her throat.

"What did you do to upset your intended? What did you say that made him change his mind?"

"Nothing. I can't imagine why he did this. All was well. After he sent the train fare, I sent him the telegram informing him of our arrival."

"Well, that's it then. You didn't write him a letter. You got what you wanted and snubbed him."

"You didn't write a letter to Wade." In fact, Maude made Nora pay for the telegram. "Whatever the reason, the fact remains that we are two destitute widows with no options. If you don't marry Wade, we don't survive."

"We'll get jobs."

Nora laughed. "Doing what? There isn't a hotel here or anything." The town, as far as Nora could see, consisted of the train depot, a church, a general store, a livery, and several scattered homes. That was about it. Up until two years ago, Maude had slaves who fulfilled her every command.

Maude paced the small platform as the train chugged out of the station. "I can't believe you put us in this situation. You're forcing me to marry a man who is ugly, backward, and—"

"You don't even know him."

"And if I agree to take you in, you must help in the running of the home and the raising of the children. I will not have you be a burden on us."

Nora sighed. "Fine. What other choice do I have?"

"Apparently very little. And neither do I, thanks to you."

Nora stood beside Maude inside the little white clapboard church. Even in May, the heat and humidity bore down on her. Sweat trickled between her shoulder blades. The freshening they did at Pastor Miles's house lasted all of ten minutes.

The reverend intoned the marriage ceremony. She should be standing in front of the church beside J. M. This was her chance to start over. No more debt. No more widowhood. No more cares. Someone to lift the burden of day-to-day living from her shoulders.

How could J. M. have done this to her? Didn't he realize the predicament he put her in by not carrying through on this promised marriage? Without Maude, she'd be forced to. . .

No sense in wondering. Living with Maude was an acceptable solution for now. Nora's temples throbbed, and her tongue stuck to the roof of her mouth. There would be time enough to figure out the future. Right now, a bath and a cool glass of water would be worth more than gold.

"I now pronounce you husband and wife." Pastor Miles slapped the small book shut.

Wade took Maude by the hand. "Guess that's about it. Are you ready to head to the ranch?"

Sweat beaded on Maude's upper lip. "You would think a town would have a hotel and restaurant for weary travelers."

"Sorry about that. This village is new, cotton farming just opening up around here since the war. The men have been busy getting their operations going. Just trying to make a living off the land. There hasn't been time for much else. Not even marrying." Wade had the audacity to wink at Maude.

"What are you doing? Stop the tomfoolery, and let's get going. This heat is even more intolerable than at home."

Wade clucked to the horses, and they bumped their way to their new place of residence. A familiar ache settled in Nora's chest. Where were the woods and rivers of Virginia? The live oaks dripping with moss?

They drove along fields bursting with cotton plants, as far as the eye could see across the prairie. Here and there, a small cabin broke the monotony.

No one spoke the entire journey to Wade's farm. Didn't the newlyweds want to get to know each other? The silence stretched on. Guess they had no intention of it.

The trip came to a merciful end when they rolled up to a cabin planted in the middle of a field. A long front porch ran the length of the single-story house. Brick chimneys rose on either end. As Wade pulled the team to a stop, four children spilled from the house and down the porch steps. Three young boys in britches that didn't quite reach to their ankles toed the dirt with their bare feet while one little girl, the smallest of the children, clung to her brother's shirttail, her thumb in her mouth.

"Children, come say hi to your new momma." Wade hopped from the wagon and held out his hand to help Maude. She climbed down on her own.

The children shuffled forward. Wade nudged the tallest, who bowed. "How do, ma'am?"

"That's Charles, followed by William and James. And the littlest there is Alice."

Maude patted each of them on the head and then marched into the house.

"Boys, this here is Miss Nora. She'll be staying with us for a while. Now help me get these trunks inside."

With a good deal of groaning and complaining, the boys pulled the trunks from the wagon and lugged them to the house. Nora bent in front of Alice, peering into the little girl's wide blue eyes. "Hello, sweetheart. How old are you?"

Alice held up three fingers.

"Oh my, aren't you a big girl? And such pretty yellow curls you have."

A grin broke out on the toddler's face. She pointed to the house and spoke around the thumb in her mouth. "Momma?"

"That's right. That's your new momma. She's here to watch over you and take care of you. And I'm going to help her. How does that sound?"

Alice stood still and sucked her thumb all the harder.

Maude flung open the cabin's door. "Nora? Nora! Get in here right now. I need you to clean up this kitchen. It's a disaster."

Nora closed her eyes and drew in a deep breath. It was Virginia all over.

Chapter 3

Morning sunlight streamed through the just-washed kitchen window. Josiah clutched his coffee, steam rising from the mug. Since he hadn't slept well last night, he downed it and poured himself a second cup.

How had Nora taken the news that he wasn't coming? Had she been angry? Distressed? His stomach clenched. Yes, it was cowardly for him to desert her. But this way was better. Once she realized what the war cost him, she would leave him. Or stay with him out of pity, which he would refuse to allow. This way, he didn't put her in a position to decide. He took the preemptive strike.

My, she had been beautiful. Just about the most gorgeous creature he'd ever beheld. To have such a woman for his wife. . . Well, it was a dream beyond his reach. Some Union soldier saw to that.

He left his cup on the table and pulled the coffeepot to the back of the stove before thumping out the door, across the porch, and down the step he'd fixed yesterday morning so his new bride wouldn't trip.

He may have been brave enough to face an army of Yankees, but he wasn't brave enough to face a single woman. A one-note laugh escaped his lips. Some kind of man he was.

Even this early, the sharecroppers were in the fields, hoeing the weeds between the green rows of cotton plants. He had plenty to support a wife and family. But he'd die a lonely old man.

In the distance, a horse and rider approached. Despite the glare of the morning sun, Josiah couldn't mistake his visitor. Wade. Josiah shuddered. Wade would give him what for. And with good reason.

Wade reined the horse to a stop in front of the house and slid from the mare's back. "Good morning to you."

"Congratulations on your new bride. I'm assuming you went through with the wedding."

"Of course. I need a mother for my children, so I had little choice but to do so."

"How is married life?"

Wade shook his head. "Well, I'll tell you, Maude isn't quite all I thought she'd be. She hasn't taken much interest in the children. But maybe that will change once she's rested. She retired early last night with a severe headache, complaining of fatigue."

Josiah wagged his eyebrows. "You don't say."

"Don't start on that. At least I had the fortitude to go through with the ceremony.

And by the way, you are missing out. Nora is another story altogether. Beautiful."

"I saw that part."

"Not only that, but she is so good with the children. She's staying with us for the time being, since she has no husband here and no home to go back to. I overheard the two of them talking, and they lost everything in the war. Anyway, Nora took right over as soon as she entered the house. So far, she's charmed Alice and gotten the boys to hold their forks right and not talk with their mouths full. And she's cleaned the kitchen so it shines."

"Quite the list of accomplishments in a short amount of time." Josiah rubbed his aching head. Maybe he had done the right thing. A beautiful, loving woman such as Nora wouldn't look twice at a man such as him.

"She's everything she said she was in her letters and more. Maybe I should have married her and not Maude. But I didn't know that when they first stepped from the train. And I thought you might change your mind about her. Any chance of it?"

"Not a one. She'd take one look at me and run home to Virginia screaming."

"Now you're exaggerating. She's not the type to do such a thing."

"You haven't even known her twenty-four hours."

"Long enough."

"Is that all you came for? To taunt me with the woman who might have been my wife?"

"That's your fault. But no, it's not. Just wondering if the town is still putting on that play. I'd like to take Maude and introduce her to some of the ladies around here. Maybe she'll feel settled if she makes a few friends. Sunday mornings are fine, but the play will allow her more time to interact with the other women, few as there are."

"Yes, it's still scheduled for Saturday evening."

"And what do you want me to do about Nora?"

"What did you say to her?"

"That you're shy and stay on your farm all the time."

"Good. Don't tell her anything else about me. And whatever you do, don't tell her who I am or where I live." If she met him and found out what he'd done, he'd die of shame.

Nora rubbed her aching lower back as she poured another pot of warm water into the metal tub in the middle of the kitchen. Time to see that four rowdy children had their Saturday evening baths. Whether they liked it or not. And it was a not with William, Charles, and James.

The large tub and shimmering water beckoned to Nora. Maude had complained every day since they'd been here of some ailment or another that kept her from caring for the house or the children. What a good soak would do for Nora's sore muscles.

Maude sailed through the kitchen, the hem of her skirt skimming the swept and scrubbed floors, her hoop bouncing as she went. Her headache cleared up in time for her to attend the play tonight. She pulled her best white gloves up to her elbows. "When we get home, we expect all the children to be tucked into bed, sound asleep, and the house to be put to rights. I don't know how late we'll be."

Poor Wade followed in her wake and shrugged. "I'm sorry you have to miss it."

Nora made an unsuccessful attempt at a smile. "I've always enjoyed theater productions. My husband would take me to Richmond several times a year so we could see a show or two."

"But we need someone to watch the children." Maude humphed. "Besides, you wouldn't want to go alone. I'm sure it's going to be nothing but couples."

Wade tugged on his waistcoat. "Actually—"

"Don't be impertinent, Wade. You know those wild children of yours can't be left unattended. Really, what are you thinking? Nora has to stay here, and that's the end of that."

Wade trailed after his wife and out the door. A few muffled words from Maude and the wagon wheels creaked as the couple drove away. Hot tears burned the back of Nora's throat.

She turned just as William pushed James into the tub, water sloshing over the floor. James came up spluttering. "You dirty, rotten—"

"Boys."

They both turned to her.

"William, you will go to the sink and start drying and putting away the dinner dishes. James, since you are already in the tub, take off your clothes, and I'll get you a bar of soap and a towel for your bath." She drew the curtain around the tub as she left to procure the promised items.

Thirty minutes later and still only James had been bathed, and William had dropped and broken one of the fine china cups Maude had shipped from Virginia. At least Nora had gotten Alice into bed.

Then someone knocked on the door. Just what she needed at this moment. Nora wiped her hands on her apron and did her best to smooth her hair back before opening the door to the caller.

A rotund older woman stood on the step, her buggy and sorrel mare behind her. "Good evening, dear. I'm Polly Turnbull. You must be either Nora or Maude. My husband heard all about what happened at the train this week and told me. May I come in for a minute?"

"I'm Nora, and well, Mr. and Mrs. Yates have gone to see the play, and I'm trying to give the boys a bath and get them to bed."

"What? You aren't going yourself?"

"Someone must see to the children."

Mrs. Turnbull laughed, her plump cheeks rosy. "We can't have that, can we? I'll watch these angels. You go pretty yourself and get over to the schoolhouse before you miss it. We may be a small community, but we have a talented group of actors."

"Have you stayed with the children before?"

"Oh, many times."

"And survived?" Nora clapped her mouth shut at her words.

Mrs. Turnbull chuckled and pulled four peppermint sticks from her apron pocket. "They'll do anything for candy. Now get going with you."

"Are you sure?"

"Don't stand here and argue with me. You'll miss the best part."

"Don't you want to see it?"

"My Henry is part of the production. I've watched practice all week. I could repeat the lines in my sleep. Hurry up. I'm not taking no for an answer."

In the tiny bedroom she shared with Alice, Nora pulled on her best gown, a brown silk windowpane dress with a long brown silk bow in the back. Peering into the small looking glass, she combed her hair and fastened it with tortoiseshell combs. On the bed, Alice curled in a ball and sighed in her sleep.

Nora returned to the kitchen. Charles pulled the curtain shut, preparing to bathe. This woman was a miracle worker.

"No jewelry?" Mrs. Turnbull oversaw William who worked sums on a slate at the kitchen table.

All sold to pay off debts. "No."

"Well then, I have just the thing." She unfastened the cameo brooch from her neckline and handed it to Nora. "Put it on, dear."

There was no sense in arguing with her. Nora did as requested.

Mrs. Turnbull took a step back. "There. You're a true beauty."

"But I don't have any way to get there."

"My horse and buggy, of course. And you'd better ride hard, or you'll miss everything."

Head whirling, Nora went to the buggy and picked up the reins. Maude would be furious if she found out Nora had left the children.

She would just have to make sure Maude never found out.

Chapter 4

O ut of breath, Nora stepped into the tiny school's coatroom just as the curtain
      rose on the play to thunderous applause. She tiptoed into the classroom and
      spied Wade and Maude near the front, close to the stage, Maude's back stiff and
straight, Wade slumped over, crushing his felt hat in his hands.

No seats remained open, so she leaned against the back wall, squeezed in between it
and the last row of chairs, and fanned herself against the warm evening.

The bedsheet-turned-curtain parted, and a large man dressed as a medieval king
stepped forward. Was this Mr. Turnbull? Though his soliloquy was lengthy, he delivered
it with aplomb and received a hearty round of applause for his efforts. The play continued and featured a regal, if not rather manly, queen, and several courtiers.

Nora relaxed against the wall and lost herself in the play. She laughed and clapped
with the rest of the audience. And then the jester entered the stage. He wore green
pants, a green shirt, and a black mask that covered his entire face. Sewn onto the hems
of his pants and the wrists of his shirt were jingle bells that tinkled every time he moved.
He gestured wide and knocked the queen over, the actor doing an admirable job of playing it up. The audience roared.

He stumbled across the stage and pulled over the king's table, tin plates and cups
flying everywhere. Then he backed up toward a flaming candelabra, acting as if he
burned his backside, screaming like a woman. The audience cheered its appreciation.
Nora couldn't help but join the merriment.

For a blink-and-you-miss-it town, they sure had a fine and talented acting company. This was as good as the last show she'd seen in Richmond. Maybe even better.

By the time the play wound down, Nora's sides ached from all the laughing, and
her hands tingled with all the clapping. Mrs. Turnbull would be sorry she missed the
theatrics.

The master of ceremonies took the stage and announced that refreshments would
be served as soon as the ladies got the tables set up. Reality crashed around Nora. That
meant Maude would leave her seat, turn around, and spy Nora.

If only she could stay and get to know some of the townswomen. There weren't
many of them, but having a friend here would ease the transition. Not that she'd have
much time for visiting with having to keep four rambunctious children in check, but at
least she could greet them by name at church on Sundays.

Maude rose, raised her shoulders, and shook her head. Probably finding something
to complain about regarding the production.

Any moment she would spin around.

Heat rose in Nora's neck. She had to get out of here, but the mingling crowd blocked the exit. She ducked behind a taller, broader man as Maude scooted toward the aisle.

"Well, it wasn't like back in Virginia, that's for sure. There we have professional theater. This just doesn't measure up to those standards."

Nora cringed. Maude's words would never ingratiate her with the local people.

Ah, a sliver of light, an opening. Nora hurried toward it. She had to get home and in bed before Maude and Wade arrived.

"Excuse me, excuse me, please." She wound her way by several gentlemen discussing something or another about their cotton crops.

"Oh, Nora? She's good with the children and handy around the kitchen. That's about all I can say for her." Was Maude's voice closer than before?

The door was right in front of Nora. She sprinted for it.

Smack. Right into something.

No, someone.

The masked, green-clad jester. He grabbed her by the elbow and steadied her. "Oh, I'm so sorry, miss."

"If you'll pardon me, I must be going." The words rushed over her lips.

He held on to her, his grasp firm. "Wouldn't you care to stay for refreshments? Pies and cakes, from what I understand."

"Please, I have to get some fresh air."

"Are you ill? Forgive my poor manners." But instead of letting go, he steered her through the door and onto the school's steps. "Is this better?"

With her free hand, she patted her flaming cheek. "Yes, thank you, but I'll feel even better when I get home." She moved to descend the stairs.

"I can't let you leave like this."

She turned to face him. "Why not?"

He cleared his throat, his voice deep and warm, his accent tinged with Virginia. "If you're unwell, you shouldn't go until you've recovered a bit. Have some pie and coffee, at the very least. I insist. Let me get you something. Promise you'll still be here when I get back?"

A desperate plea? No, just a thoughtful, concerned man. "I'll be here." Praying the entire time that Maude and Wade wouldn't decide to go home early. She suppressed a nervous giggle.

Josiah's heart pounded faster now than it had when he first stepped onstage tonight. His jester's mask hid his identity, and his green pants covered his wooden leg. But he'd almost stopped breathing when he spied Nora standing alone in the back of the room. As beautiful as the day she stepped off the train. Maybe more. Definitely more.

With shaking hands, he poured two cups of coffee. On top of the cups, he balanced two slices of Mrs. Turnbull's famous butter cake.

Just as he reached the front door, someone clapped him on the shoulder. "Where are you off to?"

Wade. "Um, just passing out refreshments."

"I thought the ladies were doing that."

"I, um. . ." Why didn't he want to tell Wade that Nora, if she kept her promise, stood just outside the door?

"Good show. In a way, your standing up your bride is working out for me. Nora is home with the kids, and so me and the missus can get out for the night."

She was supposed to be watching Wade's children? So then, who was with them?

"Wade, I need a drink. I'm positively parched." A woman called across the room.

Josiah exhaled. "Sounds like you're needed elsewhere."

Like a defeated child, Wade slunk away. Before anyone else could detain him, Josiah slipped outside. Nora stood right where he'd left her. The moonlight splashed across her cheek. He gasped at her beauty. And tripped down the last stair, balancing the plates and cups like he was part of a circus.

She turned. "Oh, be careful." The plate in his right hand teetered and tottered, and she caught it in the nick of time.

Could the earth just open up and swallow him right now? "I brought you a piece of cake." His voice squeaked.

"Thank you." Even in the dim light, he caught her soft, gentle smile. Like she didn't even notice what a fool he was making of himself. Then again, he was dressed like a jester.

"I'm Nora Green, by the way."

"Yes, I know." Pesky squeaking vocal chords. He cleared his throat and tried again. "Wade told me about you."

"You know Wade? And what about J. M. Griffin? Do you know him?"

Better than anyone in the world. "Never have met him. He keeps to himself and likes it that way. I heard of your plight, but I wouldn't go bothering him. Best just to stay on with Wade and his new wife."

Her shoulders sagged. "I was so hoping to meet him tonight. Maybe he and I could get to know each other and. . . Well, that doesn't sound like it's going to happen."

"I'm mighty sorry about that."

She waved him off. "It's not your fault. You're not the one who left me at the altar. I didn't catch your name, though."

He swallowed hard. What was he going to tell her? Quick, quick. "Just call me the jester. Everyone does." If by everyone, you meant him.

"Aren't you warm with the mask still on?"

"Not at all. The director told us to stay in costume during the refreshment time, sort of to keep the feeling of the play alive for a little while longer." Like she was going to believe that.

"Oh, I see."

Better to switch topics before he got in any deeper. "Wade told me something curious just now. He's under the impression that you are at home with his children."

"Oh, I was. And please, don't tell him I was here." She touched his forearm, and tingles raced up to his elbow and down to his fingers. "Mrs. Turnbull came over and volunteered to stay with the little ones so I could attend. Wasn't that kind of her? She even lent me this brooch and her buggy."

"She does have the kindest heart. It sounds like you're making friends already."

"Just the one. Maude, Wade's wife, hasn't been feeling well, so I've taken on the responsibility of running the household."

Muffled voices came from inside, and then one shrill one. "Really, Wade, I'm exhausted. You drag me to this second-rate production when I'm just off the train from Virginia."

Nora sucked in her breath and thrust her plate and cup at Josiah. "I have to go. Remember not to tell anyone I was here."

"Nora."

With a swish of her hoop skirt, she turned and ran to Mrs. Turnbull's buggy. Before he could sort out what was happening, she was nothing more than a puff of dust in the starlight.

The door opened, and Maude and Wade left the building.

Josiah glanced at the ground, and a white square of lacy fabric caught his eye. He picked it up. Nora's handkerchief. He sniffed it.

Her sweet rosewater scent clung to it.

Chapter 5

Nora stood at the stove stirring the oatmeal, all the while staring out the window and across the cotton fields. She sighed. All night long, she'd dreamed of the jester. Jester. Was that his name or some nickname he'd picked up somewhere? A bit strange that he didn't take off his mask or tell her much about himself, yet he knew all about her.

Then again, he was so sweet and took such good care of her when he thought she was overcome with the heat, helping her outside and getting her some refreshments. And, at least so far, he'd kept his word. Maude and Wade had returned home moments after Mrs. Turnbull left the house and Nora had fled to her room. Neither Maude nor Wade mentioned seeing her.

But who was he? When would she see him again? Maybe he could be an alternative to the reclusive J. M. Griffin.

"What is that I smell burning?"

At the sound of Maude's voice, Nora jumped and flicked the spoon so that oatmeal splattered on the wall beside her. Now she needed to add cleaning the wall to today's long list of chores.

"Aren't you paying attention to anything? I've been calling for you for the past ten minutes. Alice's hair is tangled, and she won't let me anywhere near her with a brush. And Charles wet the bed. Again. Really, I don't understand how a boy of seven can't use the chamber pot at night. For goodness' sake, pull that oatmeal off the heat. You've ruined our breakfast."

Nora grabbed the pot from the stove, but the scorched mess was beyond saving. "I'm sorry. My mind wandered."

"Well, have it hurry back here."

Pain throbbed behind Nora's right eye.

Maude rubbed her temples. "I have such a headache, I must go lie down again. Keep the children quiet so they don't disturb me."

"But..."

Before Nora could say a second word, Maude disappeared down the hall, the bedroom door slamming shut after her. Nora took a deep breath, let it out a little at a time, and wiped her hands on her apron. What had to be done had to be done.

Within half an hour, she had the sheets soaking in a tub outside, Alice dressed and combed, and a batch of pancakes on the griddle. Wade and the children had just situated themselves around the table when the front door squeaked open.

"Hello? What is that delicious smell?"

Wade scraped back his chair. "Josiah. Didn't expect to see you this morning."

A young man entered the room, Wade's junior by a few years. With his dark brown hair and strong, large hands, he held an air of familiarity. But Nora couldn't place him. She shook her head. He'd probably been one of the many men at the play last night.

He doffed his felt hat and nodded at Nora. "I'm Josiah Abbott, the Yates's neighbor."

"Nora Green, Mrs. Yates's stepsister."

"I've heard so much about you. Pleased to make your acquaintance."

"Won't you sit and have breakfast with us? And a cup of coffee?"

"Don't mind if I do." He seated himself in Maude's empty chair and dug right into a stack of flapjacks.

Nora kept the griddle going. "Were you at the play last night, Mr. Abbott?"

"No, ma'am, I didn't make it."

Wade raised one of his eyebrows. "But didn't you—"

"Ate something that didn't agree with me." Josiah flashed Wade a narrow-eyed glance. What was that all about?

Josiah leaned over to Alice and chucked her under the chin. "But I bet you went in all your finery, didn't you, Miss Yates?"

Alice giggled. "I wented to bed, like Miss Nora told me to do."

"Aren't you the little angel?" Josiah gave Nora such an intense stare that she wriggled under his gaze. "What about you, Miss Green? Did you enjoy the production?"

"Um." Heat rose up her neck, and not from the warmth of the stove. "I stayed home with the children to give Mr. and Mrs. Yates an evening together."

James opened his mouth and drew in a breath. Was he going to tattle on her? "James, could you get more milk from the cold cellar? Right now." Nora crossed her arms and glared at him. So many furtive glances this morning.

The rest of breakfast passed in an easy manner, and soon the children scattered without last night's secret being divulged. With that weight off her shoulders, Nora picked up a stack of plates to carry to the sink.

"Let me help you with those." Josiah grabbed several glasses and set them on the counter.

"Don't you and Mr. Yates have business to take care of? I'm assuming that's why you're here." Oh dear, it wasn't any of her concern why he'd shown up this morning.

"That can wait. Wade, if you need to get started without me, go ahead. I'm going to help Miss Green dry these dishes, and then I'll be out."

Wade shrugged and left.

Nora bent over her task so she didn't have to look Josiah in his warm brown eyes. He'd spent half the meal staring at her, sending her heart into palpitations. If this kept up, she'd have to take to her bed, just like Maude. "Really, you don't have to help. I have everything under control. You must have better things to do than wipe plates."

"I was sorry to hear about what happened to you."

"Really, it's fine." She waved away Josiah's words. "Honestly, I'm glad I found out about the kind of man J. M. was before I married him." Better than how she'd found out about Robert—when he was dead and the money he'd bragged about was nonexistent. "I'd rather remain a widow and live in this house than to live with a husband such as J. M. It was the Lord's gracious provision to me."

Beside her, Josiah sputtered and coughed.

"Are you all right? Let me get you a glass of water."

He shook his beet-red face. "No, that's fine. I'd better get out to Wade." And still grasping the dish towel, Josiah fled the house.

Wade was harnessing Mac, his stallion, as Josiah rushed from the house. Nora despised him, no doubt about it. She harbored no love for the man who had left her alone at the train station. Well, not quite alone, but alone enough.

Wade waved Josiah over before he leaned down to buckle a strap under the horse's stomach. "Would you care to inform me what went on in the kitchen this morning? Why are you even here?"

"I came to see her." He turned to glance at the house. Was there movement behind the kitchen curtain? Was it Nora?

"Why now? And why did you say you weren't at the play last night?"

"I—I. . ." Oh, he certainly had made things worse by coming. "I'm being ridiculous, but I'm a little embarrassed about the performance. Really, I played a jester. And it was a nothing role. Let's just keep it between the two of us."

"Not a very good reason, if you ask me, but I'll do as you say."

Josiah blew out a breath. "I thought Maude was feeling better. Didn't I see her last night?"

"You did. She was better until she demanded we leave. Wouldn't even let me get a word in edgewise. That woman." Wade pulled off his hat, smoothed back his black curls, and replaced the cap. "I don't know what I'm going to do with her."

"She hates me."

"I don't think Maude even knows you."

"Not Maude. Nora."

"I beg to differ. She stared at you through most of breakfast."

"Not me. Me. J. M. Griffin. She hates him for not holding up his, my, end of the bargain and marrying her. And I can't say I blame her. I was a real coward. But now what can I do? She's beautiful and intelligent, and more than I ever imagined her to be. She can never find out that I'm J. M. Never."

Wade leaned against the fence rail. "Are you planning on wooing her?"

Josiah scuffed the dirt with the toe of his boot. "I don't know." His wooden leg rubbed against his stump. "No. I can't. She'd never have me. Not once she knew."

"She doesn't seem the kind of woman who would be bothered by that. She's sensible and levelheaded. Real tender with the kids."

"That would change once she saw the leg. And me without it." He stared at the green cotton field beyond them, the sharecroppers hard at work in the early-morning heat. "I've gotten too many pitying looks from too many women. No, I will not be courting Nora Green." He'd have to keep his distance. No more dropping in on Wade. No talking to her at church. If he stayed far away from her, he wouldn't fall for her. He fingered the lacy handkerchief in his pocket where he'd put it for safekeeping. And for reminding him of all he could have had.

Chapter 6

ome on, boys, don't forget your hats." Nora worked to spur the children out the
door. "Alice, I'll get your bonnet. We're going into town."

Charles glanced up from the game of jacks he had spread over the kitchen floor.
Nora had stepped on two already this morning. "I don't wanna go." He stuck out his lower lip.

"That matter is not up for discussion. All four of you are coming." Nora tied her
bonnet's ribbon under her chin before bending down to do the same for Alice.

James swiped Charles's ball as it bounced up in the air. "Our real momma didn't
make us go to town. She didn't make us do anything we didn't want to do."

Nora suppressed a very unladylike snort. "I doubt that very much. I'm sure she made
you eat your green beans and scrub behind your ears."

"No she didn't." William scooped up all of Charles's jacks.

"Hey, give my stuff back."

Nora stomped her foot. "That is enough from all of you. We are going into town. I
don't care what your mother did or did not make you do. I have some business there, and
as I can't trust you out of my sight for a second, you'll be coming with me."

Maude's weak voice floated down the stairs. "Hush up, all of you. How is a woman
supposed to nurse a headache with all that hullabaloo?"

"If you behave yourselves, you'll get a peppermint stick from the store. That's our
last stop. And only if you mind me without complaint." Though the tactic smacked of
bribery, if it worked for Mrs. Turnbull, Nora was willing to give it a try.

With the carrot dangling in front of them, the boys grabbed their hats and ran to
hitch Mercy to the wagon. Nora came behind them, holding Alice by the hand. "Why
would anyone call a horse by such a name?"

"Charles told me. When Daddy brought him home, Momma said, 'Mercy, mercy,
mercy.'"

Nora chuckled. The ride to town passed in a peaceable manner. Mrs. Turnbull was
right. These children would do anything for a piece of candy. That was a nugget of information she would have to keep tucked away.

Sweat ran in rivulets down Nora's back by the time they arrived in the speck of a
town. At least Virginia had trees to shade a person from the unrelenting heat. The open
prairie held no such respite from the sun. "First stop, the parsonage." With little trouble,
Nora found the white house with blue shutters where the pastor and his wife resided.

She reined the team to a halt and climbed down.

"Morning, Mrs. Green."

Josiah stood in front of her, hat in his hands. Was he even bowing slightly? "Good day, Mr. Abbott. I was just about to pay a call on the Mileses."

"What for?"

She pulled an envelope from the pocket of her violet-sprigged cotton gown. "Mr. Yates forgot to pay the preacher for performing the wedding ceremony. I offered to bring it in, but I do have an ulterior motive for being here."

Josiah raised his eyebrows. "What might that be?"

"Well, I didn't want to say anything in front of Wade, but I did go to the play the other night. Don't worry, Mrs. Turnbull came and watched the children. She even lent me her brooch and her buggy. I spoke to a man there." She fanned her face. "He played the jester but never took off his mask. I'd like to find him."

Josiah's face turned redder than a ripe strawberry. "Well, you can't speak to the pastor right now. He's. . .he's. . .uh, he's taking a nap."

"At nine o'clock in the morning?"

"Ah, you see, that is, he gets up very early in the morning for prayers and study. So he's ready to rest just about this time."

Nora peered at him sideways. What odd behavior. "What am I supposed to do with the payment?"

Josiah snatched it from her. "I'll make sure he gets it, right away today, after his nap."

"I don't know. Wade was pretty adamant that I deliver it. Seems J. M. was supposed to pay the minister, but. . ." Would that one day haunt her forever?

"No worries there. Don't you think you can trust me?"

She flashed him her I'm-not-sure-about-this-but-I'll-go-along-with-it smile. "Fine. We also need to stop at the livery and the store. I can ask about the jester there." Nora moved to climb aboard the wagon, but Josiah stepped in her way.

"What do you need at the livery?"

"Seems Wade didn't bring enough money with him when he had Mercy shoed last week. I'm to pay the rest of that bill, also."

"I can save you the trip, since I was headed over there just now myself."

"You were? It's in the same direction you came from." What was going on with this man? Was there some reason he didn't want her to be seen in town?

Josiah's heart raced faster than a locomotive across the prairie, and sweat covered his entire body. Why did Nora insist on searching for the jester? He couldn't let her do it. He had to keep her from asking around. Not everyone knew he played the part, but enough did. It only took one to tell the tale and ruin everything.

There had been something special between them that night. A connection he'd never experienced with anyone else. He'd never forget. Would always cherish that one, special memory. Oh, to be able to relax and be himself around her like he had then. But he couldn't open himself up to that kind of rejection and pain.

He'd had enough of it in his life. A vision of Susanna flashed through his mind. His fiancée before he left for the war. The woman who spurned him when he returned to

Virginia with one less limb.

He had to keep Nora from finding out who he was. Somehow keep Paul Wilson, the store clerk and the man who played the role of the king's guard, from spilling his secret.

At least no one else in town other than Pastor Miles knew about his role in the mail-order bride fiasco. He'd been wise to keep that between himself and Wade. This was a whole new problem. "Let me walk you to the store." He'd figure out how to keep her in the dark on the way.

"I thought you were going to the livery."

"That can wait. I imagine you'll have your hands full keeping this bunch in line while making your purchases. Unless there is something I can pick up for you?"

"Alice requires material for a new dress, and James's pants are much too small."

"Ah, yes, those are items you'll have to choose for yourself. But let me accompany you."

She sighed as the children scrambled from the wagon bed. William tugged on Josiah's shirt. "We're gonna be real good. Miss Nora promised us candy if we didn't cause no trouble."

"Glad to hear that you've decided to mind her." The group of them trooped down the street and marched into the mercantile. "You'll find the bolts of cloth over there." Josiah pointed them out for Nora.

She busied herself with making her selections while he sauntered over to the counter where Paul Wilson stood tallying Mr. Zimmer's bill.

"I'll be right with you, Josiah." Paul shoved his wire-framed glasses up his nose.

Josiah pushed by Mr. Zimmer. "Sorry for the interruption. I need to borrow Paul for just a moment. He'll be right back, and you'll be on your way." He leaned over the counter, grabbed Paul by the elbow, and tugged him away from his addition problem.

"What are you doing?" Paul wrenched himself free from Josiah's grasp. "I was with a customer. One who was here before you, I might add."

"I need a huge, huge favor."

"Not another one. You won't have me writing to every confectioner in the country looking for your favorite licorice again, will you?"

"Nothing like that. A very simple favor this time."

Paul glanced at the heavens. Or at least at the ceiling. "What?"

Josiah lowered his voice to a whisper. "Just don't tell Miss Green that I was the jester in the play the other night."

"Why not? You were the best part of it."

"The jester is a fool."

"Ah, and you don't want to be a fool in the eyes of a beautiful, young, and from what I hear, available young woman, is that it?"

"Something like that." The tips of his ears burned.

"No problem. She won't hear it from me. Can't guarantee that no one else won't let the word slip."

"Only you and the others involved in the production know. I want it kept that way." Though Paul did have a point. Somehow, Josiah would have to catch each of the cast members and warn them not to say anything to Nora.

How long would he be able to keep up this charade?

Chapter 7

I can't believe they're giving an encore performance of the play." Nora almost skipped across the kitchen to place the plate of fried eggs in front of Maude.

She turned up her nose. "The edges are burned, and the yolks aren't runny." She pushed the dish away. "You know how I like them. You have your mind too much on going to the play and not enough on what you're doing."

That old, familiar headache returned with a vengeance. Nora had to go, just had to. This was her one opportunity to find the jester. No one else in town knew who played the part. He was as mysterious as the yet-to-be-seen J. M. Griffin. "Please, I'd like to attend. You went last time. Why would you need to see it again?"

Maude sniffed. "Well, it certainly wasn't as good as any of the productions we saw in Virginia, not by a long sight, but it is a way to get out of this insufferably stuffy house and away from those wretched, unruly children."

Nora clamped her lips shut before she said something she would regret. If Maude ever got out of bed, she could step outdoors and work in the garden. And, while the children were a handful, they could be sweet and even charming if they tried. They needed a firm hand and loving arms. They needed a mother.

"It's just for a little while. I'll go right before it starts and come home as soon as it's finished." As soon as she discovered the jester's identity.

"You're a single woman. You can't strut about town unaccompanied."

"This isn't Virginia. Things are different around here. Nothing will happen to me."

"No, I forbid it."

"Wade could come with me."

Maude peered down her hawkish nose as her face turned as red as a poppy. She scraped back her chair. "Are you after my husband? So jealous of me because yours doesn't want to have anything to do with you? Absolutely not. You stay away from him. If I so much as catch you looking at him, I'll cast you out of this house so fast, it will make a train look like a turtle." With her skirts swishing, Maude swept out of the room.

"You wouldn't, because then you'd be left alone with the children." Lucky for Nora, Maude was too far out of the room to hear her whispered words.

She sat in a chair with a *thunk*, the cold eggs staring back at her. What had become of her life? How could she ever meet anyone, fall in love, and escape Maude's crushing thumb if she couldn't leave the house?

The back door swung open, and Josiah entered the kitchen, a grin across his round, boyish face. "Morning, Mrs. Green."

"Good morning," she mumbled, unable to find the strength to speak out loud.

He pulled out a chair and sat across the table from her. "You look like your favorite kitten died."

She sighed and wrung the corner of her apron. "Almost as bad. Maude has been on a tirade, all because I asked if I might go to the play's encore performance. I don't wish to complain, because she and Wade have been so good to take me in, but one night out would do me a world of good."

"You're a godsend to Wade. He's told me so on more than one occasion. Without you, he'd be no better off than before, except he'd have someone else to have to care for. Maude may not be appreciative, but Wade sure is."

A warmth spread through Nora's middle. "Thank you. That's just what I needed to hear at this moment."

He patted her hand, his own cool and work-roughened. Tingles shot up her arm, much like they had when the jester touched her. He, too, had calloused fingers. Could it be? No, most of the men in the area worked hard on their plantations. Many of them had fought in the war. That would toughen any hands.

His features softened. "Nora, I . . ." And then he jerked his hand away and sat back. "What's wrong?"

"Nothing. I just, well, never mind. I've taken too much of your time. Have a good day."

He stood. Winced. Stumbled.

She hurried to him and grabbed him by the elbow to steady him. "Are you hurt? Sit down. Let me help you."

He trembled beneath her touch. "No, no, let me go."

She did as he asked. Why was he leaving in such a hurry? But, more intriguing, why had he come in the first place?

Once again, Josiah stood behind the curtain on the small stage, waiting for his entrance cue. Another chance to play the jester.

He performed the part well the other day in front of Nora. When he stood, his stump pained him, as it did from time to time. The sensation caught him off guard. But he didn't want to let her know. Refused to tell her what was wrong. He'd worked so hard and long to hide his wooden leg, practicing until what was left of his real leg bled so that he could walk without a limp.

All to no avail. Susanna never got over the sight of him missing a limb. Nora never would either.

The king spoke his cue, and Josiah entered the stage. Even as he stumbled around and played the part, he scanned the audience. Wade and Maude were there, so Nora must not be. Good. How could he face her after that embarrassing incident, even with the mask hiding his identity?

Wait. There she was, in that brown gown that highlighted the red in her auburn hair. Like last time, she stood in the back of the room, pressed against the wall, casting furtive glances at Wade and Maude every few minutes.

Dear, sweet Mrs. Turnbull had given her another night out.

The production moved along, eliciting more laughs and more cheers than the first time. After a round of shouts for encores and one last group bow, the audience broke up to move to the refreshment table.

It was as if an artist had painted the same scene twice. This time, though, Josiah wove his way through the crowd. Was he trying to hide from her or find his way to her? He paused for a moment. Yes, he could go to her. The mask protected him.

Nora ran into the jester near the back of the room. Her heart trilled. "I've found you."

"So it seems you have."

"I've been searching all over town for you. No one knows who you are."

"I like a little mystery to surround me."

"Can we speak outside again? There's someone here I'm hoping to avoid."

He nodded, and she led the way through the door and down the steps. "You look lovely."

Her cheeks warmed. "Thank you."

"Can I get you something to drink?"

With a touch to his forearm, she stopped him from turning to go inside. "No, thank you. I don't have long before I have to leave. Let's enjoy this moment together. You were very good again."

"And I thank you."

"But why all the mystery? Why not reveal your identity? At least to me. I promise not to tell anyone who you are."

"That isn't possible." He fidgeted with the sash around his waist.

"Why not?"

"It just isn't."

At his strong words, she stepped back. "I'm sorry. I didn't mean to push, but it would be nice to know who you are."

He grasped her hand. "No, I'm the one who must apologize. Forgive me for my rudeness, but I simply can't permit it. I have my reasons. Can you trust me that this is for the best?"

She nodded. Was it his familiarity that brought out this trust in her? His soft, gentle manner with her? The mystery behind the man? Whatever it was, she did trust him. He hadn't betrayed her to Wade and Maude. She wouldn't betray him.

Cicadas chirped as darkness settled around them. Fireflies danced above the cotton fields, a show that rivaled the stars twinkling in the sky.

She couldn't risk staying much longer. Maude would complain of something or another at any moment, and she and Wade would leave. But she couldn't allow the jester to slip away again. "I'd like to get to know you better."

He turned away from her, his focus on the lone tuft of grass beside him. "I wish there was a way. But there isn't."

"If we meet in the darkness, in private, we could speak without me having to know who you are." Did she reek of desperation?

He caressed her cheek, and her breath hitched in her chest. She swallowed hard. Not even with Richard had she had such butterflies in her stomach, such whirring in her head.

"You are an incredible woman. But this is nothing more than a dream. A fantasy. A fairy tale for us to enjoy just for this evening."

"I'll never see you again?"

"Not unless the next play has a jester, no."

"Are you J. M.? The man I was supposed to marry?"

"Don't ask such questions of me." He bent over.

He was going to kiss her. She pulled him close, and their lips touched. Sweet and soft then intense and fiery.

"Goodness, Wade, I don't see what was so wonderful about the production. I just need to get home before this headache blinds me."

Nora yanked away from the jester. Maude. She had to get out of here before Wade and Maude left the building. With her pulse pounding in her neck, she raced for the buggy, hopped in, and spurred Mrs. Turnbull's horse to a gallop.

Tears blurred her vision.

She'd never had a chance to tell the jester good-bye.

Chapter 8

Nora flipped another batch of flapjacks onto a plate and turned the bacon in the frying pan. For two weeks, she'd hoped and prayed the jester might reconsider, that he might come calling for her.

He hadn't.

And he wouldn't. The truth hit her in the gut. Hard.

That dream, that fantasy, came crashing to earth like a kite that lost the wind.

But was the jester somehow connected to J. M.? The little niggling in the back of her mind pestered her day and night.

No one came to the table. Where were they all? Usually the salty fragrance of frying bacon brought the boys scrambling to the table long before it was ready. Come to think of it, Wade hadn't gone to the barn this morning to do the chores.

After pulling the bacon from the pan, she went to the boys' bedroom and opened the door. "Why aren't you boys. . ."

Charles and William sat on one edge of the mattress, eyes wide, William sucking his thumb. James was stretched out, asleep on the other bed. Charles took the lead. "James is real sick, Miss Nora. He's hot and moaning."

She crossed to the little boy, his cheeks scarlet, burning with fever. "You boys go and have your breakfast. It's on the table."

Without waiting for them to scurry away, she spun and hustled to the room she shared with Alice. Instead of being happy that she got a few minutes to herself while Alice slept unusually late this morning, she should have been concerned. Sure enough, the sweet child lay curled in a ball, her cheeks as red as James's. Nora dropped to the bed and cradled the little girl. "Oh, dear one, I'm sorry. I didn't know you were so sick."

Alice peered at her with glassy eyes. "I'm thirsty." She croaked out the words.

Nora kissed her fiery forehead. "You rest. I'll get you a nice, cool glass of water."

"Nora? Nora." Maude's weak call came from the bedroom she shared with Wade. Nora tucked the covers under Alice's chin and went to her stepsister's door. She knocked, soft at first then harder.

"Get in here." Though weak, Maude's words still carried impact.

Maude and Wade lay in bed, both with the same burning cheeks as the children, both with the same fevered eyes. "Not you, too. James and Alice are ill as well."

"Then do something. I need water." Maude fussed with the sheet.

"I'll bring some for both of you." Nora stepped out of the room and clicked the door shut.

In the kitchen, Charles and William sat at the table, staring at their plates. "Have you finished already?"

Charles shook his head. "We aren't much hungry. It's. . ."

"It's what?"

A small bell tinkled from the back of the house, coming from the direction of Wade and Maude's room. Wherever had she gotten that? "Try to eat a little. You don't want to get sick, too. I have to take care of the rest of your family." A doctor. That's what they needed. But Charles and William were both too small to send out on their own. And she couldn't leave the ones who were ill.

What was she going to do?

She inhaled and let the air out in small increments. First things first. "Charles, clear the table. William, find me every towel you can." They hustled to their jobs while she went to the pump and filled a bucket with clean, clear water. As she worked, she scanned the horizon. A good number of mornings each week, Josiah appeared here for one reason or another. Today, she needed him. He could go for the doctor. Help her care for all these patients.

But the horizon remained empty.

Except for the sharecroppers in the fields. The Lord provided the answer right in front of her. She brought the bucket to the house, ladled out glasses of water, and distributed them. For ease of care, she moved Alice into the room with James and helped them both sip from the glass.

Once everyone had their fill, she returned the cups to the kitchen, but before she had a chance to get outside to speak to one of the sharecroppers, Maude's bell rang.

Nora scurried to the back of the house.

"I need some chicken broth. And help to use the chamber pot."

"I was about to send someone for the doctor. Can you wait for a moment? And the broth, well, I haven't even thought about starting that yet."

"You would leave a poor, sick woman to take care of herself? What if I get dizzy when I get up and I fall?"

Wade waved her away. "Get Doc Stephenson. I'll help Maude."

"How unseemly. Nora, please."

She finished the humiliating chore, checked on the children, and at last made her way across the fields to send someone out, when a horse and rider appeared on the horizon.

Josiah.

She ran to meet him. He reined to a halt and slid from the stallion's back when they met. "What's wrong?"

Tears pooled in her eyes. A few spilled down her cheeks. "Everything. Just everything."

Josiah pulled her into his embrace. "Hush now. Things will be fine. I'll take care of you."

And for a brief moment, she leaned against him, his embrace a refuge.

One she never wanted to leave.

Josiah cradled Nora close to his chest as she relaxed into him. He breathed in her scent, a mix of rosewater and bacon. He kissed the top of her head.

For one sliver of time, he had everything he needed.

Then she stepped back. "Wade, Maude, James, and Alice are all ill. Some kind of fever, I don't know what. I was about to send one of the sharecroppers for the doctor. And Maude keeps ringing a bell so I can't get anything done. Thank goodness you're here. What would I have done without you?"

"Tell me what you need."

"I don't know." A few tendrils of hair escaped their pins and curled around her face. "Everything. Help."

"I'll send Joe for the doctor. Have the chores been done?"

She shook her head. "The poor cow."

"One of the sharecroppers can take care of that." He grabbed the horse's reins, and together they made their way to the house. "What else do you need?"

"A chicken for broth."

"Consider it done."

She stared at him. Such a little bit of a thing, but with a strong constitution. Still, she shouldn't have to go through this alone.

He butchered the chicken, plucked it, and brought it in to her. She had just put it in the pot when the doctor's buggy pulled up to the door.

The middle-aged man with a head of gray hair entered. "Hear you have some sickness going around."

"Four down as of right now." Nora's shoulders slumped.

Josiah rubbed her back. "Let me take you to see the children first."

Nora followed them and sat beside the little ones as the doctor examined them, hemming and hawing. She held them close and whispered into their ears. As she did so, each ones' features softened. No doubt she reassured them they would be fine.

While the doctor checked on Wade and Maude, Josiah and Nora went to the kitchen. She poured him a cup of coffee.

"You should be the one sitting and letting me bring you something."

"I can't be still until I know what's going on. I should have noticed yesterday. The children were lethargic, and no one ate much supper. Silly me, I thought it was just the heat getting to everyone. And here they were coming down with an illness."

She stood beside him, and he pulled her into the chair next to him. "You are running this household, taking care of the children, and catering to Maude's every whim. How much more can you expect of yourself? You had no way of knowing they were getting sick."

"But Maude complained of not feeling well."

"Maude complains every day of the week."

Nora flashed him a small smile. "That is true."

"In my book, you're a saint for putting up with her."

"She's my stepsister. And she gave me a home when I didn't have one. I owe her a great deal."

"Do you know what a wonderful woman you are?" Josiah held his breath at his brazen words. Why had he gone and said that?

A furious blush stained her cheeks, and not from fever. Could it be that she cared just a little for him?

But no, it could never be.

The doctor emerged from the sickroom. "Mighty ill bunch you have there. Ague, most likely. I'll leave you some willow bark powder to mix into tea for them. I'm smelling chicken broth, which is good. Make sure they get plenty to drink. And Josiah, I noticed you limping. Is your stump giving you trouble?"

Nora gazed at him, her mouth open.

Why did the doctor have to say anything? Josiah squared his shoulders. "It's fine."

"Good luck to you, then." With that, the doctor breezed out of the house and left in a cloud of dust.

Nora refilled his coffee. "What did he mean by your stump?" She glanced at his legs.

"Chancellorsville cost me my right leg." If he closed his eyes, the scene played in front of him, the acrid odor of gunpowder, the heat of the ball penetrating his shin, the screams of dying men.

"Why didn't you say anything?"

"I don't like people to know. I don't want pity. Not yours, not anyone's. And now is not the time to talk about it. We have a sick family to care for."

"You're going to stay and help me? Can you do it?"

He ground his teeth together. She should never have found out. Now, even this connection he had with her was ruined.

Chapter 9

Josiah dropped a load of firewood into the box beside the stove, his stomach growling at the aroma of chicken and onions. Nora came down the hall, her steps slow, her shoulders slumped. All day, she'd been running between the two sickrooms and the kitchen.

He pulled out a chair at the table and gestured to it. "Sit down before you fall over sick."

"I can't. Maude needs—"

"At this point, I don't care what Maude needs. What I care about is what you need. Which is time off your feet and a good, strong cup of coffee."

She moved in the direction of the stove until he grabbed her and steered her toward the chair. "I can get it for you. Sit. Now."

"You're almost as demanding as Maude." In between the slow blinks of her eyes, a small light twinkled. His heart flipped.

He poured the coffee and set the cup in front of her. "How you manage to keep your sense of humor is beyond me."

"If I don't laugh, I'll probably cry."

"Well, we can't have that." From the larder, he pulled the half-eaten apple pie he'd spied earlier. Once he'd cut slices for himself and Nora, he sat beside her at the table. She clasped her delicate hands together. "You're done in." *But still beautiful.*

"I'm afraid it will be a long night."

"I'll lend you a hand."

"Oh, but you can't."

"I'm every bit as capable as anyone else." His words came out more of a growl than anything.

She sat ramrod straight, every inch the genteel Southern lady. "I didn't mean to imply—"

"No one ever does. But they always do. That's the way it works. That's why I never wanted you to find out." His fork clanked to his plate. He shot upright, knocking the chair over, and marched out the door, slamming it behind him.

He'd made it down the porch steps when the door squeaked open behind him. "Josiah, wait."

He continued stomping away from her.

"Please, stop and listen to me."

He spun around to face her. "What is it? What do you have to tell me that I haven't heard a thousand times before? This is why I left Virginia and came to Texas. To get a fresh start, away from everyone who knew me. Away from the pitying stares, the platitudes that almost drove me out of my mind."

"You're upset about nothing. I didn't mean—"

The ringing of Maude's little bell drifted through the open bedroom window.

"Go to her." He spit out the words.

"No. Not until I tell you what I need to say."

His heart thumped against his rib cage. What did she have to tell him? Did he want to hear what she had to say? No. He couldn't stand the pity anymore. He wasn't half a man. But no one understood that. "I don't want your sugary words." He turned back for the barn.

Light footsteps tapped behind him. The bell dinged once more. "Nora? Nora?" Maude's weak voice drifted through the open window.

Without turning, Josiah waved Nora away. "Go take care of her."

But the footsteps behind him continued. She wasn't going to give up.

He entered the barn, his eyes needing a moment to adjust to the dim interior.

"Josiah."

He gulped. Sooner or later, he had to face her. It might as well be sooner. Get it over with. Then get over her. "What?"

She reached him, took hold of him by his forearm, and spun him so he had to look at her. At her beautiful, oval face, her green eyes shimmering with tears, several tendrils of chestnut hair curling about her flushed face. When the pain sliced through his chest, he fought to remain upright.

If only she could be his. If only she could see past his impediment.

"Please, listen to me." She breathed hard after her sprint.

"You've said enough."

"You haven't listened enough. I wasn't finished."

"Then by all means, say what you have to say and leave me in peace."

"Your leg means nothing to me. It doesn't define who you are or what you can do. I won't stop being your friend because of it."

His friend. And nothing more. Because she had never seen him without it. When it came off, that's when horror set in.

"But you asked me if I could do it. Now, knowing what you know, you're afraid I can't be of help to you. That you'll end up having to take care of me, too."

"Only if you get sick. Maybe my words didn't come out right. I meant to ask if you could take time away from your plantation and crops and animals to be here."

He rubbed his sweaty forehead. Was she sincere? Did she mean what she said, or was she only trying to get herself out of an awkward situation?

She parted her red lips. A breeze from the open door blew a wisp of her hair in front of her eyes. She brushed it away.

He reached for her. Drew her close. Leaned in for a kiss.

"Nora?"

Something crashed outside.

He released her, and she turned and dashed for the house.

What had he almost done? Had he lost his senses?

Nora held her skirts and raced from the barn toward the house, her head whirring as she ran. Had he almost kissed her?

Had she wanted him to?

Those thoughts fled when she reached the porch. Maude lay crumpled on the top step, sweating and shaking all over.

God, forgive me for leaving her. And for all my unkind thoughts about her.

Nora scurried up the stairs to her stepsister. "Maude, oh, what are you doing out here?"

"Help me."

Josiah skidded to a stop beside them. "Maude, you should be in bed. Let's get you back there." He nodded to Nora. "I'll grab her under one arm. You take her by the other."

Together, they managed to pull Maude to her feet.

"I don't know if I can make it. I'm so weak." Maude's face was an uncharacteristic shade of white.

"We'll get you there. I'm so sorry I didn't answer the bell. I should have never left the house."

"No, you shouldn't have." The fever hadn't affected Maude's tongue.

"Now that we have her up, I can take her." Josiah swept Maude into his arms and carried her through the house to the bedroom.

Nora followed. "Thank you. I couldn't have done this on my own. This is how I know what I said in the barn is true."

He flushed and then stepped back. "You'd better get her settled. I'll make sure Charles and William are behaving themselves. Think I'll take out the cart and pony. A drive around the farm will do them some good. That way, we can check on the cotton and keep them out of trouble. If you need anything, send one of the sharecroppers for me."

She touched his hand, his skin warm to the touch. "That would be very welcome. Don't let the boys run roughshod over you."

"I have two pennies in my pocket." He winked at her.

She went soft in the knees and steadied herself against the footboard.

"Are you going to help me?"

Nora returned her attention to Maude and got her situated under the covers.

"Why didn't you answer the bell?"

"I was in the barn." She suppressed a giggle. Was it from nervousness or happiness? Who could tell? Her insides were as mixed up as cake batter.

"What were you doing out there? We need you in here. Get me a glass of water. I'm parched."

Once she had given Maude her drink and checked on the other patients, Nora returned to the kitchen to prepare the broth. As she strained out the chicken bones, the onions, carrot tops, and celery bottoms, she stared out the window. Her stomach danced as Josiah rode into view astride his gleaming black stallion, following the pony cart Charles was driving.

What the poor man must have suffered. She'd sat with Richard at the hospital in Richmond as his life ebbed away, brought water to the other men in agony, read to those well enough to sit for a while. Even though years had passed, the odors of blood and decay and death filled her nostrils, a smell she would never forget. Nor the screams and moans of the injured and dying men.

She shook off the memories, set the pot aside, and wandered to the window in the front room. Josiah and the boys made their way toward the fields, cotton balls now puffing out from the green plants. She leaned against the cool glass, her head aching.

Josiah. The jester. J. M. What was she going to do about them? J. M. was as good as a ghost. Maybe he didn't even exist. And the jester? She'd never see him again.

But Josiah was right here. More real than either of the others. She sighed and hugged herself. Could she be falling in love with him? A small laugh burst from her lips. Yes, she might be.

If only Maude hadn't interrupted their kiss.

Chapter 10

The oppressive Sunday summer afternoon heat bore down on Nora. For over a week, she'd been cooped up in the house, afraid to leave, only doing so to make brief trips to the privy. She'd neglected Maude once, and look what happened.

The fevers all broke, and the family was on the mend. It would have been nice to go to church this morning, but she didn't dare leave. The moment she did, something was sure to happen.

But maybe she could enjoy a Sabbath's rest. She wandered onto the porch and sat in the rocker overlooking the ripening cotton, the plants' leaves dying back. Soon the sharecroppers would be picking it, their dark faces shining with sweat, their songs rising and filling the air.

Her favorite time of the year. The rhythm of it moved something in her soul. Made her come alive.

A slight breeze stirred the leaves of the rosebushes along the porch rail, and she sat back in the chair with a sigh. Maybe she could close her eyes, just for a moment.

Boots clomping across the porch startled her awake. She bolted upright. Josiah stood over her, his dark brown hair parted on one side and slicked back, a grin traversing the whole of his face. "Good morning, sleepyhead."

She covered her yawn. "Oh my, I must have dozed off. I only meant to sit for a minute." In front of her, his horse stood hooked to his buggy, the fringe top pulled down. "I didn't know you had such a beautiful rig."

"Mostly I don't bother with it. Doesn't seem to be many occasions for me to have it out, since I'd be the only one in it."

"What's the special event that made you bring it?"

"I've come to take you for a ride."

At his announcement, she trembled. What did he mean by the offer? Had he come courting?

"I figure that you've been in the house long enough and you must be ready to get out for a while."

Oh. He felt sorry for her. "If only I could. Everyone is napping, but they might need me. They still aren't fully recovered."

"Recovered enough for you to take a break."

The infernal bell rang. Nora shrugged. "See what I mean?"

Josiah strode into the house. She jumped up to follow him. Without missing a beat, he marched right into Wade and Maude's bedroom, not even bothering to knock. He grabbed the small brass bell from the bedside table and chucked it out the window.

Maude and Nora both gasped. Wade sat up in the bed, wide-eyed.

"How could you do something like that? How am I to call Nora when I need her?" Maude stared narrow-eyed at Josiah.

He clenched and unclenched his fists. "Ever since you took sick, you've been running Nora ragged. She's done a wonderful job caring for you and Wade and the children. She deserves a bit of rest before she comes down with the fever herself. Then who would look after you?"

Maude's mouth opened and shut like that of a fish.

"Precisely. Now, since it's a rather warm day, I'm taking Nora out for a breath of fresh air. We'll be back in a few hours. You can fend for yourselves for that amount of time."

Wade nodded. "She's done enough for us. She deserves some fun."

Maude shot her narrow-eyed gaze at her husband. "Hush up, Wade. I'm not taking care of those kids."

Josiah grabbed Nora by the elbow and led her from the room. "We'll make our escape while we can." He chuckled, the sound as soothing as a low rumble of thunder on a steamy summer day.

Once outside, he helped her into the buggy, his hand strong and firm in hers. Richard's had been soft, like a woman's. This was better. Much better. Josiah knew the value of hard work.

He climbed in beside her and clucked to the horse. The breeze the movement generated washed over Nora's warm face. "Ah, that feels good."

"Nothing better for cooling off, unless you jump in the creek. And you don't seem to be the kind of lady who would do such a thing." The color in his cheeks heightened.

"I used to sneak out of the house and from under Mammy's nose when I was little and run to the brook behind the house. My brother and I would catch tadpoles and minnows." She pressed her middle.

"I didn't know you had a brother."

"He died when he was thirteen."

"I'm so sorry. Is that why you came out here as a mail-order bride?"

"Daddy's gone, and my husband, too. The war cost us everything."

"And there I go again, nosing into business that isn't mine. My apologies."

Richard would never have apologized for anything. In almost every way, Josiah was her late husband's opposite. She touched his hand. "Thank you, but you have nothing to be sorry for."

Nora squeezed Josiah's hand, sending tingling shivers up and down his arm. Even after she knew about his leg, she didn't treat him different than everyone else. Susanna hadn't been able to do that. No one had. "Well, I'm still sorry. I know how it is to have people pry into your private life."

"But friends can." She sat back. "When I first came, I didn't like this wide-open space at all. But I'm getting used to it. I'm finding the beauty here."

"You should see it when the bluebonnets bloom in the spring. A carpet of purply blue as far as the eye can see."

"Sounds spectacular."

"It's a sight to behold."

"Thank you for coming to my rescue with Maude."

"She doesn't treat you well."

"But I owe them. They took me in when I had nowhere else to go."

He bit his lip. That was his fault. He'd put in her a position where she was forced to live with that woman. Should he tell her his true identity? Could he do it?

What point was there? He couldn't marry her. Couldn't allow her to see him as he truly was. She might not have bolted when he told her he lost his leg. It was another thing to see him without it, hobbling around.

And if he told her the truth of his identity, she would hate him. He couldn't bear not having her in his life.

That sounded like love.

He peered at her, her eyes gleaming as the two of them raced over the prairie, her cheeks flushed, a smile curving her lips.

So beautiful.

And then the reins in his hands jerked. Rosco reared. He came down and bolted.

Josiah pulled back with all his strength. His horse refused to slow.

Nora screamed, covered her mouth with one hand, and clung to the edge of the seat with the other.

As he tugged at the reins, sweat poured down his face, stinging his eyes. His muscles cried for him to let up.

The buggy bumped over a rock and tilted to one side. "Lord, keep us upright."

With another bump, they righted. Beside him, Nora laughed, but not a chuckle of glee. More a strangled tittering. Her nervous chuckle.

Nothing but open road lay before them. As long as they didn't hit too many ruts or rocks, the best course of action might be to let Rosco have his head. Josiah loosened his hold on the reins. "Hang on."

"What are you doing?"

"Letting him run himself out."

She slid to his side and grasped his bicep with a death grip. "Are we going to crash?" She breathed hard.

"Trust me. We'll be fine."

She nodded but didn't let go of him. He had to protect her.

After a good gallop, Rosco, now lathered, slowed. This time when Josiah pulled back, the horse responded and stopped.

Josiah dropped the leather straps. His hands shook. Nora trembled beside him. He turned and stroked her cheek. "See, we're fine."

"You handled Rosco well."

"In town, it would have been a different story. I wouldn't have been able to let him go. But out here, there was no danger. Did you see what spooked him?"

"A snake. The biggest I've ever seen." She shuddered. "I think it was poised to strike."

"Then it's a good thing Rosco ran."

"You kept such a cool head."

"Compared to battle, this was nothing."

"Since we're friends, I'm going to ask. Was it awful?"

He'd never cleanse the stench of gunpowder or blood or death from his nostrils. "The worst. No matter what happens to me the rest of my life, that will always be the most horrible thing I'll ever endure."

"Does nothing frighten you anymore?" She didn't turn his way but gazed at the birds as they crisscrossed the sky and called to one another.

Only her. Only that she would hate him if she knew the truth. "A few things. But mostly, no."

She chuckled. "Spoken like a true man."

"What do you fear?"

"My biggest fear?"

He nodded.

"Loneliness."

He ground his teeth together. How could he have done this to her? Left her by herself and vulnerable. "Now you have a friend, so you shouldn't be lonely."

She gazed at him, a dimple deepening in her cheek. He'd never noticed that before. "You're right. I have you and Wade and Maude and all the children."

Once Rosco cooled down, Josiah turned the buggy toward the Yateses' home. Maude sat on the porch rocker and came to her feet as they pulled up. "It's about time you're home. Alice is crying and asking for you, and I can't get her to stop."

Josiah helped her down. She squeezed his hand once more, the warmth of it shooting straight to his heart. "Thank you for the lovely diversion. Guess I'm needed here."

All the way home, Josiah slumped in the seat.

He'd been such a fool.

Chapter 11

Just as Nora finished washing the coffeepot and storing it on the shelf, Maude swept into the kitchen, her fan flapping like a hummingbird's wings.

"Give me a cup of coffee. And some of that cake from last night."

Nora sighed. "We ate all the cake, and I just finished washing the pot. Isn't it too hot for coffee?"

"Never. It's the only thing that keeps me going."

The words *going where?* balanced on Nora's lips. She sucked them in and reached for the pot. "You'll have to wait for it to brew."

"You never have anything ready for me. I'm constantly waiting for you. Can't you be a little more organized? Maybe then the house wouldn't be such a mess."

"A mess?" Nora peered around. She'd spent the morning scrubbing the kitchen from top to bottom. Not a speck of dirt remained.

"I see crumbs all over the table."

They must be imaginary. Nora fought to keep those words from spilling from her mouth.

Josiah knocked and entered, saving her from another tongue-lashing. He smiled at her, and her afternoon brightened.

"I let Charles borrow my hammer to practice with some nails, and I think he brought it in here with him. Since I'm helping Wade with the fence, I'm in need of it."

Maude did what she did best. Screeched at the boy. "Charles Yates, you get in here right this minute with Mr. Josiah's hammer."

"No harm. It's good for the boy to learn."

"And what happened to you?" Nora nodded to Josiah's pants. A long rip ran vertically from three inches above his knee to three inches below it.

"Got it caught on a nail. That's why I need the hammer."

"You can't work like that. Let me get you a pair of Wade's, and I'll sew that rip right up for you."

Maude harrumphed. "He doesn't need to borrow anything. Next thing you know, Wade's pants will be ripped, and then what is he supposed to wear?"

"I'll go back in the room and get them for you. And stop and pry that hammer from Charles's hands."

He winked at her. Her knees went weak. Would she even be able to make it down the hall?

With Maude squawking behind her the entire time, Nora retrieved the pants and the missing tool. While Josiah changed, Maude continued her tirade. Nora allowed it to fade into the background as she measured out the coffee.

Josiah emerged from the bedroom and handed her the pants. "You're a good soul, Nora."

"It's no trouble at all." Except for the fluttering in her stomach, a sensation that plagued her every time Josiah came anywhere near her.

Once Josiah returned to work and Maude had her coffee, Nora sat with a thread and needle to repair the rip. She turned the pants inside out to hide the sewing as much as possible. As she did so, something fell out of the pocket. A folded piece of paper.

She picked it up. Her breath caught in her throat. The lavender paper. The rosy scent of it. The rounded script on it. All familiar.

Hers.

The first letter she'd sent J. M. Griffin, answering his mail-order bride advertisement. But why would Josiah have it? She crinkled her forehead. This didn't make sense.

She checked the other pockets. In one, she touched a soft piece of fabric and pulled it out. Her handkerchief. The one she'd dropped the night of the first play.

Again, why did Josiah have it?

Her heart rate kicked up until it matched that of Rosco's pounding hooves on Sunday. There was only one logical explanation to all of this.

Only one thing made sense.

She rose, dumping her sewing supplies from her lap to the floor.

Maude clucked her tongue. "What are you doing? Look at the mess you've made."

Unable to answer for the lump that clogged her throat, Nora fled the house.

Josiah swung the hammer, hit the nail on the head, and drove it into the wood. Only a few more spots to fix and Wade's fence would be good as new. With Wade just barely recovered from the fever, he needed a helping hand. At least, that's what Josiah told himself. But the truth was his appearances at the Yateses' place had more to do with a beautiful young widow than with anything else.

The front door slapping shut brought Josiah to attention. Nora marched down the porch steps and strode across the farmyard. A woman on a mission. And not a very pleasant one, judging by the scowl on her face. One of the boys must be in a heapload of trouble. Josiah chuckled. Poor kid.

But she didn't call out for one of the children. Instead, she halted right in front of him, her skirts swishing behind her with the suddenness of it. "Josiah Abbott."

"Yes, ma'am."

"Is that your real name?"

He cocked his head. "Pardon me?"

"Is Josiah Abbot your given name?"

His stomach plummeted like the teacher had called him to attention for some offense. He leaned against the fence for support. Had she figured it out? "Yes, it is."

"Then explain this." She thrust the lilac-colored paper she'd used to write to him in front of his face.

"What is it?"

"A letter I sent to J. M. Griffin, agreeing to be his bride. Strangely enough, it fell out of your pants pocket when I went to sew them."

There was no use denying it. She knew the truth. He only had to speak the words. Even though he would lose her forever, it was beyond time for the truth. He closed his eyes and puffed out a burst of air. "There's a logical reason for that."

"I'm waiting." She pinched her lips together.

"Nora, I never meant to hurt you. My initials are J. M., and Griffin is my mother's maiden name. All this mail-order bride business was Wade's idea. He persuaded me to place an advertisement, too, but I was scared."

"Of what? A woman?"

"Yes, precisely. I had a fiancée before the war. Susanna. When she learned I lost my leg, she broke off the engagement. What if I married someone and she rejected me as soon as she saw me without my wooden leg? I'd have to annul the marriage. How embarrassing for both of us."

"But you sent me the train fare. Why do that if you didn't intend to marry me?"

"Oh, but I did plan to take you as my wife."

She blinked, her lashes fluttering against her pale cheek. "Then why aren't we married?"

"I was there that day at the train station. I saw you exit the car." How did he tell her this? He toed the ground with his good foot, rolling the words around in his head, and then stared straight at her and clasped her hands. "You were, are, the most beautiful woman I've ever met. Stunning. From that one glance at your face, I knew you were too good for me. You'd never have me in this condition. When I ran away, I did so to protect both of us from broken hearts."

"You don't think my heart was broken when you didn't claim me?" Color rose in her face, and probably not from the August sun.

"What was I to do?"

She shook her head. "How about give me a chance to make up my own mind? You could have told me. Let me tell you what I thought about your leg. Our marriage."

"Don't you think it tore me in two to walk away from you?"

"You left me alone on the train platform. No money. Nowhere to go. Without Wade and Maude's kindness to me, I would be destitute, without a place to live. When I told you I lost everything in Virginia, I wasn't exaggerating."

"I'm so sorry about that. If they hadn't taken you in, I would have helped you out, at least until you found another husband."

Tears pooled in the corners of her eyes, shimmering in the bright sunlight. "I—I. . .I don't even know what to say to that." A few tears spilled over her eyelids and slid down her cheeks.

He reached out to wipe them away.

She wrenched free of his grasp and backed up two steps. "Please, don't."

"If there is anything you need, let me know. It's the least I can do for you."

"Do you think giving me money will fix this mess?"

He rubbed his forehead, pain stabbing him behind his eyes. "What am I supposed to do?"

"And what about this?" She held up her wrinkled handkerchief.

His throat tightened. No, she'd found that too?

"Were you also the jester?"

He nodded.

"Why didn't you tell me it was you?"

"For two nights, there was beauty for me. The chance to speak to you unfettered by my past. To tell you what was in my heart without having to worry about anything else. A memory for me to tuck away to last me the rest of my life."

"How could you tell me such a lie?"

Her rapid breathing, her flared nostrils, the tears in her eyes—it was too much for him, and he studied the ground. "Only my identity was a lie."

She threw the paper at him, the breeze carrying it away as it fluttered to the dirt. "Please, don't ever speak to me again."

As she stomped away, his body went cold.

What would he do without her in his life?

Chapter 12

Josiah held his breath until Nora disappeared into the house, the door slamming behind her. He slumped against the fence.

It had all been a dream, anyway. A child's fairy tale that would never be real. A woman like her could never love a man like him. He slammed the hammer into the dirt, took off his hat, and squeezed his throbbing head.

Wade emerged from the barn and wiped his glistening face with a handkerchief. "Heard a bit of squawking out here, like a mad momma hen. What's the trouble?"

"Nothing." Josiah stared at Wade, who stared back. "All right, everything."

"You got yourself into a bit of trouble?"

"More than a bit. I'd call it a heap." He sighed. Might as well tell Wade. He'd find out sooner or later. "She knows. Everything. All about the mail-order fiasco, all about the jester."

"That would explain the noise. She sounded furious."

"An understatement. I've never seen a woman so angry before. And my mammy got pretty angry with me from time to time."

"So, what are you going to do about it?"

"Do about it? She warned me never to speak to her again, so my only option is to keep my distance. Maybe I can try to find her another mail-order groom. She can't stay with you forever."

Wade grimaced. "Much as I would like her to, you're right, she can't. A woman like her needs a home and family of her own. But I think you're it."

Josiah frowned. "Me?"

"I've sat through meals and church services and such with you both. The way she gazes at you, I'd say she's smitten. And you, I can tell the feeling's mutual."

Josiah's chest squeezed. It would be less painful to lose another limb than to lose Nora. Life without her would be empty. Cold. Lonelier than ever. "But what am I supposed to do? She's sworn she'll never have anything to do with me again."

"She just said that in the heat of the moment. Give her a chance to cool down, to do some thinking. Maybe she'll take pity on you yet." Wade gave Josiah a light punch on the arm. "She's a gem. Don't let her get away."

"Maybe it's for the best. We could never have a future together. Shattering the dream now will keep me from false hope that there could be anything between us."

"You're so hung up on that leg of yours. Why not let her decide if that's something she can live with or not?"

"Because I know what her answer would be." Josiah circled Wade.

"You don't know until you ask the question."

Josiah snapped to attention. Could he gather the courage to talk to her about it? To show her what an empty pant leg looked like?

But what if she rejected him? Well, it couldn't get worse than it was now. All she could do was walk away. But if she wasn't bothered by it...

"Give her a few days to calm down, to sort through everything she's learned. To get used to the idea of you being her mail-order groom. Then talk to her."

Josiah drew in a deep breath. "It's not like I could end up in a worse position."

"That's the spirit." Wade chuckled as his three boys scampered by, chasing a barn cat to the cotton fields.

"All right. I'll do it. I'll talk to her. Thanks. You're a wise man."

A window in the house banged open. "Wade Yates, you get yourself in here right this instant."

"Maybe in some things. Not in everything." Like a naughty child, he slunk toward the house.

Josiah picked up the hammer from the ground and got back to work on the fence. Mending his relationship with Nora wouldn't be as easy as repairing this enclosure.

But if he could explain things to her, if he could make her understand, if she could see past his impediment, then maybe they had a chance to be happy together. To make that life he promised her in his letters.

What an awful lot of ifs.

Nora wrestled with her sheets, tossing and turning in bed until she found the covers twisted around her. It was too hot for them anyway. She threw them aside and slid from the mattress, even though darkness still covered the plantation. The sharecroppers wouldn't even be up yet.

In her bare feet, her shawl wrapped around her shoulders, she padded to the front door, opened it without a sound, and stepped onto the wide porch. Early morning dew clung to the rosebush beside the steps, the sweet scent hanging on the breeze. She sucked in a deep breath, the air cool and clean.

So, Josiah was both J. M. and the Jester. A few days had passed and the idea was taking root in her mind now. How blind could she have been? She should have known. He and Wade were best friends, so it made sense they would have both placed advertisements for mail-order brides. And the jester had the same uneven gait as Josiah. The mask hid his features and muffled his voice, but it didn't conceal the way he walked.

Why hadn't she picked up on those clues?

Not that it mattered.

He'd deceived her.

Those days at the military hospital rushed back to her. When Richard was delirious, she spoke to many of the soldiers. They worried what their sweethearts back home would think of them now that they'd lost an arm or a leg. One time, she'd read a letter to a young man from his girl. In it, she broke off their courtship, unable to bear the thought of being married to a man with one arm.

Josiah had mentioned a woman. His fiancée, who'd had the same reaction. How that must have stung.

She leaned against the porch rail and stared across the fields. Against the sunrise-streaked sky, a dark silhouette approached. A horse and rider. Who could be coming at this early hour?

The trot of the stallion gave her the answer.

Josiah.

Her insides danced around. She pressed her middle in a hopeless attempt to stop them. No matter the lies he'd told, there was something about him that sent her to quivering whenever he came around.

She stood without moving as he came near, right up to the steps, and slipped from his horse's back. Shivering, she pulled her shawl tighter around herself. "I didn't expect to see you this early."

"I hoped you might be up." Huskiness edged his voice. He climbed the stairs and stood beside her, overlooking the fields. "Cotton picking should be finished in the next few days."

"Wade said it was a good crop this year."

"Plenty to get by on for the winter."

A few of the hands emerged from their cabins, probably eager to get as much work done as possible before the heat of the day.

He took her by the shoulders and spun her to face him. "Nora, I am very sorry for what I did to you. Leaving you at the station. The lies. All of it. I don't know if I'll ever be able to make it up to you, but I'd sure like to try."

"That's a hard thing, Josiah."

"I don't expect you to understand why I didn't tell you the truth. My reasons, which seemed good enough to me, weren't right. It's nothing I'm proud of. In the end, instead of protecting you, I hurt you."

Now her heart joined in the fluttering. "But I think I do understand." Her words came out in a breathy whisper.

He furrowed his brows. "How can you?"

"What you don't know is that I spent three weeks at a military hospital in Richmond, tending to my husband before he died. Much of the time, he wasn't lucid. I spoke with the other soldiers. Those who had lost limbs. I know the pain they endured, both physical and emotional. What you went through was extremely difficult. I spent many hours holding these men's hands, reading the Bible to them, praying with them. And hearing how the women they loved rejected them."

His brown eyes widened. "When she broke off our engagement, Susanna shattered my heart. We grew up together. I didn't know life without her."

"Is that why you moved to Texas?"

"I had to get as far away from her and the memories as possible."

She reached out and touched his stubble-covered cheek. "I can only begin to imagine how difficult that was for you. Though you were wrong to lie, I understand why you did it."

"You do?"

Her breath came in small drafts. "Yes, I do."

"Can you forgive me?"

"I already have."

He stepped closer, pulled her to himself, and whispered into her hair. "I love you, Nora Green. You are the only woman in the world for me."

She nestled into the crook of his arm. "Josiah Abbott, I love you, too." So full of love, her chest might burst open.

He squeezed her and then released her. "Before we get carried away, I have a question to ask you."

Could it be? Was he going to propose? Had she forgiven him enough to accept him? "Go ahead."

He bent over, lifted his pants to reveal his wooden leg, and unfastened the buckles that held it to his stump. The fake leg fell away. He grabbed the porch rail. "Can you bear the sight of this?"

An unbidden tear slid from the corner of her eye. "I cared for men who had just endured amputation. I cleaned their wounds. I smoothed their brows." She drew her gaze from his leg to his face. "When I look at you, I don't see a missing leg. I see a whole man. A sweet, caring, able man. One I love with all my heart." She drew him into an embrace. "One who gave me hope again."

He kissed her forehead and each of her temples. "Then, Nora Green, there's only one thing we can do about this."

"What's that?" She held her breath.

"We have to get married."

"Is that a proposal, Mr. Abbott?"

"The way I see it, I already proposed, and you accepted. All we have to do is make it official."

"Then let's get married."

Josiah leaned over and kissed her, like she'd always dreamed the handsome prince kissed Cinderella.

Epilogue

A warm breeze from the open window caressed Nora's cheek as she waited in the Mileses' spare room for the wedding ceremony to start. Alice tugged on the skirt of Nora's dove-gray dress trimmed in red. "Are you getting married?"

Nora squatted to Alice's eye level, her voluminous skirt billowing. "I am, sweetie. But don't worry, I'm just going to move down the road to Mr. Josiah's farm. We'll still see each other all the time."

Despite the reassurance, Alice frowned. She leaned over and whispered in Nora's ear. "Is she gonna have to be my momma now?"

"What is she saying to you?" Maude, dressed all in black, squawked as she sat and fanned herself in the far corner of the room. "How you can just up and leave us like this with a mere three days' notice? Now I must deal with this pack of wild animals myself. Did you stop to think about me even once? Of course not. I do believe I'm going to swoon."

Nora didn't so much as glance in Maude's direction. With no *thunk* forthcoming, Maude must have remained upright.

Alice stuck out her bottom lip, and tears glistened in the corners of her eyes like raindrops on the cotton plants. "I don't want you to go."

Poor dears. Heaven help them. "I'll be next door. You can visit me as much as you like."

Alice's frown curved upward. "Do you promise?"

"Certainly."

Maude flipped her fan closed. "After your chores are done, and not a moment before."

Nora kissed the little girl's cheek and whispered back. "I love you, and I'll speak to your daddy. He'll let you come whenever you want."

A knock sounded at the door, and Mrs. Miles peeked inside. "The men are ready. My, oh my, Nora, you are exquisite. Josiah is a very blessed man."

The three ladies and Alice made their way across the yard to the church. As she stepped into the back room, Nora tingled from the top of her plaited hair to the soles of her satin boots. Josiah stood at the front of the church, Pastor Miles behind him, a book in his hands.

She giggled but not from nerves. Not this time.

With sure, firm steps, she marched to stand beside her groom, his hair slicked back, wearing the same suit as when she'd caught sight of him as she disembarked the train.

Her stomach fluttered. She had to be the most fortunate woman in the world.

Pastor Miles intoned the ceremony. "You two have taken quite the journey to get here. What was supposed to be a marriage of mutual benefit has turned into a union of two hearts in love. God has surely blessed both of you and brought you together in His providence and His timing."

That He had. From a jilted bride to one in love. From a destitute woman to one overflowing with joy. From forsaken to cherished.

She stared at Josiah, who stared back at her. For a moment, the rest of the world faded away, as if it didn't exist. Only Josiah. He squeezed her hand and smiled at her. She clung to him, woozy.

Around her, the ceremony continued. "Love each other every day. Don't take one another for granted. The Lord has given you a special gift from above. Cherish it. Cherish each other."

The pastor spoke some more, but Nora didn't hear him until he said, "Nora, do you take this man to be your lawfully wedded husband, to have and to hold from this day forward, for better or worse, in plenty and in want, in sickness and in health, until death do you part?"

"I do." With all her heart.

"Josiah, do you take this woman to be your lawfully wedded wife, to have and to hold from this day forward, for better or worse, in plenty and in want, in sickness and in health, until death do you part?"

A single tear escaped his eye and trickled down his cheek. She reached up and wiped it away.

"I do. I most certainly do."

"Then by the power vested in me by the church of God, I pronounce you husband and wife."

Josiah didn't wait for the pastor's go-ahead. He swept her into an embrace and kissed her until she lost her breath.

Oh, what a happy story they would write together.

Liz Tolsma is a popular speaker and an editor and the owner of the Write Direction Editing. An almost-native Wisconsinite, she resides in a quiet corner of the state with her husband and their two daughters. Her son proudly serves as a US Marine. They adopted all of their children internationally, and one has special needs. When she gets a few spare minutes, she enjoys reading, relaxing on the front porch, walking, working in her large perennial garden, and camping with her family.

The Brigand and the Bride

by Jennifer Uhlarik

Chapter 1

Meribah, Arizona Territory
November 1876

Heart pounding, Jolie Hilliard glanced back, scanned the street behind, then hurried through the afternoon crowds of Meribah. Tucking her groom's letter with instructions for their nuptials under her arm, she shifted her nearly full satchel to her other hand. She must hurry, or their carefully laid plans would be for naught.

Seeing the SEAMSTRESS shingle outside a Meribah storefront, she took another glance around. No sign of her brother, Brand, though she couldn't be lulled into complacency. He and his men were too wily to be fooled for long. A chill gripped her as she darted inside the shop.

"May I help you?" a woman called from the back of the room.

At the counter, Jolie dropped her satchel. "My name's Jolie Hilliard. I'm to pick up a suit for Mr.—"

"Oooh." The woman squealed, a broad smile lighting her face as she laid aside her sewing and approached. "You're the blushing bride."

Jolie's cheeks heated. "Yes, ma'am. How'd you know? I didn't give you his name."

"You're just as he described. That, and. . .in my business, ain't too often someone sends another to pick up their clothes."

Jolie nodded. It *was* odd, but the tight time frame between her groom's expected arrival and the preacher's impending departure meant this was the only way they could pull off the quick ceremony.

"Your man is such a charmer," the woman blathered.

Jolie glanced toward the windows, scanning for familiar faces.

"He'll make a fine husband. And so handsome, to boot."

She nodded. "Not to be rude, but. . .I'm in a bit of a hurry."

"Oh, of course. Forgive me. I love weddings." She left and returned momentarily with a paper-wrapped parcel. She snipped the string and peeled back the crinkly paper to reveal a costly looking suit coat. The woman pushed it nearer. "This'll be striking on him, won't it?"

Jolie nodded, mute. She'd trust the woman's assessment. Her groom's letters described him as slightly taller than average with blond hair and blue eyes. Until they met, she couldn't judge. She touched the fabric. "You do fine work. What do I owe?"

"He paid in advance." She retied the package and handed it over. "Best wishes on your marriage, young lady."

Young lady. Hardly. At twenty-six, she was a spinster but only for another hour. Jolie tucked the package under her arm with the letter, retrieved her satchel, and faced the door. "Thank you."

Once more, she scanned the street and, certain Brand and his men weren't around, stepped outside. She paused at a nearby bench to tuck the suit inside her bag and adjust the Colt Peacemaker she'd hidden inside for easy access.

Jolie hurried, scanning faces and shadows on every side.

Lord, help me reach the church and get married without my good-for-nothing brother finding me. I beg You.

No sooner had the prayer formed than someone hooked her elbow and spun her around. A screech clogged her throat as she fumbled for the pistol. Before she reached it, a kindly gray-headed gentleman waved a paper at her.

"Beg pardon, but you dropped this." He shrugged. "Called after you, but you didn't hear."

Heart hammering, she relaxed. "Thank you, sir."

Grinning, the gentleman handed it over and moved along. She eyed the nearby faces then glanced at the letter.

After exchanging a few notes, sweet Jolie, I'm confident I'd like to marry you. I understand our union would be in name only, but you strike me as intelligent and hardworking, and I'm successful in my chosen profession. It would be a smart match.

Could becoming a mail-order bride ever be considered *smart*? Not when she'd dreamed she'd marry for love. But with Brand's gang dominating her life, she had no other choice.

Jolie reread the directions to the church then scurried toward it, happy to see the whitewashed steeple come into view as she rounded the corner. One last time, she scanned the street then nearly ran to the double-doored entrance.

As she entered, a stout little woman pushed herself out of a ladder-backed chair. "Jolie Hilliard?"

"Mrs. Carter?"

The woman grinned. "Come. The rooms you requested are this way."

She followed. "Please take me to the groom's room first. I've brought him some things."

The woman stopped halfway down the hall. "This is his."

Jolie entered the room and placed the requested towel, razor, shears, and grooming items next to a basin of water then unwrapped the suit. She draped it over the chair to prevent wrinkles.

"And my room?" As per their agreement, she deposited her satchel near the door so her groom could store the toiletries and his clothes in it.

Mrs. Carter led her back to the first doorway and motioned her inside.

"Thank you."

"I'll be about, should you need anything."

"I appreciate your kindness."

"The reverend and I are happy to oblige where young love is concerned." She waddled from the room.

Eyes closed, Jolie squared her shoulders. There was no love. Within the hour, she would wed a stranger and hopefully leave the Hilliard name behind. Forever.

Lord, please let this man be as kind and gentlemanly as his letters portray. And please. . .please don't let Brand find me—us. Ever.

Del Adler ducked into the church, pulse galloping. He must hurry. The vestibule empty, he darted down a hallway and peeked into room after room. All empty but for some chairs or a desk. Halfway down, he hesitated. On the desk lay a basin, towel, comb, straight razor, strop, and shears, and draped over the chair, a suit. Just waiting—for him. His heart beat even faster.

He cast his silent thanks heavenward then entered. Locking the door, he removed his tattered hat and slicked his hair with water then combed it. He cut his shaggy blond locks into a neat style. Not the easiest thing, but he'd clean up as best he could—and quickly. Task accomplished, he combed his hair again then lathered his scraggly beard and shaved his whiskers. Hurrying, he wiped his face and changed clothes. The small mirror revealed a much different-looking man than when he'd entered.

"Just what I prayed for, Lord. Thank You."

He wrapped the clumps of hair he'd cut in the towel then rolled his clothes around it. Near the door, a satchel caught his attention. He unfastened the top but before cramming his clothes and hat inside, he spied the butt of a pistol peeking at him. He grasped the gun. A Colt Peacemaker. Del checked the loads, grinned, and stashed it and his things inside.

Again, Lord, thank You. You're taking better care of me than I deserve.

Bulging satchel in hand, he opened the door and scanned the hall. Empty. Tiptoeing, he headed toward the vestibule. At the intersection of the hall and foyer, he squinted through the window. He gulped as several familiar figures approached.

"Oh, goodness, you startled me!" a feminine voice blurted from behind him.

Spooked himself, he spun.

"It's a good thing you made it." A stout woman pulled him toward what had to be the sanctuary. "We've just enough time."

"Time?" He stalled, though she wouldn't be deterred.

"As my letter stated, our schedule is very tight. The reverend and I must take today's stagecoach, which leaves town in fifteen minutes. We were about to cancel. Miss Hilliard is close to tears."

For a short woman, she was mighty strong, dragging him down the aisle toward a lanky, gray-headed fella and a fetching auburn-haired beauty in a shimmering blue ensemble. Quite a good-looker, that one.

The redhead cupped a hand over her mouth, looking for all the world like she might cry but quickly composed herself and met his gaze with striking blue eyes. "Thank God you made it. Are you ready?"

Dread skittered down his spine. Ready…for *what*? Surely not what it looked like. His belly knotted.

The round woman snatched his bag and shoved him into position beside the beauty.

The redhead smiled. "It's nice to finally meet you, Frank. I'm Jolie. Hilliard." She shrugged. "I guess you knew that."

Astonished, he stared. "I. . .I. . ." He glanced at the tall drink of water facing them. Clammy sweat covered Del's skin. Good Lord above, what had he gotten into?

Heavy footsteps and familiar voices sounded at the back of the room. Fear gripped him. "Sorry 'bout the delay. Nice to meet you, Jolie. I'm. . .Frank." He clamped his eyes shut and faced the man. "Reverend? Don't wanna hold you up."

The man nodded. "I'll make this brief. Do you, Franklin Thomas Lovell, take Jolie Ann Hilliard to be your lawful wife?"

Del dared not look back as the voices drew nearer. "I do."

"Do you, Jolie Ann Hilliard, take Franklin Thomas Lovell to be your lawful husband?"

Miss Hilliard's brows furrowed as the plump woman spoke a few sharp words to the intruders behind them.

Del nudged her. "Well, my sweet? Do you?"

She raked wide blue eyes toward him before facing the reverend. "I. . .do."

"By the power vested in me by the Territory of Arizona, I pronounce you husband and wife." The preacher grinned. "You may kiss your bride."

Del faced her. One of the interlopers stood far too close for comfort. In a heartbeat, he swept the woman into his arms, angled his face toward the cross on the front wall, and pressed his mouth to hers in a deep, abiding, and passionate kiss.

She stiffened, panting, but quickly relaxed and returned the affection.

Mind spinning with the intensity, Del forced himself to focus—listening for hints the lawmen he'd escaped that morning might've moved on. *Lord, forgive my deception. You know I'd never play such a foul trick under normal circumstances. Help me, and I promise I'll make it right.*

"Deputy Kagan!" Marshal Connor Benson's voice boomed. "That's not Adler. Let's go before we lose him for good."

The deputy clomped toward the door.

When the footsteps died away, Del broke the kiss. Miss Hilliard stared, wide-eyed and breathless. Truth be told, his lungs labored to draw air, too. He grinned at her.

Stunned, she turned to the preacher.

"Congratulations, Mr. and Mrs. Lovell. Now if you'll excuse us, my wife and I have a stage to catch. Please leave so we can lock up and git."

"Happy to oblige." Del took his *bride's* hand and led the thunderstruck gal from the sanctuary, pausing only to grab the satchel.

Chapter 2

Jolie's mind raced. Frank's letters had promised their marriage would be in name only, yet the kiss he'd just given her. . .had curled her toes. Her knees were *still* weak. What was he thinking? Was he expecting more than a business partnership?

Lord, please don't let this be a mistake.

Her groom paused at the church doors. Jolie's eyes strayed to the windows flanking the double doors and found the churchyard quiet. No sign of her brother's gang.

Frank plucked the hat hanging from a hook beside the door and, tugging it low over his eyes, peered outside. With a gentle hand at her back, he guided her down the path, through the gate, and around the corner, away from the hotel she'd seen on her way to the seamstress's shop.

Jolie's thoughts churned. "That was odd, those men interrupting our wedding, wasn't it?"

He glanced her way, his hat brim shading his light-colored eyes. His Adam's apple bobbed. "Surely was." He fell silent again.

After half a block, Frank hooked her arm and turned down a small alley. His pace slowed as they reached the far end, and he peered out.

Dread traced her spine. "What's wrong?"

Silence.

Leading her from the alley to the town's livery, he stopped at a stall containing a big strawberry roan with a white blaze. The animal nickered softly, nudging Frank's chest.

Frank rubbed the horse's nose in return. "Missed you, too."

Jolie stared. He'd missed him? How, when they would've ridden into town within the last hour?

"Wait here whilst I fetch my gear." He disappeared.

She stared. They'd agreed to spend their first night in the Meribah hotel—she in the bed, he on the floor—and head to his Phoenix-area home the following day. Why ride to the hotel just blocks away?

He returned, dropped his saddle, and began bridling the roan.

Jolie's belly knotted. "I mean no disrespect, Frank, but aren't we staying in town tonight?"

He led the horse from the stall, tossed the blanket and saddle in place, and cinched it. "C'mon, we got a ride ahead."

Her jaw slackened. "Didn't you hear me?"

He led the horse toward the stable entrance.

Confused, Jolie followed. "Frank. . . ."

Just outside the wide door, he slipped the satchel's handle over the saddle horn, swung onto the horse's back, and offered her a hand.

"This is nothing like we agreed."

"So you said. I have my reasons, and I'll make 'em clear soon enough."

Hesitating, she finally took his hand and scrambled up behind him, her hands settling awkwardly at his waist.

Frank clucked his tongue and headed toward the mountains a few miles west of town.

Del's head throbbed, partly from the too-tight hat he'd *borrowed* from the church—presumably the preacher's—and partly from having to lie to Miss Hilliard. She'd be miffed once she learned his deception, but hopefully she'd grant him mercy.

Lord, I wouldn't've done this if there'd been another choice, but Marshal Benson was breathing down my neck.

"Where are we going?" Miss Hilliard asked.

He had to get her out of town before she caused a fuss. If she raised an unholy scene in Meribah, Benson might hear and recapture him. "You'll see."

Outside of town, he moved the roan into a lope, and soon they reached the foothills.

"Frank, I demand to know what's happening. I'm concerned. This is all very strange."

Del slipped from the saddle once they'd ridden into the hills. "Get down, please. . . ." He reached to help her, but for an instant, she eyed him. Eventually, she rested a hand on his shoulder and, his hands at her waist, he lifted her down.

On the ground, she searched his face. "Is everything all right?"

Holy Moses, but she was pretty. He loosed his hold and took a step back.

"No, ma'am. Not exactly."

Concern creased her porcelain skin. "What's wrong?"

"Well, um. . ." Del threw a prayer heavenward. "I'm, uh. . .not. . .Frank."

As realization dawned, Miss Hilliard's face blanched. Tears pooled against her lashes, though as quick as they came, they disappeared again, and her jaw clenched. She stormed toward him, palm smashing hard against his chest. "What do you mean, you're not Frank? Who are you?"

He backed up. "I'm real sorry. I meant no harm."

"Who in blue blazes are you, mister?" She stormed at him, shook her slim, graceful finger at him. "Why would you impersonate my groom?"

"It's a misunderstandin'. I promise."

"You'd better explain, quick, or I'll. . .I'll. . ." She looked toward the horse.

His heart seizing, Del strode toward the roan and swung onto its back.

She glared. "You brigand. What do you want from me?"

He chuckled. "Nothin'. Truly, ma'am. Iffen I had more time, I'd explain the misunderstandin'. Reckon you'd laugh iffen you knew the full story." He'd laugh but for the fact that Marshal Benson was working so hard to recapture him. Once he'd cleared his name, though, this would be worth a month of laughs.

"Find the time, mister. The real Frank Lovell will want to know why I married another man today."

"You didn't. Frank Lovell didn't take vows, and the vows I said weren't under my proper name, so. . .beggin' your pardon, but you're still plain ol' Jolie Hilliard." He backed the roan away. "Now you walk on back to Meribah—ain't but a couple miles— and have yourself a happy life. Please forget you ever met me."

He spun the roan and rode deeper into the mountains.

"Wait! I need my. . ." Her words faded under the heavy hoofbeats.

Lord, please let that pretty gal forget me, quick.

As comely as she was, it'd be hard to forget her.

Chapter 3

Belly roiling, Jolie stared after the blond interloper. Not only had he impersonated her groom, he'd taken her clothes, Frank's letters, his suit, and her Peacemaker. *Lord, can this get any worse?*

She glanced at Meribah then back the way Frank—er, the imposter—had ridden. Her frustration boiling, Jolie shrieked. This was *not* how she'd envisioned her wedding day going.

Of course, she'd never dreamed she'd marry a stranger either.

Jolie glared at the town, shimmering like a mirage, then toward the foothills covered in cactus and desert plants. Return to Meribah, or seek out the meddling fool. Her jaw clenched tighter. Somewhere, the *real* Frank Lovell would be looking for her—at least she hoped he would—but she couldn't face him until this sham marriage was resolved. Nor could she risk running into Brand's gang without her Peacemaker. They'd mistreated her for too many years. Her marriage was her ticket to freedom, but just when she'd broken their hold, this handsome rogue had used her, too. She'd have none of it. He wouldn't take advantage, nor would he undo her plans.

Grinding her teeth, she marched after the imposter.

Working his way through the dense cactus, Del ducked low to avoid the arm of a saguaro. He hadn't gotten near as far into the mountains as he'd hoped, thanks to the threat of the posse on his trail. When he'd heard men's voices, he'd hid out awhile until they'd passed, slowing his progress.

Lord, I surely didn't intend on dumpin' that pretty little gal. Please see her safely back to town.

The unusual action had so gnawed at his conscience that he'd repeated the prayer since he'd left her. Pa had taught him to escort a lady to her destination—be concerned for others, particularly his ma and sisters. Surely that gal was somebody's kin.

But his current circumstances were anything but normal.

Lord, please. . .help me get clear of the mess I'm in. . .and get Pa's ring back. He rubbed the conspicuous indentation on his right-hand ring finger. *Then let me find Miss Hilliard and make this up to her.*

It'd be downright awkward to find her with the real Frank Lovell, though. He didn't want a fight, but he might be begging trouble from the devil himself. For Miss Hilliard's sake, hopefully not. She seemed like a kind woman, not the type who deserved trouble.

He snorted. Perhaps that lightning-fast wedding had put him in a romantic mood. What could he really know of her from those few minutes?

That she was prettier than any woman he'd ever met.

That she was spunky and unafraid to give him what for.

That he'd hurt her but she was strong enough not to melt into tears like so many women would.

How could Miss Hilliard mistake him for her groom? When she thought he was Frank, she'd introduced herself, saying it was nice to *finally* meet him. What sort of courtin' process did they have?

Del scanned every direction for the marshals. Alone, he turned into a small cactus-filled canyon and slid from the saddle. He patted the horse's neck. "Let me change my clothes, and then we'll figure where to camp. Sound good?"

The horse tossed its head and nibbled on the sparse grass.

"Good enough." He seated himself on a nearby rock and set aside the borrowed hat. Satchel between his feet, he removed his worn duds and peered into the bag. Miss Hilliard's threadbare ivory and pink dress, the pistol, and a letter from Frank Lovell.

Dearest Jolie,

Thank you for your candor about your difficulties with your brother. I now understand why you'd advertise yourself as a mail-order bride and why you've asked my secrecy.

After exchanging a few notes, sweet Jolie, I'm confident I'd like to marry you. I understand our union would be in name only, but you strike me as intelligent and hardworking, and I'm successful in my chosen profession. It would be a smart match.

If you'll accept these terms, please meet me in the Meribah church at four o'clock Tuesday, the twenty-third. The schedule will be tight—I cannot arrive sooner, and the parson must leave on the afternoon stage an hour later. That leaves us a thirty-minute window to take our vows. Thus, please stop by the seamstress shop while going to the church and collect the suit I'm having made.

If that didn't beat all. He'd stampeded in on this gal's secret wedding. No wonder she hadn't realized he wasn't Frank. Their union was a mail-order arrangement. *Lord, I didn't mean to bust up her plans. Please let her reach Meribah and get hitched like she. . .*

Recalling the preacher's hurry to leave, Del scanned the letter again. Iffen Frank intended to marry her, they'd have to wait for the preacher's return.

Why would God allow him to stumble into the middle of this? He had a crime to solve, was dodging the law. . .and now he'd be worried about some poor gal getting hitched to a stranger.

"Just stop." He crammed the letter into the bag. "You got enough trouble without borrowin' more." He tucked the string tie in a pocket before stripping the suit off. He laid it neatly over the satchel. "She ain't *your* sister, Delaney Adler. Or your wife." He threaded his arms through his rumpled plaid shirtsleeves. "You don't have to save the world. Take care of this business and head home to Ma and the girls." In a wide spot in the path, he shook the wrinkles loose from his folded pants.

"Don't move. . ." The metallic click of a gun's hammer sliding into place punctuated Jolie Hilliard's steely command.

Chapter 4

Jolie rose after retrieving her gun from her satchel. The man lifted his hands, pants dangling from one fist. He was a comical sight. Bedraggled plaid shirt just covering his rump, and his legs swathed in a faded red union suit and stocking feet.

"How in the name of Pete did you track me down?" The imposter glanced over his shoulder.

"Wasn't hard. Once you got into this dense vegetation, you'd stick to areas you could traverse with a horse." She scanned the several varieties of cactus, ocotillo, yucca, and other desert plants. "You'd stay on the more traveled paths, so once I knew your direction, I cut across country and picked up your trail farther along."

"Well, I'll be. . ." His tone held a grudging respect.

"Why did you do this to me?"

"Look here, little lady, I didn't mean you no trouble. That's for sure." He started to turn.

"I said don't move!"

He faced front. "I'm sorry."

"What's your name—your *real* one? I know it's *not* Frank."

"No, ma'am, it's Delaney Aaron Adler. You can call me Del."

"Oh, there's plenty of choice names I'd rather call you."

"Reckon you'd have that right."

Yes, she would, although she wouldn't do it. She'd committed to always act like the lady Ma raised her to be, despite the rough life Brand exposed her to.

"Beggin' your pardon, ma'am, but I'm at a real disadvantage. Can I put on some britches so I ain't standin' in my drawers?"

Cheeks flaming, Jolie kept the pistol level while she reached for the bundle that must be his trousers. As the fabric unfurled, the shears, razor, and other gear clattered to the parched ground.

She scooped up the shears and razor and put them in her pocket. "You were trying to get me to hand over that shaver, weren't you?"

"No, ma'am." His voice shook a little. "I forgot that was there."

Lies. "Just for that, you can stand there in your drawers awhile longer."

His shoulders slumped. "Please, ma'a—"

"Let's get something clear, Adler. You tricked me this afternoon. To make it right, you're going to accompany me back to Meribah, and, first thing tomorrow, see a judge to be sure this mix-up isn't binding. Understand? Then I can marry Frank."

"Ain't tryin' to get your dander up, ma'am, especially with you aimin' that peashooter at me, but. . .I can't go to a judge."

Jolie scowled. "Can't. . .or won't?"

"Both, I reckon."

"Start making sense, mister, or I might just pull this trigger."

He hung his head. "It's just that. . .those men at the church were lookin' for me. I ducked inside to hide, and I found your man's suit. Figured God was offerin' me a way to change my look and slip outta town. Only the preacher's wife shoved me down the aisle and. . .the marshals came bustin' in. You didn't know I wasn't Frank, and I couldn't come clean about the mix-up without gettin' caught." He shrugged.

Her thoughts ricocheted through the hasty ceremony. One of the lawmen said a name. . .something like Adler. *Lord, of all the people to get mixed up with. . . Why did this addlepated dolt barge in on my carefully laid plans?* "You're an outlaw then?"

"No!" He shook his head fiercely. "I'm a rancher from Colorado. Came here on business some weeks back and got accused of robbin' a bank. I got railroaded, sentenced to serve time at Yuma Territorial Prison. Thing is, I never set foot in that bank."

Sure he hadn't. Criminals were practiced at professing innocence. "I'm afraid I have to insist. Once we see that judge, you can go and I'll wish you the best of luck."

Hands sinking, he shook his head. "I set foot in a courtroom, and that'll be the end of me clearin' my name and gettin' back to my kin in Colorado. Surely you understand that."

"And surely you understand that my future nuptials can't happen if I'm already hitched to you." Her belly flip-flopped at the thought.

"Like I said, those vows can't be bindin'." Again, he twisted to face her. "Not when I used a wrong na—"

She squeezed the Peacemaker's trigger, and the pistol roared, raining moist cactus flesh over him.

Adler faced front and, squatting, dropped Frank's pants to cover his head.

"Unless you want the next one aimed at your skull, don't turn around."

Slowly, he straightened. "I understand."

"Good. Now put these on." She tossed his britches, the balled fabric hitting him between the shoulder blades and falling to the ground. He slipped them on then lifted his hands again. "Can I get my boots, ma'am?"

The sky was streaked with pink and purple hues, far too late to make it to town before nightfall. Jolie had no desire to camp alone with this brigand, so she retrieved the coiled rope from his saddle. "Turn around."

He complied.

"Sit down." She pointed to the rock he'd sat on earlier then backed away, making room.

"Pardon?" His eyebrows arched.

"Sit." Jolie motioned. "I'm going to tie you to that rock, and come morning, I'll return with the posse."

"You intend to leave me tied up all night?" His voice was incredulous.

"Since you frittered away our travel time, yes." Even an extra half hour of daylight could've meant getting back to Meribah that evening. "Sit. Now."

With a harrumph, Adler complied.

She tossed the rope at his feet. "Tie your ankles."

He complied, scowling. Legs secured, she had him sit in front of the rock, his back braced against it. She bound one wrist, looped the remaining length of rope tightly around the back side of the boulder, and tied his other.

"That oughta hold you till morning."

In the waning light, his gaze reflected frustration, trepidation, and ire. "How am I supposed to defend myself? What if some varmint thinks I'm easy pickin's?"

She glared. "You should've thought of that before you crossed me."

No sooner had she spoken the words than regret enveloped her. Since when had she turned into Brand? She shoved her belongings into her satchel and strode to the horse. There, she removed the canteen from the saddle and hung the satchel in its place. Glancing at Adler, she sighed and withdrew Frank's coat. Looking at it a moment, she dropped the canteen within reach of his hand then draped the garment around his shoulders.

"Nighttime gets cold in these mountains. I'll leave you this. Try not to dirty it, please. I'll expect it back in the morning."

Del seethed as Jolie Hilliard mounted his roan and rode into the growing darkness. Blast that wicked woman, leaving him like this. He'd have no way of defending himself if a varmint wandered near. God forbid she get delayed in returning. He'd bake to a crisp in the sun. Bless her for leaving him the canteen, but. . .the way he was tied, he couldn't bring it to his lips.

Lord, this here's a predicament I hadn't planned on. I'd be obliged if You'd help me out of this fix.

He rolled each wrist, the stiff rope biting into his flesh, and his left hand struck something hard and cold. He felt the ground, fingers grazing it again. This time he latched on, fumbling to identify it.

The razor. Del cast a humble glance heavenward. "Bless You, Father."

He shrugged the suit coat from his shoulders and struggled to open the blade. After several attempts, he pried it free from its protective covering and aimed the sharp edge toward the rope.

The blade made easy work of the stiff fibers and they gave way, releasing his wrist. Drawing the rope from around the rock, Del worked the other knots loose.

He looked toward the ever-darkening sky. "Now. . .You know exactly who robbed that bank. Just how am I to clear my name?" He listened for the answer. When nothing other than Jolie Hilliard's face came to mind, he shook his head. "Forgive me for remindin' You, Lord, but I escaped the US Marshals' custody so I could take care of this. Last thing I need is trouble of the female persuasion."

Free of the ropes, he tucked the razor safely in his back pocket. Thankfully, Miss

Hilliard had left his boots. Bless her, even if it was an oversight. Her pretty porcelain features, ice-blue eyes, and auburn hair danced through his mind as he tugged his boots on and pulled his pant legs into place then rose to coil the rope. Where to? The picture of Miss Hilliard atop his roan bubbled into his thoughts. "Dad-blame it. Are You telling me to track her down?" She was likely headed to town to round up that posse.

He'd caused the woman enough grief. He'd almost be willing to let her ride away on his horse, except for the part where. . .she rode off on *his horse*. The roan was a mighty fine animal—best he'd ever owned. He blew out a long breath and snatched up ol' Frank's suit coat.

One lonely star and a sliver of a moon hung in the velvety blackness above. "Fine, Lord, I'll hunt her down, but You're gonna have to lead me iffen You expect me to catch her in this darkness."

Chapter 5

Jolie awakened to the crackle of a blazing campfire. Instantly alert, she sat up. Heart pounding, she grabbed the Peacemaker then looked around. All was still.

She hadn't built a campfire. She'd stripped the saddle from the roan and draped the saddle blanket over hersel—

The roan! The big horse wasn't where she'd tied him. She fisted the blanket in her lap, only it wasn't the scratchy blanket. It was the fine suiting material of Frank's suit coa—

"Oh, Lord Jesus, help me. . . ." Jolie bolted up, sleep fleeing as anger coursed through her veins. Land sakes, how had Delaney Adler gotten free of that rope and tracked her down? She'd forgone a fire so as not to draw attention. And with only a tiny slice of a moon, there was hardly enough light to travel this far, much less track her through the mountains. But track her he had.

Unless. . .

Her heart lurched. Was it Adler who'd built the fire, exchanged the coat and blanket, and taken the horse—or had Brand found Mr. Adler, taken the coat, and followed her here? Her brother loved to toy with her that way. Tears brimming, she examined every shadow beyond the firelight. *Lord, You know what Brand is capable of.* Her brother would be harsh with her. He might kill Mr. Adler for meanness' sake.

As firelight danced against the desert plants, Jolie kicked dirt at the flames. They flickered a moment then reignited. She tried again.

"What're ya doing?" a distant voice called, more curious than angry.

Jolie stilled, nerves primed. She gripped the heavy Peacemaker, thumb on the hammer. "Mr. Adler?" Her voice shook.

"Yeah. . .?" He strung the word out like a question. "Who else did you reckon it'd be?"

At the almost teasing question, two fat tears streaked down her cheeks. She squared her shoulders. "None of your business."

Silence stretched for an instant. "Missy, you were about as a-feared as a hen standin' eye-to-eye with the fox raidin' her house. Then, when you heard it was me, you settled some."

Jolie balled her calico dress in her fingers. "What if I did?"

When Mr. Adler spoke again, his voice was closer. "You in some kind of trouble?"

She drew back from the fire. "No."

To her left, a rock skittered across the ground, and she leveled the Peacemaker and cocked it. Del Adler appeared off to her right, hands raised in surrender.

She faced him, heart pounding, limbs shaking.

"Easy, now. I ain't lookin' to get myself shot." He took a single sliding step into the firelight. "Keep in mind, I coulda taken that peashooter when I fetched my horse. That oughta go some distance toward makin' you believe I ain't out to harm you, oughtn't it?"

Blast him, but it did. A long way.

"Just wanna talk, ma'am."

Hesitating, Jolie lowered the gun. Again, her eyes filled with tears, and she shifted to hide them, feigning it was so she could safely ease the gun's hammer down.

Adler's posture eased. "Thank you kindly, missy."

"What do you want to talk about—at this hour, especially?"

"Am I trustworthy enough to set a spell, or should I keep standin'?"

Eyes still brimming, she glanced into the darkness. "Sit if you like." She folded her arms, rubbing warmth into one arm with her free hand.

"Here. . ." He spoke directly behind her.

Startled, she spun as he attempted to drape the coat around her. "Thought you were gonna sit."

"You looked. . .cold." He cocked his head. "Why're you cryin'?"

She rubbed her eyes dry. "You're awful nosy."

Hesitating, he held out the coat as if to help her into it. "Think of it as concerned, and it's awful cold out here. Please put this on."

Jolie eyed him then slipped into the garment. The night's chill dulled. "Why do you care?"

"My pa died when I was young, makin' me the man of the house. I learned to know when my four sisters or our ma was upset, figure ways to fix it. You remind me of them."

Her brows arched. "You have. . .four sisters."

Mr. Adler nodded.

"You said you're. . .a rancher?"

"Yes, ma'am."

"And you've never robbed a bank."

He guffawed. "Never. I ain't been perfect, but I ain't done nothin' to warrant a prison stint, neither."

She gaped.

"Is that so strange?"

Jolie swallowed. "Where I come from, it is. My brother's done nothing but harm all his life."

Firelight and deep shadows couldn't mask the concern in his blue eyes. "What's that mean?"

Her fingers strayed to the knot left when her arm had healed after Brand broke it during her childhood. "Never you mind. I've said more than enough." She folded her arms, the pistol still tightly gripped in her fist. "You asked to talk. So talk."

A grin crossed Mr. Adler's pleasant face, and he nodded. "All right. I obviously ain't tied up anymore." When Jolie tried to break in, he held up a silencing hand. "Don't know how, but a straight razor got left near my hand." He produced it and held it out of her reach.

Jaw clenched, Jolie grabbed for the covered blade.

"Uh-uh." He tucked it in his pocket again. "Figure God's givin' me a chance to clear my name, but I also don't want to mess up your future, so how 'bout come mornin', you help me clear my name, and once that's finished, we'll see the judge about an annulment. Deal?"

"How on earth am I supposed to help clear your name?"

"I can't move about town with the marshals searchin' for me. You can go places I can't, like the newspaper office."

"The newspaper office?" Was he daft?

"Yes, ma'am. To buy articles pertainin' to the robbery. Might be some clues there."

He *might* have a point. . .and the element of surprise wasn't on her side this time. She'd likely have a harder time getting him tied up a second time, even if she had a rope.

She nodded. "Deal."

He crammed his hands in his pockets. "Thank you. Now iffen you'd like, I'll get my roan so you can have that saddle blanket and catch some shut-eye. Closer to daylight, you can spell me. Sound like a workable plan, pardner?"

She considered, unsure. "As long as you promise to be a gentleman."

"Keep that peashooter handy, iffen you want, but so you know, my momma raised me right. I don't know how to be anythin' but."

Thoughts warring, she agreed. "Fine."

He stalked into the darkness.

Blast him. That perfect gentleman was making it near impossible to keep her guard up.

Del awakened, groggy, and blinked heavily. Recalling where he was, he bolted into a sitting position.

"Good morning, sleepyhead." Miss Hilliard crouched near the campfire with two prickly pear pads impaled on a stick. She held them over the flames, twisting the stick to roast the opposite side.

"What're you doin'?" Del blinked away sleep.

"I was hungry, so I found some prickly pear."

Del faced her, realizing she'd draped the saddle blanket over him as he slept. "You know which plants are edible?"

"Don't you?" She shot him a teasing grin.

Was this the same little gal as the night before? She'd been all business. This one bordered on good-humored. "Reckon I could figure it out."

She pulled the stick from the flame and, inspecting the cactus, scraped away the spines with—

"Where'd you get that razor?" Del felt his pocket.

Miss Hilliard flashed him a less-than-innocent grin.

His laughter bubbled. "You wicked woman."

"Hardly." Her smile faded as she removed the cactus spines. "I know far too much about being wicked, Mr. Adler. Fortunately for you, my momma raised me right." Her words echoed his but dripped sadness.

"Is your momma still ali—"

At Miss Hilliard's glare, his question stalled.

Standing, he folded the blanket. *Lord, I hunted her down like You said. Reckon it's up to You to get her talkin'.* Since the moment he'd set out to get his horse back, the good Lord had spoken.

"Watch over her. Let no harm befall her."

He'd argued, but God won that wrestling match. "Please, ma'am. Would you do me two favors?"

"What are they?"

"One, you call me Del, and I'll call you Jolie. It'll simplify matters."

"Fine. And. . .?"

"Two, you know I got the marshals breathin' down my neck. Could be arrested, maybe hung, iffen I'm caught."

Her fine features softened. "I'm aware."

"I need to know what type o' trouble you're facin'."

"I'm not facing any—"

Del raised a silencing hand. "Mr. Lovell's letter said your brother's caused you trouble. Whatever you're runnin' from has caused you to advertise yourself as a mail-order bride."

Jolie's face went ashen, and for once, she made no sharp-tongued retort.

"Iffen we're to get through this, I need to know. Who's your brother, and what's he capable of?"

She laid aside the stick and the razor and cupped her face in her hands.

His heart seized. *Lord, I don't mean to cause her pain.* Instinct told him to gather her in his arms, but he dared not. "Jolie?"

She drew a shuddering breath. "His name is Brand. Brand Hilliard. You've likely read newspaper articles about him but under the name of Brent Hill."

Del's mouth fell open. "You're *Brent Hill's* sister?" The outlaw and his gang were well known across the Southwest, suspected of several brutal murders and robberies—not a one of 'em solved.

Hands covering her mouth, she nodded.

That explains things, doesn't it, Lord? I'm to protect her from him.

"Last night, I thought you were him coming to retrieve me." Fear etched her face. "By now, he'll have figured out I'm not coming home, but I have no idea whether. . .or when. . .he'll guess where I've gone. Mr. Lovell and I were to marry, spend one night in the Meribah hotel, and take the stage out of town. With my name changed because of the marriage, we thought I'd finally break free of his abuses and his bad reputation."

"Reckon I put a fly in that ointment." He exhaled. "I can't apologize to you enough, ma'am."

Her fear and shame were almost palpable.

Unable to stop himself, he strode up and pulled her to her feet. "Jolie, you have my word I'll make this right. Until I can, I'll protect you from that scoundrel." He tipped her chin up until her ice-blue eyes collided with his. "Understand?"

Without warning, she collapsed into his arms with a sob. "Thank you."

Chapter 6

Jolie sat behind Del as they rode back to Meribah, hands at his waist. He'd been so kind. So. . .safe. It had felt very right being in his arms, so much that she had to resist the urge to lean close and rest her cheek against his strong back. Del was *not* her intended, and cuddling close to him would give Frank good reason to be upset, should he find out. As if melting into Del's arms in camp wasn't reason enough. If it weren't for this big. . .kindhearted. . .handsome. . .lug, she'd already be Mrs. Frank Lovell. Except that Frank hadn't shown up.

However, trying to focus on either fact was nearly impossible when Del's nearness, the tender way he'd comforted her. . .the heart-pounding memory of their kiss during their sham wedding kept battering her thoughts. *Lord, I waited until twenty-six for my first kiss. I'm afraid my first has ruined me for any to follow.* Her cheeks warmed.

She willed the shameful thought—and the desire to kiss Del Adler again—from her mind. What a fool.

"You asked about my mother." The turn of conversation would free her mind from this rut. "I'm all but sure she's dead."

Del halted the roan. After an instant, he shifted his weight to one stirrup and twisted to look at her. "*All but sure?*"

She looked away and nodded.

"Missy, you'd best explain how you don't *know.*"

The plan had worked. Any vestige of romantic feelings fled, replaced by a knot in her belly. "I think my brother murdered her."

"Lord God Almighty above." He cast a glance heavenward then dismounted and helped her down. "What happened?"

The concern in his gaze was too great. Too foreign. She focused on a button on his shirt. "Ma always said she and Pa fell in love the moment they met, and she loved him so fiercely, she wouldn't marry again after he died. She did her best raising me and Brand, but Brand had a fearsome mean streak. By the time I was six and he was ten, he'd fallen in with a bad lot, doing illegal things."

She glanced up, and the compassion in his eyes nearly undid her. "I suspect Brand threatened her. . .or me, maybe. As much as she hated them, Ma let Brand's friends move in. She cooked for 'em, lied when the law came around. When I was fourteen, Brand and Ma argued. I never saw them fight so bad. Ma always sent me to the barn when they argued, but when dark fell and she hadn't come for me, I ventured into the house." She closed her eyes. "Ma wasn't there, and Brand backed me in a corner. I'll never forget what he said to me. 'Fix us something to eat, you stupid, good-for-nothin' little mouse.'" Jolie shuddered. "When I asked why Ma wasn't cooking, Brand said she was. . .not coming back." Finding a shred of courage, she met his eyes again. "Ma was a God-fearing woman. She wouldn't've left me. Not if she had a choice."

Del pulled her to his broad chest, his arms circling her frame. "Why didn't you run?"

There in his arms, she felt nothing could harm her. "I did. Many times. Brand always dragged me back. I fought him as best I could, but I eventually quit trying. There was too high a price."

He held her at arm's length. "You mean—" The question stalled in his throat as a mixture of horror and anger filled his eyes. "Did he put his hands on you?"

"Plenty of times. He broke my arm when we were kids, and that was just the start."

He gaped. "They didn't try to—"

"One tried—once." Thank God she'd kept the Peacemaker close when she saw them drinking heavily that night. "I shot him."

A stuttering breath escaped Del's chest. "Dead?"

"No. He survived. . .barely." She squared her shoulders. "They never tried *that* again, but they beat me. Kept me locked in a room some of the time." She spoke the words slowly.

He cupped her cheek in his palm and pulled her close again. "I'm so sorry. How'd you survive all these years?"

Jolie drank in the shelter of his arms, the warmth of his calloused hand caressing her cheek. "I did what they told me and prayed like Ma taught. I knew God would rescue me if I'd wait for Him, and I eventually decided to advertise myself as a mail-order bride. That's when Frank's letter arrived, and God said it was time." She pulled back and smoothed her dress. "So the sooner we clear your name, the sooner I can get on with God's plan for my life."

Del swallowed hard. "You're right."

Who was he to argue with God?

Except that God had told him to let no harm befall her, and after all she'd been through, the thought of her marrying some stranger stuck in his craw. Iffen she was his sister, he'd forbid such a union. But she wasn't, and he shouldn't assume he could hear God's will for her better than she could. "Let's get on with it, then."

Elsewise, he might share his thoughts about her getting hitched to Lovell. Or his crazy notion of her marrying *him* instead. God *had* told him to protect her, after all. . .but iffen he'd forbid his sisters from marrying except for love, surely they'd withhold their blessing from him marrying for convenience. Besides, Jolie didn't have to be his wife for him to protect her.

Why then, dad-gum it, was he struggling to put the idea out of his mind?

He strode to the roan and beckoned to Jolie. She came, and he lifted her into the saddle and took the place behind her. He took the reins and clucked his tongue.

As they rode, his mind clicked through all that had happened. He'd come to Arizona Territory to deliver horses to a fella who'd bought 'em on a trip through Colorado the month before. That business landed him in Meribah the day the bank was robbed.

He'd been arrested, tried, and convicted—railroaded—within days then sent to Yuma. Only God provided him an escape while traveling there, and he ran back to Meribah on the day Jolie Hilliard was to marry Frank Lovell.

"What kind of clues do you think you'll find in the newspaper articles?"

Del shook free of his thoughts. "Ain't rightly sure." He rubbed his thumb against the bare place where his ring normally sat. "Maybe somethin' about that banker's ring."

"How will that help clear your name?"

"I wear a ring." He wiggled his finger in her view. "When the sheriff arrested me, he took it. Said I lifted it off the dead bank owner during the robbery. Only I was never in that bank."

"What type of ring?"

"Pa's West Point ring. It has the school's symbol on the top, and Pa's name engraved inside. He wore it until illness took him when I was eleven. Once I was grown, Ma passed it to me. Didn't leave my finger till I came to Meribah."

Jolie glanced back, sunlight highlighting her fair skin. "They couldn't ask the banker's widow to identify the ring?"

His gaze wandered over her thick auburn curls. Loose tendrils brushed what looked to be silky-soft skin. She was a handsome woma—

"Del?"

Those were downright perilous thoughts. He had no right. . . . She was promised to another man, and besides, he'd only known her since the previous afternoon. "Wasn't married. No kin in town, neither. During the trial, they called the jeweler that made the ring. He vouched it was the same one."

She grunted. "Convenient. Was that the only evidence they provided?"

"That, and the fact I'm tall with blond hair and light eyes."

Jolie loosed a sardonic laugh. "That could describe any number of men in Meribah. Gracious, it could fit a third of Brand's gang, for that matter."

Del stiffened.

Startled, she glanced back. "I assure you, they weren't involved."

"Beggin' your pardon, but how can you know?"

"Brand broke his leg over a month ago. He's able to hobble some now, but the gang's been lying low while he's healing."

Del exhaled heavily. "That's too bad."

"About his leg?"

"Hardly." If even half of what she claimed about Brent Hill was true, he and his gang should rot in hell. "Too bad it wasn't him that robbed the bank. We coulda cleared my name and got your brother and his gang arrested in one. Give you back your life. . ."

"I can't imagine living without the fear of Brand and his men." A touch of wonder etched her voice.

They cleared the last hills and settled into the valley, headed toward Meribah. *Lord, that ain't right, Jolie livin' in fear. I'll do what I can to protect her like You said, but. . .once we clear my name and see that judge, she'll marry Lovell.*

The thought set his teeth on edge.

Chapter 7

I'll go to the newspaper office and collect any articles about the robbery." Jolie stared toward Meribah, about a quarter-mile ahead.

"Then bring 'em to me so's we can read 'em."

"Should I talk to the jeweler, too?"

Del shook his head. "Not now. Iffen we ask too many pointed questions, we'll draw attention."

The same thought had crossed her mind. "Will you be waiting here, or. . .?" The dusty landscape provided no place to hide from the marshals.

"Once you're in town, I'll head to the livery." His timid smile warmed her. "You helpin' me means a lot, Jolie."

"We're helping each other, remember?"

Del caught her arm as she turned. "Please. . .be careful."

"I will."

Before she turned away, he cupped her face in his hands and leaned in, lips hovering near hers. Jolie's heart pounded as he lingered then finally tipped her head to plant a firm kiss on her forehead. He took one big step backward and shoved his hands deep in his pockets. "Keep your eyes open."

Disappointment weaved through her, though she chided herself. *Fool.* "Don't worry. Where Brand is concerned, I'm always alert."

Only with Del around, her senses were dulling, her mind wandering where it shouldn't go. She smoothed her dress and turned.

"Wanna take the gun?"

Was he stalling? She looked back. "I fear I'll be more conspicuous carrying that satchel." She pulled the razor from her pocket. "This'll be enough."

She marched into Meribah. The streets weren't busy, and no one paid her any mind. Just how she wanted it. Hand fisted around the razor in her pocket, she meandered down the boardwalk toward the newspaper office two blocks beyond the livery. After she'd scanned for any sign of Brand or his men, she entered the office.

A small gent with oil-slicked hair, spectacles, and brown pants approached the long counter separating his work space from the waiting area. "How can I help you?"

"Do you keep copies of your past editions?"

"We do." He pointed to the cabinets lining the walls. "We've got copies back to six years ago."

"Oh, goodness. I don't need anything that old." She smiled, trying to ease the tension in her muscles.

"What might you be looking for?"

"I heard there was a bank robbery a few weeks ago."

His eyes widened. "Yes, there was."

Jolie shrugged sheepishly. "I was looking for articles on that event. My brother likes reading about such things." It wasn't an untruth. Brand read articles on various crimes, though Lord willing, she'd never see him again.

"I've got copies of those editions. Three papers. Five cents apiece." While he retrieved the newspapers, Jolie glanced outside. Sure no one was watching, she knelt and unpinned the hem of her dress where she'd stashed some money. Since her mother's disappearance, Jolie had pilfered small amounts of cash from Brand and sewed or pinned the money into the hems and linings of her clothing so he wouldn't catch on.

"You want the article on the robber's escape, too?" the man called.

"He escaped?" She hoped she could convincingly feign surprise.

The man nodded. "Yes, ma'am. The marshals were swarming all over town yesterday, hunting him."

"Yes, please." She'd read it to be sure Del was as trustworthy as he seemed. If the articles portrayed him as a man who'd shot and killed guards during his escape from the marshals, she'd. . .she'd. . .

Jolie stifled a laugh. If he'd killed lawmen or harmed anyone in his escape, she would march herself into the sheriff's office, explain the situation, and tell them right where to find Del. Once captured, she could have the judge annul their marriage prior to him being shipped to Yuma. In fact, little was stopping her from doing that now.

Little, other than the whole idea set her nerves on edge. Unlike Brand, Del didn't have a mean bone in his body. He was kind, gentle, and concerned. He had nothing in common with the outlaws she was used to. They were cut from much different cloth.

The newspaperman laid out the four slim editions. "This one's about the robbery, this one the capture. The trial, and the robber's escape." He pointed to each in turn.

She slid the small bill across the counter to him. He stepped away to make change.

"Did they catch the man?"

He counted her change. "No, ma'am. Some are still searching in town. The rest rode into the countryside."

Jolie's belly knotted as she folded the newspapers together. "Would a criminal really return to the scene of his crime?"

"They thought they'd cornered him at the church yesterday, but he slipped away." He stowed the cash box and approached. "They're unsure where he's gone, but they aren't giving up." The man's brows furrowed. "What'd you say your name was, ma'am?"

Wary, she took the change. "I didn't. Why do you ask?"

"You match the description of a woman the sheriff's looking for. Is your name Miss. . ."

Jolie's heart seized. Why on earth would the Meribah sheriff be asking for her by name?

". . .Holland?" He stretched out the name, unsure. "No, Miss. . .Heller? That's not it."

When he scurried to his desk for a scrap of paper, Jolie shoved through the office door.

"Hilliard. That's it. Are you Jolie Hill—?"

The door slammed, cutting off the question. Down the street, across from the stable, Del waited. At the sight, she turned and hurried the other way.

If the marshals were still searching the town, they'd be looking for Del's rumpled plaid shirt and tattered hat, so he'd changed into Lovell's suit pants and shirt and the preacher's hat. Doubtful that the change of clothes would hide his identity for long. A haircut, shave, and fresh clothes would go only so far. By now, they could've figured out he'd pretended to be the groom and be looking for a dark suit.

No matter what, it was risky, sitting in plain view. After weeks in the local jail, the Meribah sheriff would know him. The marshals were embarrassed and looking to recapture him—quick. And anyone who'd seen his joke of a trial could easily recognize him.

They'd be just as happy to spill his blood as garner his surrender.

Regardless, he'd positioned himself where he could see Jolie, protect her if Brand found her. Del shot a discreet glance toward the newspaper office. He'd seen her step into the building, but it was taking far longer than he'd expected.

Lord, is everything all right?

The office door opened and slammed shut, Jolie glancing his way. When she turned suddenly and scrambled in the opposite direction, he craned his neck to follow her path.

An instant later, a short man in a brown suit stepped out, locked up, and trotted after her.

Warning bells clanged in Del's thoughts. Something wasn't right. Pulling the preacher's hat low, he marched after them.

Chapter 8

Jolie's heart pounded. If the town's sheriff was asking for her by name, it meant trouble. Del didn't need more difficulty, especially with the marshals nearby. One problem. . .where could she go? She knew the pastor and his wife, but they'd left town.

Brand had probably tracked her here and, knowing him, he'd probably walked into the lawman's office, given a false name, and feigned concern for his dear sister. She couldn't let him find her. Nor could she lead Brand to Del. Even their mistaken attachment to each other could cost Del his life.

If, by some chance, Brand hadn't found her, the next logical explanation was they'd figured out her association with Del. Either way, this meant trouble for her unintended groom. Trouble she dared not lead to the kind Colorado gentleman.

She turned down an alley, zigzagging around crates and refuse. Glancing around, she unbuttoned her dress bodice, tucked the newspapers inside, and rebuttoned the fabric. She must think, find a way to signal Del. Once hidden in the mountains, they could make a plan. Staying in town wasn't an option—for either of them.

Jolie emerged from the alley. This street was busier than the last, two separate groups of men congregating on the boardwalk, deep in conversation. Among the nearest group, she recognized one of the marshals who'd interrupted her wedding. Perspiration prickled across her skin as the newspaperman rounded the corner a block down. She ducked back into the alley, praying neither man saw her, and retraced her steps to the previous street.

At the sight of Del only a short distance from her, she gave a tiny shake of her head and mouthed the word *run*. His brows knitted in confusion. Before they drew attention, she darted into a small mercantile.

Would he understand, do as she'd said? Doubtful.

"Can I help you, ma'am?" the clerk asked.

Jolie approached the counter, mind churning. "I. . .wonder if. . .I could borrow a pencil."

The man's face puckered. "A pencil?"

She laughed. "Something important crossed my mind. I need to write it down before I forget."

"Oh. Happens to me all the time. Here." He produced pencil and paper from behind the counter.

She scribbled. *Get out. Posse near. Meet at last night's camp.*

Paper in hand, she thanked the clerk and darted outside, crumpling the page. As suspected, Del waited nearby. Without a passing glance, she walked by and dropped the crumpled ball near his feet.

"Pardon me, ma'am," Del called as she passed. "You dropped something."

Jolie's footsteps faltered. Couldn't he just read the note? The more contact they had, the more likely someone would pair them. She turned, smiling politely. "Did I?"

"Appears so." He held out the wadded paper.

Smile faltering, she reached for it, whispering. "I'll toss it in the alley. Read it." Taking the paper, she reasserted her smile. "You're very kind, sir."

Jolie carried on, dropping the paper ball in the next alley then hurrying down the street. If she could walk out of town and straight toward the mountains, she could cover those few miles in far less than an hour. Del might even catch up to her on horseback, though if the marshals really were looking for her, it was best not to be seen together.

As Jolie reached the middle of the nearest intersection, an unfamiliar voice rang out. "Jolie Hilliard! A word, please?"

At the mouth of the alley, Del stepped into the narrow passageway and retrieved the wadded paper. He smoothed it and read, the simple message causing his heart to pound. He crumpled the paper and stood.

Jolie's skittishness made sense now. He felt it, too. Resisting the urge to scan the street, he braced a hand against the nearest building. *Lord, show me where the posse is.*

"Jolie Hilliard! A word, please?"

Sheriff Matthew Waight's familiar voice split the air from down the street, and something like lightning crackled through Del's body. He peeked at Jolie as she faced the lawman who came into view beyond the corner storefront. Del slipped deeper into the alley.

Tarnation. What'd the sheriff want with Jolie? And how'd he know her name?

How much simpler would it be to slip out of town and forget Miss Jolie Hilliard? Far too late for that. She'd captured a piece of his heart, and it was growing harder not to willingly hand her the rest.

Lord, reckon I don't have to tell You this is bad. Real bad. You want me to protect her, then You're gonna have to see to me.

Chapter 9

Jolie's limbs trembled as she faced the man who'd called out, though she cringed inwardly. She shouldn't have reacted to her real name if she wanted to keep her anonymity. *Lord, help.*

The man approached the corner of the boardwalk, star-shaped badge on his chest and a gun on his hip. Likely the Meribah sheriff.

Jolie met his gaze. "Are you speaking to me?"

"I am, Miss Hilliard." He approached.

"I'm sorry." She swallowed. No moisture reached her parched throat. "That's not my name."

Grasping her elbow, he escorted her across the intersection. "There's a gent in my office who's mighty fired up to find a woman matching your description."

She drew back, her blood curdling. *Lord, not Brand.* "I...I'm sorry, Sheriff. My name is not Josie—"

"*Jolie.* Hilliard." He skewered her with a glance.

It took concentration to steady her voice. "As I said, that's not my name."

His expression turned grim. "Hmm. Too bad. That fella's bride has gone missing, and he's mighty concerned something's befallen her."

She covered her mouth. *Frank, not Brand.* Relief washed through her, though until Del cleared his name and they saw the judge, she—

The lawman's amused expression warned she was reacting too openly. "The man's bride is missing? That's...terrible."

"Ain't it? There's an escaped prisoner roaming these parts, and the marshals witnessed a gal fitting your description getting hitched at the church yesterday." His pointed stare bored through her. "They're thinking the groom was their prisoner."

Knees soft, she fought to remain upright. "You must be joshing."

"No, Miss Hilliard, I'm not."

She swallowed. "I told you, Sheriff, I'm not Josie Hilliard."

"What's your name, then?"

Jolie's mind churned. "Katherine. Adelaide."

"Adelaide's your last name?"

"No, Cooper. Katherine Adelaide Cooper. From Texas."

The sheriff smirked. "Whereabouts in Texas?"

She must stop this. "I'm sorry, Sheriff. I'd love to continue these parlor games, but I've important business. Unless you are detaining me, I must go."

"Parlor games." He chuckled. "I get it. Twenty Questions. You're funny, Miss Hilliard."

"Cooper."

"My mistake." The smile trickled from his lips. "Be careful, what with that bank robber on the loose. Perhaps I should escort you, be sure nothing happens to you."

"That's unnecessary, Sheriff. I'm quite capable of caring for myself, thank you. I'll be on my way."

"Suit yourself, ma'am. So you know, the wanted fella's got blond hair and light eyes, about my height. When he stayed in my jail, he had a scraggly beard, but the marshals think he may've shaved."

Fear clawed her spine. They knew too much. "I'll keep watch. Good day, Sheriff." She started toward the livery.

"Good day, Miss Hilliard."

"That's Cooper." Spine straight, Jolie walked purposefully toward the stable. The newspaperman said that the marshals were combing the countryside, but there were a few left in town as well. The sheriff knew—or strongly suspected—she had ties to Del. They must find somewhere secure to plan their next steps, and fast.

At the livery, she glanced back. The sheriff watched from the corner, unabashedly. Nodding to him, she slipped inside.

"I need a horse, please," she informed the stable hand.

She chose a sturdy little paint mustang and some well-worn gear. As the stable hand saddled the horse, she removed another bill from her dress's hem. She paid then led the horse outside.

On the street, her muscles tensed. The roan still stood in the sun. Del hadn't made it back. Not good, though the lawman had finally left. She mounted and turned toward the mountains, resisting her inclination to spur the paint into a gallop.

Some distance from Meribah, she faced the town and found a suit-clad man on a chestnut horse following her. Del. He'd made it after all. Jolie turned toward the mountains, and this time, urged the animal into an easy canter. Hopefully he'd keep his distance until they were safely in the mountains.

Yet, as she rode, fast-approaching hoofbeats drummed behind her. The rider had closed the distance, and as she looked his way, he called to her.

"Jolie?"

Not Del's soothing baritone.

"Stop. It's Frank," he called. "Or would you rather I call you Katherine Adelaide Cooper?"

Del had watched the interchange between Jolie and Sheriff Waight from the alley, though their words were too distant for him to hear. She'd done a right fine job of keeping her fear tamped down, but the discussion had obviously rattled her. With good reason, given the way the sheriff watched her even after she'd moved on.

It rattled him aplenty, the sheriff standing there minutes after Jolie departed. He was trapped. His roan was tied at the far end of the street, but Waight wouldn't budge. Skin crawling, Del waited for the sheriff to look away then crossed the street to another alley. From there, he navigated to the next street and, scanning for badges, proceeded toward the livery.

As he neared, two of Waight's regular deputies rounded a corner. One had been kind enough to mail Del's letter home to his ma. Would he recognize Del? Del paused at a store window and, realizing it was a gunsmith's shop, ducked inside. They needed extra bullets for Jolie's gun anyway.

The clerk approached, but before he spoke, the door opened again, and the deputies entered, standing between him and the door. Every nerve crackled.

"Help you?" the man behind the counter asked.

Del shook his head. "Just lookin'." He spoke in a deep voice so neither deputy would recognize it.

"Let me know what ya need."

Del moved toward the far end of the counter, eyeing the newcomers. *Lord, get me out of this store. Fast.*

"What can I do for you fellers?" the man called to the deputies.

"We got an escaped prisoner, and I'm nearly out of ammunition, Eugene." The man approached. "Gimme two boxes for my Peacemaker."

Del's heart pounded as the clerk rang up the bullets. He hoped the two lawmen might go once Eugene pushed the bullets and change across the counter, but no such luck. The deputy opened a box and, drawing his Colt, loaded the gun while chattering about Del's escape.

Abandoning hope of outwaiting the deputies, Del turned toward the door.

"Didn't see anything you liked, mister?"

"Not today." He put a rasp into his voice. The lawmen glanced his way as he shoved through the door.

Had they recognized him? He couldn't tell. Nor would he wait to find out. He stalked up the street, cutting back to the road where the livery—and his roan—were. Finding no sign of Jolie, his muscles quaked.

Lord, did she get away safe? Can I skedaddle now, or. . .

In the distance, two mounted figures rode out of town. The farther, a woman—hopefully Jolie. The nearer, some gent in a dark suit, headed in the same direction.

Del tightened the cinch and, swinging into the saddle, headed after the pair.

Chapter 10

Jolie looked back. Should she stop? If she did, she'd have a *lot* to explain to Frank. He might decide she wasn't worth the trouble. If she could somehow outride him, she'd afford herself time to help Del and get the legalities sorted out, but. . .would Frank forgive her? *Lord, help. You know I never intended on marrying the wrong man. Make Frank understand this is all a mix-up.* She slowed.

Frank rode up. "Jolie?"

She gulped. "Yes, I'm Jolie."

"Thank the stars!" Relief washed over his features as he dismounted and strode to her side. He plucked Jolie from her saddle and settled her before him, hands on her shoulders. "Why'd you lie to the sheriff?"

Hesitating, Jolie shook her head. "Where were you? I waited at the church the other day, but you never showed."

"I was unavoidably detained." Cupping her hand in his, he lifted her palm to his lips. Sunlight glinted on his hand, though she couldn't discern why.

A shiver gripped her, and she tried to pull free. When he held her fast but lowered their entwined hands again, she cleared her throat. "Detained by what?" What was so all-fired important he'd missed their wedding?

Frank shook his head. "The marshals are in town searching for an escaped bank robber. They tracked him to the Meribah church and said a wedding *did* take place. A redheaded woman married a blond fella in a dark suit. When I showed up asking after you, they realized the groom was *him*, clean-shaven and hair cut. You know anything about that, Jolie?"

Her knees going weak, she reached for her saddle horn for support. "I'm sorry," she breathed. "I thought he was you. *He said* he was. . . . He was blond-haired and light-eyed, same as you, and about your same size. The suit fit him so well, I never thought to question—"

He gaped. "You *did* marry that thief."

Her hackles stood on end, and she squared her shoulders. "Del Adler's no thief. There's good reason to believe he's been framed."

"You know his name?"

The snarl that was Frank's question rubbed her all wrong. "Yes I do. In fact, I'm helping him find the real robber and clear himself."

Frank landed a backhanded blow along her cheekbone.

Jolie toppled, her pony darting sideways. Pain throbbed through her face, and her skin stung as she pressed shaky fingers to her cheekbone. When she pulled her hand back, her fingers were bloody. She glared, astonishment and anger warring for control.

"You really are a stupid, good-for-nothing little mouse, aren't you?"

Shock threaded through her at the all-too-familiar words.

He clamped a hand over her wrist, dragging her up. "I forbid you to have anything to do with that liar."

Mind swimming, Jolie dug in her heels and picked at his fingers. "Unhand me, you scoundrel. The wedding's off!"

Frank tipped his arm, and in an instant a tiny Derringer pistol appeared, so small his hand dwarfed it. He turned it on her. "I dare say it's not. Let's go."

Eyes darting from him to his gun, her eyes settled on the flashy gold ring adorning his pinky finger.

Del had only covered half the distance to the two riders before the gent roughly dragged the gal to his horse. The way she struggled, the lady didn't want to go. Del's belly churned, and he spurred his horse.

Lord, I'm all but certain that's Jolie, and iffen I'm right, I need Your help. But who was the man—one of the marshals, or a sheriff's deputy? Maybe her intended. No matter who, he didn't particularly want to make himself known. But no man had a right to manhandle a woman that way.

As the fella ahead dragged Jolie onto his horse, Del bent over his own mount's neck and rode hard. The pair lit out for the mountains another mile beyond. Del gained, though he paused long enough to catch the woman's paint pony and retrieve the Peacemaker then pushed on, praying he could catch up.

The pair neared the base of the mountains, and Del's horse, winded though it was, put on one final burst of speed to close the gap.

"Stop!" he shouted as he dropped the paint's reins and cocked the Peacemaker. When they failed to heed his command, Del fired a single shot. The pair slowed and they all stopped, the horses laboring for breath.

"Jolie?" he called.

The woman twisted, though as she did, the man whispered something, and she faced forward again.

"Unhand her, mister, and git down from that horse." Del cocked the pistol. "Slow-like."

Positioned directly behind the two, he had no safe shot. He'd hit Jolie. But the fella must not have realized that, for he slipped to the ground and faced Del.

"Jolie, darlin', you all right?"

Again, she started to turn then stalled as her gaze fell on the man. "Fine, Del."

"Then walk that horse on over here and show me."

"I. . .I. . .no. Del, this is Frank. As I've said all along, as soon as I found him, I would go with him. Remember?"

So this was Frank Lovell. About Del's own height and weight, with blond hair and a well-trimmed mustache and beard. It was her right to stay with him, though. He cocked his head. "Don't rightly recall you saying that, Jolie. You wanted to get to a judge first."

She stiffened and shifted slightly, glancing at Frank.

He also looked toward the man just as Frank raised his right arm to about shoulder height.

"No!" Jolie screamed, and kicked at Frank's arm.

A sudden pop sounded, and something smashed the left side of Del's head as the world plunged into darkness.

Chapter 11

Jolie's heart thundered as Del crumpled to the ground, blood sprouting from a spot an inch below his hat brim. *Lord, no! Please!*

Frank reached for the chestnut's reins, though Jolie gripped the saddle horn and kicked again. This time, her left boot connected solidly with Frank's head. He toppled sideways, and she spurred the chestnut into a gallop.

God, please. . .please let Del be alive! If she could just lose Frank, maybe she could circle back and check on him. But— A violent sob wrenched loose. *Lord, he can't be dead.*

The hills rose around her, and relief washed through her. There'd be plenty of places to hide here. Knowing the chestnut had already run hard, she slowed its pace, checking to see what might lie behind. Her belly clenched as Frank easily gained on her, riding Del's roan.

Jolie reined her horse to the right and raced on as the terrain grew steeper. She worked to guide the horse safely through the rocky outcroppings and difficult landscape. Seeing a break in the rocks, she turned sharply onto a worn dirt path and barreled up a small rise. As she crested the hill, the ground fell away from either side of the narrow trail and, directly ahead, a towering saguaro cactus blocked her path. She yanked on the reins, her horse skidding on the dusty ground, and finally stopped only a foot or so from the prickly giant.

Her heart pounded as she stared at the cactus then slowly looked back. Frank sat atop the rise, her own Colt Peacemaker pointed straight at her.

"Be smart and turn that horse around. And keep in mind, I'm not squeamish about shooting people."

He'd proven that. By now, Del was certainly dead, shot in the head from close range. No one else in the world would care about her, now that he was gone. With few choices left, she turned the big horse to face him. "What do want with me, Frank?"

"Your brother was growing weary of your quarrelsome attitude. He'd've killed you, but when he learned about your mail-order scheme, I offered to take you off his hands." He paused while that sunk in. "Now walk on back this way, and keep yourself in check, woman."

Del roused to fearsome pain ricocheting through his skull, like wild horses stampeding inside his head. He pried his eyes open, though something marred his vision in his left eye. Carefully, he rubbed it. Sticky. Blood stained his fingers. Recollections of where he was—or why he lay bloodied on the ground—were hazy, as if mired in fog.

He lolled his head to the side. Something moved. The fog lifted, replaced by fear. Someone or something was near, just out of his sight. Enemy—or friend? He twisted around, the pain arcing with the movement.

A horse. A little paint that nibbled the grasses that dared to grow here. Where was the owner? Bracing himself for the onslaught of thunderous hooves beating between his ears, he rolled, sat up, and scanned his surroundings. Momentary waves of agony swept over him.

Finally, he opened his eyes. Alone. Just him and the paint. In the distance lay a town, and much nearer, the mountains. He held his head in his hands. The town. *Meribah.* Where he'd been falsely convicted of bank robbery. The horse. . .Jolie's horse. Pieces slowly fell into place. He'd followed her from town, only she was with Frank. And Frank had manhandled her. He'd tried to get Jolie away from him, but something hit him in the noggin.

Lord, where's Jolie now—and my horse? And the Peacemaker he'd turned on Frank?

Del stood slowly, desert terrain swimming. A few feet behind him lay an unfamiliar hat. He tugged it on. Far too snug for his pounding skull. He removed it and shuffled toward the horse.

"Up for a ride?" He asked to bolster his confidence, but before he could lift a foot to the stirrup, he spied Jolie's satchel lying on the ground nearby. He looped it over the saddle horn then opened it. Inside, he found his tattered hat and traded it for the unfamiliar one. It was a slight bit better.

With difficulty, Del mounted then turned the horse in a slow circle. "All right, Lord, which way?"

Chapter 12

Inside." Frank shoved Jolie toward the door of a mountain cabin.

Her eye swollen from where he'd hit her, she stumbled over a stone she didn't see in her path. She righted herself and spun. "Guess you lied when you said you lived near Phoenix, huh, Frank?"

"Near enough. It's in the same territory." He shooed her toward the door with her Peacemaker. "Get moving."

Lord, don't make me go in there. Please. It had been concerning enough riding through the mountains with him. No telling what liberties he might expect once away from prying eyes.

She pressed a hand to her roiling stomach, reminded again of the folded newspapers she'd hidden inside her dress. Her throat clogged. They'd do little good now that Del was dead. He'd meant to look for clues, information on the banker's stolen ring. At least she could look into that, see if Frank's gaudy pinky ring bore any resemblance.

He pushed her to the door. "Open it."

Once she did, Frank escorted her inside. Unused to the dim light, she squinted to see two shadowy figures look up from a table.

Jolie tensed. *Lord God, two more men to contend with? You've got to get me out of here. Please.*

"Welcome back," the large, slovenly man said, amusement in his tone.

Jolie glared at Frank. "Who're they?"

"Howdy, Mrs. Lovell." A second, slim-waisted man grinned. "We're Frank's business associates. I'm Henry, and this here's my brother Al."

Al leered. "Ol' Frank musta given you quite a welcome."

"I was late, so she's not my missus yet. We'll get married when the preacher returns."

Jolie stifled a derisive laugh. Never. . .*never* would she promise to love, honor, and cherish Frank Lovell. Not after he'd hit her. Nor after admitting this was some twisted arrangement between him and Brand. Certainly not after he'd gunned Del Adler down. And then there was the ring. . . . No. She'd escape if it took her last breath.

"Move." He guided her toward a ladder leading to a second story and pointed with the pistol. "Climb up there."

Her mouth went dry. "Why?"

He traced her cheek with the cold barrel of her Peacemaker. "Because I said so, beautiful."

Trembling, Jolie complied, aching to retrieve the razor from her pocket. She dared not risk it. Not yet. Perhaps if Henry and Al left her alone with Frank, she could give him a surprise—a sharp blade to his throat.

Jolie swallowed hard. At the top of the ladder, she peered into a small loft with a sloping roof and a bed for two. She froze.

"Keep moving."

She glanced down. Frank waited as if he meant to climb the ladder also.

When she didn't move, he leveled the pistol. "I said move."

Jolie fought for composure. "The least you could do is say please, Frank."

"Move. *Please*." He snarled the last word.

She scrambled up the ladder and, feet planted on the floor, reached for the razor as Frank joined her.

"Open that door." He pointed to the left wall.

Confused, Jolie faced a doorway centered on the wall. Nerves jangling, she turned the knob. A musty garret stacked with steamer trunks and crates opened before her. A single dingy window lit the space.

Frank nudged her forward, and once she entered, he pulled the door halfway closed. "I'll bring your dinner later."

The door clapped shut, and a key turned in the lock. Instantaneously, relief washed through her. He hadn't intended what she'd feared.

She tiptoed to the window and tried to lift the glass. It went up two inches and stopped. Only then did she see the nails driven into the window jambs. Closing it, she pulled on the nail heads. Neither budged.

She was trapped, and no one in the world would care now that Del was gone.

Voices sounded nearby, warning Del someone was near. Head still pounding, he halted the paint and glanced around. The voices seemed to be approaching from beyond a bend in the forked trail to his left. Heart pounding, he scanned the terrain. Cactus and ocotillo dominated the area, none of it dense enough to hide a horse and rider. He could turn tail and retreat, but he'd leave an easy trail to follow.

Lord, You got any good ideas?

He rubbed at his forehead, trying to smooth away the ache. He focused on a clump of prickly pear, spanning a good six feet wide and four feet tall. Hardly large enough to hide a horse standing upri—

He reined the paint behind the cacti, dismounted, and unhooked the satchel from the saddle horn. His heart pounding, he led the horse a few feet away and tied one end of his rope around a front hoof. He glanced heavenward as he hoisted the horse's leg up and wrestled the animal off his hooves. The pony rolled onto his side, and Del lay across his neck to keep the horse down. One hand over the paint's nostrils to keep it from making any noise, Del shook his hat from his head.

His skull crackled with pain, but he gritted his teeth and squinted through the prickly pear. A lone rider came into view, dull silver badge pinned to his vest. Connor Benson, the territorial marshal who'd come to transport him to Yuma. The marshal stared at the ground, moving slowly.

The paint attempted to stand, and Del adjusted his bodyweight. *Lord, keep this beast still, please.* He whispered soothing words in the pony's ear.

Two more marshals appeared, trailing Benson. Del held his breath and ducked low as one man glanced his way. Benson dismounted to look at the ground. Del's heart pounded. *Lord, please don't let me be caught. Jolie needs me.* He couldn't stomach stranding her with Frank while they carted him off to Yuma. As his hazy memory had cleared, he recalled the feeling he got seeing them together. She was afraid. No way could he leave her until he knew the source of that fear. Had to be more than just her riding off with the stranger she'd promised to share her life with.

The pony flinched, drawing him from his thoughts. He willed the animal to remain still, praying hard for divine help.

The marshal finally nodded toward the other fork of the path. "We'll head that way."

"It's getting late," one of the others spoke. "This spot would make a good campsite."

Del's chest constricted. If they made camp, he'd be stuck trying to keep a fidgeting pony down and still.

Benson swung into his saddle. "We've still got an hour of daylight. We'll move on."

"You're the boss."

When he could hear no further murmuring, Del rolled off the paint, and the animal scrambled up and gave a swift shake, the wave seeming to travel from its head right out its tail. He looped the satchel over the saddle horn and mounted, patting the pony's neck.

"You did real good. Now let's go get Jolie."

Chapter 13

In the hours since Frank locked Jolie in the garret, she'd read through the newspapers and tucked them back inside her dress bodice then looked through the various steamer trunks and crates she could get into. By the time the sky turned brilliant hues of pink and orange, her mind swam with what she'd found.

The articles detailing the robbery and trial both referenced the banker's gold signet ring, though little was mentioned about it. From what she'd seen of Frank's ring, it was a gold signet ring. A coincidence?

The articles also mentioned eyewitnesses to the robbery, among them brothers Henry and Al Mabb. Each had testified that a blond-haired, blue- or green-eyed man had been seen fleeing the bank. Al Mabb testified that the culprit shot the banker and stole his ring. Hard to believe two brothers named Henry and Al would witness the robbery—and two *other* brothers with those same names would be here at the cabin. The chances were slim.

And then there was the garret full of trunks. Every last one had its lock jimmied, making it easy for her to open them. They were full of odd items—quilts, letters, clothing. Particularly women's dresses and unmentionables of various sizes. The letters were all in different handwriting, addressed to different people. These weren't the belongings of these men. They were stolen, probably from stagecoaches up and down the line from Meribah.

Footsteps sounded, and the key turned in the lock. Frank entered, balancing a tray on one arm.

"Dinner." He set it atop the nearest crate.

"Is this how you treat your bride, Frank?" She'd spent hours thinking how she could escape, return to Meribah for help, even considering cutting Frank's throat when he came in with her dinner. But even if she'd been able to do that, how far could she have gotten with the Mabb brothers downstairs? No, getting out of the room was the first step, and *then* she could escape the house. "You lock her in a room and ignore her?"

"Thought you said the wedding was off."

She ran her finger across her bruised cheekbone. "I don't take kindly to my husband hitting me."

"So you've changed your mind?" He eyed her suspiciously.

Jolie smoothed her dress. "You treat me like a lady deserves, and I'll consider the idea. But. . .no more holding me at gunpoint. No more hitting me. No expectations of marital privileges, like we agreed in our letters. And you speak to me like I have a good mind. Am I understood?"

His eyes narrowed. "What do I get in return?"

"The things I've done for Brand—cooking, cleaning, laundry. And *if* we should fall in love, then. . .maybe more. But *not* if you treat me as you have today."

Frank contemplated what she'd said. "You got a lot of rules, lady." He swung the door wide. "But we'll try it your way."

Jolie stifled a devious smile as she crossed the garret. Yes, they would.

Despite the lawmen going in exactly the direction Jolie's tracks led, Del followed their path at a cautious distance. When the marshals made camp another two miles beyond, he hesitated. Their camp was smack in the middle of a cactus-filled canyon, cutting off his best path through the area. Any alternate route through there would be in plain sight of the lawmen. The sky, streaked heavily with myriad colors, warned of the coming darkness. Little chance he'd get any farther tonight, even if he could circle around the marshals' camp.

Del rubbed his throbbing skull. *Iffen I can't find her tonight, Father. . .You protect her.*

He scanned the canyon. Navigating it on horseback would be impossible after dusk.

But iffen he *walked*. . .Hope speared his heart. He'd navigated equally tricky terrain the night Jolie tied him, and—

Had that truly been just two days ago? The way he cared for her, it felt like it'd been far longer.

Del shook away the rambling thoughts then regretted it, pain stabbing through his noggin. One hip against the rocky canyon wall, he held his skull until the pain ceased. Head clear again, he eyed the camp. He could leave the paint there, cross the canyon on foot, skirting their camp, and at least check the far end of the canyon.

Dusk took an eternity to fall, though when it came, it enveloped the terrain in deep shadows. He stripped the paint's saddle and slinked into the canyon slowly, taking time to avoid the thousands of spines and barbs. The marshals' murmured conversation reached his ears, though their words were lost. He smiled. They were probably talking about him. If they only knew how near he was.

Reaching the far end of the canyon, Del peered into the darkness beyond.

Not far off, the warm glow of lamplight pierced the night as it flooded through two cabin windows.

Chapter 14

Jolie's skin crawled as Henry and Al slipped outside, each carrying bedrolls. Would Frank remain true to his promises, or would he expect a romantic evening? For the millionth time, she felt for the straight razor in her skirt pocket. Satisfied, she paced to the table and stacked dirty plates and silverware then dropped them into a tub of hot water. Returning, she retrieved the cast-iron pan as well.

"Where's the kindhearted gentleman portrayed in your letters, Frank?" She pushed her sleeves up and scrubbed the first plate.

He leaned against the counter, arms folded. "He was a storybook character meant to draw a little mouse from her hole. That's it."

After years of Brand's abuses, Jolie had become practiced at keeping her expression neutral. She dropped the plate in the clean water and scrubbed another. "There's no gentleman in you?"

"If you're expecting to be doted on, I'm not your man."

"But you won't let me go if I prefer not to marry you, will you?"

He laughed. "The mouse ain't so stupid as she looks."

No, not stupid at all. Dropping the plate into the rinse water, she searched the wash-tub for the sharp knife at the bottom. Finding it, she stared out the window. "So what're you expecting to get out of this marr—"

Jolie's question stalled as a face, streaked with blood, bobbed into view beyond the window—there, then gone again. She dropped the knife.

Del? He'd popped into view, finger to his lips, then disappeared. But it couldn't be him. He'd been shot.

Frank grabbed her arm. "What's wrong with you?"

Startled, she stared at him. "I. . ." She blinked away shock and rubbed her wrist against her nose. "I was going to sneeze. It's so musty upstairs."

He huffed. "Watch your complaining, or you might wind up there again."

"I thought we agreed. You treat me like a lady, and I'll—"

"I'll revoke those terms any time I see fit." He turned his back to the window, arms folded.

Certain her mind was playing tricks, she searched for the knife. "You have no idea how to relate to women, do you?"

"Never heard complaints before."

If so, the women he'd seen were likely *working* women. A *lady* would complain vehemently at Frank's treatment and expectations.

Del's blood-streaked face appeared again, and she covered her mouth to stifle a gasp as he ducked from view.

Frank turned quickly and must've caught sight of Del, for he shoved past her. As he jerked the door open, Jolie grabbed the cast-iron skillet and, running after him, swung. A frightening *clang* sounded, and Frank sprawled through the doorway, unmoving. Her feet tangling with his, she also crashed into the wall.

Dazed, she tried to draw breath. Someone burst through the door and pawed at her. Panicked, she tried to raise the skillet again, though gentle hands stilled hers.

"Stop, Jolie. It's me. It's Del." He hauled her into his arms. "You're all right now."

Jolie burrowed into his embrace. It *had* to be Del. There in his arms, she felt *safe*.

"I thought you were dead. Frank shot you."

"Shhh. . ." Del pushed her back and removed his hat. "It's just a graze. I got a real skull-thumper, but I'll live." He brushed his thumb across her swollen cheekbone. "What'd he do to you?" He braced himself for an answer he wouldn't like.

She quirked a frail smile at him. "He hit me—right after I said I was helping you find the real bank robber."

His gaze flashed to Lovell, anger building in his gut. "Is that so?"

Lovell groaned, and Del dropped to a knee beside him. "Jolie, find me somethin' I can tie him up with."

"Watch him closely." She scrambled toward two narrow wooden bunks in the corner. "He's got a Derringer up his sleeve."

Awake but obviously dazed, Lovell clawed the floor planks as Del rolled him and checked his sleeves.

Once Del relieved Lovell of the weapon, he hauled him into a semiseated position by his shirt. "Didn't your ma tell you not to harm a woman?"

Lovell leered Jolie's way, evil in his eyes, before he turned to glare at Del. "Shut up, you sorry piece—"

Del struck—hard—sinking Lovell into semiconsciousness again. "You never hit a woman." He wrestled Lovell onto his belly. "Particularly *my* woman."

Across the room, Jolie flung open doors and drawers. "I don't see anything to tie him with."

Del's eyes settled on the two bunks. "Move the mattresses."

She shoved the nearest lumpy cushion onto the floor to reveal ropes crisscrossing the frame, then sawed through the fibers and tossed him a good length of rope.

As Del bound Lovell, she scooped a handgun from one of the crates, as well as a box of .45 bullets, and headed to the table. With practiced fingers, she easily spun the cylinder, ejected any spent shells, and reloaded it.

At his curious glance, she shrugged. "Frank took my Peacemaker when he shot you. Figured I'd take it back."

"Good thinkin'." Drawing Lovell's arms behind his back, Del paused as he looped the rope around the downed man's wrists. A ring adorning his pinky caught his attention. "Did you see this?"

"That and a whole lot more. You recall the brothers, Henry and Al Mabb, from your trial?"

"Yeah. . .?"

"They're here. Asleep in the barn."

Del's heart seized. "You're just tellin' me this now?"

She shrugged sheepishly. "It just came to mind."

As he bound the unconscious man's wrists, she connected Lovell's ring and the Mabb brothers being cozied up in the same cabin. While he tied Lovell's ankles, she talked of the strange collection of steamer trunks and crates in the garret above.

Done, Del listened as he searched for a gag. A dirty dishcloth on the corner of the table caught his eye. "So the Mabb brothers are in the barn?"

"Yes."

"And my roan, too?"

Her ice-blue eyes skated his way. "Unfortunately."

Blast. It'd kill him to leave such a fine mount behind, but getting Jolie to safety was his top priority. Del dropped to a knee beside Lovell, rolled him onto his back, and shoved the dishcloth between the man's teeth.

Suddenly, a bullet whizzed through the open door and struck a tin cup on the table.

"Get down!" Del's eyes darted toward a large form lumbering across the yard. He jerked Lovell free of the door and slammed it then dropped the bar into position to keep the intruder out. "Put out that lamp."

Jolie blew out the flame, plunging the room into darkness and rendering Del momentarily blind. He left Lovell's bound form in front of the doorway—another obstacle the Mabb brothers would have to overcome to enter the cabin.

"You all right in there, Frank?" a familiar voice called from outside.

"He's a little indisposed just now," Del hollered. Turning toward Jolie, he beckoned her nearer. "Stay low and bring me that pistol."

Lovell roused, shook his head, and screamed through the gag.

"Who are you, mister?" the outside voice called.

As Del peered out from behind the flour sack–covered window, Jolie crawled over and shoved the Peacemaker into his hands. The bigger of the two Mabb brothers stood in the center of the yard, backlit by a lantern shining from the barn. No sign of the other brother.

"I asked you a question!" the voice bellowed.

The chilling metallic click of a gun's cylinder rotating sent a shiver down Del's spine. He spun to find Jolie loading a second weapon. Despite the darkness, he saw her shrug. "There's more guns in the crate. Figured I'd get prepared."

Heart hammering, he blew out a breath. "You scared me."

Outside, the big man hollered and paced. The barn lantern highlighted his movements.

"Hey!" Mabb yelled. "Open up and come out. I won't hurt ya."

A whisper of sound from the cabin's back side drew Del's attention. He spun. Too late, he realized there was a second entrance—one he'd failed to secure. As the door shifted, Del launched himself at Jolie, pushing her to the floor. "Stay down," he hissed in her ear.

She trembled beneath him but made no attempt to move.

Shadows shifted near the back entrance. From near the front door, Lovell screamed through the gag again. Outside, Al Mabb hurled taunts.

Del waited, nerves prickling with danger. *Lord, keep Jolie safe. And me, iffen You're of a mind.* The dark shadow of a slim man eased in the back door, and Del took careful aim.

The Colt leaped in his hand, and the shadow jerked, fell back through the doorway. Del lunged for the door, slamming it with his shoulder. The cabin walls rattled with the force, and he slid the bar down to secure it.

A hail of gunfire rent the stillness. Bullets punched through the wooden walls and door. Glass shattered. Del hit the floor and belly-crawled toward Jolie, now huddled in a ball near the window.

When the gunshots stalled, she reared up and broke out a corner pane of glass. Firing once, then again, her aim shifted as if her target was moving.

Del peeked out as Al Mabb lumbered toward the barn, several guns in hand. The big man was probably out of bullets. Del also knocked out a windowpane and fired once as the man ducked into the barn.

Wood creaked at the back of the house as another volley rang out. Glass shattered and a bullet struck near Del's shoulder. He fired once at the wall on either side of the back window. The second shot struck its mark as the shooter cried out in pain.

"You wanna keep doin' this?" Del hollered.

More gunshots came from the direction of the barn.

One struck the window above, showering them with glass shards. Jolie covered her head. Del lunged toward her, shielding her from the shots with his body.

Lord, stop this. I don't want Jolie hurt.

"US Marshals! Put down your weapons!"

Chapter 15

In the moments after the marshals called out, Del lit the lamp and laid out Jolie's Colt, the other pistol she'd found, and Frank's Derringer. As Jolie set the razor on the table, he looked away.

"You know I'm gonna be arrested, right? And probably you too, since you're with me."

Jolie pressed her eyes shut. "Yes."

A sudden pounding on the front door startled her, and she jerked toward the sound. "Inside the house. . .this is the US Marshals. Open up, real slow. Keep your hands where we can see 'em."

Del pinned her with a concerned stare. "Do exactly as they say, and let me do the talkin'. The less you say, the less they can pin on you."

Jolie's throat knotted. She walked toward the middle of the room then realized someone had stationed himself outside the back window, barrel of a long gun pointed through the broken glass. Her head swam as she lifted her hands.

"Fellas, this is Del Adler. I'm givin' myself up. Don't want no trouble. Jolie Hilliard's with me, and Frank Lovell's tied up in front of the door. I'll have to move him before I can let you in."

"He's tellin' the truth, Benson," the man at the back hollered. "There's a body blocking the door."

Jolie faced the front, flashes of movement at both windows drawing her attention. Undoubtedly, other lawmen ready to shoot them if need be.

"Don't do anything stupid, Adler. You're in enough trouble. We got guns trained on you and the woman from three directions."

"I understand."

"Move that body and step away. Keep your hands in plain sight."

Lord, please. . .keep us safe from harm. She watched as Del dragged Frank's bound form away from the door, blood smearing across the planks.

"He's hurt pretty bad. You might wanna check on—"

"Keep quiet! No thief's gonna tell us how to do our jobs."

Del complied as he lifted the bar that secured the door. Silently, he backed away.

"Face the back of the house, both of you."

Jolie turned as the man at the back window signaled they were clear. The front door creaked open, and after seconds, rapid footsteps beat across the plank floor. Someone shoved her face-first into the wall and cuffed her wrists behind her. Rough hands spun her around and pressed her back to the wall.

"Show me your hands." A tall, dark-haired marshal held Del against the same wall, his forearm shoved against Del's shoulder blades.

Del hiked his hands higher, wincing as the marshal pressed his gun's barrel to Del's ear. "Delany Adler, you're under arrest."

"I ain't resistin'. Said I was givin' myself u—"

"Please. . .keep talking." The marshal cocked his gun and jammed it against Del's head. "Give me a reason to put an extra hole in you."

Jolie's heart nearly stalled. "Pardon me. . ."

"Jolie, quiet. . .please." Del's voice rasped.

She eyed the man handling Del then the one beside her. A third, probably from the back, had entered and checked Frank's pulse. Through the open front door, she saw Al Mabb seated on the porch, hands cuffed around one of the support posts.

"Pardon me." Jolie gulped. "Who's in charge?"

"Jolie!" Del spat her name.

The man holding Del holstered his pistol and reached for Del's hand. "That'd be me, ma'am. Connor Benson of the US Marshals." He drew Del's right arm behind his back and cuffed it then twisted his left around also.

"Do you know who I am?"

Benson turned Del to face the room. "No, ma'am. And at the moment, I don't rightly care."

She met the lawman's eyes, challenging him to listen. "My name is Jolie Hilliard. I'm the younger sister of Brand Hilliard, also known as Brent Hill."

Benson twitched at her brother's name.

"Now that I have your attention, I'd like to make a proposition."

"What kind of proposition?" Benson eyed her.

She glanced around the room, suddenly uncomfortable. "Could we speak in private?"

Benson hesitated then patted Del down before guiding him to a chair he set in the center of the room. "Emory, c'mere and secure our little jackrabbit's feet before he runs."

"Yes, sir." The deputy beside her dropped his voice. "Keep your back against this wall until you're told otherwise."

At Jolie's nod, he stepped away.

"Kagan, how's that fella?"

The one stooped over Frank shook his head. "There's a fierce lump on his head and he's been shot a couple times. Ain't holdin' out much hope. There's another fella out back, already dead."

"Do what you can for him. Miss Hilliard and I are going outside to chat." Benson took Jolie by the elbow and, not unkindly, escorted her toward the barn. Inside, he faced her. "All right, ma'am, you have my attention."

"Thank you." She whispered a prayer. "Mr. Adler and I can provide you with several interesting facts that prove he didn't rob that bank, and if you'll listen with an open mind—and look for ways to help—then I'll give you information to convict my brother once and for all."

Benson shook his head. "No deal. Tell me what you have on Brent Hill and I *might* discuss helping Adler. All depends on what you tell me, though."

Jolie inhaled deeply, mind churning, then squared her shoulders. "If I can tell you exactly where his hideout is, the names of his gang members, and at least some of his crimes, would that be enough to help Del?"

"You've piqued my interest, ma'am. Yes, it would."

The afternoon sun warmed Del's shoulders as the old farm wagon the marshals found beside the barn rumbled into Meribah. They'd shackled Del's hands to one side of the wagon bench and Al Mabb was shackled to the other. Between them, Frank Lovell clung to life, just as he had through the night. Kagan drove the wagon, Benson and Emory flanked it, rifles ready. At the back of the wagon, his roan and the other men's horses were loaded with money and stolen goods found in the cabin and barn. Jolie brought up the rear.

News of their arrests had spread like wildfire. All along Meribah's streets, townsfolk watched the wagon pass. *Lord, iffen You'll get me out of this mess, I promise I'll never set foot back in this territory again.*

As the wagon stopped outside the Meribah sheriff's office, Del's stomach churned with the thought of spending more time in a cell. Benson unhooked him from the wagon and led him inside.

Sheriff Waight looked up as they entered. "Caught him, did you?"

Benson grunted as he pushed Del into a chair near the sheriff's desk. "You still got the ring Adler supposedly stole off the banker's finger?"

Waight's brows knitted together. "What d'ya want that f—"

The office door opened as Emory pushed Al Mabb inside. "I need the keys to your jail, Sheriff."

Waight peered out the large window as his own deputies hurried up and, taking orders from Kagan, lifted Lovell down. They carried Frank inside, and Jolie trailed them.

Del attempted—and failed—to catch her eye.

"Thank you, Miss Hilliard." Benson pointed. "Have a seat over there, please."

The sheriff turned on Benson, spine stiff. "What's going on here?"

"That's what I'm trying to figure out, Sheriff. There's reason to question whether Del Adler committed that bank robbery."

Waight's face blanched. "Of course he did. I investigated it myself."

"Good. You'll be the one I direct my questions to. . .startin' with where is the ring you say he stole?"

"The ring. . .is. . ." Waight opened a desk drawer and pawed through the items inside.

The sheriff squirmed. Del had suspected from the moment he'd been accused that something was off about the lawman. The feeling had only grown the more time he spent around the sheriff.

The two sheriff's deputies, one being the fella who'd mailed Del's letter home, reentered the office after depositing Frank in a jail cell, and Waight straightened. "I remember. The ring is lost. Disappeared after the trial."

One deputy's stride faltered. Hands in pockets, the other hung his head, and both made for the door.

"You two." Benson faced them.

They turned, lookin' like boys caught elbow-deep in their ma's cookie jar.

"Is there a doctor in town?" Benson asked.

"Of a sort. Got us a barber that dabbles in medicine."

"Tell him we've a patient lying at death's door."

Waight smacked his hands on his desk, papers scattering. "Just hold on. You will *not* walk in my office and order my deputies around. I'm the sheriff in Meribah."

"Yeah? I'm the *federal* marshal that just deputized them." Benson turned to the deputies. "You. Fetch the barber, and you. . ." He turned to the deputy who'd mailed Del's letter. "Fetch me the jeweler that testified in Adler's trial."

The deputy shot an uncomfortable glance toward Waight then nodded. "Yes, sir."

Tension hung thick as fog as the deputy glanced at Waight then exited.

The sheriff's jaw clenched, and he slammed the drawer shut. "I got work to do. . ." He bolted out the door.

Benson stepped out onto the boardwalk after Waight exited. "Kagan."

The other deputy marshal hurried over.

"I don't trust that fella. Follow him. I wanna know everywhere he goes."

A weight lifted from Del's chest. *Thank You, Lord. Someone's listening.* He twisted to look at Jolie, sitting silently in the corner. "Reckon you can see the judge soon. . .like you wanted." An ache leached through his chest like nothing he'd ever felt before.

Jolie mustered a feeble smile, though it quickly trickled from her lips. "It seems so." She rubbed at her forehead. "You'll be rid of me soon."

The whispered comment stung. "Jolie, I. . ."

She shook her head, and before he could continue, Benson entered with the deputy and the barber. "Take him back to Lovell's cell and stay with him. Understood?"

Nodding, the deputy and barber disappeared into the back.

Del cleared his throat, hoping to share the thoughts spinning through his mind. Before he could speak, Jolie bolted up and approached Benson.

"Marshal, may I have a private word?"

Hesitating, the lawman waved her outside and shut the door. When he reentered moments later, he was alone. Wordless, he sat at the sheriff's desk and riffled through the drawers.

Del peered out the window. No Jolie. And Benson seemed completely unconcerned. Had she gone on some errand, or. . .? He scrambled to put the sudden tension crawling up his spine to rest.

How in blazes had he become so attached to her in a matter of days?

"Beggin' your pardon, Marshal, but is Jolie all right?"

Benson paused, glancing Del's way. "That gal's exhausted and overwhelmed." He shut one drawer to riffle through another. "This has been a lot to deal with."

Del's shoulders ached, whether from having his hands cuffed behind him or the desire to hold and comfort Jolie, he wasn't sure.

The office door swung open, and the deputy entered with a curly-haired man in tow. "Here's the jeweler."

Benson stood. "You the one that testified about the banker's ring?"

The jeweler nodded uncomfortably. "Yes."

"Can you describe the ring to me, please?"

"Don't have to." He removed a handkerchief from his pocket. Unwrapping the cloth, he produced a ring, which he offered to the lawman. "Sheriff Waight told me to melt that down the week after the trial ended."

Benson's brows arched. "Did he, now?"

The ache ricocheted through Del's skull again.

Benson fished in his own pocket, producing the ring Frank had worn. Del's muscles quivered in anticipation.

The lawman held them side by side. "They're similar but certainly not the same."

"May I see?" the jeweler asked.

The marshal handed them over as Del craned his neck to see.

"They're both signet rings, but the markings are quite different. Wouldn't be easy to mix them up."

Del glared. "You testified under oath that you made the ring they showed you."

The jeweler hung his head. "S'pose I did." He looked Del's way. "I'm sorry for the trouble it caused you."

"So you lied in court?" Marshal Benson barked.

"Didn't want to." He glanced around nervously. "Sheriff Waight threatened me. Said my shop might get burned down if I didn't say what he wanted me to. I risked everything to come west. My business fails, and I got nothing left. No way to care for my family. So I lied."

Del's thoughts roiled.

"He threatened you?" At the jeweler's vigorous nod, Benson glared at the sheriff's deputy. "You know anything about that?"

The deputy shook his head. "About Waight's threats. . .no. But I've seen things recently that haven't set right with me. I'll gladly tell you about 'em when you have some time."

Benson nodded. "I'd be real happy to hear." He shifted back to the jeweler. "What can you tell me about these rings?"

"This one." He motioned. "They showed it to me in court. If I'd told the truth, I'd have said it has a name and date engraved inside. *Lon Adler, June 1846.*" He directed the lawman's attention to the inscription. "I was born in December 1846, so I couldn't've made that ring."

Benson squinted at the ring. "And the other?"

The jeweler looked at the underside. "This one's the banker's ring. There's my mark." He shifted so the marshal could see. "And. . .the banker had uncommon small hands, sir. The two rings aren't even close in size."

Benson held them side by side. After a moment, he fished something from his pocket. "Adler, stand up."

Del complied, and the marshal unlocked his handcuffs.

"Put those on." Benson deposited both rings in his hand.

Del slipped the banker's ring on his fourth finger. It stopped above his middle knuckle. Once the men had all seen it, he slipped the other on. It settled in place easily.

Relief and vindication stirred in Del's chest.

Marshal Benson finally met Del's gaze. "Adler, never reckoned to say this, but there's enough proof here to make a monkey question how you coulda committed this crime."

Del roughed a hand over his stubbly jaw. "Thank you, Marsh—"

A sharp sob tore the quiet, and Del pivoted to see Jolie standing at the door, hand clamped over her mouth. Eyes brimming, she turned and ran.

"Jolie?" He darted toward the door.

Benson clasped his arm. "You're still under arrest."

"But—"

Benson snapped at the deputy. "Find her."

Chapter 16

Jolie swallowed hard as the deputy escorted her into the nearly empty courtroom and sat her in the last row. Del waited at the front table, hands clasped as if he were praying. The jeweler sat on the witness stand while Benson stood before the judge's bench. Silently, the judge studied something in front of him.

"You're confessing to perjury." The judge directed the statement to the jeweler.

Squirming, he nodded. "After the sheriff threatened me."

"This is the ring you made the banker?" The judge showed the jeweler a ring.

"Yes, sir. It has my mark."

He held the second ring out toward Del. "And this one is your father's ring, as evidenced by the inscription."

Del's chair scraped the floor as he stood. "Yes, sir. I rode into town wearing it and never set foot near that bank."

"Come up here and put these on."

Jolie held her breath as Del paced to the bench. *Lord, I want Del's name cleared, but . . .what about me?* Even if Frank survived and beat the robbery charges the marshal was mounting, she wouldn't marry him. And once Del's name was cleared, she would provide information to convict Brand. In moments, she'd have nowhere to go and no one to care about her. The realization left her trembling.

"Mr. Adler, a travesty of justice has been committed against you," the judge said. "There's many things that don't add up here. I'm reversing your conviction, effective immediately." He turned to Marshal Benson. "Are you charging him for the escape?"

After interminable seconds, the lawman shook his head. "I ought to. . .but I reckon this whole ordeal has been punishment enough."

"Adler, you're dismissed. Here's your ring."

Del's relief was palpable. "Thank you both." He turned sideways as he slipped the ring on then looked her way.

"You'll be investigating the robbery further, Marshal?" the judge asked.

"Yes, sir, Judge."

"Good. Anything else I can help you gents with?"

Del's gaze connected with hers. "There's one more thing, sir."

"Make it quick, Adler."

He faced the bench. "Miss Hilliard and I. . .spoke some wedding vows the other day. Only I used another man's name." He shrugged sheepishly. "Are they binding?"

The room erupted with the guffaws of judge, marshal, deputy, and jeweler.

Embarrassment blanketing her, Jolie lunged for the door, but the deputy caught her wrist and pulled her back down. If she could, she would melt into the floorboards.

The judge sobered, though an amused grin tugged at his lips. "I don't see how that could be considered binding."

"Then we're not married?"

"Nope." The judge shook his head.

"Thank you, sir." Del reached to shake the judge's hand.

Panicked, Jolie pried at the deputy's thumb. "Please, let me go."

He tightened his grip. "You gotta talk to Marshal Benson."

Tears streaked down her cheeks as the men all congratulated Del. "Please."

"No, ma'am."

Unable to free herself, she stifled a sob as Benson and Del turned her way. Clamping her free hand over her eyes, she tried to hold her emotions in check.

One set of footsteps stopped, looming over her, while another—Del's, surely—proceeded out the courtroom door. Out of her life. The deputy released her wrist and stepped away, leaving her to talk to Benson.

She couldn't bring herself to look up.

"Jolie?"

It wasn't Benson's voice.

Lowering her trembling hand, she found Del.

He sat beside her. "You all right?"

She shook her head. "No."

"What's wrong?"

"I. . .don't know. . .what to do now."

"Reckon you can do anything you want." He took her hand. "I know one thing I hope you'll do."

Jolie's breath hitched. "What?"

"The judge says the preacher's due back day after tomorrow. Kinda hoped you'd marry me proper."

"I married you five days ago." The hatless preacher balked outside the stagecoach office.

Del shrugged sheepishly. "That's a long story, sir. I'll pay you handsomely for your trouble."

Reverend Carter looked at his wife. "Oh, fine. We have to pass the church to get home anyway."

Jolie smiled, picking up her satchel. "Thank you, Reverend. You don't know how much this means."

Del took the reverend's bags, and they hurried to the church. Once inside, they took their positions at the altar.

The pastor opened his Bible. "Forgive me, but this'll be short. Do you, Franklin Thomas Lov—"

"Wait!" both he and Jolie chorused.

The reverend's eyes widened. "What?"

"The name's Delany Aaron Adler."

Confusion etched the preacher's face.

Once more, Del shrugged. "Long story. . ."

The preacher rubbed his forehead. "Sounds like it. Do you, Delaney. . .Aaron. . . Adler, take—wait." He turned to Jolie. "What's *your* name?"

She giggled. "Jolie Ann Hilliard."

"Of course it is." Reverend Carter restarted, shaking his head at the oddity of marrying the same couple twice in a week.

"I now pronounce you husband and wife. Kiss your bride."

Del swept Jolie into his arms, his left hand cupping her cheek. Her eyes danced with anticipation as he leaned in. He drank in the intoxicating scent of the flowers she'd weaved into her hair as his mouth hovered near hers. Finally, he captured her lips. Soft and tantalizing, she melted against him, a tiny moan rumbling in her throat. He breathed in her sweetness and strength. His head swam as he deepened the kiss, though before he got too lost in it, he pulled away. Breathless, he grinned.

"You brigand," Jolie whispered, blue eyes sparking.

His smile faltered. "I thought we were past all that name-calling."

"This time, it fits."

Irritation slinked down his spine. "How do you reckon?"

She blushed. "Every time you kiss me like that, you steal a piece of my heart."

The irritation dissolved, and in its place, desire grew. He leaned in again.

From behind them, someone cleared his throat roughly. They turned to find Marshal Benson. "Congratulations to the happy couple."

Del stepped down from the altar but turned back long enough to hand Reverend Carter his payment. "Thank you again, sir."

Without further conversation, they retrieved their satchel and exited the sanctuary, Marshal Benson falling in beside them.

"Just wanted you both to know. My men found your brother and his gang right where you said. They're in custody, and we're already building our case. The Brent Hill gang won't bother you again."

Jolie smiled, and Del looped an arm around her shoulders.

"Thank you. There's no better wedding gift anyone could've given me."

"You're welcome, ma'am." Benson turned Del's way. "You two are leaving town soon?"

"Tomorrow. Heading home to Colorado. You need anything from us, you can find us there."

Benson nodded. "I'll be in touch. Best wishes." He shook Del's hand and nodded to Jolie then slipped out of the church.

"Shall we go, Mrs. Adler?"

Jolie reached to unfasten the satchel's flap. From inside, she retrieved the preacher's hat and, looking back to be sure the preacher didn't see, hung it on the hook beside the door. "I'm ready, Mr. Adler."

Jennifer Uhlarik discovered the western genre as a preteen, when she swiped the only "horse" book she'd found on her older brother's bookshelf. A new love was born. Across the next ten years, she devoured Louis L'Amour westerns and fell in love with the genre. In college at the University of Tampa, she began penning her own story of the Old West. Armed with a BA in writing, she has won five writing competitions and was a finalist in two others. In addition to writing, she has held jobs as a private business owner, a schoolteacher, a marketing director, and her favorite—a full-time homemaker. Jennifer is active in American Christian Fiction Writers and is a lifetime member of the Florida Writers Association. She lives near Tampa, Florida, with her husband, teenage son, and four fur children.

The Mail-Order Mistake

by Kathleen Y'Barbo

Husbands, love your wives,
even as Christ also loved the church,
and gave himself for it.
EPHESIANS 5:25

Chapter 1

H eads up, Bingham. We've got another one."

Pinkerton Detective Jeremiah Bingham swiveled in his chair to see Alan Pinkerton headed his way. "Another fellow wondering where his bride is, boss?"

"Baroness Fleurette has stolen another rancher's dreams," Mr. Pinkerton said as he tossed a letter atop Jeremiah's desk. "To the tune of five thousand dollars and a stake in a gold mine out in California."

"So much for connubial happiness and eternal love." Jeremiah moved the letter to the growing stack on the corner of his desk. "Or whatever she called it in this ad."

For the past two years since the Pinkerton Agency signed a contract with the railroads to assist in mail fraud, they had become the owners of bags and bags of letters from men whose bought-and-paid-for brides had gone missing. By far, the largest offender of fraudulent marriage brokering using the mail system was the elusive Baroness Fleurette.

Jeremiah returned his attention to Mr. Pinkerton. "From the way you're looking at me, I am guessing you've got a plan."

"I do." His boss grinned. "Congratulations, Detective Bingham. You're about to become a gentleman of means looking for a sweet dove who will gratefully accept the arrow from Cupid's bow."

"Me?" Jeremiah shook his head. "I don't know the first thing about pretending to want a mail-order bride."

In truth, he had enough trouble trying to shake off the would-be Mrs. Binghams ever since he came into his share of the Bingham Mining fortune five years ago. Sure enough, he'd see the back side of his twenties soon, but that was no reason to hurry into sticking his head into the yoke of marital entanglement, despite his sister Stella's attempts. Especially since he'd finally found some anonymity working for the Pinkerton Agency.

"I would be willing to wager neither did those men," Mr. Pinkerton said, indicating the letters. "Now see what you can do about putting Baroness Fleurette out of business."

"Mrs. Baronne, you are a true friend." May Conrad accepted the cup of hot tea with shaking hands. "I do not know what I would have done had you not extended such kindness to me."

The elderly woman sat down across the table and offered a smile. While she always did dress to excess, today's emerald silk gown and matching turban with feathers tucked into her elaborate coiffure were in stark contrast to the simplicity of her home here on Dumont Street.

"My dear," she said as she stretched her arm across the table to rest it atop May's free hand, "your mother, rest her soul, would have done the same thing if it was my home that burned to the ground instead of yours."

Though May seriously doubted that fact, still she managed to answer in the affirmative. There was no need to let Fleurette Baronne know that well before Mama passed away back in February, she suspected the Baronnes of some sort of nefarious conduct. What other reason might there be for the unusually large deliveries of mail that arrived regularly?

Of course, should Mama have been watching out the window spying on the neighbors? That was another question altogether. But then, so was the question of what kind of awful brew this was in her cup.

May upped her smile as she set the teacup back atop the saucer. "Again, you are a godsend. I only hope I can repay you."

"My dear, I actually had it in mind to speak to you about this before now, but I don't suppose it will hurt to bring up a rather indelicate topic on the same night you've lost your home, would it? I mean, you're already distraught, so there's no harm in a distraction, is there?"

"Well now," she said as gently as she could manage given the pounding at her temples and the smell of smoke still lingering in her hair and clothing. "Yes, I suppose you're right. What is this distraction, exactly? An indelicate topic of some kind?"

The sound of footsteps caught Mrs. Baronne's attention. She pulled back her hand and swiveled to smile at her husband as he walked into the room. "Hello, love," she told him. "Look, we've got dear May here."

The gray-haired Mr. Baronne, whose first name she'd never learned, was a small man in stature but broad of shoulder and most intimidating when he turned his steely eyes in her direction as he did now. "Aye, yes, there she sits. Appears there was a bit of trouble at your place."

May stifled the urge to impudently roll her eyes, putting the impulse off to exhaustion. Mr. Baronne might be aged, but it would be impossible for anyone to miss the smoldering pile of bricks next door that had once been a lovely, if modest, home.

And to say that losing everything she owned except the clothes on her back and what little she'd managed to pull from the flames was a bit of trouble? "Indeed there was," she said as politely as possible.

"Dear, I was just about to talk to May here about the little thing you and I discussed in regard to her." At his confused face, Mrs. Baronne continued. "The letter?"

A look of recognition dawned. "Ah, yes, well then. I'll leave you to it."

He cast a brief nod in May's direction and then hurried away. A moment later, his tread on the stairs echoed creaks and groans until he arrived on the second floor.

Mrs. Baronne lifted the teapot in an offer to pour more of the bitter liquid into May's cup. "Thank you, but I don't believe I'll have any more."

"Suit yourself then," she said with a shrug. "So, as to this letter I mentioned to the mister, perhaps I should begin at the beginning, eh? Back in the old country my people were considered quite skilled at the art of matchmaking. We were known to find just the right person for anyone, even the most difficult of persons." She paused to offer May a broad grin. "It is a talent that was passed forward for so many generations that it has been forgotten just who was the first to obtain the skill."

Mrs. Baronne looked at May as if she was expecting a response. "How interesting," was all she could manage.

"It is indeed. So, when it was discovered that I could indeed perform this match-making with a great deal of success. . ." She paused to look around as if she suspected they might be overheard. "Well, as you can imagine, I set about to use my skills in a way most beneficial to mankind. It's the only right thing to do."

Mrs. Baronne continued to talk, but May's attention wandered. This morning she'd awakened thinking today would be like any other day. That the routine and tedium that was her life after years of caring for her invalid mother would go on ad nauseam.

How wrong she'd been.

"So you see, May, how I thought of you."

"Me?" May shook her head. "I'm sorry, would you mind repeating that?"

The older lady shook her head, causing the feathers in her turban to shimmy. "You've been through so much, May. First losing your mother only two years after the abandonment of your father, and now just a few months later your home. So many tragedies in such a young life."

Tears shimmered in Mrs. Baronne's eyes. "Oh May, you are an orphan with no home or family. What will you do?"

She appeared once again to be waiting for an answer, possibly some kind of grand plan that would remove the losses of the past few months and set May off on a path toward some lovely and yet unnamed future.

Unfortunately, May had none. "The Lord never gives us more than we can bear."

Words her mother not only believed but spoke at least once every day. This time when she thought of Mama, tears inexplicably threatened.

"That is so true," Mrs. Baronne said. "And I believe the Lord also provides us with others to share our burdens. And that brings me to this letter."

She pulled a letter out of her pocket and set it on the table in front of May. Though upside down, May could easily read the information contained on the front.

Someone from Chicago sent a letter to a Baroness Fleurette. Odd that the sender had gotten Mrs. Baronne's name so terribly wrong.

"This letter," she said as she slid it back toward her and then tucked it into her pocket again, "it represents the dream of someone in need of my skills. And," she said as she attempted a look of happiness, or perhaps she merely had some sort of intestinal issue, "that is where you come in."

"Me?" May shook her head and then stifled a groan at the pain it caused. "I don't understand."

"Haven't you been listening?" she demanded and then waved away any possible response with a sweep of her hand. "No matter. While you are most welcome to make your home here with us for as long as you need, I would submit that this couldn't possibly be a permanent solution. A girl your age needs a bigger life than what can be offered here."

At this moment, May cared nothing for the size of her life. It was the size of the pile of rubble next door that was foremost in her thoughts. Ridding herself of this pounding head-ache by finding a pillow and blanket and sleeping for several days was also high on her list.

"So with your permission I will write to this young man and tell him you are interested in beginning a correspondence but only if it is to lead to something other than a flirtation."

"Wait." May straightened. "What young man? What are you talking about?"

"Oh dear. You haven't heard a thing I've told you. I put it off to the extreme dis-agreeable events of this day." Mrs. Baronne shook her head. "Don't you worry about a thing. I will see all is set to rights for the daughter of my dearest friend. Now, why don't you let me see you to your room and let you get some rest?"

"That does sound lovely, but I am concerned about this letter and the young man you mentioned." She rose and allowed Mrs. Baronne to lead her up the stairs. "See, I was listening at least in part. Things just aren't making much sense. I do apologize."

Mrs. Baronne stopped in front of a door at the end of the hall and then pulled out a key ring and fumbled with the keys until she managed to unlock it. "Inside with you," she said. "Tomorrow is a brand-new day and it will all make sense then."

But it wouldn't. Nothing made sense.

May looked around the tidy but small room and then moved toward the single bed set in the corner. Bypassing the pitcher and towel she should have used to get the scent of smoke off her, instead May flopped onto the narrow mattress and laid her head on the pillow.

"Tomorrow is a brand-new day," she whispered, trying to convince herself of the truth of that statement, "and the Lord will never give me more than I can handle."

And though she likely smudged the fine silk sheets with the soot still clinging to her gown, May closed her eyes and willed sleep to hurry. So successful was she that she almost immediately dreamed she heard the lock click in the door.

Her next recollection was another click, the same sound she'd heard in her dreams. May sat bolt upright, the covers tangled around her and a curtain of hair obstructing her view. As she swiped at her eyes, a wide-eyed serving girl holding a small trunk came into view in the doorway.

"Madame says you are to bathe and dress."

She placed the trunk on the table beside the door and then stepped aside to allow two lads not much older than her to drag a small bathing tub in and place it by the fire. Two more young men brought buckets of water to quickly fill the tub.

When the door closed behind them, May tossed off her ruined clothes and gratefully scrubbed herself clean. She would still be soaking in the lavender-scented water had the girl not returned, insistent on helping her dress in a borrowed gown and pin up her hair.

When May finally arrived at Madame's parlor door, she almost felt like her old self. Then she spied the pile of rubble out the hallway window and nearly crumpled.

She was, as Madame had so clearly pointed out last night, an orphan with no home or family. Owing to Papa's advanced age, all his siblings were long deceased and any cousins lost to time and inattention. Mama had come into her marriage with Papa an orphan with no knowledge of her parents beyond the names they inscribed into the family Bible that had surely been lost to the flames.

A wave of fresh grief threatened. Steeling her backbone to ward off such unpleasantness, May slid open the parlor door and stepped inside.

"There you are, dear," Mrs. Baronne said cheerily. "Do come in. I have someone for you to meet."

A brief recollection of the older woman's matchmaking skills occurred. She pressed it away with a smile.

Madame had chosen a gown of crimson trimmed with ebony beads and cuffs. Her hair was all but hidden beneath a matching crimson turban encrusted with beads of jet and crystal and topped by two raven feathers that had been made to curl in opposite directions. In stark contrast to his host, the gentleman perched at the edge of a gilt-and-ebony settee wore a drab brown suit, a hat that appeared to cover drab brown hair, and brown shoes with more scuffs than leather showing. The fellow rose as May entered the room, unfolding arms and legs that were far too long for his body.

"Pleased to meet you, Miss Conrad," he told her. "I do hope we can get started immediately. You look quite lovely, and I believe I can capture you if we hurry."

Thoughts of matchmaking turned May's attention to Mrs. Baronne. Crimson lips were parted in a broad smile that disappeared quickly.

"May, do stop gaping."

"Yes, I do apologize," she said as she moved closer to Mrs. Baronne. "If this is about what we discussed last night, the. . ."

"Matchmaking?" the older lady supplied.

May nodded and then cut her eyes toward the man in brown before returning her attention to Mrs. Baronne. "Yes, well, I do wonder if we might speak in private."

"Don't be silly," she said. "Mr. Carstens has limited time. Now be a lamb and do as he says. His equipment has been set up in the dining room."

May knew she was gaping again but was powerless to stop. "Equipment?"

At Mrs. Baronne's nod, Mr. Carstens pressed past May then stopped to beckon May to follow. "Go on," Mrs. Baronne said, waving her bejeweled fingers at her.

"Truly it is too soon for any matchmaking efforts," she said to her hostess. "There is so much yet to do."

"First and foremost, do follow Mr. Carstens into the dining room." She added a please, but it sounded anything but cordial.

"Yes, of course," May said before hurrying to follow the man in brown. In the dining room she stopped short when she spied the aforementioned equipment. "You are a photographer?"

Mr. Carstens looked up at her, his expression neutral. "Sit there, please," he said, ignoring her question.

A half hour later, the photographer declared the session at an end and ordered her back to the parlor, where Mrs. Baronne was waiting. "You are in need of a place to stay, May. Let's talk about what will happen next, yes?"

Chapter 2

Three weeks later

At first it seemed so simple. Mrs. Baronne promised all May needed to do to earn her keep was to respond to any potential suitors who might wish to correspond. "But there are so many," May protested as she nodded toward the stack of letters littering her writing table. "How are they finding me?"

Mrs. Baronne smiled. "My dear, you are an excellent catch. And I am an excellent matchmaker."

A matchmaker, perhaps, but her claim of excellence was suspect at best. Most of the letters May got were so poorly written that it was impossible to determine much of what was said. Others were from men she found absolutely no interest in.

Of all the correspondence she'd received since Mrs. Baronne began her matchmaking, only one piqued her interest. She opened the desk drawer and pulled out the letter.

Despite Mrs. Baronne's insistence that May give all the letters to her for safekeeping, she had spirited this one away so that she might read it again. And again.

Silly since unlike the other missives, this one was simple and straightforward.

Our mutual interests might be served by a meeting to see if we are a match. I don't have much tolerance for small talk. If you feel the same, I await your letter.

Our mutual interests. No vain professions of suitability or, worse, flowery paragraphs declaring eternal love. Just a simple statement indicating they might have something to offer each other.

May flipped the paper over and took note of the name and address. "All right, Jeremiah Bingham," she said as she reached for her writing materials. "Let's see if you really want to meet."

After several attempts, May settled for a brief response.

Agreed. Please notify me of your travel plans. Telegram is preferred.

The door opened and May tossed her letter back into the drawer. The serving girl whose name she'd learned was Violet stepped inside. "You called for me?"

May beckoned her to come closer as she reached inside the drawer for one of the tintype photographs Mrs. Baronne required her to put in each response to her suitors. "If I were to say I had an errand, a very secret errand, would you be willing to take care of it without letting Madame know?" She paused to lower her voice.

"For a generous price, of course."

Violet grinned. "How generous?"

One week later

"Telegram is preferred?" Mr. Pinkerton's laughter echoed against the brick walls of the office. "Well, Bingham, it looks like you've got a fish on the line. Now go reel her in." He leaned forward to slide the picture toward him. "Is this the lucky woman?"

"Allegedly," Jeremiah said.

"Pretty girl. Too bad she's gotten herself tangled up in this mess."

Jeremiah was more of a skeptic than his boss. He'd learned firsthand that a pretty face could hide a scheming mind. "I tend to think this mess is tangled up around her."

"Then send her that telegram, Romeo," he said as he stood. "Looks like you're going to New Orleans."

The door burst open and an errand boy tumbled inside. "Urgent for Mr. Pinkerton," he managed as he climbed to his feet and thrust a note at the boss.

Mr. Pinkerton accepted the paper and then tipped the boy, who ran off as quickly as he had arrived. "Well, I'll be," he said as he shifted his attention from the note to Jeremiah. "Looks like your engagement needs to be put off awhile. I've got a tip on that mail fraud case we've been watching over in Philadelphia."

He handed Jeremiah the note. Sure enough, their contact had come through with a name and the date of the perpetrator's next attempt. Gathering up his letter from the matrimonial agency, he slipped the photograph inside and tipped his hat to the boss.

"Go get your man, son," Mr. Pinkerton told him. "Then you can come back here and get your woman."

It took the better part of two months to complete his surveillance and catch their mail fraud suspect. By the time he returned to his office in Chicago, it was the middle of June and the stack of marriage fraud letters had nearly doubled.

"What's all this?" he said as he settled onto the chair to survey the chaos that was his desktop.

"Thirteen more letters just this week. Your Miss Conrad has been quite busy in your absence."

Jeremiah reached for the letter on top of the stack. "How do you know it was her?"

Before Mr. Pinkerton could respond, a tintype fell out. He turned it over and looked into the face of the same woman who was waiting for a telegram from him.

"Same photo is in every letter," Mr. Pinkerton said. "I know you just got back, but you're needed in New Orleans. Just don't get too comfortable down there," he said. "Figuratively speaking, that is. I don't want to lose my best detective to the state of Louisiana."

Jeremiah grinned. "Never, boss. Texas maybe, but not Louisiana."

"I thought your people were from California," he said as he rose. "Isn't that where those mines are?"

He stifled a cringe. For most men, wealth on a ridiculous scale was a source of pride. For Jeremiah, it was the noose that kept trying to tighten around his neck.

"The mines are in multiple locations," he said carefully. "I leave the running of that to my sister's husband. I prefer detective work."

Mr. Pinkerton clasped a hand on Jeremiah's shoulder. "And for that, the Pinkerton Detective Agency is very thankful."

No more thankful than Jeremiah was to the Pinkerton Detective Agency for allowing him to achieve something other than having been born into the Bingham family.

One week later, Jeremiah stepped off the train in New Orleans. The heat wrapped around him as the humidity made him feel as if he were stepping into Chicago fog.

His first order of business after settling in was to walk down to the telegraph office on the corner and send a telegram to Miss May Conrad.

FORGIVE DELAY. *Stop*. MEET AT JACKSON STATUE. *Stop*. 7PM.

The telegraph operator's bushy eyebrows rose. "You could just go over and talk to the girl. Dumont Street isn't that far."

"I could," he agreed, "but I prefer this way."

So did the courts when it came to proving who said what and when it was said. Thus, he would see that he had a paper trail and an airtight case.

Jeremiah made for the door. "You'll let me know when she responds?" he said over his shoulder.

The telegraph operator tipped his cap. "Sure and for certain, sir."

Jeremiah stepped out into the early afternoon sunshine and paused to get his bearings. With the river over there and the cathedral behind him, he knew exactly where he was. He might have been raised a Texan, but his grandmother had kept a home in this city as far back as anyone could remember.

Likely that home was sitting empty now, awaiting the next Bingham's visit. It wouldn't be him, however. The last thing Jeremiah needed when he was working undercover was to be seen coming out of a mansion on Royal Street with his family crest on the door.

True to his word, the fellow at the telegraph office was correct. Dumont Street was only a short walk away. A tree-lined avenue with modest homes that once housed the playthings of wealthy planters, Dumont Street ran east to west in a straight line.

Here it was not as easy to blend in, so he tucked his hat down low and kept his surveillance as unobtrusive as possible. The rubble of a burned-out home gave him good reason to pause and pretend interest as he scribbled notes on his notepad. Any of these homes could be the one where the illegal operation was housed.

"You there, what are you doing?"

Jeremiah looked toward the direction where the question had come from and spied a serving girl staring at him over the fence. He put on his most cordial expression and headed her way.

She couldn't have been more than twelve or thirteen though her expression told him she intended to pretend she was much older. "You don't belong over there," she told him when he got close enough to see the dirt smudges on her starched apron.

"And how would you know this?" he asked as he covertly surveyed the property where the maid stood.

The home was a modest copy of all the others in this neighborhood. Nothing to indicate anything sinister going on, but then mail fraud and matrimonial larceny could happen even in the nicest places.

"Heard the lot was for sale," he said, improvising as he stopped a short distance away from her.

"You heard wrong."

The back door opened and a young man stuck his head out. "Violet, the missus is looking for you."

"Leave it be over there," she said before hurrying to the door and disappearing inside.

Jeremiah made a note of the conversation in his notebook and then tucked it into his pocket. Likely this meant nothing, but he'd been with the agency long enough to know that sometimes the biggest cases hinged on the smallest details.

Chapter 3

Sometimes detective work was difficult, and other times the work practically did itself. Jeremiah did not believe in coincidence, although the timing was certainly perfect to be standing within sight of May Conrad's home when his telegram was delivered.

If indeed her name was truly May, which he doubted. Nor did he believe she was the Baroness Fleurette, although he had decided she pretended to be.

"You there," a distinctly female voice called.

Jeremiah turned around in anticipation of seeing the surly maid again. Instead, a woman who looked like she stepped out of the marital agency tintypes hurried toward him. Though her stride was not quite unseemly, she did appear to be in a hurry.

Unlike the sepia tones of the photograph, this version of the woman was very much the opposite. From her honey-toned hair and yellow dress sprigged with tiny blue flowers, to eyes the color of his mother's favorite jade brooch, she radiated color.

She was of medium height and slender build, and she wore no jewelry or bonnet. A pink flush stained her cheeks and traveled down her neck as she seemed to be searching for something to say.

Most intriguing was how young she looked. No more than twenty or possibly a few years past. Oh, but those eyes, they held the weight of something that aged her.

Jeremiah decided to take the lead, intentionally omitting any introductions. "I suppose you're wondering why I was asking about the house next door."

"Actually," she said matter-of-factly, "I was merely wondering what amount you considered fair for making the purchase."

He certainly hadn't expected that sort of forthrightness from someone who profited from fraud. "You are the property's owner?"

"I am." She paused. "Have you an offer to make, or were you inquiring for someone else?"

He looked into her eyes and expected her to flinch. She did nothing of the sort. Instead, she returned his stare and appeared ready to wait for his response.

"What happened?" he said, intent on watching how she handled diversionary tactics.

"It is a mystery." She barely blinked as she continued to study him. "Should you decide to purchase the property, you may inquire with a note at the home next door. I would wish any discussions regarding this matter remain private between the two of us."

Either May Conrad was running yet another scam or she was just a very private person. In his experience, the former was the most likely scenario. Standing here watching her closely, he was tempted to claim the latter.

She tipped her chin slightly, a gesture that ought to have made her look haughty. It would have had her eyes not told him another story. It was almost as if they pleaded with him to help her.

In that moment, he wished with all he had that he could.

"Thank you," he said as he tipped his hat. "I will remember this. And to what name shall I inquire?"

She paused only a moment. "The owner of the property at 4310 Dumont will suffice for a name. Now if there is nothing further, I will apologize for the interruption and say good day."

"Good day to you as well," he said with a smile that May Conrad quickly returned.

Knowing he would have questions to answer should she respond to his telegram, Jeremiah tipped his hat. "May I do you the honor of escorting you home, then?"

"No need," was her hasty response. "Again, good day, sir."

She turned and walked back in the direction she came from, her back straight as a schoolteacher and her pace still quick for a woman of obvious quality. Out of courtesy as much as curiosity, Jeremiah continued to watch her until she opened the gate and stepped inside.

If she saw him, she made no indication of that fact. Rather, she continued toward the front door and stepped inside just as a buggy emerged from the side of the house. A woman of middle age sat like a queen on her throne while a lad of twelve or thirteen listened to a litany of complaints about his ability to drive the buggy.

Laden with enough jewels to embarrass a raja, the woman's garish clothing and obvious wealth were in stark contrast to the modest home where May Conrad appeared to reside. Or did she?

Jeremiah gave that question a moment's thought. If the marriage fraud business was as lucrative as the letters of complaint made it appear, then wouldn't those who profited from it live in splendor and not in simplicity?

He looked down the road to where the buggy had not yet made its turn and decided to see what he could discover. Knowing the alleys in this area of the city helped him to reach the main road first. Thus, when the poor lad and his passenger appeared a few blocks south of where Jeremiah stood, they were easily seen.

Waving down a hack, Jeremiah showed his Pinkerton credentials and gave the driver instructions to follow the buggy at a discreet distance. For the next two hours, he followed the older woman as she went about the business of dining, shopping, and finally arriving at a row house adjacent to the Jackson Square on St. Ann Street.

Jeremiah wrote the address in his notebook, paid the driver, and set off on foot toward the buggy. By the time the lad had returned from helping the flamboyant older woman inside, Jeremiah was waiting.

"A minute of your time?" he said to the boy, showing a coin as he inquired.

"Don't suppose it'd hurt," he said. "You'll have to ride with me to the Old Spanish Stables on Hospital Street. Ma'am doesn't keep a carriage house here."

Ten minutes later, Jeremiah had written three full pages of notes regarding "Ma'am" and her several homes. Though the lad wasn't certain of the old woman's name, he could say with some measure of assurance that there was a mister and that there was also a young lady who used to live next door now residing in the Dumont Street home.

Yes, he did take an overlarge amount of correspondence to be posted, and yes, he did deliver an equal amount of responses to that correspondence to Dumont Street. But no, his employer did not live on Dumont Street.

"That'd be the business house," the lad said. "This'n on St. Ann is where they live, her and the mister."

"And what of Miss Conrad?" he asked as the boy deftly steered the rig through traffic down Hospital Street. "Does she live there, too?"

"That'd be the lady who stays at the business house?" At Jeremiah's nod, the boy continued. "Nice lady, that one, but I don't know her well enough to say more than that."

"Does she run things? By that, I mean who is in charge of these letters, and more important, is she the one who profits from any responses mailed to her?"

The boy clamped his mouth shut, obviously deciding what to say. "She's a nice lady," he repeated, his eyes on the road ahead.

Jeremiah sat back and tried to decide what other information he could gain from the lad. Finally, he retrieved another coin and held it where the boy could see. "All right. Miss Conrad is a nice lady. I've met her and would likely agree. So, who is writing those letters? Is it the lady you just delivered to St. Ann Street or Miss Conrad? Or perhaps someone else?"

"Miss Conrad, of course," he said.

"So you've seen her writing to gentlemen who might wish to marry her?" The boy nodded, giving Jeremiah clearance to continue. "And you deliver those letters to be mailed?"

"Now hold on here," he said as he pulled up at the stables. "I'll talk to you all day long as you pay me for my time, but I won't be saying anything that gets me into trouble."

Jeremiah closed his palm with the coin still in it. So the boy knew there was wrongdoing occurring. Just how much he knew remained to be seen.

"And if you were guaranteed immunity from prosecution?" The lad looked confused. "What you tell me goes no further," he amended as he opened his palm. "I'm not looking to make trouble for you, but if Miss Conrad is doing something wrong, I am here to see that it stops."

"I doubt she does much wrong," he said as he climbed down from the buggy and handed the reins to the stable hand. "Seeing as Ma'am has me lock her in every night."

He climbed down and caught up to the boy. "Lock her in the house?"

"No," he said, stopping to look up at Jeremiah. "In her bedchamber. How many more questions do you have?"

Jeremiah handed him the coin. "How many more questions will you answer?"

"As many as you have coins for," he said as he nodded to a food stand adjacent to the stables. "Though I wouldn't turn down an oyster loaf and something cold to drink."

"How do I know you're not feeding me lies while I'm feeding you coins and a sandwich?" Jeremiah said, giving him a sideways look.

"Because I know things. Like why Miss Conrad's house burned to the ground and who Baroness Fleurette really is."

An hour later, Jeremiah had a signed affidavit from the lad he now knew as Damien Girourd, and he had a plan. Though Damien's knowledge of the marriage fraud was limited to what he had seen as a driver and houseboy, it was sufficient to send a coded telegram to Mr. Pinkerton to let him know there could soon be an arrest warrant issued for Madame Fleurette and her accomplices.

As he stepped outside, he allowed himself to consider what Damien told him in regard to May Conrad, the beautiful young woman with those timeworn eyes. The anger that had burned toward May was now directed at those who were using her for their own gain.

Or at least that was how things appeared. Jeremiah had learned that the only way to find out what a woman really wanted was to ignore her words and watch what she did.

He intended to use that principle to determine just which of these females was guilty. And if the Conrad woman was indeed innocent, he vowed he would do all he could to help her.

Jeremiah Bingham was here in New Orleans and he wanted to meet her. Twin feelings of anticipation and dread rose as May folded the telegram and stuffed it back into her pocket.

Rising from her desk, she upset the stack of letters awaiting her response. As she gathered up the dozen or so correspondences, she thought of how different Mr. Bingham's letters had been. Succinct and to the point, he was. A man who seemed to waste no words, unlike the flowery absurdity she received from other suitors.

She sighed. The other suitors would have to be notified that she was no longer interested in continuing correspondence with them. Even if Mr. Bingham did not end up making an offer of marriage, May knew she just couldn't imagine being yoked to any of the other men who had written to her.

May thought briefly of the handsome man who had inquired about the now-empty lot next door. If only this Bingham fellow turned out to be half as attractive as he.

As soon as the thought occurred, she pushed it away. Just as she hoped her plainness would not matter to Mr. Bingham, so she hoped she would not care about Mr. Bingham's appearance.

With that decision still taking root, she tackled the job ahead of her. Mrs. Baronne was still out when May finished writing her responses to this week's letters. All the better, for the older woman would not be happy if she read the gentle but firm letters of rejection May had written to these men.

Mrs. Baronne had put the men's gifts away for safekeeping—presents of anything from money to jewelry and even the deed to a plot of land—but May had carefully cataloged each one. She would see that each item was returned.

Perhaps not the cake one suitor had baked in hopes of not only swaying her favor but also showing his multitude of talents outside of blacksmithing and carpentry work.

Unfortunately for him, the cake had not arrived in any sort of edible manner. In truth, she hadn't known what the foul-smelling porridgelike concoction was until she read the poor man's letter boasting of using his late wife's favorite recipe.

May tucked the letters into her reticule and walked over to open the door only to find it locked. "How strange."

She tried the knob again and found it would not turn. Checking the clock on her bedside table, May decided the hour was far too early for this sort of thing.

She had discovered the disturbing fact that she was locked in at night sometime during the first week of staying in her borrowed bedchamber. Always the lock turned exactly twenty minutes after May had extinguished the lamp.

Not a minute before or a minute after.

She had mentioned her concern to Mrs. Baronne, who said seeing that all interior doors were locked was merely a safety matter owing to the suspicious fire next door. That May might be unable to escape should this home catch fire seemed not to matter to the older lady. Rather came the reminder that this was Mrs. Baronne's home and she would conduct business inside in the manner she wished.

Of course, May had agreed. To disagree meant she would be left with nothing but a pile of rubble to call home.

So May had concocted a plan that kept her from feeling like a prisoner even as she played along with Mrs. Baronne's disturbing rule. Slipping out the back window was most improper, but it was the only way to get out of her bedchamber before daylight.

Until now she had only made the attempt with the idea of learning whether it would work. This afternoon, however, she would use her newly learned skill to escape the house and post these letters.

She might even stay out long enough to meet her suitor later this evening and not tell anyone where she had gone. May smiled. Yes. Why not? How utterly scandalous.

Not that it was, really, but Mrs. Baronne would certainly find it so. But then Mrs. Baronne was so intent on seeing that nothing happened to May until she was properly wed that she did tend to be overzealous.

May tried to think of the older woman's kindness of taking her in, of seeing that she found a good match to a man who would care for her. Thinking on these things, the good things as the Bible said, kept her from dwelling on the tiny voice that told her Mrs. Baronne did not have her best interests at heart.

The afternoon was quiet, uncharacteristically so, as May carefully let herself down using the thick ropelike branches of the wisteria vine that climbed up the trellis on the back of the house. There was no sign of Violet in the outdoor kitchen or either of the young men who were also employed as servants to the Baronne household.

All the better to escape, and yet it still was decidedly odd.

When her feet touched the ground, May straightened her skirt and adjusted her sleeves. It would not do to look untidy despite the fact she'd just climbed down the back of the house using only a vine instead of a proper ladder.

Her walk to the post office proved uneventful, although May had been unprepared for the cost of posting letters. During her time of caring for her mother, no letters had been written. There had been no need.

She sighed as she stuffed the letters back into her reticule and walked back out into the afternoon sunshine. With time enough to spare until her meeting with Mr. Bingham, May decided to become a tourist in her own city.

Although she had been born here in that house that no longer existed on Dumont Street, she had seen very little of the city. With Papa gone and Mama sick, she had spent most of her life on Dumont Street.

Lifting her gaze to the sun, May closed her eyes and allowed the sound of traffic, the press of people walking past, and the warmth of the June breeze to soak in. Someone jostled her, and May opened her eyes.

"Watch out, lady," a young man in a red cap said as he slipped away in the crowd.

She saw the cap bobbing along in the sea of people and wondered what in the world might cause anyone to hurry on such a lovely day. Then she realized the reticule that should have been hanging from her wrist was gone.

Chapter 4

It didn't take a Pinkerton detective to know the boy wearing the red cap was doing something he shouldn't when he came flying by not caring whom he ran over in the process. It was a simple matter to stand between the thief and freedom and grab the arm that was gripping some woman's purse, and Jeremiah had him captured.

Three steps later, he and the thief stumbled into the police station where he handed the young man over to the first officer he found, a portly fellow named Officer Harlan. The policeman emptied the contents of the purse onto the desk in front of him while another officer hauled the lad away.

Other than a stack of letters missing their stamps and a few coins, there was nothing of value inside. He turned to leave only to spy a face that was becoming quite familiar.

She wore a dark green skirt today and a matching blouse sprigged with tiny red flowers, her honey-colored hair now tucked into a fashionable style beneath her simple green hat.

"You," Miss Conrad said as she stopped short. "Are you following me?"

"Hardly," he said. "Though I'm curious as to why you are following me."

Miss Conrad looked as though she might protest then merely shook her head and walked toward Officer Harlan. "That is mine," she said as she nodded toward the bag still on the policeman's desk. "It was stolen by a young man of slightly more than average height wearing a red cap. Have you found him or only this reticule?"

Jeremiah moved close enough to hear the policeman tell the story of how the stolen item came into his possession. As he moved closer, Miss Conrad gave him a sideways look, her expression guarded. Once again, he was struck by how young she appeared.

"This man brought my stolen reticule to you?" The suspicion in her voice was unmistakable.

"Yes, he did," Officer Harlan said, obviously noting the interaction between Jeremiah and the woman. "Along with the thief, who was wearing a red cap, just as you said he would be."

"I see." She once again turned her attention to Jeremiah. "It appears I owe you both an apology and a debt of gratitude."

"Not necessary," Jeremiah told her. "I am glad to be of service."

Harlan looked over the woman's head to meet Jeremiah's gaze. "You two give me just a minute and I'll have the lad fetched up here so you can identify him."

"I'm afraid I cannot identify anything more than his cap and perhaps the clothing he wore," she said to the officer. "I did not see his face. It all happened so fast."

"You'll do the best you can then," he told her before turning his attention to Jeremiah. "It just may be this man here who saves the day and makes the identification."

Miss Conrad nodded in the officer's direction then returned her attention to Jeremiah. "Thank you," she told him as she swayed slightly.

"Sit down." He guided Miss Conrad toward the officer's empty chair.

"It appears I continue to be in your debt," she said as she did as he told her. "I only just meant to mail some letters, and look at how that turned out."

More missives to heartsick suitors, no doubt. "Well, perhaps those letters weren't meant to be mailed," he offered along with some sarcasm of his own.

"Oh no," she said softly. "It cannot be."

"What?" Jeremiah followed the line of her sight and spied Officer Harlan returning with the prisoner. "Do you know him?"

Miss Conrad nodded, eyes wide. "That is Antoine. He works for Mrs. Baronne."

Interesting. Jeremiah watched the thief closely as the burly officer hauled him across the room. Any look of defiance was gone when he spied May Conrad.

"I didn't want to," he said before May could do anything more than rise.

"Oh Antoine," she said. "Why would you frighten me like that? I have nothing you want." She shook her head. "Have you taken up thieving because you're not being paid? I will certainly have a word with Mrs. Baronne if that is the case."

The lad she identified as Antoine ignored May to look over at Jeremiah. "You friends with her?" he asked.

"We have become acquainted," Jeremiah said.

"Then get her out of that house," he said. "Bad things are supposed to happen there."

"What kind of bad things?" Miss Conrad demanded. "If the people who reside in that home are in danger, you must tell Mrs. Baronne."

Antoine laughed. "They said you were an innocent, but I didn't believe it."

Jeremiah stepped between Antoine and Miss Conrad. "What bad things? And be specific."

A rumble went up at the far end of the room, jerking Jeremiah's attention away from the suspect. There he spied a pair of matrons pouring in the door and howling something about a fire nearby. Several officers hurried to help, but Officer Harlan only tightened his grip on the thief.

The entire group went outside, taking the excitement with them. Jeremiah tried again. "Antoine, tell us what you're talking about when you say bad things will happen."

"What time is it?" Antoine said. "Because if it is three o'clock, that fire is over on Dumont Street."

Officer Harlan retrieved his pocket watch. "It's straight up three," he said as he returned his watch to his pocket then grasped the lad by his shoulders and shook him. "Tell me what you know about a fire."

Jeremiah placed his hand on Harlan's shoulder. "Don't hurt him. It appears he has valuable information. Is there a place where he can speak to us in private?"

"I got nothing more to say," Antoine said. "Except that she was supposed to be in that house this afternoon and it was supposed to blow up. Now take her somewhere safe."

"May I?" Jeremiah said to the police officer. At Harlan's nod, Jeremiah led the boy to a quieter corner of the busy station house. "All right, Antoine, if you knew this and you saw Miss Conrad on the street, why steal her purse?"

The lad looked defeated. He sighed before looking up at Jeremiah. "Because when I saw her I realized there was hope she wouldn't be harmed if I did something. I figured she'd be smart enough to either chase me or go file a police report. Given how close the Baronne house is to the post office, I was afraid she was heading home."

"Where she would be when the house blew up." At Antoine's nod, Jeremiah continued. "So you led her here to keep her safe."

"She's a nice lady," he said, tears threatening. "Like I said, she's an innocent. She has no idea. . ." His voice trailed off as he furiously swiped at his eyes with his free hand.

"Antoine," Jeremiah said carefully. "I cannot help you unless you tell the truth. Why would Mrs. Baronne want to harm Miss Conrad?"

He let out a long breath but said nothing. Jeremiah decided to try again.

"All right, then," he said. "Tell me this. What was going on in that house that Mrs. Baronne needed to hide?" When the lad remained silent, Jeremiah continued. "Perhaps they wanted to hide the fact that they were running a marriage fraud scheme? And who better to con into helping with such a scheme than a woman who was a complete innocent?"

This time the lad's tear fell without being swiped away. "She had no idea. The old lady asked her to write those letters, but it was the old lady who got all the money from those men."

"Are you willing to testify to this in court?"

"Court?" His eyes widened. "They'd kill me for sure."

"Who are they?"

He shook his head. "The old lady and her husband. What you know about those ads is nothing compared to. . ." He clamped his lips tight.

"Then we need to make sure they don't get the chance. Will you sign a statement attesting to what you've just told me?" He paused. "In exchange for dropping all charges and letting you go, of course."

"I will," he said.

"All right, then." He led Antoine back to Officer Harlan and explained the situation, keeping his voice low. "I will need that affidavit if I am to make a case against these people," he told Officer Harlan. "Once the federal government has had their go at them, then they can be remanded back to New Orleans for your court system to take over."

"Fine by me," Officer Harlan said. "But what about the girl?"

Jeremiah stole a look at Miss Conrad. "Leave her to me. I can keep her safe until the Baronnes are in custody."

"She'll need to be willing to testify."

"I'll see to it," Jeremiah said. "You have my word."

The police officer nodded then led the lad away to write up the affidavit. Jeremiah returned to Miss Conrad and handed her the purse.

"Shall we go?" he said as casually as he could manage.

She rose but stalled. Those jade-green eyes seemed to assess him. "You weren't interested in buying my property, were you?"

Miss Conrad appeared more upset about this than about anything else that had happened since she arrived at the police station. Jeremiah looked away. He hated this part of undercover work. He hated even more the fact that he had disappointed her.

"No," he said as he swung his gaze back to her, "I was not."

"I see," whispered across the space between them. "Then who are you?"

"Where's Harlan?" an officer called from across the room. "Lady says you're holding her employee and her house is on fire."

Stepping between Miss Conrad and the officer, Jeremiah showed his badge. "Officer Harlan is with a prisoner. Tell her to come in and have a seat here at this desk. And do not let her leave. Do you understand?"

"Yes, sir," the policeman said, his brows lifted as he turned to walk away.

Jeremiah slid his arm around Miss Conrad. "Forgive the familiarity," he said as he ushered her off in the opposite direction from the front door, "but unless you want to see Mrs. Baronne get arrested, we need to get out of here. I'll tell you everything you want to know once you're safe."

After what appeared to be a moment of indecision, Miss Conrad nodded. He led her through a labyrinth of hallways and small rooms until he found a door that led outside to an alley. Immediately he smelled the acrid scent of smoke.

A fire this close would mean other structures could be involved. "This way," he told Miss Conrad as he led her through the alleys to emerge on the opposite side of the neighborhood. From there, Royal Street was a quick walk, but he did not intend to risk being seen.

"Stay here, but watch for my signal." Jeremiah hailed a cab then went back to find Miss Conrad, who was waiting right where he left her, a rare quality in a woman—at least in his experience.

May allowed herself to be jostled into a buggy. With a word of apology, the dark-haired man threw her onto the floor and removed his coat.

"Wait just a minute," she exclaimed. "Surely you do not wish me to sit on the floor."

He looked down at her, his expression broaching no argument. "I can either hide you from the persons who just attempted to murder you or you can argue about how you will be treated."

Not since the morning she stood on the lawn and watched the embers of her former home smolder did she feel so befuddled. She curled her knees up to her chest and wrapped her arms around her legs, holding on tight as the buggy bounced along.

Finally the vehicle stopped and she heard the creaking sound of an iron gate. The buggy proceeded, and then the gate shut behind them with a loud clang as the vehicle stopped.

May threw off the coat and climbed to her feet to look around. The buggy had stopped in front of a carriage house attached to a rather large home in the older part of New Orleans. The sound of a fountain echoed against the bricks and served to mostly drown out the noise of traffic and street vendors on the other side of the high wall.

She was in a place she did not know. With a man she did not know. Under the control of someone besides herself.

Again.

"You're safe now," the man said.

Ignoring the man's offer of help, she climbed down from the buggy and stalked toward the iron gates. "Safe is it?" she said, anger rising. "I would say I have traded one prison for another."

The stranger exchanged quiet words with the buggy driver along with what appeared to be a significant sum. The driver returned to the buggy, and the gate swung open to allow an exit.

May followed the carriage with the stranger a step behind. "I offer safety here," he said. "I cannot guarantee that if you leave."

The same thing Mrs. Baronne had told her. Something inside May snapped.

She whirled around, not caring if anyone on the crowded avenue saw. "Who are you?"

His expression softened. "I'm a Pinkerton detective, ma'am." He swung his gaze up to meet hers. "And my name is Jeremiah Bingham."

Jeremiah Bingham. *Oh.*

The wind went out of her and she sagged against the wall. So the man she thought she might have a future with was a Pinkerton detective.

"The same man who wrote me letters?"

He had the decency to look away. "Yes, ma'am."

"I see."

Mr. Bingham gripped her elbow and guided her back inside the gate. "I don't think you do, but we'd best talk about this inside."

She stood up to her full height, still pitifully smaller than the Pinkerton, and squared her shoulders. "Are you arresting me, Detective Bingham?"

Chapter 5

Should I be?" the detective asked.

May's eyes narrowed. "If you must. Otherwise I will take what remains of my pride and go."

He stepped in front of her. "I'm sorry, Miss Conrad, but I can't let you do that. I promised Officer Harlan I would see to your safety and guarantee you would testify."

"What does testifying entail?"

"I would expect the court will need a written statement from you regarding this whole mess with the Baronne family as well as an assurance you will attend court and answer questions if the judge requires it."

"Fair enough." May allowed herself to be ushered back into the courtyard then cringed when the gates clanged shut again. "Let's get on with it, then."

Detective Bingham gave her a sideways look. "What do you mean?"

"You need me to testify. Then I will testify with a written statement." She shrugged, avoiding his direct gaze. "As to keeping me safe, once I make my statement, I will merely leave the city and fix that problem entirely. I will keep the court informed as to where I can be found."

Where she would go was anyone's guess, for she had no idea and no close relations. Perhaps one of the gentlemen who had made an offer for her hand would be a good means of escape.

He shrugged. "All right."

May shook her head. "So it's that easy, then?"

"Yes, it is that easy." He nodded toward a side door that was obviously meant for the owners of this fine home. "Come with me."

Clutching her reticule, May followed Detective Bingham across the lushly planted courtyard to a door that appeared to open of its own accord. A servant dressed in a staid black dress and white apron stepped back to allow them through.

"Whose home is this?" she asked.

"It's a safe house."

"It's a very nice safe house." She followed the Pinkerton detective's broad back as he walked down corridors where beautiful paintings hung one after the other and the thick carpet swallowed any sound of footsteps. Emerging into a vast foyer that rose three stories to culminate in a stained-glass window depicting cherubs and clouds, she gasped.

Apparently Detective Bingham was not impressed, for he continued walking as if she were still behind him. Finally he stopped at a door and nodded for her to enter the room. It was a library of some sort, filled from floor to ceiling with volumes of all sizes and colors.

Had the Pinkerton not followed her, May would have gravitated toward the books. Instead, she did as he indicated and settled on a chair nearest to a large carved rosewood desk.

"I wish we had met under other circumstances," Detective Bingham said as he seated himself at the desk. "I do regret all of this."

She studied him a moment, watching his handsome features for signs of how he truly felt about this entire debacle. Finally, she made her decision.

"Yes," she said, "I believe you do. Nevertheless, that still leaves us with the situation at hand. I should have known I was perpetrating a fraud. I regret that I did not."

"I believe you."

May hadn't expected that. "Why?"

He toyed with the top of a silver inkwell then set it back in place. "Another employee has come forward to tell his story. He puts the blame squarely on Mrs. Baronne." Detective Bingham shrugged. "Even if he hadn't, now that I've met you I would never expect you to be involved in anything like that."

"Thank you."

He shook his head. "However, I do wonder about those letters in your bag. Tell me about them, Miss Conrad."

Heat flooded her cheeks. "I would rather not," she said.

"But you wrote them, didn't you?" At her nod, he continued. "Then humor me, Miss Conrad. Either let me read them or tell me what they say."

"Again, I prefer not to."

Detective Bingham's expression turned sour. "I could confiscate them. Or I could assume you decided to continue the fraud by sending those."

"But I just told you. . ." she managed before she collected her thoughts. "Very well. I will tell you."

He leaned forward. "Go on."

"When I received your telegram," she began, "I was, well, I had given up hope that you would respond. When you did, without telling Mrs. Baronne I wrote to the other men with whom I had been corresponding to tell them I wished to end our exchange of letters and to promise that I would return any gifts they had sent."

"How were you going to do that?"

"I hadn't exactly figured that out," she said. "Although I had a list and knew what would need to be returned to whom."

"Where did you keep that list?"

She sighed. "In my desk at Mrs. Baronne's home."

He leaned back in the chair. "So it's gone."

"Yes," was all she could manage. "Everything is gone. Again."

A knock at the door prevented his response. A different uniformed servant stepped inside to deliver some sort of note.

"Stay there," the detective told her. "I will be right back."

When Detective Bingham stepped outside and closed the door, May rose. Stay there. She'd heard that phrase all her life, first from her father who'd walked out one day and never returned. Then from her mama whose needs required May's care. Just when she'd been released from her duty of caring for her mother, she'd heard the same thing from Mrs. Baronne, the woman whose kindness had actually been anything but kind.

It was all too much. May straightened her spine and waited for the Pinkerton detective's return. When he opened the door, she was ready.

"I'm done with waiting," she told him. "And I am done with hiding and being told to stay behind. If Mrs. Baronne has been caught, then I want to see her now. I will offer my testimony at the police station. If she has not, then let's go find her."

The detective grinned. "Well now," he said as if surprised. "How long was I gone?"

"Long enough for me to realize I am tired of letting others tell me what to do. I participated in this fraud, and I intend to see those responsible punished."

He walked over to the desk and sat again. "I'm glad you said that, Miss Conrad, because we've got a situation, and the way I see it, your cooperation would go a long way toward putting an end to it."

"Let me guess. Mrs. Baronne is not in police custody."

The detective shook his head. "Apparently she was able to talk her way out of being arrested by claiming to be the victim. I suspect money changed hands but cannot prove it. In any case, the officer elected to let her go."

She walked over to the desk and leaned against the edge. "Let's catch them, then."

The timid woman who stepped into his father's library was gone, and in her place was a version of May Conrad that Jeremiah did not recognize but liked very much. Though he very much wanted to respond, all he could do was stare.

And despite it all, he still wanted to protect her.

"What?" she finally said. "Are you surprised?" She shrugged. "So am I, a little. But I have had enough, and I am ready to end this on my own terms. I was party to this fraud, and I will see that justice is done."

Jeremiah grinned. "I feel like I ought to let Mr. Pinkerton know I've deputized a new detective."

Miss Conrad's brows rose. "Can you do that?"

"I'm afraid not," he said as he watched disappointment color her lovely face. "But it's just a formality. If you're truly ready to see the Baronnes behind bars, you can start by telling me everything you know about both of them."

She nodded. "Before I do that, however, I want to tell you how sorry I am that you were caught up in this fraud. Of all the men I corresponded with, you were the only one I agreed to meet in person."

It took him a minute to realize she thought he, too, was a victim. That she expected he was romantically interested in her.

Which was preposterous, of course. And yet, had he seen her walking down the street or been introduced to her at one of his mother's parties, he would certainly have had a healthy interest in getting to know her.

"Detective?" the object of his thoughts said. "Is there something wrong?"

"Nothing, no," he quickly said. "Let me just get pen and paper so I can take notes and we will begin."

After almost an hour of work, Jeremiah rang for a maid who brought refreshments along with a response to the telegram he'd sent to Mr. Pinkerton updating him on the situation.

He unfolded the telegram as Miss Conrad reached for the teapot.

FOLLOW LEADS. *Stop*. DON'T LET SUSPECT OUT OF YOUR SIGHT. *Stop*. ASK ABOUT HER FATHER. *Stop*.

"None for me, thanks," he said when she offered. "Do you mind if we continue?"

"No, of course." She set her teacup down and began toying with the lace on her sleeve. "Where were we?"

Jeremiah folded the telegram and placed it in the desk drawer. He glanced down at his notes and then back up at her. "I think you've given me good information on the Baronnes. Let's change the subject for a minute. Tell me about you, Miss Conrad."

"Me?" Her fingers stilled. "Why?"

"Humor me," he said. "You never know when something that seems unimportant will end up being the fact that turns the case around."

"All right," she said. "I was born in the house on Dumont Street and was raised there as the only child to my parents, Cora and Theodore Conrad. My mother never completely recovered from my birth and was an invalid until her death last fall."

"And your father?" She looked away, a sure sign in his line of work that the person being interrogated did not want to answer the question. "Miss Conrad?"

"Yes, I'm sorry." Her attention returned to him, those jade-green eyes now revealing nothing of what she might be thinking. "He sailed on ships when I was a child. One day he left and didn't come back."

"I'm sorry," he said. "That must have been difficult. Have you tried to find him?"

She appeared to be considering her response. "It was, and I have not. I fail to understand how this is pertinent to the case."

Jeremiah shook his head. "I'm just trying to be thorough."

They lapsed into silence as Jeremiah scribbled notes regarding their conversation. When he finished, he looked up to find Miss Conrad had wandered over to the bookshelves and was holding a slim leather volume.

"Are you a reader?" he asked as he set the pen aside.

"Reading was my lifeline to the world for many years." She returned the volume to its place on the shelf then turned to face him. "But those days are gone. I would like very much to finish with this interview so we can get on with finding these awful people."

Jeremiah rose to walk around the desk. Resting his hip on the edge of the desk, he crossed his arms over his chest and regarded her evenly. "You really want revenge, don't you?"

"Not at all," she said, her expression showing surprise. "I merely want those men who were misled to have their gifts returned. I know she's put them away, or at least I hope she has. Even though my list burned with the house, I have their addresses and can write to find out what they've sent."

"You would do that?" He gave her a sideways look. "What if they don't tell you the truth? You could easily be taken advantage of."

"That is between them and God," she said. "It is only up to me to return what they claim they are owed."

"And if it's gone?"

"I have considered that possibility. If Mrs. Baronne has nothing left, then it will be left to me to make things right." She returned to the chair and retrieved her bag then reached inside to pull out a stack of letters. "I wonder if I might impose on you to post these after I amend them. I will keep track of anything you spend and see that you are paid back."

Despite the fact she had obviously spent her entire life dependent on others, May Conrad obviously did not accept charity easily. He let out a long breath and shook his head.

"I'm afraid I cannot do that," he said, keeping his expression neutral even as hers fell. "You see, I've got some news for you. Remember how you asked about being deputized?"

"Yes," she said softly. "You said you could not."

"Indeed at that moment, I could not," he said as he thought about how best to proceed. "However, as you might have noticed, I received a telegram." At her nod, he continued. "That telegram was from Mr. Pinkerton. I've been keeping him up to date on what has happened here. And Mr. Pinkerton has authorized me to allow you to work this case with me. His exact instructions were to follow all leads and not let you out of my sight."

Miss Conrad worried the letters still in her hand rather than respond. This told Jeremiah she was considering his statement carefully. Finally she swung her gaze up to meet his.

"So I am to be deputized to work on this case with you, then?"

"Of a sort, yes," he said. "Providing you agree to the terms, which are that you are to remain with me at all times and that we will follow all leads as instructed by Mr. Pinkerton himself."

"So I am a Pinkerton detective," she said softly. "Oh my."

How in the world would he explain this to Mr. Pinkerton? Jeremiah's best defense was to say that he was merely doing what he'd been told and keeping the suspect close at hand. Yes, he'd go with that should he be questioned.

He upped his smile. "So, since you are now officially deputized, you should know that the position does come with an allowance for expenses." He paused. "That should cover not only the postage you need but also a new wardrobe, given that yours is probably still smoldering over on Dumont Street."

"Oh," she said softly. "I suppose it is."

The mantel clock chimed. "Well, Deputy Detective Conrad, I think we've made significant progress today." He rang for a maid. "Until we catch these folks, you're safest here in this house. You will have a suite of rooms on the second floor at your disposal, but I will ask that you do not leave the property without me."

"I suppose that's fair."

The maid knocked twice then stepped inside. "Please show Deputy Detective Conrad to her rooms." He turned back to Miss Conrad. "Shall we meet back here at seven? That should give you time to settle in and write your letters."

"Yes, of course," she said, though she made no move to leave. "Detective Bingham," she finally said. "Thank you."

"No, Miss Conrad," he easily responded. "Thank *you* for agreeing to help."

Her smile was radiant as she followed the maid out of the library. Once his new deputy was gone, Jeremiah returned to the chair where his father used to sit and sank down into its depths.

"What in the world have I done?"

"I was just about to ask," came a familiar voice from the door. "But I didn't want to interrupt you and Deputy Detective Conrad while you were deep into your investigation. Is it true she is to be your mail-order bride? If it is, then congratulations. It's about time you settled down."

Jeremiah looked over at the door and groaned. Of all the family members who might have arrived unannounced at the New Orleans home, why did it have to be his matchmaking sister?

"Hello, Stella," he managed. "Do come in."

"Wouldn't dream of interrupting," his socialite sister said with a wave of her hand. "I thought I'd just go and welcome Miss Conrad to our humble home." She paused to offer another smile. "And to our family."

"How long were you listening?"

"Long enough," she said. "You ordered a mail-order bride?"

Jeremiah sighed. "As part of a Pinkerton investigation, yes. Is John here, or did you come alone?"

"My husband is handling family business in New York City, and I'll be joining him there in a week or so. But as to this bride, funny how you chose one who was perfect for you, Jeremiah."

He ignored the obvious attempt at matchmaking. "Despite what you think you heard, Miss Conrad and I are not engaged. We were discussing a case. And as to the family, she doesn't know, and I would greatly appreciate it if you didn't tell her."

"Doesn't know what?" Stella shook her head. "That this is our home? That you're ridiculously wealthy?" She giggled. "Oh Jeremiah. She doesn't know any of it, does she? This is going to be so much fun."

Chapter 6

Mmy lifted her hand to knock on the closed door of the library. Not only had she written the letters as promised, but she had also partaken of a long soak in lavender-scented bathwater.

During her soak, someone had taken May's day dress away to be laundered and left a lovely blue formal gown. The maid insisted on helping her dress and do up her hair, even insisting she wear a matching set of sapphires at her neck and ears.

The outfit seemed a bit much for a meeting in the library. Perhaps that was all that could be found on short notice.

"Miss Conrad?"

She turned toward the voice and spied a lovely dark-haired woman in a stylish crimson gown and matching garnet necklace walking toward her. "Yes. I am May Conrad."

"I'm Stella Cassidy, Jeremiah's sister." She linked arms with May. "I'm so happy you're here."

May gave the woman a sideways look. "You do know why I'm here, don't you?"

"Of course I do, but that doesn't mean we cannot have some fun," she said as she appeared to take note of May's clothing. "You look lovely. It is a pity Jeremiah cannot see you right now. He will meet us later."

May shook her head. "I'm sorry, Mrs. Cassidy, but I promised the detective I would not leave this house without him, and he told me I was to meet him in the library at seven."

Her smile was radiant. "I do understand, but he will be along shortly, and in the meantime you are in my care. You will be with me at the home of an old family friend." She paused. "But please, call me Stella. I insist."

"All right, Stella," she said with no small measure of misgiving as she followed the enigmatic young woman out to the courtyard where a carriage awaited. Stella allowed a footman to help her inside, and then May joined her.

"You're certain Detective Bingham will be following shortly?" May asked as the footman closed the carriage door.

"Trust me," she said with a grin as the carriage jerked forward. "He will."

Not long after, the carriage rolled to a stop, and they descended in front of a lovely home with lamps lit in every window. May tried not to gape as Stella led the way past the reception area and into the ballroom where an orchestra was playing some sort of waltz.

Two massive chandeliers glinted with light, bathing the room with a golden glow.

In the center of the room, elegantly dressed dancers twirled and spun in time to the music, while on the edges, people congregated in small groups to watch and converse.

"Stella," a young woman said as she stepped into their path, "where is that brother of yours tonight?" She focused her attention on May. "And who is this?"

"Genevieve Montgomery, I am pleased to present Miss May Conrad. May, this is our hostess, Gennie Montgomery, an old family friend." She smiled at the young woman. "As to my brother, Miss Conrad expects him any moment."

"Do you now?" Miss Montgomery gave her a decidedly sour look. "Well, isn't that fortunate of you?"

Uncertain how to respond, May merely smiled. A moment later, their hostess glided away on the arm of a young man who happened to be walking past.

"I'm so sorry," Stella told her. "I should have warned you that Gennie is rather fond of my brother. If given the choice, she would have joined our family ages ago." She leaned in and nodded toward a lanky young man surrounded by several admirers. "That is her brother Henry."

The man in question turned and caught them staring. Rather than showing embarrassment, Stella beckoned him to join them. Of course, he did.

Once she had made the introductions, Stella tapped Henry on the arm. "Miss Conrad has not yet danced. Perhaps you can remedy the situation?"

"Oh no, really," May protested. "I am not much of a dancer. Perhaps Stella will take my place."

"I will do nothing of the sort," Stella said. "Now go and have fun. I will watch for my brother." She paused. "If that is what you were worried about."

"Thank you. That would be a relief." May allowed their host to lead her onto the dance floor. "I warn you," she told him. "I cannot recall the last time I've danced. Won't you reconsider?"

Rather than respond, Mr. Montgomery whisked her off into the throng of dancers. After a few halting steps, she managed to decipher the pattern of moves that made up the dance.

"You're quite good at this," he told her, leaning down to whisper in her ear. "What's this I hear that you're Jeremiah Bingham's girl?"

She stopped short and nearly was tumbled by another couple dancing past. Falling back into step, May shook her head. "I am afraid you've heard wrong."

"Don't be shy, May," a familiar voice said as Jeremiah stepped between her and Mr. Montgomery to take her by the arm. "It's just that we're not announcing yet. Good to see you again, Montgomery," he said to their host. "Thank you for entertaining my fiancée in my absence. I'll take over now."

Detective Bingham swept her away before she could say a word. "Smile, Miss Conrad," he whispered against her ear as he ushered her across the room, through a set of curtains that had been pulled to one side, and out onto a balcony. "This ruse of being affianced will work in our favor."

The warmth of a June night in New Orleans enveloped them as May stepped aside to allow Detective Bingham to join her on the small balcony. Wrapped in lacy black wrought iron from the rails to the trim, the space hovered over a lush garden that included a fountain much like the one at the safe house.

"I am curious about one thing," he said when the curtains closed behind them. "What did my sister say to convince you to follow her here?"

"That you would be joining us shortly and that this was the home of old family friends," she told him even as she questioned whether she should have come here at all. "I've been had, haven't I?"

He looked down at her, his face surprisingly gentle. "We've been had, Deputy Detective Conrad. But don't feel bad. My sister is quite good at what she does."

"And what does she do?"

Matchmaking, he should have told her. Instead, he went with his second choice of response. "Stella is very good at getting people to do what she wishes. However, she also is very good at getting information about people. And that is exactly what you and I need to solve this case."

Jeremiah determined to keep his thoughts on a professional level. This was, to his own credit, a woman he'd called his deputy. And yet when he'd seen her across the room all dressed up in his sister's blue gown with his mother's sapphires around her neck, his breath had quite literally been stolen from him.

The deputy had become a thief, and for a moment he thought of rewarding her with a kiss. The idea startled him. In an instant he came up with an excellent argument against it, and an even better argument for it.

She leaned in, keeping her voice low. "So you think your sister can help us find the Baronnes?"

Good sense returned. He shrugged off the insanity of his thoughts to give her the proper response to her question.

"We're no longer looking for Mr. and Mrs. Baronne. They were found at an apartment on St. Ann this afternoon and are in custody, which is why I was not there to meet you at seven. Officers were working to open a safe in the apartment when I left."

"I do hope everything is there so it can be returned," she said with a smile that melted his heart. "That would make an excellent conclusion to the matter, don't you think?"

She looked so hopeful, so lovely in the moonlight. He hated to tell her the rest of the story.

"They did not act alone," he told her. "This assignment has become more dangerous than expected, so I'm going to have to take back your deputy status."

Miss Conrad took a step backward, anger flashing in those beautiful jade-colored eyes. "You will do no such thing," she snapped, her voice quiet but firm. "I will see this to the end, either in partnership with you or alone."

Jeremiah gave her an appraising look, noting the flush in her cheeks. "All right, then, Deputy Detective Conrad, enjoy your evening, because tomorrow we leave for Texas."

She shook her head. "Why Texas?"

"If Fleurette Baronne is to be believed, the Baronnes answer to a man named Sebastian Thomas whose crimes reach beyond marriage fraud. We can find him in Galveston."

"And how do we do that?"

"In her affidavit, she gave the police the name." He paused to look around. "And she says you can identify him."

"Me?" She shook her head. "I highly doubt that. I rarely met any of her visitors."

"Apparently you met this one." He pressed his finger to her lips to quiet her. "This discussion can wait until tomorrow, Deputy. Tonight we pretend to like each other so you are not bothered by Henry Montgomery."

She grinned up at him. "Does that mean we must dance?"

"Only if you wish," he said, returning her smile.

"I think it would help keep up pretenses, don't you?" She paused to drum her fingers on the iron rail before looking back up at him. "And I am surprised to admit I quite like it."

"Dancing? You mean you've never. . ."

"Danced?" she supplied. "With my feet firmly atop my father's in the safety of our parlor, yes. In public at an event such as this? Never."

"Then I am disappointed that Henry Montgomery was the man who made dancing possible for you." He offered her his arm, reminding himself that he must walk a tight line between keeping May Conrad safe and falling in love with her. "I will make it my business to be the man who made dancing memorable for you."

Her laughter followed him back into the ballroom where he held May Conrad against him and showed her just how dancing could be. They danced every dance, and by the end of the evening, when he walked ahead of Miss Conrad and his infuriating sister to the carriage, Jeremiah had lost track of just who was making memories for whom.

"Thank you for making our little party the talk of New Orleans," Gennie Montgomery told him as he offered his good-byes. "Who would have thought that the great Jeremiah Bingham would be felled by a nobody?"

He spied Miss Conrad walking toward them, and anger rose. "I assure you she is not a nobody."

"Well no, of course not," she said, eyes wide. "I find her, well, delightful. And I am so happy for you."

Miss Conrad joined them and offered Gennie a smile. "Thank you so very much for your hospitality. I have never danced like I did tonight."

"Nor have I," Jeremiah said as he linked arms with his deputy. "We're going now, Stella," he called to his sister.

"You two go ahead. I'll be right out."

Jeremiah led her to the carriage and helped her inside then closed the door and took a seat across from her. The silence enveloped them, as did the faint scent of lavender.

"Detective Bingham, I know I am supposed to be on duty, but I had such a wonderful time tonight." She wrapped her arms around her waist and giggled. "I danced, can you believe it?"

"First, if we are going to work together, I insist you call me Jeremiah."

She smiled. "Only if you will call me May."

"Done," he said. "Now as to your question. What I cannot believe is that you have never danced before tonight." He paused to study her. "You should dance regularly, May."

"I should," she agreed. "Now tell me again about our case. You say Mrs. Baronne expects I will recognize the man at the top of the operation?"

"That is her testimony." Jeremiah shifted positions. "Whether any of it is true, who is to say? She and her husband may be trying to cast blame elsewhere to try and limit their responsibility."

Her gaze found his across the space between them. "Then it will be up to us to investigate, won't it?"

"This deputy work suits you."

"Yes," she said as she leaned forward and rested her palms on her knees. "I had no idea I would like it so much."

"I had no idea I would like you so much, May."

She laughed. "We didn't have the best start, did we?"

"I think we've remedied that."

"Yes, we have," she said, gazing at him with eyes that no longer looked old or tired. Rather, there was a light there that had been sorely missing before.

If dancing did this, then he would see that May Conrad danced every day.

Jeremiah reached over to press his palms atop her hands. She moved closer.

He did the same and then lifted one hand to trace the line of her jaw. "Moonlight suits you, May."

"Oh," she said softly, her lips near to his. "Would you just kiss me now?"

Jeremiah leaned back and grinned. "From our first correspondence, I have admired how plainspoken you are."

May rested her chin in her hands and offered a disappointed look. "And until now I admired how you appeared to prefer to use few words. Why are you still talking?"

He laughed as he leaned forward. Never had he met a woman like May Conrad. If he wasn't careful, he'd be sunk.

And that was without his sister's matchmaking efforts.

Jeremiah wrapped his arm around May's shoulder. Slowly, gently their lips touched.

The carriage door jerked open. "I am so sorry. I was just leaving when that awful Isabella Seward called me over to ask me if I had heard the latest about. . ." Stella froze, half in and half out of the carriage. "Oh." She looked from Jeremiah to May and then back to Jeremiah. "Oh."

Chapter 7

"Get inside, Stella," Jeremiah said as he leaned back against the seat and watched May do the same.

His sister complied, her grin almost as broad as May's as she settled across from Jeremiah. "You two were the talk of the party," she told him.

"Then it worked," May said cheerily. "Your brother and I were using the ruse of being a couple to further our investigation."

"I see," Stella said. "And what were you investigating at the Montgomery's party?" she said as she turned her attention back to Jeremiah. "How long two people could remain on the dance floor without dancing with anyone else?"

Jeremiah shrugged. "Yes, and now we know."

Stella gave him her I-can't-believe-you-said-that look and then turned to May. "I don't know if my brother told you, but you looked so beautiful tonight, May. I hope you don't mind that I picked that dress out for you, but I just knew it was perfect for you."

"I felt like a princess," she said.

"You should always feel like a princess," Stella told her. "And I know just how to fix that."

His sister chattered away, allowing May only the occasional response. Meanwhile Jeremiah thought about that kiss, or what that kiss might have been, had they not been interrupted. When he heard Stella promise their guest a shopping trip tomorrow, he immediately put a stop to that.

"Her clothing has all burned except for the dress she was wearing when she arrived," Stella reminded him. "And I understand as a deputy, May has an expense account for such essentials."

His sister's eyes twinkled as she dared him to deny this. Jeremiah was, in fact, caught with his own words. Or was he?

"I won't allow it," he told them both. "We'll send someone out for clothes. Or have a seamstress come in."

"That's ridiculous. Tonight was fine, and tomorrow will be fine, too," Stella said.

"Tonight was fine because obnoxious as Henry Montgomery is, he runs a tight ship and would allow no one of any danger near May. But a shopping trip? Not until this man we're going after in Galveston is caught."

"If he's in Galveston, then how can he hurt her here?"

"We are taking the word of an admitted criminal. I won't be convinced of her safety until the case is concluded."

"Oh Jeremiah," Stella said. "Relax. It'll be fun."

"No. Absolutely not."

Those were his final words, and yet somehow the next morning Jeremiah found himself supervising the purchase of a new wardrobe for his deputy detective. Three hours into what appeared to be an endless day of shopping, he declared an end to it all.

"Whatever has not been purchased, ordered, or promised is not needed," he said as he ushered the women into the carriage. "At this rate your trunks will sink the ship."

"Don't joke about that, Jeremiah," Stella said. "Your deputy has never been on a sailing ship. That's why I thought I would come along instead of joining John in New York."

For once, Jeremiah was glad for his sister's interference. Having her around in Galveston would be helpful.

"Another first?" he asked May, lightening his tone as he saw her expression. "There's nothing to it. Just walk aboard here, settle into your cabin, and wake up at your destination."

Her weak smile told him that if she was indeed afraid, she would never admit it. Miss Conrad kept up that bravado all the way to their final destination of Galveston, Texas. Even then, she emerged from the cabin where she'd been hiding since they reached open water looking fresh as if she'd actually enjoyed the trip.

Had his nosy sister not insisted on telling him of Miss Conrad's seasickness, he never would have guessed as she straightened her back and walked down the gangplank of the Vanderbilt steamship *Daniel Webster* to the docks and the buggy waiting nearby. Maybe she would make a good Pinkerton detective after all.

Once the buggy was in motion, his deputy's facade disappeared. "Fresh air at last," she said as she inhaled deeply of the salt-scented air. "This is wonderful."

"You've never been to a beach town either?" Stella asked. "Amazing."

"Not really," she said. "Although I have a distant memory of this very familiar scent. Perhaps it only came from my father's descriptions."

The carriage rolled to a stop in front of the Bingham home. While the driver saw to their trunks, Jeremiah helped the ladies down. "The Pinkerton Agency certainly spares no expense in its safe houses," she said.

Stella exchanged a glance with him behind May's back but remained silent. Once inside, he left May in Stella's capable hands and went off to read the stack of mail he'd been handed upon arrival.

Topmost was a letter from Mr. Pinkerton letting him know that local law enforcement had been enlisted to watch a man that was under suspicion as being a partner in the mail fraud crimes. He set that letter aside and retrieved a note that appeared to have been hand delivered.

The author of the message proved to be the man Mr. Pinkerton had recommended in his letter. This man's note indicated Sebastian Thomas had booked passage on a ship leaving for New Orleans tomorrow.

Though he knew he should wait until the ladies settled in, the letter indicated that time was of the essence. He sent a maid up to fetch Miss Conrad.

"I apologize for the urgency," he said when she returned to the parlor. "But we've got some detective work to do. Unless you prefer I go alone."

"You're joking, right?" She followed him out to the buggy. "What is the plan?"

He settled her onto the seat and climbed inside. "I've got information that the man the Baronnes identified as the ringleader has booked passage on a ship for New Orleans tomorrow."

"Do we know where he can be found?"

"The Ayres & Perry Wholesale Grocery on Strand."

Never one to ignore the obvious, May reached over to touch Jeremiah's hand. "About that kiss in the carriage after the Montgomery party."

He swiveled to face her. "That was the beginning of a kiss," he said, his expression unreadable. "I can do much better if given the opportunity."

"Does that happen often with your partners?" Soon as she said the words, May wanted to reel them back in. Certainly this was none of her business.

"I assure you it has not." He leaned toward her.

"Jeremiah," she said, putting space between them. "Do you think this sort of thing is advisable considering we're in the process of following up on an important lead?"

He sighed. "All right, Deputy Detective Conrad. You're right." He reached for the reins. "Let's go catch this man."

They rode in silence until May decided to give voice to a concern she'd had since before they left New Orleans. "This Sebastian Thomas, what has he done exactly?"

"The Baronnes claim Thomas is the mastermind behind marriage fraud schemes in several states. People like Fleurette Baronne act as contacts for men who pay heavy prices for brides they will never see." He paused and May guessed Jeremiah was trying to figure out how to soften his words.

"I'll save you the effort of making things sound nicer than they are," she said. "The contacts find gullible women like me to pose as potential brides."

Jeremiah reached over to touch her hand. "You had no way of knowing you were being used, May. Given the timing of it all, I think the Baronnes realized you were living alone and used that to their advantage by setting fire to your home and causing you to depend on their kindness for a place to live."

She sighed. "Yes, that is all true, but why did they burn down their own home? That just doesn't make any sense."

"Think about it," he said. "What if someone tipped the Baronnes off that the Pinkerton Detective Agency was investigating them for mail fraud? The only way to get rid of the evidence and the one person who could link them to that fraud was to burn down the house with you inside."

May shivered despite the heat of the day. "I suppose I should have known that Mrs. Baronne was not as she claimed. I just had no experience with things like that, and I felt so helpless after I lost everything." She slid Jeremiah a sideways glance. "I have you to thank for giving me a purpose again. If you hadn't deputized me and given me a job with the agency, I might never have known that I had any value to give."

Jeremiah grimaced. "About that. I should be totally honest and tell you—"

"Stop!" May swiveled around to watch an elderly fellow disappear inside a storefront beneath a sign that proclaimed the establishment as B. SHERIDAN, WATCHMAKER.

Jeremiah pulled the buggy over to the curb and jumped out to help May down. "I saw someone. . . ." She shook her head, unable to credit her own eyes. "He went into the watchmaker's shop."

"Who did you see, May?" he demanded.

"I'd rather not say until I'm sure."

She hurried inside the watchmaker's store, a narrow but long room with brick walls covered in shelves that contained watches of all sorts and advertisements for watch fobs and other items, but found it empty of customers. A dark-haired man came out from behind a curtain in the back and regarded her with a smile.

"May I help you?" he asked.

"We're looking for a customer who might have just come in," Jeremiah told the watchmaker.

"I am sorry," he said. "But you're the first ones who've come in since I opened this morning."

May shook her head. "You mean there was no man about this tall with sandy-colored hair?" She lifted her hand to a spot above her head to indicate the man's height.

"As I said, you're the only ones I've seen today." He shrugged. "Perhaps if someone comes in, I could alert you? For whom are you looking?"

Her gaze swept the small space and then returned to the watchmaker. "No need," she told him. "I must have been mistaken."

Pressing past Jeremiah, she walked back out into the morning sunshine. Jeremiah caught up to her and matched his pace with hers.

He stepped in front of her, halting her progress. "We're a team, remember."

"Yes, I remember," she said, "but this was personal, not anything that has to do with our case."

He nodded. "All right. Since we're just around the corner from the wholesale grocery, why don't we leave the buggy where it is and walk?"

"Yes, that's a good idea." Walking would help her to return her focus to the case. Still, she wondered, did she see the man she thought she saw?

Impossible. And yet. . .

So intent on puzzling out the mystery was she that May kept walking as Jeremiah turned. She only realized this when his hand jerked her back a moment before a wagon team of mules nearly ran her down.

"You're distracted, Deputy," he told her. "Either focus or tell me why."

"I choose to focus," she said. "Maybe later I will tell you why."

"Fair enough, but remember we're partners." At her nod, Jeremiah gestured toward a cluster of buildings straight ahead. "We're here. Now before we go in, I suggest we devise a plan."

He led her around to the side of the building into an alley. May forced her attention away from her runaway thoughts as they stopped in the cool shade.

"I've been thinking about this, and you're the only one who can identify our suspect, May." Jeremiah looked away. "I'm just trying to figure out how to keep you safe if the suspect sees you first. I know time is of the essence, but I'm reluctant to proceed right now."

"Nonsense." May walked over to stand in front of him. "My guess is anyone I might know is someone who probably would not know me."

He reached up to tuck an errant strand of hair behind her ear. "And if you're wrong?"

"I am not wrong." She smiled. "Face it, Detective. You're not in charge right now. I am."

Jeremiah laughed. "The deputy detective is never in charge."

"We can debate that," she said lightly, "or we can go in and get our man."

"After you, boss," Jeremiah said.

"All right. I will go in first with you following a few steps behind. If our man is in there, I think there's power in him believing I am alone, don't you think?"

"Not happening," he said. "I won't give our suspect any opportunity to harm you. Besides, we are a team."

"All right, then," she said, stifling a smile. "When I have identified our man, how do you want me to let you know that?"

"If you can tell me without drawing his attention, then that's plan A. If you can't, then walk out and I will follow." He paused. "Either way, once the suspect has been identified, you will proceed back to this alley until I tell you the situation is under control. Understand?"

She quirked a brow and looked up at him. "What happened to us being partners, Jeremiah?"

"Partners work together using their expertise to get the job done," he said. "Unless you have training I do not know about, then we'll rely on mine to get us out of any potentially dangerous situations."

"I will concede your point this time," she told him. "But we do not move from this spot until you promise me that once this case is over, I will get the same training as you."

Jeremiah hesitated. "I promise," he finally said.

Chapter 8

Jeremiah's promise stung. He'd have to figure out some way to make that training happen. In the meantime, he had work to do, although watching the determined deputy march across the sidewalk and into the entrance of the grocer's felt like anything but work.

As soon as she disappeared inside, however, his instincts kicked in, and he hurried to catch up to her. The building's interior was vast and decently lit, owing to the windows that marched along the tops of the brick walls on two sides.

Long expanses of glass counters filled with items for sale ran along either side of the space, and low shelves filled the center of the room. Along the backs of the walls behind the counters were more shelves. Several dozen employees stood behind the counters, and another half dozen milled around interacting with customers.

Thus, their man could be one of more than twenty people, possibly more if those who worked behind the scenes were taken into account. By habit, Jeremiah touched the stock of the pistol he kept hidden beneath his coat and then followed May as she blended in with the other customers.

When she froze, he immediately looked around to determine the cause. Three men, two that were no more than Jeremiah's age and another much older, stood together in the back corner. The two younger men appeared to be arguing while the older fellow merely watched.

Though May had gone back to an appearance of browsing, she continued to sneak covert glances at the men. One of the younger men broke away from the other two and walked toward May, causing Jeremiah to move in closer.

"May I help you?" he asked her.

He took note of the younger man's well-cut suit and expensive gold watch chain. If he had to guess, Jeremiah would take him for a partner in this enterprise.

"Thank you, no," May said, turning her back on the stranger.

Jeremiah tipped his hat and hurried to follow May. "Was that our suspect?" he whispered against her ear when he was certain the man was out of earshot.

"Him?" She shook her head. "I have never seen that man or any of the others at Mrs. Baronne's home. That was her accusation, right?"

"Yes, I think it was." He shrugged. "I believe we've seen everyone here. If you don't believe there is someone who could be the missing suspect, then we're left with staking out the docks tomorrow and hoping you see him before he gets on the ship."

"Yes, all right," she said, though her words didn't quite match her expression.

He linked arms with May and led her away from the grocer's. "Since we have the rest of the day free, how about a few Pinkerton training lessons?"

She looked up at him with those jade eyes and almost smiled. "Yes," she said with a little more enthusiasm. "What is my first lesson?"

Jeremiah thought a moment. "A Pinkerton detective must practice situational awareness and learn how to take evasive action should the situation call for it." He paused to give his lofty statement the proper effect. "For example," he said as he gathered May close and then gestured to the busy street in front of them. "What do you see when you look that direction?"

May seemed to consider the question a moment. "People, carts, buildings." She looked up at him as if asking for his response. "A Pinkerton agent who should be more specific?"

"All right. What *specifically* do you see when you look with a detective's eye? Look at the details, for example, that wagon. What could be under the tarp? Supplies, maybe? Or something else? And what about that building over there? See the second-floor window where two people are having a conversation? A detective would wonder why they chose to stand by the window. He might wonder what they were up to."

"Or *she* might read the sign hanging above that window that indicated the owner of that office was a dentist." May grinned. "Which might also account for the fact that one of them appears to be looking into the mouth of the other."

"Good job, Deputy," he said. "What else do you see?"

She grinned. "Your sister."

"Where?"

Stella tapped him on the shoulder. "What did I miss?"

"The question is, what did your brother miss?" May said. "And that would be your approach."

Stella shook her head. "I don't understand."

"How did you do that?" Jeremiah asked her.

"I looked at the details," she said with a grin. "Namely, our reflection in the window below the dentist's office. The window acted like a mirror, making it easy for me to see your sister approach even though she was behind us."

"Oh, you're very good at this Pinkerton detective thing," Stella said. "Isn't she brilliant, Jeremiah?"

He had to admit she was. She was also distracted by something.

"What is it, May?" he asked as he searched the perimeter in the direction where she appeared to be staring.

"Nothing. Or maybe something." She looked up at him. "Are we done here for now?"

"Yes, I suppose," he said. "Why?"

"I need to do something." May paused. "Alone."

"No," he said, still looking around to see what she might be considering. To his trained eye, nothing looked amiss. And yet something had caught her interest.

"Yes." He looked down at May, her expression defiant. "You need me to identify our suspect tomorrow. If you want me to do that, then you have to let me do this."

"Do whatever you need to do, May, but I will not let you go anywhere alone. It isn't safe." He reached over to capture her hands. "Let's not forget you were meant to go up in flames along with the Baronnes' home. If they've gotten word to their operative here, then you're still in danger."

Everything Jeremiah said was true, and yet May wasn't worried. Not this time. "I appreciate your concern," she said as she tried to ignore just how nice it felt to have this man appoint himself as her protector. "But this is personal. And I won't be a minute. I promise."

"Oh, let her go, Jeremiah," Stella urged. "I've been wanting to speak to you in private anyway, but you always seem to be with Miss Conrad." She grinned at May. "Not that I am not extremely happy that the two of you have developed such a close relationship."

"We are partners," May said.

"Indeed," Jeremiah responded. "And as your partner, May, I cannot allow this."

"Jeremiah," she said gently, "as your partner, you have my word I will not jeopardize our case and I will not do anything dangerous."

He looked over at Stella and said, "Go back to the carriage and wait for us, please."

Stella looked as if she might argue and then smiled. "Of course. Take your time."

When they were relatively alone, given the crowd milling around them, Jeremiah took May into his arms. "If something were to happen. . ."

She smiled. "It won't. Trust me, please."

Jeremiah seemed to consider this. "All right. I trust you."

He took a step backward as if to watch her go, but she shook her head. "Back to the carriage with you."

"May," he told her. "Be careful."

She forced a laugh. "You're worried for nothing, Jeremiah."

But even as she watched him reluctantly walk away, May wasn't so sure. Once Jeremiah disappeared around the corner, she turned and walked the opposite direction until she came to an alley that ran behind the buildings.

Ducking into the alley, she counted the storefronts until she reached the one she sought and stepped inside. There she found a gray-haired gentleman hunched over his work at a table strewn with watch parts. His hands moved deliberately, his head bent to his work beneath the glow of a brass lamp.

May stilled her racing heart. "Mr. Sheridan?"

He paused in his motions and then turned around slowly until he faced May. "I wondered how long it would take for you to find me."

Streams of sunlight slanted across a face that was timeworn but still so very familiar. "Where did you go before here?" was all she could think to say.

His laughter held no humor. "Anyone else would ask why I left."

She stilled her shaking hands by lacing her fingers together as she walked toward him. "That is not how you and Mama raised me, Papa."

"Your mother completed what I abandoned." Her father's gaze swept the length of her then returned to her eyes. "And a fine job it appears she's done."

Ignoring the mention of her mother, May pressed her point. "You haven't answered my question."

"To answer would mean putting you and your mother in grave danger," he said. "Keeping you and your mother safe was my reason for staying away." His eyes narrowed. "You must believe there was nothing more than that."

May searched his face. "I do believe that," she finally said. "But there is no reason to fear for Mama's safety. She is with Jesus now almost half a year."

"Oh," escaped softly as he looked away.

"And I cannot be in any more danger from something you tell me than I already am," she added.

"What is this danger that has come to you, Mary Margaret?"

The sound of her full name in his voice sent her spiraling back to a time when her father was more than just the man who had left them. Unexpected tears threatened. She shrugged them away with a roll of her shoulders.

"I depended on the kindness of a friend who turned out not to be a friend at all," she told him. "I'll tell you nothing more until I hear your story."

"Fair enough," he said, "but will you come closer so I may better see you?"

May moved toward her father but stopped just outside his reach. Her fingers itched to touch him, to wrap her arms around the man whom she thought she would never see again.

"I, too, depended on the kindness of a friend," he began, his voice soft but firm. "Your mother was ill and there was no extra money for medicine. Then just like that, my friend offered a solution. All the money I needed plus much more in exchange for one condition."

"That you leave Mama and me?"

His eyes, so like her own, showed only sadness. "No, nothing like that. I sailed on ships that carried cargo. I only had to add their cargo to the ship's hold. So I did. It was so simple. Until they asked again, offering more money. Soon I was ensnared in a trap of my own making. There were threats made against your mother." He paused. "And against you."

"So you disappeared rather than continue to ship whatever cargo they demanded."

"A friend in Galveston needed help in this shop. The watchmaker taught me his craft, and I took over when he passed on." He dipped his head, shoulders sinking. "I wanted to return, but I was afraid. She would have killed you both."

"Mrs. Baronne?"

Papa looked up sharply. "How did you know?"

May told him everything, including the allegations Mrs. Baronne made against a man to whom she claimed to answer. She added her own guess that not only had the woman set fire to her own home, but she likely had done the same to the Conrad family home.

"What I don't understand is why you purchased a ticket to New Orleans under a false name if you were planning to stay away."

"He didn't."

May turned to see Jeremiah at the door. "Papa, this is Pinkerton Detective Bingham. How long have you been standing there, Jeremiah?"

"Long enough." He moved toward her and placed a protective hand on the small of her back. "The Baronnes paid for that ticket to make it look like your father was coming back to New Orleans. According to Mr. Baronne, who apparently is having no trouble testifying against his wife, she wanted us to believe the man who ran things was coming back to claim control."

"So even now I'm blamed for something that woman is doing?" Papa said.

"No, sir," Jeremiah responded. "My employer had a tip that your name was among those given by Mrs. Baronne to the men who complained when she did not provide a bride after payment."

"Of all the nerve," Papa said, his expression indignant.

"She and her husband are in jail. The information you've given May regarding shipments and coercion will be added to their list of charges. Will you testify?"

"Of course. But I am to blame as well," he said. "It would be their word against mine, and me a man who left his wife and daughter."

"For a reason your daughter understands," May said.

Papa rose and took her hands in his. "I have done nothing to deserve this of you, May," he said. "Will you forgive the mistakes of an old man? Anything I did was done out of love."

"I understand, Papa," she said as she gave in to tears. "But I missed you."

He closed the distance between them and captured May in his arms. "Oh, my Mary Margaret, I did miss you so."

May melted into her father's arms. She stepped back only reluctantly after she'd soaked his shoulder with her tears.

"How do we proceed, Detective?" Papa said to Jeremiah.

"With a Pinkerton detective for a daughter, you shouldn't worry. You'll find evidence to prove his story, won't you, May?"

"Pinkerton detective?" She shook her head. "I thought I was just a deputy."

"There's a letter in my pocket from Mr. Pinkerton authorizing me to hire you on his behalf." He shrugged. "As long as you don't mind he's assigned me to see to your training."

"Stella will be thrilled," May said to cover her excitement.

Jeremiah looked down at her, a smile on his handsome face. "I had rather hoped you would be too."

Epilogue

Pinkerton Headquarters, Chicago
One year later

Jeremiah stepped into Mr. Pinkerton's office and closed the door behind him. His boss looked up from his reading. "Trouble with the new recruit, Bingham?"

"Always," he said, "although not professionally. She's every bit as good a detective as I imagined she would be. As a future wife, I expect she will bring the best kind of trouble, however."

Mr. Pinkerton folded his newspaper and gave Jeremiah his full attention. "So she has accepted your proposal."

"Not yet, but I feel certain she will." Jeremiah shrugged. "I've got her father's permission and a plan. That should suffice." He paused. "One question before I leave, though. I've always wondered why your telegram requested I ask May about her father."

"A hunch, mostly," Mr. Pinkerton said. "Where a key figure in the family is missing, I tend to wonder why. Just like when a man has millions at his disposal and he neither acknowledges it nor tells the woman he loves, I have to wonder why."

"I thought I would get to that eventually, but the subject never came up. For some strange reason, my sister has cooperated." Jeremiah frowned. "I will tell her, but not until I know she would marry me even though I am a destitute Pinkerton detective."

Mr. Pinkerton's brows rose. "Have a care, Bingham. I pay my detectives well."

Jeremiah laughed. "Which is why I will not worry if you fire me. We'll live off May's paycheck." He stopped to consider his words carefully. "She will be able to continue as a detective after our marriage, won't she? If she wants to, that is."

"In my experience, marriage neither decreases a woman's ability to reason nor to act as a detective for my organization. Miss Conrad may remain in my employ so long as she wishes, even after she becomes Mrs. Bingham."

"Thank you, sir." The mantel clock chimed. "Wish me luck."

"No luck needed," he said as he went back to his paper. "God bless the both of you."

After two weeks of nothing but conversation and walks on the Galveston beach with her father, May was stunned to see Jeremiah at her doorstep this evening. Even more stunned when Papa welcomed him in like an old friend.

Ever since she agreed to an assignment with the Pinkerton Agency, Papa had been wary of the handsome Texan. He'd warned her there was more to Jeremiah Bingham than she knew about. Of course, he was right, although what she learned through her detective skills made no difference in how she felt about the man standing before her.

Because somehow, despite her best efforts to the contrary, she had fallen madly, crazy in love with the fellow who had taught her to reason out puzzles, interview suspects, and shoot better than he could.

So in that regard, Papa had every right to be concerned.

"Let's walk," Jeremiah said as he led her down toward the beach where the sun was setting, leaving faint smudges of orange and purple on the horizon.

With the sand beneath them and a carpet of stars thrown across the sky above, Jeremiah took her into his arms. He smelled of soap and sunshine, distinctly him. "Moonlight suits you, May," he said against her ear.

"Seems I've heard that before." She snuggled against his broad shoulder. "Would you just kiss me now?"

Jeremiah leaned back and grinned. "Since our first case, I have admired how plain-spoken you are. But not yet. I have something to discuss with you."

"And until now I admired how you appeared to prefer to use few words." May offered a disappointed look. "Why are you still talking?"

"Because we've got another case, an important one."

"So that's why you've interrupted my visit with Papa." She stifled a groan. And this had been going so well. "What kind of assignment does Mr. Pinkerton bring this time?"

"More of a blessing, actually," he said. "But I should begin at the beginning. I've withheld some things from you, May, and I should admit to them."

"You should," she said, "especially the parts about me not really being a Pinkerton detective at first. An expense account? Really, Jeremiah, I am still waiting to be reimbursed and so are the dressmakers in New Orleans."

"They are not," he said with mock horror. "They were paid the next day."

"No doubt with funds from Bingham Mining," she said with a grin.

He shook his head. "When did you find me out?"

"Well, after I fell in love with you, if that's what you're worried about," she said. "And the fact you live on a detective's salary might horrify your sister, but I personally think it's merely interesting."

"Merely interesting?" He shook his head. "I don't follow."

"No, you wouldn't. A man who pays his own way in the world? I find that quite. . ." She paused, searching for the word.

Jeremiah stepped out of her embrace and knelt before her on the sand. "Worthy of marriage, which I have on good authority will not disqualify you from your continued employment by the Pinkerton Agency?"

"You spoke to Mr. Pinkerton about this?"

He shrugged. "Him and your father. Both offered us their blessings."

"Oh Jeremiah, stand up and kiss me," she exclaimed.

"Not until you answer the question."

"Then I shall come to you." She laughed and tumbled beside him onto the sand, taking Jeremiah with her. "Of course I will marry you, Detective Bingham. Now please shut up and kiss me."

And he did.

Bent Facts: An Author's Note

I hope you have enjoyed your historical trip through one of my favorite cities in the world, New Orleans, Louisiana. Because I am a historian at heart, I take the factual events of history very seriously. On occasion, however, I have had to bend the facts slightly to allow my fictional characters to live, work, and fall in love in a "real" world. Did you notice the following bent facts in *Mail-Order Mistake*?

Despite the fact that tintypes of May were sent to her suitors, in reality, they were not widely available until two or three years later.

A New Orleans sandwich made up of fried oysters and crispy French bread was called an oyster loaf until the early 1900s. That sandwich would evolve into the famous po'boy sandwich.

Although telegrams are exchanged between Jeremiah and his boss, Mr. Pinkerton, in this story, actual widespread use of telegrams did not happen until a few years later due to high costs.

One fact that *was not* bent was the use of female detectives by the Pinkerton Detective Agency, most notably the detective Kate Warne who went on to save the life of the incumbent president Abraham Lincoln.

Bestselling author **Kathleen Y'Barbo** is a multiple Carol Award and RITA nominee of over eighty novels with more than two million copies in print in the United States and abroad. She has been nominated for a Career Achievement Award as well as a Reader's Choice Award and is the winner of the 2014 Inspirational Romance of the Year by *Romantic Times* magazine. Kathleen is a paralegal, a proud military wife, and a tenth-generation Texan, who recently moved back to cheer on her beloved Texas Aggies. Connect with her through social media at www.kathleenybarbo.com.

If You Liked This Book, You'll Also Like...

Of Rags and Riches Romance Collection

Nine couples meet during the transforming era of America's Gilded Age and work to build a future together through fighting for social reform, celebrating new opportunities for leisure activities, taking advantage of economic growth and new inventions, and more. Soon romances develop and legacies of faith and love are formed.

Paperback / 978-1-68322-263-7 / $14.99

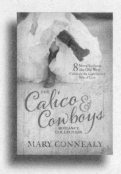

The Calico and Cowboys Romance Collection

In the American Old West from Texas across the Plains to Montana, love is sneaking into the lives of eight couples who begin their relationships on the wrong foot. Faced with the challenges of taming the land, enduring harsh weather, and outsmarting outlaws, these couples' faith and love will be tested in exciting ways.

Paperback / 978-1-68322-402-0 / $14.99

Seven Brides for Seven Mail-Order Husbands Romance Collection

A small Kansas town is dying after the War Between the States took its best men. Seven single women are determined to see their town revived, so they devise a plan to advertise for husbands. But how can each make the best practical choice when her heart cries out to be loved?

Paperback / 978-1-68322-132-6 / $14.99